Camilla by Frances Burney

or A Picture of Youth

VOLUMES I, II & III

Frances Burney was born on June 13th, 1752 in Lynn Regis (now King's Lynn). By the age of 8 Frances had still not learned the alphabet and couldn't read. She now began a period of self-education, which included devouring the family library and to begin her own 'scribblings', these journal writings would document her life and cover the next 72 years.

Her journal writing was accepted but writing novels was frowned upon by her family and friends. Feeling that she had been improper, she burnt her first manuscript, The History of Caroline Evelyn, which she had written in secret.

It was only in 1778 with the anonymous publication of Evelina that her talents were available to the wider world. She was now a published and admired author.

Despite this success and that of her second novel, Cecilia, in 1785, Frances travelled to the court of King George III and Queen Charlotte and was offered the post of "Keeper of the Robes". Frances hesitated. She had no wish to be separated from her family, nor to anything that would restrict her time in writing. But, unmarried at 34, she felt obliged to accept and thought that improved social status and income might allow her greater freedom to write.

The years at Court were fruitful but took a toll on her health, writing and relationships and in 1790 she prevailed upon her father to request her release from service. He was successful.

The ideals of the French Revolution had brought support from many English literates for the ideals of equality and social justice. Frances quickly became attached to General Alexandre D'Arblay, an artillery officer who had fled to England. In spite of the objections of her father they were married on July 28th, 1793.

On December 18th, 1794, Frances gave birth to their only child, a son, Alexander.

Frances's third novel, Camilla, in 1796 earned her £2000 and was enough for them to build a house in Westhumble; Camilla Cottage.

In 1801 D'Arblay was offered service with the government of Napoleon in France, and in 1802 Frances and her son followed him to Paris, where they expected to remain for a year. The outbreak of the war between France and England meant their stay extended for ten years.

In August 1810 Frances developed breast cancer and underwent a mastectomy performed by "7 men in black". Frances was later able to write about the operation in detail, being conscious through most of it, anesthetics not yet being in use.

With the death of D'Arblay, in 1818, of cancer, Frances moved to London to be near her son. Tragically he died in 1837. Frances, in her last years, was by now retired but entertained many visits from younger members of the Burney family, who gathered to listen to her fascinating accounts and her talents for imitating the people she described.

Frances Burney died on January 6th, 1840.

Index of Contents

DEDICATION

TO THE QUEEN

MADAM,

That Goodness inspires a confidence, which, by divesting respect of terror, excites attachment to Greatness, the presentation of this little Work to Your Majesty must truly, however humbly, evince; and though a public manifestation of duty and regard from an obscure Individual may betray a proud ambition, it is, I trust, but a venial—I am sure it is a natural one.

In those to whom Your Majesty is known but by exaltation of Rank, it may raise, perhaps, some surprise, that scenes, characters, and incidents, which have reference only to common life, should be brought into so august a presence; but the inhabitant of a retired cottage, who there receives the benign permission which at Your Majesty's feet casts this humble offering, bears in mind recollections which must live there while 'memory holds its seat,' of a benevolence withheld from no condition, and delighting in all ways to speed the progress of Morality, through whatever channel it could flow, to whatever port it might steer. I blush at the inference I seem here to leave open of annexing undue importance to a production of apparently so light a kind—yet if my hope, my view—however fallacious they may eventually prove, extended not beyond whiling away an idle hour, should I dare seek such patronage?

With the deepest gratitude, and most heart-felt respect, I am,

MADAM,

Your MAJESTY'S

Most obedient, most obliged,
And most dutiful servant,
F. d'ARBLAY.
BOOKHAM,
June 28, 1796

ADVERTISEMENT

The Author of this little Work cannot, in the anxious moment of committing it to its fate, refuse herself the indulgence of expressing some portion of the gratitude with which she is filled, by the highly favourable reception given to her TWO former attempts in this species of composition; nor forbear pouring forth her thanks to the many Friends whose kind zeal has forwarded the present undertaking:—from amongst whom she knows not how to resist selecting and gratifying herself by naming the Hon. Mrs. BOSCAWEN, Mrs. CREWE, and Mrs. LOCKE.

VOLUME I

BOOK I

The historian of human life finds less of difficulty and of intricacy to develop, in its accidents and adventures, than the investigator of the human heart in its feelings and its changes. In vain may Fortune wave her many-coloured banner, alternately regaling and dismaying, with hues that seem glowing with all the creation's felicities, or with tints that appear stained with ingredients of unmixt horrors; her most rapid vicissitudes, her most unassimilating eccentricities, are mocked, laughed at, and distanced by the wilder wonders of the Heart of man; that amazing assemblage of all possible contrarieties, in which one thing alone is steady—the perverseness of spirit which grafts desire on what is denied. Its qualities are indefinable, its resources unfathomable, its weaknesses indefensible. In our neighbours we cannot judge, in ourselves we dare not trust it. We lose ere we learn to appreciate, and ere we can comprehend it we must be born again. Its capacity o'er-leaps all limit, while its futility includes every absurdity. It lives its own surprise—it ceases to beat—and the void is inscrutable! In one grand and general view, who can display such a portrait? Fairly, however faintly, to delineate some of its features, is the sole and discriminate province of the pen which would trace nature, yet blot out personality.

CHAPTER I

A Family Scene

Repose is not more welcome to the worn and to the aged, to the sick and to the unhappy, than danger, difficulty, and toil to the young and adventurous. Danger they encounter but as the forerunner of success; difficulty, as the spur of ingenuity; and toil, as the herald of honour. The experience which teaches the lesson of truth, and the blessings of tranquillity, comes not in the shape of warning nor of wisdom; from such they turn aside, defying or disbelieving. 'Tis in the bitterness of personal proof alone, in suffering and in feeling, in erring and in repenting, that experience comes home with conviction, or impresses to any use.

In the bosom of her respectable family resided Camilla. Nature, with a bounty the most profuse, had been lavish to her of attractions; Fortune, with a moderation yet kinder, had placed her between luxury and indigence. Her abode was in the parsonage-house of Etherington, beautifully situated in the unequal county of Hampshire, and in the vicinity of the varied landscapes of the New Forest. Her father, the rector, was the younger son of the house of Tyrold. The living, though not considerable, enabled its incumbent to attain every rational object of his modest and circumscribed wishes; to bestow upon a deserving wife whatever her own forbearance declined not; and to educate a lovely race of one son and three daughters, with that expansive propriety, which unites improvement for the future with present enjoyment.

In goodness of heart, and in principles of piety, this exemplary couple was bound to each other by the most perfect unison of character, though in their tempers there was a contrast which had scarce the gradation of a single shade to smooth off its abrupt dissimilitude. Mr. Tyrold, gentle with wisdom, and benign in virtue, saw with compassion all imperfections but his own, and there doubled the severity which to others he spared. Yet the mildness that urged him to pity blinded him not to approve; his equity was unerring, though his judgment was indulgent. His partner had a firmness of mind which nothing could shake: calamity found her resolute; even prosperity was powerless to lull her duties asleep. The exalted character of her husband was the pride of her existence, and the source of her happiness. He was not merely her standard of excellence, but of endurance, since her sense of his worth was the criterion for her opinion of all others. This instigated a spirit of comparison, which is almost always uncandid, and which here could rarely escape proving injurious. Such, at its very best, is the unskilfulness of our fallible nature, that even the noble principle which impels our love of right, misleads us but into new deviations, when its ambition presumes to point at perfection. In this instance, however, distinctness of disposition stifled not reciprocity of affection—that magnetic concentration of all marriage felicity;—Mr. Tyrold revered while he softened the rigid virtues of his wife, who adored while she fortified the melting humanity of her husband.

Thus, in an interchange of happiness the most deserved, and of parental occupations the most promising, passed the first married years of this blest and blessing pair. An event then came to pass extremely interesting at the moment, and yet more important in its consequences. This was the receipt of a letter from the elder brother of Mr. Tyrold, containing information that he meant to remove into Hampshire.

Sir Hugh Tyrold was a baronet, who resided upon the hereditary estate of the family in Yorkshire. He was many years older than Mr. Tyrold, who had never seen him since his marriage; religious duties, prudence, and domestic affairs having from that period detained him at his benefice; while a passion for field sports had, with equal constancy, kept his brother stationary.

The baronet began his letter with kind enquiries after the welfare of Mr. Tyrold and his family, and then entered upon the state of his own affairs, briefly narrating, that he had lost his health, and, not knowing what to do with himself, had resolved to change his habitation, and settle near his relations. The Cleves' estate, which he heard was just by Etherington, being then upon sale, he desired his brother to make the purchase for him out of hand; and then to prepare Mrs. Tyrold, with whom he was yet unacquainted, though he took it for granted she was a woman of great learning, to receive a mere poor country squire, who knew no more of hic, hæc, hoc, than the baby unborn. He begged him to provide a proper apartment for their niece Indiana Lynmere, whom he should bring with him, and another for their nephew Clermont, who was to follow at the next holidays; and not to forget Mrs. Margland, Indiana's governess, she being rather the most particular in point of pleasing amongst them.

Mr. Tyrold, extremely gratified by this unexpected renewal of fraternal intercourse, wrote the warmest thanks to his brother, and executed the commission with the utmost alacrity. A noble mansion, with an extensive pleasure-ground, scarce four miles distant from the parsonage-house of Etherington, was bought, fitted up, and made ready for his reception in the course of a few months. The baronet, impatient to take possession of his new territory, arrived speedily after, with his niece Indiana, and was welcomed at the gate of the park by Mr. Tyrold and his whole family.

Sir Hugh Tyrold inherited from his ancestors an unincumbered estate of £.5000 per annum; which he enjoyed with ease and affluence to himself, and disseminated with a good will so generous, that he appeared to think his personal prosperity, and that of all who surrounded him, bestowed but to be shared in common, rather from general right, than through his own dispensing bounty. His temper was unalterably sweet, and every thought of his breast was laid open to the world with an almost infantine artlessness. But his talents bore no proportion to the goodness of his heart, an insuperable want of quickness, and of application in his early days, having left him, at a later period, wholly uncultivated, and singularly self-formed.

A dearth of all sedentary resources became, when his youth passed away, his own constant reproach. Health failed him in the meridian of his life, from the consequences of a wound in his side, occasioned by a fall from his horse; exercise, therefore, and active diversions, were of necessity relinquished, and as these had hitherto occupied all his time, except that portion which he delighted to devote to hospitality and neighbourly offices, now equally beyond his strength, he found himself at once deprived of all employment, and destitute of all comfort. Nor did any plan occur to him to solace his misfortunes, till he accidentally read in the newspapers that the Cleves' estate was upon sale.

Indiana, the niece who accompanied him, a beautiful little girl, was the orphan daughter of a deceased sister, who, at the death of her parents, had, with Clermont, an only brother, been left to the guardianship of Sir Hugh; with the charge of a small estate for the son of scarce £.200 a-year, and the sum of £.1000 for the fortune of the daughter.

The meeting was a source of tender pleasure to Mr. Tyrold; and gave birth in his young family to that eager joy which is so naturally attached, by our happiest early prejudices, to the first sight of near relations. Mrs. Tyrold received Sir Hugh with the complacency due to the brother of her husband; who now rose higher than ever in her estimation, from a fraternal comparison to the unavoidable disadvantage of the baronet; though she was not insensible to the fair future prospects of her children, which seemed the probable result of his change of abode.

Sir Hugh himself, notwithstanding his best affections were all opened by the sight of so many claimants to their kindness, was the only dejected person of the group.

Though too good in his nature for envy, a severe self-upbraiding followed his view of the happiness of his brother; he regretted he had not married at the same age, that he might have owned as fine a family, and repined against the unfortunate privileges of his birth-right, which, by indulging him in his first youth with whatever he could covet, drove from his attention that modest foresight, which prepares for later years the consolation they are sure to require.

By degrees, however, the satisfaction spread around him found some place in his own breast, and he acknowledged himself sensibly revived by so endearing a reception; though he candidly avowed, that if he had not been at a loss what to do, he should never have had a thought of taking so long a journey. 'But the not having made,' cried he, 'the proper proficiency in my youth for the filling up my time, has put me quite behind-hand.'

He caressed all the children with great fondness, and was much struck with the beauty of his three nieces, particularly with that of Camilla, Mr. Tyrold's second daughter; 'yet she is not,' he cried, 'so pretty as her little sister Eugenia, nor much better than t'other sister Lavinia; and not one of the three is half so great a beauty as my little Indiana; so I can't well make out what it is that's so catching in her; but there's something in her little mouth that quite wins me; though she looks as if she was half laughing at me too: which can't very well be, neither; for I suppose, as yet, at least, she knows no more of books and studying than her uncle. And that's little enough, God knows, for I never took to them in proper season; which I have been sorry enough for, upon coming to discretion.'

Then addressing himself to the boy, he exhorted him to work hard while yet in his youth, and related sundry anecdotes of the industry and merit of his father when at the same age, though left quite to himself, as, to his great misfortune, he had been also, 'which brought about,' he continued, 'my being this present ignoramus that you see me; which would not have happened, if my good forefathers had been pleased to keep a sharper look out upon my education.'

Lionel, the little boy, casting a comic glance at Camilla, begged to know what his uncle meant by a sharper look out?

'Mean, my dear? why correction, to be sure; for all that, they tell me, is to be done by the rod; so there, at least, I might have stood as good a chance as my neighbours.'

'And pray, uncle,' cried Lionel, pursing up his mouth to hide his laughter, 'did you always like the thoughts of it so well?'

'Why no, my dear, I can't pretend to that; at your age I had no more taste for it than you have: but there's a proper season for every thing. However, though I tell you this for a warning, perhaps you may do without it; for, by what I hear, the rising generation's got to a much greater pitch since my time.'

He then added, he must advise him, as a friend, to be upon his guard, as his Cousin, Clermont Lynmere, who was coming home from Eton school next Christmas for the holidays, would turn out the very mirror of scholarship; for he had given directions to have him study both night and day, except what might be taken off for eating and sleeping: 'Because,' he continued, 'having proved the bad of knowing nothing in my own case, I have the more right to intermeddle with others. And he will thank me enough when once he has got over his classics. And I hope, my dear little boy, you see it in the same light too; which, however, is what I can't expect.'

The house was now examined; the fair little Indiana took possession of her apartment; Miss Margland was satisfied with the attention that had been paid her; and Sir Hugh was rejoiced to find a room for Clermont that had no window but a skylight, by which means his studies, he observed, would receive no interruption from gaping and staring about him. And, when the night advanced, Mr. Tyrold had the happiness of leaving him with some prospect of recovering his spirits.

The revival, however, lasted but during the novelty of the scene; depression returned with the feelings of ill health; and the happier lot of his brother, though born to almost nothing, filled him with incessent repentance of his own mismanagement.

In some measure to atone for this, he resolved to collect himself a family in his own house; and the young Camilla, whose dawning archness of expression had instinctively caught him, he now demanded of her parents, to come and reside with him and Indiana at Cleves; 'for certainly,' he said, 'for such a young little thing, she looks full of amusement.'

Mrs. Tyrold objected against reposing a trust so precious where its value could so ill be appreciated. Camilla was, in secret, the fondest hope of her mother, though the rigour of her justice scarce permitted the partiality to beat even in her own breast. Nor did the happy little person need the avowed distinction. The tide of youthful glee flowed jocund from her heart, and the transparency of her fine blue veins almost shewed the velocity of its current. Every look was a smile, every step was a spring, every thought was a hope, every feeling was joy! and the early felicity of her mind was without allay. O blissful state of innocence, purity, and delight, why must it fleet so fast? why scarcely but by retrospection is its happiness known?

Mr. Tyrold, while his tenderest hopes encircled the same object, saw the proposal in a fairer light, from the love he bore to his brother. It seemed certain such a residence would secure her an ample fortune; the governess to whom Indiana was entrusted would take care of his little girl; though removed from the hourly instructions, she would still be within reach of the general superintendance of her mother, into whose power he cast the uncontrolled liberty to reclaim her, if there started any occasion. His children had no provision ascertained, should his life be too short to fulfil his own personal schemes of economy in their favour: and while to an argument so incontrovertible Mrs. Tyrold was silent, he begged her also to reflect, that, persuasive as were the attractions of elegance and refinement, no just parental expectations could be essentially disappointed, where the great moral lessons were practically inculcated, by a uniform view of goodness of heart, and firmness of principle. These his brother possessed in an eminent degree; and if his character had nothing more from which their daughter could derive benefit, it undoubtedly had not a point from which she could receive injury.

Mrs. Tyrold now yielded; she never resisted a remonstrance of her husband; and as her sense of duty impelled her also never to murmur, she retired to her own room, to conceal with how ill a grace she complied.

Had this lady been united to a man whom she despised, she would yet have obeyed him, and as scrupulously, though not as happily, as she obeyed her honoured partner. She considered the vow taken at the altar to her husband, as a voluntary vestal would have held one taken to her Maker; and no dissent in opinion exculpated, in her mind, the least deviation from his will.

But here, where an admiration almost adoring was fixt of the character to which she submitted, she was sure to applaud the motives which swayed him, however little their consequences met her sentiments: and even where the contrariety was wholly repugnant to her judgment, the genuine warmth of her just affection made every compliance, and every forbearance, not merely exempt from pain, but if to him any satisfaction, a sacrifice soothing to her heart.

Mr. Tyrold, whose whole soul was deeply affected by her excellencies, gratefully felt his power, and religiously studied not to abuse it: he respected what he owed to her conscience, he tenderly returned what he was indebted to her affection. To render her virtues conducive to her happiness, to soften her duties by the highest sense of their merit, were the first and most sacred objects of his solicitude in life.

When the lively and lovely little girl, mingling the tears of separation with all the childish rapture which novelty, to a much later period inspires, was preparing to change her home, 'Remember,' cried Mr. Tyrold, to her anxious mother, 'that on you, my Georgiana, devolves the sole charge, the unlimited judgment, to again bring her under this roof, the first moment she appears to you in any danger from having quitted it.'

The prompt and thankful acceptance of Mrs. Tyrold did justice to the sincerity of this offer: and the cheerful acquiescence of lessened reluctance, raised her higher in that esteem to which her constant mind invariably looked up, as the summit of her chosen ambition.

CHAPTER II

Comic Gambols

Delighted with this acquisition to his household, Sir Hugh again revived. 'My dear brother and sister,' he cried, when next the family visited Cleves, 'this proves the most fortunate step I have ever taken since I was born. Camilla's a little jewel; she jumps and skips about till she makes my eyes ache with looking after her, for fear of her breaking her neck. I must keep a sharp watch, or she'll put poor Indiana's nose quite out of joint, which God forbid. However, she's the life of us all, for I'm sorry to say it, but I think, my dear brother, poor Indiana promises to turn out rather dull.'

The sprightly little girl, thus possessed of the heart, soon guided the will of her uncle. He could refuse nothing to her endearing entreaty, and felt every indulgence repaid by the enchantment of her gaiety. Indiana, his first idol, lost her power to please him, though no essential kindness was abated in his conduct. He still acknowledged that her beauty was the most complete; but he found in Camilla a variety that was captivation. Her form and her mind were of equal elasticity. Her playful countenance rekindled his spirits, the cheerfulness of her animated voice awakened him to its own joy. He doated upon detaining her by his side, or delighted to gratify her if she wished to be absent. She exhilarated him with pleasure, she supplied him with ideas, and from the morning's first dawn to the evening's latest close, his eye followed her light springing figure, or his ear vibrated with her sportive sounds; catching, as it listened, in successive rotation, the spontaneous laugh, the unconscious bound, the genuine glee of childhood's fearless happiness, uncurbed by severity, untamed by misfortune.

This ascendance was soon pointed out by the servants to Indiana, who sometimes shewed her resentment in unexplained and pouting sullenness, and at others, let all pass unnoticed, with unreflecting forgetfulness. But her mind was soon empoisoned with a jealousy of more permanent seriousness; in less than a month after the residence of Camilla at Cleves, Sir Hugh took the resolution of making her his heiress.

Even Mr. Tyrold, notwithstanding his fondness for Camilla, remonstrated against a partiality so injurious to his nephew and niece, as well as to the rest of his family. And Mrs. Tyrold, though her secret heart subscribed, without wonder, to a predilection in favour of Camilla, was maternally disturbed for her other children, and felt her justice sensibly shocked at a blight so unmerited to the hopes cherished by Indiana and Clermont Lynmere: for though the fruits of this change of plan would be reaped by her little darling, they were robbed of all their sweetness to a mind so correct, by their undeserved bitterness towards the first expectants.

Sir Hugh, however, was immoveable; he would provide handsomely, he said, for Indiana and Clermont, by settling a thousand pounds a year between them; and he would bequeath capital legacies amongst the rest of his nephews and nieces: but as to the bulk of his fortune, it should all go to Camilla; for how else could he make her amends for having amused him? or how, when he was gone, should he prove to her he loved her the best?

Sir Hugh could keep nothing secret; Camilla was soon informed of the riches she was destined to inherit; and servants, who now with added respect attended her, took frequent opportunities of impressing her with the expectation, by the favours they begged from her in reversion.

The happy young heiress heard them with little concern: interest and ambition could find no room in a mind, which to dance, sing, and play could enliven to rapture. Yet the continued repetition of requests soon made the idea of patronage familiar to her, and though wholly uninfected with one thought of power or consequence, she sometimes regaled her fancy with the presents she should make amongst her friends; designing a coach for her mamma, that she might oftener go abroad; an horse for her brother Lionel, which she knew to be his most passionate wish; a new bureau, with a lock and key, for her eldest sister Lavinia; innumerable trinkets for her cousin Indiana; dolls and toys without end for her little sister Eugenia; and a new library of new books, finely bound and gilt, for her papa. But these munificent donations looked forward to no other date than the anticipation of womanhood. If an hint were surmised of her surviving her uncle, an impetuous shower of tears dampt all her gay schemes, deluged every airy castle, and shewed the instinctive gratitude which kindness can awaken, even in the unthinking period of earliest youth, in those bosoms it has ever the power to animate.

Her ensuing birth-day, upon which she would enter her tenth year, was to announce to the adjoining country her uncle's splendid plan in her favour. Her brother and sisters were invited to keep it with her at Cleves; but Sir Hugh declined asking either her father or mother, that his own time, without restraint, might be dedicated to the promotion of her festivity; he even requested of Miss Margland, that she would not appear that day, lest her presence should curb the children's spirits.

The gay little party, consisting of Lavinia, who was two years older, and Eugenia, who was two years younger than Camilla, with her beautiful cousin, who was exactly of her own age, her brother Lionel, who counted three years more, and Edgar Mandlebert, a ward of Mr. Tyrold's, all assembled at Cleves upon this important occasion, at eight o'clock in the morning, to breakfast.

Edgar Mandlebert, an uncommonly spirited and manly boy, now thirteen years of age, was heir to one of the finest estates in the county. He was the only son of a bosom friend of Mr. Tyrold, to whose guardianship he had been consigned almost from his infancy, and who superintended the care of his education with as much zeal, though not as much oeconomy, as that of his own son. He placed him under the tuition of Dr. Marchmont, a man of consummate learning, and he sent for him to Etherington twice in every year, where he assiduously kept up his studies by his own personal instructions. 'I leave him rich, my dear friend,' said his father, when on his death-bed he recommended him to Mr. Tyrold, 'and you, I trust, will make him good, and see him happy; and should hereafter a daughter of your own, from frequent intercourse, become mistress of his affections, do not oppose such a union from a disparity of fortune, which a daughter of yours, and of your incomparable partner's, can hardly fail to counterbalance in merit.' Mr. Tyrold, though too noble to avail himself of a declaration so generous, by forming any plan to bring such a connection to bear, felt conscientiously absolved from using any measures of frustration, and determined, as the young people grew up, neither to promote nor impede any rising regard.

The estate of Beech Park was not all that young Mandlebert inherited; the friendship of its late owner for Mr. Tyrold, seemed instinctively transfused into his breast, and he paid back the parental tenderness with which he was watched and cherished, by a fondness and veneration truly filial.

Whatever could indulge or delight the little set was brought forth upon this joyous meeting; fruits, sweetmeats, and cakes; cards, trinkets, and blind fiddlers, were all at the unlimited command of the fairy mistress of the ceremonies. But unbounded as were the transports of the jovial little group, they could scarcely keep pace with the enjoyment of Sir Hugh; he entered into all their plays, he forgot all his pains, he laughed because they laughed, and suffered his darling little girl to govern and direct him at her pleasure. She made him whiskers of cork, powdered his brown bob, and covered a thread paper with black ribbon to hang to it for a queue. She metamorphosed him into a female, accoutring him with her fine new cap, while she enveloped her own small head in his wig; and then, tying the maid's apron round his waist, put a rattle into his hand, and Eugenia's doll upon his lap, which she told him was a baby that he must nurse and amuse.

The excess of merriment thus excited spread through the whole house. Lionel called in the servants to see this comical sight, and the servants indulged their numerous guests with a peep at it from the windows. Sir Hugh, meanwhile, resolved to object to nothing, performed every part assigned him, joined in their hearty laughs at the grotesque figure they made of him, and cordially encouraged all their proceedings, assuring them he had not been so much diverted himself since his fall from his horse, and advising them, with great zeal, to be merry while they could: 'For you will never, my dears,' said he, 'be younger, never while you live; no more, for that matter, shall I, neither, for all I am so much older, which, in that point, makes no difference.'

He grew weary, however, first; and stretching himself his full length, with a prodigious yawn, 'Heigh ho!' he cried, 'Camilla, my dear, do take away poor Doll, for fear I should let it slip.'

The little gigglers, almost in convulsions of laughter, entreated him to nurse it some time longer; but he frankly answered, 'No, my dears, no; I can play no more now, if I'd ever so fain, for I'm tired to death, which is really a pity; so you must either go out with me my airing, for a rest to your merry little sides, or stay and play by yourselves till I come back, which I think will put you all into fevers; but, however, nobody shall trouble your little souls with advice to-day; there are days enough in the year for teazing, without this one.'

Camilla instantly decided for the airing, and without a dissentient voice: so entirely had the extreme good humour of Sir Hugh won the hearts of the little party, that they felt as if the whole of their entertainment depended upon his presence. The carriage, therefore, was ordered for the baronet and his four nieces, and Lionel and Edgar Mandlebert, at the request of Camilla, were gratified with horses.

Camilla was desired to fix their route, and while she hesitated from the variety in her choice, Lionel proposed to Edgar that they should take a view of his house, park, and gardens, which were only three miles from Cleves. Edgar referred the matter to Indiana, to whose already exquisite beauty his juvenile admiration paid its most early obeisance. Indiana approved; the little heroine of the day assented with pleasure and they immediately set out upon the happy expedition.

The two boys the whole way came with offerings of wild honeysuckle and sweetbriar, the grateful nosegays of all-diffusing nature, to the coach windows, each carefully presenting the most fragrant to Indiana; for Lionel, even more than sympathising with Edgar, declared his sisters to be mere frights in comparison with his fair cousin. Their partiality, however, struggled vainly against that of Sir Hugh, who still, in every the most trivial particular, gave the preference to Camilla.

The baronet had ordered that his own garden chair should follow him to young Mandlebert's park, that he might take Camilla by his side, and go about the grounds without fatigue; the rest were to walk. Here Indiana received again the homage of her two young beaus; they pointed out to her the most beautiful prospects, they gathered her the fairest flowers, they loaded her with the best and ripest fruits.

This was no sooner observed by Sir Hugh, than hastily stopping his chair, he called after them aloud, 'Holloa! come hither, my boys! here, you Mr. young Mandlebert, what are you all about? Why don't you bring that best bunch of grapes to Camilla?'

'I have already promised it to Miss Lynmere, Sir.'

'O ho, have you so? well, give it her then if you have. I have no right to rob you of your choice. Indiana, my dear, how do you like this place?'

'Very much, indeed, uncle; I never saw any place I liked so much in my life.'

'I am sure else,' said Edgar, 'I should never care for it again myself.'

'O, I could look at it for ever,' cried Indiana, 'and not be tired!'

Sir Hugh gravely paused at these speeches, and regarded them in turn with much steadiness, as if settling their future destinies; but ever unable to keep a single thought to himself, he presently burst forth aloud with his new mental arrangement, saying: 'Well, my dears, well; this is not quite the thing I had taken a fancy to in my own private brain, but it's all for the best, there's no doubt; though the estate being just in my neighbourhood, would have made it more suitable for Camilla; I mean provided we could have bought, among us, the odd three miles between the Parks; which how many acres they make, I can't pretend to say, without the proper calculation; but if it was all joined, it would be the finest domain in the county, as far as I know to the contrary: nevertheless, my dear young Mr. Mandlebert, you have a right to choose for yourself; for as to beauty, 'tis mere fancy; not but what Indiana has one or other the prettiest face I ever saw, though I think Camilla's so much prettier; I mean in point of winningness. However, there's no fear as to my consent, for nothing can be a greater pleasure to me than having two such good girls, both being cousins, live so near that they may overlook one another from park to park, all day long, by the mode of a telescope.'

Edgar, perfectly understanding him, blushed deeply, and, forgetting what he had just declared, offered his grapes to Lavinia. Indiana, conceiving herself already mistress of so fine a place, smiled with approving complacency; and the rest were too much occupied with the objects around them, to listen to so long a speech.

They then all moved on; but, soon after, Lionel, flying up to his uncle's chair, informed Camilla he had just heard from the gardener, that only half a mile off, at Northwick, there was a fair, to which he begged she would ask to go. She found no difficulty in obliging him; and Sir Hugh was incapable of hesitating at whatever she could desire. The carriage and the horses for the boys were again ordered, and to the regret of only Edgar and Indiana, the beautiful plantations of Beech Park were relinquished for the fair.

They had hardly proceeded twenty yards, when the smiles that had brightened the face of Lavinia, the eldest daughter of Mr. Tyrold, were suddenly overcast, giving place to a look of dismay, which seemed the effect of some abruptly painful recollection; and the moment Sir Hugh perceived it, and enquired the cause, the tears rolled fast down her cheeks, and she said she had been guilty of a great sin, and could never forgive herself.

They all eagerly endeavoured to console her, Camilla fondly taking her hand, little Eugenia sympathetically crying over and kissing her, Indiana begging to know what was the matter, and Sir Hugh, holding out to her the finest peach from his stores for Camilla, and saying, 'Don't cry so, my dear, don't cry: take a little bit of peach; I dare say you are not so bad as you think for.'

The weeping young penitent besought leave to get out of the coach with Camilla, to whom alone she could explain herself. Camilla almost opened the door herself, to hasten the discovery; and the moment they had run up a bank by the road side, 'Tell me what it is, my dear Lavinia,' she cried, 'and I am sure my uncle will do anything in the world to help you.'

'O Camilla,' she answered, 'I have disobeyed mamma! and I did not mean it in the least—but I have forgot all her commands!—She charged me not to let Eugenia stir out from Cleves, because of the small pox—and she has been already at Beech Park—and now, how can I tell the poor little thing she must not go to the fair?'

'Don't vex yourself about that,' cried Camilla, kindly kissing the tears off her cheeks, 'for I will stay behind, and play with Eugenia myself, if my uncle will drive us back to Beech Park; and then all the rest may go to the fair, and take us up again in the way home.'

With this expedient she flew to the coach, charging the two boys, who with great curiosity had ridden to the bank side, and listened to all that had passed, to comfort Lavinia.

'Lionel,' cried Edgar, 'do you know, while Camilla was speaking so kindly to Lavinia, I thought she looked almost as pretty as your cousin?' Lionel would by no means subscribe to this opinion, but Edgar would not retract.

Camilla, jumping into the carriage, threw her arms around the neck of her uncle, and whispered to him all that had passed. 'Poor innocent little dear!' cried he, 'is that all?' it's just nothing, considering her young age.'

Then, looking out of the window, 'Lavinia,' he said, 'you have done no more harm than what's quite natural; and so I shall tell your mamma; who is a woman of sense, and won't expect such a young head as yours to be of the same age as hers and mine. But come into the coach, my dear; we'll just drive as far as Northwick, for an airing, and then back again.'

The extreme delicacy of the constitution of Eugenia had hitherto deterred Mrs. Tyrold from innoculating her; she had therefore scrupulously kept her from all miscellaneous intercourse in the neighbourhood: but as the weakness of her infancy was now promising to change into health and strength, she meant to give to that terrible disease its best chance, and the only security it allows from perpetual alarm, immediately after the heats of the present autumn should be over.

Lavinia, unused to disobedience, could not be happy in practising it: she entreated, therefore, to return immediately to Cleves. Sir Hugh complied; premising only that they must none of them expect him to be of their play-party again till after dinner.

The coachman then received fresh orders: but, the moment they were communicated to the two boys, Lionel, protesting he would not lose the fair, said he should soon overtake them, and, regardless of all remonstrances, put spurs to his horse, and galloped off.

Sir Hugh, looking after him with great alarm, exclaimed, 'Now he is going to break all his bones! which is always the case with those young boys, when first they get a horseback.'

Camilla, terrified that she had begged this boon, requested that the servant might directly ride after him.

'Yes, my dear, if you wish it,' answered Sir Hugh; 'only we have but this one man for us all, because of the rest staying to get the ball and supper ready; so that if we should be overturned ourselves, here's never a soul to pick us up.'

Edgar offered to ride on alone, and persuade the truant to return.

'Thank you, my dear, thank you,' answered Sir Hugh, 'you are as good a boy as any I know, but, in point of horsemanship, one's as ignorant as t'other, as far as I can tell; so we may only see both your sculls fractured instead of one, in the midst of your galloping; which God forbid for either.'

'Then let us all go together,' cried Indiana, 'and bring him back.'

'But do not let us get out of the coach, uncle,' said Lavinia; 'pray do not let us get out!'

Sir Hugh agreed; though he added, that as to the small pox, he could by no means see it in the same light, for he had no notion of people's taking diseases upon themselves. 'Besides,' continued he, 'she will be sure to have it when her time comes, whether she is moped up or no; and how did people do before these new modes of making themselves sick of their own accord?'

Pitying, however, the uneasiness of Lavinia, when they came near the town, he called to the footman, and said, 'Hark'ee, Jacob, do you ride on first, and keep a sharp look out that nobody has the small pox.'

The fair being held in the suburbs, they soon arrived at some straggling booths, and the coach, at the instance of Lavinia, was stopt.

Indiana now earnestly solicited leave to alight and see the fair; and Edgar offered to be her esquire. Sir Hugh consented, but desired that Lavinia and Camilla might be also of the party. Lavinia tried vainly to excuse herself; he assured her it would raise her spirits, and bid her be under no apprehension, for he would stay and amuse the little Eugenia himself, and take care that she came to no harm.

They were no sooner gone, however, than the little girl cried to follow; Sir Hugh, compassionately kissing her, owned she had as good a right as any of them, and declared it was a hard thing to have her punished for other people's particularities. This concession served only to make her tears flow the faster; till, unable to bear the sight, he said he could not answer to his conscience the vexing such a young thing, and, promising she should have whatever she liked, if she would cry no more, he ordered the coachman to drive to the first booth where there were any toys to be sold.

Here, having no footman to bring the trinkets to the coach, he alighted, and, suffering the little girl, for whom he had not a fear himself, to accompany him, he entered the booth, and told her to take whatever hit her fancy, for she should have as many playthings as she could carry.

Her grief now gave way to ecstasy, and her little hands could soon scarcely sustain the loaded skirt of her white frock. Sir Hugh, determining to make the rest of the children equally happy, was selecting presents for them all, when the little group, ignorant whom they should encounter, advanced towards the same booth: but he had hardly time to exclaim, 'Oho! have you caught us?' when the innocent voice of Eugenia, calling out, 'Little boy; what's the matter with your face, little boy?' drew his attention another way, and he perceived a child apparently just recovering from the small pox.

Edgar, who at the same instant saw the same dreaded sight, darted forward, seized Eugenia in his arms, and, in defiance of her playthings and her struggles, carried her back to the coach; while Lavinia, in an agony of terror, ran up to the little boy, and, crying out, 'O go away! go away!' dragged him out of the booth, and, perfectly unconscious what she did, covered his head with her frock, and held him fast with both her hands.

Sir Hugh, all aghast, hurried out of the booth, but could scarce support himself from emotion; and, while he leaned upon his stick, ejaculating, 'Lord help us! what poor creatures we are, we poor mortals!' Edgar had the presence of mind to make Indiana and Camilla go directly to the carriage. He then prevailed with Sir Hugh to enter it also, and ran back for Lavinia. But when he perceived the situation into which distress and affright had driven her, and saw her sobbing over the child, whom she still held confined, with an idea of hiding him from Eugenia, he was instantly sensible of the danger of her joining her little sister. Extremely perplexed for them all, and afraid, by going from the sick child, he might himself carry the infection to the coach, he sent a man to Sir Hugh to know what was to be done.

Sir Hugh, totally overset by the unexpected accident, and conscience-struck at his own wilful share in risking it, was utterly helpless, and could only answer, that he wished young Mr. Edgar would give him his advice.

Edgar, thus called upon, now first felt the abilities which his short life had not hitherto brought into use: he begged Sir Hugh would return immediately to Cleves, and keep Eugenia there for a few days with Camilla and her cousin; while he undertook to go himself in search of Lionel, with whose assistance he would convey Lavinia back to Etherington, without seeing her little sister; since she must now be as full of contagion as the poor object who had just had the disease.

Sir Hugh, much relieved, sent him word he had no doubt he would become the first scholar of the age; and desired he would get a chaise for himself and Lavinia, and let the footman take charge of his horse.

He then ordered the coach to Cleves.

Edgar fulfilled the injunctions of Sir Hugh with alacrity; but had a very difficult task to find Lionel, and one far more painful to appease Lavinia, whose apprehensions were so great as they advanced towards Etherington, that, to sooth and comfort her, he ordered the postilion to drive first to a farm-house near Cleves, whence he forwarded a boy to Sir Hugh, with entreaties that he would write a few lines to Mrs. Tyrold, in exculpation of her sorrowing daughter.

Sir Hugh complied, but was so little in the habit of writing, that he sent over a messenger to desire they would dine at the farm-house, in order to give him time to compose his epistle.

Early in the afternoon, he conveyed to them the following letter:

To Mrs. Tyrold at the Parsonage House, belonging to the Reverend Rector, Mr. Tyrold, for the Time being, at Etherington in Hampshire.

DEAR SISTER,

I am no remarkable good writer, in comparison with my brother, which you will excuse from my deficiencies, as it is my only apology. I beg you will not be angry with little Lavinia, as she did nothing in the whole business, except wanting to do right, only not mentioning it in the beginning, which is very excusable in the light of a fault; the wisest of us having been youths ourselves once, and the most learned being subject to do wrong, but how much so the ignorant? of which I may speak more properly. However, as she would certainly have caught the small pox herself, except from the lucky circumstance of having had it before, I think it best to keep Eugenia a few days at Cleves, for the sake of her infection. Not but what if she should have it, I trust your sense won't fret about it, as it is only in the course of Nature; which, if she had been innoculated, is more than any man could say; even a physician. So the whole being my own fault, without the least meaning to offend, if any thing comes of it, I hope, my dear sister, you won't take it ill, especially of poor little Lavinia, for 'tis hard if such young things may not be happy at their time of life, before having done harm to a human soul. Poor dears! 'tis soon enough to be unhappy after being wicked; which, God knows, we are all liable to be in the proper season. I beg my love to my brother; and remain,

Dear sister,

Your affectionate brother,

HUGH TYROLD.

P.S. It is but justice to my brother to mention that young Master Mandlebert's behaviour has done the greatest honour to the classics; which must be a great satisfaction to a person having the care of his education.

The rest of the day lost all its delights to the young heiress from this unfortunate adventure. The deprivation of three of the party, with the well-grounded fear of Mrs. Tyrold's just blame, were greater mortifications to those that remained, than even the ball and supper could remove. And Sir

Hugh, to whom their lowered spirits were sufficiently depressing, had an additional, though hardly to himself acknowledged, weight upon his mind, relative to Eugenia and the small pox.

The contrition of the trembling Lavinia could not but obtain from Mrs. Tyrold the pardon it deserved: but she could make no allowance for the extreme want of consideration in Sir Hugh; and anxiously waited the time when she might call back Eugenia from the management of a person whom she considered as more childish than her children themselves.

CHAPTER III

Consequences

Every precaution being taken with regard to Lavinia and her clothes, for warding off infection to Eugenia, if as yet she had escaped it; Mrs. Tyrold fixed a day for fetching her little daughter from Cleves. Sir Hugh, at the earnest entreaty of Camilla, invited the young party to come again early that morning, that some amends might be made them for their recent disappointment of the ball and supper, by a holiday, and a little sport, previous to the arrival of Mrs. Tyrold; to whom he voluntarily pledged his word, that Eugenia should not again be taken abroad, nor suffered to appear before any strangers.

Various gambols were now again enacted by the once more happy group; but all was conducted with as much security as gaiety, till Lionel proposed the amusement of riding upon a plank in the park.

A plank was immediately procured by the gardener, and placed upon the trunk of an old oak, where it parted into two thick branches.

The boys and the three eldest girls balanced one another in turn, with great delight and dexterity; but Sir Hugh feared committing the little Eugenia, for whom he was grown very anxious, amongst them, till the repinings of the child demolished his prudence. The difficulty how to indulge her with safety was, nevertheless, considerable: and, after various experiments, he resolved to trust her to nobody but himself; and, placing her upon his lap, occupied one end of the plank, and desired that as many of the rest as were necessary to make the weight equal, would seat themselves upon the other.

This diversion was short, but its consequences were long. Edgar Mandlebert, who superintended the balance, poised it with great exactness; yet no sooner was Sir Hugh elevated, than, becoming exceedingly giddy, he involuntarily loosened his hold of Eugenia, who fell from his arms to the ground.

In the agitation of his fright, he stooped forward to save her, but lost his equilibrium; and, instead of rescuing, followed her.

The greatest confusion ensued; Edgar, with admirable adroitness, preserved the elder girls from suffering by the accident; and Lionel took care of himself by leaping instantly from the plank: Sir Hugh, extremely bruised, could not get up without pain; but all concern and attention soon centred in the little Eugenia, whose incessant cries raised apprehensions of some more than common mischief.

She was carried to the house in the arms of Edgar, and delivered to the governess. She screamed the whole time she was undressing; and Edgar, convinced she had received some injury, galloped off, unbid, for a surgeon: but what was the horror of Sir Hugh, upon hearing him pronounce, that her left shoulder was put out, and that one of her knees was dislocated!

In an agony of remorse, he shut himself up in his room, without power to issue a command, or listen to a question: nor could he be prevailed upon to open his door, till the arrival of Mrs. Tyrold.

Hastily then rushing out, he hurried to meet her; and, snatching both her hands, and pressing them between his own, he burst into a passionate flood of tears, and sobbed out: 'Hate me, my dear sister, for you can't help it! for I am sorry to tell it you, but I believe I have been the death of poor Eugenia, that never hurt a fly in her life!'

Pale, and struck with dread, yet always possessing her presence of mind, Mrs. Tyrold disengaged herself, and demanded where she might find her? Sir Hugh could make no rational answer; but Edgar, who had run down stairs, purposing to communicate the tidings more gently, briefly stated the misfortune, and conducted her to the poor little sufferer.

Mrs. Tyrold, though nearly overpowered by a sight so affecting, still preserved her faculties for better uses than lamentation. She held the child in her arms while the necessary operations were performing by the surgeon; she put her to bed, and watched by her side the whole night; during which, in defiance of all precautions, a high fever came on, and she grew worse every moment.

The next morning, while still in this alarming state, the unfortunate little innocent exhibited undoubted symptoms of the small pox.

Mr. Tyrold now also established himself at Cleves, to share the parental task of nursing the afflicted child, whose room he never left, except to give consolation to his unhappy brother, who lived wholly in his own apartment, refusing the sight even of Camilla, and calling himself a monster too wicked to look at any thing that was good; though the affectionate little girl, pining at the exclusion, continually presented herself at his door.

The disease bore every prognostic of fatal consequences, and the fond parents soon lost all hope, though they redoubled every attention.

Sir Hugh then gave himself up wholly to despair: he darkened his room, refused all food but bread and water, permitted no one to approach him, and reviled himself invariably with the contrition of a wilful murderer.

In this state of self-punishment he persevered, till the distemper unexpectedly took a sudden and happy turn, and the surgeon made known, that his patient might possibly recover.

The joy of Sir Hugh was now as frantic as his grief had been the moment before: he hastened to his drawing-room, commanded that the whole house should be illuminated; promised a year's wages to all his servants; bid his house-keeper distribute beef and broth throughout the village; and sent directions that the bells of the three nearest parish churches should be rung for a day and a night. But when Mr. Tyrold, to avert the horror of any wholly unprepared disappointment, represented the still precarious state of Eugenia, and the many changes yet to be feared; he desperately reversed all his orders, returned sadly to his dark room, and protested he would never more rejoice, till Mrs. Tyrold herself should come to him with good news.

This anxiously waited æra at length arrived; Eugenia, though seamed and even scarred by the horrible disorder, was declared out of danger; and Mrs. Tyrold, burying her anguish at the alteration, in her joy for the safety of her child, with an heart overflowing from pious gratitude, became the messenger of peace; and, holding out her hand to Sir Hugh, assured him the little Eugenia would soon be well.

Sir Hugh, in an ecstasy which no power could check, forgot every pain and infirmity to hurry up to the apartment of the little girl, that he might kneel, he said, at her feet, and there give thanks for her recovery: but the moment he entered the room, and saw the dreadful havoc grim disease had made on her face; not a trace of her beauty left, no resemblance by which he could have known her; he shrunk back, wrung his hands, called himself the most sinful of all created beings, and in the deepest despondence, sunk into a chair and wept aloud.

Eugenia soon began to cry also, though unconscious for what cause; and Mrs. Tyrold remonstrated to Sir Hugh upon the uselessness of such transports, calmly beseeching him to retire and compose himself.

'Yes, sister,' he answered, 'yes, I'll go away, for I am sure, I do not want to look at her again; but to think of its being all my doing!—O brother! O sister! why don't you both kill me in return? And what amends can I make her? what amends, except a poor little trifle of money?—And as to that, she shall have it, God knows, every penny I am worth, the moment I am gone; ay, that she shall, to a single shilling, if I die tomorrow!'

Starting up with revived courage from this idea, he ventured again to turn his head towards Eugenia, exclaiming: 'O, if she does but get well! does but ease my poor conscience by making me out not to be a murderer, a guinea for every pit in that poor face will I settle on her out of hand; yes, before I so much as breathe again, for fear of dying in the mean time!'

Mrs. Tyrold scarce noticed this declaration; but his brother endeavoured to dissuade him from so sudden and partial a measure: he would not, however, listen; he made what speed he could down stairs, called hastily for his hat and stick, commanded all his servants to attend him, and muttering frequent ejaculations to himself, that he would not trust to changing his mind, he proceeded to the family chapel, and approaching with eager steps to the altar, knelt down, and bidding every one hear and witness what he said, made a solemn vow, 'That if he might be cleared of the crime of murder, by the recovery of Eugenia, he would atone what he could for the ill he had done her, by bequeathing to her every thing he possessed in the world, in estate, cash, and property, without the deduction of a sixpence.'

He told all present to remember and witness this, in case of an apoplexy before his new will could be written down.

Returning then to the house, lightened, he said, from a load of self-reproach, which had rendered the last fortnight insupportable to him, he sent for the attorney of a neighbouring town, and went upstairs, with a firmer mind, to wait his arrival in the sick room.

'O my dear uncle,' cried his long banished Camilla, who hearing him upon the stairs, skipt lightly after him, 'how glad I am to see you again! I almost thought I should see you no more!'

Here ended at once the just acquired tranquility of Sir Hugh; all his satisfaction forsook him at the appearance of his little darling; he considered her as an innocent creature whom he was preparing to injure; he could not bear to look at her; his heart smote him in her favour; his eyes filled with tears; he was unable to go on, and with slow and trembling steps, he moved again towards his own room.

'My dearest uncle!' cried Camilla, holding by his coat, and hanging upon his arm, 'won't you speak to me?'

'Yes, my dear, to be sure I will,' he answered, endeavouring to hide his emotion, 'only not now; so don't follow me Camilla, for I'm going to be remarkably busy!'

'O uncle!' she cried, plaintively, 'and I have not seen you so long! And I have wished so to see you! and I have been so unhappy about Eugenia! and you have always locked your door; and I would not rap hard at it, for fear you should be asleep: But why would you not see me, uncle? and why will you send me away?'

'My dear Camilla,' he replied, with increased agitation, 'I have used you very ill; I have been your worst enemy, which is the very reason I don't care to see you; so go away, I beg, for I am bad enough without all this. But I give you my thanks for all your little playful gambols, having nothing better now to offer you; which is but a poor return from an uncle to a niece!'

He then shut himself into his room, leaving Camilla drowned in tears at the outside of the door.

Wretched in reflecting upon the shock and disappointment which the new disposition of his affairs must occasion her, he had not fortitude to inform her of his intention. He desired to speak with Edgar Mandlebert, who, with all the Tyrold family, resided, for the present, at Cleves, and abruptly related to him the new destination he had just vowed of his wealth; beseeching that he would break it in the softest manner to his poor little favourite, assuring her she would be always the first in his love, though a point of mere conscience had forced him to make choice of another heiress.

Edgar, whose zeal to serve and oblige had never been put to so severe a test, hesitated how to obey this injunction; yet he would not refuse it, as he found that all the servants of the house were enabled, if they pleased, to anticipate more incautiously the ill news. He followed her, therefore, into the garden, whither she had wandered to weep unobserved; but he stopt short at sight of her distress, conceiving his errand to be already known to her, and determined to consult with Indiana, to whom he communicated his terrible embassy, entreating her to devise some consolation for her poor cousin.

Indiana felt too much chagrined at her own part in this transaction, to give her attention to Camilla; she murmured without scruple at the deprivation of what she had once expected for herself, and at another time for her brother; and expressed much resentment at the behaviour of her uncle, mingled with something very near repining, not merely at his late preference of Camilla, but even at the recovery of the little Eugenia. Edgar heard her with surprise, and wondered to find how much less her beauty attracted him from the failure of her good nature.

He now pursued the weeping Camilla, who, dispersing her tears at his approach, pretended to be picking some lavender, and keeping her eyes steadfastly upon the bush, asked him if he would have any? He took a sprig, but spoke to her in a voice of such involuntary compassion, that she soon lost her self-command, and the big drops again rolled fast down her cheeks. Extremely concerned, he strove gently to sooth her; but the expressions of regret at her uncle's avoidance, which then escaped her, soon convinced him his own task was still to be performed. With anxious fear of the consequences of a blow so unlooked for, he executed it with all the speed, yet all the consideration in his power. Camilla, the moment she understood him, passionately clasped her hands, and exclaimed: 'O if that is all! If my uncle indeed loves me as well as before all this; I am sure I can never, never be so wicked, as to envy poor little Eugenia, who has suffered so much, and almost been dying, because she will be richer than I shall be!'

Edgar, delighted and relieved, thought she was grown a thousand times more beautiful than Indiana; and eagerly taking her hand, ran with her to the apartment of the poor disconsolate Sir Hugh; where his own eyes soon overflowed from tenderness and admiration, at the uncommon scene he witnessed, of the generous affection with which Camilla consoled the fond distress of her uncle, though springing from her own disappointment and loss.

They stayed till the arrival of the attorney, who took the directions of Sir Hugh, and drew up, for his immediate satisfaction, a short deed, making over, according to his vow, all he should die possessed of, without any let or qualification whatsoever, to his niece Eugenia. This was properly signed and sealed, and Sir Hugh hastened up stairs with a copy of it to Mr. Tyrold.

All remonstrance was ineffectual; his conscience, he protested, could no other way be appeased; his noble little Camilla had forgiven him her ill usage, and he could now bear to look at the change for the worse in Eugenia, without finding his heart-strings ready to burst at the sight. 'You,' he cried, 'brother, who do not know what it is I have suffered through my conscience, can't tell what it is to get a little ease; for if she had died, you might all have had the comfort to say 'twas I murdered her, which would have given you the satisfaction of having had no hand in it. But then, what would have become of poor me, having it all upon my own head? However, now thank Heaven, I have no need to care about the matter; for as to the mere loss of beauty, pretty as it is to look at, I hope it is no such great injury, as she'll have a splendid fortune, which is certainly a better thing, in point of lasting. For as to beauty, Lord help us! what is it? except just to the eye.'

He then walked up to the child, intending to kiss her, but stopt and sighed involuntarily as he looked at her, saying: 'After all, she's not like the same thing! no more than I am myself. I shall never think I know her again, never as long as I live! I can't so much as believe her to be the same, though I am sure of its being true. However, it shall make no change in my love for her, poor little dear, for it's all my own doing; though innocently enough, as to any meaning, God knows!'

It was still some time before the little girl recovered, and then a new misfortune became daily more palpable, from some latent and incurable mischief, owing to her fall, which made her grow up with one leg shorter than the other, and her whole figure diminutive and deformed: These additional evils reconciled her parents to the partial will of her uncle, which they now, indeed, thought less wanting in equity, since no other reparation could be offered to the innocent sufferer for ills so insurmountable.

CHAPTER IV

Studies of a Grown Gentleman

When the tumult of this affair subsided, Mr. Tyrold and his family prepared to re-establish themselves at Etherington; and Mrs. Tyrold, the great inducement for the separation being over, was earnest to take home again the disinherited Camilla. Sir Hugh, whose pleasure in her sight was how embittered by regret and remorse, had not courage to make the smallest opposition; yet he spent the day of her departure in groans and penitence. He thought it right, however, to detain Eugenia, who, as his decided heiress, was left to be brought up at Cleves.

The loss of the amusing society of his favourite; the disappointment he had inflicted upon her, and the sweetness with which she had borne it, preyed incessantly upon his spirits; and he knew not how to employ himself, which way to direct his thoughts, nor in what manner to beguile one moment of his time, after the children were gone to rest.

The view of the constant resources which his brother found in literature, augmented his melancholy at his own imperfections; and the steady industry with which Mr. Tyrold, in early youth, had attained them, and which, while devoted to field sports, he had often observed with wonder and pity, he now looked back to with self-reproach, and recognised in its effect with a reverence almost awful.

His imagination, neither regulated by wisdom, nor disciplined by experience, having once taken this turn, he soon fancied that every earthly misfortune originated in a carelessness of learning, and that all he wished, and all he wanted, upbraided him with his ignorance. If disease and pain afflicted him, he lamented the juvenile inattention that had robbed him of acquirements which might have taught him not to regard them; if the word scholar was named in his presence, he heaved the deepest sigh; if an article in a newspaper, with which he was unacquainted, was discussed, he reviled his early heedlessness of study; and the mention of a common pamphlet, which was unknown to him, gave him a sensation of disgrace: even inevitable calamities he attributed to the negligence of his education, and construed every error, and every evil of his life, to his youthful disrespect of Greek and Latin.

Such was the state of his mind, when his ordinary maladies had the serious aggravation of a violent fit of the gout.

In the midst of the acute anguish, and useless repentance, which now alternately ravaged his happiness, it suddenly occurred to him, that, perhaps, with proper instruction, he might even yet obtain a sufficient portion of this enviable knowledge, to enable him to pass his evenings with some similarity to his brother.

Revived by this suggestion, he sent for Mr. Tyrold, to communicate to him his idea, and to beg he would put him into a way to recover his lost time, by recommending to him a tutor, with whom he might set about a course of studies:—'Not that I want,' cried he, 'to make any particular great figure as a scholar; but if I could only learn just enough to amuse me at odd hours, and make me forget the gout, it's as much as I desire.'

The total impossibility that such a project should answer its given purpose, deterred not Mr. Tyrold from listening to his request. The mild philosophy of his character saw whatever was lenient to human sufferings as eligible, and looked no further for any obstacles to the wishes of another, than to investigate if their gratification would be compatible with innocence. He wrote, therefore, to a college associate of his younger years, whom he knew to be severely embarrassed in his affairs, and made proposals for settling him in the house of his brother. These were not merely gratefully accepted by his old friend, but drew forth a confession that he was daily menaced with a public arrest for debts, which he had incurred without luxury or extravagance, from mere ignorance of the value of money, and of oeconomy.

In the award of cool reason, to attend to what is impracticable, appears a folly which no inducement can excuse. Mrs. Tyrold treated this scheme with calm, but complete contempt. She allowed no palliation for a measure of which the abortive end was glaring; to hearken to it displeased her, as a false indulgence of childish vanity; and her understanding felt shocked that Mr. Tyrold would deign to humour his brother in an enterprise which must inevitably terminate in a fruitless consumption of time.

Sir Hugh soon, but without anger, saw her disapprobation of his plan; her opinions, from a high superiority to all deceit, were as unreserved as those of the baronet, from a nature incapable of caution. He told her he was sorry to perceive that she thought he should make no proficiency, but entreated her to take notice there was at least no great presumption in his attempt, as he meant to begin with the very beginning, and to go no farther at the first than any young little school-boy; for he should give himself fair play, by trying his hand with the rudiments, which would no sooner be run over, than the rest would become plain sailing: 'And if once,' he added, 'I should conquer the mastery of the classics, I shall make but very short work of all the rest.'

Mr. Tyrold saw, as forcibly as his wife, the utter impossibility that Sir Hugh could now repair the omissions of his youth; but he was willing to console his want of knowledge, and sooth his mortifications; and while he grieved for his bodily infirmities, and pitied his mental repinings, he considered his idea as not illaudable, though injudicious, and in favour of its blamelessness, forgave its absurdity.

He was gratified, also, in offering an honourable provision to a man of learning in distress, whose time and attention could not fail to deserve it, if dedicated to his brother, in whatever way they might be bestowed.

He took care to be at Cleves on the day Dr. Orkborne, this gentleman, was expected, and he presented him to Sir Hugh with every mark of regard, as a companion in whose conversation, he flattered himself, pain might be lightened, and seclusion from mixt company cheerfully supported.

Dr. Orkborne expressed his gratitude for the kindness of Mr. Tyrold, and promised to make it his first study to merit the high consideration with which he had been called from his retirement.

A scholastic education was all that had been given to Dr. Orkborne by his friends; and though in that their hopes were answered, no prosperity followed. His labours had been seconded by industry, but not enforced by talents; and they soon found how wide the difference between acquiring stores, and bringing them into use. Application, operating upon a retentive memory, had enabled him to lay by the most ample hoards of erudition; but these, though they rendered him respectable amongst the learned, proved nearly nugatory in his progress through the world, from a total want of skill and penetration to know how or where they might turn to any account. Nevertheless, his character was unexceptionable, his manners were quiet, and his fortune was ruined. These were the motives which induced rather the benevolence than the selection of Mr. Tyrold to name him to his brother, in the hope that, while an asylum at Cleves would exonerate him from all pecuniary hardships, his very deficiency in brilliancy of parts, and knowledge of mankind, which though differently modified, was equal to that of Sir Hugh himself, would obviate regret of more cultivated society, and facilitate their reciprocal satisfaction.

The introduction over, Mr. Tyrold sought by general topics to forward their acquaintance, before any allusion should be made to the professed plan of Sir Hugh; but Sir Hugh was too well pleased with its ingenuity to be ashamed of its avowal; he began, therefore, immediately to descant upon the indolence of his early years, and to impeach the want of timely severity in his instructors: 'For there is an old saying,' he cried, 'but remarkably true, That learning is better than house or land; which I am an instance of myself, for I have house and land plenty, yet don't know what to do with them properly, nor with myself neither, for want of a little notion of things to guide me by.' His brother, he added, had been too partial in thinking him already fitted for such a master as Dr. Orkborne; though he promised, notwithstanding his time of life, to become the most docile of pupils, and he hoped before long to do no discredit to the Doctor as his tutor.

Mr. Tyrold, whose own benign countenance could scarce refrain from a smile at this unqualified opening, endeavoured to divert to some other subject the grave astonishment of Dr. Orkborne, who, previously aware of the age and ill health of the baronet, naturally concluded himself called upon to solace the privacy of his life by reading or discourse, but suggested not the most distant surmise he could be summoned as a preceptor.

Sir Hugh, however, far from palliating any design, disguised not even a feeling; he plunged deeper and deeper in the acknowledgment of his ignorance, and soon set wholly apart the delicate circumspection of his brother, by demanding of Dr. Orkborne what book he thought he had best buy for a beginning?

Receiving from the wondering Doctor no answer, he good humouredly added, 'Come, don't be ashamed to name the easiest, for this reason; you must know my plan is one of my own, which it is right to tell you. As fast as I get on, I intend, for the sake of remembering my lesson, to send for one of my nephews, and teach it all over again to him myself; which will be doing service to us all at once.'

Mr. Tyrold now, though for a few moments he looked down, thought it best to leave the matter to its own course, and Dr. Orkborne to his own observations; fully persuaded, that the smiles Sir Hugh might excite would be transient, and that no serious or lasting ridicule could be attached to his character, in the mind of a worthy man, to whom time and opportunity would be allowed for an acquaintance with its habitual beneficence. He excused himself, therefore, from staying any longer, somewhat to the distress of Dr. Orkborne, but hardly with the notice of the baronet, whose eagerness in his new pursuit completely engrossed him.

His late adventure, and his new heiress, now tormented him no more; Indiana was forgotten, Camilla but little thought of, and his whole mind became exclusively occupied by this fruitful expedient for retrieving his lost time.

Dr. Orkborne, whose life had been spent in any study rather than that of human nature, was so little able to enter into the character of Sir Hugh, that nothing less than the respect he knew to be due to Mr. Tyrold, could have saved him, upon his first reception, from a suspicion that he had been summoned in mere mockery. The situation, however, was peculiarly desirable to him, and the experiment, in the beginning, corresponded with the hopes of Mr. Tyrold. Placed suddenly in ease and affluence, Dr. Orkborne, with the most profound desire to please, sought to sustain so convenient a post, by obliging the patron, whom he soon saw it would be vain to attempt improving; while Sir Hugh, in return, professed himself the most fortunate of men, that he had now met with a scholar who had the good nature not to despise him.

Relief from care thus combining with opportunity, Dr. Orkborne was scarce settled, ere he determined upon the execution of a long, critical, and difficult work in philology, which he had often had in contemplation, but never found leisure to undertake. By this means he had a constant resource for himself; and the baronet, observing that time never hung heavy upon his hands, conceived a yet higher admiration of learning, and felt his spirits proportionably re-animated by the fair prospect of participating in such advantages.

From this dream, however, he was soon awakened; a parcel, by the direction of Dr. Orkborne, arrived from his bookseller, with materials for going to work.

Sir Hugh then sent off a message to the parsonage-house, informing his brother and his family, that they must not be surprised if they did not see or hear of him for some time, as he had got his hands quite full, and should be particularly engaged for a week or two to come.

Dr. Orkborne, still but imperfectly conceiving the extent, either of the plan, or of the simplicity of his new pupil, proposed, as soon as the packet was opened, that they should read together; but Sir Hugh replied, that he would do the whole in order, and by no means skip the rudiments.

The disappointment which followed, may be easily imagined; with neither quickness to learn, nor memory to retain, he aimed at being initiated in the elements of a dead language, for which youth only can find time and application, and even youth but by compulsion. His head soon became confused, his ideas were all perplexed, his attention was vainly strained, and his faculties were totally disordered.

Astonished at his own disturbance, which he attributed solely to not getting yet into the right mode, he laughed off his chagrin, but was steady in his perseverance; and continued wholly shut up from his family and friends, with a zeal worthy better success.

Lesson after lesson, however, only aggravated his difficulties, till his intellects grew so embarrassed he scarce knew if he slept or waked. His nights became infected by the perturbation of the day; his health visibly suffered from the restlessness of both, and all his flattering hopes of new and unknown happiness were ere long exchanged for despair.

He now sent for his brother, and desired to speak with him alone; when, catching him fast by the hand, and looking piteously in his face, 'Do you know, my dear brother,' he cried, 'I find myself turning out as sheer a blockhead as ever, for all I have got so many more years over my head than when I began all this hard jingle jangle before?'

Mr. Tyrold, with greater concern than surprise, endeavoured to re-assure and console him, by pointing out a road more attainable for reaping benefit from the presence of Dr. Orkborne, than the impracticable path into which he had erroneously entered.

'Ah! no, my dear brother,' he answered; 'if I don't succeed this way, I am sure I shall succeed no other; for as to pains, I could not have taken more if I had been afraid to be flogged once a-day: and that gentleman has done all he can, too, as far as I know to the contrary. But I really think whatever's the meaning of it, there's some people can't learn.'

Then, shaking his head, he added, in a low voice: 'To say the truth, I might as well have given it up from the very first, for any great comfort I found in it, if it had not been for fear of hurting that gentleman; however, don't let the poor gentleman know that; for I've no right to turn him off upon nothing, merely for the fault of my having no head, which how can he help?'

Mr. Tyrold agreed in the justice of this reflection, and undertook to deliberate upon some conciliatory expedient.

Sir Hugh heartily thanked him; 'But only in the mean time that you are thinking,' cried he, 'how shall I bring it about to stop him from coming to me with all those books for my study? For, do you know, my dear brother, because I asked him to buy me one for my beginning, he sent for a full score? And when he comes to me about my lesson, he brings them all upon me together: which is one thing, for ought I know, that helps to confuse me; for I am wondering all the while when I shall get through with them. However, say nothing of all this before the poor gentleman, for fear he should take it as a hint; which might put him out of heart: for which reason I'd rather take another lesson, Lord help me!—than vex him.'

Mr. Tyrold promised his best consideration, and to see him again the next morning. But he had hardly left Cleves ten minutes, when a man and horse came galloping after him, with a petition that he would return without delay.

The baronet received him with a countenance renovated with self-complacency. 'I won't trouble you,' he cried, 'to think any more; for now I have got a plan of my own, which I will tell you. Not to throw this good gentleman entirely away, I intend having a sort of a kind of school set up here in my sick room, and so to let all my nephews come, and say their tasks to him in my hearing; and then, who knows but I may pick up a little amongst them myself, without all this hard study?'

Mr. Tyrold stated the obvious objections to so wild a scheme; but he besought him not to oppose it, as there was no other way for him to get rid of his tutoring, without sending off Dr. Orkborne. He desired, therefore, that Lionel might come instantly to Cleves; saying, 'I shall write myself to Eton, by the means of the Doctor, to tell the Master I shall take Clermont entirely home after the next holidays, for the sake of having him study under my own eye.'

He then entreated him to prepare Dr. Orkborne for his new avocation.

Mr. Tyrold, who saw that in this plan the inventor alone could be disappointed, made no further remonstrance, and communicated the design to Dr. Orkborne; who, growing now deeply engaged in his own undertaking, was perfectly indifferent to whom or to what his occasional attendance might be given.

CHAPTER V

Schooling of a Young Gentleman

Mrs. Tyrold expressed much astonishment that her husband could afford any countenance to this new plan. 'Your expectations from it,' she cried, 'can be no higher than my own; you have certainly some influence with your brother; why, then, will you suffer him thus egregiously to expose himself?'

'I cannot protect his pride,' answered Mr. Tyrold, 'at the expence of his comfort. His faculties want some object, his thoughts some employment. Inaction bodily and intellectual pervading the same character, cannot but fix disgust upon every stage and every state of life. Vice alone is worse than such double inertion. Where mental vigour can be kept alive without offence to religion and virtue, innocence as well as happiness is promoted; and the starter of difficulties with regard to the means which point to such an end, inadvertently risks both. To save the mind from preying inwardly upon itself, it must be encouraged to some outward pursuit. There is no other way to elude apathy, or escape discontent; none other to guard the temper from that quarrel with itself, which ultimately ends in quarrelling with all mankind.'

'But may you not, by refusing to send him your son, induce him to seek recreation in some more rational way?'

'Recreation, my dear Georgiana, must be spontaneous. Bidden pleasures fly the perversity of our tastes. Let us take care, then, scrupulously, of our duties, but suffer our amusements to take care of themselves. A project, a pastime, such as this, is, at least, as harmless as it is hopeless, since the utmost sport of wit, or acrimony of malice, can only fasten a laugh upon it: and how few are the diversions of the rich and indolent that can so lightly be acquitted!'

Lionel, the new young student, speedily, though but little to her satisfaction, abetted the judgment of his mother. He was no sooner summoned to Cleves, than, enchanted to find himself a fellow-pupil with his uncle, he conceived the highest ideas of his own premature genius: and when this vanity, from the avowed ignorance of the artless baronet, subsided, it was only replaced by a sovereign contempt of his new associate. He made the most pompous display of his own little acquirements; he took every opportunity to ask questions of Sir Hugh which he knew he could not answer; and he would sometimes, with an arch mock solemnity, carry his exercise to him, and beg his assistance.

Sir Hugh bore this juvenile impertinence with unshaken good humour. But the spirits of Lionel were too mutinous for such lenity: he grew bolder in his attacks, and more fearless of consequences; and in a very short time, his uncle seemed to him little more than the butt at which he might level the shafts of his rising triumph; till tired, at length, though not angry, the baronet applied to Dr. Orkborne, and begged he would teach him, out of hand, some small little smattering of Latin sentences, by which he might make the young pedant think better of him.

Dr. Orkborne complied, and wrote him a few brief exercises; but these, after toiling day and night to learn, he pronounced so ill, and so constantly mis-applied, that, far from impressing his fellow-labourer with more respect, the moment he uttered a single word of his new lesson, the boy almost rolled upon the floor with convulsive merriment.

Sir Hugh, with whom these phrases neither lost nor gained by mistaking one word for another, appealed to Dr. Orkborne to remedy what he conceived to be an unaccountable failure. Dr. Orkborne, absorbed in his new personal pursuit, to which he daily grew more devoted, was earnest to be as little as possible interrupted, and therefore only advised him to study his last lesson, before he pressed for any thing new.

Study, however, was unavailing, and he heard this injunction with despair; but finding it constantly repeated upon every application for help, he was seized again with a horror of the whole attempt, and begged to consult with Mr. Tyrold.

'This gentleman you have recommended to me for my tutor,' he cried, 'is certainly a great scholar; I don't mean to doubt that the least in the world, being no judge: and he is complaisant enough too, considering all that; but yet I have rather a suspicion he is afraid I shall make no hand of it; which is a thing so disheartening to a person in the line of improvement, that, to tell you the honest truth, I am thinking of giving the whole up at a blow; for, Lord help me! what shall I be the better for knowing Latin and Greek? It's not worth a man's while to think of it, after being a boy. And so, if you please, I'd rather you'd take Lionel home again.'

Mr. Tyrold agreed; but asked what he meant to do further concerning the Doctor?

'Why that, brother, is the very thing my poor ignorant head wants your advice for: because, as to that plan about our learning all together, I see it won't do; for either the boys will grow up to be no better scholars than their uncle, which is to say, none at all; or else they'll hold everybody cheap, when they meet with a person knowing nothing; so I'll have no more hand in it. And I shall really be glad enough to get such a thing off my mind; for it's been weight enough upon it from the beginning.'

He then desired the opinion of Mr. Tyrold what step he should take to prevent the arrival of Clermont Lynmere, whom, he said, he dreaded to see, being determined to have no more little boys about him for some time to come.

Mr. Tyrold recommended re-settling him at Eton: but Sir Hugh declared he could not possibly do that, because the poor little fellow had written him word he was glad to leave school. 'And I don't doubt,' he added, 'but he'll make the best figure of us all; because I had him put in the right mode from the first; though, I must needs own, I had as lieve see him a mere dunce all his life, supposing I should live so long, which God forbid in regard to his dying, as have him turn out a mere coxcomb of a pedant, laughing and grinning at everybody that can't spell a Greek noun.'

Mr. Tyrold promised to take the matter into consideration; but early the next morning, the baronet again summoned him, and joyfully made known, that a scheme had come into his own head, which answered all purposes. In the first place, he said, he had really taken so prodigious a dislike to learning, that he was determined to send Clermont over the seas, to finish his Greek and Latin; not because he was fond of foreign parts, but for fear, if he should let him come to Cleves, the great distaste he had now conceived against those sort of languages, might disgust the poor boy from his book. And he had most luckily recollected, in the middle of the night, that he had a dear friend, one Mr. Westwyn, who was going the very next month to carry his own son to Leipsic; which was just what had put the thought into his head; because, by that means, Clermont might be removed from one studying place to t'other, without loss of time.

'But for all that,' he continued, 'as this good gentleman here has been doing no harm, I won't have him become a sufferer for my changing my mind: and so, not to affront him by giving him nothing to do, which would be like saying, "You may go your ways," I intend he should try Indiana.'

Observing Mr. Tyrold now look with the extremest surprise, he added; 'To be sure, being a girl, it is rather out of the way; but as there is never another boy, what can I do? Besides I shan't so much mind her getting a little learning, because she's not likely to make much hand of it. And this one thing, I can tell you, which I have learnt of my own accord; I'll never press a person to set about studying at my time of life as long as I live, knowing what a plague it is.'

Lionel returned to Etherington with his father, and the rest of the scheme was put into execution without delay. Mr. Westwyn conveyed Clermont from Eton to Leipsic, where he settled him with the preceptor and masters appointed for his own son; and Dr. Orkborne was desired to become the tutor of Indiana.

At first, quitting his learned residence, the Doctor might indignantly have blushed at the proposition of an employment so much beneath his abilities: but he now heard it without the smallest emotion; sedately revolving in his mind, that his literary work would not be affected by the ignorance or absurdity of his several pupils.

CHAPTER VI

Tuition of a Young Lady

The fair Indiana participated not in the philosophy of her preceptor. The first mention of taking lessons produced an aversion unconquerable to their teacher; and the first question he asked her at the appointed hour for study, was answered by a burst of tears.

To Dr. Orkborne this sorrow would have proved no impediment to their proceeding, as he hardly noticed it; but Sir Hugh, extremely affected, kindly kissed her, and said he would beg her off for this time. The next day, however, gave rise but to a similar scene; and the next which followed would precisely have resembled it, had not the promise of some new finery of attire dispersed the pearly drops that were preparing to fall.

The uncommon beauty of Indiana had made her infancy adored, and her childhood indulged by almost all who had seen her. The brilliant picture she presented to the eye by her smiles and her spirits, rendered the devastation caused by crying, pouting, or fretfulness so striking, and so painful to behold, that not alone her uncle, but every servant in the house, and every stranger who visited it, granted to her lamentations whatever they demanded, to relieve their own impatience at the loss of so pleasing an image. Accustomed, therefore, never to weep without advantage, she was in the constant habit of giving unbridled vent to her tears upon the smallest contradiction, well knowing that not to spoil her pretty eyes by crying, was the current maxim of the whole house.

Unused, by this means, to any trouble or application, the purposed tuition of Dr. Orkborne appeared a burden to her intolerable; yet weeping, her standing resource, was with him utterly vain; her tears were unimportant to one who had taken no notice of her smiles; and intent upon his own learned ruminations, he never even looked at her.

Bribery, day after day, could procure but a few instants' attention, given so unwillingly, and so speedily withdrawn, that trinkets, dress, and excursions were soon exhausted, without the smallest advancement. The general indulgence of the baronet made partial favours of small efficacy; and Indiana was sooner tired of receiving, than he of presenting his offerings.

She applied, therefore, at length, to the governess, whose expostulations, she knew by experience, were precisely what Sir Hugh most sedulously aimed to avoid.

Miss Margland was a woman of family and fashion, but reduced, through the gaming and extravagance of her father, to such indigence, that, after sundry failures in higher attempts, she was compelled to acquiesce in the good offices of her friends, which placed her as a governess in the house of Sir Hugh.

To Indiana, however, she was but nominally a tutress; neglected in her own education, there was nothing she could teach, though, born and bred in the circle of fashion, she imagined she had nothing to learn. And, while a mind proudly shallow kept her unacquainted with her own deficiencies, her former rank in society imposed an equal ignorance of them upon Sir Hugh. But, notwithstanding he implicitly gave her credit for possessing whatever she assumed, he found her of a temper so unpleasant, and so irritable to offence, that he made it a rule never to differ from her. The irksomeness of this restraint induced him to keep as much as possible out of her way; though respect and pity for her birth and her misfortunes, led him to resolve never to part with her till Indiana was married.

The spirit of Miss Margland was as haughty as her intellects were weak; and her disposition was so querulous, that, in her constant suspicion of humiliation, she seemed always looking for an affront, and ready primed for a contest.

She seized with pleasure the opportunity offered her by Indiana, of remonstrating against this new system of education; readily allowing, that any accomplishment beyond what she had herself acquired, would be completely a work of supererogation. She represented dictatorily her objections to the baronet. Miss Lynmere, she said, though both beautiful and well brought up, could never cope with so great a disadvantage as the knowledge of Latin: 'Consider, Sir,' she cried, 'what an obstacle it will prove to her making her way in the great world, when she comes to be of a proper age for thinking of an establishment. What gentleman will you ever find that will bear with a learned wife? except some mere downright fogrum, no young lady of fashion could endure.'

She then spoke of the danger of injuring her beauty by study; and ran over all the qualifications really necessary for a young lady to attain, which consisted simply of an enumeration of all she had herself attempted; a little music, a little drawing, and a little dancing; which should all, she added, be but slightly pursued, to distinguish a lady of fashion from an artist.

Sir Hugh, a good deal disturbed, because unable to answer her, thought it would be best to interest Dr. Orkborne in his plan, and to beg him to reconcile her to its execution. He sent, therefore, a message to the Doctor, to beg to speak with him immediately.

Dr. Orkborne promised to wait upon him without delay: but he was at that moment hunting for a passage in a Greek author, and presently forgot both the promise and the request.

Sir Hugh, concluding nothing but sickness could detain him, went to his apartment; where, finding him perfectly well, he stared at him a moment; and then, sitting down, begged him to make no apology, for he could tell his business there as well as any where else.

He gave a long and copious relation of the objections of Miss Margland, earnestly begging Dr. Orkborne would save him from such another harangue, it being bad for his health, by undertaking to give her the proper notion of things himself.

The Doctor, who had just found the passage for which he had been seeking, heard not one word that he said.

Sir Hugh, receiving no answer, imagined him to be weighing the substance of his narration; and, therefore, bidding him not worry his brain too much, offered him half an hour to fix upon what should be done; and returned quietly to his own room.

Here he sat, counting the minutes, with his watch in his hand, till the time stipulated arrived: but finding Dr. Orkborne let it pass without any notice, he again took the trouble of going back to his apartment.

He then eagerly asked what plan he had formed?

Dr. Orkborne, much incommoded by this second interruption, coldly begged to know his pleasure.

Sir Hugh, with great patience, though much surprise, repeated the whole, word for word, over again: but the history was far too long for Dr. Orkborne, whose attention, after the first sentence or two, was completely restored to his Greek quotation, which he was in the act of transcribing when Sir Hugh re-entered the room.

The baronet, at length, more categorically said, 'Don't be so shy of speaking out, Doctor; though I am afraid, by your silence, you've rather a notion poor Indiana will never get on; which, perhaps, makes you think it not worth while contradicting Mrs. Margland? Come, speak out!—Is that the case with the poor girl?'

'Yes, sir,' answered Dr. Orkborne, with great composure; though perfectly unconscious of the proposition to which he assented.

'Lack a-day! if I was not always afraid she had rather a turn to being a dunce! So it's your opinion it won't do, then?'

'Yes, sir,' again replied the Doctor; his eye the whole time fastened upon the passage which occupied his thoughts.

'Why then we are all at a stand again! This is worse than I thought for! So the poor dear girl has really no head?—Hay, Doctor?—Do speak, pray?—Don't mind vexing me. Say so at once, if you can't help thinking it.'

Another extorted, 'Yes, sir,' completely overset Sir Hugh; who, imputing the absent and perplexed air with which it was pronounced to an unwillingness to give pain, shook him by the hand, and, quitting the room, ordered his carriage, and set off for Etherington.

'Oh, brother,' he cried; 'Indiana's the best girl in the world, as well as the prettiest; but, do you know, Dr. Orkborne says she has got no brains! So there's an end of that scheme! However, I have now thought of another that will settle all differences.'

Mr. Tyrold hoped it was an entire discontinuance of all pupilage and tutorship; and that Dr. Orkborne might henceforth be considered as a mere family friend.

'No, no, my dear brother, no! 'tis a better thing than that, as you shall hear. You must know I have often been concerned to think how glum poor Clermont will look when he hears of my will in favour of Eugenia; which was my chief reason in my own private mind, for not caring to see him before he went abroad; but I have made myself quite easy about him now, by resolving to set little Eugenia upon learning the classics.'

'Eugenia! and of what benefit will that prove to Clermont?'

'Why, as soon as she grows a little old, that is to say, a young woman, I intend, with your good will and my sister's, to marry her to Clermont.'

Mr. Tyrold smiled, but declared his entire concurrence, if the young people, when they grew up, wished for the alliance.

'As to that,' said he, 'I mean to make sure work, by having them educated exactly to fit one another. I shall order Clermont to think of nothing but his studies till the proper time; and as to Eugenia, I shall make her a wife after his own heart, by the help of this gentleman; for I intend to bid him teach her just like a man, which, as she's so young, may be done from the beginning, the same as if she was a boy.'

He then enumerated the advantages of this project, which would save Clermont from all disappointment, by still making over to him his whole fortune, with a wife ready formed into a complete scholar for him into the bargain. It would also hinder Eugenia from being a prey to some sop for her money, who, being no relation, could not have so good a right to it; and it would prevent any affront to Dr. Orkborne, by keeping him a constant tight task in hand.

Mr. Tyrold forbore to chagrin him with any strong expostulation, and he returned, therefore, to Cleves in full glee. He repaired immediately to the apartment of the Doctor, who, only by what was now said, was apprized of what had passed before. Somewhat, therefore, alarmed, to understand that the studies of Indiana were to be relinquished, he exerted all the alacrity in his power for accepting his new little pupil: not from any idea of preference; for he concluded that incapacity of Indiana to be rather that of her sex than of an individual; but from conceiving that his commodious abode at Cleves depended upon his retaining one scholar in the family. Eugenia therefore was called, and the lessons were begun.

The little girl, who was naturally of a thoughtful turn, and whose state of health deprived her of most childish amusements, was well contented with the arrangement, and soon made a progress so satisfactory to Dr. Orkborne, that Sir Hugh, letting his mind now rest from all other schemes, became fully and happily occupied by the prosecution of his last suggestion.

CHAPTER VII

Lost Labour

From this period, the families of Etherington and Cleves lived in the enjoyment of uninterrupted harmony and repose, till Eugenia, the most juvenile of the set, had attained her fifteenth year.

Sir Hugh then wrote to Leipsic, desiring his nephew Lynmere to return home without delay. 'Not that I intend,' he said to Mr. Tyrold, 'marrying them together at this young age, Eugenia being but a child, except in point of Latin; though I assure you, my dear brother, she's the most sensible of the whole, poor Indiana being nothing to her, for all her prettiness; but the thing is, the sooner Clermont comes over, the sooner they may begin forming the proper regard.'

The knowledge of this projected alliance was by no means confined to Sir Hugh and Mr. and Mrs. Tyrold; it was known throughout the family, though never publicly announced, and understood from her childhood by Eugenia herself, though Mrs. Tyrold had exerted her utmost authority to prevent Sir Hugh from apprizing her of it in form. It was nevertheless, the joy of his heart to prepare the young people for each other: and his scheme received every encouragement he could desire, from the zeal and uncommon progress in her studies made by Eugenia; which most happily corresponded with all his injunctions to Leipsic, for the application and acquirements of Clermont.

Thus circumstanced, it was a blow to him the most unexpected, to receive from the young bridegroom elect, in answer to his summons home, a petition to make the tour of Europe, while yet on the continent.

'What!' cried Sir Hugh, 'and is this all his care for us? after so many years separation from his kin and kind, has he no natural longings to see his native land? no yearnings to know his own relations from strangers?'

Eugenia, notwithstanding her extreme youth, secretly applauded and admired a search of knowledge she would gladly have participated in; though she was not incurious to see the youth she considered as her destined partner for life, and to whom all her literary labours had been directed:

for the never-failing method of Sir Hugh to stimulate her if she was idle, had been to assure her that, unless she worked harder, her cousin Clermont would eclipse her.

She had now acquired a decided taste for study, which, however unusual for her age, most fortunately rescued from weariness or sadness the sedentary life, which a weak state of health compelled her to lead. This induced her to look with pleasure upon Clermont as the object of her emulation, and to prosecute every plan for her improvement, with that vigour which accompanies a pursuit of our own choice; the only labour that asks no relaxation.

Steady occupations, such as these, kept off all attention to her personal misfortunes, which Sir Hugh had strictly ordered should never be alluded to; first, he said, for fear they should vex her; and next, lest they should make her hate him, for being their cause. Those incidents, therefore, from never being named, glided imperceptibly from her thoughts; and she grew up as unconscious as she was innocent, that, though born with a beauty which surpassed that of her lovely sisters, disease and accident had robbed her of that charm ere she knew she possessed it. But neither disease nor accident had power over her mind; there, in its purest proportions, moral beauty preserved its first energy. The equanimity of her temper made her seem, though a female, born to be a practical philosopher; her abilities and her sentiments were each of the highest class, uniting the best adorned intellects with the best principled virtues.

The dissatisfaction of Sir Hugh with his nephew reached not to prohibition: his consent was painful, but his remittances were generous, and Clermont had three years allowed him for his travels through Europe.

Yet this permission was no sooner granted than the baronet again became dejected. Three years appeared to him to be endless: he could hardly persuade himself to look forward to them with expectation of life; and all the learned labours he had promoted seemed vain and unpromising, ill requiting his toils, and still less answering his hopes. Even the studious turn of Eugenia, hitherto his first delight, he now thought served but to render her unsociable; and the time she devoted to study, he began to regret as lost to himself; nor could he suggest any possible consolation for his drooping spirits, till it occurred to him that Camilla might again enliven him.

This idea, and the order for his carriage, were the birth of the same moment; and, upon entering the study of Mr. Tyrold, he abruptly exclaimed, 'My dear brother, I must have Camilla back! Indiana says nothing to amuse me; and Eugenia is so bookish, I might as well live with an old woman; which God forbid I should object to, only I like Camilla better.'

This request was by no means welcome to Mr. Tyrold, and utterly distasteful to his lady. Camilla was now just seventeen years of age, and attractively lovely; but of a character that called for more attention to its developement than to its formation; though of a disposition so engaging, that affection kept pace with watchfulness, and her fond parents knew as little for their own sakes as for her's how to part with her.

Her qualities had a power which, without consciousness how, or consideration why, governed her whole family. The airy thoughtlessness of her nature was a source of perpetual amusement; and, if sometimes her vivacity raised a fear for her discretion, the innocence of her mind reassured them after every alarm. The interest which she excited served to render her the first object of the house; it was just short of solicitude, yet kept it constantly alive. Her spirits were volatile, but her heart was tender; her gaiety had a fascination; her persuasion was irresistible.

To give her now up to Sir Hugh, seemed to Mrs. Tyrold rather impossible than disagreeable; but he was too urgent with his brother to be wholly refused. She was granted him, therefore, as a guest, for the three ensuing months, to aid him to dissipate his immediate disappointment, from the procrastinated absence of Clermont.

Sir Hugh received back his first favourite with all the fond glee of a ductile imagination, which in every new good sees a refuge from every past or present evil. But, as the extremest distaste of all literature now succeeded those sanguine views which had lately made it his exclusive object, the first words he spoke upon her arrival were, to inform her she must learn no Latin; and the first step which followed her welcome, was a solemn charge to Dr. Orkborne, that he must give her no lessons.

The gaiety, the spirit, the playful good humour of Camilla, had lost nothing of their charm by added years, though her understanding had been sedulously cultivated, and her principles modelled by the pure and practical tenets of her exemplary parents. The delight of Sir Hugh in regaining her, consisted not merely of the renovation of his first prejudice in her favour; it was strengthened by the restoration it afforded his own mind to its natural state, and the relief of being disburthened of a task he was so ill calculated to undertake, as superintending, in any sort, intellectual pursuits.

BOOK II

CHAPTER I

New Projects

The baronet would, at length, have enjoyed perfect contentment, had he not been molested by the teasing spirit of Miss Margland, now daily at work in proposing a journey to London, and in representing as an indispensable duty, that the young ladies should see and be seen, in a manner suitable to their situation in life.

Miss Margland, equally void either of taste or of resources for the country, had languished and fretted away twelve years in its bosom, with no other opening to any satisfaction beyond a maintenance, except what she secretly nourished in her hopes, that, when her beautiful pupil was grown up, she should accompany her to the metropolis. Her former connections and acquaintance in high life still continued to be the stationary pride of her heart, the constant theme of her discourse, and the perpetual allusion of some lamentation and regret. This excursion, therefore, in prospect, had been her sole support during her retirement; nor had she failed to instruct her fair disciple to aid her scheme, though she had kept from her its private motive.

Most successfully, indeed, had she instilled into the youthful breast of Indiana, a wondering curiosity to see the place which she described as the sole residence of elegance and fashion, and an eager impatience to exhibit there a person which she was assured would meet with universal homage.

But neither the exhortations of the governess, nor the wishes of her pupil, could in this point move Sir Hugh. He had a fixt aversion to London, and to all public places, and had constantly some disaster to relate of every visit he had accidentally made to them. The amusements which had decided his partiality for the country were now, indeed, no longer within his reach; but his sanguine temper, which occasionally entertained him with hopes of a recovery, determined him always to keep upon the right spot, he said, for sport, in the case of any sudden and favourable change in his health.

Upon the visit of Camilla, Miss Margland grew yet more urgent, expecting through her powerful influence to gain her point. She strove, therefore, to engage her intercession, but Camilla, careless, easy, and gay, had no wish about the matter, and could not be brought into the cabal.

This disappointment so much soured and provoked Miss Margland, that she lost the usual discretion she had hitherto practised, of confining her remonstrances to those times when she saw Sir Hugh alone. Such opportunities, indeed, weary of the use she made of them, the baronet contrived daily to lessen; but every meeting now, whether public or private, was seized alike for the same purpose, and the necessity of bringing the young ladies out, and the duty of thinking of their establishment, were the sentences with which he was so regularly assailed, that the moment he saw her he prepared to hear them, and commonly with a heavy sigh anticipated their fatigue to his spirits.

No arguments, however, relative to disposing of the young ladies, had any weight with him; he had long planned to give Eugenia to Clermont Lynmere, and he depended upon Edgar Mandlebert for Indiana, while with regard to Camilla, to keep her unmarried, that he might detain her under his own roof, was the favourite wish of his heart. Nevertheless, this perpetual persecution became by degrees insupportable, and, unused to be deaf to any claimant, he was upon the point of constrained compliance, when his passion for forming schemes came again to his aid, upon hearing that Edgar Mandlebert, after a twelvemonth's absence, was just returned to Etherington.

This youth had been making the tour of England, Wales, and Scotland, with Dr. Marchmont, who had been induced by Mr. Tyrold to relinquish all other avocations, and devote to him his whole time.

Sir Hugh hastening, upon this news, to the parsonage-house, said: 'Don't imagine, brother, I am going to make any complaint against Mrs. Margland, for she is an excellent governess, and I have no fault to find with her, except her making too many objections, which I take to be her worst part; but as every body has something, it would be very unfair to quarrel with her for such a mere nothing, especially as she can't help it, after so many years going on the same way, without coming to a stop; but the thing I have thought of now may set it all to rights, which I hope you'll approve, and especially my sister.'

He then explained, that as he had fixt upon marrying Eugenia to Clermont Lynmere, she was put so completely under the care of Dr. Orkborne, in order to make her fit for the young scholar, that Miss Margland was of little or no use to her. He meant, therefore, to bring forward immediately the marriage of Indiana with young Mandlebert, and then to ask Miss Margland to go and live with them entirely, as he could very well spare her: 'This,' he continued, 'Indiana can't object to, from the point of having had her so long; and young Mr. Edgar's remarkably complaisant, for such a young youth, which I saw a great while ago. By this means, Mrs. Margland will get her main end of going to London, which she may show off to the young bride, without my budging from home, Lord help me! being a thing I don't much like, to be taken about to dances and shews, now that I am not a boy; so then Camilla will be left to stay with me, for my own companion; which I assure you I desire no better, though she knows no more, as the Doctor tells me, of the classics, than my old spaniel; which, to give every one his due, is much the same with myself.'

Mr. Tyrold, with a very unpleasant astonishment, enquired further into his meaning concerning Mandlebert; but his surprise ended in a smile, when he heard the juvenile circumstances upon which alone Sir Hugh built his expectations. To argue with him, however, was always fruitless; he had found out, he said, the intentions of Edgar from the first, and he came now to invite him to pass a month at Cleves, for the sake of cutting the courtship short, by letting him see Indiana every day, so that no time might be lost in coming to the conclusion.

The first wish of the secret heart of Mr. Tyrold was, that one of his own daughters should be the choice of his ward; he did not, therefore, totally unmoved, hear this project for Indiana, though its basis was so little alarming.

Edgar, who was now just of age, was receiving the last cares of his guardian, and taking into his own hands his fortune and affairs. He was at Etherington, at present, only for that purpose, Beech Park being already fitted up for his residence.

Sir Hugh, desiring to speak with him, most cordially made his invitation: 'Besides myself,' he cried, 'whom I only mention first, as being master of the house, which I hope is my excuse for it, you will meet three very good young girls, not to mention Dr. Orkborne and Miss Margland, who are rather not of the youngest at present, whatever they may have been in former times; and they will all, myself included, make you as welcome as themselves.'

Edgar accepted the proposal with pleasure, and agreed to wait upon him the next day, Mr. Tyrold consenting that they should transact their mutual business at Etherington, by morning rides.

At dinner Sir Hugh told the family at Cleves the new guest they were so soon to expect, assuring them he was become a very fine young gentleman, and bidding Indiana, with a significant nod, hold up her head.

Indiana wanted no charge upon this subject; she fully understood the views of her uncle, and it was now some years since she had heard the name of Beech Park without a smile or a blush.

Upon the arrival of the young man, Sir Hugh summoned his household to meet him in the hall, where he received him with an hearty welcome, and, in the flutter of his spirits, introduced him to them all, as if this had been his first appearance in the family; remarking, that a full week of shyness might be saved, by making acquaintance with the whole set in a clump.

From eagerness irrepressible, he began with Indiana, apologising when he had done, by saying it was only because she was oldest, having the advantage of three weeks over Camilla: 'For which, however,' he added, 'I must beg pardon of Mrs. Margland and Dr. Orkborne, who, to be sure, must be pretty much older.'

He next presented him to Camilla; and then, taking him apart, begged, in a whisper, that he would not seem to notice the ugliness of Eugenia, which, he said, was never mentioned in her hearing, by his particular order; 'though, to be sure,' he added, 'since that small-pox, she's grown plain enough, in point of beauty, considering how pretty she was before. However, she's a remarkable good girl, and with regard to Virgil and those others will pose you in a second, for aught I know to the contrary, being but an indifferent judge in things of that sort, from leaving off my own studies rather short, on account of the gout; besides some other reasons.'

Edgar assured him these introductions were by no means necessary, a single twelvemonth's absence being very insufficient to obliterate from his memory his best and earliest friends.

Edgar Mandlebert was a young man who, if possessed neither of fortune nor its expectations, must from his person and his manners have been as attractive to the young, as from his morals and his conduct to those of riper years. His disposition was serious and meditative; but liberal, open, and candid. He was observant of the errors of others, and watched till he nearly eradicated his own. But though with difficulty he bestowed admiration, he diffused, both in words and deeds, such general amity and good will, that if the strictness of his character inspired general respect, its virtues could no less fail engaging the kinder mede of affection. When to merit of a species so rare were added a fine estate and a large independent fortune, it is not easy to decide whether in prosperity or desert he was most distinguished.

The first week which he spent at Cleves, was passed with a gaiety as unremitting as it was innocent. All parties felt his arrival as an acquisition: Indiana thought the hour of public exhibition, long promised by Miss Margland, at length fast approaching; Camilla, who escaped all expectation for herself, from being informed of what was entertained by her cousin, enjoyed the tranquil pleasure of undesigning friendship, unchequered either by hope or fear; Eugenia met with a respect for her acquirements that redoubled her ambition to increase them; Sir Hugh looked forward with joy to the happy disposal of Indiana, and a blameless riddance of Miss Margland; who, on her part, with an almost boundless satisfaction, saw her near return to a town life, from the high favour in which she stood with the supposed bride elect; even Dr. Orkborne, though he disdained with so young a scholar to enter into much philological disquisition, was gratified by a presence which afforded a little relief to the stores of his burdened memory, from authorizing some occasional utterance of the learned recollections, which for many years had encumbered it without vent. Edgar, meanwhile, obliging and obliged, received pleasure from them all; for though not blind to any of their imperfections, they had not a merit which he failed to discern.

The second week opened with a plan which promised a scene more lively, though it broke into the calm retirement of this peaceful party. Lionel, who was now at Etherington, to spend his university vacation, rode over to Cleves, to inform Edgar, that there would be a ball the next evening at Northwick, at which the officers of the — regiment, which was quartered in the neighbourhood, and all the beaux and belles of the county, were expected to assemble.

Miss Margland, who was present, struck with a desire that Indiana might make her first public appearance in the county, at a ball where Edgar might be her partner, went instantly to Sir Hugh to impart the idea. Sir Hugh, though averse to all public places, consented to the plan, from the hope of accelerating the affair; but declared, that if there was any amusement, his little Camilla should not be left out. Eugenia, won by the novelty of a first expedition of this sort, made her own request to be included; Lionel undertook to procure tickets, and Miss Margland had the welcome labour of arranging their dress, for which Sir Hugh, to atone for the shortness of the time, gave her powers unlimited.

Indiana was almost distracted with joy at this event. Miss Margland assured her, that now was the moment for fixing her conquest of Mandlebert, by adroitly displaying to him the admiration she could not but excite, in the numerous strangers before whom she would appear; she gave her various instructions how to set off her person to most advantage, and she delighted Sir Hugh with assurances of what this evening would effect: 'There is nothing, Sir,' said she, 'so conducive towards a right understanding between persons of fashion, as a ball. A gentleman may spend months and months in this drowsy way in the country, and always think one day will do as well as another for his declaration; but when he sees a young lady admired and noticed by others, he falls naturally into making her the same compliments, and the affair goes into a regular train, without his almost thinking of it.'

Sir Hugh listened to this doctrine with every desire to give it credit; and though the occupations of the toilette left him alone the whole of the assembly day, he was as happy in the prospect of their diversion, as they were themselves in its preparation.

When the young ladies were ready, they repaired to the apartment of the baronet, to shew themselves, and to take leave. Edgar and Lionel were waiting to meet them upon the stairs. Indiana had never yet looked so lovely; Camilla, with all her attractions, was eclipsed; and Eugenia could only have served as a foil, even to those who had no pretensions to beauty.

Edgar, nevertheless, asked Camilla to dance with him; she willingly, though not without wonder, consented. Lionel desired the hand of his fair cousin; but Indiana, self-destined to Edgar, whose address to Camilla, she had not heard, made him no answer, and ran on to present herself to her uncle; who, struck with admiration as he beheld her, cried, 'Indiana, my dear, you really look prettier than I could even have guessed; and yet I always knew there was no fault to be found with the outside; nor indeed with the inside neither, Mr. Mandlebert, so I don't mean anything by that; only, by use, one is apt to put the outside first.'

Lionel was now hurrying them away, when Sir Hugh calling to Edgar, said: 'Pray, young Mr. Mandlebert, take as much care of her as possible; which I am sure you will do of your own accord.'

Edgar, with some surprise, answered, he should be happy to take whatever care was in his power of all the ladies; 'but,' added he, 'for my own particular charge to-night, I have engaged Miss Camilla.'

'And how came you to do that? Don't you know I let them all go on purpose for the sake of your dancing with Indiana, which I mean as a particular favour?'

'Sir,' replied Edgar, a little embarrassed, 'you are very good; but as Lionel cannot dance with his sisters, he has engaged Miss Lynmere himself.'

'Pho, pho, what do you mind Lionel for? not but what he's a very good lad; only I had rather have you and Indiana dance together, which I dare say so had she.'

Edgar, somewhat distressed, looked at Camilla: 'O, as to me,' cried she, gaily, 'pray let me take my chance; if I should not dance at all, the whole will be so new to me, that I am sure of entertainment.'

'You are the best good girl, without the smallest exception,' said Sir Hugh, 'that ever I have known in the world; and so you always were; by which I mean nothing as to Indiana, who is just such another, except in some points; and so here's her hand, young Mr. Mandlebert, and if you think you shall meet a prettier partner at the ball, I beg when you get her there, you will tell her so fairly, and give her up.'

Edgar, who had hardly yet looked at her, was now himself struck with the unusual resplendence of her beauty, and telling Camilla he saw she was glad to be at liberty, protested he could not but rejoice to be spared a decision for himself, where the choice would have been so difficult.

'Well then, now go,' cried the delighted baronet; 'Lionel will find himself a partner, I have no doubt, because he is nothing particular in point of shyness; and as to Camilla, she'll want nothing but to hear the fiddlers to be as merry as a grig, which what it is I never knew: so I have no concern,' added he, in a low voice, to Edgar, 'except for little Eugenia, and poor Mrs. Margland; for Eugenia being so plain, which is no fault of her's, on account of the small-pox, many a person may overlook her from that objection; and as to Mrs. Margland, being with all these young chickens, I am afraid people will think her rather one of the oldest for a dancing match; which I say in no disrespect, for oldness gives one no choice.'

CHAPTER II

New Characters

The dancing was not yet begun, but the company was met, and the sprightly violins were employed to quicken their motions, when the Cleves party entered the ball room. They were distinguished immediately by a large party of officers, who assured Lionel, with whom they were acquainted, that they had impatiently been expected.

'I shall recompense you for waiting,' answered he, in a whisper, 'by introducing you to the rich heiress of Cleves, who now makes her first appearance from the nursery; though no! upon farther thoughts, I will only tell you she is one of our set, and leave it to your own ingenuity to find her out.'

While this was passing, Indiana, fluttering with all the secret triumph of conscious beauty, attended by Edgar, and guarded by Miss Margland, walked up the room, through a crowd of admiring spectators; in whom a new figure, without half her loveliness, would have excited the same curiosity, that her extreme inexperience attributed solely to her peculiar charms. Camilla and Eugenia followed rather as if in her train, than of her party; but Lionel kept entirely with the officers, insisting upon their guessing which was the heiress; to whom, while he purposely misled their conjectures, he urged them to make their court, by enumerating the present possessions of Sir Hugh, and her future expectations.

Camilla, however, passed not long unnoticed, though the splendor of Indiana's appearance cast her at first on the back ground; a circumstance which, by impressing her with a sensation of inferiority, divested her mind of all personal considerations, and gave to her air and countenance a graceful simplicity, a disengaged openness, and a guileless freedom from affectation, that rendered her, to the observant eye, as captivating upon examination, as Indiana, from the first glance, was brilliant and alluring. And thus, as they patrolled the room, Indiana excited an unmixt admiration, Camilla awakened an endless variety of remark; while each being seen for the first time, and every one else of the company for at least the second, all attention was their own, whether for criticism or for praise. To Indiana this answered, in fulfilling her expectations; by Camilla, it was unheeded, for, not awaiting, she did not perceive it; yet both felt equal satisfaction. The eyes of Camilla sparkled with delight as she surveyed all around her the gay novelty of the scene; the heart of Indiana beat with a pleasure wholly new, as she discovered that all surrounding her regarded her as the principal object.

Eugenia, meanwhile, had not even the negative felicity to pass unobserved; impertinent witticisms upon her face, person, and walk, though not uttered so audibly as to be distinctly heard, ran round the room in a confused murmur, and produced a disposition for sneering in the satirical, and for tittering in the giddy, that made her as valuable an acquisition to the company at large, who collect for any amusement, indifferent to its nature, as her fair cousin proved to the admirers of beauty, and her sister to the developers of expression. She was shielded, however, herself, from all undeserved mortifications, by not suspecting any were meant for her, and by a mind delightedly pre-occupied with that sudden expansion of ideas, with which new scenery and new objects charm a youthful imagination.

When they had taken two or three turns up and down the room, the saunterers were called upon to give place to the dancers. Edgar then led out Indiana, and the master of the ceremonies brought Major Cerwood to Camilla.

Eugenia, wholly left out, became the exclusive charge of Miss Margland; she felt no resentment of neglect, for she had formed no species of expectation. She looked on with perfect contentment, and the motley and quick changing group afforded her ample entertainment.

Miss Margland was not so passive; she seized the opportunity of inveighing very angrily against the mismanagement of Sir Hugh: 'If you had all,' she cried, 'been taken to town, and properly brought out, according to my advice, such a disgrace as this could never have happened; everybody would have known who you were, and then, there is no doubt, you might have had partners enough; however, I heartily hope you won't be asked to dance all the evening, that he may be convinced who was in the right; besides, the more you are tired, the more you may see, against another time, Miss Eugenia, that it is better to listen a little to people's opinions, when they speak only for your own advantage, than to go on with just the same indifference, as if you had no proper person to consult with.'

Eugenia was too well amused to heed this remonstrance; and long accustomed to hear the voice of Miss Margland without profit or pleasure, her ear received its sound, but her attention included not its purpose.

Indiana and Camilla, in this public essay, acquitted themselves with all the merits, and all the faults common to a first exhibition. The spectators upon such occasions, though never equally observant, are never afterwards so lenient. Whatever fails is attributed to modesty, more winning than the utmost success of excellence. Timidity solicits that mercy which pride is most gratified to grant; the blushes of juvenile shame atone for the deficiencies which cause them; and awkwardness itself, in the unfounded terrors of youth, is perhaps more interesting than grace.

Indiana could with difficulty keep to the figure of the dance, from the exulting, yet unpractised certainty of attracting all eyes; and Camilla perpetually turned wrong, from the mere flutter of fear, which made her expect she should never turn right. Major Cerwood, her partner, with a view to encourage her, was profuse in his compliments; but, as new to what she heard as what she performed, she was only the more confused by the double claim to her attention.

Edgar, meanwhile, was most assiduous to aid his fair partner. Miss Margland, though scarcely even superficial in general knowledge, was conversant in the practical detail of the hackneyed mode of forming matrimonial engagements; she judged, therefore, rightly, that her pupil would be seen to most advantage, in the distinction of that adulation by which new beholders would stamp new value on her charms. From the time of his first boyish gallantry, on the ill-fated birth-day of Camilla, Indiana had never so much struck young Mandlebert, as while he attended her up the assembly-room. Miss Margland observed this with triumph, and prophesied the speediest conclusion to her long and weary sojourn at Cleves, in the much wished-for journey to London, with a bride ready made, and an establishment ready formed.

When the two first dances were over, the gentlemen were desired to change partners. Major Cerwood asked the hand of Indiana, and Edgar repaired to Camilla: 'Do you bear malice?' he cried, with a smile, 'or may I now make the claim that Sir Hugh relinquished for me?'

'O yes,' answered she, with alacrity, when informed of the plan of change; 'and I wish there was any body else, that would dance with me afterwards, instead of that Major.'

'I dare believe,' said he, laughing 'there are many bodies else, who would oblige you, if your declaration were heard. But what has the Major done to you? Has he admired you without knowing how to keep is own counsel?'

'No, no; only he has treated me like a country simpleton, and made me as many fine speeches, as if he had been talking to Indiana.'

'You think, then, Indiana would have swallowed flattery with less difficulty?'

'No, indeed! but I think the same things said to her would no longer have been so extravagant.'

Edgar, to whom the sun-beams of the mind gave a glow which not all the sparkling rays of the brightest eyes could emit, respected her modesty too highly to combat it, and, dropping the subject, enquired what was become of Eugenia.

'O poor Eugenia!' cried she, 'I see nothing of her, and I am very much afraid she has had no better partner all this time than Miss Margland.'

Edgar, turning round, presently discerned her; she was still looking on, with an air of the most perfect composure, examining the various parties, totally without suspicion of the examination she was herself sustaining; while Miss Margland was vainly pouring in her ears observations, or exhortations, evidently of a complaining nature.

'There is something truly respectable,' said Edgar, 'in the innate philosophy with which she bears such neglect.'

'Yet I wish it were put less to the proof;' said Camilla. 'I would give the world somebody would take her out!'

'You don't think she would dance?'

'O yes she would! her lameness is no impediment; for she never thinks of it. We all learnt together at Cleves. Dancing gives her a little more exertion, and therefore a little more fatigue than other people, but that is all.'

'After these two dances then—'

'Will you be her partner?' interrupted Camilla, 'O go to her at once! immediately! and you will give me twenty times more pleasure than I can have in dancing myself.'

She then flew to a form, and eagerly seated herself where she perceived the first vacancy, to stop any debate, and enforce his consent.

The dance, which had been delayed by a dispute about the tune, was now beginning. Edgar, looking after her with affected reproach, but real admiration, asked the hand of Eugenia; who gave it with readiness and pleasure; for, though contented as a spectatress, she experienced an agreeable surprise in becoming a party engaged.

Camilla, happy in her own good humour, now looked at her neighbours; one of which was an elderly lady, who, wholly employed in examining and admiring the performance of her own daughters, saw nothing else in the room. The other was a gentleman, much distinguished by his figure and appearance, and dressed so completely in the extreme of fashion, as more than to border upon foppery. The ease and negligence of his air denoted a self-settled superiority to all about him; yet, from time to time, there was an archness in the glance of his eye, that promised, under a deep and wilful veil of conceit and affectation, a secret disposition to deride the very follies he was practising. He was now lounging against the wainscoat; with one hand on his side, and the other upon his eye-lids, occupying the space, without using the seat, to the left of Camilla.

Miss Margland, perceiving what she regarded as a fair vacancy, made up to the spot, and saying, 'Sir, by your leave,' was preparing to take possession of the place, when the gentleman, as if without seeing her, dropt suddenly into it himself, and, pouring a profusion of eau suave upon his handkerchief, exclaimed: 'What a vastly bad room this is for dancing!'

Camilla, concluding herself addressed, turned round to him; but, seeing he was sniffing up the eau suave, without looking at her, imagined he meant to speak to Miss Margland.

Miss Margland was of the same opinion, and, with some pique at his seizing thus her intended seat, rather sharply answered: 'Yes, sir, and it's a vast bad room for not dancing; for if every body would dance that ought, there would be accommodation sufficient for other people.'

'Incomparably well observed!' cried he, collecting some bonbons from a bonboniere, and swallowing one after another with great rapidity: 'But won't you sit down? You must be enormously tired. Let me supplicate you to sit down.'

Miss Margland, supposing he meant to make amends for his inattention, by delivering up the place, civilly thanked him, and said she should not be sorry, for she had stood a good while.

'Have you, indeed?' cried he, sprinkling some jessamine drops upon his hands; 'how horribly abominable? Why don't some of those Mercuries, those Ganymedes, those waiters, I believe you call them, get you a chair?'

Miss Margland, excessively affronted, turned her back to him; and Camilla made an offer of her own seat; but, as she had been dancing, and would probably dance again, Miss Margland would not let her rise.

'Shall I call to one of those Barbarians, those Goths, those Vandals?' cried the same gentleman, who now was spirting lavender water all about him, with grimaces that proclaimed forcibly his opinion of the want of perfume in the room: 'Do pray let me harangue them a little for you upon their inordinate want of sensibility.'

Miss Margland deigned not any answer; but of that he took no notice, and presently called out, though without raising his voice, 'Here, Mr. Waiter! Purveyor, Surveyor, or whatsoever other title "please thine ear," art thou deaf? why dost not bring this lady a chair? Those people are most amazing hard of hearing! Shall I call again? Waiter, I say!' still speaking rather lower than louder; 'Don't I stun you by this shocking vociferation?'

'Sir, you're vastly—obliging!' cried Miss Margland, unable longer to hold silence, yet with a look and manner that would much better have accorded with vastly—impertinent.

She then pursued a waiter herself, and procured a chair.

Casting his eyes next upon Camilla, he examined her with much attention. Abashed, she turned away her head; but not choosing to lose his object, he called it back again, by familiarly saying, 'How is Sir Hugh?'

A good deal surprised, she exclaimed, 'Do you know my uncle, sir?'

'Not in the least, ma'am,' he coolly answered.

Camilla, much wondering, was then forced into conversation with Miss Margland: but, without paying any regard to her surprise, he presently said, 'It's most extremely worth your while to take a glance at that inimitably good figure. Is it not exquisite? Can you suppose any thing beyond it?'

Camilla, looking at the person to whom he pointed, and who was sufficiently ludicrous, from an air of vulgar solemnity, and a dress stiffly new, though completely old-fashioned, felt disposed to join in his laugh, had she not been disconcerted by the mingled liberty and oddity of his attack.

'Sir,' said Miss Margland, winking at her to be silent, though eager to answer in her stead, 'the mixt company one always meets at these public balls, makes them very unfit for ladies of fashion, for there's no knowing who one may either dance with or speak to.'

'Vastly true, ma'am,' cried he, superciliously dropping his eyes, not to look at her.

Miss Margland, perceiving this, bridled resentfully, and again talked on with Camilla; till another exclamation interrupted them. 'O pray,' cried he, 'I do entreat you look at that group! Is it not past compare? If ever you held a pencil in your life, I beg and beseech you to take a memorandum of that tall may-pole. Have you ever seen any thing so excessively delectable?'

Camilla could not forbear smiling; but Miss Margland, taking all reply upon herself, said: 'Caricatures, sir, are by no means pleasing for young ladies to be taking, at their first coming out: one does not know who may be next, if once they get into that habit!'

'Immeasurably well spoken, ma'am,' returned he; and, rising with a look of disgust, he sauntered to another part of the room.

Miss Margland, extremely provoked, said she was sure he was some Irish fortune-hunter, dressed out in all he was worth; and charged Camilla to take no manner of notice of him.

When the two second dances were over, Edgar, conducting Eugenia to Miss Margland, said to Camilla: 'Now, at least, if there is not a spell against it, will you dance with me?'

'And if there is one, too,' cried she, gaily; 'for I am perfectly disposed to help breaking it.'

She rose, and they were again going to take their places, when Miss Margland, reproachfully calling after Edgar, demanded what he had done with Miss Lynmere?

At the same moment, led by Major Cerwood, who was paying her in full all the arrears of that gallantry Miss Margland had taught her to regret hitherto missing, Indiana joined them; the Major, in making his bow, lamenting the rules of the assembly, that compelled him to relinquish her hand.

'Mr. Mandlebert,' said Miss Margland, 'you see Miss Lynmere is again disengaged.'

'Yes, ma'am,' answered Edgar, drawing Camilla away; 'and every gentleman in the room will be happy to see it too.'

'Stop, Miss Camilla!' cried Miss Margland; 'I thought, Mr. Mandlebert, Sir Hugh had put Miss Lynmere under your protection?'

'O it does not signify!' said Indiana, colouring high with a new raised sense of importance; 'I don't at all doubt but one or other of the officers will take care of me.'

Edgar, though somewhat disconcerted, would still have proceeded; but Camilla, alarmed by the frowns of Miss Margland, begged him to lead out her cousin, and, promising to be in readiness for the next two dances, glided back to her seat. He upbraided her in vain; Miss Margland looked pleased, and Indiana was so much piqued, that he found it necessary to direct all his attention to appeasing her, as he led her to join the dance.

A gentleman now, eminently distinguished by personal beauty, approached the ladies that remained, and, in the most respectful manner, began conversing with Miss Margland; who received his attentions so gratefully, that, when he told her he only waited to see the master of the ceremonies at leisure, in order to have the honour of begging the hand of one of her young ladies, his civilities so conquered all her pride of etiquette, that she assured him there was no sort of occasion for such a formality, with a person of his appearance and manners; and was bidding Camilla rise, who was innocently preparing to obey, when, to the surprise of them all, he addressed himself to Eugenia.

'There!' cried Miss Margland, exultingly, when they were gone; 'that gentleman is completely a gentleman. I saw it from the beginning. How different to that impertinent fop that spoke to us just now! He has the politeness to take out Miss Eugenia, because he sees plainly nobody else will think of it, except just Mr. Mandlebert, or some such old acquaintance.'

Major Cerwood was now advancing towards Camilla, with that species of smiling and bowing manner, which is the usual precursor of an invitation to a fair partner; when the gentleman whom Miss Margland had just called an impertinent fop, with a sudden swing, not to be eluded, cast himself between the Major and Camilla, as if he had not observed his approach; and spoke to her in a voice so low, that, though she concluded he asked her to dance, she could not distinctly hear a word he said.

A good deal confused, she looked at him for an explanation; while the Major, from her air of attention, supposing himself too late, retreated.

Her new beau then, carelessly seating himself by her side, indolently said: 'What a heat! I have not the most distant idea how you can bear it!'

Camilla found it impossible to keep her countenance at such a result of a whisper, though she complied with the injunctions of Miss Margland, in avoiding mutual discourse with a stranger of so showy an appearance.

'Yet they are dancing on,' he continued, 'just as if the Greenland snows were inviting their exercise! I should really like to find out what those people are made of. Can you possibly imagine their composition?'

Heedless of receiving no answer, he soon after added: 'I am vastly glad you don't like dancing.'

'Me?' cried Camilla, surprised out of her caution.

'Yes; you hold it in antipathy, don't you?'

'No, indeed! far from it.'

'Don't you really?' cried he, starting back; 'that's amazingly extraordinary! surprising in the extreme! Will you have the goodness to tell me what you like in it?'

'Sir,' interfered Miss Margland, 'there's nothing but what's very natural in a young lady's taking pleasure in an elegant accomplishment; provided she is secure from any improper partner, or company.'

'Irrefragably just, ma'am!' answered he; affecting to take a pinch of snuff, and turning his head another way.

Here Lionel, hastily running up to Camilla, whispered, 'I have made a fine confusion among the red-coats about the heiress of Cleves! I have put them all upon different scents.'

He was then going back, when a faint laugh from the neighbour of Camilla detained him; 'Look, I adjure you,' cried he, addressing her, 'if there's not that delightful creature again, with his bran-new clothes? and they sit upon him so tight, he can't turn round his vastly droll figure, except like a puppet with one jerk for the whole body. He is really an immense treat: I should like of all things in nature, to know who he can be.'

A waiter then passing with a glass of water for a lady, he stopt him in his way, exclaiming: 'Pray, my extremely good friend, can you tell me who that agreeable person is, that stands there, with the air of a poker?'

'Yes, sir,' answered the man; 'I know him very well. His name is Dubster. He's quite a gentleman to my knowledge, and has very good fortunes.'

'Camilla,' cried Lionel, 'will you have him for a partner?' And, immediately hastening up to him, he said two or three words in a low voice, and skipped back to the dance.

Mr. Dubster then walked up to her, and, with an air conspicuously aukward, solemnly said, 'So you want to dance, ma'am?'

Convinced he had been sent to her by Lionel, but by no means chusing to display herself with a figure distinguished only as a mark for ridicule; she looked down to conceal her ever-ready smiles, and said she had been dancing some time.

'But if you like to dance again, ma'am,' said he, 'I am very ready to oblige you.'

She now saw that this offer had been requested as a favour; and, while half provoked, half diverted, grew embarrassed how to get rid of him, without involving a necessity to refuse afterwards Edgar, and every other; for Miss Margland had informed her of the general rules upon these occasions. She looked, therefore, at that lady for counsel; while her neighbour, sticking his hands in his sides, surveyed him from head to foot, with an expression of such undisguised amusement, that Mr. Dubster, who could not help observing it, cast towards him, from time to time, a look of the most angry surprise.

Miss Margland approving, as well understanding the appeal, now authoritatively interfered, saying: 'Sir, I suppose you know the etiquette in public places?'

'The what, ma'am?' cried he, staring.

'You know, I suppose, sir, that no young lady of any consideration dances with a gentleman that is a stranger to her, without he's brought to her by the master of the ceremonies?'

'O as to that, ma'am, I have no objection. I'll go see for him, if you've a mind. It makes no difference to me.'

And away he went.

'So you really intend dancing with him?' cried Camilla's neighbour. ''Twill be a vastly good sight. I have not the most remote conception how he will bear the pulling and jostling about. Bend he cannot; but I am immensely afraid he will break. I would give fifty guineas for his portrait. He is indubitably put together without joints.'

Mr. Dubster now returned, and, with a look of some disturbance, said to Miss Margland: 'Ma'am, I don't know which is the master of the ceremonies. I can't find him out; for I don't know as ever I see him.'

'O pray,' cried Camilla eagerly, 'do not take the trouble of looking for him; 'twill answer no purpose.'

'Why I think so too, ma'am,' said he, misunderstanding her; 'for as I don't know the gentleman myself, he could go no great way towards making us better acquainted with one another: so we may just as well take our skip at once.'

Camilla now looked extremely foolish; and Miss Margland was again preparing an obstacle, when Mr. Dubster started one himself. 'The worst is,' cried he, 'I have lost one of my gloves, and I am sure I had two when I came. I suppose I may have dropt it in the other room. If you shan't mind it, I'll dance without it; for I don't mind those things myself of a straw.'

'O! sir,' cried Miss Margland, 'that's such a thing as never was heard of. I can't possibly consent to let Miss Camilla dance in such a manner as that.'

'Why then, if you like it better, ma'am, I'll go back and look for it.'

Again Camilla would have declined giving him any trouble; but he seemed persuaded it was only from shyness, and would not listen. 'Though the worst is,' he said, 'you're losing so much time. However, I'll give a good hunt; unless, indeed, that gentleman, who is doing nothing himself, except looking on at us all, would be kind enough to lend me his.'

'I rather fancy, sir,' cried the gentleman, immediately recovering from a laughing fit, and surveying the requester with supercilious contempt; 'I rather suspect they would not perfectly fit you.'

'Why then,' cried he, 'I think I'll go and ask Tom Hicks to lend me a pair; for it's a pity to let the young lady lose her dance for such a small trifle as that.'

Camilla began remonstrating; but he tranquilly walked away.

'You are superlatively in the good graces of fortune to-night,' cried her new friend, 'superlatively to a degree: you may not meet with such an invaluably uncommon object in twenty lustres.'

'Certainly,' said Miss Margland, 'there's a great want of regulation at balls, to prevent low people from asking who they will to dance with them. It's bad enough one can't keep people one knows nothing of from speaking to one.'

'Admirably hit off! admirable in the extreme!' he answered; suddenly twisting himself round, and beginning a whispering conversation with a gentleman on his other side.

Mr. Dubster soon came again, saying, somewhat dolorously, 'I have looked high and low for my glove, but I am no nearer. I dare say somebody has picked it up, out of a joke, and put it in their pocket. And as to Tom Hicks, where he can be hid, I can't tell, unless he has hanged himself; for I can't find him no more than my glove. However, I've got a boy to go and get me a pair; if all the shops a'n't shut up.'

Camilla, fearing to be involved in a necessity of dancing with him, expressed herself very sorry for this step; but, again misconceiving her motive, he begged her not to mind it; saying, 'A pair of gloves here or there is no great matter. All I am concerned for is, putting you off so long from having a little pleasure, for I dare say the boy won't come till the next two batches; so if that gentleman that looks so particular at me, has a mind to jig it with you a bit himself, in the interim, I won't be his hindrance.'

Receiving no answer, he bent his head lower down, and said, in a louder voice, 'Pray, sir, did you hear me?'

'Sir, you are ineffably good!' was the reply; without a look, or any further notice.

Much affronted, he said no more, but stood pouting and stiff before Camilla, till the second dance was over, and another general separation of partners took place. 'I thought how it would be, ma'am,' he then cried; 'for I know it's no such easy matter to find shops open at this time of night; for if people's 'prentices can't take a little pleasure by now, they can't never.'

Tea being at this time ordered, the whole party collected to remove to the next room. Lionel, seeing Mr. Dubster standing by Camilla, with a rapturous laugh, cried, 'Well, sister, have you been dancing?'

Camilla, though laughing too, reproachfully shook her head at him; while Mr. Dubster gravely said, 'It's no fault of mine, sir, that the lady's sitting still; for I come and offered myself to her the moment you told me she wanted a partner; but I happened of the misfortune of losing one of my gloves, and not being able to find Tom Hicks, I've been waiting all this while for a boy as has promised to get me a pair; though, I suppose he's fell down in the dark and broke his skull, by his not coming. And, indeed, if that elderly lady had not been so particular, I might as well have done without; for, if I had one on, nobody would have been the wiser but that t'other might have been in my pocket.'

This speech, spoken without any ceremony in the hearing of Miss Margland, to the visible and undisguised delight of Lionel, so much enraged her, that, hastily calling him aside, she peremptorily demanded how he came to bring such a vulgar partner to his sister?

'Because you took no care to get her a better,' he answered, heedlessly.

Camilla also began to remonstrate; but, without hearing her, he courteously addressed himself to Mr. Dubster, and told him he was sure Miss Margland and his sister would expect the pleasure of his company to join their party at tea.

Miss Margland frowned in vain; Mr. Dubster bowed, as at a compliment but his due; observing he should then be close at hand for his partner; and they were proceeding to the tea-room, when the finer new acquaintance of Camilla called after Mr. Dubster: 'Pray, my good sir, who may this Signor Thomaso be, that has the honour to stand so high in your good graces?'

'Mine, sir?' cried Mr. Dubster; 'I know no Signor Thomaso, nor Signor nothing else neither: so I don't know what you mean.'

'Did not I hear you dilating, my very good sir, upon a certain Mr. Tom somebody?'

'What, I suppose then, sir, if the truth be known, you would say Tom Hicks?'

'Very probably, sir: though I am not of the first accuracy as the gentleman's nomenclator.'

'What? don't you know him, sir? why he's the head waiter!'

Then, following the rest of the party, he was placed, by the assistance of Lionel, next to Camilla, in utter defiance of all the angry glances of Miss Margland, who herself invited the handsome partner of Eugenia to join their group, and reaped some consolation in his willing civilities; till the attention of the whole assembly was called, or rather commanded by a new object.

A lady, not young, but still handsome, with an air of fashion easy almost to insolence, with a complete but becoming undress, with a work-bag hanging on her arm, whence she was carelessly knotting, entered the ball-room alone, and, walking straight through it to the large folding glass doors of the tea-room, there stopt, and took a general survey of the company, with a look that announced a decided superiority to all she saw, and a perfect indifference to what opinion she incurred in return.

She was immediately joined by all the officers, and several other gentlemen, whose eagerness to shew themselves of her acquaintance marked her for a woman of some consequence; though she took little other notice of them, than that of giving to each some frivolous commission; telling one to hold her work-bag; bidding another fetch her a chair; a third, ask for a glass of water; and a fourth, take care of her cloak. She then planted herself just without the folding-doors, declaring there could be no breathing in the smaller apartment, and sent about the gentlemen for various refreshments; all which she rejected when they arrived, with extreme contempt, and a thousand fantastic grimaces.

The tea-table at which Miss Margland presided being nearest to these folding-doors, she and her party heard, from time to time, most of what was said, especially by the newly arrived lady; who, though she now and then spoke for several minutes in a laughing whisper, to some one she called to her side, uttered most of her remarks, and all her commands quite aloud, with that sort of deliberate ease which belongs to the most determined negligence of who heard, or who escaped hearing her, who were pleased, or who were offended.

Camilla and Eugenia were soon wholly engrossed by this new personage; and Lionel, seeing her surrounded by the most fashionable men of the assembly, forgot Mr. Dubster and his gloves, in an eagerness to be introduced to her.

Colonel Andover, to whom he applied, willingly gratified him: 'Give me leave, Mrs. Arlbery,' cried he, to the lady, who was then conversing with General Kinsale, 'to present to you Mr. Tyrold.'

'For Heaven's sake don't speak to me just now,' cried she; 'the General is telling me the most interesting thing in the world. Go on, dear General!'

Lionel, who, if guided by his own natural judgment, would have conceived this to be the height of ill-breeding or of ignorance, no sooner saw Colonel Andover bow in smiling submission to her orders, than he concluded himself all in the dark with respect to the last licences of fashion: and, while contentedly he waited her leisure for his reception, he ran over in his own mind the triumph with which he should carry to Oxford the newest flourish of the bon ton.

In a few minutes, after gaily laughing with the General, she turned suddenly to Colonel Andover, and, striking him on the arm with her fan, exclaimed: 'Well, now, Colonel, what is it you would say?'

'Mr. Tyrold,' he answered, 'is very ambitious of the honour of being introduced to you.'

'With all my heart. Which is he?' And then, nodding to Lionel's bow, 'You live, I think,' she added, 'in this neighbourhood? By the way, Colonel, how came you never to bring Mr. Tyrold to me before? Mr. Tyrold, I flatter myself you intend to take this very ill.'

Lionel was beginning to express his sense of the loss he had suffered by the delay, when, again, patting the Colonel, 'Only look, I beg you,' she cried, 'at that insupportable Sir Sedley Clarendel! how he sits at his ease there! amusing his ridiculous fancy with every creature he sees. Yet what an elegant posture the animal has found out! I make no doubt he would as soon forfeit his estate as give up that attitude. I must make him come to me immediately for that very reason;—do go to him, good Andover, and say I want him directly.'

The Colonel obeyed; but not so the gentleman he addressed, who was the new acquaintance of Camilla. He only bowed to the message, and, kissing his hand across the room to the lady, desired the Colonel to tell her he was ineffably tired; but would incontestably have the honour to throw himself at her feet the next morning.

'O, intolerable!' cried she, 'he grows more conceited every hour. Yet what an agreeable wretch it is! There's nothing like him. I cannot possibly do without him. Andover, tell him if he does not come this moment he kills me.'

'And is that a message,' said General Kinsale, 'to cure him of being conceited?'

'O, Heaven forbid, my good General, I should cure him! That would utterly spoil him. His conceit is precisely what enchants me. Rob him of that, and you lose all hold of him.'

'Is it then necessary to keep him a fop, in order to retain him in your chains?'

'O, he is not in my chains, I promise you. A fop, my dear General, wears no chains but his own. However, I like to have him, because he is so hard to be got; and I am fond of conversing with him, because he is so ridiculous. Fetch him, therefore, Colonel, without delay.'

This second embassy prevailed; he shrugged his shoulders, but arose to follow the Colonel.

'See, madam, your victory!' said the General. 'What would not a military man give for such talents of command?'

'Ay, but look with what magnificent tardiness he obeys orders! There is something quite irresistible in his impertinence; 'tis so conscious and so piquant. I think, General, 'tis a little like my own.'

Sir Sedley now advancing, seized the back of a chair, which he twirled round for a resting place to his elbow, and exclaimed, 'You know yourself invincible!' with an air that shewed him languidly prepared for her reproaches: but, to his own surprise, and that of all around him, she only, with a smile and a nod, cried, 'How do do?' and immediately turning wholly away from him, addressed herself to Colonel Andover, desiring him to give her the history of who was in the tea-room.

At this time a young Ensign, who had been engaged at a late dinner in the neighbourhood, stroamed into the ballroom, with the most visible marks of his unfitness for appearing in it; and, in total ignorance of his own condition, went up to Colonel Andover, and, clapping him upon the back, called out, with a loud oath, 'Colonel, I hope you have taken care to secure to me the prettiest little young angel in the room? You know with what sincerity I despise an old hag.'

The Colonel, with some concern, advised him to retire; but, insensible to his counsel, he uttered oath upon oath, and added, 'I'm not to be played upon, Colonel. Beauty in a pretty girl is as necessary an ingredient, as honour in a brave soldier; and I could find in my heart to sink down to the bottom of the Channel every fellow without one, and every dear creature without the other.'

Then, in defiance of all remonstrance, he staggered into the tea-room; and, after a short survey, stopt opposite to Indiana, and, swearing aloud she was the handsomest angel he had ever beheld, begged her hand without further ceremony; assuring her he had broken up the best party that had yet been made for him in the county, merely for the joy of dancing with her.

Indiana, to whom not the smallest doubt of the truth of this assertion occurred; and who, not suspecting he was intoxicated, thought his manner the most spirited and gallant she had ever seen, was readily accepting his offer; when Edgar, who saw her danger, started up, and exclaimed: 'This lady, sir, is engaged to dance the next two dances with me.'

'The lady did not tell me so, sir!' cried the Ensign, firing.

'Miss Lynmere,' replied Edgar, coolly, 'will pardon me, that on this occasion, my memory has an interest to be better than her's. I believe it is time for us to take our places.'

He then whispered a brief excuse to Camilla, and hurried Indiana to the ballroom.

The Ensign, who knew not that she had danced with him the last time, was obliged to submit; while Indiana, not conjecturing the motive that now impelled Edgar, was in a yet brighter blaze of beauty, from an exhilarating notion that there was a contest for the honour of her hand.

Camilla, once more disappointed of Edgar, had now no resource against Mr. Dubster, but the non-arrival of the gloves; for he had talked so publicly of waiting for them to dance with her, that every one regarded her as engaged.

No new proposition being made for Eugenia, Miss Margland permitted her again to be led out by the handsome stranger.

When she was gone, Mr. Dubster, who kept constantly close to Camilla, said: 'They tell me, ma'am, that ugly little body's a great fortune.'

Camilla very innocently asked who he meant.

'Why that little lame thing, that was here drinking tea with you. Tom Hicks says she'll have a power of money.'

Camilla, whose sister was deservedly dear to her, looked much displeased; but Mr. Dubster, not perceiving it, continued: 'He recommended it to me to dance with her myself, from the first, upon that account. But I says to him, says I, I had no notion that a person, who had such a hobble in their gait, would think of such a thing as going to dancing. But there I was out, for as to the women, asking your pardon, ma'am, there's nothing will put 'em off from their pleasure. But, however, for my part, I had no thought of dancing at all, if it had not been for that young gentleman's asking me; for I'm not over fond of such jiggets, as they've no great use in 'em; only I happened to be this way, upon a little matter of business, so I thought I might as well come and see the hop, as Tom Hicks could contrive to get me a ticket.'

This was the sort of discourse with which Camilla was regaled till the two dances were over; and then, begging her to sit still till he came back, he quitted her, to see what he could do about his gloves.

Edgar, when he returned with Indiana, addressed himself privately to Miss Margland, whom he advised to take the young ladies immediately home; as it would not be possible for him, a second time, to break through the rules of the assembly, and Indiana must, therefore, inevitably accept the young Ensign, who already was following and claiming her, and whose condition was obviously improper for the society of ladies.

Miss Margland, extremely pleased with him, for thus protecting her pupil, instantly agreed; and, collecting her three young charges, hastened them down stairs; though the young Ensign, inflamed with angry disappointment, uttered the most bitter lamentations at their sudden departure; and though Mr. Dubster, pursuing them to the coach door, called out to Camilla, in a tone of pique and vexation, 'Why, what are you going for now, ma'am, when I have just got a new pair of gloves, that I have bought o' purpose?'

CHAPTER III

A Family Breakfast

In their way home, Edgar apologised to Camilla for again foregoing the promised pleasure of dancing with her, by explaining the situation of the Ensign.

Camilla, internally persuaded that any reason would suffice for such an arrangement, where Indiana was its object, scarce listened to an excuse which she considered as unnecessary.

Indiana was eager to view in the glass how her dress and ornaments had borne the shaking of the dance, and curiously impatient to look anew at a face and a figure of which no self-vanity, nor even the adulation of Miss Margland, had taught her a consciousness, such as she had acquired from the adventures of this night. She hastened, therefore, to her apartment as soon as she arrived at Cleves, and there indulged in an examination which forbade all surprise, and commanded equal justice for the admirers and the admired.

Miss Margland, anxious to make her own report to Sir Hugh, accompanied Camilla and Eugenia to his room, where he was still sitting up for them.

She expatiated upon the behaviour of young Mandlebert, in terms that filled the baronet with satisfaction. She exulted in the success of her own measures; and, sinking the circumstance of the intended impartiality of Edgar, enlarged upon his dancing, out of his turn, with Indiana, as at an event which manifested his serious designs beyond all possibility of mistake.

Sir Hugh, in the fulness of his content, promised that when the wedding day arrived, they should all have as fine new gowns as the bride herself.

The next morning, not considering that every one else would require unusual repose, he got up before his customary hour, from an involuntary hope of accelerating his favourite project; but he had long the breakfast parlour to himself, and became so fatigued and discomfited by fasting and waiting, that when Indiana, who appeared last, but for whom he insisted upon staying, entered the room, he said: 'My dear, I could really find a pleasure in giving you a little scold, if it were not for setting a bad example, which God forbid! And, indeed, it's not so much your fault as the ball's, to which I can never be a sincere friend, unless it be just to answer some particular purpose.'

Miss Margland defended her pupil, and called upon Mandlebert for assistance, which he readily gave. Sir Hugh then was not merely appeased but gratified, and declared, the next moment, with a marked smile at Indiana, that his breakfast he had not relished so well for a twelvemonth, owing to the advantage of not beginning till he had got an appetite.

Soon after, Lionel, galloping across the park, hastily dismounted, and scampered into the parlour.

The zealot for every species of sport, the candidate for every order of whim, was the light-hearted mirthful Lionel. A stranger to reflection, and incapable of care, laughter seemed not merely the bent of his humour, but the necessity of his existence: he pursued it at all seasons, he indulged it upon all occasions. With excellent natural parts, he trifled away all improvement; without any ill temper, he spared no one's feelings. Yet, though not radically vicious, nor deliberately malevolent, the egotism which urged him to make his own amusement his first pursuit, sacrificed his best friends and first duties, if they stood in its way.

'Come, my little girls, come!' cried he, as he entered the room; 'get your hats and cloaks as fast as possible; there is a public breakfast at Northwick, and you are all expected without delay.'

This sudden invitation occasioned a general commotion. Indiana gave an involuntary jump; Camilla and Eugenia looked delighted; and Miss Margland seemed ready to second the proposition; but Sir Hugh, with some surprise, exclaimed: 'A public breakfast, my dear boy! why where's the need of that, when we have got so good a private one?'

'O, let us go! let us go, uncle!' cried Indiana. 'Miss Margland, do pray speak to my uncle to let us go!'

'Indeed, sir,' said Miss Margland, 'it is time now, in all conscience, for the young ladies to see a little more of the world, and that it should be known who they are. I am sure they have been immured long enough, and I only wish you had been at the ball last night, sir, yourself!'

'Me, Mrs. Margland! Lord help me! what should I do at such a thing as that, with all this gout in my hip?'

'You would have seen, sir, the fine effects of keeping the young ladies out of society in this manner. Miss Camilla, if I had not prevented it, would have danced with I don't know who; and as to Miss Eugenia, she was as near as possible to not dancing at all, owing to nobody's knowing who she was.'

Sir Hugh had no time to reply to this attack, from the urgency of Indiana, and the impetuosity of Lionel, who, applying to Camilla, said: 'Come, child, ask my uncle yourself, and then we shall go at once.'

Camilla readily made it her own request.

'My dear,' answered Sir Hugh, 'I can't be so unnatural to deny you a little pleasure, knowing you to be such a merry little whirligig; not but what you'd enjoy yourself just as much at home, if they'd let you alone. However, as Indiana's head is so much turned upon it, for which I beg you won't think the worse of her, Mr. Mandlebert, it being no more than the common fault of a young person no older than her; why, you must all go, I think, provided you are not satisfied already, which, by the breakfast you have made, I should think likely enough to be the case.'

They then eagerly arose, and the females hastened to make some change in their dress. Sir Hugh, calling Eugenia back, said: 'As to you, my little classic, I make but small doubt you will be half ready to break your heart at missing your lesson, knowing hic, hæc, hoc, to be dearer to you, and for good reasons enough, too, in the end, than all the hopping and skipping in the world; so if you had rather stay away, don't mind all those dunces; for so I must needs call them, in comparison to you and Dr. Orkborne, though without the least meaning to undervalue them.'

Eugenia frankly acknowledged she had been much amused the preceding evening, and wished to be again of the party.

'Why then, if that's the case,' said the baronet, the best way will be for Dr. Orkborne to be your squire; by which means you may have a little study as you go along, to the end that the less time may be thrown away in doing nothing.'

Eugenia, who perceived no objection to this idea, assented, and went quietly up stairs, to prepare for setting out. Sir Hugh, by no means connecting the laughter of Lionel, nor the smile of Edgar, with his proposal, gravely repeated it to Dr. Orkborne, adding: 'And if you want a nice pair of gloves, Doctor, not that I make the offer in any detriment to your own, but I had six new pair come home just before my gout, which, I can assure you, have never seen the light since, and are as much at your service as if I had bespoke them on purpose.'

The mirth of Lionel grew now so outrageous, that Dr. Orkborne, much offended, walked out of the room without making any answer.

'There is something,' cried Sir Hugh, after a pause, 'in these men of learning, prodigious nice to deal with; however, not understanding them, in point of their maxims, it's likely enough I may have done something wrong; for he could not have seemed much more affronted, if I had told him I had six new pair of gloves lying by me, which he should be never the better for.'

When they were all ready, Sir Hugh calling to Edgar, said: 'Now as I don't much chuse to have my girls go to these sort of places often, which is a prudence that I dare say you approve as much as myself, I would wish to have the most made of them at once; and, therefore, as I've no doubt but they'll strike up a dance, after having eat what they think proper, why I would advise you, Mr. Mandlebert, to let Indiana trip it away till she's heartily tired, for else she'll never give it up, with a good grace, of her own accord.'

'Certainly, sir,' answered Edgar, 'I shall not hurry the ladies.'

'O, as to any of the rest,' interrupted Sir Hugh, 'they'll be as soon satisfied as yourself, except,' lowering his voice, 'Mrs. Margland, who, between friends, seems to me as glad of one of those freaks, as when she was but sixteen; which how long it is since she was no more I can't pretend to say, being a point she never mentions.'

Then addressing them in general: 'I wish you a good breakfast,' he cried, 'with all my heart, which I think you pretty well deserve, considering you go so far for it, with one close at your elbow, but just swallowed. And so, my dear Indiana, I hope you won't tire Mr. Mandlebert more than can't be avoided.'

'How came you to engage Indiana again, Mandlebert?' cried Lionel, in their way to the carriage.

'Because,' said Miss Margland, finding he hesitated, 'there is no other partner so proper for Miss Lynmere.'

'And pray what's the matter with me? why am not I as proper as Mandlebert?'

'Because you are her relation, to be sure!'

'Well,' cried he, vaulting his horse, 'if I meet but the charming widow, I shall care for none of you.'

CHAPTER IV

A Public Breakfast

The unfitting, however customary, occasion of this speedy repetition of public amusement in the town of Northwick, was, that the county assizes were now held there; and the arrival of the Judges of the land, to hear causes which kept life or death suspended, was the signal for entertainment to the surrounding neighbourhood: a hardening of human feelings against human crimes and human miseries, at which reflection revolts, however habit may persevere.

The young men, who rode on first, joined the ladies as they entered the town, and told them to drive straight to the ballroom, where the company had assembled, in consequence of a shower of rain which had forced them from the public garden intended for the breakfast.

Here, as they stopt, a poor woman, nearly in rags, with one child by her side, and another in her arms, approached the carriage, and presenting a petition, besought the ladies to read or hear her case. Eugenia, with the ready impulse of generous affluence, instantly felt for her purse; but Miss Margland, angrily holding her hand, said, with authority: 'Miss Eugenia, never encourage beggars; you don't know the mischief you may do by it.' Eugenia reluctantly desisted, but made a sign to her footman to give something for her. Edgar then alighting, advanced to hand them from the coach, while Lionel ran forward to settle their tickets of admittance.

The woman now grew more urgent in her supplications, and Miss Margland in her remonstrances against attending to them.

Indiana, who was placed under the care of Edgar, enchanted to again display herself where sure of again being admired, neither heard nor saw the petitioner; but dimpling and smiling, quickened her motions towards the assembly room: while Camilla, who was last, stopping short, said: 'What is the matter, poor woman?' and took her paper to examine.

Miss Margland, snatching it from her, threw it on the ground, peremptorily saying: 'Miss Camilla, if once you begin such a thing as that, there will be no end to it; so come along with the rest of your company, like other people.'

She then haughtily proceeded; but Camilla, brought up by her admirable parents never to pass distress without inquiry, nor to refuse giving at all, because she could give but little, remained with the poor object, and repeated her question. The woman, shedding a torrent of tears, said she was wife to one of the prisoners who was to be tried the next day, and who expected to lose his life, or be transported, for only one bad action of stealing a leg of mutton; which, though she knew it to be a sin, was not without excuse, being a first offence, and committed in poverty and sickness. And this, she was told, the Judges would take into consideration; but her husband was now so ill, that he could not feed on the gaol allowance, and not having wherewithal to buy any other, would either die before his trial, or be too weak to make known his sad story in his own behalf, for want of some wine or some broth to support him in the meanwhile.

Camilla, hastily giving her a shilling, took one of her petitions, and promising to do all in her power to serve her, left the poor creature almost choaked with sobbing joy. She was flying to join her party, when she perceived Edgar at her side. 'I came to see,' cried he, with glistening eyes, 'if you were running away from us; but you were doing far better in not thinking of us at all.'

Camilla, accustomed from her earliest childhood to attend to the indigent and unhappy, felt neither retreating shame, nor parading pride in the office; she gave him the petition of the poor woman, and begged he would consider if there was any thing that could be done for her husband.

'I have received a paper from herself,' he answered, 'before you alighted; and I hope I should not have neglected it: but I will now take yours, that my memory may run no risk.'

They then went on to the assembly room.

The company, which was numerous, was already seated at breakfast. Indiana and Camilla, now first surveyed by daylight, again attracted all eyes; but, in the simplicity of undress, the superiority of Indiana was no longer wholly unrivalled, though the general voice was still strongly in her favour.

Indiana was a beauty of so regular a cast, that her face had no feature, no look to which criticism could point as susceptible of improvement, or on which admiration could dwell with more delight than on the rest. No statuary could have modelled her form with more exquisite symmetry; no painter have harmonised her complexion with greater brilliancy of colouring. But here ended the liberality of nature, which, in not sullying this fair workmanship by inclosing in it what was bad, contentedly left it vacant of whatever was noble and desirable.

The beauty of Camilla, though neither perfect nor regular, had an influence so peculiar on the beholder, it was hard to catch its fault; and the cynic connoisseur, who might persevere in seeking it, would involuntarily surrender the strict rules of his art to the predominance of its loveliness. Even judgment itself, the coolest and last betrayed of our faculties, she took by surprise, though it was not till she was absent the seizure was detected. Her disposition was ardent in sincerity, her mind untainted with evil. The reigning and radical defect of her character—an imagination that submitted to no control—proved not any antidote against her attractions; it caught, by its force and fire, the quick-kindling admiration of the lively; it possessed, by magnetic pervasion, the witchery to create sympathy in the most serious.

In their march up the room, Camilla was spoken to by a person from the tea-table, who was distinct from every other, by being particularly ill dressed; and who, though she did not know him, asked her how she did, with a familiar look of intimacy. She slightly curtsied, and endeavoured to draw her party more nimbly on; when another person, equally conspicuous, though from being accoutred in the opposite extreme of full dress, quitting his seat, formally made up to her, and drawing on a stiff pair of new gloves as he spoke, said: 'So you are come at last, ma'am! I began to think you would not come at all, begging that gentleman's pardon, who told me to the contrary last night, when I thought, thinks I, here I've bought these new gloves, for no reason but to oblige the young lady, and now I might as well not have bought 'em at all.'

Camilla, ready to laugh, yet much provoked at this renewed claim from her old persecutor, Mr. Dubster, looked vainly for redress at the mischievous Lionel, who archly answered: 'O, ay, true, sister; I told the gentleman, last night, you would be sure to make him amends this morning for putting him to so much expence.'

'I'm sure, Sir,' said Mr. Dubster, 'I did not speak for that, expence being no great matter to me at this time; only nobody likes to fool away their money for nothing.'

Edgar having now, at the end of one of the tables, secured places for the ladies, Lionel again, in defiance of the frowns of Miss Margland, invited Mr. Dubster to join them: even the appealing looks of Camilla served but to increase her brother's ludicrous diversion, in coupling her with so ridiculous a companion; who, without seeming at all aware of the liberty he was taking, engrossed her wholly.

'So I see, ma'am,' he cried, pointing to Eugenia, 'you've brought that limping little body with you again? Tom Hicks had like to have took me in finely about her! He thought she was the great fortune of these here parts; and if it had not been for the young gentleman, I might have known no better neither, for there's half the room in the same scrape at this minute.'

Observing Camilla regard him with an unpleasant surprise, he more solemnly added: 'I ask pardon, ma'am, for mentioning the thing, which I only do in excuse for what I said last night, not knowing then you was the fortune yourself.'

An eager sign of silence from Lionel, forbade her explaining this mistake; Mr. Dubster, therefore, proceeded:

'When Tom Hicks told me about it, I said at the time, says I, she looks more like to some sort of a humble young person, just brought out of a little good-nature to see the company, and the like of that; for she's not a bit like a lady of fortunes, with that nudging look; and I said to Tom Hicks, by way of joke, says I, if I was to think of her, which I don't think I shall, at least she would not be much in my way, for she could not follow a body much about, because of that hitch in her gait, for I'm a pretty good walker.'

Here the ill dressed man, who had already spoken to Camilla, quitting his seat, strolled up to her, and fastening his eyes upon her face, though without bowing, made some speech about the weather, with the lounging freedom of manner of a confirmed old acquaintance. His whole appearance had an air of even wilful slovenliness: His hair was uncombed; he was in boots, which were covered with mud; his coat seemed to have been designedly immersed in powder, and his universal negligence was not only shabby but uncleanly. Astonished and offended by his forwardness, Camilla turned entirely away from him.

Not disconcerted by this distance, he procured a chair, upon which he cast himself, perfectly at his ease, immediately behind her.

Just as the general breakfast was over, and the waiters were summoned to clear away the tables, and prepare the room for dancing, the lady who had so strikingly made her appearance the preceding evening, again entered. She was alone, as before, and walked up the room with the same decided air of indifference to all opinion; sometimes knotting with as much diligence and earnestness as if her subsistence depended upon the rapidity of her work; and at other times stopping short, she applied to her eye a near-sighted glass, which hung to her finger, and intently examined some particular person or group; then, with a look of absence, as if she had not seen a creature, she hummed an opera song to herself, and proceeded. Her rouge was remarkably well put on, and her claim to being still a fine woman, though past her prime, was as obvious as it was conscious: Her dress was more fantastic and studied than the night before, in the same proportion as that of every other person present was more simple and quiet; and the commanding air of her countenance, and the easiness of her carriage, spoke a confirmed internal assurance, that her charms and her power were absolute, wherever she thought their exertion worth her trouble.

When she came to the head of the room, she turned about, and, with her glass, surveyed the whole company; then smilingly advancing to the sloven, whom Camilla was shunning, she called out: 'O! are you there? what rural deity could break your rest so early?'

'None!' answered he, rubbing his eyes; 'I am invulnerably asleep at this very moment! In the very centre of the morphetic dominions. But how barbarously late you are! I should never have come to this vastly horrid place before my ride, if I had imagined you could be so excruciating.'

Struck with a jargon of which she could not suspect two persons to be capable, Camilla turned round to her slighted neighbour, and with the greatest surprise recognised, upon examination, the most brilliant beau of the preceding evening, in the worst dressed man of the present morning.

The lady now, again holding her glass to her eye, which she directed without scruple towards Camilla and her party, said: 'Who have you got there?'

Camilla looked hastily away, and her whole set, abashed by so unseasoned an inquiry, cast down their eyes.

'Hey!' cried he, calmly viewing them, as if for the first time himself: 'Why, I'll tell you!' Then making her bend to hear his whisper, which, nevertheless, was by no means intended for her own ear alone, he added: 'Two little things as pretty as angels, and two others as ugly as—I say no more!'

'O, I take in the full force of your metaphor!' cried she, laughing; 'and acknowledge the truth of its contrast.'

Camilla alone, as they meant, had heard them; and ashamed for herself, and provoked to find Eugenia coupled with Miss Margland, she endeavoured to converse with some of her own society; but their attention was entirely engaged by the whispers; nor could she, for more than a minute, deny her own curiosity the pleasure of observing them.

They now spoke together for some time in low voices, laughing immoderately at the occasional sallies of each other; Sir Sedley Clarendel sitting at his ease, Mrs. Arlbery standing, and knotting by his side.

The officers, and almost all the beaux, began to crowd to this spot; but neither the gentleman nor the lady interrupted their discourse to return or receive any salutations. Lionel, who with much eagerness had quitted an inside seat at a long table, to pay his court to Mrs. Arlbery, could catch neither her eye nor her ear for his bow or his compliment.

Sir Sedley, at last, looking up in her face and smiling, said: 'A'n't you shockingly tired?'

'To death!' answered she, coolly.

'Why then, I am afraid, I must positively do the thing that's old fashioned.'

And rising, and making her a very elegant bow, he presented her his seat, adding: 'There, ma'am! I have the honour to give you my chair—at the risk of my reputation.'

'I should have thought,' cried Lionel, now getting forward, 'that omitting to give it would rather have risked your reputation.'

'It is possible you could be born before all that was over?' said Mrs. Arlbery, dropping carelessly upon the chair as she perceived Lionel, whom she honoured with a nod: 'How do do, Mr. Tyrold? are you just come in?' But turning again to Sir Sedley, without waiting for his answer, 'I swear, you barbarian,' she cried, 'you have really almost killed me with fatigue.'

'Have I indeed?' said he, smiling.

Mr. Dubster now, leaning over the table, solemnly said: 'I am sure I should have offered the lady my own place, if I had not been so tired myself; but Tom Hicks over-persuaded me to dance a bit before you came in, ma'am,' addressing Camilla, 'for you have lost a deal of dancing by coming so late; for they all fell to as soon as ever they come; and, as I'm not over and above used to it, it soon makes one a little stiffish, as one may say; and indeed, the lady's much better off in getting a chair, for one sits mighty little at one's ease on these here benches, with nothing to lean one's back against.'

'And who's that?' cried Mrs. Arlbery to Sir Sedley, looking Mr. Dubster full in the face.

Sir Sedley made some answer in a whisper, which proved highly entertaining to them both. Mr. Dubster, with an air much offended, said to Camilla: 'People's laughing and whispering, which one don't know what it's about, is not one of the politest things, I know, for polite people to do; and, in my mind, they ought to be above it.'

This resentment excited Lionel to join in the laugh; and Mr. Dubster, with great gravity of manner, rose, and said to Camilla: 'When you are ready to dance, ma'am, I am willing to be your partner, and I shan't engage myself to nobody else; but I shall go to t'other end of the room till you choose to stand up; for I don't much care to stay here, only to be laughed at, when I don't know what it's for.'

They now all left the table; and Lionel eagerly begged permission to introduce his sisters and cousin to Mrs. Arlbery, who readily consented to the proposal.

Indiana advanced with pleasure into a circle of beaux, whose eyes were most assiduous to welcome her. Camilla, though a little alarmed in being presented to a lady of so singular a deportment, had yet a curiosity to see more of her, that willingly seconded her brother's motion. And Eugenia, to whose early reflecting mind every new character and new scene opened a fresh fund for thought, if not for knowledge, was charmed to take a nearer view of what promised such food for observation. But Miss Margland began an angry remonstrance against the proceedings of Lionel, in thus taking out of her hands the direction of her charges. What she urged, however, was vain: Lionel was only diverted by her wrath, and the three young ladies, as they had not requested the introduction, did not feel themselves responsible for its taking effect.

Lionel led them on: Mrs. Arlbery half rose to return their curtsies; and gave them a reception so full of vivacity and good humour, that they soon forgot the ill will with which Miss Margland had suffered them to quit her; and even lost all recollection that it belonged to them to return to her. The satisfaction of Indiana, indeed, flowed simply from the glances of admiration which every where met her eye; but Eugenia attended to every word, and every motion of Mrs. Arlbery, with that sort of earnestness which marks an intelligent child at a first play; and Camilla, still more struck by the novelty of this new acquaintance, scarce permitted herself to breathe, lest she should lose anything she said.

Mrs. Arlbery perceived their youthful wonder, and felt a propensity to increase it, which strengthened all her powers, and called forth all her faculties. Wit she possessed at will; and, with exertions which rendered it uncommonly brilliant, she displayed it, now to them, now to the gentlemen, with a gaiety so fantastic, a raillery so arch, a spirit of satire so seasoned with a delight in coquetry, and a certain negligence of air so enlivened by a whimsical pleasantry, that she could not have failed to strike with admiration even the most hackneyed seekers of character; much less the inexperienced young creatures now presented to her; who, with open eyes and ears, regarded her as a phenomenon, upon finding that the splendor of her talents equalled the singularity of her manners.

When the room was prepared for dancing, Major Cerwood brought to Indiana Mr. Macdersey, the young Ensign who had so improperly addressed her at the ball; and, after a formal apology, in his name, for what had passed, begged the honour of her hand for him this morning. Indiana, flattered and fluttered together by this ceremony, almost forgot Edgar, who stood quietly but watchfully aloof, and was actually giving her consent when, meeting his eye, she recollected she was already engaged. Mr. Macdersey hoped for more success another time, and Edgar advanced to lead his fair partner to her place.

Major Cerwood offered himself to Camilla; but Mr. Dubster coming forward, pulled him by the elbow, and making a stiff low bow, said: 'Sir, I ask your pardon for taking the liberty of giving you such a jog, but the young lady's been engaged to me ever so long.' The Major looked surprised; but, observing that Camilla coloured, he bowed respectfully and retreated.

Camilla, ashamed of her beau, determined not to dance at all: though she saw, with much vexation, upon the general dispersion, Miss Margland approach to claim her. Educated in all the harmony of contentment and benevolence, she had a horror of a temper so irascible, that made it a penance to remain a moment in its vicinity. Mr. Dubster, however, left her not alone to it: when she positively refused his hand, he said it was equal agreeable to him to have only a little dish of chat with her; and composedly stationed himself before her. Eugenia had already been taken out by the handsome stranger, with whom she had danced the evening before; and Lionel, bewitched with Mrs. Arlbery, enlisted himself entirely in her train; and with Sir Sedley Clarendel, and almost every man of any consequence in the room, declined all dancing for the pleasure of attending her.

Mr. Dubster, unacquainted with the natural high spirits of Camilla, inferred nothing to his own disadvantage from her silence, but talked incessantly himself with perfect complacency. 'Do you know, ma'am,' cried he, 'just as that elderly lady, that, I suppose, is your mamma, took you all away in that hurry last night, up comes the boy with my new pair of gloves! but, though I run down directly to tell you of it, there was no making the old lady stop; which I was fool to try at; for as to women, I know their obstinacy of old. But what I grudged the most was, as soon as I come up again, as ill luck would have it, Tom Hicks finds me my own t'other glove! So there I had two pair, when I might as well have had never a one!'

Observing that Eugenia was dancing, 'Lack a-day!' he exclaimed, 'I'll lay a wager that poor gentleman has been took in, just as I was yesterday! He thinks that young lady that's had the small-pox so bad, is you, ma'am! 'Twould be a fine joke if such a mistake as that should get the little lame duck, as I call her, a husband! He'd be in a fine hobble when he found he'd got nothing but her ugly face for his bargain. Though, provided she'd had the rhino, it would not much have signified: for, as to being pretty or not, it's not great matter in a wife. A man soon tires of seeing nothing but the same face, if it's one of the best.'

Camilla here, in the midst of her chagrin, could not forbear asking him if he was married? 'Yes, ma'am,' answered he calmly, 'I've had two wives to my share already; so I know what I'm speaking of; though I've buried them both. Why it was all along of my wives, what with the money I had with one, and what with the money I had with the other, that I got out of business so soon.'

'You were very much obliged to them, then?'

'Why, yes, ma'am, as to that, I can't say to the contrary, now that they're gone: but I can't say I had much comfort with 'em while they lived. They was always a thinking they had a right to what they had a mind, because of what they brought me; so that I had enough to do to scrape a little matter together, in case of outliving them. One of 'em has not been dead above a twelvemonth, or there about; these are the first clothes I've bought since I left off my blacks.'

When Indiana past them, he expressed his admiration of her beauty. 'That young lady, ma'am,' he said, 'cuts you all up, sure enough. She's as fine a piece of red and white as ever I see. I could think of such a young lady as that myself, if I did not remember that I thought no more of my wife that was pretty, than of my wife that was ugly, after the first month or so. Beauty goes for a mere nothing in matrimony, when once one's used to it. Besides, I've no great thoughts at present of entering into the state again of one while, at any rate, being but just got to be a little comfortable.'

The second dance was now called, when Mrs. Arlbery, coming suddenly behind Camilla, said, in a low voice, 'Do you know who you are talking with?'

'No, ma'am!'

'A young tinker, my dear! that's all!' And, with a provoking nod, she retreated.

Camilla, half ready to laugh, half to cry, restrained herself with difficulty from running after her; and Mr. Dubster, observing that she abruptly turned away, and would listen no more, again claimed her for his partner; and, upon her absolute refusal, surprised and affronted, walked off in silence. She was then finally condemned to the morose society of Miss Margland: and invectives against Sir Hugh for mismanagement, and Lionel, with whom now that lady was at open war, for impertinence, filled up the rest of her time, till the company was informed that refreshments were served in the card-room.

Thither, immediately, every body flocked, with as much speed and avidity, as if they had learnt to appreciate the blessing of plenty, by the experience of want. Such is the vacancy of dissipated pleasure, that, never satisfied with what it possesses, an opening always remains for something yet to be tried, and, on that something still to come, all enjoyment seems to depend.

The day beginning now to clear, the sashes of a large bow-window were thrown up. Sir Sedley Clarendel sauntered thither, and instantly everybody followed, as if there were no breathing anywhere else; declaring, while they pressed upon one another almost to suffocation, that nothing was so reviving as the fresh air: and, in a minute, not a creature was to be seen in any other part of the room.

Here, in full view, stood sundry hapless relations of the poorer part of the prisoners to be tried the next morning, who, with supplicating hands and eyes, implored the compassion of the company, whom their very calamities assembled for amusement.

Nobody took any notice of them; nobody appeared even to see them: but, one by one, all glided gently away, and the bow-window was presently the only empty space in the apartment.

Camilla, contented with having already presented her mite, and Eugenia, with having given her's in commission, retired unaffectedly with the rest; while Miss Margland, shrugging up her shoulders, and declaring there was no end of beggars, pompously added, 'However, we gave before we came in.'

Presently, a paper was handed about, to collect half guineas for a raffle. A beautiful locket, set round with pearls, ornamented at the top with a little knot of small brilliants, and very elegantly shaped, with a space left for a braid of hair, or a cypher, was produced; and, as if by magnetic power, attracted into almost every hand the capricious coin, which distress, but the moment before had repelled.

Miss Margland lamented she had only guineas or silver, but suffered Edgar to be her paymaster; privately resolving, that, if she won the locket, she would remember the debt: Eugenia, amused in seeing the humour of all that was going forward, readily put in; Indiana, satisfied her uncle would repay the expences of the day, with a heart panting from hope of the prize, did the same; but Camilla hung back, totally unused to hazard upon what was unnecessary the little allowance she had been taught to spend sparingly upon herself, that something might be always in her power to bestow upon others. The character of this raffle was not of that interesting nature which calls forth from the affluent and easy respect as well as aid: the prize belonged to no one whom adversity compelled to change what once was an innocent luxury, into the means of subsistence; it was the mere common mode of getting rid of a mere common bauble, which no one had thought worth the full price affixed to it by its toyman. She knew not, however, till now, how hard to resist was the contagion of example, and felt a struggle in her self-denial, that made her, when she put the locket down, withdraw from the crowd, and resolve not to look at it again.

Edgar, who had observed her, read her secret conflict with an emotion which impelled him to follow her, that he might express his admiration; but he was stopt by Mrs. Arlbery, who just then hastily attacked her with, 'What have you done with your friend the tinker, my dear?'

Camilla, laughing, though extremely ashamed, said, she knew nothing at all about him.

'You talked with him, then, by way of experiment, to see how you might like him?'

'No, indeed! I merely answered him when I could not help it; but still I thought, at a ball, gentlemen only would present themselves.'

'And how many couple,' said Mrs. Arlbery, smiling, 'do you calculate would, in that case, stand up?'

She then ordered one of the beaux who attended her, to bring her a chair, and told another to fetch her the locket. Edgar was again advancing to Camilla, when Lionel, whose desire to obtain the good graces of Mrs. Arlbery, had suggested to him an anticipation of her commands, pushed forward with the locket.

'Well, really, it is not ugly,' cried she, taking it in her hand: 'Have you put in yet, Miss Tyrold?'

'No, ma'am.'

'O, I am vastly glad of that; for now we will try our fortune together.'

Camilla, though secretly blushing at what she felt was an extravagance, could not withstand this invitation: she gave her half guinea.

Edgar, disappointed, retreated in silence.

The money being collected, and the names of the rafflers taken down, information was given, that the prize was to be thrown for in three days time, at one o'clock at noon, in the shop of a bookseller at Northwick.

Some of the company now departed; others prepared for a last dance. Miss Margland desired Lionel to see for their carriage; but Lionel had no greater joy than to disregard her. Indiana asked earnestly to stay longer; Miss Margland said, she could only give way to her request, upon condition her partner should be Mr. Mandlebert. It was in vain she urged that she was already engaged to Colonel Andover; Miss Margland was inexorable, and Edgar, laughing, said, he should certainly have the whole corps upon his back; but the honour was sufficient to counterbalance the risk, and he would, therefore, beg the Colonel's patience.

'Mr. Mandlebert,' said Miss Margland, 'I know enough of quarrels at balls about partners, and ladies changing their minds, to know how to act pretty well in those cases: I shall desire, therefore, to speak to the Colonel myself, and not trust two gentlemen together upon such a nice matter.'

She then beckoned to the Colonel, who stood at a little distance, and, taking him apart, told him, she flattered herself he would not be offended, if Miss Lynmere should dance again with Mr. Mandlebert, though rather out of rule, as there were particular reasons for it.

The Colonel, with a smile, said he perceived Mr. Mandlebert was the happy man, and acquiesced.

A general murmur now ran buzzing round the room, that Mr. Mandlebert and Miss Lynmere were publicly contracted to each other; and, amongst many who heard with displeasure that the young beauty was betrothed before she was exhibited to view, Mr. Macdersey appeared to suffer the most serious mortification.

As soon as this dance was over, Edgar conducted his ladies to an apartment below stairs, and went in search of the carriage.

He did not return for some time. Miss Margland, as usual, grumbled; but Camilla, perceiving Mrs. Arlbery, rejoiced in the delay; and stationed herself by her side, all alive in attending to the pleasantry with which she was amusing herself and those around her.

When Edgar, who seemed out of breath from running, came back, he made but short answers to the murmurs of Miss Margland; and, hastening to Camilla, said: 'I have been with your petitioner:—she has all that can comfort her for the present; and I have learnt the name of her husband's counsel. You will be so good as to excuse me at dinner to Sir Hugh. I shall remain here till I can judge what may be done.'

The attention of Camilla was now effectually withdrawn from Mrs. Arlbery, and the purest delight of which human feelings are susceptible, took sudden and sole possession of her youthful mind, in the idea of being instrumental to the preservation of a fellow-creature.

Edgar saw, in the change, yet brightness of her countenance, what passed within;—and his disappointment concerning the raffle was immediately forgotten.

A short consultation followed, in which both spoke with so much energy, as not only to overpower the remonstrances of Miss Margland for their departure, but to catch the notice of Mrs. Arlbery, who, coming forward, and leaning her hand on the shoulder of Camilla, said: 'Tell me what it is that has thus animated you? Have you heard any good tidings of your new friend?'

Camilla instantly and eagerly related the subject that occupied them, without observing that the whole company around were smiling, at her earnestness in a cause of such common distress.

'You are new, my dear,' said Mrs. Arlbery, patting her cheek, 'very new; but I take the whim sometimes of being charitable myself, for a little variety. It always looks pretty; and begging is no bad way of shewing off one's powers. So give me your documents, and I'll give you my eloquence.'

Camilla presented her the petition, and she invited Mandlebert to dine with her. Miss Margland then led the way, and the female party returned to Cleves.

CHAPTER V

A Raffle

It was late when Edgar returned to Cleves. Camilla flew to meet him. He told her everything relative to her petitioner was in the most prosperous train; he had seen the prisoner, heard the particulars of his story, which all tended to his exculpation; and Mrs. Arlbery had contrived to make acquaintance with his counsel, whom she found perfectly well disposed to exert himself in the cause, and whom she had invited to a splendid supper. The trial was to take place the next morning.

Camilla, already powerfully struck with Mrs. Arlbery, was enchanted to find her thus active in benevolence.

Edgar was to dine with that lady the next day, and to learn the event of their joint exertions.

This proved all that could be wished. The prosecution had been mild: the judge and jury had been touched with compassion; and the venial offender had been released with a gentle reprimand.

Mandlebert returned to communicate these tidings to Camilla, with a pleasure exactly in unison with her own. Mrs. Arlbery, he avowed, had been as zealous as himself; and had manifested a charity of disposition which the flightiness of her manners had not let him to expect.

The next object of attention was the raffle, which was to take place the following morning.

Sir Hugh was averse to letting his nieces go abroad again so soon: but Miss Margland, extremely anxious about her own chance for the prize, solemnly asserted its necessity; inveighed against the mismanagement of everything at Cleves, stifled all her complaints of Lionel, and pronounced a positive decision, that, to carry Indiana to public places, was the sole method of promoting the match.

Sir Hugh then, willing to believe, and yet more willing to get rid of disputing with her, no longer withheld his consent.

They were advanced within half a mile of Northwick, when a sick man, painfully supported by a woman with a child in her arms, caught their eyes. The ready hand of Eugenia was immediately in her pocket; Camilla, looking more intently upon the group, perceived another child, and presently recognised the wife of the prisoner. She called to the coachman to stop, and Edgar, at the same moment, rode up to the carriage.

Miss Margland angrily ordered the man to drive on, saying, she was quite sick of being thus for ever infested with beggars; who really came so often, they were no better than pick-pockets.

'O, don't refuse to let me speak to them!' cried Camilla; 'it will be such a pleasure to see their joy!'

'O yes! they look in much joy indeed! they seem as if they had not eat a morsel these three weeks! Drive on, I say, coachman! I like no such melancholy sights, for my part. They always make me ill. I wonder how any body can bear them.'

'But we may help them; we may assist them!' said Camilla, with increasing earnestness.

'And pray, when they have got all our money, who is to help us?'

Eugenia, delighted to give, but unhabituated to any other exertion, flung half a crown to them; and Indiana, begging to look out, said, 'Dear! I never saw a prisoner before!'

Encouraged by an expressive look from Camilla, Edgar dismounted to hand her from the carriage, affecting not to hear the remonstrances of Miss Margland, though she scrupled not to deliver them very audibly. Eugenia languished to join them, but could not venture to disobey a direct command; and Indiana, observing the road to be very dusty, submitted, to save a pair of beautiful new shoes.

Camilla had all the gratification she promised herself, in witnessing the happiness of the poor petitioner. He was crawling to Cleves, with his family, to offer thanks. They were penniless, sick, and wretched; yet the preservation of the poor man seemed to make misery light to them all. Edgar desired to know what were their designs for the future. The man answered that he should not dare go back to his own country, because there his disgrace was known, and he should procure no work; nor, indeed, was he now able to do any. 'So we must make up our minds to beg from door to door, and in the streets, and on the high road,' he continued; 'till I get back a little strength; and can earn a living more creditably.'

'But as long as we have kept you alive, and saved you from being transported,' said his wife, 'for which all thanks be due to this good gentleman, we shall mind no hardships, and never go astray again, in wicked unthinkingness of this great mercy.'

Edgar inquired what had been their former occupations; they answered, they had both been day-workers in the field, till a fit of sickness had hindered the poor man from getting his livelihood: penury and hunger then pressing hard upon them all, he had been tempted to commit the offence for which he was taken, and brought to death's door. 'But as now,' he added, 'I have been saved, I shall make it a warning for the time to come, and never give myself up to so bad a course again.'

Edgar asked the woman what money she had left.

'Ah, sir, none! for we had things to pay, and people to satisfy, and so everything you and the good ladies gave us, is all gone; for, while anything was left us, they would not be easy. But this is no great mischief now, as my husband is not taken away from us, and is come to a right sense.'

'I believe,' said Edgar, 'you are very good sort of people, however distress had misguided you.'

He then put something into the man's hand, and Eugenia, who from the carriage window heard what passed, flung him another half crown; Camilla added a shilling, and turning suddenly away, walked a few paces from them all.

Edgar, gently following, inquired if anything was the matter; her eyes were full of tears: 'I was thinking,' she cried, 'what my dear father would have said, had he seen me giving half a guinea for a toy, and a shilling to such poor starving people as these!'

'Why, what would he have said?' cried Edgar, charmed with her penitence, though joining in the apprehended censure.

'He would more than ever have pitied those who want money, in seeing it so squandered by one who should better have remembered his lessons! O, if I could but recover that half guinea!'

'Will you give me leave to get it back for you?'

'Leave? you would lay me under the greatest obligation! How far half a guinea would go here, in poverty such as this!'

He assured her he could regain it without difficulty; and then, telling the poor people to postpone their walk to Cleves till the evening, when Camilla meant to prepare her uncle, also, to assist them, he handed her to the coach, with feelings yet more pleased than her own, and galloped forward to execute his commission.

He was ready at the door of the library to receive them. As they alighted, Camilla eagerly cried: 'Well! have you succeeded?'

'Can you trust yourself to this spot, and to a review of the allurement,' answered he, smiling, and holding half a guinea between his fingers, 'yet be content to see your chance for the prize withdrawn?'

'O give it me! give it me!' cried she, almost seizing it from him, 'my dear father will be so glad to hear I have not spent it so foolishly.'

The rafflers were not yet assembled; no one was in the shop but a well dressed elegant young man, who was reading at a table, and who neither raised his eyes at their entrance, nor suffered their discourse to interrupt his attention; yet though abstracted from outward objects, his studiousness was not of a solemn cast; he seemed wrapt in what he was reading with a pleasure amounting to ecstasy. He started, acted, smiled, and looked pensive in turn, while his features were thrown into a thousand different expressions, and his person was almost writhed with perpetually varying gestures. From time to time his rapture broke forth into loud exclamations of 'Exquisite! exquisite!' while he beat the leaves of the book violently with his hands, in token of applause, or lifting them up to his lips, almost devoured with kisses the passages that charmed him. Sometimes he read a few words aloud, calling out 'Heavenly!' and vehemently stamping his approbation with his feet; then suddenly shutting up the book, folded his arms, and casting his eyes towards the ceiling, uttered: 'O too much! too much! there is no standing it!' yet again, the next minute, opened it and resumed the lecture.

The youthful group was much diverted with this unintended exhibition. To Eugenia alone it did not appear ridiculous; she simply envied his transports, and only wished to discover by what book they were excited. Edgar and Camilla amused themselves with conjecturing various authors; Indiana and Miss Margland required no such aid to pass their time, while, with at least equal delight, they contemplated the hoped-for prize.

Lionel now bounced in: 'Why what,' cried he, 'are you all doing in this musty old shop, when Mrs. Arlbery and all the world are enjoying the air on the public walks?'

Camilla was instantly for joining that lady; but Eugenia felt an unconquerable curiosity to learn the running title of the book. She stole softly round to look over the shoulder of the reader, and her respect for his raptures increased, when she saw they were raised by Thomson's Seasons.

Neither this approach, nor the loud call of Lionel, had interrupted the attention of the young student, who perceived and regarded nothing but what he was about; and though occasionally he ceased reading to indulge in passionate ejaculations, he seemed to hold everything else beneath his consideration.

Lionel, drawn to observe him from the circuit made by Eugenia, exclaimed: 'What, Melmond! why, how long have you been in Hampshire?'

The youth, surprised from his absence of mind by the sound of his own name, looked up and said: 'Who's that?'

'Why, when the deuce did you come into this part of the world?' cried Lionel, approaching him to shake hands.

'O! for pity's sake,' answered he, with energy, 'don't interrupt me!'

'Why not? have not you enough of that dry work at Oxford? Come, come, have done with this boyish stuff, and behave like a man.'

'You distract me,' answered Melmond, motioning him away; 'I am in a scene that entrances me to Elysium! I have never read it since I could appreciate it.'

'What! old Thomson?' said Lionel, peeping over him; 'why, I never read him at all. Come, man! (giving him a slap on the shoulder) come along with me, and I'll shew you something more worth looking at.'

'You will drive me mad, if you break in upon this episode! 'tis a picture of all that is divine upon earth! hear it, only hear it!'

He then began the truly elegant and feeling description that concludes Thomson's Spring; and though Lionel, with a loud shout, cried: 'Do you think I come hither for such fogrum stuff as that?' and ran out of the shop; the 'wrapt enthusiast' continued reading aloud, too much delighted with the pathos of his own voice in expressing the sentiments of the poet, to deny himself a regale so soothing to his ears.

Eugenia, enchanted, stood on tiptoe to hear him, her uplifted finger petitioning silence all around, and her heart fondly repeating, O just such a youth be Clermont! just such his passion for reading! just such his fervour for poetry! just such his exaltation of delight in literary yet domestic felicity!

Mandlebert, also, caught by the rehearsal of his favourite picture of a scheme of human happiness, which no time, no repetition can make vapid to a feeling heart, stood pleased and attentive to hear him; even Indiana, though she listened not to the matter, was struck by the manner in which it was delivered, which so resembled dramatic recitation, that she thought herself at a play, and full of wonder, advanced straight before him, to look full in his face, and watch the motions of his right arm, with which he acted incessantly, while the left held his book. Miss Margland concluded he was a strolling player, and did not suffer him to draw her eyes from the locket. But when, at the words

—content,
Retirement, rural quiet, friendship, books,
Ease and alternate labour, useful life,
Progressive virtue, and approving Heaven,

Mandlebert turned softly round to read their impression on the countenance of Camilla—she was gone!

Attracted by her wish to see more of Mrs. Arlbery, she had run out of the shop after Lionel, before she either knew what was reading, or was missed by those the reader had engaged. Edgar, though disappointed, wondered he should have stayed himself to listen to what had long been familiar to him, and was quietly gliding away when he saw her returning. He then went back to his post, wondering, with still less satisfaction, how she could absent herself from hearing what so well was worth her studying.

The young man, when he came to the concluding line:

To scenes where love and bliss immortal reign!

rose, let fall the book, clasped his hands with a theatrical air, and was casting his eyes upwards in a fervent and willing trance, when he perceived Indiana standing immediately before him.

Surprised and ashamed, his sublimity suddenly forsook him; his arms dropt, and his hands were slipt into his waistcoat pockets.

But, the very next moment, the sensation of shame and of self was superseded by the fair object that had thus aroused him. Her beauty, her youth, her attitude of examination, struck him at first with an amazement that presently gave place to an admiration as violent as it was sudden. He started back, bowed profoundly, without any pretence for bowing at all, and then rivetting his eyes, in which his whole soul seemed centred, on her lovely face, stood viewing her with a look of homage, motionless, yet enraptured.

Indiana, still conceiving this to be some sort of acting, unabashed kept her post, expecting every moment he would begin spouting something more. But the enthusiasm of the young Oxonian had changed its object; the charms of poetry yielded to the superior charms of beauty, and while he gazed on the fair Indiana, his fervent mind fancied her some being of celestial order, wonderfully accorded to his view: How, or for what purpose, he as little knew as cared. The play of imagination, in the romance of early youth, is rarely interrupted with scruples of probability.

This scene of dumb transport and unfixed expectation, was broken up neither by the admirer nor the admired, but by the entrance of Mrs. Arlbery, Sir Sedley Clarendel, Lionel, the officers, and many of the rest of the company that had been present at the public breakfast: Nor would even this intrusion have disengaged the young Oxonian from his devout and ecstatic adoration, had it been equally indifferent to Indiana; but the appearance of a party of gay officers was not, to her, a matter of little moment. Eager for the notice in which she delighted, she looked round in full confidence of receiving it. The rapture of the Oxonian, as she had seen it kindled while he was reading, she attributed to something she did not understand, and took in it, therefore, no part; but the adulation of the officers was by no means ambiguous, and its acceptance was as obvious as its presentation.

Willingly, therefore, as well as immediately encompassed, she received a thousand compliments, and in the gratification of hearing them, completely forgot her late short surprise; but the Oxonian, more forcibly struck, ardently followed her with his eyes, started back theatrically at every change of attitude which displayed her fine figure, and at her smiles smiled again, from the uncontrollable sympathy of a fascinated imagination.

Miss Margland felt not small pride in seeing her pupil thus distinguished, since it marked the shrewdness of her capacity in foretelling the effect of bringing her forth. Anxious to share in a consequence to which she had industriously contributed, she paradingly forced her way through the group, and calling the attention of Indiana to herself, said: 'I am glad you came away, my dear; for I am sure that man is only a poor strolling player.'

'Dear! let me look at him again!' cried Indiana; 'for I never saw a player before; only at a play.'

She then turned back to examine him.

Enchanted to again meet her eyes, the youth bowed with intense respect, and advanced a few paces, as if with intention to speak to her, though immediately and with still more precipitance he retreated, from being ready with nothing to say.

Lionel, going up to him, and pulling him by the arm, cried: 'Why, man! what's come to you? These are worse heroics than I have seen you in yet.'

The bright eyes of Indiana being still fixed upon him, he disdained all notice of Lionel, beyond a silent repulse.

Indiana, having now satisfied her curiosity, restored her attention to the beaux that surrounded her. The Oxonian, half sighing, unfolded his clasped hands, one of which he reposed upon the shoulder of Lionel.

'Come, prithee, be a little less in alt,' cried Lionel, 'and answer a man when he speaks to you. Where did you leave Smythson?'

'Who is that divinity; can you tell me?' said the Oxonian in a low and respectful tone of inquiry.

'What divinity?'

'What divinity? insensible Tyrold! tasteless! adamantine! Look, look yonder, and ask me again if you can!'

'O what; my cousin Indiana?'

'Your cousin? have you any affinity with such a creature as that? O Tyrold! I glory in your acquaintance! she is all I ever read of! all I ever conceived! she is beauty in its very essence! she is elegance, delicacy, and sensibility personified!'

'All very true,' said Lionel; 'but how should you know anything of her besides her beauty?'

'How? by looking at her! Can you view that countenance and ask me how? Are not those eyes all soul? Does not that mouth promise every thing that is intelligent? Can those lips ever move but to diffuse sweetness and smiles? I must not look at her again! another glance may set me raving!'

'May?' cried Lionel, laughing; 'why what have you been doing all this time? However, be a little less in the sublime, and I'll introduce you to her.'

'Is it possible? shall I owe to you so celestial a happiness? O Tyrold! you bind me to you for life!'

Lionel, heartily hallowing, then brought him forward to Indiana: 'Miss Lynmere,' he cried, 'a fellow student of mine, though somewhat more given to study than your poor cousin, most humbly begs the honour of kissing your toe.'

The uncommon lowness of the bow which the Oxonian, ignorant of what Lionel would say, was making, led Miss Margland to imagine he was really going to perform that popish ceremony; and hastily pulling Lionel by the sleeve, she angrily said: 'Mr. Lionel, I desire to know by whose authority you present such actor-men to a young lady under my care.'

Lionel, almost in convulsions, repeated this aloud; and the young student, who had just, in a voice of the deepest interest and respect, begun, 'The high honour, madam;' hearing an universal laugh from the company, stopt short, utterly disconcerted, and after a few vainly stammering attempts, bowed again, and was silent.

Edgar, who in this distress, read an ingenuousness of nature that counterpoised its romantic enthusiasm, felt for the young man, and taking Lionel by the arm, said: 'Will you not introduce me also to your friend?'

'Mr. Melmond of Brazen Nose! Mr. Mandlebert of Beech Park!' cried Lionel, flourishing, and bowing from one to the other.

Edgar shook hands with the youth, and hoped they should be better acquainted.

Camilla, gliding round, whispered him: 'How like my dear father was that! to give relief to embarrassment, instead of joining in the laugh which excites it!'

Edgar, touched by a comparison to the person he most honoured, gratefully looked his acknowledgment; and all displeasure at her flight, even from Thomson's scene of conjugal felicity, was erased from his mind.

The company grew impatient for the raffle, though some of the subscribers were not arrived. It was voted, at the proposition of Mrs. Arlbery, that the master of the shop should represent, as their turns came round, those who were absent.

While this was settling, Edgar, in some confusion, drew Camilla to the door, saying: 'To avoid any perplexity about your throwing, suppose you step into the haberdasher's shop that is over the way?'

Camilla, who already had felt very awkward with respect to her withdrawn subscription, gladly agreed to the proposal, and begging him to explain the matter to Miss Margland, tript across the street, while the rafflers were crowding to the point of action.

Here she sat, making some small purchases, till the business was over: The whole party then came forth into the street, and all in a body poured into the haberdasher's shop, smiling, bowing, and of one accord wishing her joy.

Concluding this to be in derision of her desertion, she rallied as well as she was able; but Mrs. Arlbery, who entered the last, and held the locket in her hand, said: 'Miss Tyrold, I heartily wish you equally brilliant success, in the next, and far more dangerous lottery, in which, I presume, you will try your fate.' And presented her the prize.

Camilla, colouring, laughing, and unwillingly taking it, said: 'I suppose, ma'am—I hope—it is yours?' And she looked about for Edgar to assist her; but, he was gone to hasten the carriage.

Every body crowded round her to take a last sight of the beautiful locket. Eager to get rid of it, she put it into the hands of Indiana, who regarded it with a partiality which her numerous admirers had courted, individually, in vain; though the young Oxonian, by his dramatic emotions, had engaged more of her attention than she had yet bestowed elsewhere. Eugenia too, caught by his eccentricity, was powerfully impelled to watch and admire him; and not the less, in the unenvying innocency of her heart, for his evident predilection in favour of her cousin. This youth was not, however, suffered to engross her; the stranger by whom she had already been distinguished at the ball and public breakfast, was one in the group, and resumed a claim upon her notice, too flattering in its manner to be repulsed, and too new to her extreme inexperience to be obtrusive.

Meanwhile, Camilla gathered from Major Cerwood, that the prize had really fallen to her lot. Edgar had excused her not staying to throw for herself, but the general proxy, the bookseller, had been successful in her name.

In great perplexity how to account for this incident, she apprehended Edgar had made some mistake, and determined, through his means, to restore the locket to the subscription.

The carriage of Mrs. Arlbery was first ready; but, pushing away the throng of beaux offering assistance, she went up to Camilla, and said: 'Fair object of the spleen of all around, will you bring a little of your influence with good fortune to my domain, and come and dine with me?'

Delighted at the proposal, Camilla looked at Miss Margland; but Miss Margland, not being included in the invitation, frowned a refusal.

Edgar now entered and announced the coach of Sir Hugh.

'Make use of it as you can,' said Mrs. Arlbery; 'there is room for one more to go back than it brought; so pray do the honours prettily. Clarendel! take care of Miss Tyrold to my coach.'

Sir Sedley smiled, and played with his watch chain, but did not move.

'O you laziest of all lazy wretches!' cried Mrs. Arlbery.

'I shall reverse the epithet, and be the alertest of the alert,' said Major Cerwood; 'if the commission may be devolved to myself.'

'Positively not for the world! there is nothing so pleasant as working the indolent; except, indeed, making the restless keep quiet; so, come forth, Clarendel! be civil, and strike us all with astonishment!'

'My adored Mrs. Arlbery!' cried he, (hoisting himself upon the shop counter, and swinging a switch to and fro, with a languid motion) your maxims are all of the first superlative, except this; but nobody's civil now, you know; 'tis a fogramity quite out.'

'So you absolutely won't stir, then?'

'O pray! pray!' answered he, putting on his hat and folding his arms, 'a little mercy! 'tis so vastly insufferably hot! Calcutta must be in the frigid zone to this shop! a very ice-house!'

Camilla, who never imagined rudeness could make a feature of affectation, internally attributed this refusal to his pique that she had disregarded him at the public breakfast, and would have made him some apology, but knew not in what manner to word it.

The Major again came forward, but Miss Margland, advancing also, said: 'Miss Camilla! you won't think of dining out unknown to Sir Hugh?'

'I am sure,' cried Mrs. Arlbery, 'you will have the goodness to speak for me to Sir Hugh.' Then, turning to Lionel, 'Mr. Tyrold,' she added, 'you must go with us, that you may conduct your sister safe home. Don't be affronted; I shall invite you for your own sake another time. Come, you abominable Clarendel! awake! and give a little spring to our motions.'

'You are most incommodiously cruel!' answered he; 'but I am bound to be your slave.' Then calling to one of the apprentices in the shop: 'My vastly good boy,' he cried, 'do you want to see me irrecoverably subdued by this immensely inhuman heat?'

The boy stared; and said, 'Sir.'

'If not, do get me a glass of water.'

'O worse and worse!' said Mrs. Arlbery; 'your whims are insupportable. I give you up! Major! advance.'

The Major, with alacrity, offered his hand; Camilla hesitated; she wished passionately to go, yet felt she had no authority for such a measure. The name, though not the person of Mrs. Arlbery, was known both at Cleves and at Etherington, as belonging to the owner of a capital house in the neighbourhood; and though the invitation was without form, Camilla was too young to be withheld by ceremony. Her uncle, she was sure, could refuse her nothing; and she thought, as she was only a visitor at Cleves, Miss Margland had no right to control her; the pleasure, therefore, of the scheme, soon conquered every smaller difficulty, and, looking away from her party, she suffered herself to be led to the coach.

Miss Margland as she passed, said aloud: 'Remember! I give no consent to this!'

But Eugenia, on the other side, whispered: 'Don't be uneasy; I will explain to my uncle how it all happened.'

Mrs. Arlbery was following, when Indiana exclaimed: 'Cousin Camilla, what am I to do with your locket?'

Camilla had wholly forgotten it; she called to Edgar, who slowly, and with a seriousness very unusual, obeyed her summons.

'There has been some great mistake,' said she, 'about the locket. I suppose they neglected to scratch out my name from the subscription; for Major Cerwood says it really came to me. Will you be so good as to return it to the bookseller?'

The gravity of Edgar immediately vanished: 'Are you so ready,' he said, 'even when it is in your possession, to part with so pretty a trinket?'

'You know it cannot be mine, for here is my half guinea.'

Mrs. Arlbery then got into the coach; but Camilla, still farther recollecting herself, again called to Edgar, and holding out the half guinea, said: 'How shall I get this to the poor people?'

'They were to come,' he answered, 'to Cleves this afternoon.'

'Will you, then, give it them for me?'

'No commission to Mr. Mandlebert!' interrupted Mrs. Arlbery; 'for he must positively dine with us.'

Mandlebert bowed a pleased assent, and Camilla applied to Eugenia; but Miss Margland, in deep wrath, refused to let her move a step.

Mrs. Arlbery then ordered the coach to drive home. Camilla, begging a moment's delay, desired Edgar to approach nearer, and said, in a low voice: 'I cannot bear to let those poor expectants toil so far for nothing. I will sooner go back to Cleves myself. I shall not sleep all night if I disappoint them. Pray, invent some excuse for me.'

'If you have set your heart upon this visit,' answered Mandlebert, with vivacity, though in a whisper, 'I will ride over myself to Cleves, and arrange all to your wishes; but if not, certainly there can need no invention, to decline an invitation of which Sir Hugh has no knowledge.'

Camilla, who at the beginning of this speech felt the highest glee, sunk involuntarily at its conclusion, and turning with a blank countenance to Mrs. Arlbery, stammeringly said: 'Can you, will you—be so very good, as not to take it ill if I don't go with you?'

Mrs. Arlbery, surprised, very coldly answered: 'Certainly not! I would be no restraint upon you. I hate restraint myself.' She then ordered the footman to open the door; and Camilla, too much abashed to offer any apology, was handed out by Edgar.

'Amiable Camilla!' said he, in conducting her back to Miss Margland, 'this is a self-conquest that I alone, perhaps, expected from you!'

Cheered by such approbation, she forgot her disappointment, and regardless of Miss Margland and her ill humour, jumped into her uncle's coach, and was the gayest of the party that returned to Cleves.

Edgar took the locket from Indiana, and promised to rectify the mistake; and then, lest Mrs. Arlbery should be offended with them all, rode to her house without any fresh invitation, accompanied by Lionel; whose anger against Camilla, for suffering Miss Margland to gain a victory, was his theme the whole ride.

CHAPTER VI

A Barn

The first care of Camilla was to interest Sir Hugh in the misfortunes of the prisoner and his family; her next, to relate the invitation of Mrs. Arlbery, and to beg permission that she might wait upon the lady the next morning, with apologies for her abrupt retreat, and with acknowledgments for the services done to the poor woman; which first the Oxonian, and then the raffle, had driven from her mind. Sir Hugh readily consented, blaming her for supposing it possible he could ever hesitate in what could give her any pleasure.

Before the tea-party broke up, Edgar returned. He told Camilla he had stolen away the instant the dinner was over, to avoid any mistake about the poor people, whom he had just overtaken by the park-gate, and conducted to the great barn, where he had directed them to wait for orders.

'I'll run to them immediately,' cried she, 'for my half guinea is in an agony to be gone!'

'The barn! my dear young Mr. Mandlebert!' exclaimed Sir Hugh; 'and why did you not bring them to the servants' hall? My little girl has been telling me all their history; and, God forbid, I should turn hard-hearted, because of their wanting a leg of mutton, in preference to being starved; though they might have no great right to it, according to the forms of law; which, however, is not much impediment to the calls of nature, when a man sees a butcher's stall well covered, and has got nothing within him, except his own poor craving appetite; which is a thing I always take into consideration; though, God forbid, I should protect a thief, no man's property being another's, whether he's poor or rich.'

He then gave Camilla three guineas to deliver to them from himself, to set them a little a-going in an honest way, that they might not, he said, repent leaving off bad actions. Her joy was so excessive, that she passionately embraced his knees: and Edgar, while he looked on, could nearly have bent to her his own, with admiration of her generous nature. Eugenia desired to accompany her; and Indiana, rising also, said: 'Dear! I wonder how they will look in the barn! I should like to see them too.'

Miss Margland made no opposition, and they set out.

Camilla, leading the way, with a fleetness that mocked all equality, ran into the barn, and saw the whole party, according to their several powers, enjoying themselves. The poor man, stretched upon straw, was resting his aching limbs; his wife, by his side, was giving nourishment to her baby; and the other child, a little boy of three years old, was jumping and turning head over heels, with the true glee of unspoilt nature, superior to poverty and distress.

To the gay heart of Camilla whatever was sportive was attractive; she flew to the little fellow, whose skin was clean and bright, in the midst of his rags and wretchedness, and, making herself his play-mate, bid the woman finish feeding her child, told the man to repose himself undisturbed, and began dancing with the little boy, not less delighted than himself at the festive exercise.

Miss Margland cast up her hands and eyes as she entered, and poured forth a warm remonstrance against so demeaning a condescension: but Camilla, in whose composition pride had no share, though spirit was a principal ingredient, danced on unheeding, to the equal amaze and enchantment of the poor man and woman, at the honour done to their little son.

Edgar came in last; he had given his arm to Eugenia, who was always in the rear if unassisted. Miss Margland appealed to him upon the impropriety of the behaviour of Camilla, adding, 'If I had had the bringing up a young lady who could so degrade herself, I protest I should blush to shew my face: but you cannot, I am sure, fail remarking the difference of Miss Lynmere's conduct.'

Edgar attended with an air of complacency, which he thought due to the situation of Miss Margland in the family, yet kept his eyes fixt upon Camilla, with an expression that, to the least discernment, would have evinced his utmost approbation of her innocent gaiety: but Miss Margland was amongst that numerous tribe, who, content as well as occupied with making observations upon others, have neither the power, nor thought, of developing those that are returned upon themselves.

Camilla at length, wholly out of breath, gave over; but perceiving that the baby was no longer at its mother's breast, flew to the poor woman, and, taking the child in her arms, said: 'Come, I can nurse and rest at the same time; I assure you the baby will be safe with me, for I nurse all the children in our neighbourhood.' She then fondled the poor little half-starved child to her bosom, quieting, and kissing, and cooing over it.

Miss Margland was still more incensed; but Edgar could attend to her no longer. Charmed with the youthful nurse, and seeing in her unaffected attitudes, a thousand graces he had never before remarked, and reading in her fondness for children the genuine sweetness of her character, he could not bear to have the pleasing reflections revolving in his mind interrupted by the spleen of Miss Margland, and, slipping away, posted himself behind the baby's father, where he could look on undisturbed, certain it was a vicinity to which Miss Margland would not follow him.

Had this scene lasted till Camilla was tired, its period would not have been very short; but Miss Margland, finding her exhortations vain, suddenly called out: 'Miss Lynmere! Miss Eugenia! come away directly! It's ten to one but these people have all got the gaol distemper!'

Edgar, quick as lightning at this sound, flew to Camilla, and snatched the child from her arms. Indiana, with a scream, ran out of the barn; Miss Margland hurried after; and Eugenia, following, earnestly entreated Camilla not to stay another moment.

'And what is there to be alarmed at?' cried she; 'I always nurse poor children when I see them at home; and my father never prohibits me.'

'There may be some reason, however,' said Edgar, while still he tenderly held the baby himself, 'for the present apprehension: I beg you, therefore, to hasten away.'

'At least,' said she, 'before I depart, let me execute my commission.' And then, with the kindest good wishes for their better fortune, she put her uncle's three guineas into the hands of the poor man, and her own rescued half guinea into those of his wife; and, desiring Edgar not to remain himself where he would not suffer her to stay, ran to give her arm to Eugenia; leaving it a doubtful point, whether the good humour accompanying her alms, made the most pleased impression upon their receivers, or upon their observer.

CHAPTER VII

A Declaration

At night, while they were enjoying the bright beams of the moon, from an apartment in the front of the house, they observed a strange footman, in a superb livery, ride towards the servants hall; and presently a letter was delivered to Miss Margland.

She opened it with an air of exulting consequence; one which was inclosed, she put into her pocket, and read the other three or four times over, with looks of importance and complacency. She then pompously demanded a private audience with Sir Hugh, and the young party left the room.

'Well, sir!' she cried, proudly, 'you may now see if I judged right as to taking the young ladies a little into the world. Please to look at this letter, sir:'

To Miss Margland, at Sir Hugh Tyrold's, Bart.
Cleves, Hampshire.

MADAM,

With the most profound respect I presume to address you, though only upon the strength of that marked politeness which shines forth in your deportment. I have the highest ambition to offer a few lines to the perusal of Miss Eugenia Tyrold, previous to presenting myself to Sir Hugh. My reasons will be contained in the letter which I take the liberty to put into your hands. It is only under your protection, madam, I can aim at approaching that young lady, as all that I have either seen or heard convinces me of her extraordinary happiness in being under your direction. Your influence, madam, I should therefore esteem as an honour, and I leave it wholly to your own choice, whether to read what I have addressed to that young lady before or after she has deigned to cast an eye upon it herself. I remain, with the most profound respect,

Madam,
your most obedient,
and obliged servant,
ALPHONSO BELLAMY.

I shall take the liberty to send my servant for an answer tomorrow evening.

'This, sir,' continued Miss Margland, when Sir Hugh had read the letter; 'this is the exact conduct of a gentleman; all open, all respectful. No attempt at any clandestine intercourse. All is addressed where it ought to be, to the person most proper to superintend such an affair. This is that very same gentleman whose politeness I mentioned to you, and who danced with Miss Eugenia at Northwick, when nobody else took any notice of her. This is—'

'Why then this is one of the most untoward things,' cried Sir Hugh, who, vainly waiting for a pause, began to speak without one, 'that has ever come to bear; for where's the use of Eugenia's making poor young fellows fall in love with her for nothing? which I hold to be a pity, provided it's sincere, which I take for granted.'

'As to that, sir, I can't say I see the reason why Miss Eugenia should not be allowed to look about her, and have some choice; especially as the young gentleman abroad has no fortune; at least none answerable to her expectations.'

'But that's the very reason for my marrying them together. For as he has not had the small-pox himself, that is, not in the natural way; which, Lord help me! I thought the best, owing to my want of knowledge; why he'll the more readily excuse her face not being one of the prettiest, for her kindness in putting up with his having so little money; being a thing some people think a good deal of.'

'But, sir, won't it be very hard upon poor Miss Eugenia, if a better offer should come, that she must not listen to it, only because of a person she has never seen, though he has no estate?'

'Mrs. Margland,' said Sir Hugh, (with some heat,) 'this is the very thing that I would sooner have given a crown than have had happen! Who knows but Eugenia may take a fancy to this young jackanapes? who, for aught I know, may be as good a man as another, for which I beg his pardon; but, as he is nothing to me, and my nephew's my nephew, why am I to have the best scheme I ever made knocked on the head, for a person I had as lieve were twitched into the Red Sea? which, however, is a thing I should not say, being what I would not do.'

Miss Margland took from her pocket the letter designed for Eugenia, and was going to break the seal; but Sir Hugh, preventing her, said: 'No, Miss Margland; Eugenia shall read her own letters. I have not had her taught all this time, by one of the first scholars of the age, as far as I can tell, to put that affront upon her.'

He then rang the bell, and sent for Eugenia.

Miss Margland stated the utter impropriety of suffering any young lady to read a letter of that sort, till proposals had been laid before her parents and guardians. But Sir Hugh spoke no more till Eugenia appeared.

'My dear,' he then said, 'here is a letter just come to put your education to the trial; which, I make no doubt, will stand the test properly: therefore, in regard to the answer, you shall write it all yourself, being qualified in a manner to which I have no right to pretend; though I shall go to-morrow to my brother, which will give me a better insight; his head being one of the best.'

Eugenia, greatly surprised, opened the letter, and read it with visible emotion.

'Well, my dear, and what do you say to it?'

Without answering, she read it again.

Sir Hugh repeated the question.

'Indeed, sir,' said she, (in a tone of sadness,) 'it is something that afflicts me very much!'

'Lord help us!' cried Sir Hugh, 'this comes of going to a ball! which, begging Miss Margland's pardon, is the last time it shall be done.'

Miss Margland was beginning a vehement defence of herself; but Sir Hugh interrupted it, by desiring to see the letter.

Eugenia, with increased confusion, folded it up, and said: 'Indeed, sir—Indeed, uncle—it is a very improper letter for me to shew.'

'Well, that,' cried Miss Margland, 'is a thing I could never have imagined! that a gentleman, who is so much the gentleman, should write an improper letter!'

'No, no,' interrupted she, 'not improper—perhaps—for him to write,—but for me to exhibit.'

'O, if that's all, my dear,' said Sir Hugh, 'if it's only because of a few compliments, I beg you not to mind them, because of their having no meaning; which is a thing common enough in the way of making love, by what I hear; though such a young thing as you can know nothing of the matter, your learning not going in that line; nor Dr. Orkborne's neither, if one may judge; which, God forbid I should find fault with, being no business of mine.'

He then again asked to see the letter; and Eugenia, ashamed to refuse, gave it, and went out of the room.

To Miss Eugenia Tyrold, Cleves.

MADAM,

The delicacy of your highly cultivated mind awes even the violent passion which you inspire. And to this I entreat you to attribute the trembling fear which deters me from the honour of waiting upon Sir Hugh, while uncertain, if my addressing him might not raise your displeasure. I forbear, therefore, to lay before him my pretensions for soliciting your favour, from the deepest apprehension you might think I presumed too far, upon an acquaintance, to my unhappiness, so short; yet, as I feel it to have excited in me the most lasting attachment, from my fixed admiration of your virtues and talents, I cannot endure to run the risk of incurring your aversion. Allow me then, once more, under the sanction of that excellent lady in whose care I have had the honour of seeing you, to entreat one moment's audience, that I may be graced with your own commands about waiting upon Sir Hugh, without which, I should hold myself ungenerous and unworthy to approach him; since I should blush to throw myself at your feet from an authority which you do not permit. I beseech you, madam, to remember, that I shall be miserable till I know my doom; but still, that the heart, not the hand, can alone bestow happiness on a disinterested mind.

I have the honour to be, Madam,
your most devoted and obedient humble servant,
ALPHONSO BELLAMY.

Sir Hugh, when he had finished the letter, heaved a sigh, and leant his head upon his hand, considering whether or not to let it be seen by Miss Margland; who, however, not feeling secure what his determination might be, had so contrived to sit at the table as to read it at the same time with himself. Nor had she weighed the interest of her curiosity amiss; Sir Hugh, dreading a debate with her, soon put the letter into his pocket-book, and again sent for Eugenia.

Eugenia excused herself from returning, pleaded a head-ache, and went to bed.

Sir Hugh was in the deepest alarm; though the evening was far advanced, he could scarce refrain from going to Etherington directly; he ordered his carriage to be at the door at eight o'clock the next morning; and sent a second order, a moment after, that it should not be later than half past seven.

He then summoned Camilla, and, giving her the letter, bid her run with it to her sister, for fear it was that she was fretting for. And soon after, he went to bed, that he might be ready in the morning.

Eugenia, meanwhile, felt the placid composure of her mind now for the first time shaken. The assiduities of this young man had already pleased and interested her; but, though gratified by them in his presence, they occurred to her no more in his absence. With the Oxonian she had been far more struck; his energy, his sentiments, his passion for literature, would instantly have riveted him in her fairest favour, had she not so completely regarded herself as the wife of Clermont Lynmere, that she denied her imagination any power over her reason.

This letter, however, filled her with sensations wholly new. She now first reflected seriously upon the nature of her situation with regard to Clermont, for whom she seemed bespoken by her uncle, without the smallest knowledge how they might approve or suit each other. Perhaps he might dislike her; she must then have the mortification of being refused: perhaps he might excite her own antipathy; she must then either disappoint her uncle, or become a miserable sacrifice.

Here, on the contrary, she conceived herself an elected object. The difference of being accepted, or being chosen, worked forcibly upon her mind; and, all that was delicate, feminine, or dignified in her notions, rose in favour of him who sought, when opposed to him who could only consent to receive her. Generous, too, he appeared to her, in forbearing to apply to Sir Hugh, without her permission; disinterested, in declaring he did not wish for her hand without her heart; and noble, in not seeking her in a clandestine manner, but referring every thing to Miss Margland.

The idea also of exciting an ardent passion, lost none of its force from its novelty to her expectations. It was not that she had hitherto supposed it impossible; she had done less; she had not thought of it all. Nor came it now with any triumph to her modest and unassuming mind; all it brought with it was gratitude towards Bellamy, and a something soothing towards herself, which, though inexplicable to her reason, was irresistible to her feelings.

When Camilla entered with the letter, she bashfully asked her, if she wished to read it? Camilla eagerly cried: 'O, yes.' But, having finished it, said: 'It is not such a letter as Edgar Mandlebert would have written.'

'I am sure, then,' said Eugenia, colouring, 'I am sorry to have received it.'

'Do you not observe every day,' said Camilla, 'the distance, the delicacy of his behaviour to Indiana, though Miss Margland says their marriage is fixed; how free from all distinction that might confuse her? This declaration, on the contrary, is so abrupt—and from so new an acquaintance—'

'Certainly, then, I won't answer it,' said Eugenia, much discomposed; 'it had not struck me thus at first reading; but I see now all its impropriety.'

She then bid good night to Camilla; who, concluding her the appropriated wife of Clermont, had uttered her opinion without scruple.

Eugenia now again read the letter; but not again with pleasure. She thought it forward and presumptuous; and the only gratification that remained upon her mind, was an half conscious scarce admitted, and, even to herself, unacknowledged charm, in a belief, that she possessed the power to inspire an animated regard.

CHAPTER VIII

An Answer

Mr. and Mrs. Tyrold and Lavinia were at breakfast when Sir Hugh entered their parlour, the next morning. 'Brother,' he cried, 'I have something of great importance to tell you, which it is very fit my sister should hear too; for which reason, I make no doubt but my dear Lavinia's good sense will leave the room, without waiting for a hint.'

Lavinia instantly retired.

'O, my dear brother,' continued the baronet; 'do you know here's a young chap, who appears to be a rather good sort of man, which is so much the worse, who has been falling in love with Eugenia?'

He then delivered the two letters to Mr. Tyrold.

'Now the only thing that hurts me in this business is, that this young man, who Miss Margland calls a person of fashion, writes as well as Clermont would do himself; though that is what I shall never own to Eugenia, which I hope is no sin being all for her own sake; that is to say, for Clermont's.'

Mr. Tyrold, after attentively reading the letters, gave them to his wife, and made many inquiries concerning their writer, and his acquaintance with Eugenia and Miss Margland.

'Why it was all brought about,' said Sir Hugh, 'by their going to a ball and a public breakfast; which is a thing my little Camilla is not at all to blame for, because if nobody had put it in her head, she would not have known there was a thing of the kind. And, indeed, it was but natural in poor Lionel neither, to set her agog, the chief fault lying in the assizes; to which my particular objection is against the lawyers, who come into a town to hang and transport the poor, by way of keeping the peace, and then encourage the rich to make all the noise and riot they can, by their own junkettings; for which, however, being generally, I believe, pretty good scholars, I make no doubt but they have their own reasons.'

'I flatter myself,' said Mrs. Tyrold, scarce deigning to finish the letters, 'Eugenia, young as she is, will need no counsel how to estimate a writer such as this. What must the man be, who, presuming upon his personal influence, ventures to claim her concurrence in an application to her friends, though he has seen her but twice, and knows her to be destitute of the smallest knowledge of his principles, his character, or his situation in life?'

'Good lack!' cried the baronet, 'what a prodigious poor head I must have! here I could hardly sleep all night, for thinking what a fine letter this jackanapes, which I shall make no more apology for calling him, had been writing, fearing it would cut up poor Clermont in her opinion, for all his grand tour.'

Perfectly restored to ease, he now bad them good morning; but Mr. Tyrold entreated him to stay till they had settled how to get rid of the business.

'My dear brother,' he answered, 'I want no more help now, since I have got your opinion, that is, my sister's, which I take it for granted is the same. I make no doubt but Eugenia will pretty near have writ her foul copy by the time I get home, which Dr. Orkborne may overlook for her, to the end that this Mr. Upstart may have no more fault to find against it.'

They both desired to dine at Cleves, that they might speak themselves with Eugenia.

'And how,' said Mr. Tyrold, with a strong secret emotion, 'how goes on Edgar with Indiana?'

'Vastly well, vastly well indeed! not that I pretend to speak for myself, being rather too dull in these matters, owing to never entering upon them in the right season, as I intend to tell other young men doing the same.'

He then, in warm terms, narrated the accounts given him by Miss Margland of the security of the conquest of Indiana.

Mr. Tyrold fixed his hour for expecting the carriage, and the baronet desired that Lavinia should be of the party; 'because,' he said, 'I see she has the proper discretion, when she is wanted to go out of the way; which must be the same with Camilla and Indiana, too, to-day, as well as with young Mr. Edgar; for I don't think it prudent to trust such new beginners with every thing that goes on, till they get a little older.'

The anxiety of Mr. Tyrold, concerning Bellamy, was now mingled with a cruel regret in relation to Mandlebert. Even his own upright conduct could scarce console him for the loss of his favourite hope, and he almost repented that he had not been more active in endeavouring to preserve it.

All that passed in his mind was read and participated in by his partner, whose displeasure was greater, though her mortification could but be equal. 'That Edgar,' said she, 'should have kept his heart wholly untouched, would less have moved my wonder; he has a peculiar, though unconscious delicacy in his nature, which results not from insolence nor presumption, but from his own invariable and familiar exercise of every virtue and of every duty: the smallest deviation is offensive, and even the least inaccuracy is painful to him. Was it possible, then, to be prepared for such an election as this? He has disgraced my expectations; he has played the common part of a mere common young man, whose eye is his sole governor.'

'My Georgiana,' said Mr. Tyrold, 'I am deeply disappointed. Our two eldest girls are but slightly provided for; and Eugenia is far more dangerously circumstanced, in standing so conspicuously apart, as a prize to some adventurer. One of these three precious cares I had fondly concluded certain of protection and happiness; for which ever I might have bestowed upon Edgar Mandlebert, I should have considered as the most fortunate of her sex. Let us, however, rejoice for Indiana; no one can more need a protector; and, next to my own three girls, there is no one for whom I am so much interested. I grieve, however, for Edgar himself, whose excellent judgment will, in time, assert its rights, though passion, at this period, has set it aside.'

'I am too angry with him for pity,' said Mrs. Tyrold; 'nor is his understanding of a class that has any claim to such lenity: I had often thought our gentle Lavinia almost born to be his wife, and no one could more truly have deserved him. But the soft perfection of her character relieves me from any apprehension for her conduct, and almost all my solicitude devolves upon Camilla. For our poor Eugenia I had never indulged a hope of his choice; though that valuable, unfortunate girl, with every unearned defect about her, intrinsically merits him, with all his advantages, his accomplishments, and his virtues: but to appreciate her, uninfluenced by pecuniary views, to which he is every way superior, was too much to expect from so young a man. My wishes, therefore, had guided him to our Camilla, that sweet, open, generous, inconsiderate girl, whose feelings are all virtues, but whose impulses have no restraints: I have not a fear for her, when she can act with deliberation; but fear is almost all I have left, when I consider her as led by the start of the moment. With him, however, she would have been the safest, and with him—next alone to her mother, the happiest of her sex.'

The kindest acknowledgments repaid this sympathy of sentiment, and they agreed that their felicity would have been almost too complete for this lower world, if such an event had come to pass. 'Nevertheless its failure,' added Mrs. Tyrold, 'is almost incredible, and wholly unpardonable. That Indiana should vanquish where Lavinia and Camilla have failed! I feel indignant at such a triumph of mere external unintelligent beauty.'

Eugenia received her parents with the most bashful confusion; yet they found, upon conversing with her, it was merely from youthful shame, and not from any dangerous prepossession. The observations of Camilla had broken that spell with which a first declaration of regard is apt to entangle unreflecting inexperience; and by teaching her to less value the votary, had made the conquest less an object of satisfaction. She was gratified by the permission of her uncle to write her own answer, which was now produced.

To Alphonso Bellamy, Esq.

SIR,

I am highly sensible to the honour of your partiality, which I regret it is not possible for me to deserve. Be not, therefore, offended, and still less suffer yourself to be afflicted, when I confess I have only my poor thanks to offer, and poor esteem to return, for your unmerited goodness. Dwell not, sir, upon this disappointment, but receive my best wishes for your restored happiness; for never can I forget a distinction to which I have so little claim. Believe me,

Sir, Your very much obliged,
and most grateful humble servant,
EUGENIA TYROLD.

Mr. Tyrold, who delighted to see how completely, in her studies with Dr. Orkborne, she had escaped any pedantry or affectation, and even preserved all the native humility of her artless character, returned her the letter with an affectionate embrace, and told her he could desire no alteration but that of omitting the word grateful at the conclusion.

Mrs. Tyrold was far less satisfied. She wished it to be completely re-written; protesting, that a man who, in all probability, was a mere fortune-hunter, would infer from so gentle a dismission encouragement rather than repulse.

Sir Hugh said there was one thing only he desired to have added, which was a hint of a pre-engagement with a relation of her own.

Eugenia, at this, coloured and retreated; and Mrs. Tyrold reminded the baronet, with some displeasure, of his promise to guard the secret of his project. Sir Hugh, a little disturbed, said it never broke out from him but by accident, which he would take care should never get the upper hand again. He would not, however, consent to have the letter altered, which he said would be an affront to the learning of Eugenia, unless it were done by Dr. Orkborne himself, who, being her master, had a right to correct her first penmanship.

Dr. Orkborne, being called upon, slightly glanced his eye over the letter, but made no emendation, saying: 'I believe it will do very sufficiently; but I have only concerned myself with the progress of Miss Eugenia in the Greek and Latin languages; any body can teach her English.'

The fond parents finished their visit in full satisfaction with their irreproachable Eugenia, and with the joy of seeing their darling Camilla as happy and as disengaged as when she had left them; but Mandlebert had spent the day abroad, and escaped, therefore, the observations with which they had meant to have investigated his sentiments. Indiana, with whom they conversed more than usual, and with the most scrutinizing attention, offered nothing either in manner or matter to rescue his decision from their censure: Mrs. Tyrold, therefore, rejoiced at his absence, lest a coolness she knew not how to repress, should have led him to surmise her disappointment. Her husband besought her to be guarded: 'We had no right,' he said, 'to the disposal of his heart; and Indiana, however he may find her inadequate to his future expectations, will not disgrace his present choice. She is beautiful, she is young, and she is innocent; this in early life is sufficient for felicity; and Edgar is yet too new in the world to be aware how much of life remains when youth is gone, and too unpractised to foresee, that beauty loses its power even before it loses its charms, and that the season of declining nature sighs deeply for the support which sympathy and intelligence can alone bestow.'

CHAPTER IX

An Explication

The visit which Camilla had designed this morning to Mrs. Arlbery, she had been induced to relinquish through a speech made to her by Lionel. 'You have done for yourself, now!' said he, exultingly; 'so you may be governed by that scare-crow, Miss Margland, at your leisure. Do you know you were not once mentioned again at the Grove, neither by Mrs. Arlbery nor any body else? and they all agreed Indiana was the finest girl in the world.'

Camilla, though of the same opinion with respect to Indiana, concluded Mrs. Arlbery was offended by her retreat, and lost all courage for offering any apology.

Edgar did not return to Cleves till some time after the departure of Mr. and Mrs. Tyrold, when he met Miss Margland and the young ladies strolling in the park.

Camilla, running to meet him, asked if he had restored the locket to the right owner.

'No,' answered he, smiling, 'not yet.'

'What can be done then? my half guinea is gone; and, to confess the truth, I have not another I can well spare!'

He made no immediate reply; but, after speaking to the rest of the party, walked on towards the house.

Camilla, in some perplexity, following him, exclaimed: 'Pray tell me what I must do? indeed I am quite uneasy.'

'You would really have me give the locket to its rightful proprietor?'

'To be sure I would!'

'My commission, then, is soon executed.' And taking a little shagreen case from his waistcoat pocket, he put it into her hand.

'What can you mean? is there still any mistake?'

'None but what you may immediately rectify, by simply retaining your own prize.'

Camilla, opening the case, saw the locket, and perceived under the crystal a light knot of braided hair. But while she looked at it, he hurried into the house.

She ran after him, and insisted upon an explanation, declaring it to be utterly impossible that the locket and the half guinea should belong to the same person.

'You must not then,' he said, 'be angry, if you find I have managed, at last, but aukwardly. When I came to the library, the master of the raffle told me it was against all rule to refund a subscription.' He stopt.

'The half guinea you put into my hand, then,' cried she, colouring, 'was your own?'

'My dear Miss Camilla, there is no other occasion upon which I would have hazarded such a liberty; but as the money was for a charity, and as I had undertaken what I could not perform, I rather ventured to replace it, than suffer the poor objects for whom it was destined, to miss your kind intention.'

'You have certainly done right,' said she (feeling for her purse); 'but you must not, for that reason, make me a second time do wrong.'

'You will not so much hurt me?' replied he, gravely; 'you will not reprove me as if I were a stranger, a mere common acquaintance? Where could the money have been so well bestowed? It is not you, but those poor people who are in my debt. So many were the chances against your gaining the prize, that it was an event I had not even taken into consideration: I had merely induced you to leave the shop, that you might not have the surprise of finding your name was not withdrawn; the rest was accident; and surely you will not punish me that I have paid to the poor the penalty of my own ill weighed officiousness?'

Camilla put up her purse, but, with some spirit, said: 'There is another way to settle the matter which cannot hurt you; if I do not pay you my half guinea, you must at least keep the fruits of your own.' And she returned him the locket.

'And what,' cried he, laughing 'must I do with it? would you have me wear it myself?'

'Give it,' answered she, innocently, 'to Indiana.'

'No;' replied he, (reddening and putting it down upon a table,) but you may, if you believe her value will be greater than your own for the hair of your two sisters.'

Camilla, surprised, again looked at it, and recognized the hair of Lavinia and Eugenia.

'And how in the world did you get this hair?'

'I told them both the accident that had happened, and begged them to contribute their assistance to obtain your pardon.'

'Is it possible,' cried she, with vivacity, 'you could add to all your trouble so kind a thought?' and, without a moment's further hesitation, she accepted the prize, returning him the most animated thanks, and flying to Eugenia to inquire further into the matter, and then to her uncle, to shew him her new acquisition.

Sir Hugh, like herself, immediately said: 'But why did he not give it to Indiana?'

'I suppose,' said Eugenia, 'because Camilla had herself drawn the prize, and he had only added our hair to it.'

This perfectly satisfied the baronet; but Indiana could by no means understand why it had not been managed better; and Miss Margland, with much ill will, nourished a private opinion that the prize might perhaps have been her own, had not Mandlebert interfered. However, as there seemed some collusion which she could not develope, her conscience wholly acquitted her of any necessity to refund her borrowed half guinea.

Camilla, meanwhile, decorated herself with the locket, and had nothing in her possession which gave her equal delight.

Miss Margland now became, internally, less sanguine, with regard to the preference of Edgar for Indiana; but she concealed from Sir Hugh a doubt so unpleasant, through an unconquerable repugnance to acknowledge it possible she could have formed a wrong judgment.

CHAPTER X

A Panic

Upon the ensuing Sunday, Edgar proposed that a party should be made to visit a new little cottage, which he had just fitted up. This was agreed to; and as it was not above a mile from the parish church, Sir Hugh ordered that his low garden phaeton should be in readiness, after the service, to convey himself and Eugenia thither. The rest, as the weather was fine, desired to walk.

They went to the church, as usual, in a coach and a chaise, which were dismissed as soon as they alighted: but before that period, Eugenia, with a sigh, had observed, that Melmond, the young Oxonian, was strolling the same way, and had seen, with a blush, that Bellamy was by his side.

The two gentlemen recognised them as they were crossing the church-yard. The Oxonian bowed profoundly, but stood aloof: Bellamy bowed also, but immediately approached; and as Sir Hugh, at that moment, accidentally let fall his stick, darted forward to recover and present it him.

The baronet, from surprise at his quick motion, dropt his handkerchief in receiving his cane; this also Bellamy, attentively shaking, restored to him: and Sir Hugh, who could accept no civility unrequited, said: 'Sir, if you are a stranger, as I imagine, not knowing your face, you are welcome to a place in my pew, provided you don't get a seat in a better; which I'm pretty much afraid you can't, mine being the best.'

The invitation was promptly accepted.

Miss Margland, always happy to be of consequence, was hastening to Sir Hugh, to put him upon his guard; when a respectful offer from Bellamy to assist her down the steps, induced her to remit her design to a future opportunity. Any attentions from a young man were now so new to her as to seem a call upon her gratitude; nor had her charms ever been so attractive as to render them common.

Edgar and Indiana, knowing nothing of his late declaration, thought nothing of his present admission; to Dr. Orkborne he was an utter stranger; but Camilla had recourse to her fan to conceal a smile; and Eugenia was in the utmost confusion. She felt at a loss how to meet his eyes, and seated herself as much as possible out of his way.

A few minutes after, looking up towards the gallery, she perceived, in one of the furthest rows, young Melmond; his eyes fixt upon their pew, but withdrawn the instant he was observed, and his air the most melancholy and dejected.

Again a half sigh escaped the tender Eugenia. How delicate, how elegant, thought she, is this retired behaviour! what refinement results from a true literary taste! O such be Clermont! if he resemble not this Oxonian—I must be wretched for life!

These ideas, which unavoidably, though unwillingly, interrupted her devotion, were again broken in upon, when the service was nearly over, by the appearance of Lionel. He had ridden five miles to join them, merely not to be thought in leading-strings, by staying at Etherington to hear his father; though the name and the excellence of the preaching of Mr. Tyrold, attracted to his church all strangers who had power to reach it:—so vehement in early youth is the eagerness to appear independant, and so general is the belief that all merit must be sought from a distance.

The deeper understanding of Mandlebert rendered him superior to this common puerility: and, though the preacher at Cleves church was his own tutor, Dr. Marchmont, from whom he was scarce yet emancipated, he listened to him with reverence, and would have travelled any distance, and taken cheerfully any trouble, that would in the best and strongest manner have marked the respect with which he attended to his doctrine.

Dr. Marchmont was a man of the highest intellectual accomplishments, uniting deep learning with general knowledge, and the graceful exterior of a man of the world, with the erudition and science of a fellow of a college. He obtained the esteem of the scholar wherever he was known, and caught the approbation of the most uncultivated wherever he was seen.

When the service was over, Edgar proposed that Dr. Marchmont should join the party to the cottage. Sir Hugh was most willing, and they sauntered about the church, while the Doctor retired to the vestry to take off his gown.

During this interval, Eugenia, who had a passion for reading epitaphs and inscriptions, became so intently engaged in decyphering some old verses on an antique tablet, that she perceived not when Dr. Marchmont was ready, nor when the party was leaving the church: and before any of the rest missed her, Bellamy suddenly took the opportunity of her being out of sight of all others, to drop on one knee, and passionately seize her hand, exclaiming: 'O madam!—' When hearing an approaching step, he hastily arose; but parted not with her hand till he had pressed it to his lips.

The astonished Eugenia, though at first all emotion, was completely recovered by this action. His kneeling and his 'O madam!' had every chance to affect her; but his kissing her hand she thought a liberty the most unpardonable. She resented it as an injury to Clermont, that would risk his life should he ever know it, and a blot to her own delicacy, as irreparable as it was irremediable.

Bellamy, who, from her letter, had augured nothing of hardness of heart, tenderly solicited her forgiveness; but she made him no answer; silent and offended she walked away, and, losing her timidity in her displeasure, went up to her uncle, and whispered: 'Sir, the gentleman you invited into your pew, is Mr. Bellamy!'

The consternation of Sir Hugh was extreme: he had concluded him a stranger to the whole party because a stranger to himself; and the discovery of his mistake made him next conclude, that he had risked a breach of the marriage he so much desired by his own indiscretion. He took Eugenia immediately under his arm, as if fearful she might else be conveyed away for Scotland before his eyes, and hurrying to the church porch, called aloud for his phaeton.

The phaeton was not arrived.

Still more dismayed, he walked on with Eugenia to the railing round the church-yard, motioning with his left hand that no one should follow.

Edgar, Lionel, and Bellamy marched to the road, listening for the sound of horses, but they heard none; and the carriages of the neighbouring gentry, from which they might have hoped any assistance, had been driven away while they had waited for Dr. Marchmont.

Meanwhile, the eyes of Eugenia again caught the young Oxonian, who was wandering around the church-yard: neither was he unobserved by Indiana, who, though she participated not in the turn of reasoning, or taste for the romantic, which awakened in Eugenia so forcible a sympathy, was yet highly gratified by his apparent devotion to her charms: and had not Miss Margland narrowly watched and tutored her, would easily have been attracted from the cold civilities of Edgar, to the magnetism of animated admiration.

In these circumstances, a few minutes appeared many hours to Sir Hugh, and he presently exclaimed: 'There's no possibility of waiting here the whole day long, not knowing what may be the end!' Then, calling to Dr. Orkborne, he said to him in a low voice, 'My good friend, here's happened a sad thing; that young man I asked into my pew, for which I take proper shame to myself, is the same person that wanted to make Eugenia give up Clermont Lynmere, her own natural relation, and mine into the bargain, for the sake of a stranger to us all; which I hold to be rather uncommendable, considering we know nothing about him; though there's no denying his being handsome enough to look at; which, however, is no certainty of his making a good husband; so I'll tell you a mode I've thought of, which I think to be a pretty good one, for parting them out of hand.'

Dr. Orkborne, who had just taken out his tablets, in order to enter some hints relative to his great work, begged him to say no more till he had finished his sentence. The baronet looked much distressed, but consented: and when he had done, went on:

'Why, if you will hold Eugenia, I'll go up to the rest, and send them on to the cottage; and when they are gone, I shall get rid of this young chap, by telling him Eugenia and I want to be alone.'

Dr. Orkborne assented; and Sir Hugh, advancing to the group, made his proposition, adding: 'Eugenia and I will overtake you as soon as the garden-chair comes, which, I dare say, won't be long, Robert being so behind-hand already.' Then, turning to Bellamy, 'I am sorry, sir,' he said, 'I can't possibly ask you to stay with us, because of something my little niece and I have got to talk about, which we had rather nobody should hear, being an affair of our own: but I thank you for your civility, sir, in picking up my stick and my pocket handkerchief, and I wish you a very good morning and a pleasant walk, which I hope you won't take ill.'

Bellamy bowed, and, saying he by no means intended to intrude himself into the company, slowly drew back.

Edgar then pointed out a path through the fields that would considerably abridge the walk, if the ladies could manage to cross over a dirty lane on the other side of the church-yard.

The baronet, who was in high spirits at the success of his scheme, declared that if there was a short cut, they should not part company, for he could walk it himself. Edgar assured him it could not be more than half a mile, and offered him the use of his arm.

'No, no, my good young friend,' answered he, smiling significantly; 'take care of Indiana! I have got a good stick, which I hold to be worth any arm in Christendom, except for not being alive; so take care of Indiana, I say.'

Edgar bowed, but with a silence and gravity not unmixt with surprise; and Sir Hugh, a little struck, hastily added, 'Nay, nay, I mean no harm!'

'No, sir,' said Edgar, recovering, 'you can mean nothing but good, when you give me so fair a charge.' And he placed himself at the side of Indiana.

'Well then, now,' cried Sir Hugh, 'I'll marshal you all; and, first, for my little Camilla, who shall come to my proper share; for she's certainly the best companion of the whole; which I hope nobody will take for a slight, all of us not being the same, without any fault of our own. Dr. Orkborne shall keep to Eugenia, because, if there should be a want of conversation, they can go over some of their lessons. Lionel shall take the care of Mrs. Margland, it being always right for the young to help people a little stricken; and as for the odd one, Dr. Marchmont, why he may join little Camilla and me; for as she's none of the steadiest, and I am none of the strongest, it is but fair the one over should be between us.'

Everybody professed obedience but Lionel; who, with a loud laugh, called to Edgar to change partners.

'We are all under orders,' answered he, quietly, 'and I must not be the first to mutiny.'

Indiana smiled with triumph; but Miss Margland, firing with anger, declared she wanted no help, and would accept none.

Sir Hugh was now beginning an expostulation with his nephew; but Lionel preferred compliance to hearing it; yet, to obviate the ridicule which he was persuaded would follow such an acquiescence, he strided up to Miss Margland with hasty steps, and dropping on one knee, in the dust, seized and kissed her hand; but precipitately rising, and shaking himself, called out: 'My dear ma'am, have you never a little cloaths-brush in your pocket? I can't kneel again else!'

Miss Margland wrathfully turned from him; and the party proceeded to a small gate, at the back of the church, that opened to the lane mentioned by Edgar, over which, when the rest of the company had passed, into a beautiful meadow, Lionel offered his hand for conducting Miss Margland, who rejected it disdainfully.

'Then, you will be sure to fall,' said he.

'Not unless you do something to make me.'

'You will be sure to fall,' he repeated coolly.

Much alarmed, she protested she would not get over before him.

He absolutely refused to go first.

The whole party stopt; and Bellamy, who had hitherto stood still and back, now ventured to approach, and in the most courteous manner, to offer his services to Miss Margland. She looked victoriously around her; but as he had spoken in a low voice, only said: 'Sir?' to make him repeat his proposal more audibly. He complied, and the impertinencies of Lionel rendered his civility irresistible: 'I am glad,' she cried, 'there is still one gentleman left in the world!' And accepted his assistance, though her persecutor whispered that her spark was a dead man! and strutted significantly away.

Half frightened, half suspecting she was laughed at, she repeated softly to Sir Hugh the menace of his nephew, begging that, to prevent mischief, she might still retain Bellamy.

'Lord be good unto me!' cried he, 'what amazing fools the boys of now a-days are grown! with all their learning, and teaching, and classics at their tongue's end for nothing! However, not to set them together by the ears, till they grow a little wiser, which, I take it, won't be of one while, why you must e'en let this strange gentleman walk with you till t'other boy's further off. However, this one thing pray mind! (lowering his voice,) keep him all to yourself! if he does but so much as look at Eugenia, give him to understand it's a thing I sha'n't take very kind of him.'

Beckoning then to Dr. Orkborne, he uneasily said: 'As I am now obliged to have that young fellow along with us, for the sake of preventing an affray, about nobody knows what, which is the common reason of quarrels among those raw young fry, I beg you to keep a particular sharp look out, that he does not take the opportunity to run off with Eugenia.'

The spirit of the baronet had over-rated his strength; and he was forced to sit upon the lower step of a broad stile at the other end of the meadow: while Miss Margland, who leant her tall thin figure against a five-barred gate, willingly obviated his solicitude about Eugenia, by keeping Bellamy in close and unabating conference with herself.

A circumstance in the scenery before him now struck Dr. Orkborne with some resemblance to a verse in one of Virgil's Eclogues, which he thought might be happily applied to illustrate a passage in his own work; taking out, therefore, his tablets, he begged Eugenia not to move, and wrote his quotation; which, leading him on to some reflections upon the subject, soon drove his charge from his thoughts, and consigned him solely to his pencil.

Eugenia willingly kept her place at his side: offended by Bellamy, she would give him no chance of speaking with her, and the protection under which her uncle had placed her she deemed sacred.

Here they remained but a short time, when their ears received the shock of a prodigious roar from a bull in the field adjoining. Miss Margland screamed, and hid her face with her hands. Indiana, taught by her lessons to nourish every fear as becoming, shriekt still louder, and ran swiftly away, deaf to all that Edgar, who attended her, could urge. Eugenia, to whom Bellamy instantly hastened, seeing the beast furiously make towards the gate, almost unconsciously accepted his assistance, to accelerate her flight from its vicinity; while Dr. Orkborne, intent upon his annotations, calmly wrote on, sensible there was some disturbance, but determining to evade inquiring whence it arose, till he had secured what he meant to transmit to posterity from the treachery of his memory.

Camilla, the least frightened, because the most enured to such sounds, from the habits and the instruction of her rural life and education, adhered firmly to Sir Hugh, who began blessing himself with some alarm; but whom Dr. Marchmont re-assured, by saying the gate was secured, and too high for the bull to leap, even supposing it a vicious animal.

The first panic was still in its meridian, when Lionel, rushing past the beast, which he had secretly been tormenting, skipt over the gate, with every appearance of terror, and called out: 'Save yourselves all! Miss Margland in particular; for here's a mad bull!'

A second astounding bellow put a stop to any question, and wholly checked the immediate impulse of Miss Margland to ask why she was thus selected; she snatched her hands from her face, not doubting she should see her esquire soothingly standing by her side; but, though internally surprised and shocked to find herself deserted, she gathered strength to run from the gate with the nimbleness of youth, and, flying to the stile, regardless of Sir Hugh, and forgetting all her charges, scrambled over it, and ran on from the noise, without looking to the right or the left.

Sir Hugh, whom Lionel's information, and Miss Margland's pushing past him, had extremely terrified, was now also getting over the stile, with the assistance of Dr. Marchmont, ejaculating: 'Lord help us! what a poor race we are! No safety for us! if we only come out once in a dozen years, we must meet with a mad bull!'

He had, however, insisted that Camilla should jump over first, saying, 'There's no need of all of us being tost, my dear girl, because, of my slowness, which is no fault of mine, but of Robert's not being in the way; which must needs make the poor fellow unhappy enough, when he hears of it: which, no doubt, I shall let him do, according to his deserts.'

The other side of the stile brought them to the high road. Lionel, who had only wished to torment Miss Margland, felt his heart smite him, when he saw the fright of his uncle, and flew to acquaint him that he had made a mistake, for the bull was only angry, not mad.

The unsuspicious baronet thanked him for his good news, and sat upon a bank till the party could be collected.

This, however, was not soon to be done; the dispersion from the meadow having been made in every possible direction.

CHAPTER XI

Two Lovers

Indiana, intent but upon running on, had nearly reached the church-yard, without hearkening to one word of the expostulating Mandlebert; when, leaning over a tombstone, on which she had herself leant while waiting for the carriage, she perceived the young Oxonian. An instinctive spirit of coquetry made her now increase her pace; he heard the rustling of female approach, and looked up: her beauty, heightened by her flight, which animated her complexion, while it displayed her fine form, seemed more than ever celestial to the enamoured student; who darted forward from an impulse of irresistible surprise. 'O Heaven!' she cried, panting and stopping as he met her; 'I shall die! I shall die!—I am pursued by a mad bull!'

Edgar would have explained, that all was safe; but Melmond neither heard nor saw him.—'O, give me, then,' he cried, emphatically; 'give me the ecstasy to protect—to save you!'

His out-spread arms shewed his intention to bear her away; but Edgar, placing himself between them, said: 'Pardon me, sir! this lady is under my care!'

'O don't fight about me! don't quarrel!' cried Indiana, with an apprehension half simple, half affected.

'No, Madam!' answered Melmond, respectfully retreating; 'I know too—too well! my little claim in such a dispute!—Permit me, however, to assist you, Mr. Mandlebert, in your search of refuge; and deign, madam, to endure me in your sight, till this alarm passes away.'

Indiana, by no means insensible to this language, looked with some elation at Edgar, to see how he bore it.

Edgar was not surprised; he had already observed the potent impression made by the beauty of Indiana upon the Oxonian; and was struck, in defiance of its romance and suddenness, with its air of sincerity; he only, therefore, gently answered, that there was not the least cause of fear.

'O, how can you say so?' said Indiana; 'how can you take so little interest in me?'

'At least, at least,' cried Melmond, trembling with eagerness, 'condescend to accept a double guard!—Refuse not, Mr. Mandlebert, to suffer any attendance!'

Mandlebert, a little embarrassed, answered: 'I have no authority to decide for Miss Lynmere: but, certainly, I see no occasion for my assistance.'

Melmond fervently clasped his hands, and exclaimed: 'Do not, do not, madam, command me to leave you till all danger is over!'

The little heart of Indiana beat high with triumph; she thought Mandlebert jealous: Miss Margland had often told her there was no surer way to quicken him: and, even independently of this idea, the spirit, the ardour, the admiration of the Oxonian, had a power upon her mind that needed no auxiliary for delighting it.

She curtsied her consent; but declared she would never go back the same way. They proceeded, therefore, by a little round to the high road, which led to the field in which the party had been dispersed.

Indiana was full of starts, little shrieks, and palpitations; every one of which rendered her, in the eyes of the Oxonian, more and more captivating; and, while Edgar walked gravely on, reflecting, with some uneasiness, upon being thus drawn in to suffer the attendance of a youth so nearly a stranger, upon a young lady actually under his protection; Melmond was continually ejaculating in return to her perpetual apprehensions, 'What lovely timidity!—What bewitching softness!—What feminine, what beautiful delicacy!—How sweet in terror!—How soul-piercing in alarm!'

These exclamations were nearly enchanting to Indiana, whose only fear was, lest they should not be heard by Edgar; and, whenever they ceased, whenever a pause and respectful silence took their place, new starts, fresh palpitations, and designed false steps, again called them forth; while the smile with which she repaid their enthusiastic speaker, was fuel to his flame, but poison to his peace.

They had not proceeded far, when they were met by Miss Margland, who, in equal trepidation from anger and from fear, was still making the best of her way from the bellowing of the bull. Edgar inquired for Sir Hugh, and the rest of the party; but she could speak only of Lionel; his insolence and his ill usage; protesting nothing but her regard for Indiana, could induce her to live a moment longer under his uncle's roof.

'But where,' again cried Edgar, 'where is Sir Hugh? and where are the ladies?'

'Tossed by the bull,' answered she, pettishly, 'for aught I know; I did not choose to stay and be tossed myself; and a person like Mr. Lionel can soon make such a beast point at one, if he takes it into his humour.'

Edgar then begged they might hasten to their company; but Miss Margland positively refused to go back: and Indiana, always ready to second any alarm, declared, she should quite sink with fright, if they went within a hundred yards of that horrid field. Edgar still pleaded that the baronet would expect them; but Melmond, in softer tones, spoke of fears, sensibility, and dangers; and Edgar soon found he was talking to the winds.

All now that remained to prevent further separations was, that Edgar should run on to the party, and acquaint them that Miss Margland and Indiana would wait for them upon the high road.

Melmond, meanwhile, felt in paradise; even the presence of Miss Margland could not restrain his rapture, upon a casualty that gave him such a charge, though it forced him to forbear making the direct and open declaration of his passion, with which his heart was burning, and his tongue quivering. He attended them both with the most fervent respect, evidently very gratifying to the object of his adoration, though not noticed by Miss Margland, who was wholly absorbed by her own provocations.

Edgar soon reached the bank by the road's side, upon which the baronet, Dr. Marchmont, Lionel, and Camilla were seated. 'Lord help us!' exclaimed Sir Hugh, aghast at his approach, 'if here is not young Mr. Edgar without Indiana! This is a thing I could never have expected from you, young Mr. Edgar! that you should leave her, I don't know where, and come without her!'

Edgar assured him she was safe, and under the care of Miss Margland, but that neither of them could be prevailed with to come farther: he had, therefore, advanced to inquire after the rest of the party, and to arrange where they should all assemble.

'You have done very right, then, my dear Mr. Edgar, as you always do, as far as I can make out, when I come to the bottom. And now I am quite easy about Indiana. But as to Eugenia, what Dr. Orkborne has done with her is more than I can devise; unless, indeed, they are got to studying some of their Greek verbs, and so forgot us all, which is likely enough; only I had rather they had taken another time, not much caring to stay here longer than I can help.'

Edgar said, he would make a circuit in search of them; but, first, addressing Camilla, 'You alone,' he cried, with an approving smile, 'have remained thus quiet, while all else have been scampering apart, making confusion worse confounded.'

'I have lived too completely in the country to be afraid of cattle,' she answered; 'and Dr. Marchmont assured me there was no danger.'

'You can listen, then, even when you are alarmed,' said he, expressively, 'to the voice of reason!'

Camilla raised her eyes, and looked at him, but dropt them again without making any answer: Can you, she thought, have been pleading it in vain? How I wonder at Indiana?

He then set out to seek Eugenia, recommending the same office to Lionel by another route; but Lionel no sooner gathered where Miss Margland might be met with, than his repentance was forgotten, and he quitted everything to encounter her.

Edgar spent near half an hour in his search, without the smallest success; he was then seriously uneasy, and returning to the party, when a countryman, to whom he was known, told him he had seen Miss Eugenia Tyrold, with a very handsome fine town gentleman, going into a farm house.

Edgar flew to the spot, and through a window, as he advanced, perceived Eugenia seated, and Bellamy kneeling before her.

Amazed and concerned, he abruptly made his way into the apartment. Bellamy rose in the utmost confusion, and Eugenia, starting and colouring, caught Edgar by the arm, but could not speak.

He told her that her uncle and the whole company were waiting for her in great anxiety.

'And where, where,' cried she, 'are they? I have been in agonies about them all! and I could not prevail—I could not—this gentleman said the risk was so great—he would not suffer me—but he has sent for a chaise, though I told him I had a thousand times rather hazard my life amongst them, and with them, than save it alone!'

'They are all perfectly safe, nor has there ever been any danger.'

'I was told—I was assured—' said Bellamy, 'that a mad bull was running wild about the country; and I thought it, therefore, advisable to send for a chaise from the nearest inn, that I might return this young lady to her friends.'

Edgar made no answer, but offered his arm to conduct Eugenia to her uncle. She accepted it, and Bellamy attended on her other side.

Edgar was silent the whole way. The attitude in which he had surprised Bellamy, by assuring him of the nature of his pretensions, had awakened doubts the most alarming of the destination in view for the chaise which he had ordered; and he believed that Eugenia was either to have been beguiled, or betrayed, into a journey the most remote from the home to which she belonged.

Eugenia increased his suspicions by the mere confusion which deterred her from removing them. Bellamy had assured her she was in the most eminent personal danger, and had hurried her from field to field, with an idea that the dreaded animal was in full pursuit. When carried, however, into the farm house, she lost all apprehension for herself in fears for her friends, and insisted upon sharing their fate. Bellamy, who immediately ordered a chaise, then cast himself at her feet, to entreat she would not throw away her life by so rash a measure.

Exhausted, from her lameness, she was forced to sit still, and such was their situation at the entrance of Edgar. She wished extremely to explain what had been the object of the solicitation of Bellamy, and to clear him, as well as herself, from any further surmises; but she was ashamed to begin the subject. Edgar had seen a man at her feet, and she thought, herself, it was a cruel injury to Clermont, though she knew not how to refuse it forgiveness, since it was merely to supplicate she would save her own life.

Bellamy, therefore, was the only one who spoke; and his unanswered observations contributed but little to enliven the walk.

When they came within sight of the party, the baronet was again seized with the extremest dismay. 'Why now, what's this?' cried he; 'here's nothing but blunders. Pray, Sir, who gave you authority to take my niece from her own tutor? for so I may call him, though more properly speaking, he came amongst us to be mine; which, however, is no affair but of our own.'

'Sir,' answered Bellamy, advancing and bowing; 'I hope I have had the happiness of rather doing service than mischief; I saw the young lady upon the point of destruction, and I hastened her to a place of security, from whence I had ordered a post-chaise, to convey her safe to your house.'

'Yes, my dear uncle,' said Eugenia, recovering from her embarrassment; 'I have occasioned this gentleman infinite trouble; and though Mr. Mandlebert assures us there was no real danger, he thought there was, and therefore I must always hold myself to be greatly obliged to him.'

'Well, if that's the case, I must be obliged to him too; which, to tell you the truth, is not a thing I am remarkably fond of having happened. But where's Dr. Orkborne? I hope he's come to no harm, by his not shewing himself?'

'At the moment of terror,' said Eugenia, 'I accepted the first offer of assistance, concluding we were all hurrying away at the same time; but I saw Dr. Orkborne no more afterwards.'

'I can't say that was over and above kind of him, nor careful neither,' cried Sir Hugh, 'considering some particular reasons; however, where is he now?'

Nobody could say; no one had seen or observed him.

'Why then, ten to one, poor gentleman!' exclaimed the baronet, 'but he's the very person himself who's tossed, while we are all of us running away for nothing!'

A suspicion now occurred to Dr. Marchmont, which led him to return over the stile into the field where the confusion had begun; and there, on the exact spot where he had first taken out his tablets, calmly stood Dr. Orkborne; looking now upon his writing, now up to the sky, but seeing nothing any where, from intense absorption of thought upon the illustration he was framing.

Awakened from his reverie by the Doctor, his first recollection was of Eugenia; he had not doubted her remaining quietly by his side, and the moment he looked round and missed her, he felt considerable compunction. The good Doctor, however, assured him all were safe, and conducted him to the group.

'So here you are,' said the baronet, 'and no more tossed than myself, for which I am sincerely thankful, though I can't say I think you have taken much care of my niece, nobody knowing what might have become of her, if it had not been for that strange gentleman, that I never saw before.'

He then formally placed Eugenia under the care of Dr. Marchmont.

Dr. Orkborne, piqued by this transfer, sullenly followed, and now gave to her, pertinaciously, his undivided attention. Drawn by a total revulsion of ideas from the chain of thinking that had led him to composition, he relinquished his annotations in resentment of this dismission, when he might have pursued them uninterruptedly without neglect of other avocations.

CHAPTER XII

Two Doctors

A council was now held upon what course must next be taken. Both Sir Hugh and Eugenia were too much fatigued to walk any further; yet it was concluded that the garden chair, by some mistake, was gone straight to the cottage. Edgar, therefore, proposed running thither to bring it round for them, while Dr. Orkborne should go forward for Miss Margland and Indiana, and conduct them by the high road to the same place; where the whole party might at length re-assemble. Sir Hugh approved the plan, and he set off instantly.

But not so Dr. Orkborne; he thought himself disgraced by being sent from one post to another; and though Eugenia was nothing to him, in competition with his tablets and his work, his own instructions had so raised her in his mind, that he thought her the only female worthy a moment of his time. Indiana he looked upon with ineffable contempt; the incapacity she had shewn during the short time she was under his pupillage, had convinced him of the futility of her whole sex, from which he held Eugenia to be a partial exception; and Miss Margland, who never spoke to him but in a voice of haughty superiority, and whom he never answered, but with an air of solemn superciliousness, was his rooted aversion. He could not brook being employed in the service of either; he stood, therefore, motionless, till Sir Hugh repeated the proposition.

Not caring to disoblige him, he then, without speaking, slowly and unwillingly moved forwards.

'I see,' said the baronet, softened rather than offended, 'he does not much like to leave his little scholar, which is but natural; though I took it rather unkind his letting the poor thing run against the very horns of the bull, as one may say, if it had not been for a mere accidental passenger. However, one must always make allowance for a man that takes much to his studies, those things generally turning the head pretty much into a narrow compass.'

He then called after him, and said if the walk would tire him, he would wait till they came of themselves, which no doubt they would soon do, as Lionel was gone for them.

Dr. Orkborne gladly stopt; but Dr. Marchmont, seeing little likelihood of a general meeting without some trouble, offered to take the commission upon himself, with a politeness that seemed to shew it to be a wish of his own.

Sir Hugh accepted his kindness with thanks; and Dr. Orkborne, though secretly disconcerted by such superior alacrity in so learned a man, was well content to reinstate himself by the side of his pupil.

Sir Hugh, who saw the eyes of Bellamy constantly turned towards Eugenia, thought his presence highly dangerous, and with much tribulation, said: 'As I find, sir, we may all have to stay here, I don't know how long, I hope you won't be affronted, after my best thanks for your keeping my niece from the bull, if I don't make any particular point of begging the favour of you to stay much longer with us.'

Bellamy, extremely chagrined, cast an appealing look at Eugenia, and expressing his regret that his services were inadmissible, made his retreat with undisguised reluctance.

Eugenia, persuaded she owed him a serious obligation for his care, as well as for his partiality, felt the sincerest concern at his apparent distress, and contributed far more than she intended to its removal, by the gentle countenance with which she received his sorrowful glance.

Bellamy, hastily overtaking Dr. Marchmont, darted on before him in search of Miss Margland and Indiana, who, far from advancing, were pacing their way back to the church-yard. Lionel had joined them, and the incensed Miss Margland had encouraged the glad attendance of the Oxonian, as a protection to herself.

The sight of Bellamy by no means tended to disperse the storm: She resented his deserting her while she was in danger, and desired to see no more of him. But when he had respectfully suffered her wrath to vent itself, he made apologies, with an obsequiousness so rare to her, and a deference so strikingly contrasted with the daring ridicule of Lionel, that she did not long oppose the potent charm of adulation—a charm which, however it may be sweetened by novelty, seldom loses its effect by any familiarity.

During these contests, Indiana was left wholly to young Melmond, and the temptation was too strong for his impassioned feelings to withstand: 'O fairest,' he cried, 'fairest and most beautiful of all created beings! Can I resist—no! this one, one effusion—the first and the last! The sensibility of your mind will plead for me—I read it in those heavenly eyes—they emit mercy in their beauty! they are as radiant with goodness as with loveliness! alas! I trespass—I blush and dare not hope your forgiveness.'

He stopt, terrified at his own presumption; but the looks of Indiana were never more beautiful, and never less formidable. A milder doom, therefore, seemed suddenly to burst upon his view. Elated and enraptured, he vehemently exclaimed: 'Oh, were my lot not irrevocably miserable! were the smallest ray of light to beam upon my despondence!'—

Indiana still spoke not a word, but she withdrew not her smiles; and the enraptured student, lifted into the highest bliss by the permission even of a doubt, walked on, transported, by her side, too happy in suspence to wish an explanation.

In this manner they proceeded, till they were joined by Dr. Marchmont. The task he had attempted was beyond his power of performance; Miss Margland was inexorable; she declared nothing should induce her to go a step towards the field inhabited by the bull, and every assurance of safety the Doctor could urge was ineffectual.

He next assailed Indiana; but her first terror, soothed by the compassion and admiration of Melmond, was now revived, and she protested, almost with tears, that to go within a hundred yards of that dreadful meadow would make her undoubtedly faint away. The tender commiseration of Melmond confirmed her apprehensions, and she soon looked upon Dr. Marchmont as a barbarian for making the proposal.

The Doctor then commended them to the care of Lionel, and returned with this repulse to Sir Hugh.

The baronet, incapable of being angry with any one he conceived to be frightened, said they should be pressed no more, for he would give up going to the cottage, and put his best foot forward to walk on to them himself; adding he was so overjoyed to have got rid of that young spark, that he had no fear but that he, and poor Eugenia, too, should both do as well as they could.

They proceeded very slowly, the baronet leaning upon Dr. Marchmont, and Eugenia upon Dr. Orkborne, who watchful, with no small alarm, of the behaviour of the only man he had yet seen with any internal respect, since he left the university, sacrificed completely his notes and his tablets to emulate his attentions.

When they approached the church-yard, in which Miss Margland and her party had halted, Sir Hugh perceived Bellamy. He stopt short, calling out, with extreme chagrin, 'Lord help us! what a thing it is to rejoice! which one never knows the right season to do, on the score of meeting with disappointments!'

Then, after a little meditation, 'There is but one thing,' he cried, 'to be done, which is to guard from the first against any more mischief, having already had enough of it for one morning, not to say more than I could have wished by half: So do you, good Dr. Marchmont, take Eugenia under your own care, and I'll make shift with Dr. Orkborne for myself; for, in the case he should take again to writing or thinking, it will be nothing to me to keep still till he has done; provided it should happen at a place where I can sit down.'

Dr. Orkborne had never felt so deeply hurt; the same commission transferred to Edgar, or to Lionel, would have failed to affect him; he considered them as of an age fitted for such frivolous employment, which he thought as much below his dignity, as the young men themselves were beneath his competition; but the comfort of contempt, a species of consolation ever ready to offer itself to the impulsive pride of man, was here an alleviation he could not call to his aid; the character of Dr. Marchmont stood as high in erudition as his own; and, though his acquaintance with him was merely personal, the fame of his learning, the only attribute to which fame, in his conception, belonged, had reached him from authority too unquestionable for doubt. The urbanity, therefore, of his manners, his general diffusion of discourse, and his universal complaisance, filled him with astonishment, and raised an emotion of envy which no other person would have been deemed worthy of exciting.

But though his long and fixed residence at Cleves had now removed the timid circumspection with which he first sought to ensure his establishment, he yet would not venture any positive refusal to the baronet; he resigned, therefore, his young charge to his new and formidable opponent, and even exerted himself to mark some alacrity in assisting Sir Hugh. But his whole real attention was upon Dr. Marchmont, whom his eye followed in every motion, to discover, if possible, by what art unknown he had acquired such a command over his thoughts and understanding, as to bear patiently, nay pleasantly, with the idle and unequal companions of general society.

Dr. Marchmont, who was rector of Cleves, had been introduced to Sir Hugh upon the baronet's settling in the large mansion-house of that village; but he had not visited at the house, nor had his company been solicited. Sir Hugh, who could never separate understanding from learning, nor want of education from folly, concluded that such a man as Dr. Marchmont must necessarily despise him; and though the extreme sweetness of his temper made him draw the conclusion without resentment, it so effectually prevented all wish of any intercourse, that they had never conversed together till this morning; and his surprise, now, at such civilities and good humour in so great a scholar, differed only from that of Dr. Orkborne, in being accompanied with admiration instead of envy.

Eugenia thus disposed of, they were proceeding, when Sir Hugh next observed the young Oxonian: He was speaking with Indiana, to whom his passionate devotion was glaring from his looks, air, and whole manner.

'Lord held me!' exclaimed he; 'if there is not another of those new chaps, that nobody knows anything about, talking to Indiana! and, for aught I can tell to the contrary, making love to her! I think I never took such a bad walk as this before, since the hour I was born, in point of unluckiness. Robert will have enough to answer for, which he must expect to hear; and indeed I am not much obliged to Mrs. Margland herself, and so I must needs tell her, though it is not what I much like to do.'

He then made a sign to Miss Margland to approach him: 'Mrs. Margland,' he cried, 'I should not have taken the liberty to beckon you in this manner, but that I think it right to ask you what those two young gentlemen, that I never saw before, do in the church-yard; which is a thing I think rather odd.'

'As to that gentleman, sir,' she answered, bridling, 'who was standing by me, he is the only person I have found to protect me from Mr. Lionel, whose behaviour, sir, I must freely tell you—'

'Why certainly, Mrs. Margland, I can't deny but he's rather a little over and above giddy; but I am sure your understanding won't mind it, in consideration of his being young enough to be your son, in the case of your having been married time enough.'

He then desired Indiana would come to him.

The rapture of the Oxonian was converted into torture by this summons; and the suspence which the moment before he had gilded with the gay colours of hope, he felt would be no longer supportable when deprived of the sight of his divinity. Scarce could he refrain from casting himself publicly at her feet, and pouring forth the wishes of his heart. But when again the call was repeated, and he saw her look another way, as if desirous not to attend to it, the impulse of quick rising joy dispersed his small remains of forbearance, and precipitately clasping his hands, 'O go not!' he passionately exclaimed; 'leave me not in this abyss of suffering! Fairest and most beautiful! tell me at least, if my death is inevitable! if no time—no constancy—no adoration—may ever dare hope to penetrate that gentlest of bosoms!'

Indiana herself was now, for the first time, sensible of a little emotion; the animation of this address delighted her; it was new, and its effect was highly pleasing. How cold, she thought, is Edgar! She made not any answer, but permitted her eyes to meet his with the most languishing softness.

Melmond trembled through his whole frame; despair flew him, and expectation wore her brightest plumage: 'O pronounce but one word,' he cried, 'one single word!—are, are you—O say not yes!—irrevocably engaged?—lost to all hope—all possibility for ever?'

Indiana again licensed her fine eyes with their most melting powers, and all self-control was finally over with her impassioned lover; who, mingling prayers for her favour, with adoration of her beauty, heeded not who heard him, and forgot every presence but her own.

Miss Margland, who, engrossed by personal resentment and debates, had not remarked the rising courage and energy of Melmond, had just turned to Indiana, upon the second call of Sir Hugh, and became now utterly confounded by the sight of her willing attention: 'Miss Lynmere,' cried she, angrily, 'what are you thinking of? Suppose Mr. Mandlebert should come, what might be the consequence?'

'Mandlebert?' repeated Melmond, while the blood forsook his cheeks; 'is it then even so?—is all over?—all decided? is my destiny black and ireful for ever?'

Indiana still more and more struck with him, looked down, internally uttering: Ah! were this charming youth but master of Beech Park!

At this instant, the rapid approach of a carriage caught their ears; and eager to avoid making a decisive reply, she ran to the church-yard gate to look at it, exclaiming: 'Dear! what an elegant chariot.' When it came up to the party, it stopt, and, opening the door himself, Edgar jumped hastily out of it.

The Oxonian stood aghast: but Indiana, springing forward, and losing in curiosity every other sensation, cried: 'Dear! Mr. Mandlebert, whose beautiful new carriage is that?'

'Yours,' answered he, gallantly, 'if you will honour it with any commands.'

She then observed his crest and cypher were on the panels; and another entire new set of ideas took instant possession of her mind. She received literally an answer which he had made in gay courtesy, and held out her hand to be helped into the chariot.

Edgar, though surprised and even startled at this unexpected appropriation of his civility, could not recede; but the moment he had seated her, hastily turned round, to inquire who else was most fatigued.

The Oxonian now felt lost! suddenly, abruptly, but irretrievably lost! The cypher he saw—the question 'whose carriage is that?' he heard—the answer 'yours' made him gasp for breath, and the instantaneous acceptance stung him to the soul. Wholly in desperation, he rushed to the opposite window of the chariot, and calling out, 'enough, cruel!—cruel!—enough—I will see you no more!' hurried out of sight.

Indiana, who, for the first time, thought herself mistress of a new and elegant equipage, was so busily employed in examining the trappings and the lining, that she bore his departure without a sigh; though but an instant before it might have cost her something near one.

Eugenia had been touched more deeply. She was ignorant of what had passed, but she had seen the agitation of Melmond, and the moment he disappeared, she ejaculated secretly: 'Ah! had he conceived the prepossession of Bellamy! where had been my steadiness? where, O Clermont! thy security!—'

The scrupulous delicacy of her mind was shocked at this suggestion, and she rejoiced she had not been put to such a trial.

Edgar now explained, that when he arrived at the cottage, he found, as he had foreseen, the garden chair waiting there, by mistake, and Robert in much distress, having just discovered that an accident had happened to one of the wheels. He had run on, therefore, himself, to Beech Park, for his own new chariot, which was lately arrived from town, making Robert follow with Sir Hugh's horses, as his own were out at grass.

It was dinner-time, and Sir Hugh, equally vexed and fatigued, resolved to return straight home. He accepted, therefore, a place in the chariot, bid Eugenia follow him, and Robert make haste; solemnly adding to the latter: 'I had fully intended making you the proper lecture upon your not coming in time; but as it has turned out not to be your fault, on account of an accident, I shall say no more; except to give you a hint not to do such a thing again, because we have all been upon the point of being tossed by a mad bull; which would certainly have happened, but for the lucky chance of its turning out a false alarm.'

The remainder of the party proceeded without further adventure. Edgar attended Camilla; Miss Margland adhered to Bellamy: Lionel, who durst not venture at any new frolic, but with whom time lingered when none was passing, retreated; Dr. Marchmont, who was near his home, soon also made his bow; and Dr. Orkborne, who was glad to be alone, ruminated with wonder upon what appeared to him a phenomenon, a man of learning who could deign to please and seem pleased where books were not the subject of discourse, and where scholastic attainments were not required to elucidate a single sentence.

CHAPTER XIII

Two Ways of Looking at the Same Thing

When the party arrived at Cleves, Camilla, who had observed that Edgar seemed much disappointed by the breaking up of the cottage expedition, proposed that it should take place in the evening; and her uncle, though too much fatigued to venture out again himself, consented, or rather insisted, that the excursion should be made without him.

Before they set out, Edgar desired to speak with Sir Hugh in private.

Sir Hugh concluded it was to make his proposals of marriage for Indiana; and had not patience to step into his own apartment, but told them all to retire, with a nod at Indiana, which prepared not only herself but Miss Margland, Camilla, and Eugenia to join in his expectation.

Indiana, though a good deal fluttered, flew to a window, to see if the new chariot was in sight; and then, turning to Miss Margland, asked, 'Pray, should I refuse him at first?'

Miss Margland spared not for proper instructions; and immediately began a negociation with the fair questioner, for continuing to live with her.

Eugenia was occupied in reflecting with pity upon the idleness of Indiana, which so ill had fitted her for becoming the companion of Mandlebert.

Camilla, unusually thoughtful, walked alone into the garden, and sought a path least in sight.

Sir Hugh, meanwhile, was most unpleasantly undeceived. Edgar, without naming Indiana, informed him of the situation in which he had surprised Bellamy, and of his suspicions with regard to the destination of the chaise, but for his own timely arrival at the farm-house; adding, that his gratitude to Mr. Tyrold, his respect for himself, and his affection for all the family, made him think it is duty to reveal these circumstances without delay.

The baronet shuddered with horror; and declared he would instantly send an express to bring Clermont home, that Eugenia might be married out of hand; and, in the mean time, that he would have every window in the house barred, and keep her locked up in her room.

Edgar dissuaded him from so violent a measure; but advised him to speak with his niece upon the danger she had probably escaped, and of which she seemed wholly unconscious; to prevail with her not to go out again this evening, and to send for Mr. Tyrold, and acquaint him with the affair.

Sir Hugh thanked him for his counsel, and implicitly acted by his opinion.

He then ordered the coach for Miss Margland, Indiana, and Camilla.

Dr. Orkborne, finding neither Sir Hugh nor Eugenia of the party, declined joining it. Lionel was returned to Etherington; and Edgar rode on before, to invite Dr. Marchmont, with the consent of the Baronet, to take the fourth place in the carriage.

Arrived at the rectory, he went straight, by prescriptive privilege, into the study of Dr. Marchmont, whom he found immersed in books and papers, which, immediately, at the request of Edgar, he put aside; not without regret to quit them, though wholly without reluctance to oblige.

Edgar had ridden so hard, that they had some time to wait for the coach. But he did not appear anxious for its arrival; though he wore a look that was far from implying him to be free from anxiety.

He was silent,—he hemmed,—he was silent again,—and again he hemmed,—and then, gently laying his hand upon the shoulder of the Doctor, while his eyes, full of meaning, were fixed upon his face; 'Doctor,' he cried, 'you would hardly have known these young ladies?—they are all grown from children into women since you saw them last.'

'Yes,' answered the Doctor, 'and very charming women. Indiana has a beauty so exquisite, it is scarce possible to look away from it a moment: Eugenia joins so much innocence with information, that the mind must itself be deformed that could dwell upon her personal defects, after conversing with her: Camilla'—

He paused, and Edgar hastily turned another way, not to look at him, nor be looked at, while he proceeded:

'Camilla,' he presently continued, 'seems the most inartificially sweet, the most unobtrusively gay, and the most attractively lovely of almost any young creature I ever beheld.'

With a heart all expanded, and a face full of sensibility, Edgar now turned to him, and seizing, involuntarily, his hand, which he eagerly shook, 'You think her, then,'—he cried,—but suddenly stopt, dropt his hand, coughed two or three times; and, taking out his pocket handkerchief, seemed tormented with a violent cold.

Dr. Marchmont affectionately embraced him. 'My dear young young friend,' he cried, 'I see the situation of your mind—and think every possible happiness promises to be yours; yet, if you have taken no positive step, suffer me to speak with you before you proceed.'

'Far from having taken any positive step, I have not yet even formed any resolution.'

Here the carriage stopt for the Doctor, who repeated, 'Yes! I think every possible happiness promises to be yours!' before he went on to the ladies. Edgar, in a trepidation too great to be seen by them, kept behind till they drove off, though he then galloped so fast, that he arrived at the cottage before them: the words, 'I think every possible happiness promises to be yours,' vibrating the whole time in his ears.

When the coach arrived, Edgar handed out Miss Margland and Indiana; leaving Camilla to the Doctor; willing to let him see more of her, and by no means displeased to avoid his eyes at that moment himself.

Indiana was in the most sprightly spirits she had ever experienced; she concluded herself on the verge of becoming mistress of a fine place and a large fortune; she had received adulation all the morning that had raised her beauty higher than ever in her own estimation; and she secretly revolved, with delight, various articles of ornament and of luxury, which she had long wished to possess, and which now, for her wedding clothes, she should have riches sufficient to purchase.

Miss Margland, too, was all smoothness, complacency, and courtesy.

Camilla, alone, was grave; Camilla, who, by nature, was gay.

'Dear! is this the cottage we have been coming to all this time?' cried Indiana, upon entering; 'Lord! I thought it would have been something quite pretty.'

'And what sort of prettiness,' said Edgar, 'did you expect from a cottage?'

'Dear, I don't know—but I thought we were come on purpose to see something extraordinary?'

Camilla, who followed, made an exclamation far different; an exclamation of pleasure, surprise, and vivacity, that restored for an instant, all her native gaiety: for no sooner had she crossed the threshold, than she recognised, in a woman who was curtsying low to receive her, and whom Indiana had passed without observing, the wife of the poor prisoner for whom she had interceded with Mandlebert.

'How I rejoice to see you!' cried she, 'and to see you here! and how much better you look! and how comfortable you seem! I hope you are now all well?'

'Ah, madam,' answered the woman; 'we owe everything to that good young gentleman! he has put us in this nice new cottage, and employs us in his service. Blessings on his head! I am sure he will be paid for it!'

Edgar, somewhat agitated, occupied himself with jumping the little boy; Camilla looked round with rapture; Indiana seemed wonder-struck, without knowing why; Dr. Marchmont narrowly watched them all; and Miss Margland, expecting a new collection would be next proposed for setting them up, nimbly re-crossed the threshold, to examine the prospect without.

The husband, now in decent garb, and much recovered, though still weak and emaciated, advanced to Camilla, to make his humble acknowledgments, that she had recommended them to their kind benefactor.

'No!' cried Camilla; 'you owe me nothing! your own distress recommended you;—your own distress—and Mr. Mandlebert's generosity.'

Then, going up to Edgar, 'It is your happy fate,' she said, in an accent of admiration, 'to act all that my father so often plans and wishes, but which his income will not allow him to execute.'

'You see,' answered he, gratefully, 'how little suffices for content! I have scarce done anything—yet how relieved, how satisfied are these poor people! This hut was fortunately vacant'—

'O, madam!' interrupted the poor woman, 'if you knew but how that good gentleman has done it all! how kindly he has used us, and made everybody else use us! and let nobody taunt us with our bad faults!—and what good he has done to my poor sick husband! and how he has clothed my poor little half naked children! and, what is more than all, saved us from the shame of an ill life.'—

Camilla felt the tears start into her eyes;—she hastily snatched the little babe into her arms; and, while her kisses hid her face, Happy, and thrice happy Indiana! with a soft sigh, was the silent ejaculation of her heart.

She seated herself on a stool, and, without speaking or hearing any thing more, devoted herself to the baby.

Indiana, meanwhile, whose confidence in her own situation gave her courage to utter whatever first occurred to her, having made a general survey of the place and people, with an air of disappointment, now amused herself with an inspection more minute, taking up and casting down everything that was portable, without any regard either to deranging its neatness, or endangering its safety:—exclaiming, as she made her round of investigation, 'Dear! Crockery ware! how ugly!—Lord, what little mean chairs!—Is that your best gown, good woman?—Dear, what an ugly pattern!—Well, I would not wear such a thing to save my life!—Have you got nothing better than this for a floor-cloth?—Only look at those curtains! Did you ever see such frights?—Lord! do you eat off these platters? I am sure I could sooner die! I should not mind starving half as much!'

Miss Margland, hoping the collection was now either made or relinquished, ventured to re-enter, and inquire if they never meant to return home? Camilla unwillingly gave up the baby; but would not depart without looking over the cottage, where everything she saw excited a sensation of pleasure. 'How neat is this! How tidy that!' were her continual exclamations; 'How bright you have rubbed your saucepans! How clean every thing is all round! How soon you will all get well in this healthy and comfortable little dwelling!'

Edgar, in a low voice, then told Dr. Marchmont the history of his new cottagers, saying: 'You will not, I hope, disapprove what I have done? Their natures seemed so much disposed to good, I could not bear to let their wants turn them again to evil.'

'You have certainly done right,' answered the Doctor; 'to give money without inquiry, or further aid, to those who have adopted bad practices, is, to them, but temptation, and to society an injury; but to give them both the counsel and the means to pursue a right course, is, to them, perhaps, salvation, and to the community, the greatest service.'

Indiana and Miss Margland, quite wearied, both got into the carriage; Edgar, having deposited them, returned to Camilla, who kissed both the children, poured forth good wishes upon the father and mother; and, then, gave him her hand. Enchanted, he took it, exclaiming; 'Ah! who is like you! so lively—yet so feeling!'

Struck and penetrated, she made no answer: Alas! she thought, I fear he is not quite satisfied with Indiana!

Dr. Marchmont was set down at his own house; where, he begged to have a conference with Edgar the next morning.

The whole way home, the benevolence of Edgar occupied the mind of Camilla; and, not in the present instance, the less, that its object had been originally of her own pointing out.

CHAPTER XIV

Two Retreats

Mr. and Mrs. Tyrold had obeyed the summons of Sir Hugh, whom they found in extreme tribulation; persuaded by his fears not only of the design of Bellamy, but of its inevitable success. His brother, however, who knew his alarms to be generally as unfounded as his hopes; and Mrs. Tyrold, who almost undisguisedly despised both; no sooner heard his account, than, declining to discuss it, they sent for Eugenia. She related the transaction with a confusion so innocent, that it was easy to discern shame alone had hitherto caused her silence; and with a simplicity so unaffected, that not a doubt could rest upon their minds, but that her heart was as disengaged as her intentions had been irreproachable. Yet they were not the less struck with the danger she had incurred; and, while her father blessed Mandlebert for her preservation, her mother was so sensible to his care for the family welfare and honour, that the anger she had conceived against him subsided, though the regret to which it had owed its birth increased.

Mr. Tyrold gave his daughter some slight cautions and general advice; but thought it wisest, since he found her tranquil and unsuspicious, not to raise apprehensions that might disturb her composure, nor awaken ideas of which the termination must be doubtful.

Her mother deemed the matter to be undeserving the least serious alarm. The man had appeared to her from the beginning to be a despicable adventurer; and her lofty contempt of all low arts made her conclude her well-principled Eugenia as superior to their snares as to their practice.

This conference completely quieted the fears of Sir Hugh; who relinquished his design of sending for Clermont, and imagined Edgar to have been too severe in his judgment of Bellamy, who had only knelt in pure compassion, to prevail with Eugenia to take care of her life.

The rector and his lady were already gone before the cottage group came home. Edgar was anxious to inquire of Sir Hugh what had passed. The three females, concluding he had still something to say relative to his proposals, by tacit agreement, retired to their own rooms.

They were not, however, as concurrent in their eagerness to re-assemble. Miss Margland and Indiana watched the moment when they might appease their burning curiosity by descending: but Eugenia wished to prolong her absence, that she might recover from the embarrassment she had just suffered; and Camilla determined not to appear again till the next morning.

For the first time in her life after the shortest separation, she forbore to seek Eugenia, who she supposed would have gathered all the particular of the approaching nuptials. She felt no desire to hear them. It was a period to which, hitherto, she had looked forward as to a thing of course; but this day it had struck her that Edgar and Indiana could not be happy together.—She had even surmised, from his last speech, that he lamented, in secret, the connexion he had formed.

The gentlest pity took possession of her breast; an increasing admiration succeeded to her pity. She could not bear to witness so unequal a scene, as the full satisfaction of Sir Hugh contrasted with the seriousness, perhaps repentance, of Edgar. She pleaded an head-ache, and went to bed.

The morning did not find her less averse to hear the confirmation of the suspected news. On the contrary, her repugnance to have it ascertained became stronger. She did not ask herself why; she did not consider the uselessness of flying for one hour what she must encounter the next. The present moment was all she could weigh; and, to procrastinate any evil, seemed, to her ardent and active imagination, to conquer it. Again, therefore, she planned a visit to Mrs. Arlbery; though she had given it up so long, from the discouragement of Lionel, that she felt more of shame than of pleasure in the idea of making so tardy an apology; but she could think of no other place to which the whole party would not accompany her; and to avoid them and their communications, for however short a space of time, was now her sole aim.

Before breakfast, she repaired to the apartment of her uncle; her request was granted, as soon as heard; and she ordered the chaise.

Indiana and Miss Margland, meanwhile, had learnt from the baronet, that the proposals were not yet made. Miss Margland softened the disappointment of Indiana, by suggesting that her admirer was probably waiting the arrival of some elegant trinket, that he destined to present her upon his declaration: but she was by no means free from doubt and suspicion herself. She languished to quit Cleves, and Sir Hugh had almost thought her accountable for the slowness of Mandlebert's proceedings. To keep up her own consequence, she had again repeated her assurances, that all was in a prosperous train; though she had frequently, with strong private uneasiness, observed the eyes of Edgar fixed upon Camilla, with an attention far more pointed than she had ever remarked in them when their direction was towards her fair pupil.

Camilla hurried over her breakfast in expectation of the chaise, and in dread continual, lest her cousin should call her aside, to acquaint her that all was arranged. Edgar perceived, with surprise, that she was going out alone; and, no sooner gathered whither, than, drawing her to one of the windows, he earnestly said: 'Is it by appointment you wait upon Mrs. Arlbery?'

'No.'

'Does she at all expect you this morning?'

'No.'

'Would it, then, be asking too much, if I should entreat you to postpone your visit for a short time?'

The whole design of Camilla was to absent herself immediately; yet she hated to say no. She looked disturbed, and was silent.

'Have you made any further acquaintance with her since the morning of the raffle?'

'No, none; but I wish excessively to know more of her.'

'She is certainly, very—agreeable,' said he, with some hesitation; 'but, whether she is all Mrs. Tyrold would approve'—

'I hope you know no harm of her?—If you do, pray keep it to yourself!—for it would quite afflict me to hear anything to her disadvantage.'

'I should be grieved, indeed, to be the messenger of affliction to you; but I hope there may be no occasion; I only beg a day or two's patience; and, in the meanwhile, I can give you this assurance; she is undoubtedly a woman of character. I saw she had charmed you, and I made some immediate inquiries. Her reputation is without taint.'

'A thousand, thousand thanks,' cried Camilla, gaily, 'for taking so much trouble; and ten thousand more for finding it needless!'

Edgar could not forbear laughing, but answered, he was not yet so certain it was needless; since exemption from actual blemish could only be a negative recommendation: he should very soon, he added, see a lady upon whose judgment he could rely, and who would frankly satisfy him with respect to some other particulars, which, he owned, he considered as essential to be known, before any intimacy should be formed.

Wishing to comply with his request, yet impatient to leave the house, Camilla stood suspended till the chaise was announced.

'I think,' cried she, with a look and tone of irresolution, 'my going this once can draw on no ill consequence?'

Edgar only dropt his eyes.

'You are not of that opinion?'

'I have a very particular engagement this morning,' he replied; 'but I will readily give it up, and ride off instantly to make my application to this lady, if it is possible you can defer only till tomorrow your visit. Will you suffer me to ask such a delay? It will greatly oblige me.'

'Why, then,—I will defer it till to-morrow,—or till to-morrow week!' cried she, wholly vanquished; 'I insist, therefore, that you do not postpone your business.'

She then desired the servant, who was taking away the breakfast equipage, to order the chaise to be put up.

Edgar, subdued in his turn, caught her hand: but, instantly, recollecting himself, hastily let it go; and, throwing up the window sash, abruptly exclaimed: 'I never saw such fine weather:—I hope it will not rain!'

He then rapidly wished them all good morning, and mounted his horse.

Miss Margland, who, sideling towards the window, on pretence of examining a print, had heard and seen all that had passed, was almost overpowered with rage, by the conviction she received that her apprehensions were not groundless. She feared losing all weight both with the baronet and with Indiana, if she made this acknowledgment, and retreated, confounded, to her own room, to consider what path to pursue at so dangerous a crisis; wearing a scowl upon her face, that was always an indication she would not be followed.

Camilla also went to her chamber, in a perturbation at once pleasing and painful. She was sorry to have missed her excursion, but she was happy to have obliged Edgar; she was delighted he could take such interest in her conduct and affairs, yet dreaded, more than ever, a private conversation with Indiana;—Indiana, who, every moment, appeared to her less and less calculated to bestow felicity upon Edgar Mandlebert.

She seated herself at a window, and soon, through the trees, perceived him galloping away. 'Too—too amiable Edgar!' she cried, earnestly looking after him, with her hands clasped, and tears starting into her eyes.

Frightened at her own tenderness, she rose, shut the window, and walked to another end of the apartment.

She took up a book; but she could not read: 'Too—too amiable Edgar!' again escaped her. She went to her piano-forte; she could not play: 'Too—too amiable Edgar!' broke forth in defiance of all struggle.

Alarmed and ashamed, even to herself, she resolved to dissipate her ideas by a long walk; and not to come out of the park, till the first dinner-bell summoned her to dress.

CHAPTER XV

Two Sides of a Question

The intention of Edgar had been to ride to Mrs. Needham, the lady of whom he meant to ask the information to which he had alluded; but a charm too potent for resistance demanded his immediate liberation from the promise to Dr. Marchmont, which bound him to proceed no further till they had again conversed together.

He galloped, therefore, to the parsonage-house of Cleves, and entering the study of the Doctor, and taking him by the hand, with the most animated gesture; 'My dear and honoured friend,' he cried, 'I come to you now without hesitation, and free from every painful embarrassment of lurking irresolution! I come to you decided, and upon grounds which cannot offend you, though the decision anticipates your counsel. I come to you, in fine, my dear Doctor, my good and kind friend, to confess that yesterday you saw right, with regard to the situation of my mind, and that, to-day, I have only your felicitations to beg, upon my confirmed, my irrevocable choice!'

Dr. Marchmont embraced him: 'May you then,' he cried, 'be as happy, my dear young friend, as you deserve! I can wish you nothing higher.'

'Last night,' continued Edgar, 'I felt all doubt die away: captivating as I have ever thought her, so soft, so gentle, so touchingly sweet, as last night, I had never yet beheld her; you witnessed it, my dear Doctor? you saw her with the baby in her arms? how beautiful, how endearing a sight!'

The Doctor looked assentingly, but did not speak.

'Yet even last night was short of the feelings she excited this morning. My dear friend! she was upon the point of making an excursion from which she had promised herself peculiar pleasure, and to see a lady for whom she had conceived the warmest admiration—I begged her to postpone—perhaps relinquish entirely the visit—she had obtained leave from Sir Hugh—the carriage was at the door—would you, could you believe such sweetness with such vivacity? she complied with my request, and complied with a grace that has rivetted her—I own it—that has rivetted her to my soul!'

Doctor Marchmont smiled, but rather pensively than rejoicingly; and Edgar, receiving no answer, walked for some time about the room, silently enjoying his own thoughts.

Returning then to the Doctor, 'My dear friend,' he cried, 'I understood you wished to speak with me?'

'Yes—but I thought you disengaged.'

'So, except mentally, I am still.'

'Does she not yet know her conquest?'

'She does not even guess it.'

Dr. Marchmont now rising, with much energy said: 'Hear me then, my dear and most valued young friend; forbear to declare yourself, make no overtures to her relations, raise no expectations even in her own breast, and let not rumour surmise your passion to the world, till her heart is better known to you.'

Edgar, starting and amazed, with great emotion exclaimed: 'What do you mean, my good Doctor? do you suspect any prior engagement? any fatal prepossession?'—

'I suspect nothing. I do not know her. I mean not, therefore, the propensities alone, but the worth, also, of her heart; deception is easy, and I must not see you thrown away.'

'Let me, then, be her guarantee!' cried Edgar, with firmness; 'for I know her well! I have known her from her childhood, and cannot be deceived. I fear nothing—except my own powers of engaging her regard. I can trace to a certainty, even from my boyish remarks, her fair, open, artless, and disinterested character.'

He then gave a recital of the nobleness of her sentiments and conduct when only nine years old; contrasting the relation with the sullen and ungenerous behaviour of Indiana at the same age.

Dr. Marchmont listened to the account with attention and pleasure, but not with an air of that full conviction which Edgar expected. 'All this,' he said, 'is highly prophetic of good, and confirms me in the opinion I expressed last night, that every possible happiness promises to be yours.'

'Yet, still,' said Edgar, a little chagrined, 'there seems some drawback to your entire approbation?'

'To your choice I have none.'

'You perplex me, Doctor! I know not to what you object, what you would intimate, nor what propose?'

'All I have to suggest may be comprised in two points: First, That you will refuse confirmation even to your own intentions, till you have positively ascertained her actual possession of those virtues with which she appears to be endowed: and secondly, That if you find her gifted with them all, you will not solicit her acceptance till you are satisfied of her affection.'

'My dear Doctor,' cried Edgar, half laughing, 'from what an alarm of wild conjecture has your explanation relieved me! Hear me, however, in return, and I think I can satisfy you, that, even upon your own conditions, not an obstacle stands in the way of my speaking to Mr. Tyrold this very evening.

'With regard to your first article, her virtues, I have told you the dawning superiority of her most juvenile ideas of right; and though I have latterly lost sight of her, by travelling during our vacations, I know her to have always been under the superintendence of one of the first of women; and for these last three weeks, which I have spent under the same roof with her, I have observed her to be all that is amiable, sweet, natural, and generous. What then on this point remains? Nothing. I am irrefragably convinced of her worth.

'With respect to your second condition, I own you a little embarrass me; yet how may I inquire into the state of her affections, without acknowledging her mistress of mine?'

'Hold! hold!' interrupted the Doctor, 'you proceed too rapidly. The first article is all unsettled, while you are flying to the last.

'It is true, and I again repeat it, every promise is in your favour; but do not mistake promise for performance. This young lady appears to be all excellence; for an acquaintance, for a friend, I doubt not you have already seen enough to establish her in your good opinion; but since it is only within a few hours you have taken the resolution which is to empower her to colour the rest of your life, you must study her, from this moment, with new eyes, new ears, and new thoughts. Whatever she does, you must ask yourself this question: "Should I like such behaviour in my wife?" Whatever she says, you must make yourself the same demand. Nothing must escape you; you must view as if you had never seen her before; the interrogatory, Were she mine? must be present at every look, every word, every motion; you must forget her wholly as Camilla Tyrold, you must think of her only as Camilla Mandlebert; even justice is insufficient during this period of probation, and instead of inquiring, "Is this right in her?" you must simply ask, "Would it be pleasing to me?"'

'You are apprehensive, then, of some dissimilitude of character prejudicial to our future happiness?'

'Not of character; you have been very peculiarly situated for obviating all risk upon that first and most important particular. I have no doubt of her general worthiness; but though esteem hangs wholly upon character, happiness always links itself with disposition.'

'You gratify me, Doctor, by naming disposition, for I can give you the most unequivocal assurance of her sweetness, her innocence, her benevolence, joined to a spirit of never-dying vivacity—an animation of never-ceasing good humour!'

'I know you, my dear Mandlebert, to be, by nature, penetrating and minute in your observations; which, in your general commerce with the world, will protect both your understanding and your affections from the usual snares of youth: But here—to be even scrupulous is not enough; to avoid all danger of repentance, you must become positively distrustful.'

'Never, Doctor, never! I would sooner renounce every prospect of felicity, than act a part so ungenerous, where I am conscious of such desert! Upon this article, therefore, we have done; I am already and fully convinced of her excellence. But, with respect to your second difficulty, that I will not seek her acceptance, till satisfied of her regard—there—indeed, you start an idea that comes home to my soul in its very inmost recesses! O Doctor!—could I hope—however distantly—durst I hope—the independent, unsolicited, involuntary possession of that most ingenuous, most inartificial of human hearts!—'

'And why not? why, while so liberally you do justice to another, should you not learn to appreciate yourself?'

A look of elation, delight, and happiness conveyed to Dr. Marchmont his pupil's grateful sense of this question.

'I do not fear making you vain,' he continued; 'I know your understanding to be too solid, and your temperament too philosophic, to endanger your running into the common futility of priding yourself upon the gifts of nature, any more than upon those of fortune; 'tis in their uses only you can claim any applause. I will not, therefore, scruple to assert, you can hardly any where propose yourself with much danger of being rejected. You are amiable and accomplished; abounding in wealth, high in character; in person and appearance unexceptionable; you can have no doubt of the joyful approbation of her friends, nor can you entertain a reasonable fear of her concurrence; yet, with all this, pardon me, when I plainly, explicitly add, it is very possible you may be utterly indifferent to her.'

'If so, at least,' said Edgar, in a tone and with a countenance whence all elation was flown, 'she will leave me master of myself; she is too noble to suffer any sordid motives to unite us.'

'Do not depend upon that; the influence of friends, the prevalence of example, the early notion which every female imbibes, that a good establishment must be her first object in life—these are motives of marriage commonly sufficient for the whole sex.'

'Her choice, indeed,' said Edgar, thoughtfully, 'would not, perhaps, be wholly uninfluenced;—I pretend not to doubt that the voice of her friends would be all in my favour.'

'Yes,' interrupted Dr. Marchmont, 'and, be she noble as she may, Beech Park will be also in your favour! your mansion, your equipage, your domestics, even your table, will be in your favour—'

'Doctor,' interrupted Edgar, in his turn, 'I know you think ill of women.—'

'Do not let that idea weaken what I urge; I have not had reason to think well of them; yet I believe there are individuals who merit every regard: your Camilla may be one of them. Take, however, this warning from my experience; whatever is her appearance of worth, try and prove its foundation, ere you conclude it invulnerable; and whatever are your pretensions to her hand, do not necessarily connect them with your chances for her heart.'

Mandlebert, filled now with a distrust of himself and of his powers, which he was incapable of harbouring of Camilla and her magnanimity, felt struck to the soul with the apprehension of failing to gain her affection, and wounded in every point both of honour and delicacy, from the bare suggestion of owing his wife to his situation in the world. He found no longer any difficulty in promising not to act with precipitance; his confidence was gone; his elevation of sentiment was depressed; a general mist clouded his prospects, and a suspensive discomfort inquieted his mind. He shook Dr. Marchmont by the hand, and assuring him he would weigh well all he had said, and take no measure till he had again consulted with him, remounted his horse, and slowly walked it back to Cleves.

VOLUME II

BOOK III

CHAPTER I

A Few Kind Offices

With deep concern Edgar revolved in his mind the suggestions of Dr. Marchmont; and meditation, far from diminishing, added importance to the arguments of his friend. To obtain the hand of an object he so highly admired, though but lately his sole wish, appeared now an uncertain blessing, a suspicious good, since the possession of her heart was no longer to be considered as its inseparable appendage. His very security of the approbation of Mr. and Mrs. Tyrold became a source of solicitude; and, secret from them, from her, and from all, he determined to guard his views, till he could find some opportunity of investigating her own unbiased sentiments.

Such were his ruminations, when, on re-entering the Park, he perceived her wandering alone amidst the trees. Her figure looked so interesting, her air so serious, her solitude so attractive, that every maxim of tardy prudence, every caution of timid foresight, would instantly have given way to the quick feelings of generous impulse, had he not been restrained by his promise to Dr. Marchmont. He dismounted, and giving his horse to his groom, re-traced her footsteps.

Camilla, almost without her own knowledge, had strolled towards the gate, whence she concluded Edgar to have ridden from the Park, and, almost without consciousness, had continued sauntering in its vicinity; yet she no sooner descried him, than, struck with a species of self-accusation for this appearance of awaiting him, she crossed over to the nearest path towards the house, and, for the first time, was aware of the approach of Edgar without hastening to meet him.

He slackened his pace, to quiet his spirits, and restore his manner to its customary serenity, before he permitted himself to overtake her. 'Can you,' he then cried, 'forgive me, when you hear I have been fulfilling my own appointment, and have postponed my promised investigation?'

'Rather say,' she gently answered, 'could I have forgiven you, if you had shewn me you thought my impatience too ungovernable for any delay?'

To find her thus willing to oblige him, was a new delight, and he expressed his acknowledgments in terms the most flattering.

An unusual seriousness made her hear him almost without reply; yet peace and harmony revisited her mind, and, in listening to his valued praise, she forgot her late alarm at her own sensations, and without extending a thought beyond the present instant, again felt tranquil and happy: while to Edgar she appeared so completely all that was adorable, that he could only remember to repent his engagement with Dr. Marchmont.

Her secret opinion that he was dissatisfied with his lot, gave a softness to her accents that enchanted him; while the high esteem for his character, which mingled with her pity, joined to a lowered sense of her own, from a new-born terror lest that pity were too tender, spread a charm wholly new over her native fire and vivacity.

In a few minutes, they were overtaken by Mandlebert's gardener, who was bringing from Beech Park a basket of flowers for his master. They were selected from curious hot-house plants, and Camilla stopt to admire their beauty and fragrance.

Edgar presented her the basket; whence she simply took a sprig of myrtle and geranium, conceiving the present to be designed for Indiana. 'If you are fond of geraniums,' said he, 'there is an almost endless variety in my greenhouse, and I will bring you tomorrow some specimens.'

She thanked him, and while he gave orders to the gardener, Miss Margland and Indiana advanced from the house.

Miss Margland had seen them from her window, where, in vain deliberation, she had been considering what step to take. But, upon beholding them together, she thought deliberation and patience were hopeless, and determined, by a decisive stroke, to break in its bud the connection she supposed forming, or throw upon Camilla all censure, if she failed, as the sole means she could devise to exculpate her own sagacity from impeachment. She called upon Indiana, therefore, to accompany her into the Park, exclaiming, in an angry tone, 'Miss Lynmere, I will shew you the true cause why Mr. Mandlebert does not declare himself—your cousin, Miss Camilla, is wheedling him away from you.'

Indiana, whose belief in almost whatever was said, was undisturbed by any species of reflection, felt filled with resentment, and a sense of injury, and readily following, said—'I was sure there was something more in it than I saw, because Mr. Melmond behaved so differently. But I don't take it very kind of my cousin, I can tell her!'

They then hurried into the Park; but, as they came without any plan, they were no sooner within a few yards of the meeting, than they stopt short, at a loss what to say or do.

Edgar, vexed at their interruption, continued talking to the gardener, to avoid joining them; but seeing Camilla, who less than ever wished for their communications, walk instantly another way, he thought it would be improper to pursue her, and only bowing to Miss Margland and Indiana, went into the house.

'This is worse than ever,' cried Miss Margland, 'to stalk off without speaking, or even offering you any of his flowers, which, I dare say, are only to be put into the parlour flower-pots, for the whole house.'

'I'm sure I'm very glad of it,' said Indiana, for I hate flowers; but I'm sure Mr. Melmond would not have done so; nor Colonel Andover; nor Mr. Macdersey more than all.'

'No, nor any body else, my dear, that had common sense, and their eyes open; nor Mr. Mandlebert neither, if it were not for Miss Camilla. However, we'll let her know we see what she is about; and let Sir Hugh know too: for as to the colonels, and the ensigns, and that young Oxford student, they won't at all do; officers are commonly worth nothing; and scholars, you may take my word for it, my dear, are the dullest men in the world. Besides, one would not give such a fine fortune as Mr. Mandlebert's without making a little struggle for it. You don't know how many pretty things you may do with it. So let us shew her we don't want for spirit, and speak to her at once.'

These words, reviving in the mind of Indiana her wedding clothes, the train of servants, and the new equipage, gave fresh pique to her provocation: but finding some difficulty to overtake the fleet Camilla, whose pace kept measure with her wish to avoid them, she called after her, to desire she would not walk so fast.

Camilla reluctantly loitered, but without stopping or turning to meet them, that she might still regale herself with the perfume of the geranium presented her by Edgar.

'You're in great haste, ma'am,' said Miss Margland, 'which I own I did not observe to be the case just now!'

Camilla, in much surprize, asked, what she meant.

'My meaning is pretty plain, I believe, to any body that chose to understand it. However, though Miss Lynmere scorns to be her own champion, I cannot, as a friend, be quite so passive, nor help hinting to you, how little you would like such a proceeding to yourself, from any other person.'

'What proceeding?' cried Camilla, blushing, from a dawning comprehension of the subject, though resenting the manner of the complaint.

'Nay, only ask yourself, ma'am, only ask yourself, Miss Camilla, how you should like to be so supplanted, if such an establishment were forming for yourself, and every thing were fixt, and every body else refused, and nobody to hinder its all taking place, but a near relation of your own, who ought to be the first to help it forward. I should like to know, I say, Miss Camilla, how you would feel, if it were your own case?'

Astonished and indignant at so sudden and violent an assault, Camilla stood suspended, whether to deign any vindication, or to walk silently away: yet its implications involuntarily filled her with a thousand other, and less offending emotions than those of anger, and a general confusion crimsoned her cheeks.

'You cannot but be sensible, ma'am,' resumed Miss Margland, 'for sense is not what you want, that you have seduced Mr. Mandlebert from your cousin; you cannot but see he takes hardly the smallest notice of her, from the pains you are at to make him admire nobody but yourself.'

The spirit of Camilla now rose high to her aid, at a charge thus impertinent and unjust. 'Miss Margland,' she cried, 'you shock and amaze me! I am at a loss for any motive to so cruel an accusation: but you, I hope at least, my dear Indiana, are convinced how much it injures me.' She would then have taken the hand of Indiana, but disdainfully drawing it back, 'I shan't break my heart about it, I assure you,' she cried, 'you are vastly welcome to him for me; I hope I am not quite so odious, but I may find other people in the world besides Mr. Mandlebert!'

'O, as to that,' said Miss Margland, 'I am sure you have only to look in order to chuse; but since this affair has been settled by your uncle, I can't say I think it very grateful in any person to try to overset his particular wishes. Poor old gentleman! I'm sure I pity him! It will go hard enough with him, when he comes to hear it! Such a requital!—and from his own niece!'

This was an attack the most offensive that Camilla could receive; nothing could so nearly touch her as an idea of ingratitude to her uncle, and resting upon that, the whole tide of those feelings which were, in fact, divided and subdivided into many crossing channels, she broke forth, with great eagerness, into exclaiming, 'Miss Margland, this is quite barbarous! You know, and you, Indiana, cannot but know, I would not give my uncle the smallest pain, to be mistress of a thousand universes!'

'Why, then,' said Miss Margland, 'should you break up a scheme which he has so much set his heart upon? Why are you always winning over Mr. Mandlebert to yourself, by all that flattery? Why are you always consulting him? always obliging him? always of his opinion? always ready to take his advice?'

'Miss Margland,' replied Camilla, with the extremest agitation, 'this is so unexpected—so undeserved an interpretation,—my consultation, or my acquiescence have been merely from respect; no other thought, no other motive—Good God! what is it you imagine?—what guilt would you impute to me?'

'O dear,' cried Indiana, 'pray don't suppose it signifies. If you like to make compliments in that manner to gentlemen, pray do it. I hope I shall always hold myself above it. I think it's their place to make compliments to me.'

A resentful answer was rising to the tongue of Camilla, when she perceived her two little sprigs, which in her recent disorder she had dropt, were demolishing under the feet of Indiana, who, with apparent unmeaningness, but internal suspicion of their giver, had trampled upon them both. Hastily stooping she picked them up, and, with evident vexation, was blowing from them the dust and dirt, when Indiana scoffingly said, 'I wonder where you got that geranium?'

'I don't wonder at all,' said Miss Margland, 'for Sir Hugh has none of that species; so one may easily guess.'

Camilla felt herself blush, and letting the flowers fall, turned to Indiana, and said, 'Cousin, if on my account, it is possible you can suffer the smallest uneasiness, tell me but what I shall do—you shall dictate to me—you shall command me.'

Indiana disclaimed all interest in her behaviour; but Miss Margland cried, 'What you can do, ma'am, is this, and nothing can be easier, nor fairer: leave off paying all that court to Mr. Mandlebert, of asking his advice, and follow your own way, whether he likes it or not, and go to see Mrs. Arlbery, and Mrs. every body else, when you have a mind, without waiting for his permission, or troubling yourself about what he thinks of it.'

Camilla now trembled in every joint, and with difficulty restrained from tears, while, timidly, she said—'And do you, my dear Indiana, demand of me this conduct? and will it, at least, satisfy you?'

'Me? O dear no! I demand nothing, I assure you. The whole matter is quite indifferent to me, and you may ask his leave for every thing in the world, if you chuse it. There are people enough ready to take my part, I hope, if you set him against me ever so much.'

'Indeed, indeed, Indiana,' said Camilla, overpowered with conflicting sensations, 'this is using me very unkindly!' And, without waiting to hear another word, she hurried into the house, and flew to hide herself in her own room.

This was the first bitter moment she had ever known. Peace, gay though uniform, had been the constant inmate of her breast, enjoyed without thought, possessed without struggle; not the subdued gift of accommodating philosophy, but the inborn and genial produce of youthful felicity's best aliment, the energy of its own animal spirits.

She had, indeed, for some time past, thought Edgar, of too refined and too susceptible a character for the unthinking and undistinguishing Indiana; and for the last day or two, her regret at his fate had strengthened itself into an averseness of his supposed destination, that made the idea of it painful, and the subject repugnant to her; but she had never, till this very morning, distrusted the innoxiousness either of her pity or her regard; and, startled at the first surmise of danger, she had wished to fly even from herself, rather than venture to investigate feelings so unwelcome; yet still and invariably, she had concluded Edgar the future husband of Indiana.

To hear there were any doubts of the intended marriage, filled her with emotions indefinable; to hear herself named as the cause of those doubts, was alarming both to her integrity and her delicacy. She felt the extremest anger at the unprovoked and unwarrantable harshness of Miss Margland, and a resentment nearly equal at the determined petulance, and unjustifiable aspersions of Indiana.

Satisfied of the innocence of her intentions, she knew, not what alteration she could make in her behaviour; and, after various plans, concluded, that to make none would best manifest her freedom from self-reproach. At the summons therefore to dinner, she was the first to appear, eager to shew herself unmoved by the injustice of her accusers, and desirous to convince them she was fearless of examination.

Yet, too much discomposed to talk in her usual manner, she seized upon a book till the party was seated. Answering then to the call of her uncle, with as easy an air as she could assume, she took her accustomed place by his side, and began, for mere employment, filling a plate from the dish that was nearest to her; which she gave to the footman, without any direction whither to carry, or enquiry if any body chose to eat it.

It was taken round the table, and, though refused by all, she heaped up another plate, with the same diligence and speed as if it had been accepted.

Edgar, who had been accidentally detained, only now entered, apologizing for being so late.

Engrossed by the pride of self-defence, and the indignancy of unmerited unkindness, the disturbed mind of Camilla had not yet formed one separate reflexion, nor even admitted a distinct idea of Edgar himself, disengaged from the accusation in which he stood involved. But he had now amply his turn. The moment he appeared, the deepest blushes covered her face; and an emotion so powerful beat in her breast, that the immediate impulse of her impetuous feelings, was to declare herself ill, and run out of the room.

With this view she rose; but ashamed of her plan, seated herself the next moment, though she had first overturned her plate and a sauce-boat in the vehemence of her haste.

This accident rather recovered than disconcerted her, by affording an unaffected occupation, in begging pardon of Sir Hugh, who was the chief sufferer, changing the napkins, and restoring the table to order.

'What upon earth can be the matter with Miss Camilla, I can't guess!' exclaimed Miss Margland, though with an expression of spite that fully contradicted her difficulty of conjecture.

'I hope,' said Edgar surprized, 'Miss Camilla is not ill?'

'I can't say I think my cousin looks very bad!' said Indiana.

Camilla, who was rubbing a part of her gown upon which nothing had fallen, affected to be too busy to hear them: which Sir Hugh, concluding her silent from shame, entreated her not to think of his cloaths, which were worth no great matter, not being his best by two or three suits. Her thoughts had not waited this injunction; yet it was in vain she strove to behave as if nothing had happened. Her spirit instigated, but it would not support her; her voice grew husky, she stammered, forgot, as she went on, what she designed to say when she began speaking, and frequently was forced to stop short, with a faint laugh at herself, and with a colour every moment encreasing. And the very instant the cloth was removed, she rose, unable to constrain herself any longer, and ran up stairs to her own room.

There all her efforts evaporated in tears. 'Cruel, cruel, Miss Margland,' she cried, 'unjust, unkind Indiana! how have I merited this treatment! What can Edgar think of my disturbance? What can I devise to keep from his knowledge the barbarous accusation which has caused it?'

In a few minutes she heard the step of Eugenia.

Ashamed, she hastily wiped her eyes; and before the door could be opened, was at the further end of the room, looking into one of her drawers.

'What is it that has vexed my dearest Camilla?' cried her kind sister, 'something I am sure has grieved her.'

'I cannot guess what I have done with—I can no where find—' stammered Camilla, engaged in some apparent search, but too much confused to name anything of which she might probably be in want.

Eugenia desired to assist her, but a servant came to the door, to tell them that the company was going to the summer-house, whither Sir Hugh begged they would follow.

Camilla besought Eugenia to join them, and make her excuses: but, fearing Miss Margland would attribute her absconding to guilt, or cowardice, she bathed her eyes in cold water, and overtook her sister at the stairs of the little building.

In ascending them, she heard Miss Margland say, 'I dare believe nothing's the matter but some whim; for to be sure as to whims, Miss Camilla has the most of any creature I ever saw, and Miss Lynmere the least; for you may imagine, Mr. Mandlebert, I have pretty good opportunity to see all these young people in their real colours.'

Overset by this malignancy, she was again flying to the refuge of her own room, and the relief of tears, when the conviction of such positive ill-will in Miss Margland, for which she could assign no reason, but her unjust and exclusive partiality to Indiana, checked her precipitancy. She feared she would construe to still another whim her non-appearance, and resuming a little fresh strength from fresh resentment, turned back; but the various keen sensations she experienced as she entered the summer-house, rendered this little action the most severe stretch of fortitude, her short and happy life had yet called upon her to make.

Sir Hugh addressed her some kind enquiries, which she hastily answered, while she pretended to be busy in preparing to wind some sewing silk upon cards.

She could have chosen no employment less adapted to display the cool indifference she wished to manifest to Miss Margland and Indiana. She pulled the silk the wrong way, twisted, twirled, and entangled it continually; and while she talked volubly of what she was about, as if it were the sole subject of her thoughts, her shaking hands shewed her whole frame disordered, and her high colour betrayed her strong internal emotion.

Edgar looked at her with surprize and concern. What had dropt from Miss Margland of her whims, he had heard with disdain; for, without suspecting her of malice to Camilla, he concluded her warped by her prejudice in favour of Indiana. Dr. Marchmont, however, had bid him judge by proof, not appearance; and he resolved therefore to investigate the cause of this disquiet, before he acted upon his belief in its blamelessness.

Having completely spoilt one skein, she threw it aside, and saying 'the weather's so fine, I cannot bear to stay within,'—left her silk, her winders, and her work-bag, on the first chair, and skipt down the stairs.

Sir Hugh declined walking, but would let nobody remain with him. Edgar, as if studying the clouds, glided down first. Camilla, perceiving him, bent her head, and began gathering some flowers. He stood by her a moment in silence, and then said: 'To-morrow morning, without fail, I will wait upon Mrs. Needham.'

'Pray take your own time. I am not in any haste.'

'You are very good, and I am more obliged to you than I can express, for suffering my officious interference with such patience.'

A rustling of silk made Camilla now look up, and she perceived Miss Margland leaning half out of the window of the summer-house, from earnestness to catch what she said.

Angry thus to be watched, and persuaded that both innocence and dignity called upon her to make no change in her open consideration for Edgar, she answered, in a voice that strove to be more audible, but that irresistibly trembled, 'I beg you will impartially consult your own judgment, and decide as you think right.'

Edgar, now, became as little composed as herself: the power with which she invested him, possessed a charm to dissolve every hesitating doubt; and when, upon her raising her head, he perceived the redness of her eyes, and found that the perturbation which had perplexed him was mingled with some affliction, the most tender anxiety filled his mind, and though somewhat checked by the vicinity of Miss Margland, his voice expressed the warmest solicitude, as he said, 'I know not how to thank you for this sweetness; but I fear something disturbs you?—I fear you are not well, or are not happy?'

Camilla again bent over the flowers; but it was not to scent their fragrance; she sought only a hiding place for her eyes, which were gushing with tears; and though she wished to fly a thousand miles off, she had not courage to take a single step, nor force to trust her voice with the shortest reply.

'You will not speak? yet you do not deny that you have some uneasiness?—Could I give it but the smallest relief, how fortunate I should think myself!—And is it quite impossible?—Do you forbid me to ask what it is?—forbid me the indulgence even to suggest—'

'Ask nothing! suggest nothing! and think of it no more!' interrupted Camilla, 'if you would not make me quite—'

She stopt suddenly, not to utter the word unhappy, of which she felt the improper strength at the moment it was quivering on her lips, and leaving her sentence unfinished, abruptly walked away.

Edgar could not presume to follow, yet felt her conquest irresistible. Her self-denial with regard to Mrs. Arlbery won his highest approbation; her compliance with his wishes convinced him of her esteem; and her distress, so new and so unaccountable, centered every wish of his heart in a desire to solace, and to revive her.

To obtain this privilege hastened at once and determined his measures; he excused himself, therefore, from walking, and went instantly to his chamber, to reclaim, by a hasty letter to Dr. Marchmont, his procrastinating promise.

CHAPTER II

A Pro and a Con

With a pen flowing quick from feelings of the most generous warmth, Edgar wrote the following letter:

To Dr. Marchmont.

Accuse me not of precipitance, my dear Doctor, nor believe me capable of forgetting the wisdom of your suggestions, nor of lightly weighing those evils with which your zeal has encompassed me, though I write at this instant to confess a total contrariety of sentiment, to call back every promise of delay, and to make an unqualified avowal, that the period of caution is past! Camilla is not happy—something, I know not what, has disturbed the gay serenity of her bosom: she has forbid me to enquire the cause;—one way only remains to give me a claim to her confidence.—O Doctor! wonder not if cold, tardy, suspicious—I had nearly said unfeeling, caution, shrinks at such a moment, from the rising influence of warmer sympathy, which bids me sooth her in distress, shield her from danger, strengthen all her virtues, and participate in their emanations!

You will not do me the injustice to think me either impelled or blinded by external enchantments; you know me to have withstood their yet fuller blaze in her cousin: O no! were she despoiled of all personal attraction by the same ravaging distemper that has been so fierce with her poor sister; were a similar cruel accident to rob her form of all symmetry, she would yet be more fascinating to my soul, by one single look, one single word, one sweet beaming smile, diffusing all the gaiety it displays, than all of beauty, all of elegance, all of rank, all of wealth, the whole kingdom, in some wonderful aggregate, could oppose to her.

Her face, her form, however penetrating in loveliness, aid, but do not constitute, her charms; no, 'tis the quick intelligence of soul that mounts to her eyes, 'tis the spirit checked by sweetness, the sweetness animated by spirit, the nature so nobly above all artifice, all study—O Doctor! restore to me immediately every vestige, every trait of any promise, any acquiescence, any idea the most distant, that can be construed into a compliance with one moment's requisition of delay!

EDGAR MANDLEBERT.

Cleves Park, Friday Evening.

Camilla, meanwhile, shut up in her room, wept almost without cessation, from a sense of general unhappiness, though fixed to no point, and from a disturbance of mind, a confusion of ideas and of feelings, that rendered her incapable of reflection. She was again followed by Eugenia, and could no longer refuse, to her tender anxiety, a short detail of the attack which occasioned her disorder; happy, at least, in reciting it, that by unfolding the cause, there no longer remained any necessity to repress the effects of her affliction.

To her great surprise, however, Eugenia only said: 'And is this all, my dear Camilla?'

'All!' exclaimed Camilla.

'Yes, is it all?—I was afraid some great misfortune had happened.'

'And what could happen more painful, more shocking, more cruel?'

'A thousand things! for this is nothing but a mere mistake; and you should not make yourself unhappy about it, because you are not to blame.'

'Is it then nothing to be accused of designs and intentions so criminal?'

'If the accusation were just, it might indeed make you wretched: but it is Miss Margland only who has any reason to be afflicted; for it is she alone who has been in the wrong.'

Struck with this plain but uncontrovertible truth, Camilla wiped her eyes, and strove to recover some composure; but finding her tears still force their way, 'It is not,' she cried, with some hesitation, 'it is not the aspersions of Miss Margland alone that give me so much vexation—the unkindness of Indiana—'

'Indeed she is highly reprehensible; and so I will tell her;—but still, if she has any fears, however ill-founded, of losing Edgar, you cannot but pardon—you must even pity her.'

Struck again, and still more forcibly, by this second truth, Camilla, ashamed of her grief, made a stronger and more serious effort to repress it; and receiving soon afterwards a summons from her uncle, her spirit rose once more to the relief of her dejection, upon seeing him seated between Miss Margland and Indiana, and discerning that they had been making some successful complaint, by the air of triumph with which they waited her approach.

'My dear Camilla,' he cried, with a look of much disturbance, 'here's a sad ado, I find; though I don't mean to blame you, nor young Mr. Mandlebert neither, taste being a fault one can't avoid; not but what a person's changing their mind is what I can't commend in any one, which I shall certainly let him know, not doubting to bring him round by means of his own sense: only, my dear, in the meanwhile, I must beg you not to stand in your cousin's way.'

'Indeed, my dear uncle, I do not merit this imputation; I am not capable of such treachery!' indignantly answered Camilla.

'Treachery! Lord help us! treachery!' cried Sir Hugh, fondly embracing her, 'don't I know you are as innocent as the baby unborn? and more innocent too, from the advantage of having more sense to guide you by! treachery, my dear Camilla! why, I think there's nobody so good in the wide world!—by which I mean no reflections, never thinking it right to make any.'

Indiana, sullenly pouting, spoke not a word; but Miss Margland, with a tone of plausibility that was some covert to its malice, said 'Why then all may be well, and the young ladies as good friends as ever, and Mr. Mandlebert return to the conduct of a gentleman, only just by Miss Camilla's doing as she would be done by; for nothing that all of us can say will have any effect, if she does not discourage him from dangling about after her in the manner he does now, speaking to nobody else, and always asking her opinion about every trifle, which is certainly doing no great justice to Miss Lynmere.'

Indiana, with a toss of the head, protested his notice was the last thing she desired.

'My dear Indiana,' said Sir Hugh, 'don't mind all that outward shew. Mr. Mandlebert is a very good boy, and as to your cousin Camilla, I am sure I need not put you in mind how much she is the same; but I really think, whatever's the reason, the young youths of now-a-days grow backwarder and backwarder. Though I can't say but what in my time it was just the same; witness myself; which is what I have been sorry for often enough, though I have left off repenting it now, because it's of no use; age being a thing there's no getting ahead of.'

'Well, then, all that remains is this,' said Miss Margland, 'let Miss Camilla keep out of Mr. Mandlebert's way; and let her order the carriage, and go to Mrs. Arlbery's to-morrow, and take no notice of his likings and dislikings; and I'll be bound for it he will soon think no more of her, and then, of course, he will give the proper attention to Miss Lynmere.'

'O, if that's all,' cried Sir Hugh, 'my dear Camilla, I am sure, will do it, and as much again too, to make her cousin easy. And so now, I hope, all is settled, and my two good girls will kiss one another, and be friends; which I am sure I am myself, with all my heart.'

Camilla hung her head, in speechless perturbation, at a task which appeared to her equally hard and unjust; but while fear and shame kept her silent, Sir Hugh drew her to Indiana, and a cold, yet unavoidable salute, gave a species of tacit consent to a plan which she did not dare oppose, from the very strength of the desire that urged her opposition.

They then separated; Sir Hugh delighted, Miss Margland triumphant, Indiana half satisfied, half affronted, and Camilla with a mind so crowded, a heart so full, she scarcely breathed. Sensations the most contrary, of pain, pleasure, hope, and terror, at once assailed her. Edgar, of whom so long she had only thought as of the destined husband of Indiana, she now heard named with suspicions of another regard, to which she did not dare give full extension; yet of which the most distant surmise made her consider herself, for a moment, as the happiest of human beings, though she held herself the next as the most culpable for even wishing it.

She found Eugenia still in her room, who, perceiving her increased emotion, tenderly enquired, if there were any new cause.

'Alas! yes, my dearest Eugenia! they have been exacting from me the most cruel of sacrifices! They order me to fly from Edgar Mandlebert—to resist his advice—to take the very measures I have promised to forbear—to disoblige, to slight, to behave to him even offensively! my uncle himself, lenient, kind, indulgent as he is, my uncle himself has been prevailed with to inflict upon me this terrible injunction.'

'My uncle,' answered Eugenia, 'is incapable of giving pain to any body, and least of all to you, whom he loves with such fondness; he has not therefore comprehended the affair; he only considers, in general, that to please or to displease Edgar Mandlebert can be a matter of no moment to you, when compared with its importance to Indiana.'

'It is a thousand and a thousand, a million and a million times more important to me, than it can ever be to her!' exclaimed the ardent Camilla, 'for she values not his kindness, she knows not his worth, she is insensible to his virtues!'

'You judge too hastily, my dear Camilla; she has not indeed your warmth of heart; but if she did not wish the union to take place, why would she shew all this disquiet in the apprehension of its breach?'

Camilla, surprised into recollection, endeavoured to become calmer.

'You, indeed,' continued the temperate Eugenia, 'if so situated, would not so have behaved; you would not have been so unjust; and you could not have been so weak; but still, if you had received, however causelessly, any alarm for the affection of the man you meant to marry, and that man were as amiable as Edgar, you would have been equally disturbed.'

Camilla, convinced, yet shocked, felt the flutter of her heart give a thousand hues to her face, and walking to the window, leaned far out to gasp for breath.

'Weigh the request more coolly, and you cannot refuse a short compliance. I am sure you would not make Indiana unhappy.'

'O, no! not for the world!' cried she, struggling to seem more reasonable than she felt.

'Yet how can she be otherwise, if she imagines you have more of the notice and esteem of Edgar than herself?'

Camilla now had not a word to say; the subject dropt; she took up a book, and by earnest internal remonstrances, commanded herself to appear at tea-time with tolerable serenity.

The evening was passed in spiritless conversation, or in listening to the piano-forte, upon which Indiana, with the utmost difficulty, played some very easy lessons.

At night, the following answer arrived from Dr. Marchmont:

To Edgar Mandlebert, Esq.

Parsonage House, Cleves,
Friday Night.

MY DEAR FRIEND,

I must be thankful, in a moment of such enthusiasm, that you can pay the attention of even recollecting those evils with which my zeal only has, you think, encompassed you. I cannot insist upon the practice of caution which you deem unfounded; but as you wait my answer, I will once more open upon my sentiments, and communicate my wishes. It is now only I can speak them; the instant you have informed the young lady of your own, silences them for ever. Your honour and her happiness become then entangled in each other, and I know not which I would least willingly assail. What in all men is base, would to you, I believe, be impossible—to trifle with such favour as may be the growth of your own undisguised partiality.

Your present vehemence to ascertain the permanent possession of one you conceive formed for your felicity, obscures, to your now absorbed faculties, the thousand nameless, but tenacious, delicacies annexed by your species of character to your powers of enjoyment. In two words, then, let me tell you, what, in a short time, you will daily tell yourself: you cannot be happy if not exclusively loved; for you cannot excite, you cannot bestow happiness.

By exclusively, I do not mean to the exclusion of other connections and regard; far from it; those who covet in a bride the oblivion of all former friendships, all early affections, weaken the finest ties of humanity, and dissolve the first compact of unregistered but genuine integrity. The husband, who would rather rationally than with romance be loved himself, should seek to cherish, not obliterate the kind feelings of nature in its first expansions. These, where properly bestowed, are the guarantees to that constant and respectable tenderness, which a narrow and selfish jealousy rarely fails to convert into distaste and disgust.

The partiality which I mean you to ascertain, injures not these prior claims; I mean but a partiality exclusive of your situation in life, and of all declaration of your passion: a partiality, in fine, that is appropriate to yourself, not to the rank in the world with which you may tempt her ambition, nor to the blandishments of flattery, which only soften the heart by intoxicating the understanding.

Observe, therefore, if your general character, and usual conduct, strike her mind; if her esteem is yours without the attraction of assiduity and adulation; if your natural disposition and manners make your society grateful to her, and your approbation desirable.

It is thus alone you can secure your own contentment; for it is thus alone your reflecting mind can snatch from the time to come the dangerous surmises of a dubious retrospection.

Remember, you can always advance; you can never, in honour, go back; and believe me when I tell you, that the mere simple avowal of preference, which only ultimately binds the man, is frequently what first captivates the woman. If her mind is not previously occupied, it operates with such seductive sway, it so soothes, so flatters, so bewitches her self-complacency, that while she listens, she imperceptibly fancies she participates in sentiments, which, but the minute before, occurred not even to her imagination; and while her hand is the recompence of her own eulogy, she is not herself aware if she has bestowed it where her esteem and regard, unbiassed by the eloquence of acknowledged admiration, would have wished it sought, or if it has simply been the boon of her own gratified vanity.

I now no longer urge your acquiescence, my dear friend; I merely entreat you twice to peruse what I have written, and then leave you to act by the result of such perusal.

I remain
Your truly faithful and obliged
GABRIEL MARCHMONT.

Edgar ran through this letter with an impatience wholly foreign to his general character. 'Why,' cried he, 'will he thus obtrude upon me these fastidious doubts and causeless difficulties? I begged but the restitution of my promise, and he gives it me in words that nearly annihilate my power of using it.'

Disappointed and displeased, he hastily put it into his pocket-book, resolving to seek Camilla, and commit the consequences of an interview to the impulses it might awaken.

He was half way down stairs, when the sentence finishing with, 'you cannot excite, you cannot bestow happiness,' confusedly recurred to him: 'If in that,' thought he, 'I fail, I am a stranger to it myself, and a stranger for ever;' and, returning to his room, he re-opened the letter to look for the passage.

The sentence lost nothing by being read a second time; he paused upon it dejectedly, and presently re-read the whole epistle.

'He is not quite wrong!' cried he, pensively; 'there is nothing very unreasonable in what he urges: true, indeed, it is, that I can never be happy myself, if her happiness is not entwined around my own.'

The first blight thus borne to that ardent glee with which the imagination rewards its own elevated speculations, he yet a third time read the letter.

'He is right!' he then cried; 'I will investigate her sentiments, and know what are my chances for her regard; what I owe to real approbation; and what merely to intimacy of situation. I will postpone all explanation till my visit here expires, and devote the probationary interval, to an examination which shall obviate all danger of either deceiving my own reason, or of beguiling her inconsiderate acceptance.'

This settled, he rejoiced in a mastery over his eagerness, which he considered as complete, since it would defer for no less than a week the declaration of his passion.

CHAPTER III

An Author's Notion of Travelling

The next morning Camilla, sad and unwilling to appear, was the last who entered the breakfast-parlour. Edgar instantly discerned the continued unhappiness, which an assumed smile concealed from the unsuspicious Sir Hugh, and the week of delay before him seemed an outrage to all his wishes.

While she was drinking her first cup of tea, a servant came in, and told her the carriage was ready.

She coloured, but nobody spoke, and the servant retired. Edgar was going to ask the design for the morning, when Miss Margland said—'Miss Camilla, as the horses have got to go and return, you had better not keep them waiting.'

Colouring still more deeply, she was going to disclaim having ordered them, though well aware for what purpose they were come, when Sir Hugh said—'I think, my dear, you had best take Eugenia with you, which may serve you as a companion to talk to, in case you want to say anything by the way, which I take for granted; young people not much liking to hold their tongues for a long while together, which is very natural, having so little to think of.'

'Miss Eugenia, then,' cried Miss Margland, before Camilla could reply, 'run for your cloak as soon as you have finished your breakfast.'

Eugenia, hoping to aid her sister in performing a task, which she considered as a peace-offering to Indiana, said, she had already done.

Camilla now lost all courage for resistance; but feeling her chagrin almost intolerable, quitted the room with her tea undrunk, and without making known if she should return or not.

Eugenia followed, and Edgar, much amazed, said, he had forgotten to order his horse for his morning's ride, and hastily made off: determined to be ready to hand the sisters to the carriage, and learn whither it was to drive.

Camilla, who, in flying to her room, thought of nothing less than preparing for an excursion which she now detested, was again surprised in tears by Eugenia.

'What, my dearest Camilla,' she cried, 'can thus continually affect you? you cannot be so unhappy without some cause!—why will you not trust your Eugenia?'

'I cannot talk,' she answered, ashamed to repeat reasons which she knew Eugenia held to be inadequate to her concern—'If there is no resource against this persecution—if I must render myself hateful to give them satisfaction, let us, at least, be gone immediately, and let me be spared seeing the person I so ungratefully offend.'

She then hurried down stairs; but finding Edgar in waiting, still more quickly hurried back, and in an agony, for which she attempted not to account, cast herself into a chair, and told Eugenia, that if Miss Margland did not contrive to call Edgar away, the universe could not prevail with her to pass him in such defiance.

'My dear Camilla,' said Eugenia, surprized, yet compassionately, 'if this visit is become so painful to you, relinquish it at once.'

'Ah, no! for that cruel Miss Margland will then accuse me of staying away only to follow the counsel of Edgar.'

She stopt; for the countenance of Eugenia said—'And is that not your motive?' A sudden consciousness took place of her distress; she hid her face, in the hope of concealing her emotion, and with as calm a voice as she could attain, said, the moment they could pass unobserved she would set off.

Eugenia went downstairs.

'Alas! alas!' she then cried, 'into what misery has this barbarous Miss Margland thrown me! Eugenia herself seems now to suspect something wrong; and so, I suppose, will my uncle; and I can only convince them of my innocence by acting towards Edgar as a monster.—Ah! I would sooner a thousand times let them all think me guilty!'

Eugenia had met Miss Margland in the hall, who, impatient for their departure, passed her, and ascended the stairs.

At the sound of her footsteps, the horror of her reproaches and insinuations conquered every other feeling, and Camilla, starting up, rushed forward, and saying 'Good morning!' ran off.

Edgar was still at the door, and came forward to offer her his hand. 'Pray take care of Eugenia,' she cried, abruptly passing him, and darting, unaided, into the chaise. Edgar, astonished, obeyed, and gave his more welcome assistance to Eugenia; but when both were seated, said—'Where shall I tell the postillion to drive?'

Camilla, who was pulling one of the green blinds up, and again letting it down, twenty times in a minute, affected not to hear him; but Eugenia answered, 'to the Grove, to Mrs. Arlbery's.'

The postillion had already received his orders from Miss Margland, and drove off; leaving Edgar mute with surprise, disappointment and mortification.

Miss Margland was just behind him, and conceived this the fortunate instant for eradicating from his mind every favourable pre-possession for Camilla; assuming, therefore, an air of concern, she said—'So, you have found Miss Camilla out, in spite of all her precautions! she would fain not have had you know her frolic.'

'Not know it! has there, then, been any plan? did Miss Camilla intend—'

'O, she intends nothing in the world for two minutes together! only she did not like you should find out her fickleness. You know, I told you, before, she was all whim; and so you will find. You may always take my opinion, be assured. Miss Lynmere is the only one among them that is always the same, always good, always amiable.'

'And is not Miss—' he was going to say Camilla, but checking himself, finished with—'Miss Eugenia, at least, always equal, always consistent?'

'Why, she is better than Miss Camilla; but not one among them has any steadiness, or real sweetness, but Miss Lynmere. As to Miss Camilla, if she has not her own way, there's no enduring her, she frets, and is so cross. When you put her off, in that friendly manner, from gadding after a new acquaintance so improper for her, you set her into such an ill humour, that she has done nothing but cry, as you may have seen by her eyes, and worry herself and all of us round, except you, ever since; but she was afraid of you, for fear you should take her to task, which she hates of all things.'

Half incredulous, yet half shocked, Edgar turned from this harangue in silent disgust. He knew the splenetic nature of Miss Margland, and trusted she might be wrong; but he knew, too, her opportunities for observation, and dreaded lest she might be right. Camilla had been certainly low spirited, weeping, and restless; was it possible it could be for so slight, so unmeaning a cause? His wish was to follow her on horseback; but this, unauthorized, might betray too much anxiety: he tried not to think of what had been said by Dr. Marchmont, while this cloud hung over her disposition and sincerity; for whatever might be the malignity of Miss Margland, the breach of a promise, of which the voluntary sweetness had so lately proved his final captivation, could not be doubted, and called aloud for explanation.

He mounted, however, his horse, to make his promised enquiries of Mrs. Needham; for though the time was already past for impeding the acquaintance from taking place, its progress might yet be stopt, should it be found incompatible with propriety.

The young ladies had scarce left the Park, when Sir Hugh, recollecting a promise he had made to Mr. and Mrs. Tyrold, of never suffering Eugenia to go abroad unattended by some gentleman, while Bellamy remained in the country, sent hastily to beg that Edgar would follow the carriage.

Edgar was out of sight, and there was no chance of overtaking him.

'Lack-a-day!' said Sir Hugh, 'those young folks can never walk a horse but full gallop!' He then resolved to ask Dr. Orkborne to go after his pupil, and ride by the side of the chaise. He ordered a horse to be saddled; and, to lose no time by messages, the tardiness of which he had already experienced with this gentleman, he went himself to his apartment, and after several vain rappings at his door, entered the room unbid, saying—'Good Dr. Orkborne, unless you are dead, which God forbid! I think it's something uncomfortable that you can't speak to a person waiting at your door; not that I pretend to doubt but you may have your proper reasons, being what I can't judge.'

He then begged he would get booted and spurred instantly, and follow his two nieces to Mrs. Arlbery's, in order to take care of Eugenia; adding, 'though I'm afraid, Doctor, by your look, you don't much listen to me, which I am sorry for; my not being able to speak like Horace and Virgil being no fault of mine, but of my poor capacity, which no man can be said to be answerable for.'

He then again entreated him to set off.

'Only a moment, sir! I only beg you'll accord me one moment!' cried the Doctor, with a fretful sigh; while, screening his eyes with his left hand, he endeavoured hastily to make a memorandum of his ideas, before he forced them to any other subject.

'Really, Dr. Orkborne,' said Sir Hugh, somewhat displeased, 'I must needs remark, for a friend, I think this rather slow: however, I can't say I am much disappointed, now, that I did not turn out a scholar myself, for I see, plain enough, you learned men think nothing of any consequence but Homer and such; which, however, I don't mean to take ill, knowing it was like enough to have been my own case.'

He then left the room, intending to send a man and horse after the chaise, to desire his two nieces to return immediately.

Dr. Orkborne, who, though copiously stored with the works of the ancients, had a sluggish understanding, and no imagination, was entirely overset by this intrusion. The chain of his observations was utterly broken; he strove vainly to rescue from oblivion the slow ripening fruits of his tardy conceptions, and, proportioning his estimation of their value by their labour, he not only considered his own loss as irreparable, but the whole world to be injured by so unfortunate an interruption.

The recollection, however, which refused to assist his fame, was importunate in reminding him that the present offender was his patron; and his total want of skill in character kept from him the just confidence he would otherwise have placed in the unalterable goodness of heart of Sir Hugh, whom, though he despised for his ignorance, he feared for his power.

Uneasy, therefore, at his exit, which he concluded to be made in wrath, he uttered a dolorous groan over his papers, and compelled himself to follow, with an apology, the innocent enemy of his glory.

Sir Hugh, who never harboured displeasure for two minutes in his life, was more inclined to offer an excuse himself for what he had dropt against learning, than to resist the slightest concession from the Doctor, whom he only begged to make haste, the horse being already at the door. But Dr. Orkborne, as soon as he comprehended what was desired, revived from the weight of sacrificing so much time; he had never been on horseback since he was fifteen years of age, and declared, to the wondering baronet, he could not risk his neck by undertaking such a journey.

In high satisfaction, he would then have returned to his room, persuaded that, when his mind was disembarrassed, a parallel between two ancient authors which, with much painful stretch of thought, he had suggested, and which, with the most elaborate difficulty, he was arranging and drawing up, would recur again to his memory: but Sir Hugh, always eager in expedients, said, he should follow in the coach, which might be ready time enough for him to arrive at Mrs. Arlbery's before the visit was over, and to bring Eugenia safe back; 'which,' cried he, 'is the main point, for the sake of seeing that she goes no where else.'

Dr. Orkborne, looking extremely blank at this unexpected proposition, stood still.

'Won't you go, then, my good friend?'

The Doctor, after a long pause, and in a most dejected tone, sighed out, 'Yes, sir, certainly, with the greatest—alacrity.'

Sir Hugh, who took everything literally that seemed right or good-natured, thanked him, and ordered the horses to be put to the coach with all possible expedition.

It was soon at the door, and Dr. Orkborne, who had spent in his room the intervening period, in moaning the loss of the time that was to succeed, and in an opinion that two hours of this morning would have been of more value to him than two years when it was gone, reluctantly obeyed the call that obliged him to descend: but he had no sooner entered the carriage, and found he was to have it to himself, than leaping suddenly from it, as the groom, who was to attend him, was preparing to shut the door, he hastened back to his chamber to collect a packet of books and papers, through the means of which he hoped to recall those flowers of rhetoric, upon which he was willing to risk his future reputation.

The astonished groom, concluding something had frightened him, jumped into the coach to find the cause of his flight; but Sir Hugh, who was advancing to give his final directions, called out, with some displeasure 'Hollo, there, you Jacob! if Dr. Orkborne thinks to get you to go for my nieces in place of himself, it's what I don't approve; which, however, you need not take amiss, one man being no more born with a livery upon his back than another; which God forbid I should think otherwise. Nevertheless, my little girls must have a proper respect shewn them; which, it's surprising Dr. Orkborne should not know as well as me.'

And, much disconcerted, he walked to the parlour, to ruminate upon some other measure.

'I am sure, your honour,' said Jacob, following him, 'I got in with no ill intention; but what it was as come across the Doctor I don't know; but just as I was a going to shut the door, without saying never a word, out he pops, and runs upstairs again; so I only got in to see if something had hurt him; but I can't find nothing of no sort.'

Then, putting to the door, and looking sagaciously, 'Please your honour,' he continued, 'I dare say it's only some maggot got into his brain from over reading and writing; for all the maids think he'll soon be cracked.'

'That's very wrong of them, Jacob; and I desire you'll tell them they must not think any such thing.'

'Why, your honour don't know half, or you'd be afraid too,' said Jacob, lowering his voice; 'he's like nothing you ever see. He won't let a chair nor a table be dusted in his room, though they are covered over with cobwebs, because he says, it takes him such a time to put his things to rights again; though all the while what he calls being to rights is just the contrary; for it's a mere higgledy piggledy, one thing heaped o'top of t'other, as if he did it for fun.'

The baronet gravely answered, that if there were not the proper shelves for his books he would order more.

'Why, your honour, that's not the quarter, as I tell you! why, when they're cleaning out his room, if they happen but to sweep away a bit of paper as big as my hand, he'll make believe they've done him as much mischief as if they'd stole a thousand pound. It would make your honour stare to hear him. Mary says, she's sure he has never been quite right ever since he come to the house.'

'But I desire you'll tell Mary I don't approve of that opinion. Dr. Orkborne is one of the first scholars in the world, as I am credibly informed; and I beg you'll all respect him accordingly.'

'Why, your honour, if it i'n't owing to something of that sort, why does he behave so unaccountable? I myself heard him making such a noise at the maids one day, that I spoke to Mary afterwards, and asked her what was the matter?—"Laws, nobody knows," says she, "but here's the Doctor been all in a huff again; I was just a dusting his desk (says she) and so I happened to wipe down a little bundle of papers, all nothing but mere scraps, and he took on as if they'd been so many guineas (says she) and he kept me there for an hour looking for them, and scolding, and telling such a heap of fibs, that if he was not out of his head, would be a shame for a gentleman to say" (says she).'

'Fie, fie, Jacob! and tell Mary fie, too. He is a very learned gentleman, and no more a story-teller than I am myself; which God forbid.'

'Why, your honour, how could this here be true? he told the maids how they had undone him, and the like, only because of their throwing down them few bits of papers; though they are ready to make oath they picked them up, almost every one; and that they were all of a crump, and of no manner of use.'

'Well, well, say no more about it, good Jacob, but go and give my compliments to Dr. Orkborne, and ask him, what's the reason of his changing his mind; I mean, provided it's no secret.'

Jacob returned in two minutes, with uplifted hands and eyes; 'your honour,' cried he, 'now you'll believe me another time! he is worse than ever, and I'll be bound he'll break out before another quarter.'

'Why, what's the matter?'

'Why, as sure as I'm here, he's getting together ever so many books, and stuffing his pockets, and cramming them under his arms, just as if he was a porter! and when I gave him your honour's message, I suppose it put him out, for he said, "Don't hurry me so, I'm a coming;" making believe as if he was only a preparing for going out, in the stead of making that fool of himself.'

Sir Hugh, now really alarmed, bid him not mention the matter to anyone; and was going upstairs himself, when he saw Dr. Orkborne, heavily laden with books in each hand, and bulging from both coat pockets, slowly and carefully coming down.

'Bless me,' cried he, rather fearfully, 'my dear sir, what are you going to do with all that library?'

Dr. Orkborne, wishing him good morning, without attending to his question, proceeding to the carriage, calling to Jacob, who stood aloof, to make haste and open the door.

Jacob obeyed, but with a significant look at his master, that said, 'you see how it is, sir!'

Sir Hugh following him, gently put his hand upon his shoulder, and mildly said, 'My dear friend, to be sure you know best, but I don't see the use of loading yourself in that manner for nothing.'

'It is a great loss of time, sir, to travel without books,' answered the Doctor, quietly arranging them in the coach.

'Travel, my good friend? Why, you don't call it travelling to go four or five miles? why, if you had known me before my fall—However, I don't mean to make any comparisons, you gentlemen scholars being no particular good horsemen. However, if you were to go one hundred miles instead of four or five, you could not get through more than one of those books, read as hard as you please; unless you skip half, which I suppose you solid heads leave to the lower ignoramusses.'

'It is not for reading, sir, that I take all these books, but merely to look into. There are many of them I shall never read in my life, but I shall want them all.'

Sir Hugh now stared with increased perplexity; but Dr. Orkborne, as eager to go, since his books were to accompany him, as before to stay, told Jacob to bid the coachman make haste. Jacob looked at his master, who ordered him to mount his mare, and the carriage drove off.

The baronet, in some uneasiness, seated himself in the hall, to ruminate upon what he had just heard. The quietness and usual manner of speaking and looking of Dr. Orkborne, which he had remarked, removed any immediate apprehensions from the assertions of Jacob and Mary; but still he did not like the suggestion; and the carrying off so many books, when he acknowledged he did not mean to read one of them, disturbed him.

In every shadow of perplexity, his first wish was to consult with his brother; and if he had not parted with both his carriages, he would instantly have set off for Etherington. He sent, however, an express for Mr. Tyrold, begging to see him at Cleves with all speed.

CHAPTER IV

An Internal Detection

When the chaise drove from Cleves Park, all attempt at any disguise was over with Camilla, who alive only to the horror of appearing ungrateful to Edgar, wept without controul; and, leaning back in the carriage, entreated Eugenia to dispense with all conversation.

Eugenia, filled with pity, wondered, but complied, and they travelled near four miles in silence; when, perceiving, over the paling round a paddock, Mrs. Arlbery and a party of company, Camilla dried her eyes, and prepared for her visit, of which the impetuosity of her feelings had retarded all previous consideration.

Eugenia, with true concern, saw the unfitness of her sister to appear, and proposed walking the rest of the way, in the hope that a little air and exercise might compose her spirits.

She agreed; they alighted, and bidding the footman keep with the carriage, which they ordered should drive slowly behind, they proceeded gently, arm in arm, along a clean raised bank by the side of the road, with a pace suiting at once the infirmity of Eugenia, and the wish of delay in Camilla.

The sound of voices reached them from within the paddock, though a thick shrubbery prevented their seeing the interlocutors.

'Can you make out the arms?' said one.

'No,' answered another, 'but I can see the postillion's livery, and I am certain it is Sir Hugh Tyrold's.'

'Then it is not coming hither,' said a third voice, which they recollected for Mrs. Arlbery's; 'we don't visit: though I should not dislike to see the old baronet. They tell me he is a humorist; and I have a taste for all oddities: but then he has a house full of females, and females I never admit in a morning, except when I have secured some men to take the entertaining them off my hands.'

'Whither is Bellamy running?' cried another voice, 'he's off without a word.'

'Gone in hopes of a rencounter, I doubt not,' answered Mrs. Arlbery; 'he made palpable aim at one of the divinities of Cleves at the ball.'

Eugenia now grew uneasy. 'Let us be quick,' she whispered 'and enter the house!'

'Divinities! Lord! are they divinities?' said a girlish female voice; 'pray how old are they?'

'I fancy about seventeen.'

'Seventeen! gracious! I thought they'd been quite young; I wonder they a'n't married!'

'I presume, then, you intend to be more expeditious?' said another, whose voice spoke him to be General Kinsale.

'Gracious! I hope so, for I hate an old bride. I'll never marry at all, if I stay till I am eighteen.'

'A story goes about,' said the General, 'that Sir Hugh Tyrold has selected one of his nieces for his sole heiress; but no two people agree which it is; they have asserted it of each.'

'I was mightily taken with one of the girls,' said Mrs. Arlbery; 'there was something so pleasant in her looks and manner, that I even felt inclined to forgive her being younger and prettier than myself; but she turned out also to be more whimsical—and that there was no enduring.'

Camilla, extremely ashamed, was now upon the point of begging Eugenia to return, when a new speech seized all her attention.

'Do you know, General, when that beautiful automaton, Miss Lynmere, is to marry young Mandlebert?'

'Immediately, I understand; I am told he has fitted up his house very elegantly for her reception.'

A deep sigh escaped Camilla at such publicity in the report and belief of the engagement of Edgar with her cousin, and brought with it a consciousness too strong for any further self-disguise, that her distress flowed not all from an unjust accusation: the sound alone of the union struck as a dagger at her heart, and told her, incontrovertibly, who was its master.

Her sensations were now most painful: she grew pale, she became sick, and was obliged, in her turn, to lean upon Eugenia, who, affrighted to see her thus strangely disordered, besought her to go back to the chaise.

She consented, and begged to pass a few minutes there alone. Eugenia therefore stayed without, walking slowly upon the bank.

Camilla, getting into the carriage, pulled up the blinds, and, no longer self-deceived, lamented in a new burst of sorrow, her unhappy fate, and unpropitious attachment.

This consciousness, however, became soon a call upon her integrity, and her regret was succeeded by a summons upon propriety. She gave herself up as lost to all personal felicity, but hoped she had discovered the tendency of her affliction, in time to avoid the dangers, and the errors to which it might lead. She determined to struggle without cessation for the conquest of a partiality she deemed it treachery to indulge; and to appease any pain she now blushed to have caused to Indiana, by strictly following the hard prescription of Miss Margland, and the obvious opinion of Eugenia, in shunning the society, and no longer coveting the approbation of Edgar. 'Such, my dear father,' she cried, 'would be your lesson, if I dared consult you! such, my most honoured mother, would be your conduct, if thus cruelly situated!'

This thought thrilled through every vein with pleasure, in a sense of filial desert, and her sole desire was to return immediately to those incomparable parents, under whose roof she had experienced nothing but happiness, and in whose bosoms she hoped to bury every tumultuous disturbance.

These ideas and resolutions, dejecting, yet solacing, occupied her to the forgetfulness of her intended visit, and even of Eugenia, till the words: 'Pray let me come to you, my dear Camilla!' made her let down the blinds.

She then perceived Mr. Bellamy earnestly addressing her sister.

He had advanced suddenly towards her, by a short cut from the paddock, of which she was not aware, when she was about twenty yards from the chaise.

She made an effort to avoid him; but he planted himself in the way of her retreat, though with an air of supplication, with which she strove in vain to be angry.

He warmly represented the cruelty of thus flying him, entreated but the privilege of addressing her as a common acquaintance; and promised, upon that condition, to submit unmurmuring to her rejection.

Eugenia, though in secret she thought this request but equitable, made him no answer.

'O madam,' he cried, 'what have I not suffered since your barbarous letter! why will you be so amiable, yet so inexorable?'

She attempted to quicken her pace; but again, in the same manner, stopping her, he exclaimed: 'Do not kill me by this disdain! I ask not now for favour or encouragement—I know my hard doom—I ask only to converse with you—though, alas! it was by conversing with you I lost my heart.'

Eugenia felt softened; and her countenance, which had forfeited nothing of expression, though every thing of beauty, soon shewed Bellamy his advantage. He pursued it eagerly; depicted his passion, deprecated her severity, extolled her virtues and accomplishments, and bewailed his unhappy, hopeless flame.

Eugenia, knowing that all she said, and believing that all she heard issued from the fountain of truth, became extremely distressed. 'Let me pass, I conjure you, Sir,' she cried, 'and do not take it ill—but I cannot hear you any longer.'

The vivacity of bright hope flashed into the sparkling eyes of Bellamy, at so gentle a remonstrance; and entreaties for lenity, declarations of passion, professions of submission, and practice of resistance, assailed the young Eugenia with a rapidity that confounded her: she heard him with scarce any opposition, from a fear of irritating his feelings, joined to a juvenile embarrassment how to treat with more severity so sincere and so humble a suppliant.

From this situation, to the extreme provocation of Bellamy, she was relieved by the appearance of Major Cerwood, who having observed, from the paddock, the slow motion of the carriage, had come forth to find out the cause.

Eugenia seized the moment of interruption to press forward, and make the call to her sister already mentioned; Bellamy accompanying and pleading, but no longer venturing to stop her: he handed her, therefore, to the chaise, where Major Cerwood also paid his compliments to the two ladies; and hearing they were going to the seat of Mrs. Arlbery, whither Camilla now forced herself, though more unwillingly than ever, he ran on, with Bellamy, to be ready to hand them from the carriage.

They were shewn into a parlour, while a servant went into the garden to call his mistress.

This interval was not neglected by either of the gentlemen, for Bellamy was scarce more eager to engage the attention of Eugenia, than the Major to force that of Camilla. By Lionel he had been informed she was heiress of Cleves; he deemed, therefore, the opportunity by no means to be thrown away, of making, what he believed required opportunity alone, a conquest of her young heart. Accustomed to think compliments always welcome to the fair, he construed her sadness into softness, and imputed her silence to the confusing impression made upon an inexperienced rural beauty, by the first assiduities of a man of figure and gallantry.

In about a quarter of an hour the servant of Mrs. Arlbery slowly returned, and, with some hesitation, said his lady was not at home. The gentlemen looked provoked, and Camilla and Eugenia, much disconcerted at so evident a denial, left their names, and returned to their carriage.

The journey back to Cleves was mute and dejected: Camilla was shocked at the conscious state of her own mind, and Eugenia was equally pensive. She began to think with anxiety of a contract with a person wholly unknown, and to consider the passion and constancy of Bellamy as the emanations of a truly elevated mind, and meriting her most serious gratitude.

At the hall door they were eagerly met by Sir Hugh, who, with infinite surprise, enquired where they had left Dr. Orkborne.

'Dr. Orkborne?' they repeated, 'we have not even seen him.'

'Not seen him? did not he come to fetch you?'

'No, Sir.'

'Why, he went to Mrs. Arlbery's on purpose! And what he stays for at that lady's, now you are both come away, is a thing I can't pretend to judge of; unless he has stopt to read one of those books he took with him; which is what I dare say is the case.'

'He cannot be at Mrs. Arlbery's, Sir,' said Eugenia, 'for we have but this moment left her house.'

'He must be there, my dear girls, for he's no where else. I saw him set out myself, which, however, I shan't mention the particulars of, having sent for my brother, whom I expect every minute.'

They then concluded he had gone by another road, as there were two ways to the Grove.

Edgar did not return to Cleves till the family were assembling to dinner. His visit to Mrs. Needham had occasioned him a new disturbance. She had rallied him upon the general rumour of his approaching marriage; and his confusion, from believing his partiality for Camilla detected, was construed into a confirmation of the report concerning Indiana. His disavowal was rather serious than strong, and involuntarily mixt with such warm eulogiums of the object he imagined to be meant, that Mrs. Needham, who had only named a certain fair one at Cleves, laughed at his denial, and thought the engagement undoubted.

With respect to his enquiries relative to Mrs. Arlbery, Mrs. Needham said, that she was a woman far more agreeable to the men, than to her own sex; that she was full of caprice, coquetry, and singularity; yet, though she abused the gift, she possessed an excellent and uncommon understanding. She was guilty of no vices, but utterly careless of appearances, and though her character was wholly unimpeached, she had offended or frightened almost all the county around, by a wilful strangeness of behaviour, resulting from an undaunted determination to follow in every thing the bent of her own humour.

Edgar justly deemed this a dangerous acquaintance for Camilla, whose natural thoughtlessness and vivacity made him dread the least imprudence in the connexions she might form; yet, as the reputation of Mrs. Arlbery was unsullied, he felt how difficult would be the task of demonstrating the perils he feared.

Sir Hugh, during the dinner, was exceedingly disturbed. 'What Dr. Orkborne can be doing with himself,' said he, 'is more than any man can tell, for he certainly would not stay at the lady's, when he found you were both come away; so that I begin to think it's ten to one but he's gone nobody knows where! for why else should he take all those books? which is a thing I have been thinking of ever since; especially as he owned himself he should never read one half of them. If he has taken something amiss, I am very ready to ask his pardon; though what it can be I don't pretend to guess.'

Miss Margland said, he was so often doing something or other that was ill-bred, that she was not at all surprised he should stay out at dinner time. He had never yet fetched her a chair, nor opened the door for her, since he came to the house; so that she did not know what was too bad to expect.

As they were rising from the table, a note arrived from Mr. Tyrold, with an excuse, that important business would prevent his coming to Cleves till the next day. Camilla then begged permission to go in the chaise that was to fetch him, flattering herself something might occur to detain her, when at Etherington. Sir Hugh readily assented, and composing himself for his afternoon nap, desired to be awaked if Dr. Orkborne came back.

All now left the room except Camilla, who, taking up a book, stood still at a window, till she was aroused by the voice of Edgar, who, from the Park, asked her what she was reading.

She turned over the leaves, ashamed at the question, to look for the title; she had held the book mechanically, and knew not what it was.

He then produced the promised nosegay, which had been brought by his gardener during her excursion. She softly lifted up the sash, pointing to her sleeping uncle; he gave it her with a silent little bow, and walked away; much disappointed to miss an opportunity from which he had hoped for some explanation.

She held it in her hand some time, scarcely sensible she had taken it, till, presently, she saw its buds bedewed with her falling tears.

She shook them off, and pressed the nosegay to her bosom. 'This, at least,' she cried, 'I may accept, for it was offered me before that barbarous attack. Ah! they know not the innocence of my regard, or they would not so wrong it! The universe could not tempt me to injure my cousin, though it is true, I have valued the kindness of Edgar—and I must always value it!—These flowers are more precious to me, coming from his hands, and reared in his grounds, than all the gems of the East could be from any other possessor. But where is the guilt of such a preference? And who that knows him could help feeling it?'

Sir Hugh now awakening from a short slumber, exclaimed—'I have just found out the reason why this poor gentleman has made off; I mean, provided he is really gone away, which, however, I hope not: but I think, by his bringing down all those books, he meant to give me a broad hint, that he had got no proper book-case to keep them in; which the maids as good as think too.'

Then, calling upon Camilla, he asked if she was not of that opinion.

'Y—e—s, Sir,' she hesitatingly answered.

'Well, then, my dear, if we all think the same, I'll give orders immediately for getting the better of that fault.'

Miss Margland, curious to know how Camilla was detained, now re-entered the room. Struck with the fond and melancholy air with which she was bending over her nosegay, she abruptly demanded—'Pray, where might you get those flowers?'

Covered with shame, she could make no answer.

'O, Miss Camilla! Miss Camilla!—ought not those flowers to belong to Miss Lynmere?'

'Mr. Mandlebert had promised me them yesterday morning,' answered she, in a voice scarce audible.

'And is this fair, Ma'am?—can you reckon it honourable?—I'll be judged by Sir Hugh himself. Do you think it right, Sir, that Miss Camilla should accept nosegays every day from Mr. Mandlebert, when her cousin has had never a one at all?'

'Why, it's not her fault, you know, Miss Margland, if young Mr. Mandlebert chuses to give them to her. However, if that vexes Indiana, I'm sure my niece will make them over to her with the greatest pleasure; for I never knew the thing she would not part with, much more a mere little smell at the nose, which, whether one has it or not, can't much matter after it's over.'

Miss Margland now exultingly held out her hand: the decision was obliged to be prompt; Camilla delivered up the flowers, and ran into her own room.

The sacrifice, cried she, is now complete! Edgar will conclude I hate him, and believe Indiana loves him!—no matter!—it is fitting he should think both. I will be steady this last evening, and to-morrow I will quit this fatal roof!

CHAPTER V

An Author's Opinion of Visiting

When summoned to tea, Camilla, upon entering the parlour, found Sir Hugh in mournful discourse with Edgar upon the non-appearance of Dr. Orkborne. Edgar felt a momentary disappointment that she did not honour his flowers with wearing them; but consoled himself with supposing she had preserved them in water. In a few minutes, however, Indiana appeared with them in her bosom.

Almost petrified, he turned towards Camilla, who, affecting an air of unconcern, amused herself with patting a favourite old terrier of her uncle's.

As soon as he could disengage himself from the Baronet, he leant also over the dog, and, in a low voice, said—'You have discarded, then, my poor flowers?'

'Have I not done right?' answered she, in the same tone; 'are they not where you must be far happier to see them?'

'Is it possible,' exclaimed he, 'Miss Camilla Tyrold can suppose—'. He stopt, for surprised off his guard, he was speaking loud, and he saw Miss Margland approaching.

'Don't you think, Mr. Mandlebert,' said she, 'that Miss Lynmere becomes a bouquet very much? she took a fancy to those flowers, and I think they are quite the thing for her.'

'She does them,' he coldly answered, 'too much honour.'

Ah, Heaven! he loves her not! thought Camilla, and, while trembling between hope and terror at the suggestion, determined to redouble her circumspection, not to confirm the suspicion that his indifference was produced by her efforts to attach him to herself.

She had soon what she conceived to be an occasion for its exertion. When he handed her some cakes, he said—'You would think it, I conclude, impertinent to hear anything more concerning Mrs. Arlbery, now you have positively opened an acquaintance with her?'

She felt the justice of this implied reproach of her broken promise; but she saw herself constantly watched by Miss Margland, and repressing the apology she was sighing to offer, only answered—'You have nothing, you own, to say against her reputation—and as to any thing else—'

'True,' interrupted he, 'my information on that point is all still in her favour: but can it be Miss Camilla Tyrold, who holds that to be the sole question upon which intimacy ought to depend? Does she account as nothing manners, disposition, way of life?'

'No, not absolutely as nothing,' said she, rising; 'but taste settles all those things, and mine is entirely in her favour.'

Edgar gravely begged her pardon, for so officiously resuming an irksome subject; and returning to Sir Hugh, endeavoured to listen to his lamentations and conjectures about Dr. Orkborne.

He felt, however, deeply hurt. In naming Mrs. Arlbery, he had flattered himself he had opened an opportunity for which she must herself be waiting, to explain the motives of her late visit; but her light answer put an end to that hope, and her quitting her seat shewed her impatient of further counsel.

Not a word that fell from Sir Hugh reached his ear: but he bowed from time to time, and the good Baronet had no doubt of his attention. His eyes were perpetually following Camilla, though they met not a glance from her in return. She played with the terrier, talked with Eugenia, looked out of the window, turned over some books, and did everything with an air of negligence, that while it covered absence and anxiety, displayed a studied avoidance of his notice.

The less he could account for this, the more it offended him. And dwells caprice, thought he, while his eye followed her, even there! in that fair composition!—where may I look for singleness of mind, for nobleness of simplicity, if caprice, mere girlish, unmeaning caprice, dwell there!

The moment she had finished her tea, she left the room, to shorten her cruel task. Struck with the broken sentence of 'is it possible Miss Camilla Tyrold can suppose—' the soft hope that his heart was untouched by Indiana, seized her delighted imagination; but the recollection of Miss Margland's assertions, that it was the real right of her cousin, soon robbed the hope of all happiness, and she could only repeat—To-morrow I will go!—I ought not to think of him!—I had rather be away—to-morrow I will go!

She had hardly quitted the parlour, when the distant sound of a carriage roused Sir Hugh from his fears; and, followed by Edgar and the ladies, he made what haste he could into the courtyard, where, to his infinite satisfaction, he saw his coach driving in.

He ordered it should stop immediately, and called out—'Pray, Dr. Orkborne, are you there?'

Dr. Orkborne looked out of the window, and bowed respectfully.

'Good lack, I could never have thought I should be so glad to see you! which you must excuse, in point of being no relation. You are heartily welcome, I assure you; I was afraid I should never see you again; for, to tell you the honest truth, which I would not say a word of before, I had got a notion you were going out of your mind.'

The Doctor took not the smallest heed of his speech, and the carriage drove up to the door. Sir Hugh then seating himself under the portico, said—'Pray, Dr. Orkborne, before you go to your studies, may I just ask you how you came to stay out all day? and why you never fetched Eugenia? for I take it for granted it's no secret, on the account Jacob was with you; besides the coachman and horses.'

Dr. Orkborne, though not at all discomposed by these questions, nor by his reception, answered, that he must first collect his books.

'The poor girls,' continued the Baronet, 'came home quite blank; not that they knew a word of my asking you to go for them, till I told them; which was lucky enough, for the sake of not frightening them. However, where you can have been, particularly with regard to your dinner, which, I suppose, you have gone without, is what I can't guess; unless you'd be kind enough to tell me.'

The Doctor, too busy to hear him, was packing up his books.

'Come, never mind your books,' said Sir Hugh; 'Jacob can carry them for you, or Bob, or any body. Here, Bob, (calling to the postillion, who, with all the rest of the servants, had been drawn by curiosity into the courtyard) whisk me up those books, and take them into the Doctor's room; I mean, provided you can find a place for them, which I am sorry to say there is none; owing to my not knowing better in point of taking the proper care; which I shall be sure to do for the future.'

The boy obeyed, and mounting one step of the coach, took what were within his reach; which, when the Doctor observed, he snatched away with great displeasure, saying, very solemnly, he had rather at any time be knocked down, than see any body touch one of his books or papers.

Jacob, coming forward, whispered his master not to interfere; assuring him, he was but just got out of one of his tantrums.

Sir Hugh, a little startled, rose to return to the parlour, begging Dr. Orkborne to take his own time, and not hurry himself.

He then beckoned Jacob to follow him.

'There is certainly something in all this,' said he to Edgar, 'beyond what my poor wit can comprehend: but I'll hear what Jacob has to say before I form a complete judgment; though, to be sure, his lugging out all those books to go but four or five miles, has but an odd look; which is what I don't like to say.'

Jacob now was called upon to give a narrative of the day's adventures. 'Why, your Honour,' said he, 'as soon as we come to the Grove, I goes up to the coach door, to ask the Doctor if he would get out, or only send in to let the young ladies know he was come for them; but he was got so deep into some of his larning, that, I dare say, I bawled it three good times in his ears, before he so much as lifted up his head; and then it was only to say, I put him out! and to it he went again, just as if I'd said never a word; till, at last, I was so plaguy mad, I gives the coach such a jog, to bring him to himself like, that it jerked the pencil and paper out of his hand. So then he went straight into one of his takings, pretending I had made him forget all his thoughts, and such like out of the way talk, after his old way. So when I found he was going off in that manner, I thought it only time lost to say no more to him, and so I turned me about not to mind him; when I sees a whole heap of company at a parlour window, laughing so hearty, that I was sure they had heard us. And a fine comely lady, as clever as ever you see, that I found after was the lady of the house, bid me come to the window, and asked what I wanted. So I told her we was come for two of the Miss Tyrolds. Why, says she, they've been gone a quarter of an hour, by the opposite road. So then I was coming away, but she made me a sign to come into the parlour, for all it was brimful of fine company, dressed all like I don't know what. It was as pretty a sight as you'd wish to see. And then, your honour, they all begun upon me at once! there was such a clatter, I thought I'd been turned into a booth at a fair; and merry enough they all was sure!—'specially the lady, who never opened her lips, but what they all laughed: but as to all what they asked me, I could as soon conjure a ghost as call a quarter of it to mind.'

'Try, however,' said Edgar, curious for further information of whatever related to Mrs. Arlbery.

'Why as to that, 'squire,' answered Jacob, with an arch look, 'I am not so sure and certain you'd like to hear it all.'

'No? and why not?'

'O! pray tell, Jacob,' cried Miss Margland; 'did they say anything of Mr. Mandlebert?'

'Yes, and of more than Mr. Mandlebert,' said Jacob, grinning.

'Do tell, do tell,' cried Indiana, eagerly.

'I'm afeard, Miss!'

Every body assured him no offence should be taken.

'Well, then, if you must needs know, there was not one of you, but what they had a pluck at.—Pray, says one of them, what does the old gentleman do with all those books and papers in the coach?—That's what nobody knows, says I, unless his head's cracked, which is Mary's opinion.—Then they all laughed more and more, and the lady of the house said:—Pray can he really read?—Whoo! says I, why he does nothing else; he's at it from morning till night, and Mary says she's sure before long he'll give up his meat and drink for it.—I've always heard he was a quiz, says another, or a quoz, or some such word; but I did not know he was such a book-worm.—The old quoz is generous, however, I hear, says another, pray do you find him so?—As to that, I can't say, says I, for I never see the colour of his money.—No! then, what are you such a fool as to serve him for?—So, then, your honour, I found, owing to the coach and the arms, and the like, they thought all the time it was your honour was in the coach. I hope your honour don't take it amiss of me?'

'Not at all Jacob; only I don't know why they call me an old quiz and quoz for; never having offended them; which I take rather unkind; especially not knowing what it means.'

'Why, your honour, they're such comical sort of folks; they don't mind what they say of nobody. Not but what the lady of the house is a rare gentlewoman. Your honour could not help liking her. I warrant she's made many a man's heart ache, and then jumped for joy when she'd done. And as to her eyes, I think in my born days I never see nothing like 'em: they shines like two candles on a dark night afar off on the common—.'

'Why Jacob,' said Sir Hugh, 'I see you have lost your heart. However, go on.'

'Why, as soon as I found out what they meant—That my master? says I, no, God be thanked! What should I have to live upon if a was? Not so much as a cobweb! for there would not be wherewithal for a spider to make it.'

Here Sir Hugh, with much displeasure, interrupted him; 'As to the poor gentleman's being poor,' said he, 'it's no fault of his own, for he'd be rich if he could, I make no doubt; never having heard he was a gambler. Besides which, I always respect a man the more for being poor, knowing how little a rich man may have in him; which I can judge by my own case.'

Jacob proceeded.

'Well, if it is not Sir Hugh, says one of them, who is it?—Why, it's only our Latin master, says I; upon which they all set up as jolly a laugh again as ever I heard in my days. Jobbins, they're pure merry!—And who learns Latin! says one, I hope they don't let him work at poor old Sir Hugh? No, says I, they tried their hands with him at first, but he thanked 'em for nothing. He soon grew tired on't.—So then they said, who learns now, says they, do you?—Me! says I, no, God be praised, I don't know A from B, which is the way my head's so clear, never having muddled it with what I don't understand.—And so then they all said I was a brave fellow; and they ordered me a glass of wine.'

What a set! thought Edgar, is this, idle, dissipated, curious—for Camilla to associate with!—the lively, the unthinking, the inexperienced Camilla!

'So then they asked me, says they, does Miss Lynmere learn, says they?—Not, as I know of, says I, she's no great turn for her book, as ever I heard of; which I hope Miss you won't take ill, for they all said, no, to be sure, she's too handsome for that.'

Indiana looked uncertain whether to be flattered or offended.

'But you have not told us what they said of Mr. Mandlebert yet?' cried Miss Margland.

'No, I must come to you first, Miss,' answered he, 'for that's what they come upon next. But mayhap I must not tell?'

'O yes, you may;' said she, growing a little apprehensive of some affront, but determined not to seem hurt by it; 'I am very indifferent to any thing they can say of me, assure yourself!'

'Why, I suppose, says they, this Latin master studies chiefly with the governess?—They'd study fisty-cuffs I believe, if they did, says I, for she hates him like poison; and there's no great love lost between them.'

'And what right had you to say that, Mr. Jacob? I did not ask what you said. Not that I care, I promise you!'

'Why, some how, they got it all out; they were so merry and so full of their fun, I could not be behind hand. But I hope no offence?'

'O dear no! I'm sure it's not worth while.'

'They said worse than I did,' resumed Jacob, 'by a deal; they said, says they, she looks duced crabbed—she looks just as if she was always eating a sour apple, says the lady; she looks—'

'Well, well, I don't want to hear any more of their opinions. I may look as I please I hope. I hate such gossiping.'

'So then they said, pray does Miss Camilla learn? says they;—Lord love her, no! says I.'

'And what said they to that?' cried Edgar.

'Why, they said, they hoped not, and they were glad to hear it, for they liked her the best of all. And what does the ugly one do? says they.—'

'Come, we have heard enough now,' interrupted Edgar, greatly shocked for poor Eugenia, who fortunately, however, had retired with Camilla.

Sir Hugh too, angrily broke in upon him, saying: 'I won't have my niece called ugly, Jacob! you know it's against my commands such a thing's being mentioned.'

'Why, I told 'em so, sir,' said Jacob; 'ugly one, says I, she you call the ugly one, is one of the best ladies in the land. She's ready to lend a hand to every mortal soul; she's just like my master for that. And as to learning, I make no quæry she can talk you over the Latin grammar as fast as e'er a gentleman here. So then they laughed harder than ever, and said they should be afeard to speak to her, and a deal more I can't call to mind.—So then they come to Mr. Mandlebert. Pray, says they, what's he doing among you all this time?—Why, nothing particular, says I, he's only squiring about our young ladies.—But when is this wedding to be? says another. So then I said—'

'What did you say?' cried Edgar hastily.

'Why—nothing,' answered Jacob, drawing back.

'Tell us, however, what they said,' cried Miss Margland.

'Why, they said, says they, everything has been ready some time at Beech Park;—and they'll make as handsome a couple as ever was seen.'

'What stuff is this!' cried Edgar, 'do prithee have done.'—

'No, no,' said Miss Margland; 'go on, Jacob!'

Indiana, conscious and glowing at the words handsome couple, could not restrain a simper; but Edgar, thinking only of Camilla, did not understand it.

'He'll have trouble enough, says one of the gentlemen,' continued Jacob, 'to take care of so pretty a wife.—She'll be worth a little trouble, says another, for I think she is the most beautifullest girl I ever see—Take my word of it, says the lady of the house, young Mandlebert is a man who won't be made a fool of; he'll have his own way, for all her beauty.'

'What a character to give of me to young ladies!' cried Edgar, doubtful, in his turn, whether to be hurt or gratified.

'O she did not stop at that, sir,' resumed Jacob, 'for she said, I make no question, says she, but in half a year he'll lock her up.'

Indiana, surprized, gave an involuntary little shriek: but Edgar, not imputing it to any appropriate alarm, was filled with resentment against Mrs. Arlbery. What incomprehensible injustice! he said to himself: O Camilla! is it possible any event, any circumstance upon earth, could induce me to practise such an outrage? to degenerate into such a savage?

'Is this all?' asked Miss Margland.

'No, ma'am; but I don't know if Miss will like to hear the rest.'

'O yes,' said Indiana, 'if it's about me, I don't mind.'

'Why, they all said, Miss, you'd make the most finest bride that ever was seen, and they did not wonder at Mr. Mandlebert's chusing you; but for all that—.'

He stopt, and Edgar, who, following the bent of his own thoughts, had till now concluded Camilla to be meant, was utterly confounded by discovering his mistake. The presence of Indiana redoubled the awkwardness of the situation, and her blushes, and the increased lustre of her eyes, did not make the report seem either unwelcome, or perfectly new to her.

Miss Margland raised her head triumphantly. This was precisely such a circumstance as she flattered herself would prove decisive.

The Baronet, equally pleased, returned her nod of congratulation, and nodding himself towards Edgar, said; 'you're blown, you see! but what matters secrets about nothing? which, Lord help me, I never knew how to keep.'

Edgar was now still more disconcerted, and, from mere distress what to say or do, bid Jacob go on.

'Why then, they said a deal more, how pretty she was, he continued, but they did not know how it would turn out, for the young lady was so much admired, that her husband had need look sharp after her; and if—'

'What complete impertinence!' cried Edgar, walking about the room; 'I really can listen no longer.'

'If he had done wisely, says the lady of the house, he would have left the professed beauty, and taken that pretty Camilla.'

Edgar surprized, stopt short; this seemed to him less impertinent.

'Camilla is a charming creature, says she; though she may want a little watching too; but so does every thing that is worth having.'

That woman does not want discernment, thought Edgar, nor she does not want taste.—I can never totally dislike her, if she does such justice to Camilla.

He now again invited Jacob to proceed; but Indiana, with a pouting lip, walked out of the room, and Miss Margland said, there was not need to be hearing him all night.

Jacob, therefore, when no more either interrupted or encouraged, soon finished his narrative. Mrs. Arlbery, amused by watching Dr. Orkborne, had insisted, for an experiment, that Jacob should not return to the coach till he was missed and called for; and so intense was the application of the Doctor to what he was composing, that this did not happen till the whole family had dined; Jacob and the coachman, at the invitation of Mrs. Arlbery, having partaken of the servants' fare, equally pleased with the regale and the joke. Dr. Orkborne then, suddenly recollecting himself, demanded why the young ladies were so late, and was much discomposed and astonished when he heard they were gone. Mrs. Arlbery invited him into the house, and offered him refreshments, while she ordered water and a feed of corn for the horses; but he only fretted a little, and then went on again with his studies.

Sir Hugh now sent some cold dinner into the Doctor's room, and declared he should always approve his niece's acquaintance with Mrs. Arlbery, as she was so kind to his servants and his animals.

CHAPTER VI

An Author's Idea of Order

Not a bosom of the Cleves party enjoyed much tranquillity this evening. Miss Margland, though to the Baronet she would not recede from her first assertions, strove vainly to palliate to herself the ill grace and evident dissatisfaction with which Edgar had met the report. To save her own credit, however, was always her primary consideration; she resolved, therefore, to cast upon unfair play in Camilla, or upon the instability of Edgar, all the blame really due to her own undiscerning self-sufficiency.

Indiana thought so little for herself, that she adopted, of course, every opinion of Miss Margland; yet the immoveable coldness of Edgar, contrasted frequently in her remembrance by the fervour of Melmond and of Macdersey, became more and more distasteful to her; and Mrs. Arlbery's idea, that she should be locked up in half a year, made her look upon him alternately as something to shun or to over-reach. She even wished to refuse him:—but Beech Park, the equipage, the servants, the bridal habiliment.—No! she could enjoy those, if not him. And neither her own feelings, nor the lessons of Miss Margland, had taught her to look upon marriage in any nobler point of view.

But the person most deeply dissatisfied this evening was Edgar. He now saw that, deceived by his own consciousness, he had misunderstood Mrs. Needham, who, as well as Mrs. Arlbery, he was convinced concluded him engaged to Indiana. He had observed with concern the approving credulity of Sir Hugh, and though glad to find his real plan, and all his wishes unsuspected, the false report excited his fears, lest Indiana should give it any credit, and secretly hurt his delicacy for the honour of his taste.

All the influence of pecuniary motives to which he deemed Camilla superior, occurred to him in the very words of Dr. Marchmont for Indiana; whose capacity he saw was as shallow as her person was beautiful. Yet the admiration with which she had already made her first appearance in the world, might naturally induce her belief of his reported devotion. If, therefore, his situation appeared to her to be eligible, she had probably settled to accept him.

The most timid female delicacy was not more scrupulous, than the manly honour of Edgar to avoid this species of misapprehension; and though perfectly confident his behaviour had been as irreproachable as it was undesigning, the least idea of any self-delusion on the part of Indiana, seemed a call upon his integrity for the most unequivocal manifestation of his intentions. Yet any declaration by words, with whatever care selected, might be construed into an implication that he concluded the decision in his own hands. And though he could scarcely doubt the fact, he justly held nothing so offensive as the palpable presumption. One only line of conduct appeared to him, therefore, unexceptionable; which was wholly to avoid her, till the rumour sunk into its own nothingness.

This demanded from him a sacrifice the most painful, that of retiring from Cleves in utter ignorance of the sentiments of Camilla; yet it seemed the more necessary, since he now, with much uneasiness, recollected many circumstances which his absorbed mind had hitherto suffered to pass unnoticed, that led him to fear Sir Hugh himself, and the whole party, entertained the same notion.

He was shocked to consider Camilla involved in such a deception, though delighted by the idea he might perhaps owe to an explanation, some marks of that preference for which Dr. Marchmont had taught him to wait, and which he now hoped might lie dormant from the persuasion of his engagement. To clear this mistake was, therefore, every way essential, as otherwise the very purity of her character must be in his disfavour.

Still, however, the visit to the Grove hung upon his mind, and he resolved to investigate its cause the following morning, before he made his retreat.

Early the next day, Camilla sent to hasten the chaise which was to fetch Mr. Tyrold, and begged leave of her uncle to breakfast at Etherington. His assent was always ready; and believing every evil would yield to absence, she eagerly, and even with happiness set off.

When the rest of the party assembled without her, Edgar, surprised, enquired if she were well? Miss Margland answered yes; but for the sake of what she loved best in the world, a frolic, she was gone in the chaise to Etherington. Edgar could not prevail with himself to depart till he had spoken with her, and privately deferred his purposed leave-taking till noon.

During this report, Sir Hugh was anxiously engaged in some business he seemed to wish to conceal. He spoke little, but nodded frequently to himself, with an air of approving his own ideas; he summoned Jacob to him repeatedly, with whom he held various whispering conferences; and desired Miss Margland, who made the tea, not to pour it out too fast, as he was in no hurry to have breakfast over.

When nothing he could urge succeeded, in making any of the company eat or drink any thing more, he pulled Edgar by the sleeve; and, in an eager but low voice, said, 'My dear Mr. Edgar, I have a great favour to beg of you, which is only that you will do something to divert Dr. Orkborne.'

'I should be very happy, Sir,' cried Edgar, smiling, 'but I much doubt my capability.'

'Why, my dear Mr. Edgar, it's only to keep him from finding out my new surprise till it's got ready. And if you will but just spout out to him a bit or two of Virgil and Horace, or some of those Greek and Latin language-masters, he'll be in no hurry to budge, I promise you.'

A request from Sir Hugh, who with the most prompt alacrity met the wishes of everyone, was by Edgar held to be indisputable. He advanced, therefore, to Dr. Orkborne, who was feeling for his tablets, which he commonly examined in his way up the stairs, and started a doubt, of which he begged an exposition, upon a passage of Virgil.

Dr. Orkborne willingly stopt, and displayed, with no small satisfaction, an erudition, that did him nearly as much honour in the ears of the ignorant and admiring Sir Hugh, as in those of the cultivated and well-judging Edgar. 'Ah!' said the Baronet, sighing, though addressing himself to no one, 'if I had but addicted myself to these studies in due season, I might have understood all this too! though now I can't for my life make out much sense of what they're talking of; nor a little neither, indeed, as to that; thanks to my own idleness; to which, however, I am not much obliged.'

Unfortunately, the discussion soon led to some points of comparison, that demanded a review of various authors, and the doctor proposed adjourning to his own apartment. The Baronet winked at Edgar, who would have changed the discourse, or himself have sought the books, or have been satisfied without them; but Dr. Orkborne was as eager here, as in other matters he was slow and phlegmatic; and, regardless of all opposition, was making off, when Sir Hugh, catching him by the arm, exclaimed, 'My good friend, I beg it as a particular favour, you won't stir a step!'

'Not stir a step, Sir?' repeated the doctor, amazed.

'That is, not to your own room.'

'Not go to my own room, Sir?'

The Baronet gently begged him not to take it amiss, and presently, upon the appearance of Jacob, who entered with a significant smile, said, he would keep him no longer.

Dr. Orkborne, to whom nothing was so irksome as a moment's detention from his books and papers, instantly departed, inviting Edgar to accompany him; but without troubling himself to inquire for what end he had been held back.

When they were gone, Sir Hugh, rubbing his hands, said, 'Well, I think this good gentleman won't go about the country again, with all his books fastened about him, to shew he has nowhere to put them: for as to his telling me he only took them to look at, I am not quite such an ignoramus, with all my ignorance, as to believe such a thing as that, especially of a regular bred scholar.'

A loud and angry sound of voices from above here interrupted the pleased harangue of the Baronet; Miss Margland opened the door to listen, and, with no small delight, heard words, scarce intelligible for rage, breaking from Dr. Orkborne, whose anger, while Edgar was endeavouring to moderate, Jacob and Mary were vociferously resenting.

Sir Hugh, all astonished, feared there was some mistake. He had sent, the preceding day, as far as Winchester, for two bookcases, which he had ordered should arrive early, and be put up during the breakfast; and he had directed Mary to place upon the shelves, with great care, all the loose books and papers she found dispersed about the room, as neatly as possible: after which Jacob was to give notice when all was arranged.

The words now 'If I must have my manuscripts rummaged at pleasure, by every dunce in the house, I would rather lie in the street!' distinctly caught their ears. Sir Hugh was thunderstruck with amazement and disappointment, but said nothing. Miss Margland looked all spite and pleasure, and Eugenia all concern.

Louder yet, and with accents of encreasing asperity, the Doctor next exclaimed 'A twelvemonth's hard labour will not repair this mischief! I should have been much more obliged to you if you had blown out my brains!'

The Baronet, aghast, cried, 'Lord help us! I think I had best go and get the shelves pulled down again, what I have done not being meant to offend, being what will cost me ten pounds and upwards.'

He then, though somewhat irresolute, whether or not to proceed, moved towards the foot of the stairs; but there a new storm of rage startled him. 'I wish you had been all of you annihilated ere ever you had entered my room! I had rather have lost my ears than that manuscript! I wish with all my heart you had been at the bottom of the sea, every one of you, before you had touched it!'

'If you won't believe me, it can't be helped,' said Mary; 'but if I was to tell it you over and over, I've done nothing to no mortal thing. I only just swept the room after the carpenter was gone, for it was all in such a pickle it was a shame to be seen.'

'You have ruined me!' cried he, 'you have swept it behind the fire, I make not a moment's doubt; and I had rather you had given me a bowl of poison! you can make me no reparation; it was a clue to a whole section.'

'Well, I won't make no more words about it,' said Mary, angrily; 'but I'm sure I never so much as touched it with a pair of tongs, for I never see it; nor I don't so much as know it if I do.'

'Why, it's a piece of paper written all over; look! just such another as this: I left it on the table, by this corner—'

'O! that?' cried Mary; 'yes, I remember that.'

'Well, where is it? What have you done with it?'

'Why, I happened of a little accident about that;—for as I was a sweeping under the table, the broom knocked the ink down; but, by good luck, it only fell upon that little morsel of paper.'

'Little morsel of paper? it's more precious than a whole library! But what did you do with it? what is become of it? whatever condition it is in, if you have but saved it—where is it, I say?'

'Why—it was all over ink, and good for nothing, so I did not think of your missing it—so I throwed it behind the fire.'

'I wish you had been thrown there yourself with all my heart! But if ever you bring a broom into my room again—'

'Why, I did nothing but what my master ordered—'

'Or if ever you touch a paper, or a book of mine, again—'

'My master said himself—'

'Your master's a blockhead! and you are another—go away, I say!'

Mary now hurried out of the room, enraged for her master, and frightened for herself; and Edgar, not aware Sir Hugh was within hearing, soon succeeded in calming the doctor, by mildly listening to his lamentations.

Sir Hugh, extremely shocked, sat upon the stairs to recover himself. Miss Margland, who never felt so virtuous, and never so elated, as when witnessing the imperfections or improprieties of others, descanted largely against ingratitude; treating an unmeaning sally of passion as a serious mark of turpitude: but Eugenia, ashamed for Dr. Orkborne, to whom, as her preceptor, she felt a constant disposition to be partial, determined to endeavour to induce him to make some apology. She glided, therefore, past her uncle, and tapped at the doctor's door.

Mary, seeing her master so invitingly in her way, could by no means resist her desire of appeal and complaint; and, descending the stairs, begged his honour to hear her.

'Mary,' said he, rising, and returning to the parlour, 'you need not tell me a word, for I have heard it all myself; by which it may be truly said, listeners never hear good of themselves; so I've got the proper punishment; for which reason, I hope you won't look upon it as an example.'

'I am sure, Sir,' said Mary, 'if your honour can excuse his speaking so disrespectful, it's what nobody else can; and if it was not for thinking as his head's got a crack in it, there is not a servant among us as would not affront him for it.'

The Baronet interrupted her with a serious lecture upon the civility he expected for all his guests; and she promised to restrain her wrath; 'But only, sir,' she continued, 'if your honour had seen the bit of paper as he made such a noise at me for, your honour would not have believed it. Not a soul could have read it. My Tom would ha' been well licked if he'd wrote no better at school. And as to his being a twelvemonth a scrawling such another, I'll no more believe it than I'll fly. It's as great a fib as ever was told.'

Sir Hugh begged her to be quiet, and to think no more of the matter.

'No, your honour, I hope I'm not a person as bears malice; only I could not but speak of it, because he behaves more comical every day. I thought he'd ha' beat me over and over. And as to the stories he tells about them little bits of paper, mortal patience can't bear it no longer.'

The remonstrance of Eugenia took immediate effect. Dr. Orkborne, shocked and alarmed at the expression which had escaped him, protested himself willing to make the humblest reparation, and truly declared, he had been so greatly disturbed by the loss he had just sustained, that he not merely did not mean, but did not know what he had said.

Edgar was the bearer of his apology, which Sir Hugh accepted with his usual good humour. 'His calling me a blockhead,' cried he, 'is a thing I have no right to resent, because I take it for granted, he would not have said it, if he had not thought it; and a man's thoughts are his castle, and ought to be free.'

Edgar repeated the protestation, that he had been hurried on by passion, and spoke without meaning.

'Why, then, my dear Mr. Edgar, I must fairly own I don't see the great superiorness of learning, if it can't keep a man's temper out of a passion. However, say nothing of the sort to poor Clermont, upon his coming over, who I expect won't speak one word in ten I shall understand; which, however, as it's all been done for the best, I would not have the poor boy discouraged in.'

He then sent a kind message by Edgar to Dr. Orkborne, desiring him not to mind such a trifle.

This conciliating office was congenial to the disposition of Edgar, and softened his impatience for the return of Camilla, but when, soon after, a note arrived from Mr. Tyrold, requesting Sir Hugh to dispense with seeing him till the next day, and apologising for keeping his daughter, he felt equally disappointed and provoked, though he determined not to delay any longer his departure. He gave orders, therefore, for his horses immediately, and with all the less regret, for knowing Camilla no longer in the circle he was to quit.

The ladies were in the parlour with Sir Hugh, who was sorrowfully brooding over his brother's note, when he entered it to take leave. Addressing himself somewhat rapidly to the Baronet, he told him he was under an unpleasant necessity, to relinquish some days of the month's sojourn intended for him. He made acknowledgments full of regard for his kindness and hospitality; and then, only bowing to the ladies, left the room, before the astonished Sir Hugh comprehended he was going.

'Well,' cried Miss Margland, 'this is curious indeed! He has flown off from everything, without even an apology!'

'I hope he is not really gone?' said Eugenia, walking to the window.

'I'm sure I don't care what he does,' cried Indiana, 'he's welcome to go or to stay. I'm grown quite sick of him, for my part.'

'Gone?' said Sir Hugh, recovering breath; 'it's impossible! Why, he never has said one word to me of the day, nor the settlements, nor all those things!'

He then rang the bell, and sent to desire Mr. Mandlebert might be called immediately.

Edgar, who was mounting his horse, obeyed with some chagrin. As soon as he re-entered the room, Sir Hugh cried; 'My dear Mr. young Edgar, it's something amazing to me you should think of going away without coming to an explanation?'

'An explanation, sir?'

'Yes, don't you know what I mean?'

'Not in the least, sir,' cried Edgar, staggered by a doubt whether he suspected what he felt for Camilla, or referred to what was reported of Indiana.

'Why, then, my pretty dear,' said Sir Hugh to Indiana, 'you won't object, I hope, to taking a little walk in the garden, provided it is not disagreeable to you; for you had better not hear what we are going to talk about before your face.'

Indiana, pouting her beautiful under lip, and scornfully passing Edgar, complied. Eugenia accompanied her; but Miss Margland kept her ground.

Sir Hugh, always unwilling to make any attack, and at a loss how to begin, simply said; 'Why, I thought Mr. Mandlebert, you would stay with us till next year?'

Edgar only bowed.

'Why, then, suppose you do?'

'Most probably, sir, I shall by that time be upon the Continent. If some particular circumstance does not occur, I purpose shortly making the tour of Europe.'

Sir Hugh now lost all guard and all restraint, and with undisguised displeasure exclaimed; 'So here's just the second part of Clermont! at the moment I sent for him home, thinking he would come to put the finish to all my cares about Eugenia, he sends me word he must travel!—And though the poor girl took it very well, from knowing nothing of the matter, I can't say I take it very kind of you, Mr. young Edgar, to come and do just the same by Indiana!'

The surprize of Edgar was unspeakable: that Sir Hugh should wish the relation of Jacob, with respect to Indiana, confirmed, he could not wonder; but that his wishes should have amounted to expectations, and that he should deem his niece ill used by their failure, gave him the most poignant astonishment.

Miss Margland, taking advantage of his silent consternation, began now to pour forth very volubly, the most pointed reflections upon the injury done to young ladies by reports of this nature, which were always sure to keep off all other offers. There was no end, she said, to the admirers who had deserted Indiana in despair; and she questioned if she would ever have any more, from the general belief of her being actually pre-engaged.

Edgar, whose sense of honour was tenaciously delicate, heard her with a mixture of concern for Indiana, and indignation against herself, that kept her long uninterrupted; for though burning to assert the integrity of his conduct, the fear of uttering a word that might be offensive to Indiana, embarrassed and checked him.

Sir Hugh, who in seeing him overpowered, concluded he was relenting, now kindly took his hand, and said: 'My dear Mr. Mandlebert, if you are sorry for what you were intending, of going away, and leaving us all in the lurch, why, you shall never hear a word more about it, for I will make friends for you with Indiana, and beg of Miss Margland that she'll do us the favour to say no more.'

Edgar, affectionately pressing the hand of the Baronet, uttered the warmest expressions of personal regard, and protested he should always think it an honour to have been held worthy of pretending to any alliance in his family; but he knew not how the present mistake had been made, or report had arisen: he could boast of no partiality from Miss Lynmere, nor had he ever addressed her with any particular views: yet, as it was the opinion of Miss Margland, that the rumour, however false, might prevent the approach of some deserving object, he now finally determined to become, for awhile, a stranger at Cleves, however painful such self-denial must prove.

He then precipitately left the room, and, in five minutes, had galloped out of the Park.

The rest of the morning was spent by Sir Hugh in the utmost discomposure; and by Miss Margland in alternate abuse of Camilla and of Edgar; while Indiana passed from a piqued and short disappointment, to the consolatory idea that Melmond might now re-appear.

Edgar rode strait to Beech Park, where he busied himself the whole day in viewing alterations and improvements; but where nothing answered his expectations, since Camilla had disappointed them. That sun-beam, which had gilded the place to his eyes, was now over-clouded, and the first possession of his own domain, was his first day of discontent.

CHAPTER VII

A Maternal Eye

The vivacity with which Camilla quitted Cleves, was sunk before she reached Etherington. She had quitted also Edgar, quitted him offended, and in doubt if it might ever be right she should vindicate herself in his opinion. Yet all seemed strange and unintelligible that regarded the asserted nuptials: his indifference was palpable; she believed him to have been unaccountably drawn in, and her heart softly whispered, it was herself he preferred.

From this soothing but dangerous idea, she struggled to turn her thoughts. She anticipated the remorse of holding the affections of the husband of her cousin, and determined to use every possible method to forget him—unless, which she strove vainly not to hope, the reported alliance should never take place.

These reflections so completely engrossed her the whole way, that she arrived at the Parsonage House, without the smallest mental preparation how to account for her return, or how to plead for remaining at Etherington. Foresight, the offspring of Judgment, or the disciple of Experience, made no part of the character of Camilla, whose impetuous disposition was open to every danger of indiscretion, though her genuine love of virtue glowed warm with juvenile ardour.

She entered, therefore, the breakfast parlour in a state of sudden perplexity what to say; Mr. Tyrold was alone and writing. He looked surprized, but embraced her with his accustomed affection, and enquired to what he owed her present sight.

She made no answer; but embraced him again, and enquired after her mother.

'She is well,' he replied: 'but, tell me, is your uncle impatient of my delay? It has been wholly unavoidable. I have been deeply engaged; and deeply chagrined. Your poor mother would be still more disturbed, if the nobleness of her mind did not support her.'

Camilla, extremely grieved, earnestly enquired what had happened.

He then informed her that Mrs. Tyrold, the very next morning, must abruptly quit them all and set out for Lisbon to her sick brother, Mr. Relvil.

'Is he so much worse?'

'No: I even hope he is better. An act of folly has brought this to bear. Do not now desire particulars. I will finish my letter, and then return with you for a few minutes to Cleves. The carriage must wait.'

'Suffer me first to ask, does Lavinia go with my mother?'

'No, she can only take old Ambrose. Lavinia must supply her place at home.'

'Ah! my dearest father, and may not I, too, stay with you and assist her?'

'If my brother will spare you, my dear child, there is nothing can so much contribute to wile away to me your mother's absence.'

Enchanted thus, without any explanation, to have gained her point, she completely revived; though when Mrs. Tyrold, whom she almost worshipped, entered the room, in all the hurry of preparing for her long journey, she shed a torrent of tears in her arms.

'This good girl,' said Mr. Tyrold, 'is herself desirous to quit the present gaieties of Cleves, to try to enliven my solitude till we all may meet again.'

The conscious and artless Camilla could not bear this undeserved praise. She quitted her mother, and returning to Mr. Tyrold, 'O my father!' she cried, 'if you will take me again under your beloved roof, it is for my sake—not your's—I beg to return!'

'She is right,' said Mrs. Tyrold; 'there is no merit in having an heart; she could have none, if to be with you were not her first gratification.'

'Yes, indeed, my dear mother, it would always be so, even if no other inducement—.' She stopt short, confused.

Mr. Tyrold, who continued writing, did not heed this little blunder; but his wife, whose quickness of apprehension and depth of observation, were always alive, even in the midst of business, cares, and other attentions, turned hastily to her daughter, and asked to what 'other inducement' she alluded.

Camilla, distressed, hung her head, and would have forborne making any answer.

Mrs. Tyrold, then, putting down various packets which she was sorting and selecting, came suddenly up to her, and taking both her hands, looked earnestly in her face, saying: 'My Camilla! something has disquieted you?—your countenance is not itself. Tell me, my dear girl, what brought you hither this morning? and what is it you mean by some other inducement?'

'Do not ask me now, my dearest mother,' answered she, in a faltering voice; 'when you come back again, no doubt all will be over; and then—'

'And is that the time, Camilla, to speak to your best friends? would it not be more judicious to be explicit with them, while what affects you is still depending?'

Camilla, hiding her face on her mother's bosom, burst afresh into tears.

'Alas!' cried Mrs. Tyrold, 'what new evil is hovering? If it must invade me again through one of my children, tell me, at least, Camilla, it is not wilfully that you, too, afflict me? and afflict the best of fathers?'

Mr. Tyrold, dropping his pen, looked at them both with the most apprehensive anxiety.

'No, my dearest mother,' said Camilla, endeavouring to meet her eyes; 'not wilfully,—but something has happened—I can hardly myself tell how or what—but indeed Cleves, now—' she hesitated.

'How is my brother?' demanded Mr. Tyrold.

'O! all that is good and kind! and I grieve to quit him—but, indeed, Cleves, now—' Again she hesitated.

'Ah, my dear child!' said Mrs. Tyrold, 'I always feared that residence!—you are too young, too inconsiderate, too innocent, indeed, to be left so utterly to yourself.—Forgive me, my dear Mr. Tyrold; I do not mean to reflect upon your brother, but he is not you!—and with you alone, this dear inexperienced girl can be secure from all harm. Tell me, however, what it is—?'

Camilla, in the extremest confusion changed colour, but tried vainly to speak. Mr. Tyrold, suspended from all employment, waited fearfully some explanation.

'We have no time,' said Mrs. Tyrold, 'for delay;—you know I am going abroad,—and cannot ascertain my return; though all my heart left behind me, with my children and their father, will urge every acceleration in my power.'

Camilla wept again, fondly folding her arms round her mother; 'I had hoped,' she cried, 'that I should have come home to peace, comfort, tranquillity! to both of you, my dearest father and mother, and to all my unbroken happiness under your roof!—How little did I dream of so cruel a separation!'

'Console yourself, my Camilla, that you have not been its cause; may Heaven ever spare me evil in your shape at least!—you say it is nothing wilful? I can bear everything else.'

'We will not,' said Mr. Tyrold, 'press her; she will tell us all in her own way, and at her own time. Forced confidence is neither fair nor flattering. I will excuse her return to my brother, and she will the sooner be able to give her account for finding herself not hurried.'

'Calm yourself, then,' said Mrs. Tyrold, 'as your indulgent father permits, and I will proceed with my preparations.'

Camilla now, somewhat recovering, declared she had almost nothing to say; but her mother continued packing up, and her father went on with his letter.

She had now time to consider that her own fears and emotion were involving her in unnecessary confessions; she resolved, therefore, to repress the fulness of her heart, and to acknowledge only the accusation of Miss Margland. And in a few minutes, without waiting for further enquiry, she gathered courage to open upon the subject; and with as much ease and quietness as she could command, related, in general terms, the charge brought against her, and her consequent desire to quit Cleves, 'till,—till—' Here she stopt for breath. Mr. Tyrold instantly finished the sentence, 'till the marriage has taken place?'

She coloured, and faintly uttered, 'Yes.'

'You are right, my child,' said he, 'and you have acted with a prudence which does you honour. Neither the ablest reasoning, nor the most upright conduct, can so completely obliterate a surmise of this nature, from a suspicious mind, as absence. You shall remain, therefore, with me, till your cousin is settled in her new habitation. Do you know if the day is fixed?'

'No, sir,' she answered, while the roses fled her cheeks at a question which implied so firm a belief of the union.

'Do not suffer this affair to occasion you any further uneasiness,' he continued; 'it is the inherent and unalienable compact of Innocence with Truth, to hold themselves immovably superior to the calumny of false imputations. But I will go myself to Cleves, and set this whole matter right.'

'And will you, too, sir, have the goodness—' She was going to say, to make my peace with Edgar; but the fear of misinterpretation checked her, and she turned away.

He gently enquired what she meant; she avoided any explanation, and he resumed his writing.

Ah me! thought she, will the time ever come, when with openness, with propriety, I may clear myself of caprice to Edgar?

Less patient, because more alarmed than her husband, Mrs. Tyrold followed her to the window. She saw a tear in her eye, and again she took both her hands: 'Have you, my Camilla,' she cried, 'have you told us all? Can unjust impertinence so greatly have disturbed you? Is there no sting belonging to this wound that you are covering from our sight, though it may precisely be the spot that calls most for some healing balm?'

Again the cheeks of Camilla received their fugitive roses. 'My dearest mother,' she cried, 'is not this enough?—to be accused—suspected—and to fear—'

She stammered, and would have withdrawn her hands; but Mrs. Tyrold, still holding them, said, 'To fear what? speak out, my best child! open to us your whole heart!—Where else will you find repositories so tender?'

Tears again flowed down the burning cheeks of Camilla, and dropping her eyes, 'Ah, my mother!' she cried, 'you will think me so frivolous—you will blush so for your daughter—if I own—if I dare confess—'

Again she stopped, terrified at the conjectures to which this opening might give birth; but when further and fondly pressed by her mother, she added, 'It is not alone these unjust surmises,—nor even Indiana's unkind concurrence in them—but also—I have been afraid—I must have made a strange—a capricious—an ungrateful appearance in the eyes of Edgar Mandlebert.'

Here her voice dropt; but presently recovering, she rapidly continued, 'I know it is very immaterial—and I am sensible how foolish it may sound—but I shall also think of it no more now,—and therefore, as I have told the whole—'

She looked up, conscience struck at these last words, to see if they proved satisfactory; she caught, in the countenance of her mother, an expression of deep commiseration, which was followed by a thousand maternal caresses of unusual softness, though unaccompanied by any words.

Penetrated, yet distressed, she gratefully received them, but rejoiced when, at length, Mr. Tyrold, rising, said, 'Go, my love, upstairs to your sister; your mother, else, will never proceed with her business.'

She gladly ran off, and soon, by a concise narration, satisfied Lavinia, and then calmed her own troubled mind.

Mr. Tyrold now, though evidently much affected himself, strove to compose his wife. 'Alas!' cried she, 'do you not see what thus has touched me? Do you not perceive that our lovely girl, more just to his worth than its possessor, has given her whole heart to Edgar Mandlebert?'

'I perceived it through your emotion, but I had not discovered it myself. I grieve, now, that the probability of such an event had not struck me in time to have kept them apart for its prevention.'

'I grieve for nothing,' cried she, warmly, 'but the infatuated blindness of that self-lost young man. What a wife would Camilla have made him in every stage of their united career! And how unfortunately has she sympathised in my sentiments, that he alone seemed worthy to replace the first and best protector she must relinquish when she quits this house! What will he find in Indiana but a beautiful doll, uninterested in his feelings, unmoved by his excellencies, and incapable of comprehending him if he speaks either of business or literature!'

'Yet many wives of this description,' replied Mr. Tyrold, 'are more pleasing in the eyes of their husbands than women who are either better informed in intellect, or more alive in sensation; and it is not an uncommon idea amongst men, that where, both in temper and affairs, there is least participation, there is most repose. But this is not the case with Edgar.'

'No! he has a nobler resemblance than this portrait would allow him; a resemblance which made me hope from him a far higher style of choice. He prepares himself, however, his own ample punishment; for he has too much understanding not to sicken of mere personal allurements, and too much generosity to be flattered, or satisfied, by mere passive intellectual inferiority. Neither a mistress nor a slave can make him happy; a companion is what he requires; and for that, in a very few months, how vainly his secret soul may sigh, and think of our Camilla!'

They then settled, that it would be now essential to the peace of their child to keep her as much as possible from his sight; and determined not to send her back to Cleves to apologize for the new plan, but to take upon themselves that whole charge. 'Her nature,' said Mrs. Tyrold, 'is so gay, so prompt for happiness, that I have little fear but in absence she will soon cease to dwell upon him. Fear, indeed, I have, but it is of a deeper evil than this early impression; I fear for her future lot! With whom can we trust her?—She will not endure negligence; and those she cannot respect she will soon despise. What a prospect for her, then, with our present race of young men! their frivolous fickleness nauseates whatever they can reach; they have a weak shame of asserting, or even listening to what is right, and a shallow pride in professing what is wrong. How must this ingenuous girl forget all she has yet seen, heard, or felt, ere she can encounter wickedness, or even weakness, and disguise her abhorrence or contempt?'

'My dear Georgiana, let us never look forward to evil.'

'Will it not be doubly hard to bear, if it come upon us without preparation?'

'I think not. Terror shakes, and apprehension depresses: hope nerves as well as gladdens us. Remember always, I do not by hope mean presumption; I mean simply a cheerful trust in heaven.'

'I must always yield,' cried Mrs. Tyrold, 'to your superior wisdom, and reflecting piety; and if I cannot conquer my fears, at least I will neither court nor indulge them.'

The thanks of a grateful husband repaid this compliance. They sent for Camilla, to acquaint her they would make her excuses at Cleves: she gave a ready though melancholy consent, and the virtue of her motives drew tears from her idolizing mother, as she clasped her to her heart.

They then set out together, that Mr. Tyrold might arrange this business with Sir Hugh, of whom and of Eugenia Mrs. Tyrold was to take leave.

CHAPTER VIII

Modern Ideas of Duty

Camilla now felt more permanently revived, because better satisfied with the rectitude of her conduct. She could no longer be accused of interfering between Edgar and Indiana; that affair would take its natural course, and, be it what it might, while absent from both parties, she concluded she should at least escape all censure.

Peaceably, therefore, she returned to take possession of her usual apartment, affectionately accompanied by her eldest sister.

The form and the mind of Lavinia were in the most perfect harmony. Her polished complexion was fair, clear, and transparent; her features were of the extremest delicacy, her eyes of the softest blue, and her smile displayed internal serenity. The unruffled sweetness of her disposition bore the same character of modest excellence. Joy, hope, and prosperity, sickness, sorrow, and disappointment, assailed alike in vain the uniform gentleness of her temper: yet though thus exempt from all natural turbulence, either of pleasure or of pain, the meekness of her composition degenerated not into insensibility; it was open to all the feminine feelings of pity, of sympathy, and of tenderness.

Thus copiously gifted with 'all her sex's softness,' her society would have contributed to restore Camilla to repose, had they continued together without interruption; but, in a few minutes, the room door was opened, and Lionel, rushing into the apartment, called out, 'How do, do, my girls? how do, do?' and shook them each by the hand, with a swing that nearly brought them to the ground.

Camilla always rejoiced at his sight; but Lavinia gravely said, 'I thought, brother, you had been at Dr. Marchmont's?'

'All in good time, my dear! I shall certainly visit the old gentleman before long.'

'Did you not sleep there, then, last night?'

'No, child.'

'Good God, Lionel!—if my mother—'

'My dear little Lavinia,' cried he, chucking her under the chin, 'I have a vast notion of making visits at my own time, instead of my mamma's.'

'O Lionel! and can you, just now—'

'Come, come,' interrupted he, 'don't let us waste our precious minutes in old moralizing. If I had not luckily been hard by, I should not have known the coast was clear. Pray where are they gone, tantivying?'

'To Cleves.'

'To Cleves! what a happy escape! I was upon the point of going thither myself. Camilla, what is the matter with thee?'

'Nothing—I am only thinking—pray when do you go to Oxford?'

'Pho, pho,—what do you talk of Oxford for? you are grown quite stupid, girl. I believe you have lived too long with Miss Margland. Pray how does that dear creature do? I am afraid she will grow melancholy from not seeing me so long. Is she as pretty as she used to be? I have some notion of sending her a suitor.'

'O brother,' said Lavinia, 'is it possible you can have such spirits?'

'O hang it, if one is not merry when one can, what is the world good for? besides, I do assure you, I fretted so consumed hard at first, that for the life of me I can fret no longer.'

'But why are you not at Dr. Marchmont's?'

'Because, my dear, you have no conception the pleasure those old doctors take in lecturing a youngster who is in any disgrace.'

'Disgrace!' repeated Camilla.

'At all events,' said Lavinia, 'I beseech you to be a little careful; I would not have my poor mother find you here for the world.'

'O, as to that, I defy her to desire the meeting less than I do. But come, let's talk of something else. How go on the classics? Is my old friend, Dr. Orkborne, as chatty and amusing as ever?'

'My dear Lionel,' said Camilla, 'I am filled with apprehension and perplexity. Why should my mother wish not to see you? And why—and how is it possible you can wish not to see her?'

'What, don't you know it all?'

'I know only that something must be wrong; but how, what, or which way, I have not heard.'

'Has not Lavinia told you, then?

'No,' answered Lavinia; 'I could be in no haste to give her pain.'

'You are a good girl enough. But how came you hither, Camilla? and what is the reason you have not seen my mother yourself?'

'Not seen her! I have been with her this half hour.'

'What! and in all that time did not she tell you?'

'She did not name you.'

'Is it possible!—Well, she's a noble creature! I wonder how she could ever have such a son as me. And I am still less like my father than her. I suppose I was changed in the cradle. Will you countenance me, young ladies, if some villainous attorney or exciseman should by and by come to own me?'

'Dear Lionel,' cried Camilla, 'do explain to me what has happened. You make me think it important and trifling twenty times in a minute.'

'O, a horrid business!—Lavinia must tell it you. I'll go away till she has done. Don't despise me, Camilla; I am confounded sorry, I promise you.'

He then hurried out of the room, evidently feeling more emotion than he cared to display.

Yet Lavinia had but just begun her relation, when he abruptly returned. 'Come, I had better tell it you myself,' cried he, 'for she'll make such a dismal ditty of it, that it won't be over this half year; the sooner we have done with it the better; it will only put you out of spirits.'

Then, sitting down, and taking her hand, he began, 'You must know I was in rather a bad scrape at Oxford last year—'

'Last year! and you never told us of it before!'

'O, 'twas about something you would not understand, so I shall not mention particulars now. It is enough for you to know that two or three of us wanted a little cash!—well, so—in short, I sent a letter—somewhat of a threatening sort—to poor old uncle Relvil!'—

'O Lionel!'

'O, I did not sign it,—it was only begging a little money, which he can afford to spare very well; and just telling him, if he did not come to a place I mentioned, he would have his brains blown out.'—

'How horrible!'

'Pho, pho,—he had only to send the money, you know, and then his brains might keep their place; besides, you can't suppose there was gunpowder in the words. So I got this copied, and took the proper measures for concealment, and,—would you believe it! the poor old gull was fool enough actually to send the money where he was bid?'

'Fie, Lionel!' cried Lavinia; 'do you call him a fool because you terrified him?'

'Yes, to be sure, my dear; and you both think him so too, only you don't hold it pretty to say so. Do you suppose, if he had had half the wit of his sister, he would have done it? I believe, in my conscience, there was some odd mistake in their births, and that my mother took away the brains of the man, and left the woman's for the noddle of my poor uncle.'

'Fie, fie, brother!' said Lavinia again; 'you know how sickly he has always been from his birth, and how soon therefore he might be alarmed.'

'Why, yes, Lavinia—I believe it was a very bad thing—and I would give half my little finger I had not done it. But it's over, you know; so what signifies making the worst of it?'

'And did he not discover you?'

'No; I gave him particular orders, in my letter, not to attempt anything of that sort, assuring him there were spies about him to watch his proceedings. The good old ass took it all for gospel. So there the matter dropt. However, as ill luck would have it, about three months ago we wanted another sum—'

'And could you again—'

'Why, my dear, it was only taking a little of my own fortune beforehand, for I am his heir; so we all agreed it was merely robbing myself; for we had several consultations about it, and one of us is to be a lawyer.'

'But you give me some pleasure here,' said Camilla; 'for I had never heard that my uncle had made you his heir.'

'No more have I neither, my dear; but I take it for granted. Besides, our little lawyer put it into my head. Well, we wrote again, and told the poor old gentleman—for which I assure you I am heartily repentant—that if he did not send me double the sum, in the same manner, without delay, his house was to be burnt to the ground the first night that he and all his family were asleep in bed.—Now don't make faces and shruggings, for, I promise you, I think already I deserve to be hanged for giving him the fright; though I would not really have hurt him, all the time, for half his fortune. And who could have guessed he would have bit so easily? The money, however, came, and we thought it all secure, and agreed to get the same sum annually.'

'Annually!' repeated Camilla, with uplifted hands.

'Yes, my dear. You have no conception how convenient it would have been for our extra expenses. But, unluckily, uncle grew worse, and went abroad, and then consulted with some crab of a friend, and that friend with some demagogue of a magistrate, and so all is blown!—However, we had managed it so cleverly, it cost them near three months to find it out, owing, I must confess, to poor uncle's cowardice in not making his enquiries before the money was carried off, and he himself over the seas and far away. The other particulars Lavinia must give you; for I have talked of it now till I have made myself quite sick. Do tell me something diverting to drive it a little out of my head. Have you seen any thing of my enchanting widow lately?'

'No, she does not desire to be seen by me. She would not admit me.'

'She is frankness itself, and does not pretend to care a fig for any of her own sex.—O, but, Camilla, I have wanted to ask you this great while, if you think there is any truth in this rumour, that Mandlebert intends to propose to Indiana?'

'To propose! I thought it had all long since been settled.'

'Ay, so the world says; but I don't believe a word of it. Do you think, if that were the case, he would not have owned it to me? There's nothing fixed yet, depend upon it.'

Camilla, struck, amazed, and delighted, involuntarily embraced her brother; though, recollecting herself almost at the same moment, she endeavoured to turn off the resistless impulse into taking leave, and hurrying him away.

Lionel, who to want of solidity and penetration principally owed the errors of his conduct, was easily put upon a wrong scent, and assured her he would take care to be off in time. 'But what,' cried he, 'has carried them to Cleves? Are they gone to tell tales? Because I have lost one uncle by my own fault, must I lose another by their's?'

'No,' answered Lavinia, 'they have determined not to name you. They have settled that my uncle Hugh shall never be told of the affair, nor anybody else, if they can help it, except your sisters, and Dr. Marchmont.'

'Well, they are good souls,' cried he, attempting to laugh, though his eyes were glistening; 'I wish I deserved them better; I wish, too, it was not so dull to be good. I can be merry and harmless here at the same time,—and so I can at Cleves;—but at Oxford—or in London,—your merry blades there—I can't deny it, my dear sisters—your merry blades there are but sad fellows. Yet there is such fun, such spirit, such sport amongst them, I cannot for my life keep out of their way. Besides, you have no conception, young ladies, what a bye word you become among them if they catch you flinching.'

'I would not for the world say anything to pain you, my dear brother,' cried Lavinia; 'but yet I must hope that, in future, your first study will be to resist such dangerous examples, and to drop such unworthy friends?'

'If it is not to tell tales, then, for what else are they gone to Cleves, just at this time?'

'For my mother to take leave of Eugenia and my uncle before her journey.'

'Journey! Why whither is she going?'

'Abroad.'

'The deuce she is!—And what for?'

'To try to make your peace with her brother; or at least to nurse him herself till he is tolerably recovered.'

Lionel slapped his hat over his eyes, and saying, 'This is too much!—if I were a man I should shoot myself!'—rushed out of the room.

The two sisters rapidly followed him, and caught his arm before he could quit the house. They earnestly besought him to return, to compose himself, and to promise he would commit no rash action.

'My dear sisters,' cried he, 'I am worked just now only as I ought to be; but I will give you any promise you please. However, though I have never listened to my father as I ought to have listened, he has implanted in my mind a horror of suicide, that will make me live my natural life, be it as good for nothing as it may.'

He then suffered his sisters to lead him back to their room, where he cast himself upon a chair, in painful rumination upon his own unworthiness, and his parents' excellence; but the tender soothings of Lavinia and Camilla, who trembled lest his remorse should urge him to some act of violence, soon drew him from reflections of which he hated the intrusion; and he attended, with complacency, to their youthful security of perfect reconciliations, and re-established happiness.

With reciprocal exultation, the eyes of the sisters congratulated each other on having saved him from despair: and seeing him now calm, and, they hoped, safe, they mutually, though tacitly, agreed to obtrude no further upon meditations that might be useful to him, and remained silently by his side.

For some minutes all were profoundly still; Lionel then suddenly started up; the sisters, affrighted, hastily arose at the same instant; when stretching himself and yawning, he called out, 'Pr'ythee, Camilla, what is become of that smug Mr. Dubster?'

Speechless with amazement, they looked earnestly in his face, and feared he was raving.

They were soon, however undeceived; the tide of penitence and sorrow was turned in his buoyant spirits, and he was only restored to his natural volatile self.

'You used him most shabbily,' he continued, 'and he was a very pretty fellow. The next time I have nothing better to do, I'll send him to you, that you may make it up.'

This quick return of gaiety caused a sigh to Lavinia, and much surprise to Camilla; but neither of them could prevail with him to depart, till Mr. and Mrs. Tyrold were every moment expected; they then, though with infinite difficulty, procured his promise that he would go straight to Dr. Marchmont, according to an arrangement made for that purpose by Mrs. Tyrold herself.

Lavinia, when he was gone, related some circumstances of this affair which he had omitted. Mr. Relvil, the elder brother of Mrs. Tyrold, was a country gentleman of some fortune, but of weak parts, and an invalid from his infancy. He had suffered these incendiary letters to prey upon his repose, without venturing to produce them to any one, from a terror of the menaces hurled against him by the writer, till at length he became so completely hypochondriac, that his rest was utterly broken, and, to preserve his very existence, he resolved upon visiting another climate.

The day that he set out for Lisbon, his destined harbour, he delivered his anonymous letters to a friend, to whom he left in charge to discover, if possible, their author.

This discovery, by the usual means of enquiries and rewards, was soon made; but the moment Mr. Relvil learnt that the culprit was his nephew, he wrote over to Mrs. Tyrold a statement of the transaction, declaring he should disinherit Lionel from every shilling of his estate. His health was so much impaired, he said, by the disturbance this had given to his mind, that he should be obliged to spend the ensuing year in Portugal; and he even felt uncertain if he might ever return to his own country.

Mrs. Tyrold, astonished and indignant, severely questioned her son, who covered, with shame, surprise, and repentance, confessed his guilt. Shocked and grieved in the extreme, she ordered him from her sight, and wrote to Dr. Marchmont to receive him. She then settled with Mr. Tyrold the plan of her journey and voyage, hoping by so immediately following, and herself nursing her incensed brother, to soften his wrath, and avert its final ill consequences.

CHAPTER IX

A Few Embarrassments

Mr. and Mrs. Tyrold returned to Etherington somewhat relieved in their spirits, though perplexed in their opinions. They had heard from Sir Hugh, that Edgar had decidedly disavowed any pretensions to Indiana, and had voluntarily retreated from Cleves, that his disavowal might risk no misconstruction, either in the family or the neighbourhood.

This insensibility to beauty the most exquisite wanted no advocate with Mrs. Tyrold. Once more she conceived some hope of what she wished, and she determined upon seeing Edgar before her departure. The displeasure she had nourished against him vanished, and justice to his general worth, with an affection nearly maternal to his person, took again their wonted place in her bosom, and made her deem herself unkind in having purposed to quit the kingdom without bidding him farewell.

Mr. Tyrold, whom professional duty and native inclination alike made a man of peace, was ever happy to second all conciliatory measures, and the first to propose them, where his voice had any chance of being heard. He sent a note, therefore, to invite Edgar to call the next morning; and Mrs. Tyrold deferred her hour of setting off till noon.

Her own natural and immediate impulse, had been to carry Camilla with her abroad; but when she considered that her sole errand was to nurse and appease an offended sick man, whose chamber she meant not to quit till she returned to her family, she gave up the pleasure she would herself have found in the scheme, to her fears for the health and spirits of her darling child, joined to the superior joy of leaving such a solace with her husband.

Sir Hugh had heard the petition for postponing the further visit of Camilla almost with despondence; but Mr. Tyrold restored him completely to confidence, with respect to his doubts concerning Dr. Orkborne, with whom he held a long and satisfactory conversation; and his own benevolent heart received a sensible pleasure, when, upon examining Indiana with regard to Edgar, he found her, though piqued and pouting, untouched either in affection or happiness.

Early the next morning Edgar came. Mrs. Tyrold had taken measures for employing Camilla upstairs, where she did not even hear that he entered the house.

He was received with kindness, and told of the sudden journey, though not of its motives. He heard of it with unfeigned concern, and earnestly solicited to be the companion of the voyage, if no better male protector were appointed.

Mr. Tyrold folded his arms around him at this grateful proposal, while his wife, animated off her guard, warmly exclaimed—'My dear, excellent Edgar! you are indeed the model, the true son of your guardian!'

Sorry for what had escaped her, from her internal reference to Lionel, she looked anxiously to see if he comprehended her; but the mantling blood which mounted quick into his cheeks, while his eyes sought the ground, soon told her there was another mode of affinity, which at that moment had struck him.

Willing to establish whether this idea were right, she now considered how she might name Camilla; but her husband, who for no possible purpose could witness distress without seeking to alleviate it, declined his kind offer, and began a discourse upon the passage to Lisbon.

This gave Edgar time to recover, and, in a few seconds, something of moment seemed abruptly to occur to him, and scarcely saying adieu, he hurried to remount his horse.

Mrs. Tyrold was perplexed; but she could take not steps towards an explanation, without infringing the delicacy she felt due to her daughter: she suffered him, therefore, to depart.

She then proceeded with her preparations, which entirely occupied her till the chaise was at the gate; when, as the little party, their eyes and their hearts all full, were taking a last farewell, the parlour door was hastily opened, and Dr. Marchmont and Edgar entered the room.

All were surprised, but none so much as Camilla, who, forgetting, in sudden emotion, every thing but former kindness and intimacy, delightedly exclaimed—'Edgar! O how happy, my dearest mother!—I was afraid you would go without seeing him!'

Edgar turned to her with a quickness that could only be exceeded by his pleasure; her voice, her manner, her unlooked-for interest in his appearance, penetrated to his very soul. 'Is it possible,' he cried, 'you could have the goodness to wish me this gratification? At a moment such as this, could you—?' think of me, he would have added; but Dr. Marchmont, coming forward, begged him to account for their intrusion.

Almost overpowered by his own sudden emotion, he could scarce recollect its motive himself; while Camilla, fearful and repentant that she had broken her deliberate and well-principled resolutions, retreated to the window.

Mr. and Mrs. Tyrold witnessed the involuntary movements which betrayed their mutual regard with the tenderest satisfaction; and the complacency of their attention, when Edgar advanced to them, soon removed his embarrassment.

He then briefly acquainted them, that finding Mrs. Tyrold would not accept him for her chevalier, he had ridden hard to the parsonage of Cleves, whence he hoped he had brought her one too unexceptionable for rejection.

Dr. Marchmont, with great warmth, then made a proffer of his services, declaring he had long desired an opportunity to visit Portugal; and protesting that, besides the pleasure of complying with any wish of Mr. Mandlebert's, it would give him the most serious happiness to shew his gratitude for the many kind offices he owed to Mr. Tyrold, and his high personal respect for his lady; he should require but one day for his preparations, and for securing the performance of the church duty at Cleves during his absence.

Mr. and Mrs. Tyrold were equally struck by the goodness of Dr. Marchmont, and the attentive kindness of Edgar. Mrs. Tyrold, nevertheless, would immediately have declined the scheme; but her husband interposed. Her travelling, he said, with such a guard, would be as conducive to his peace at home, as to her safety abroad. 'And with respect,' cried he, 'to obligation, I hold it as much a moral duty not to refuse receiving good offices, as not to avoid administering them. That species of independence, which proudly flies all ties of gratitude, is inimical to the social compact of civilized life, which subsists but by reciprocity of services.'

Mrs. Tyrold now opposed the scheme no longer, and the chaise was ordered for the next day.

Dr. Marchmont hurried home to settle his affairs; but Edgar begged a short conference with Mr. Tyrold.

Every maternal hope was now awake in Mrs. Tyrold, who concluded this request was to demand Camilla in marriage; and her husband himself, not without trepidation, took Edgar into his study.

But Edgar, though his heart was again wholly Camilla's, had received a look from Dr. Marchmont that guarded him from any immediate declaration. He simply opened upon the late misconception at Cleves; vindicated himself from any versatility of conduct, and affirmed, that both his attentions and his regard for Indiana had never been either more or less than they still continued. All this was spoken with a plainness to which the integrity of his character gave a weight superior to any protestations.

'My dear Edgar,' said Mr. Tyrold, 'I am convinced of your probity. The tenor of your life is its guarantee, and any other defence is a degradation. There is, indeed, no perfidy so unjustifiable, as that which wins but to desert the affections of an innocent female. It is still, if possible, more cowardly than it is cruel; for the greater her worth, and the more exquisite her feelings, the stronger will be the impulse of her delicacy to suffer uncomplaining; and the deluder of her esteem commonly confides, for averting her reproach, to the very sensibility through which he has ensnared her good opinion.'

'No one,' said Edgar, 'can more sincerely concur in this sentiment than myself; and, I trust, there is no situation, and no character, that could prompt me to deviate in this point. Here, in particular, my understanding must have been as defective as my morals, to have betrayed me into such an enterprise.'

'How do you mean?'

'I beg pardon, my dear sir; but, though I have a sort of family regard for Miss Lynmere, and though I think her beauty is transcendent, her heart, I believe—' he hesitated.

'Do you think her heart invulnerable?'—

'Why—no—not positively, perhaps,' answered he, embarrassed, 'not positively invulnerable; but certainly I do not think it composed of those finely subtle sensations which elude all vigilance, and become imperceptibly the prey of every assailing sympathy; for itself, therefore, I believe it not in much danger; and, for others—I see not in it that magnetic attraction which charms away all caution, beguiles all security, enwraps the imagination, and masters the reason!—'

The chain of thinking which, from painting what he thought insensible in Indiana, led him to describe what he felt to be resistless in Camilla, made him finish the last sentence with an energy that surprised Mr. Tyrold into a smile.

'You seem deeply,' he said, 'to have studied the subject.'

'But not under the guidance of Miss Lynmere,' he answered, rising, and colouring, the moment he had spoken, in the fear he had betrayed himself.

'I rejoice, then, the more,' replied Mr. Tyrold, calmly, 'in her own slackness of susceptibility.'

'Yes,' cried Edgar, recovering, and quietly re-placing himself; 'it is her own security, and it is the security of all who surround her; though to those, indeed, there was also another, a still greater, in the contrast which—' he stopt, confused at his own meaning; yet presently, almost irresistibly, added—'Not that I think the utmost vivacity of sentiment, nor all the charm of soul, though eternally beaming in the eyes, playing in every feature, glowing in the complection, and brightening every smile—' he stopt again, overpowered with the consciousness of the picture he was portraying; but Mr. Tyrold continuing silent, he was obliged, though he scarce knew what he said, to go on. 'Nothing, in short, so selfishly are we formed,—that nothing, not even the loveliest of the lovely, can be truly bewitching, in which we do not hope or expect some participation.—I believe I have not made myself very clear?—However, it is not material—I simply meant to explain my retreat from Cleves. And, indeed, it is barbarous, at a season such as this, to detain you a moment from your family.'

He then hastily took leave.

Mr. Tyrold was sensibly touched by this scene. He saw, through a discourse so perplexed, and a manner so confused, that his daughter had made a forcible impression upon the heart of Mandlebert, but could not comprehend why he seemed struggling to conceal it. What had dropt from him appeared to imply a distrust of exciting mutual regard; yet this, after his own observations upon Camilla, was inconceivable. He regretted, that at a period so critical, she must part with her mother, with whom again he now determined to consult.

Edgar, who hitherto had opened his whole heart upon every occasion to Mr. Tyrold, felt hurt and distressed at this first withholding of confidence. It was, however, unavoidable, in his present situation.

He went back to the parlour to take leave once more of Mrs. Tyrold; but, opening the door, found Camilla there alone. She was looking out of the window, and had not heard his entrance.

This was not a sight to still his perturbed spirits; on the contrary, the moment seemed to him so favourable, that it irresistibly occurred to him to seize it for removing every doubt.

Camilla, who had not even missed her mother and sister from the room, was contemplating the horse of Edgar, and internally arraigning herself for the dangerous pleasure she had felt and manifested at the sight of his master.

He gently shut the door, and approaching her, said, 'Do I see again the same frank and amiable friend, who in earliest days, who always, indeed, till—'

Camilla, turning round, startled to behold him so near, and that no one else remained in the room, blushed excessively, and without hearing what he said, shut the window; yet opened it the same minute, stammering out something, but she herself knew not what, concerning the weather.

The gentlest thoughts crossed the mind of Edgar at this evident embarrassment, and the most generous alacrity prompted him to hasten his purpose. He drew a chair near her, and, in penetrating accents, said: 'Will you suffer me, will you, can you permit me, to take the privilege of our long friendship, and honestly to speak to you upon what has passed within these last few days at Cleves?'

She could not answer: surprise, doubt, fear of self-deception, and hope of some happy explanation, all suddenly conspired to confound and to silence her.

'You cannot, I think, forget,' he soon resumed, 'that you had condescended to put into my hands the management and decision of the new acquaintance you are anxious to form? My memory, at least, will never be unfaithful to a testimony so grateful to me, of your entire reliance upon the deep, the unspeakable interest I have ever taken, and ever must take, in my invaluable guardian, and in every branch of his respected and beloved family.'

Camilla now began to breathe. This last expression, though zealous in friendliness, had nothing of appropriate partiality; and in losing her hope she resumed her calmness.

Edgar observed, though he understood not, the change; but as he wished to satisfy his mind before he indulged his inclination, he endeavoured not to be sorry to see her mistress of herself during the discussion. He wished her but to answer him with openness: she still, however, only listened, while she rose and looked about the room for some work. Edgar, somewhat disconcerted, waited for her again sitting down; and after a few minutes spent in a useless search, she drew a chair to a table at some distance.

Gravely then following, he stood opposite to her, and, after a little pause, said, 'I perceive you think I go too far? you think that the intimacy of childhood, and the attachment of adolescence, should expire with the juvenile sports and intercourse which nourished them, rather than ripen into solid friendship and permanent confidence?'

'Do not say so,' cried she, with emotion; 'believe me, unless you knew all that had passed, and all my motives, you should judge nothing of these last few days, but think of me only, whether well or ill, as you thought of me a week ago.'

The most laboured and explicit defence could not more immediately have satisfied his mind than this speech. Suspicion vanished, trust and admiration took its place, and once more drawing a chair by her side, 'My dear Miss Camilla,' he cried, 'forgive my having thus harped upon this subject; I here promise you I will name it no more.'

'And I,' cried she, delighted, 'promise you'—she was going to add, that she would give up Mrs. Arlbery, if he found reason to disapprove the acquaintance; but the parlour door opened, and Miss Margland stalked into the room.

Sir Hugh was going to send a messenger to enquire how and when Mrs. Tyrold had set out; but Miss Margland, from various motives of curiosity, offered her services, and came herself. So totally, however, had both Edgar and Camilla been engrossed by each other, that they had not heard the carriage drive up to the garden gate, which, with the door of the house, being always open, required neither knocker nor bell.

A spectre could not more have startled or shocked Camilla. She jumped up, with an exclamation nearly amounting to a scream, and involuntarily seated herself at the other end of the room.

Edgar, though not equally embarrassed, was still more provoked; but he rose, and got her a chair, and enquired after the health of Sir Hugh.

'He is very poorly, indeed,' answered she, with an austere air, 'and no wonder!'

'Is my uncle ill?' cried Camilla, alarmed.

Miss Margland deigned no reply.

The rest of the family, who had seen the carriage from the windows, now entered the room, and during the mutual enquiries and account which followed, Edgar, believing himself unobserved, glided round to Camilla, and in a low voice, said, 'The promise—I think I guess its gratifying import—I shall not, I hope, lose, through this cruel intrusion?'

Camilla, who saw no eyes but those of Miss Margland, which were severely fastened upon her, affected not to hear him, and planted herself in the group out of his way.

He anxiously waited for another opportunity to put in his claim; but he waited in vain; Camilla, who from the entrance of Miss Margland had had the depressing feel of self-accusation, sedulously avoided him; and though he loitered till he was ashamed of remaining in the house at a period so busy, Miss Margland, by indications not to be mistaken, shewed herself bent upon out-staying him; he was obliged, therefore, to depart; though, no sooner was he gone, than, having nothing more to scrutinize, she went also.

But little doubt now remained with the watchful parents of the mutual attachment of Edgar and Camilla, to which the only apparent obstacle seemed, a diffidence on the part of Edgar with respect to her internal sympathy. Pleased with the modesty of such a fear in so accomplished a young man, Mr. Tyrold protested that, if the superior fortune were on the side of Camilla, he would himself clear it up, and point out the mistake. His wife gloried in the virtuous delicacy of her daughter, that so properly, till it was called for, concealed her tenderness from the object who so deservingly inspired it; yet they agreed, that though she could not, at present, meet Edgar too often, she should be kept wholly ignorant of their wishes and expectations, lest they should still be crushed by any unforeseen casualty: and that, meanwhile, she should be allowed every safe and innocent recreation, that might lighten her mind from its depression, and restore her spirits to their native vivacity.

Early the next morning Dr. Marchmont came to Etherington, and brought with him Lionel, by the express direction of his father, who never objected to admit the faulty to his presence; his hopes of doing good were more potent from kindness than from severity, from example than from precept: yet he attempted not to conquer the averseness of Mrs. Tyrold to an interview; he knew it proceeded not from an inexorable nature, but from a repugnance insurmountable to the sight of a beloved object in disgrace.

Mrs. Tyrold quitted her husband with the most cruel regret, and her darling Camilla with the tenderest inquietude; she affectionately embraced the unexceptionable Lavinia, with whom she left a message for her brother, which she strictly charged her to deliver, without softening or omitting one word.

And then, attended by Dr. Marchmont, she set forward on her journey towards Falmouth: whence a packet, in a few days, she was informed, would sail for Lisbon.

CHAPTER X

Modern Ideas of Life

Grieved at this separation, Mr. Tyrold retired to his study; and his two daughters went to the apartment of Lionel, to comfort him under the weight of his misconduct.

They found him sincerely affected and repentant; yet eager to hear that his mother was actually gone. Ill as he felt himself to deserve such an exertion for his future welfare, and poignant as were his shame and sorrow to have parted her from his excellent father, he thought all evil preferable to encountering her eye, or listening to her admonitions.

Though unaffectedly beloved, Mrs. Tyrold was deeply feared by all her children, Camilla alone excepted; by Lionel, from his horror of reproof; by Lavinia, from the timidity of her humility; and by Eugenia, from her high sense of parental superiority. Camilla alone escaped the contagion; for while too innocent, too undesigning, wilfully to excite displeasure, she was too gay and too light-hearted to admit apprehension without cause.

The gentle Lavinia knew not how to perform her painful task of delivering the message with which she was commissioned. The sight of Lionel in dejection was as sad as it was new to her, and she resolved, in conjunction with Camilla, to spare him till the next day, when his feelings might be less acute. They each sat down, therefore, to work, silent and compassionate; while he, ejaculating blessings upon his parents, and calling for just vengeance upon himself, stroamed up and down the room, biting his knuckles, and now and then striking his forehead.

This lasted about ten minutes: and then, suddenly advancing to his sisters, and snatching a hand of each: 'Come, girls,' he cried, 'now let's talk of other things.'

Too young to have developed the character of Lionel, they were again as much astonished as they had been the preceding day: but his defects, though not originally of the heart, were of a species that soon tend to harden it. They had their rise in a total aversion to reflection, a wish to distinguish himself from his retired, and, he thought, unfashionable relations, and an unfortunate coalition with some unprincipled young men, who, because flashy and gay, could lead him to whatever they proposed. Yet, when mischief or misfortune ensued from his wanton faults, he was always far more sorry than he thought it manly to own; but as his actions were without judgment, his repentance was without principle; and he was ready for some new enterprise the moment the difficulties of an old one subsided.

Camilla, who, from her affection to him, read his character through the innocence of her own, met his returning gaiety with a pleasure that was proportioned to her pain at his depression; but Lavinia saw it with discomfort, as the signal for executing her charge, and, with extreme reluctance, gave him to understand she had a command to fulfil to him from his mother.

The powers of conscience were again then instantly at work; he felt what he had deserved, he dreaded to hear what he had provoked; and trembling and drawing back, entreated her to wait one half hour before she entered upon the business.

She chearfully consented; and Camilla proposed extending the reprieve to the next day: but not two minutes elapsed, before Lionel protested he could not bear the suspense, and urged an immediate communication.

'She can have said nothing,' cried he, 'worse than I expect, or than I merit. Probe me then without delay. She is acting by me like an angel, and if she were to command me to turn anchoret, I know I ought to obey her.'

With much hesitation, Lavinia then began. 'My mother says, my dear Lionel, the fraud you have practised—'

'The fraud! what a horrid word! why it was a mere trick! a joke! a frolic! just to make an old hunks open his purse-strings for his natural heir. I am astonished at my mother! I really don't care if I don't hear another syllable.'

'Well, then, my dear Lionel, I will wait till you are calmer: my mother, I am sure did not mean to irritate, but to convince.'

'My mother,' continued he, striding about the room, 'makes no allowances. She has no faults herself, and for that reason she thinks nobody else should have any. Besides, how should she know what it is to be a young man? and to want a little cash, and not know how to get it?'

'But I am sure,' said Lavinia, 'if you wanted it for any proper purpose, my father would have denied himself everything, in order to supply you.'

'Yes, yes; but suppose I want it for a purpose that is not proper, how am I to get it then?'

'Why, then, my dear Lionel, surely you must be sensible you ought to go without it,' cried the sisters, in a breath.

'Ay, that's as you girls say, that know nothing of the matter. If a young man, when he goes into the world, was to make such a speech as that, he would be pointed at. Besides, who must he live with? You don't suppose he is to shut himself up, with a few musty books, sleeping over the fire, under pretence of study, all day long, do you? like young Melmond, who knows no more of the world than one of you do?'

'Indeed,' said Camilla, 'he seemed to me an amiable and modest young man, though very romantic.'

'O, I dare say he did! I could have laid any wager of that. He's just a girl's man, just the very thing, all sentiment, and poetry and heroics. But we, my little dear, we lads of spirit, hold all that amazing cheap. I assure you, I would as soon be seen trying on a lady's cap at a glass, as poring over a crazy old author when I could help it. I warrant you think, because one is at the university, one must all be book-worms?'

'Why, what else do you go there for but to study?'

'Every thing in the world, my dear.'

'But are there not sometimes young men who are scholars without being book-worms?' cried Camilla, half colouring; 'is not—is not Edgar Mandlebert—'

'O yes, yes; an odd thing of that sort happens now and then. Mandlebert has spirit enough to carry it off pretty well, without being ridiculous; though he is as deep, for his time, as e'er an old fellow of a college. But then this is no rule for others. You must not expect an Edgar Mandlebert at every turn.'

Ah no! thought Camilla.

'But, Edgar,' said Lavinia, 'has had an extraordinary education, as well as possessing extraordinary talents and goodness: and you, too, my dear Lionel, to fulfil what may be expected from you, should look back to your father, who was brought up at the same university, and is now considered as one of the first men it has produced. While he was respected by the learned for his application, he was loved even by the indolent for his candour and kindness of heart. And though his income, as you know, was so small, he never ran in debt, and by an exact but open oeconomy, escaped all imputation of meanness: while by forbearing either to conceal, or repine at his limited fortune, he blunted even the raillery of the dissipated, by frankly and good humouredly meeting it half way. How often have I heard my dear mother tell you this!'

'Yes; but all this, child, is nothing to the purpose; my father is no more like other men than if he had been born in another planet, and my attempting to resemble him, is as great a joke, as if you were to dress up Miss Margland in Indiana's flowers and feathers, and then expect people to call her a beauty.'

'We do not say you resemble my father, now,' said Camilla, archly; 'but is there any reason why you should not try to do it by and by?'

'O yes! a little one! nature, nature, my dear, is in the way. I was born a bit of a buck. I have no manner of natural taste for study, and poring, and expounding, and black-letter work. I am a light, airy spark, at your service, not quite so wise as I am merry;—but let that pass. My father, you know, is firm as a rock. He minds neither wind nor weather, nor fleerer nor sneerer: but this firmness, look ye, he has kept all to himself; not a whit of it do I inherit; every wind that blows veers me about, and makes me look some new way.'

Soon after, gathering courage from curiosity, he desired to hear the message at once.

Lavinia, unwillingly complying, then repeated: 'The fraud which you have practised, my mother says, whether from wanton folly to give pain, or from rapacious discontent to gain money, she will leave without comment, satisfied that if you have any heart at all, its effects must bring its remorse, since it has dangerously encreased the infirmities of your uncle, driven him to a foreign land, and forced your mother to forsake her home and family in his pursuit, unless she were willing to see you punished by the entire disinheritance with which you are threatened. But—'

'O, no more! no more! I am ready to shoot myself already! My dear, excellent mother! what do I not owe you! I had never seen, never thought of the business in this solemn way before. I meant nothing at first but a silly joke, and all this mischief has followed unaccountably. I assure you, I had no notion at the beginning he would have minded the letter; and afterwards, Jack Whiston persuaded me, the money was as good as my own, and that it was nothing but a little cribbing from myself. I will never trust him again; I see the whole now in its true and atrocious colours.—I will devote myself in future to make all the amends in my power to my dear incomparable mother.'

The sisters affectionately encouraged this idea, which produced near a quarter of an hour's serious thinking and penitence.

He then begged to hear the rest; and Lavinia continued.

'But since you are re-admitted, said my mother, to Etherington, by the clemency of your forbearing father, she charges you to remember, you can only repay his goodness by an application the most intense to those studies you have hitherto neglected, and of which your neglect has been the cause of all your errors; by committing to idle amusements the time that innocently, as well as profitably, ought to have been dedicated to the attainment of knowledge. She charges you also to ask yourself, since, during the vacation, your father himself is your tutor, upon what pretext you can justify wasting his valuable time, however little you may respect your own?—Finally—'

'I never wasted his time! I never desired to have any instruction in the vacations. 'Tis the most deuced thing in life to be studying so hard incessantly. The waste of time is all his own affair;—his own choice—not mine, I assure you! Go on, however.'

'Finally, she adjures you to consider, that if you still persevere to consume your time in wilful negligence, to bury all thought in idle gaiety, and to act without either reflection or principle, the career of faults which begins but in unthinking folly, will terminate in shame, in guilt, and in ruin! And though such a declension of all good, must involve your family in your affliction, your disgrace, she bids me say, will ultimately fall but where it ought; since your own want of personal sensibility to the horror of your conduct, will neither harden nor blind any human being besides yourself. This is all.'

'And enough too,' cried he, reddening: 'I am a very wretch!—I believe that—though I am sure I can't tell how; for I never intend any harm, never think, never dream of hurting any mortal! But as to study—I must own to you, I hate it most deucedly. Anything else—if my mother had but exacted any thing else—with what joy I would have shewn my obedience!—If she had ordered me to be horse-ponded, I do protest to you, I would not have demurred.'

'How always you run into the ridiculous!' cried Camilla.

'I was never so serious in my life; not that I should like to be horse-ponded in the least, though I would submit to it for a punishment, and out of duty: but then, when it was done, it would be over: now the deuce of study is, there is no end of it! And it does so little for one! one can go through life so well without it! There is not above here and there an old codger that asks one a question that can bring it into any play. And then, a turn upon one's heel, or looking at one's watch, or wondering at one's short memory, or happening to forget just that one single passage, carries off the whole in two minutes, as completely as if one had been working one's whole life to get ready for the assault. And pray, now, tell me, how can it be worth one's best days, one's gayest hours, the very flower of one's life—all to be sacrificed to plodding over musty grammars and lexicons, merely to cut a figure just for about two minutes once or twice in a year?'

The sisters, brought up with an early reverence for learning, as forming a distinguished part of the accomplishments of their father, could not subscribe to this argument. But they laughed; and that was ever sufficient for Lionel, who, though sincerely, in private, he loved and honoured his father, never bestowed upon him one voluntary moment that frolic or folly invited elsewhere.

Lavinia and Camilla, perfectly relieved now from all fears for their brother, repaired to the study of their father, anxious to endeavour to chear him, and to accelerate a meeting and reconciliation for Lionel; but they found him desirous to be alone, though kindly, and unsolicited, he promised to admit his son before dinner.

Lionel heard this with a just awe; but gave it no time for deep impression. It was still very early, and he could settle himself to nothing during the hours yet to pass before the interview. He persuaded his sisters, therefore, to walk out with him, to while away at once expectation and retrospection.

CHAPTER XI

Modern Notions of Penitence

They set out with no other plan than to take a three hours' stroll. Lionel led the way, and they journeyed through various pleasant lanes and meadows, till, about three miles distance from Etherington, upon ascending a beautiful little hill, they espied, fifty yards off, the Grove, and a party of company sauntering round its grounds.

He immediately proposed making a visit to Mrs. Arlbery; but Lavinia declined presenting herself to a lady who was unknown to her mother; and Camilla, impressed with the promise she had intended for Edgar, which she was sure, though unpronounced, he had comprehended, dissented also from the motion.

He then said he would go alone; for his spirits were so low from vexation and regret, that they wanted recruit; and he would return to them by the time they would be sufficiently rested to walk home.

To this they agreed; and amused themselves with watching to see him join the group; in which, however, they were no sooner gratified, than, to their great confusion, they perceived that he pointed them out, and that all eyes were immediately directed towards the hill.

Vexed and astonished at his quick passing penitence, they hastened down the declivity, and ran on till a lane, with an high hedge on each side, sheltered them from view.

But Lionel, soon pursuing them, said he brought the indisputable orders of his invincible widow to convoy them to the mansion. She never, she had owned, admitted formal visitors, but whatever was abrupt and out of the way, won her heart.

To the prudent Lavinia, this invitation was by no means alluring. Mrs. Tyrold, from keeping no carriage, visited but little, and the Grove was not included in her small circle; Lavinia, therefore, though she knew not how to be peremptory, was steady in refusal; and Camilla, who would naturally with pleasure have yielded, had a stronger motive for firmness, than any with which she was gifted by discretion, in her wish to oblige Mandlebert. But Lionel would listen to neither of them; and when he found his insistance insufficient, seized Lavinia by one arm, and Camilla by the other, and dragged them up the hill, in defiance of their entreaties, and in full view of the party. He then left the more pleading, though less resisting, Lavinia alone; but pulled Camilla down by the opposite side, with a velocity that, though meant but to bring her to the verge of a small rivulet, forced her into the midst of it so rapidly that he could not himself at last stop: and wetted her so completely, that she could with difficulty, when she got across it, walk on.

The violent spirits of Lionel always carried him beyond his own intentions; he was now really sorry for what he had done: and Lavinia, who had quietly followed, was uneasy from the fear of some ill consequence to her sister.

Mrs. Arlbery, who had seen the transaction, came forth now herself, to invite them all into her house, and offer a fire and dry clothing to Camilla; not sparing, however, her well-merited raillery at the awkward exploit of young Tyrold.

Camilla, ashamed to be thus seen, would have hidden herself behind her sister, and retreated; but even Lavinia now, fearing for her health, joined in the request, and she was obliged to enter the house.

Mrs. Arlbery took her upstairs, to her own apartment, and supplied her immediately with a complete change of apparel; protesting that Lionel should be punished for his frolic, by a solitary walk to Etherington, to announce that she would keep his two sisters for the day.

Opposition was vain; she was gay, good humoured, and pleasant, but she would not be denied. She meant not, however, to inflict the serious penalty which the face of Lionel proclaimed him to be suffering, when he prepared to depart; and the sisters, who read in it his dread of meeting Mr. Tyrold alone, in the present circumstances of his affairs, conferred together, and agreed that Lavinia should accompany him, both to intercede for returning favour from his father, and to explain the accident of Camilla's staying at the Grove. Mrs. Arlbery, meanwhile, promised to restore her young guest safe at night in her own carriage.

Notwithstanding the pleasure with which Camilla, in any other situation, would have renewed this acquaintance, was now changed into reluctance, she was far from insensible to the flattering kindness with which Mrs. Arlbery received and entertained her, nor to the frankness with which she confessed, that her invisibility the other morning, had resulted solely from pique that the visit had not been made sooner.

Camilla would have attempted some apology for the delay, but she assured her apologies were what she neither took nor gave; and then laughingly added—'We will try one another to day, and if we find it won't do—we will shake hands and part. That, you must know, is my mode; and is it not vastly better than keeping up an acquaintance that proves dull, merely because it has been begun?'

She then ordered away all her visitors, without the smallest ceremony; telling them, however, they might come back in the evening, only desiring they would not be early. Camilla stared; but they all submitted as to a thing of course.

'You are not used to my way, I perceive,' cried she, smiling; 'yet, I can nevertheless assure you, you can do nothing so much for your happiness as to adopt it. You are made a slave in a moment by the world, if you don't begin life by defying it. Take your own way, follow your own humour, and you and the world will both go on just as well, as if you ask its will and pleasure for everything you do, and want, and think.'

She then expressed herself delighted with Lionel, for bringing them together by this short cut, which abolished a world of formalities, not more customary than fatiguing. 'I pass, I know,' continued she, 'for a mere creature of whim; but, believe me, there is no small touch of philosophy in the composition of my vagaries. Extremes, you know, have a mighty knack of meeting. Thus I, like the sage, though not with sage-like motives, save time that must otherwise be wasted; brave rules that would murder common sense; and when I have made people stare, turn another way that I may laugh.'

She then, in a graver strain, and in a manner that proved the laws of politeness all her own, where she chose, for any particular purpose, or inclination, to exert them, hoped this profession of her faith would plead her excuse, that she had thus incongruously made her fair guest a second time enter her house, before her first visit was acknowledged; and enquired whether it were to be returned to Etherington or at Cleves.

Camilla answered, she was now at home, on account of her mother's being obliged to make a voyage to Lisbon.

Mrs. Arlbery said, she would certainly, then, wait upon her at Etherington; and very civilly regretted having no acquaintance with Mrs. Tyrold; archly, however, adding: 'As we have no where met, I could not seek her at her own house without running too great a risk; for then, whether I had liked her or not, I must have received her, you know, into mine. So, you see, I am not quite without prudence, whatever the dear world says to the contrary.'

She then spoke of the ball, public breakfast, and raffle; chatting both upon persons and things with an easy gaiety, and sprightly negligence, extremely amusing to Camilla, and which soon, in despite of the unwillingness with which she had entered her house, brought back her original propensity to make the acquaintance, and left no regret for what Lionel had done, except what rested upon the repugnance of Edgar to his intercourse. As he could not, however, reproach what was begun without her concurrence, he would see, she hoped, like herself, that common civility henceforward would exact its continuance.

In proportion as her pleasure from this accidental commerce was awakened, and her early partiality revived, her own spirits re-animated, and, in the course of the many hours they now spent completely together, she was set so entirely at her ease, by the good humour of Mrs. Arlbery, that she lost all fear of her wit. She found it rather playful than satirical; rather seeking to amuse than to disconcert; and though sometimes, from the resistless pleasure of uttering a bon mot she thought more of its brilliancy than of the pain it might inflict, this happened but rarely, and was more commonly succeeded by regret than by triumph.

Camilla soon observed she had, personally, nothing to apprehend, peculiar partiality supplying the place of general delicacy, in shielding her from every shaft that even pleasantry could render poignant. The embarrassment, therefore, which, in ingenuous youth, checks the attempt to please, by fear of failure, or shame of exertion, gave way to natural spirits, which gaily rising from entertainment received, restored her vivacity, and gradually, though unconsciously, enabled her to do justice to her own abilities, by unaffectedly calling forth the mingled sweetness and intelligence of her character; and Mrs. Arlbery, charmed with all she observed, and flattered by all she inspired, felt such satisfaction in her evident conquest, that before the tête-à-tête was closed, their admiration was become nearly mutual.

When the evening party was announced, they both heard with surprise that the day was so far advanced. 'They can wait, however,' said Mrs. Arlbery, 'for I know they have nothing to do.'

She then invited Camilla to return to her the next day for a week.

Camilla felt well disposed to comply, hoping soon to reason from Edgar his prejudice against a connection that afforded her such singular pleasure; but to leave her father at this period was far from every wish. She excused herself, therefore, saying, she had still six weeks due to her uncle at Cleves, before any other engagement could take place.

'Well, then, when you quit your home for Sir Hugh, will you beg off a few days from him, and set them down to my account?'

'If my uncle pleases—'

'If he pleases?' repeated she, laughing; 'pray never give that If into his decision; you only put contradiction into people's heads, by asking what pleases them. Say at once, My good uncle, Mrs. Arlbery has invited me to indulge her with a few days at the Grove; so to-morrow I shall go to her. Will you promise me this?'

'Dear madam, no! my uncle would think me mad.'

'And suppose he should! A little alarm now and then keeps life from stagnation. They call me mad, I know, sometimes; wild, flighty, and what not; yet you see how harmless I am, though I afford food for such notable commentary.'

'But can you really like such things should be said of you?'

'I adore the frankness of that question! why, n—o,—I rather think I don't. But I'm not sure. However, to prevent their minding me, I must mind them. And it's vastly more irksome to give up one's own way, than to hear a few impertinent remarks. And as to the world, depend upon it, my dear Miss Tyrold, the more you see of it, the less you will care for it.'

She then said she would leave her to re-invest herself in her own attire, and go downstairs, to see what the poor simple souls, who had had no more wit than to come back thus at her call, had found to do with themselves.

Camilla, having only her common morning dress, and even that utterly spoilt, begged that her appearance might be dispensed with; but Mrs. Arlbery, exclaiming, 'Why, there are only men; you don't mind men, I hope!' ashamed, she promised to get ready; yet she had not sufficient courage to descend, till her gay hostess came back, and accompanied her to the drawing room.

CHAPTER XII

Airs and Graces

Upon entering the room, Camilla saw again the Officers who had been there in the morning, and who were now joined by Sir Sedley Clarendel. She was met at the door by Major Cerwood, who seemed waiting for her appearance, and who made her his compliments with an air that studiously proclaimed his devotion. She seated herself by the side of Mrs. Arlbery, to look on at a game of chess, played by Sir Sedley and General Kinsale.

'Clarendel,' said Mrs. Arlbery, 'you have not the least in the world the air of knowing what you are about.'

'Pardon me, ma'am,' said the General, 'he has been at least half an hour contemplating this very move,—for which, as you see, I now check-mate him. Pray, Sir Sedley, how came you, at last, to do no better?'

'Thinking of other things, my dear General. 'Tis impossible in the extreme to keep one's faculties pinioned down to the abstruse vagaries of this brain-besieging game. My head would be deranged past redress, if I did not allow it to visit the four quarters of the globe once, at least, between every move.'

'You do not play so slow, then, from deliberating upon your chances, but from forgetting them?'

'Defined, my dear General, to scrupulosity! Those exquisite little moments we steal from any given occupation, for the pleasure of speculating in secret upon something wholly foreign to it, are resistless to deliciousness.'

'I entreat, and command you then,' cried Mrs. Arlbery, 'to make your speculations public. Nothing will more amuse me, than to have the least intimation of the subjects of your reveries.'

'My dear Mrs. Arlbery! your demand is the very quintessence of impossibility! Tell the subject of a reverie! know you not it wafts one at once out of the world, and the world's powers of expression? while all it substitutes is as evanescent as it is delectable. To attempt the least description would be a presumption of the first monstrousness.'

'O never heed that! presumption will not precisely be a novelty to you; answer me, therefore, my dear Clarendel, without all this conceit. You know I hate procrastination; and procrastinators still worse.'

'Softly, dearest madam, softly! There is nothing in nature so horribly shocking to me as the least hurry. My poor nerves seek repose after any turbulent words, or jarring sounds, with the same craving for rest that my body experiences after the jolts, and concussions of a long winded chase. By the way, does anybody want a good hunter? I have the first, perhaps, in Europe; but I would sell it a surprising bargain, for I am excruciatingly tired of it.'

All the gentlemen grouped round him to hear further particulars, except Mr. Macdersey, the young Ensign, who had so unguardedly exposed himself at the Northwick ball, and who now, approaching Camilla, fervently exclaimed; 'How happy I should have been, madam, if I had had the good fortune to see you meet with that accident this morning, instead of being looking another way! I might then have had the pleasure to assist you. And O! how much more if it had been your divine cousin! I hope that fair angel is in perfect health! O what a beautiful creature she is! her outside is the completest diamond I ever saw! and if her inside is the same, which I dare say it is, by her smiles and delicate dimples, she must be a paragon upon earth!'

'There is at least something very inartificial in your praise,' said General Kinsale, 'when you make your panegyric of an absent lady to a present one.'

'O General, there is not a lady living can bear any comparison with her. I have never had her out of my thoughts from the first darling moment that ever I saw her, which has made me the most miserable of men ever since. Her eyes so beautiful, her mouth so divine, her nose so heavenly!—'

'And how,' cried Sir Sedley, 'is the tip of her chin?'

'No joking, sir!' said the Ensign, reddening; 'she is a piece of perfection not to be laughed at; she has never had her fellow upon the face of the earth; and she never will have it while the earth holds, upon account of there being no such person above ground.'

'And pray,' cried Sir Sedley, carelessly, 'how can you be sure of that?'

'How! why by being certain,' answered the inflamed admirer; 'for though I have been looking out for pretty women from morning to night, ever since I was conscious of the right use of my eyes, I never yet saw her parallel.'

A servant was now bringing in the tea; but his lady ordered him to set it down in the next room, whence the gentlemen should fetch it as it was wanted.

Major Cerwood took in charge all attendance upon Camilla; but he was not, therefore, exempt from the assiduities required by Mrs. Arlbery, for whom the homage of the General, the Colonel, and the Ensign, were insufficient; and who, had a score more been present, would have found occupation for them all. Sir Sedley alone was excepted from her commands; for knowing they would be issued to him in vain, she contented herself with only interchanging glances of triumph with him, at the submission of every vassal but himself.

'Heavens!' cried she, to Colonel Andover, who had hastened to present her the first cup, 'you surely think I have nerves for a public orator! If I should taste but one drop of this tea, I might envy the repose of the next man who robs on the highway. Major Cerwood, will you try if you can do any better for me?'

The Major obeyed, but not with more success. 'What in the world have you brought me?' cried she; 'Is it tea? It looks prodigiously as if just imported out of the slop bason. For pity sake, Macdersey, arise, and give me your help; you will at least never bring me such maudlin stuff as this. Even your tea will have some character; it will be very good or very bad; very hot or very cold; very strong or very weak; for you are always in flames of fire, or flakes of snow.'

'You do me justice, ma'am; there is nothing upon the face of the earth so insipid as a medium. Give me love or hate! a friend that will go to jail for me, or an enemy that will run me through the body!

Riches to chuck guineas about like halfpence, or poverty to beg in a ditch! Liberty wild as the four winds, or an oar to work in a galley! Misery to tear my heart into an hundred thousand millions of atoms, or joy to make my soul dance into my brain! Every thing has some gratification, except a medium. 'Tis a poor little soul that is satisfied between happiness and despair.'

He then flew to bring her a dish of tea.

'My dear Macdersey,' cried she, in receiving it, 'this is according to your system indeed; for 'tis a compound of strong, and rich, and sweet, to cloy an alderman, making altogether so luscious a syrup, that our spring would be exhausted before I could slake my thirst, if I should taste it only a second time. Do, dear General, see if it is not possible to get me some beverage that I can swallow.'

The youngest man present was not more active than the General in this service; but Mrs. Arlbery, casting herself despondingly back the moment she had tasted what he brought her, exclaimed, 'Why this is worst of all! If you can do no better for me, General, than this, tell me, at least, for mercy's sake, when some other regiment will be quartered here?'

'What a cruelty,' said the Major, looking with a sigh towards Camilla, 'to remind your unhappy prey they are but birds of passage!'

'O, all the better, Major. If you understand your own interest you will be as eager to break up your quarters, as I can be to see your successors march into them. I have now heard all your compliments, and you have heard all my repartees; both sides, therefore, want new auditors. A great many things I have said to you will do vastly well again for a new corps; and, to do you justice, some few things you have said yourselves may do again in a new county.'

Then, addressing Camilla, she proposed, though without moving, that they should converse with one another, and leave the men to take care of themselves. 'And excessively they will be obliged to me,' she continued, without lowering her voice, 'for giving this little holiday to their poor brains; for, I assure you, they have not known what to say this half hour. Indeed, since the first fortnight they were quartered here, they have not, upon an average, said above one new thing in three days. But one's obliged to take up with Officers in the country, because there's almost nothing else. Can you recommend me any agreeable new people?'

'O no, ma'am! I have hardly any acquaintance, except immediately round the rectory; but, fortunately, my own family is so large, that I have never been distressed for society.'

'O, ay, true! your own family, begin with that; do, pray, give me a little history of your own family?'

'I have no history, ma'am, to give, for my father's retired life—'

'O, I have seen your father, and I have heard him preach, and I like him very much. There's something in him there's no turning into ridicule.'

Camilla, though surprised, was delighted by such a testimony to the respectability of her father; and, with more courage, said—'And, I am sure, if you knew my mother, you would allow her the same exemption.'

'So I hear; therefore, we won't talk of them. It's a delightful thing to think of perfection; but it's vastly more amusing to talk of errors and absurdities. To begin with your eldest sister, then—but no; she seems in just the same predicament as your father and mother: so we'll let her rest, too.'

'Indeed she is; she is as faultless—'

'O, not a word more then; she won't do for me at all. But, pray, is there not a single soul in all the round of your large family, that can afford a body a little innocent diversion?'

'Ah, madam,' said Camilla, shaking her head; 'I fear, on the contrary, if they came under your examination, there is not one in whom you would not discern some foible!'

'I should not like them at all the worse for that; for, between ourselves, my dear Miss Tyrold, I am half afraid they might find a foible or two in return in me; so you must not be angry if I beg the favour of you to indulge me with a few of their defects.'

'Indulge you!'

'Yes, for when so many of a family are perfect, if you can't find me one or two that have a little speck of mortality, you must not wonder if I take flight at your very name. In charity, therefore, if you would not drop my acquaintance, tell me their vulnerable parts.'

Camilla laughed at this ridiculous reasoning, but would not enter into its consequences.

'Well, then, if you will not assist me, don't take it ill that I assist myself. In the first place, there's your brother; I don't ask you to tell me any thing of him; I have seen him! and I confess to you he does not put me into utter despair! he does not alarm me into flying all his race.'

Camilla tried vainly to look grave.

'I have seen another, too, your cousin, I think; Miss Lynmere, that's engaged to young Mandlebert.'

Camilla now tried as vainly to look gay.

'She's prodigiously pretty. Pray, is not she a great fool?'

'Ma'am?'

'I beg your pardon! but I don't suppose you are responsible for the intellects of all your generation. However, she'll do vastly well; you need not be uneasy for her. A face like that will take very good care of itself. I am glad she is engaged, for your sake, though I am sorry for Mandlebert; that is, if, as his class of countenance generally predicts, he marries with any notion of expecting to be happy.'

'But why, ma'am,' cried Camilla, checking a sigh, 'are you glad for my sake?'

'Because there are two reasons why she would be wonderfully in your way; she is not only prettier than you, but sillier.'

'And would both those reasons,' cried Camilla, again laughing, 'make against me?'

'O, intolerably, with the men! They are always enchanted with something that is both pretty and silly; because they can so easily please and so soon disconcert it; and when they have made the little blooming fools blush and look down, they feel nobly superior, and pride themselves in victory. Dear creatures! I delight in their taste; for it brings them a plentiful harvest of repentance, when it is their connubial criterion; the pretty flies off, and the silly remains, and a man then has a choice companion for life left on his hands!'

The young Ensign here could no longer be silent: 'I am sure and certain,' cried he, warmly, 'Miss Lynmere is incapable to be a fool! and when she marries, if her husband thinks her so, it's only a sign he's a blockhead himself.'

'He'll be exactly of your opinion for the first month or two,' answered Mrs. Arlbery, 'or even if he is not, he'll like her just as well. A man looks enchanted while his beautiful young bride talks nonsense; it comes so prettily from her ruby lips, and she blushes and dimples with such lovely attraction while she utters it; he casts his eyes around him with conscious elation to see her admirers, and his enviers; but he has amply his turn for looking like a fool himself, when youth and beauty take flight, and when his ugly old wife exposes her ignorance or folly at every word.'

'The contrast of beginning and end,' said the General, 'is almost always melancholy. But how rarely does any man,—nay, I had nearly said, or any woman—think a moment of the time to come, or of any time but the present day, in marrying?'

'Except with respect to fortune!' cried Mrs. Arlbery, 'and there, methinks, you men, at least, are commonly sufficiently provident. I don't think reflection is generally what you want in that point.'

'As to reflection,' exclaimed Mr. Macdersey, ''tis the thing in the world I look upon to be the meanest! a man capable of reflection, where a beautiful young creature is in question, can have no soul nor vitals. For my part, 'tis my only misfortune that I cannot get at that lovely girl, to ask her for her private opinion of me at once, that I might either get a licence tomorrow, or drive her out of my head before sleep overtakes me another night.'

'Your passions, my good Macdersey,' said Mrs. Arlbery, 'considering their violence, seem tolerably obedient. Can you really be so fond, or so forgetful at such short warning?'

'Yes, but it's with a pain that breaks my heart every time.'

'You contrive, however, to get it pretty soon mended!'

'That, madam, is a power that has come upon me by degrees; I have paid dear enough for it!—nobody ever found it harder than I did at the beginning; for the first two or three times I took my disappointments so to heart, that I should have been bound for ever to any friend that would have had the good nature to blow my brains out.'

'But now you are so much in the habit of experiencing these little failures, that they pass on as things of course?'

'No, madam, you injure me, and in the tenderest point; for, as long as I have the least hope, my passion's as violent as ever; but you would not be so unreasonable as to have a man love on, when it can answer no end? It's no better than making him unhappy for a joke. There's no sense in such a thing.'

'By the way, my dear Miss Tyrold, and apropos to this Miss Lynmere,' said Mrs. Arlbery, 'do tell me something about Mr. Mandlebert—what is he?—what does he do always amongst you?'

'He—he!—' cried Camilla, stammering, 'he was a ward of my father's—'

'O, I don't mean all that; but what is his style?—his class?—is he agreeable?'

'I believe—he is generally thought so.'

'If he is, do pray, then, draw him into my society, for I am terribly in want of recruits. These poor gentlemen you see here are very good sort of men; but they have a trick of sleeping with their eyes wide open, and fancy all the time they are awake; and, indeed, I find it hard to persuade them to the contrary, though I often ask them for their dreams. By the way, can't you contrive, some or other amongst you, to make the room a little cooler?'

'Shall I open this window?' said the Major.

'Nay, nay, don't ask me; I had rather bear six times the heat, than give my own directions: nothing in the world fatigues me so much as telling stupid people how to set about things. Colonel, don't you see I have no fan?'

'I'll fetch it directly—have you left it in the dining-parlour?'

'Do you really think I would not send a footman at once, if I must perplex myself with all that recollection? My dear Miss Tyrold, did you ever see any poor people, that pretended at all to walk about, and mingle with the rest of the world, like living creatures, so completely lethargic?—'tis really quite melancholy! I am sure you have good nature enough to pity them. It requires my utmost ingenuity to keep them in any employment; and if I left them to themselves, they would stand before the fire all the winter, and lounge upon sofas all the summer. And that indolence of body so entirely unnerves the mind, that they find as little to say as to do. Upon the whole, 'tis really a paltry race, the men of the present times. However, as we have got no better, and as the women are worse, I do all I can to make them less insufferable to me.'

'And do you really think the women are worse?' cried Camilla.

'Not in themselves, my dear; but worse to me, because I cannot possibly take the same liberties with them. Macdersey, I wish I had my salts.

'It shall be the happiness of my life to find them, be they hid where they may; only tell me where I may have the pleasure to go and look for them.'

'Nay, that's your affair.'

'Why, then, if they are to be found from the garret to the cellar, be sure I am a dead man, if I do not bring them you!'

This mode of displaying airs and graces was so perfectly new to Camilla, that the commands issued, and the obedience paid, were equally amusing to her. Brought up herself to be contented with whatever came in her way, in preference either to giving trouble, or finding fault, the ridiculous, yet playful wilfulness with which she saw Mrs. Arlbery send every one upon her errands, yet object to what every one performed, presented to her a scene of such whimsical gaiety, that her concern at the accident which had made her innocently violate her intended engagement with Edgar, was completely changed into pleasure, that thus, without any possible self blame, an acquaintance she had so earnestly desired was even by necessity established: and she returned home at night with spirits all revived, and eloquent in praise of her new favourite.

CHAPTER XIII

Attic Adventures

Mr. Tyrold, according to the system of recreation which he had settled with his wife, saw with satisfaction the pleasure with which Camilla began this new acquaintance, in the hope it would help to support her spirits during the interval of suspense with regard to the purposes of Mandlebert. Mrs. Arlbery was unknown to him, except by general fame; which told him she was a woman of reputation as well as fashion, and that though her manners were lively, her heart was friendly, and her hand ever open to charity.

Upon admitting Lionel again to his presence, he spoke forcibly, though with brevity, upon the culpability of his conduct. What he had done, he said, let him colour it to himself with what levity he might, was not only a robbery, but a robbery of the most atrocious and unjustifiable class; adding terror to violation of property, and playing upon the susceptibility of the weakness and infirmities, which he ought to have been the first to have sheltered and sheathed. Had the action contained no purpose but a frolic, even then the situation of the object on whom it fell, rendered it inhuman; but as its aim and end was to obtain money, it was dishonourable to his character, and criminal by the laws of his country. 'Yet shudder no more,' continued he, 'young man, at the justice to which they make you amenable, than at having deserved, though you escape it! From this day, however, I will name it no more. Feeble must be all I could utter, compared with what the least reflection must make you feel! Your uncle, in a broken state of health, is sent abroad; your mother, though too justly incensed to see you, sacrifices her happiness to serve you!'

Lionel, for a few hours, was in despair after this harangue; but as they passed away, he strove to drive it from his mind, persuading himself it was useless to dwell upon what was irretrievable.

Mrs. Arlbery, the following day, made her visit at Etherington, and invited the two sisters to a breakfast she was to give the next morning. Mr. Tyrold, who with surprize and concern at a coldness so dilatory, found a second day wearing away without a visit from Mandlebert, gladly consented to allow of an amusement, that might shake from Camilla the pensiveness into which, at times, he saw her falling.

Mrs. Arlbery had declared she hated ceremony in the summer; guarded, therefore, by Lionel, the sisters walked to the Grove. From the little hill they had again to pass, they observed a group of company upon the leads of her house, which were flat, and balustraded round; and when they presented themselves at the door, they were met by Major Cerwood, who conducted them to the scene of business.

It was the end of July, and the weather was sultry; but though the height of the place upon which the present party was collected, gave some freshness to the air, the heat reflected from the lead would have been nearly intolerable, had it not been obviated by an awning, and by matts, in the part where seats and refreshments were arranged. French horns and clarinets were played during the repast.

This little entertainment had for motive a young lady's quitting her boarding school. Miss Dennel, a niece, by marriage, of Mrs. Arlbery, who, at the age of fourteen, came to preside at the house and table of her father, had begged to be felicitated by her aunt, upon the joyful occasion, with a ball:

but Mrs. Arlbery declared she never gave any entertainments in which she did not expect to play the principal part herself; and that balls and concerts were therefore excluded from her list of home diversions. It was vastly well to see others shine superior, she said, elsewhere, but she could not be so accommodating as to perform Nobody under her own roof. She offered her, however, a breakfast, with full choice of its cakes and refreshments; which, with leave to fix upon the spot where it should be given, was all the youthful pleader could obtain.

The Etherington trio met with a reception the most polite, and Camilla was distinguished by marks of peculiar favour. Few guests were added to the party she had met there before, except the young lady who was its present foundress; and whose voice she recollected to have heard, in the enquiries which had reached her ear from within the paddock.

Miss Dennel was a pretty, blooming, tall girl, but as childish in intellect as in experience; though self-persuaded she was a woman in both, since she was called from school to sit at the head of her father's table.

Camilla required nothing further for entertainment than to listen to her new friend; Lavinia, though more amazed than amused, always modestly hung back as a mere looker on; and the company in general made their diversion from viewing, through various glasses, the seats of the neighbouring gentlemen, and reviewing, with yet more scrutiny, their characters and circumstances. But Lionel, ever restless, seized the opportunity to patrol the attic regions of the house, where, meeting with a capacious lumber room, he returned to assure the whole party it would make an admirable theatre, and to ask who would come forth to spout with him.

Mr. Macdersey said, he did not know one word of any part, but he could never refuse anything that might contribute to the company's pleasure.

Away they sped together, and in a few minutes reversed the face of everything. Old sofas, bedsteads, and trunks, large family chests, deal boxes and hampers, carpets and curtains rolled up for the summer, tables with two legs, and chairs without bottoms, were truckled from the middle to one end of the room, and arranged to form a semi-circle, with seats in front, for a pit. Carpets were then uncovered and untied, to be spread for the stage, and curtains, with as little mercy, were unfurled, and hung up to make a scene.

They then applied to Miss Dennel, who had followed to peep at what they were about, and asked if she thought the audience might be admitted.

She declared she had never seen any place so neat and elegant in her life.

Such an opinion could not but be decisive; and they prepared to re-ascend; when the sight of a small door, near the entrance of the large apartment, excited the ever ready curiosity of Lionel, who, though the key was on the outside, contrived to turn it wrong; but while endeavouring to rectify by force what he had spoilt by aukwardness, a sudden noise from within startled them all, and occasioned quick and reiterated screams from Miss Dennel, who, with the utmost velocity burst back upon the company on the leads, calling out; 'O Lord! how glad I am I'm coming back alive! Mr. Macdersey and young Mr. Tyrold are very likely killed! for they've just found I don't know how many robbers shut up in a dark closet!'

The gentlemen waited for no explanation to this unintelligible story, but hastened to the spot; and Mrs. Arlbery ordered all the servants who were in waiting to follow and assist.

Miss Dennel then entreated to have the trap door through which they ascended, from a small staircase, to the leads, double locked till the gentlemen should declare upon their honours that the thieves were all dead.

Mrs. Arlbery would not listen to this, but waited with Lavinia and Camilla the event.

The gentlemen, meanwhile, reached the scene of action, at the moment when Macdersey, striking first his foot, and then his whole person against the door, had forced it open with such sudden violence, that he fell over a pail of water into the adjoining room.

The servants arriving at the same time, announced that this was merely a closet for mops, brooms, and pails, belonging to the housemaid: and it appeared, upon examination, that the noise from within, had simply been produced by the falling down of a broom, occasioned by their shaking the door in endeavouring to force the lock.

The Ensign, wetted or splashed all over, was in a fury; and, turning to Lionel, who laughed vociferously, whilst the rest of the gentlemen were scarce less moderate, and the servants joined in the chorus, peremptorily demanded to know if he had put the pail there on purpose; 'In which case, sir,' said he, 'you must never let me see you laugh again to the longest hour you have to live!'

'My good Macdersey,' said the General, 'go into another room, and have your cloaths wiped and dried; it will be time enough then to settle who shall laugh longest.'

'General,' said he, 'I scorn to mind being either wet or dry; a soldier ought to be above such delicate effeminacy: it is not, therefore, the sousing I regard, provided I can once be clear it was not done for a joke.'

Lionel, when he could speak, declared, that far from placing the pail there on purpose, he had not known there was such a closet in the house, nor had ever been up those stairs till they all mounted them together.

'I am perfectly satisfied, then, my good friend,' said the Ensign, shaking him by the hand with an heartiness that gave him no small share of the pail's contents; 'when a gentleman tells me a thing seriously, I make it a point to believe him; especially if he has a good honest countenance, that assures me he would not refuse me satisfaction, in the case he had meant to make game of me.'

'And do you always terminate your jests with the ceremony of a tilting match?' cried Sir Sedley.

'Yes, Sir! if I'm made a joke of by a man of any honour. For, to tell you a piece of my mind, there's no one thing upon earth I hate like a joke; unless it's against another person; and then it only gives me a little joy inwardly; for I make it a point of complaisance not to laugh out: except where I happen to wish for a little private conversation with the person that gives me the diversion.'

'Facetious in the extreme!' cried Sir Sedley, 'an infallibly excellent mode to make a man die of laughter? Droll to the utmost!'

'With regard to that, Sir, I have no objection to a little wit or humour, provided a person has the politeness to laugh only at himself, and his own particular friends and relations; but if once he takes the liberty to turn me into ridicule, I look upon it as an affront, and expect the proper reparation.'

'O, to refuse that would be without bowels to a degree!'

Lionel now ran up stairs, to beg the ladies would come and see the theatre; but suddenly exclaimed, as he looked around, 'Ah ha!' and hastily galloped down, and to the bottom of the house. Mrs. Arlbery descended with her young party, and the Ensign, in mock heroics, solemnly prostrated himself to Miss Dennel, pouring into her delighted ears, from various shreds and scraps of different tragedies, the most high flown and egregiously ill-adapted complements: while the Major, less absurdly, though scarce less passionately, made Camilla his Juliet, and whispered the tenderest lines of Romeo.

Lionel presently running, out of breath, up stairs again, cried: 'Mrs. Arlbery, I have drawn you in a new beau.'

'Have you?' cried she, coolly; 'why then I permit you to draw him out again. Had you told me he had forced himself in, you had made him welcome. But I foster only willing slaves. So off, if you please, with your boast and your beau.'

'I can't, upon my word, ma'am, for he is at my heels.'

Mandlebert, at the same moment, not hearing what passed, made his appearance.

The surprised and always unguarded Camilla, uttered an involuntary exclamation, which instantly catching his ear, drew his eye towards the exclaimer, and there fixed it; with an astonishment which suspended wholly his half made bow, and beginning address to Mrs. Arlbery.

Lionel had descried him upon the little hill before the house; where, as he was passing on, his own attention had been caught by the sound of horns and clarinets, just as, without any explanation, Lionel flew to tell him he was wanted, and almost forced him off his horse, and up the stairs.

Mrs. Arlbery, in common with those who dispense with all forms for themselves, exacted them punctiliously from all others. The visit therefore of Mandlebert not being designed for her, afforded her at first no gratification, and produced rather a contrary feeling, when she observed the total absence of all pleasure in the surprise with which he met Camilla at her house. She gave him a reception of cold civility, and then chatted almost wholly with the General, or Sir Sedley.

Edgar scarce saw whether he was received or not; his bow was mechanical, his apology for his intrusion was unintelligible. Amazement at seeing Camilla under this roof, disappointment at her breach of implied promise, and mortification at the air of being at home, which he thought he remarked in her situation, though at an acquaintance he had taken so much pains to keep aloof from her, all conspired to displease and perplex him; and though his eyes could with difficulty look any other way, he neither spoke to nor approached her.

Nor was even thus meeting her all he had to give him disturbance; the palpable devoirs of Major Cerwood incensed as well astonished him; for, under pretext of only following the humour of the day, in affecting to act the hero in love, the Major assailed her, without reserve, with declarations of his passion, which though his words passed off as quotations, his looks and manner made appropriate. How, already, thought Edgar, has he obtained such a privilege? such confidence? To have uttered one such sentence, my tongue would have trembled, my lips would have quivered!

Camilla felt confounded by his presence, from the consciousness of the ill opinion she must excite by this second apparent disregard of a given engagement. She would fain have explained to him it's history; but she could not free herself from the Major, whose theatrical effusions were not now to be repressed, since, at first, she had unthinkingly attended to them.

Lionel joined with Macdersey in directing similar heroics to Miss Dennel, who, simply enchanted, called out: 'I'm determined when I've a house of my own, I'll have just such a room as this at the top of it, on purpose to act a play every night.'

'And when, my dear,' said Mrs. Arlbery, 'do you expect to have a house of your own?'

'O, as soon as I am married, you know.'

'Is your marrying, then, already decided?'

'Dear no, not that I know of, aunt. I'm sure I never trouble myself about it; only I suppose it will happen some day or other.'

'And when it does, you are very sure your husband will approve your acting plays every night?'

'O, as to that, I shan't ask him. Whenever I'm married I'll be my own mistress, that I'm resolved upon. But papa's so monstrous cross, he says he won't let me act plays now.'

'Papas and mamas,' cried Sir Sedley, 'are ever most egregiously in the way. 'Tis prodigiously surprising they have never yet been banished society. I know no mark more irrefragable of the supineness of mankind.'

Then rising, and exclaiming: 'What savage heat! I wish the weather had a little feeling!' he broke up the party by ordering his curricle, and being the first to depart.

'That creature,' cried Mrs. Arlbery, 'if one had the least care for him, is exactly an animal to drive one mad! He labours harder to be affected than any ploughman does for his dinner. And, completely as his conceit obscures it, he has every endowment nature can bestow, except common sense!'

They now all descended to take leave, except the Ensign and Lionel, who went, arm in arm, prowling about, to view all the garrets, followed on tip-toe by Miss Dennel. Lavinia called vainly after her brother; but Camilla, hoping every instant she might clear her conduct to Edgar, was not sorry to be detained.

They had not, however, been five minutes in the parlour, before a violent and angry noise from above, induced them all to remount to the top of the house; and there, upon entering a garret whence it issued, they saw Miss Dennel, decorated with the Ensign's cocked hat and feather, yet looking pale with fright; Lionel accoutred in the maid's cloaths, and almost in a convulsion of laughter; and Macdersey, in a rage utterly incomprehensible, with the coachman's large bob-wig hanging loose upon his head.

It was sometime before it was possible to gather, that having all paraded into various garrets, in search of adventures, Lionel, after attiring himself in the maid's gown, cap, and apron, had suddenly deposited upon Miss Dennel's head the Ensign's cocked hat, replacing it with the coachman's best wig upon the toupee of Macdersey; whose resentment was so violent at this liberty, that it was still some minutes before he could give it articulation.

The effect of this full buckled bob-jerom which stuck hollow from the young face and powdered locks of the Ensign, was irresistibly ludicrous; yet he would have deemed it a greater indignity to take it quietly off, than to be viewed in it by thousands; though when he saw the disposition of the whole company to sympathise with Lionel, his wrath rose yet higher, and stamping with passion, he fiercely said to him—'Take it off, sir!—take it off my head!'

Lionel, holding this too imperious a command to be obeyed, only shouted louder. Macdersey then, incensed beyond endurance, lowered his voice with stifled choler, and putting his arms a-kimbo, said—'If you take me for a fool, sir, I shall demand satisfaction; for it's what I never put up with!'

Then, turning to the rest, he solemnly added—'I beg pardon of all the worthy company for speaking this little whisper, which certainly I should scorn to do before ladies, if it had not been a secret.'

Mrs. Arlbery, alarmed at the serious consequences now threatening this folly, said—'No, no; I allow of no secrets in my house, but what are entrusted to myself. I insist, therefore, upon being umpire in this cause.'

'Madam,' said Macdersey, 'I hope never to become such a debased brute of the creation, as to contradict the commands of a fair lady: except when it's upon a point of honour. But I can't consent to pass for a fool; and still more not for a poltroon—You'll excuse the little hint.'

Then, while making a profound and ceremonious bow, his wig fell over his head on the ground.

'This is very unlucky,' cried he, with a look of vexation; 'for certainly, and to be sure no human mortal should have made me take it off myself, before I was righted.'

Camilla, picking it up, to render the affair merely burlesque, pulled off the maid's cap from her brother's head, and put on the wig in its place, saying—'There, Lionel, you have played the part of Lady Wrong Head long enough; be so good now as to perform that of Sir Francis.'

This ended the business, and the whole party, in curricles, on horseback, or on foot, departed from the Grove.

BOOK IV

CHAPTER I

A Few Explanations

The last words of Dr. Marchmont, in taking leave of Edgar, were injunctions to circumspection, and representations of the difficulty of drawing back with honour, if once any incautious eagerness betrayed his partiality. To this counsel he was impelled to submit, lest he should risk for Camilla a report similar to that which for Indiana had given him so much disturbance. There, indeed, he felt himself wholly blameless. His admiration was but such as he always experienced at sight of a beautiful picture, nor had it ever been demonstrated in any more serious manner. He had distinguished her by no particular attention, singled her out by no pointed address, taken no pains to engage her good opinion, and manifested no flattering pleasure at her approach or presence.

His sense of right was too just to mislead him into giving himself similar absolution with respect to Camilla. He had never, indeed, indulged a voluntary vent to his preference; but the candour of his character convinced him that what so forcibly he had felt, he must occasionally have betrayed. Yet the idea excited regret without remorse; for though it had been his wish, as well as intention, to conceal his best hopes, till they were ratified by his judgment, he had the conscious integrity of knowing that, should her heart become his prize, his dearest view in life would be to solicit her hand.

To preserve, therefore, the appearance of an undesigning friend of the house, he had forced himself to refrain, for two days, from any visit to the rectory, whither he was repairing, when thus, unlooked and unwished for, he surprized Camilla at the Grove.

Disappointed and disapproving feelings kept him, while there, aloof from her; by continual suggestions, that her character was of no stability, that Dr. Marchmont was right in his doubts, and Miss Margland herself not wrong in accusing her of caprice; and when he perceived, upon her preparing to walk home with her brother and sister, that Major Cerwood stept forward to attend her, he indignantly resolved to arrange without delay his continental excursion. But again, when, as she quitted the room, he saw her head half turned round, with an eye of enquiry if he followed, he determined frankly, and at once, in his capacity of a friend, to request some explanation of this meeting.

The assiduities of the Major made it difficult to speak to her; but the aid of her desire for a conversation, which was equally anxious, and less guarded than his own, anticipated his principal investigation, by urging her, voluntarily to seize an opportunity of relating to him the history of her first visit to Mrs. Arlbery; and of assuring him that the second was indispensably its consequence.

Softened by this apparent earnestness for his good opinion, all his interest and all his tenderness for her returned; and though much chagrined at the accident, or rather mischief, which had thus established the acquaintance, he had too little to say, whatever he had to feel, of positive weight against it, to propose its now being relinquished. He thanked her impressively for so ready an explanation; and then gently added; 'I know your predilection in favour of this lady, and I will say nothing to disturb it; but as she is yet new to you, and as all residence, all intercourse, from your own home or relations, is new to you also—tell me, candidly, sincerely tell me, can you condescend to suffer an old friend, though in the person of but a young man, to offer you, from time to time, a hint, a little counsel, a few brief words of occasional advice? and even, perhaps, now and then, to torment you into a little serious reflection?'

'If you,' cried she, gaily, 'will give me the reflection, I promise, to the best of my power, to give you in return, the seriousness; but I can by no means engage for both!'

'O, never, but from your own prudence,' he answered, gratefully, 'may your delightful vivacity know a curb! If now I seem myself to fear it, it is not from moroseness, it is not from insensibility to its charm—'

He was stopt here by Macdersey, who, suddenly overtaking him, entreated an immediate short conference upon a matter of moment.

Though cruelly vexed by the interruption, he could not refuse to turn back with him; and Camilla again was left wholly to the gallant Major; but her heart felt so light that she had thus cleared herself to Edgar, so gratified by his request to become himself her monitor, and so enchanted to find her acquaintance with Mrs. Arlbery no longer disputed, that she was too happy to admit any vexation;

and the Major had never thought her so charming, though of the Major she thought not one moment.

Macdersey, with a long, ceremonious, and not very clear apology, confessed he had called Mandlebert aside only to enquire into the certain truth, if it were not a positive secret, of his intended nuptials with the beautiful Miss Lynmere. Mandlebert, with surprize, but without any hesitation, declared himself wholly without any pretensions to that lady. Macdersey then embraced him, and they parted mutually satisfied.

It seemed now too late to Mandlebert to go to Etherington till the next day, whither, as soon as he had breakfasted, he then rode.

According to his general custom, he went immediately to the study, where he met with a calm, but kind reception from Mr. Tyrold; and after half an hour's conversation, upon Lisbon, Dr. Marchmont, and Mrs. Tyrold, he left him to seek his young friends.

In the parlour, he found Lavinia alone; but before he could enquire for her sister, who was accidentally up stairs, Lionel, just dismounted from his horse, appeared.

'O, ho, Edgar!' cried he, 'you are here, are you? this would make fine confusion, if that beauty of nature, Miss Margland, should happen to call. They've just sent for you to Beech Park. I don't know what's to be done to you; but if you have an inclination to save poor Camilla's eyes, or cap, at least, from that meek, tender creature, you'll set off for Cleves before they know you are in this house.'

Edgar amazed, desired an explanation; but he protested the wrath of Miss Margland had been so comical, and given him so much diversion, that he had not been able to get at any particulars; he only knew there was a great commotion, and that Edgar was declared in love with some of his sisters or cousins, and Miss Margland was in a rage that it was not with herself; and that, in short, because he only happened to drop a hint of the latter notion, that delectable paragon had given him so violent a blow with her fine eyes, that in order to vent an ungovernable fit of laughter, without the risk of having the house pulled about his ears, he had hastily mounted his horse, and galloped off.

The contempt of Edgar for Miss Margland would have made him disdain another question, if the name of Camilla had not been mingled in this relation; no question, however, could procure further information. Lionel, enchanted that he had tormented Miss Margland, understood nothing more of the matter, and could only repeat his own merry sayings, and their effect.

Lavinia expressed, most innocently, her curiosity to know what this meant; and was going for Camilla, to assist in some conjecture; but Edgar, who by this strange story had lost his composure, felt unequal to hearing it discussed in her presence, and, pleading sudden haste, rode away.

He did not, however, go to Cleves; he hardly knew if Lionel had not amused him with a feigned story; but he no sooner arrived at Beech Park, then he found a message from Sir Hugh, begging to see him with all speed.

The young Ensign was the cause of this present summons and disturbance. Elated by the declaration of Mandlebert, that the rumour of his contract was void of foundation, and buoyed up by Mrs. Arlbery, to whom he returned with the communication, he resolved to make his advances in form. He presented himself, therefore, at Cleves, where he asked an audience of Sir Hugh, and at once, with his accustomed vehemence, declared himself bound eternally, life and soul, to his fair niece,

Miss Lynmere; and desired that, in order to pay his addresses to her, he might be permitted to see her at odd times, when he was off duty.

Sir Hugh was scarce able to understand him, from his volubility, and the extravagance of his phrases and gestures; but he imputed them to his violent passion, and therefore answered him with great gentleness, assuring him he did not mean to doubt his being a proper alliance for his niece, though he had never heard of him before; but begging he would not be affronted if he could not accept him, not knowing yet quite clearly if she were not engaged to a young gentleman in the neighbourhood.

The Ensign now loudly proclaimed his own news: Mandlebert had protested himself free, and the whole county already rang with the mistake.

Sir Hugh, who always at a loss how to say no, thought this would have been a good answer, now sent for Miss Margland, and desired her to speak herself with the young gentleman.

Miss Margland, much gratified, asked Macdersey if she could look at his rent roll.

He had nothing of the kind at hand, he said, not being yet come to his estate, which was in Ireland, and was still the property of a first cousin, who was not yet dead.

Miss Margland, promising he should have an answer in a few days, then dismissed him; but more irritated than ever against Mandlebert, from the contrast of his power to make settlements, she burst forth into her old declarations of his ill usage of Miss Lynmere; attributing it wholly to the contrivances of Camilla, whom she had herself, she said, surprized wheedling Edgar into her snares, when she called last at Etherington; and who, she doubted not, they should soon hear was going to be married to him.

Sir Hugh always understood literally whatever was said; these assertions therefore of ill humour, merely made to vent black bile, affected him deeply for the honour and welfare of Camilla, and he hastily sent a messenger for Edgar, determining to beg, if that were the case, he would openly own the whole, and not leave all the blame to fall all upon his poor niece.

At this period, Lionel had called, and, by inflaming Miss Margland, had aggravated the general disturbance.

When Edgar arrived, Sir Hugh told him of the affair, assuring him he should never have taken amiss his preferring Camilla, which he thought but natural, if he had only done it from the first.

Edgar, though easily through all this he saw the malignant yet shallow offices of Miss Margland, found himself, with infinite vexation, compelled to declare off equally from both the charges; conscious, that till the very moment of his proposals, he must appear to have no preference nor designs. He spoke, therefore, with the utmost respect of the young ladies, but again said it was uncertain if he should not travel before he formed any establishment.

The business thus explicitly decided, nothing more could be done: but Miss Margland was somewhat appeased, when she heard that her pupil was not so disgracefully to be supplanted.

Indiana herself, to whom Edgar had never seemed agreeable, soon forgot she had ever thought of him; and elated by the acquisition of a new lover, doubted not, but, in a short time, the publication of her liberty would prove slavery to all mankind.

Early the next morning, the carriage of Sir Hugh arrived at the rectory for Camilla. She never refused an invitation from her uncle, but she felt so little equal to passing a whole day in the presence of Miss Margland, after the unaccountable, yet alarming relation she had gathered from Lionel, that she entreated him to accompany her, and to manage that she should return with him as soon as the horses were fed and rested.

Lionel, ever good humoured, and ready to oblige, willingly complied; but demanded that she should go with him, in their way back, to see a new house which he wanted to examine.

Sir Hugh received her with his usual affection, Indiana with indifference, and Miss Margland with a malicious smile: but Eugenia, soon taking her aside, disclosed to her that Edgar, the day before, had publicly and openly disclaimed any views upon Indiana, and had declared himself without any passion whatever, and free from all inclination or intention but to travel.

The blush of pleasure, with which Camilla heard the first sentence of this speech, became the tingle of shame at the second, and whitened into surprise and sorrow at the last.

Eugenia, though she saw some disturbance, understood not these changes. Early absorbed in the study of literature and languages, under the direction of a preceptor who had never mingled with the world, her capacity had been occupied in constant work for her memory; but her judgment and penetration had been wholly unexercised. Like her uncle, she concluded every body, and every thing to be precisely what they appeared; and though, in that given point of view, she had keener intellects to discern, and more skill to appreciate persons and characters, she was as unpractised as himself in those discriminative powers, which dive into their own conceptions to discover the latent springs, the multifarious and contradictory sources of human actions and propensities.

Upon their return to the company, Miss Margland chose to relate the history herself. Mr. Mandlebert, she said, had not only thought proper to acknowledge his utter insensibility to Miss Lynmere, but had declared his indifference for every woman under the sun, and protested he held them all cheap alike. 'So I would advise nobody,' she continued, 'to flatter themselves with making a conquest of him, for they may take my word for it, he won't be caught very easily.'

Camilla disdained to understand this but in a general sense, and made no answer. Indiana, pouting her lip, said she was sure she did not want to catch him: she did not fear having offers enough without him, if she should happen to chuse to marry.

'Certainly,' said Miss Margland, 'there's no doubt of that; and this young officer's coming the very moment he heard of your being at liberty, is a proof that the only reason of your having had no more proposals, is owing to Mr. Mandlebert. So I don't speak for you, but for any body else, that may suppose they may please the difficult gentleman better.'

Camilla now breathed hard with resentment; but still was silent, and Indiana, answering only for herself, said: 'O, yes! I can't say I'm much frightened. I dare say if Mr. Melmond had known, ... but he thought like everybody else ... however, I'm sure, I'm very glad of it, only I wish he had spoke a little sooner, for I suppose Mr. Melmond thinks me as much out of his reach as if I was married. Not that I care about it; only it's provoking.'

'No, my dear,' said Miss Margland, 'it would be quite below your dignity to think about him, without knowing better who he is, or what are his expectations and connexions. As to this young officer, I shall take proper care to make enquiries, before he has his answer. He belongs to a very good family; for he's related to Lord O'Lerney, and I have friends in Ireland who can acquaint me with his situation and fortune. There's time enough to look about you; only as Mr. Mandlebert has behaved so unhandsomely, I hope none of the family will give him their countenance. I am sure it will be to no purpose, if any body should think of doing it by way of having any design upon him. It will be lost labour, I can tell them.'

'As to that, I am quite easy,' said Indiana, tossing her head, 'any body is welcome to him for me;—my cousin, or any body else.'

Camilla, now, absolutely called upon to speak, with all the spirit she could assume, said, 'With regard to me, there is no occasion to remind me how much I am out of the question; yet suffer me to say, respect for myself would secure me from forming such plans as you surmise, if no other sense of propriety could save me from such humiliation.'

'Now, my dear, you speak properly,' said Miss Margland, taking her hand; 'and I hope you will have the spirit to shew him you care no more for him than he cares for you.'

'I hope so too,' answered Camilla, turning pale; 'but I don't suppose—I can't imagine—that it is very likely he should have mentioned anything good or bad—with regard to his care for me?'

This was painfully uttered, but from a curiosity irrepressible.

'As to that, my dear, don't deceive yourself; for the question was put home to him very properly, that you might know what you had to expect, and not keep off other engagements from a false notion.'

'This indeed,' said Camilla, colouring with indignation, 'this has been a most useless, a most causeless enquiry!'

'I am very glad you treat the matter as it deserves, for I like to see young ladies behave with dignity.'

'And pray, then, what—was there any—did he make—was there any—any answer—to this—to—.'

'O, yes, he answered without any great ceremony, I can assure you! He said, in so many words, that he thought no more of you than of our cousin, and was going abroad to divert and amuse himself, better than by entering into marriage, with either one or other of you; or with any body else.'

Camilla felt half killed by this answer; and presently quitting the room, ran out into the garden, and to a walk far from the house, before she had power to breathe, or recollection to be aware of the sensibility she was betraying.

She then as hastily went back, secretly resolving never more to think of him, and to shew both to himself and to the world, by every means in her power, her perfect indifference.

She could not, however, endure to encounter Miss Margland again, but called for Lionel, and begged him to hurry the coachman.

Lionel complied—she took a hasty leave of her uncle, and only saying, 'Good by, good by!' to the rest, made her escape.

Sir Hugh, ever unsuspicious, thought her merely afraid to detain her brother; but Eugenia, calm, affectionate, and divested of cares for herself, saw evidently that something was wrong, though she divined not what, and entreated leave to go with her sister to Etherington, and thence return, without keeping out the horses.

Sir Hugh was well pleased, and the two sisters and Lionel set off together.

CHAPTER II

Specimens of Taste

The presence of Lionel stifled the enquiries of Eugenia; and pride, all up in arms, absorbed every softer feeling in Camilla.

When they had driven half a mile, 'Now, young ladies,' said he, 'I shall treat you with a frolic.' He then stopt the carriage, and told the coachman to drive to Cornfield; saying, 'Tis but two miles about, and Coachy won't mind that; will you Coachy?'

The coachman, looking forward to half a crown, said his horses would be all the better for a little more exercise; and Jacob, familiarly fond of Lionel from a boy, made no difficulty.

Lionel desired his sisters to ask no questions, assuring them he had great designs, and a most agreeable surprise in view for them.

In pursuance of his directions, they drove on till they came before a small house, just new fronted with deep red bricks, containing, on the ground floor, two little bow windows, in a sharp triangular form, enclosing a door ornamented with small panes of glass, cut in various shapes; on the first story, a little balcony, decorated in the middle and at each corner with leaden images of Cupids; and, in the attic story, a very small venetian window, partly formed with minute panes of glass, and partly with glazed tiles; representing, in blue and white, various devices of dogs and cats, mice and birds, rats and ferrets, as emblems of the conjugal state.

'Well, young ladies, what say you to this?' cried he, 'does it hit your fancy? If it does, 'tis your own!'

Eugenia asked what he meant.

'Mean? to make a present of it to which ever is the best girl, and can first cry bo! to a goose. Come, don't look disdainfully. Eugenia, what say you? won't it be better to be mistress of this little neat, tight, snug box, and a pretty little tidy husband, that belongs to it, than to pore all day long over a Latin theme with old Dr. Orkborne? I have often thought my poor uncle was certainly out of his wits, when he set us all, men, women, and children, to learn Latin, or else be whipt by the old doctor. But we all soon got our necks out of the collar, except poor Eugenia, and she's had to work for us all. However, here's an opportunity—see but what a pretty place—not quite finished, to be sure, but look at that lake? how cool, how rural, how refreshing!'

'Lake?' repeated Eugenia, 'I see nothing but a very dirty little pond, with a mass of rubbish in the middle. Indeed I see nothing else but rubbish all round, and every where.'

'That's the very beauty of the thing, my dear; it's all in the exact state for being finished under your own eye, and according to your own taste.'

'To whom does it belong?'

'It's uninhabited yet; but it's preparing for a very spruce young spark, that I advise you both to set your caps at. Hold! I see somebody peeping; I'll go and get some news for you.'

He then jumped from the coach, and ran up five deep narrow steps, formed of single large rough stones, which mounted so much above the threshold of the house, that upon opening the door, there appeared a stool to assist all comers to reach the floor of the passage.

Eugenia, with some curiosity, looked out, and saw her brother, after nearly forcing his entrance, speak to a very mean little man, dressed in old dirty cloaths, who seemed willing to hide himself behind the door, but whom he almost dragged forward, saying aloud, 'O, I can take no excuse, I insist upon your shewing the house. I have brought two young ladies on purpose to see it; and who knows but one of them may take a fancy to it, and make you a happy man for life.'

'As to that, sir,' said the man, still endeavouring to retreat, 'I can't say as I've quite made my mind up yet as to the marriage ceremony. I've known partly enough of the state already; but if ever I marry again, which is a moot point, I sha'n't do it hand over head, like a boy, without knowing what I'm about. However, it's time enough o'conscience to think of that, when my house is done, and my workmen is off my hands.'

Camilla now, by the language and the voice, gathered that this was Mr. Dubster.

'Pho, pho,' answered Lionel, 'you must not be so hard-hearted when fair ladies are in the case. Besides, one of them is that pretty girl you flirted with at Northwick. She's a sister of mine, and I shall take it very ill if you don't hand her out of the coach, and do the honours of your place to her.'

Camilla, much provoked, earnestly called to her brother, but utterly in vain.

'Lauk-a-day! why it is not half finished,' said Mr. Dubster; 'nor a quarter neither: and as to that young lady, I can't say as it was much in my mind to be over civil to her any more, begging pardon, after her giving me the slip in that manner. I can't say as I think it was over and above handsome, letting me get my gloves. Not that I mind it in the least, as to that.'

'Pho, pho, man, you must never bear malice against a fair lady. Besides, she's come now on purpose to make her excuses.'

'O, that's another thing; if the young lady's sorry, I sha'n't think of holding out. Besides, I can't say but what I thought her agreeable enough, if it had not been for her behaving so comical just at the last. Not that I mean in the least to make any complaint, by way of getting of the young lady scolded.'

'You must make friends now, man, and think no more of it;' cried Lionel, who would have drawn him to the carriage; but he protested he was quite ashamed to be seen in such a dishabille, and should go first and dress himself. Lionel, on the contrary, declaring nothing so manly, nor so becoming, as a neglect of outward appearance, pulled him to the coach door, notwithstanding all his efforts to disengage himself, and the most bashful distortions with which he strove to sneak behind his conductor.

'Ladies,' said he, 'Mr. Dubster desires to have the honour of walking over his house and grounds with you.'

Camilla declared she had no time to alight; but Lionel insisted, and soon forced them both from the coach.

Mr. Dubster, no longer stiff, starched, and proud, as when full dressed, was sunk into the smallest insignificance; and when they were compelled to enter his grounds, through a small Chinese gate, painted of a deep blue, would entirely have kept out of sight; but for a whisper from Lionel, that the ladies had owned they thought he looked to particular advantage in that careless attire.

Encouraged by this, he came boldly forward, and suddenly facing them, made a low bow saying: 'Young ladies, your humble.'

They courtsied slightly, and Camilla said she was very sorry to break in upon him.

'O, it don't much matter,' cried he, extremely pleased by this civility, 'I only hope, young ladies, you won't take umbrage at my receiving you in this pickle; but you've popt upon me unawares, as one may say. And my best coat is at this very minute at Tom Hicks's, nicely packed and papered up, and tied all round, in a drawer of his, up stairs, in his room. And I'd have gone for it with the greatest pleasure in life, to shew my respect, if the young gentleman would have let me.'

And then, recollecting Eugenia, 'Good lauk, ma'am,' said he, in a low voice to Camilla, 'that's that same lame little lady as I saw at the ball?'

'That lady, sir,' answered she, provoked, 'is my sister.'

'Mercy's me!' exclaimed he, lifting up his hands, 'I wish I'd known as much at the time. I'm sure, ma'am, if I'd thought the young lady was any ways related to you, I would not have said a word disrespectful upon no account.'

Lionel asked how long he had had this place.

'Only a little while. I happened of it quite lucky. A friend of mine was just being turned out of it, in default of payment, and so I got it a bargain. I intend to fit it up a little in taste, and then, whether I like it or no, I can always let it.'

They were now, by Lionel, dragged into the house, which was yet unfurnished, half papered, and half white washed. The workmen, Mr. Dubster said, were just gone to dinner, and he rejoiced that they had happened to come so conveniently, when he should be no loser by leaving the men to themselves, in order to oblige the young ladies with his company.

He insisted upon shewing them not only every room, but every closet, every cupboard, every nook, corner, and hiding place; praising their utility, and enumerating all their possible appropriations, with the most minute encomiums.

'But I'm quite sorry,' cried he, 'young ladies, to think as I've nothing to offer you. I eats my dinner always at the Globe, having nobody here to cook. However I'd have had a morsel of cake or so, if the young gentleman had been so kind as to give me an item beforehand of your intending me the favour. But as to getting things into the house hap hazard, really everything is so dear—it's quite out of reason.'

The scampering of horses now carrying them to a window, they saw some hounds in full cry, followed by horse-men in full gallop. Lionel declared he would borrow Jacob's mare, and join them, while his sisters walked about the grounds: but Camilla, taking him aside, made a serious expostulation, protesting that her father, with all his indulgence, and even her uncle himself, would be certainly displeased, if he left them alone with this man; of whom they knew nothing but his very low trade.

'Why what is his trade?'

'A tinker's: Mrs. Arlbery told me so.'

He laughed violently at this information, protesting he was rejoiced to find so much money could be made by the tinkering business, which he was determined to follow in his next distress for cash: yet added, he feared this was only the malice of Mrs. Arlbery, for Dubster, he had been told, had kept a shop for ready made wigs.

He gave up, however, his project, forgetting the chace when he no longer heard the hounds, and desired Mr. Dubster to proceed in shewing his lions?

'Lauk a day! sir, I've got no lions, nor tygers neither. It's a deal of expence keeping them animals; and though I know they reckon me near, I sha'n't do no such thing; for if a man does not take a little care of his money when once he has got it, especially if it's honestly, I think he's a fool for his pains; begging pardon for speaking my mind so freely.'

He then led them again to the front of the house, where he desired they would look at his pond. 'This,' said he, 'is what I value the most of all, except my summer house and my labyrinth. I shall stock it well; and many a good dinner I hope to eat from it. It gets me an appetite, sometimes, I think, only to look at it.'

''Tis a beautiful piece of water,' said Lionel, 'and may be useful to the outside as well as the inside, for, if you go in head foremost, you may bathe as well as feed from it.'

'No, I sha'n't do that, sir, I'm not over and above fond of water at best. However, I shall have a swan.'

'A swan? why sure you won't be contented with only one?'

'O yes, I shall. It will only be made of wood, painted over in white. There's no end of feeding them things if one has 'em alive. Besides it will look just as pretty; and won't bite. And I know a friend of mine that one of them creatures flew at, and gave him such a bang as almost broke his leg, only for throwing a stone at it, out of mere play. They are mortal spiteful, if you happen to hurt them when you're in their reach.'

He then begged them to go over to his island, which proved to be what Eugenia had taken for a mass of rubbish. They would fain have been excused crossing a plank which he called a bridge, but Lionel would not be denied.

'Now here,' said he, 'when my island's finished, I shall have something these young ladies will like; and that's a lamb.'

'Alive, or dead?' cried Lionel.

'Alive,' he replied, 'for I shall have good pasture in a little bit of ground just by, where I shall keep me a cow; and here will be grass enough upon my island to keep it from starving on Sundays, and for now and then, when I've somebody come to see me. And when it's fit for killing, I can change it with the farmer down the lane, for another young one, by a bargain I've agreed with him for already; for I don't love to run no risks about a thing for mere pleasure.'

'Your place will be quite a paradise,' said Lionel.

'Why, indeed, sir, I think I've earned having a little recreeting, for I worked hard enough for it, before I happened of meeting with my first wife.'

'O, ho! so you began with marrying a fortune?'

'Yes, sir, and very pretty she was too, if she had not been so puny. But she was always ailing. She cost me a mort of money to the potecary before she went off. And she was a tedious while a dying, poor soul!'

'Your first wife? surely you have not been twice married already?'

'Yes, I have. My second wife brought me a very pretty fortune too. I can't say but I've rather had the luck of it, as far as I've gone yet awhile.'

They now repassed the plank, and were conducted to an angle, in which a bench was placed close to the chinese rails, which was somewhat shaded by a willow, that grew in a little piece of stagnant water on the other side. A syringa was planted in front, and a broom-tree on the right united it with the willow; in the middle there was a deal table.

'Now, young ladies,' said Mr. Dubster, 'if you have a taste to breathe a little fresh country air, here's where I advise you to take your rest. When I come to this place first, my arbour, as I call this, had no look out, but just to the fields, so I cut away them lilacs, and now there's a good pretty look out. And it's a thing not to be believed what a sight of people and coaches, and gentlemen's whiskeys and stages, and flys, and wagons, and all sorts of things as ever you can think of, goes by all day long. I often think people's got but little to do at home.'

Next, he desired to lead them to his grotto, which he said was but just begun. It was, indeed, as yet, nothing but a little square hole, dug into a chalky soil, down into which, no steps being yet made, he slid as well as he could, to the no small whitening of his old brown coat, which already was thread bare.

He begged the ladies to follow, that he might shew them the devices he had marked out with his own hand, and from his own head, for fitting up the inside. Lionel would not suffer his sisters to refuse compliance, though Mr. Dubster himself cautioned them to come carefully, 'in particular,' he said, 'the little lady, as she has happened of an ugly accident already, as I judge, in one of her hips, and 'twould be pity, at her time of life, if she should happen of another at t'other side.'

Eugenia, not aware this misfortune was so glaring, felt much hurt by this speech; and Camilla, very angry with its speaker, sought to silence him by a resentful look; but not observing it; 'Pray, ma'am,' he continued, 'was it a fall? or was you born so?'

Eugenia looked struck and surprized; and Camilla hastily whispered it was a fall, and bid him say no more about it; but, not understanding her, 'I take it, then,' he said, 'that was what stinted your growth so, Miss? for, I take it, you're not much above the dwarf as they shew at Exeter Change? Much of a muchness, I guess. Did you ever see him, ma'am?'

'No, sir.'

'It would be a good sight enough to see you together. He'd think himself a man in a minute. You must have had the small pox mortal bad, ma'am. I suppose you'd the conflint sort?'

Camilla here, without waiting for help, slid down into the intended grotto, and asked a thousand questions to change the subject; while Eugenia, much disconcerted, slowly followed, aided by Lionel.

Mr. Dubster then displayed the ingenious intermixture of circles and diamonds projected for the embellishment of his grotto; the first of which were to be formed with cockle-shells, which he meant to colour with blue paint; and the second he proposed shaping with bits of shining black coal. The spaces between would each have an oyster-shell in the middle, and here and there he designed to leave the chalk to itself, which would always, he observed, make the grotto light and cheery. Shells he said, unluckily, he did not happen to have; but as he had thoughts of taking a little pleasure some summer at Brighthelmstone or Margate, for he intended to see all those places, he should make a collection then; being told he might have as curious shells, and pebbles too, as a man could wish to look at, only for the trouble of picking them up off the shore.

They next went to what he called his labyrinth, which was a little walk he was cutting, zig-zag, through some brushwood, so low that no person above three foot height could be hid by it. Every step they took here, cost a rent to some lace or some muslin of one of the sisters; which Mr. Dubster observed with a delight he could not conceal; saying this was a true country walk, and would do them both a great deal of good; and adding: 'we that live in town, would give our ears for such a thing as this.' And though they could never proceed a yard at a time, from the continual necessity of disentangling their dress from thorns and briars, he exultingly boasted that he should give them a good appetite for their dinner; and asked if this rural ramble did not make them begin to feel hungry. 'For my part,' continued he, 'if once I get settled a bit, I shall take a turn in this zig-zag every day before dinner, which may save me my five grains of rhubarb, that the doctor ordered me for my stomach, since my having my illness, which come upon me almost as soon as I was a gentleman; from change of life, I believe, for I never knew no other reason; and none of the doctors could tell me nothing about it. But a man that's had a deal to do, feels quite unked at first, when he's only got to look and stare about him, and just walk from one room to another, without no employment.'

Lionel said he hoped, at least, he would not require his rhubarb to get down his dinner to day.

'I hope so too, 'squire,' answered he, licking his lips, 'for I've ordered a pretty good one, I can tell you; beef steaks and onions; and I don't know what's better. Tom Hicks is to dine with me at the Globe, as soon as I've give my workmen their tasks, and seen after a young lad that's to do me a job there, by my grotto. Tom Hicks is a very good fellow; I like him best of any acquaintance I've made in these here parts. Indeed, I've made no other, on account of the unconvenience of dressing, while I'm so much about with my workmen. So I keep pretty incog from the genteel; and Tom does well enough in the interim.'

He then requested them to make haste to his summer-house, because his workmen would be soon returned, and he could not then spare a moment longer, without spoiling his own dinner.

'My summer-house,' said he, 'is not above half complete yet; but it will be very pretty when it's done. Only I've got no stairs yet to it; but there's a very good ladder, if the ladies a'n't afraid.'

The ladies both desired to be excused mounting; but Lionel protested he would not have his friend affronted; and as neither of them were in the habit of resisting him, nor of investigating with seriousness any thing that he proposed, they were soon teized into acquiescence, and he assisted them to ascend.

Mr. Dubster followed.

The summer-house was, as yet, no more than a shell; without windows, scarcely roofed, and composed of lath and plaister, not half dry. It looked on to the high road, and Mr. Dubster assured them, that, on market days, the people passed so thick, there was no seeing them for the dust.

Here they had soon cause to repent their facility,—that dangerous, yet venial, because natural fault of youth;—for hardly had they entered this place, ere a distant glimpse of a fleet stag, and a party of sportsmen, incited Lionel to scamper down; and calling out: 'I shall be back presently,' he made off towards the house, dragging the ladder after him.

The sisters eagerly and almost angrily remonstrated; but to no purpose; and while they were still entreating him to return and supposing him, though out of sight, within hearing, they suddenly perceived him passing the window by the high road, on horse-back, switch in hand, and looking in the utmost glee. 'I have borrowed Jacob's mare,' he cried, 'for just half an hour's sport, and sent Jacob and Coachy to get a little refreshment at the next public house; but don't be impatient; I shan't be long.'

Off then, he galloped, laughing; in defiance of the serious entreaties of his sisters, and without staying to hear even one sentence of the formal exhortations of Mr. Dubster.

CHAPTER III

A Few Compliments

The two young ladies and Mr. Dubster, left thus together, and so situated that separation without assistance was impossible, looked at one another for some time in nearly equal dismay; and then Mr. Dubster, with much displeasure, exclaimed—'Them young gentlemen are as full of mischief, as an egg's full of meat! Who'd have thought of a person's going to do such a thing as this?—it's mortal convenient, making me leave my workmen at this rate; for I dare say they're come, or coming, by this time. I wish I'd tied the ladder to this here rafter.'

The sisters, though equally provoked, thought it necessary to make some apology for the wild behaviour of their brother.

'O, young ladies,' said he, formally waving his hand by way of a bow, 'I don't in the least mean to blame you about it, for you're very welcome to stay as long as it's agreeable; only I hope he'll come back by my dinner time; for a cold beef-steak is one or other the worst morsel I know.'

He then kept an unremitting watch from one window to another, for some passenger from whom he could claim aid; but, much as he had boasted of the numbers perpetually in sight, he now dolorously confessed, that, sometimes, not a soul came near the place for half a day together: 'And, as to my workmen,' continued he, 'the deuce can't make 'em hear if once they begin their knocking and hammering.'

And then, with a smirk at the idea, he added—'I'll tell you what; I'd best give a good squall at once, and then if they are come, I may catch 'em; in the proviso you won't mind it, young ladies.'

This scheme was put immediately into practice; but though the sisters were obliged to stop their ears from his vociferation, it answered no purpose.

'Well, I'll bet you what you will,' cried he, 'they are all deaf: however, it's as well as it is, for if they was to come, and see me hoisted up in this cage, like, they'd only make a joke of it; and then they'd mind me no more than a pin never again. It's surprising how them young gentlemen never think of nothing. If he'd served me so when I was a 'prentice, he'd have paid pretty dear for his frolic; master would have charged him half a day's work, as sure as a gun.'

Soon after, while looking out of the window, 'I do think,' he exclaimed, 'I see somebody!—It shall go hard but what I'll make 'em come to us.'

He then shouted with great violence; but the person crossed a stile into a field, without seeing or hearing him.

This provoked him very seriously; and turning to Camilla, rather indignantly, he said—'Really, ma'am, I wish you'd tell your brother, I should take it as a favour he'd never serve me o' this manner no more!'

She hoped, she said, he would in future be more considerate.

'It's a great hindrance to business, ma'am, such things; and it's a sheer love of mischief, too, begging pardon, for it's of no manner of use to him, no more than it is to us.'

He then desired, that if any body should pass by again, they might all squall out at once; saying, it was odds, then, but they might be heard.

'Not that it's over agreeable, at the best,' added he; 'for if one was to stop any poor person, and make 'em come round, and look for the ladder, one could not be off giving them something: and as to any of the gentlefolks, one might beg and pray as long as one would before they'd stir a step for one: and as to any of one's acquaintance, if they was to go by, it's ten to one but they'd only fall a laughing. People's generally ill-natured when they sees one in jeopardy.'

Eugenia, already thoughtful and discomposed, now grew uneasy, lest her uncle should be surprised at her long absence; this a little appeased Mr. Dubster, who, with less resentment, said—'So I see, then, we're all in the same quandary! However, don't mind it, young ladies; you can have no great matters to do with your time, I take it; so it does not so much signify. But a man's quite different. He looks like a fool, as one may say, poked up in such a place as this, to be stared at by all comers and goers; only nobody happens to pass by.'

His lamentations now were happily interrupted by the appearance of three women and a boy, who, with baskets on their heads, were returning from the next market town. With infinite satisfaction, he prepared to assail them, saying, he should now have some chance to get a bit of dinner: and assuring the ladies, that if they should like a little scrap for a relish, he should be very willing to send 'em it by their footman; 'For it's a long while,' said he, 'young ladies, to be fasting, that's the truth of it.'

The market women now approached, and were most clamourously hailed, before their own loud discourse, and the singing and whistling of the boy, permitted their hearing the appeal.

'Pray, will you be so kind,' said Mr. Dubster, when he had made them stop, 'as to step round by the house, and see if you can see the workmen; and if you can, tell 'em a young gentleman, as come here while they was at dinner, has taken away the ladder, and left us stuck up here in the lurch.'

The women all laughed, and said it was a good merry trick; but were preparing to follow his directions, when Mr. Dubster called after the boy, who loitered behind, with an encouraging nod: 'If you'll bring the ladder with you upon your shoulders, my lad, I'll give you a half-penny!'

The boy was well contented; but the women, a little alarmed, turned back and said—'And what will you give to us, master?' 'Give?' repeated he, a little embarrassed; 'why, I'll give—why I'll thank you kindly; and it won't be much out of your way, for the house is only round there.'

'You'll thank us kindly, will you?' said one of the women; it's like you may! But what will you do over and above?'

'Do? why it's no great matter, just to stop at the house as you go by, and tell 'em—'

Here Eugenia whispered she would herself satisfy them, and begged he would let them make their own terms.

'No, Miss, no; I don't like to see nobody's money fooled away, no more than my own. However, as you are so generous, I'll agree with 'em to give 'em a pot of beer.'

He then, with some parade, made this concession; but said, he must see the ladder, before the money should be laid down.

'A pot of beer for four!—a pot of beer for four!' they all exclaimed in a breath; and down everyone put her basket, and set her arms a-kembo, unanimously declaring, they would shame him for such stinginess.

The most violent abuse now followed, the boy imitating them, and every other sentence concluding with—'A pot of beer for four!—ha!'

Camilla and Eugenia, both frightened, besought that they might have any thing, and every thing, that could appease them; but Mr. Dubster was inflexible not to submit to imposition, because of a few foul words; 'For, dear heart,' said he, 'what harm will they do us!—they an't of no consequence.'

Then, addressing them again, 'As to four,' he cried, 'that's one over the bargain, for I did not reckon the boy for nothing.'

'You didn't, didn't you?' cried the boy; 'i'cod, I hope I'm as good as you, any day in the year!'

'You'll thank us kindly, will you?' said one of the women; 'I'fackens, and so you shall, when we're fools enough to sarve you!—A pot of beer for four!'

'We help you down!—we get you a ladder!' cried another; 'yes, forsooth, it's like we may!—no, stay where you are like a toad in a hole as you be!'

Camilla and Eugenia now, tired of vain application to Mr. Dubster, who heard all this abuse with the most sedate unconcern, advanced themselves to the window; and Eugenia, ever foremost where money was to be given, began—'Good women—' when, with a violent loud shout, they called out—'What! are you all in Hob's pound? Well, they as will may let you out for we; so I wish you a merry time of it!'

Eugenia began again her—'Good women—' when the boy exclaimed—'What were you put up there for, Miss? to frighten the crows?'

Eugenia, not understanding him, was once more re-commencing; but the first woman said—'I suppose you think we'll sarve you for looking at?—no need to be paid?'

'Yes, yes,' cried the second, 'Miss may go to market with her beauty; she'll not want for nothing if she'll shew her pretty face!'

'She need not be afeard of it, however,' said the third, 'for 'twill never be no worse. Only take care, Miss, you don't catch the small pox!'

'O fegs, that would be pity!' cried the boy, 'for fear Miss should be marked.'

Eugenia, astonished and confounded, made no farther attempt; but Camilla, though at that moment she could have inflicted any punishment upon such unprovoked assailants, affected to give but little weight to what they said, and gently drew her away.

'Hoity, toity!' cried one of the women, as she moved off, 'why, Miss, do you walk upon your knees?'

'Why my Poll would make two of her,' said another, 'though she's only nine years old.'

'She won't take much for cloaths,' cried another, 'that's one good thing.'

'I'd answer to make her a gown out of my apron,' said the third.

'Your apron?' cried another, 'your pocket handkerchief you mean!—why she'd be lost in your apron, and you might look half an hour before you'd find her.'

Eugenia, to whom such language was utterly new, was now in such visible consternation, that Camilla, affrighted, earnestly charged Mr. Dubster to find any means, either of menace or of reward, to make them depart.

'Lauk, don't mind them, ma'am,' cried he, following Eugenia, 'they can't do you no hurt; though they are rather rude, I must needs confess the truth, to say such things to your face. But one must not expect people to be over polite, so far from London. However, I see the sporting gentry coming round, over that way, yonder; and I warrant they'll gallop 'em off. Hark'ee, Mistresses! them gentlemen that are coming here, shall take you before the justice, for affronting Sir Hugh's Tyrold's Heiresses to all his fortunes.

The women, to whom the name and generous deeds of Sir Hugh Tyrold were familiar, were now quieted and dismayed. They offered some aukward apologies, of not guessing such young ladies could be posted up in such a place; and hoped it would be no detriment to them at the ensuing Christmas, when the good Baronet gave away beef and beer; but Mr. Dubster pompously ordered them to make off, saying, he would not accept the ladder from them now, for the gentry that were coming would get it for nothing: 'So troop off,' cried he; 'and as for you,' to the boy, 'you shall have your jacket well trimmed, I promise you: I know who you are, well enough; and I'll tell your master of you, as sure as you're alive.'

Away then, with complete, though not well-principled repentance, they all marched.

Mr. Dubster, turning round with exultation, cried—'I only said that to frighten them, for I never see 'em before, as I know of. But I don't mind 'em of a rush; and I hope you don't neither. Though I can't pretend it's over agreeable being made fun of. If I see anybody snigger at me, I always ask 'em what it's for; for I'd as lieve they'd let it alone.'

Eugenia, who, as there was no seat, had sunk upon the floor for rest and for refuge, remained silent, and seemed almost petrified; while Camilla, affectionately leaning over her, began talking upon other subjects, in hopes to dissipate a shock she was ashamed to console.

She made no reply, no comment; but, sighed deeply.

'Lauk!' cried Mr. Dubster, 'what's the matter with the young lady! I hope she don't go for to take to heart what them old women says? she'll be never the worse to look at, because of their impudence. Besides, fretting does no good to nothing. If you'll only come and stand here, where I do, Miss, you may have a peep at ever so many dogs, and all the gentlemen, riding helter skelter round that hill. It's a pretty sight enough for them as has nothing better to mind. I don't know but I might make one among them myself, now and then, if it was not for the expensiveness of hiring of a horse.'

Here some of the party came galloping towards them; and Mr. Dubster made so loud an outcry, that two or three of the sportsmen looked up, and one of them, riding close to the summer-house, perceived the two young ladies, and, instantly dismounting, fastened his horse to a tree, and contrived to scramble up into the little unfinished building.

Camilla then saw it was Major Cerwood. She explained to him the mischievous frolick of her brother, and accepted his offered services to find the ladder and the carriage.

Eugenia meanwhile rose and courtsied in answer to his enquiries after her health, and then, gravely fixing her eyes upon the ground, took no further notice of him.

The object of the Major was not Eugenia; her taciturnity therefore did not affect him; but pleased to be shut up with Camilla, he soon found out that though to mount had been easy, to descend would be difficult; and, after various mock efforts, pronounced it would be necessary to wait till some assistance arrived from below: adding, young Mr. Tyrold would soon return, as he had seen him in the hunt.

Camilla, whose concern now was all for her sister, heard this with indifference; but Mr. Dubster lost all patience. 'So here,' said he, 'I may stay, and let Tom Hicks eat up all my dinner! for I can't expect him to fast, because of this young gentleman's comical tricks. I've half a mind to give a jump down myself, and go look for the ladder; only I'm not over light. Besides, if one should break one's leg, it's but a hard thing upon a man to be a cripple in the middle of life. It's no such great hindrance to a lady, so I don't say it out of disrespect; because ladies can't do much at the best.'

The Major, finding Dubster was his host, thought it necessary to take some notice of him, and ask him if he never rode out.

'Why no, not much of that, Sir,' he answered; 'for when a man's not over used to riding, one's apt to get a bad tumble sometimes. I believe it's as well let alone. I never see as there was much wit in breaking one's neck before one's time. Besides, half them gentlemen are no better than sharpers, begging pardon, for all they look as if they could knock one down.'

'How do you mean sharpers, Sir?'

'Why they don't pay everyone his own, not one in ten of them. And they're as proud as Lucifer. If I was to go among them to-morrow, I'll lay a wager they'd take no notice of me: unless I was to ask them to dinner. And a man may soon eat up his substance, if he's so over complaisant.'

'Surely, Major,' cried Camilla, 'my brother cannot be much longer before he joins us?—remembers us rather.'

'Who else could desert or forget you?' cried the Major.

'It's a moot point whether he'll come or no, I see that,' said Mr. Dubster, quite enraged; 'them young 'squires never know what to do for their fun. I must needs say I think it's pity but what he'd been brought up to some calling. 'Twould have steadied him a little, I warrant. He don't seem to know much of the troubles of life.'

A shower of rain now revived his hopes that the fear of being wet might bring him back; not considering how little sportsmen regard wet jackets.

'However,' continued he, 'it's really a piece of good luck that he was not taken with a fancy to leave us upon my island; and then we might all have been soused by this here rain: and he could just as well have walked off with my bridge as with the ladder.'

Here, to his inexpressible relief, Lionel, from the road, hailed them; and Camilla, with emotion the most violent, perceived Edgar was by his side.

Mr. Dubster, however, angry as well as glad, very solemnly said, 'I wonder, Sir, what you think my workmen has been doing all this time, with nobody to look after them? Besides that I promised a pot o'beer to a lad to wheel me away all that rubbish that I'd cut out of my grotto; and it's a good half day's work, do it who will; and ten to one if they've stirred a nail, all left to themselves so.'

'Pho, pho, man, you've been too happy, I hope, to trouble your mind about business. How do do my little girls? how you have been entertained?'

'This is a better joke to you than to us 'squire; but pray, Sir, begging pardon, how come you to forget what I told you about the Globe? I know very well that they say it's quite alley-mode to make fun, but I can't pretend as I'm over fond of the custom.'

He then desired that, at least, if he would not get the ladder himself, he would tell that other gentleman, that was with him, what he had done with it.

Edgar, having met Lionel, and heard from him how and where he had left his sisters, had impatiently ridden with him to their relief; but when he saw that the Major made one in the little party, and that he was standing by Camilla, he felt hurt and amazed, and proceeded no farther.

Camilla believed herself careless of his opinion; what she had heard from Miss Margland of his professed indifference, gave her now as much resentment, as at first it had caused her grief. She thought such a declaration an unprovoked indignity; she deigned not even to look at him, resolved for ever to avoid him; yet to prove herself, at the same time, unmortified and disengaged, talked cheerfully with the Major.

Lionel now, producing the ladder, ran up it to help his sisters to descend; and Edgar, dismounting, could not resist entering the grounds, to offer them his hand as they came down.

Eugenia was first assisted; for Camilla talked on with the Major, as if not hearing she was called: and Mr. Dubster, his complaisance wholly worn out, next followed, bowing low to everyone separately, and begging pardon, but saying he could really afford to waste no more time, without going to give a little look after his workmen, to see if they were alive or dead.

At this time the horse of the Major, by some accident, breaking loose, his master was forced to run down, and Lionel scampered after to assist him.

Camilla remained alone; Edgar, slowly mounting the ladder, gravely offered his services; but, hastily leaning out of the window, she pretended to be too much occupied in watching the motions of the Major and his horse, to hear or attend to any thing else.

A sigh now tore the heart of Edgar, from doubt if this were preference to the Major, or the first dawn of incipient coquetry; but he called not upon her again; he stood quietly behind, till the horse was seized, and the Major re-ascended the ladder. They then stood at each side of it, with offers of assistance.

This appeared to Camilla a fortunate moment for making a spirited display of her indifference: she gave her hand to the Major, and, slightly courtesying to Edgar as she passed, was conducted to the carriage of her uncle.

Lionel again was the only one who spoke in the short route to Etherington, whence Eugenia, without alighting, returned to Cleves.

CHAPTER IV

The Danger of Disguise

Edgar remained behind, almost petrified: he stood in the little building, looking after them, yet neither descending nor stirring, till one of the workmen advanced to fetch the ladder. He then hastily quitted the spot, mounted his horse, and galloped after the carriage; though without any actual design to follow it, or any formed purpose whither to go.

The sight, however, of the Major, pursuing the same route, made him, with deep disgust, turn about, and take the shortest road to Beech Park.

He hardly breathed the whole way from indignation; yet his wrath was without definition, and nearly beyond comprehensibility even to himself, till suddenly recurring to the lovely smile with which Camilla had accepted the assistance of Major Cerwood, he involuntarily clasped his hands and called out: 'O happy Major!'

Awakened by his ejaculation to the true state of his feelings, he started as from a sword held at his breast. 'Jealousy!' he cried, 'am I reduced to so humiliating a passion? Am I capable of love without trust? Unhappy enough to cherish it with hope? No! I will not be such a slave to the delusions of inclination. I will abandon neither my honour nor my judgment to my wishes. It is not alone even her heart that can fully satisfy me; its delicacy must be mine as well as its preference. Jealousy is a passion for which my mind is not framed, and which I must not find a torment, but an impossibility!'

He now began to fear he had made a choice the most injudicious, and that coquetry and caprice had only waited opportunity, to take place of candour and frankness.

Yet, recollecting the disclaiming speeches he had been compelled to make at Cleves, he thought, if she had heard them, she might be actuated by resentment. Even then, however, her manner of shewing it was alarming, and fraught with mischief. He reflected with fresh repugnance upon the gay and dissipated society with which she was newly mixing, and which, from her extreme openness and facility, might so easily, yet so fatally, sully the fair artlessness of her mind.

He then felt tempted to hint to Mr. Tyrold, who, viewing all things, and all people in the best light, rarely foresaw danger, and never suspected deception, the expediency of her breaking off this intercourse, till she could pursue it under the security of her mother's penetrating protection. But it occurred to him next, it was possible the Major might have pleased her. Ardent as were his own views, they had never been declared, while those of the Major seemed proclaimed without reserve. He felt his face tingle at the idea, though it nearly made his heart cease to beat; and determined to satisfy his conjecture ere he took any measure for himself.

To speak to her openly, he thought the surest as well as fairest way, and resolved, with whatever anguish, should he find the Major favoured, to aid her choice in his fraternal character, and then travel till he should forget her in every other.

For this purpose, it was necessary to make immediate enquiry into the situation of the Major, and then, if she would hear him, relate to her the result; well assured to gather the state of her heart upon this subject, by her manner of attending to the least word by which it should be introduced.

Camilla, meanwhile, was somewhat comforted by the exertion she had shewn, and by her hopes it had struck Edgar with respect.

The next morning, Sir Hugh sent for her again, and begged she would pass the whole day with her sister Eugenia, and use all her pretty ways to amuse her; for she had returned home, the preceding morning, quite moped with melancholy, and had continued pining ever since; refusing to leave her room, even for meals, yet giving no reason for her behaviour. What had come to her he could not tell; but to see her so, went to his heart; for she had always, he said, till now, been chearful and even tempered, though thinking over her learning made her not much of a young person.

Camilla flew up stairs, and found her, with a look of despondence, seated in a corner of her room, which she had darkened by nearly shutting all the shutters.

She knew but too well the rude shock she had received, and sought to revive her with every expression of soothing kindness. But she shook her head, and continued mute, melancholy, and wrapt in meditation.

More than an hour was spent thus, the strict orders of Sir Hugh forbidding them any intrusion: but when, at length, Camilla ventured to say, 'Is it possible, my dearest Eugenia, the passing insolence of two or three brutal wretches can affect you thus deeply?' She awakened from her silent trance, and raising her head, while something bordering upon resentment began to kindle in her breast, cried, 'Spare me this question, Camilla, and I will spare you all reproach.'

'What reproach, my dear sister,' cried Camilla, amazed, 'what reproach have I merited?'

'The reproach,' answered she, solemnly; 'that, from me, all my family merit! the reproach of representing to me, that thousands resembled me! of assuring me I had nothing peculiar to myself, though I was so unlike all my family—of deluding me into utter ignorance of my unhappy defects, and then casting me, all unconscious and unprepared, into the wide world to hear them!'

She would now have shut herself into her book-closet; but Camilla, forcing her way, and almost kneeling to be heard, conjured her to drive such cruel ideas from her mind, and to treat the barbarous insults that she had suffered with the contempt they deserved.

'Camilla,' said she, firmly; 'I am no longer to be deceived nor trifled with. I will no more expose to the light a form and face so hideous:—I will retire from all mankind, and end my destined course in a solitude that no one shall discover.'

Camilla, terrified, besought her to form no such plan, bewailed the unfortunate adventure of the preceding day, inveighed against the inhuman women, and pleaded the love of all her family with the most energetic affection.

'Those women,' said she, calmly, 'are not to blame; they have been untutored, but not false; and they have only uttered such truths as I ought to have learnt from my cradle. My own blindness has been infatuated; but it sprung from inattention and ignorance.—It is now removed!—Leave me, Camilla; give notice to my Uncle he must find me some retreat. Tell all that has passed to my father. I will myself write to my mother—and when my mind is more subdued, and when sincerely and unaffectedly I can forgive you all from my heart, I may consent to see you again.'

She then positively insisted upon being left.

Camilla, penetrated with her undeserved, yet irremediable distress, still continued at her door, supplicating for re-admittance in the softest terms; but without any success till the second dinner bell summoned her down stairs. She then fervently called upon her sister to speak once more, and tell her what she must do, and what say?

Eugenia steadily answered: 'You have already my commission: I have no change to make in it.'

Unable to obtain anything further, she painfully descended: but the voice of her Uncle no sooner reached her ears from the dining parlour, than, shocked to convey to him so terrible a message, she again ran up stairs, and casting herself against her sister's door, called out 'Eugenia, I dare not obey you! would you kill my poor Uncle? My Uncle, who loves us all so tenderly? Would you afflict—would you make him unhappy?'

'No, not for the universe!' she answered, opening the door; and then, more gently, yet not less steadfastly, looking at her, 'I know,' she continued, 'you are all very good; I know all was meant for the best; I know I must be a monster not to love you for the very error to which I am a victim.—I forgive you therefore all! and I blush to have felt angry.—But yet—at the age of fifteen—at the instant of entering into the world—at the approach of forming a connection which—O Camilla! what a time, what a period, to discover—to know—that I cannot even be seen without being derided and offended!'

Her voice here faltered, and, running to the window curtain, she entwined herself in its folds, and called out: 'O hide me! hide me! from every human eye, from every thing that lives and breathes! Pursue me, persecute me no longer, but suffer me to abide by myself, till my fortitude is better strengthened to meet my destiny!'

The least impatience from Eugenia was too rare to be opposed; and Camilla, who, in common with all her family, notwithstanding her extreme youth, respected as much as she loved her, sought only to appease her by promising compliance. She gave to her, therefore, an unresisted, though unreturned embrace, and went to the dining-parlour.

Sir Hugh was much disappointed to see her without her sister; but she evaded any account of her commission till the meal was over, and then begged to speak with him alone.

Gently and gradually she disclosed the source of the sadness of Eugenia: but Sir Hugh heard it with a dismay that almost overwhelmed him. All his contrition for the evils of which, unhappily, he had been the cause, returned with severest force, and far from opposing her scheme of retreat, he empowered Camilla to offer her any residence she chose; and to tell her he would keep out of her sight, as the cause of all her misfortunes; or give her the immediate possession and disposal of his whole estate, if that would make her better amends than to wait till his death.

This message was no sooner delivered to Eugenia, than losing at once every angry impression, she hastened down stairs, and casting herself at the knees of her Uncle, begged him to pardon her design, and promised never to leave him while she lived.

Sir Hugh, most affectionately embracing her, said—'You are too good, my dear, a great deal too good, to one who has used you so ill, at the very time when you were too young to help yourself. I have not a word to offer in my own behalf; except to hope you will forgive me, for the sake of its being all done out of pure ignorance.'

'Alas, my dearest Uncle! all I owe to your intentions, is the deepest gratitude; and it is your's from the bottom of my heart. Chance alone was my enemy; and all I have to regret is, that no one was sincere enough, kind enough, considerate enough, to instruct me of the extent of my misfortunes, and prepare me for the attacks to which I am liable.'

'My dear girl,' said he, while tears started into his eyes, 'what you say nobody can reply to; and I find I have been doing you one wrong after another, instead of the least good: for all this was by my own order; which it is but fair to your brothers and sisters, and father and mother, and the servants, to confess. God knows, I have faults enough of my own upon my head, without taking another of pretending to have none!'

Eugenia now sought to condole him in her turn, voluntarily promising to mix with the family as usual, and only desiring to be excused from going abroad, or seeing any strangers.

'My dear,' said he, 'you shall judge just what you think fit, which is the least thing I can do for you, after your being so kind as to forgive me; which I hope to do nothing in future not to deserve more; meaning always to ask my brother's advice; which might have saved me all my worst actions, if I had done it sooner: for I've used poor Camilla no better; except not giving her the small pox, and that bad fall. But don't hate me, my dears, if you can help it, for it was none of it done for want of love; only not knowing how to shew it in the proper manner; which I hope you'll excuse for the score of my bad education.'

'O, my Uncle!' cried Camilla, throwing her arms round his neck, while Eugenia embraced his knees, 'what language is this for nieces who owe so much to your goodness, and who, next to their parents, love you more than anything upon earth!'

'You are both the best little girls in the world, my dears, and I need have nothing upon my conscience if you two pass it over; which is a great relief to me; for there's nobody else I've used so bad as you two young girls; which, God knows, goes to my heart whenever I think of it.—Poor little innocents!—what had you ever done to provoke me?'

The two sisters, with the most virtuous emulation, vied with each other in demonstrative affection, till he was tolerably consoled.

The rest of the day was ruffled but for one moment; upon Sir Hugh's answering, to a proposition of Miss Margland for a party to the next Middleton races,—that there was no refusing to let Eugenia take that pleasure, after her behaving so nobly: her face was then again overcast with the deepest gloom; and she begged not to hear of the races, nor of any other place, public or private, for going abroad, as she meant during the rest of her life, immoveably to remain at home.

He looked much concerned, but assured her she should be mistress in every thing.

Camilla left them in the evening, with a promise to return the next day; and with every anxiety of her own, lost in pity for her innocent and unfortunate sister.

She was soon, however, called back to herself, when, with what light yet remained, she saw Edgar ride up to the coach door.

With indefatigable pains he had devoted the day to the search of information concerning the Major. Of Mrs. Arlbery he had learned, that he was a man of fashion, but small fortune; and from the Ensign he had gathered, that even that small fortune was gone, and that the estate in which it was vested, had been mortgaged for three thousand pounds, to pay certain debts of honour.

Edgar had already been to the Parsonage House, but hearing Camilla was at Cleves, had made a short visit, and determined to walk his horse upon the road till he met the carriage of Sir Hugh; believing he could have no better opportunity of seeing her alone.

Yet when the coach, upon his riding up to the door, stopt, he found himself in an embarrassment for which he was unprepared. He asked how she did; desired news of the health of all the family one by one; and then, struck by the coldness of her answers, suffered the carriage to drive on.

Confounded at so sudden a loss of all presence of mind, he continued, for a minute or two, just where she left him; and then galloped after the coach, and again presented himself at its window.

In a voice and manner the most hurried, he apologised for this second detention. 'But, I believe,' he said, 'some genius of officiousness has to-day taken possession of me, for I began it upon a Quixote sort of enterprise, and a spirit of knight-errantry seems willing to accompany me through it to the end.'

He stopt; but she did not speak. Her first sensation at his sight had been wholly indignant: but when she found he had something to say which he knew not how to pronounce, her curiosity was awakened, and she looked earnest for an explanation.

'I know,' he resumed, with considerable hesitation, 'that to give advice and to give pain is commonly the same thing:—I do not, therefore, mean—I have no intention—though so lately you allowed me a privilege never to be forgotten'—

He could not get on; and his embarrassment, and this recollection, soon robbed Camilla of every angry emotion. She looked down, but her countenance was full of sensibility, and Edgar, recovering his voice, proceeded—

'My Quixotism, I was going to say, of this morning, though for a person of whom I know almost nothing, would urge me to every possible effort—were I certain the result would give pleasure to the person for whom alone—since with regard to himself,—I—it is merely—'

Involved in expressions he knew not how to clear or to finish, he was again without breath: and Camilla, raising her eyes, looked at him with astonishment.

Endeavouring then to laugh, 'One would think,' cried he, 'this same Quixotism had taken possession of my intellects, and rendered them as confused as if, instead of an agent, I were a principal.'—

Still wholly in the dark as to his aim, yet, satisfied by these last words, it had no reference to himself, she now lost enough of the acuteness of her curiosity to dare avow what yet remained; and begged him, without further preface, to be more explicit.

Stammering, he then said, that the evident admiration with which a certain gentleman was seen to sigh in her train, had awakened for him an interest, which had induced some inquiries into the state of his prospects and expectations. 'These,' he continued, 'turn out to be, though not high, nor by any means adequate to—to—however they are such as some previous friendly exertions, with settled future oeconomy, might render more propitious: and for those previous exertions—Mr. Tyrold has a claim which it would be the pride and happiness of my life to see him honour;—if—if—'

The if almost dropt inarticulated: but he added—'I shall make some further enquiries before I venture to say any more.'

'For yourself, then, be they made, Sir!' cried she, suddenly seizing the whole of the meaning—'not for me?—whoever this person may be to whom you allude—to me he is utterly indifferent.'

A flash of involuntary delight beamed in the eyes of Edgar at these words: he had almost thanked her, he had almost dropt the reins of his horse to clasp his hands: but filled only with her own emotions, without watching his, or waiting for any answer, she coldly bid him good night, and called to the coachman to drive fast home.

Edgar, however, was left with a sunbeam of the most lively delight. 'He is wholly indifferent to her,' he cried, 'she is angry at my interference; she has but acted a part in the apparent preference—and for me, perhaps, acted it!'

Momentary, however, was the pleasure such a thought could afford him;—'O, Camilla,' he cried, 'if, indeed, I might hope from you any partiality, why act any part at all?—how plain, how easy, how direct your road to my heart, if but straightly pursued!'

CHAPTER V

Strictures on Deformity

Camilla went on to Etherington in deep distress; every ray of hope was chaced from her prospects, with a certainty more cruel, though less offensive, to her feelings, than the crush given them by Miss Margland. He cares not for me! she cried; he even destines me for another! He is the willing agent of the Major; he would portion me, I suppose, for him, to accelerate the impossibility of ever thinking of me! And I imagined he loved me!—what a dream!—what a dream!—how has he deceived me!—or, alas! how have I deceived myself!

She rejoiced, however, that she had made so decided an answer with regard to Major Cerwood, whom she could not doubt to be the person meant, and who, presented in such a point of view, grew utterly odious to her.

The tale she had to relate to Mr. Tyrold, of the sufferings and sad resolution of Eugenia, obviated all comment upon her own disturbance. He was wounded to the heart by the recital. 'Alas!' he cried, 'your wise and excellent mother always foresaw some mischief would ensue, from the extreme caution used to keep this dear unfortunate child ignorant of her peculiar situation. This dreadful shake might have been palliated, at least, if not spared, by the lessons of fortitude that noble woman would have inculcated in her young and ductile mind. But I could not resist the painful entreaties of my poor brother, who, thinking himself the author of her calamities, believed he was responsible for saving her from feeling them; and, imagining all the world as soft-hearted as himself, concluded, that what her own family would not tell her, she could never hear elsewhere. But who should leave any events to the caprices of chance, which the precautions of foresight can determine?'

These reflections, and the thoughts of her sister, led at once and aided Camilla to stifle her own unhappiness; and for three days following, she devoted herself wholly to Eugenia.

On the morning of the fourth, instead of sending the carriage, Sir Hugh arrived himself to fetch Camilla, and to tell his brother, he must come also, to give comfort to Eugenia; for, though he had thought the worst was over, because she appeared quiet in his presence, he had just surprised her in tears, by coming upon her unawares. He had done all he could, he said, in vain; and nothing remained but for Mr. Tyrold to try his hand himself: 'For it is but justice,' he added, 'to Dr. Orkborne, to say she is wiser than all our poor heads put together; so that there is no answering her for want of sense.' He then told him to be sure to put one of his best sermons in his pocket to read to her.

Mr. Tyrold was extremely touched for his poor Eugenia, yet said he had half an hour's business to transact in the neighbourhood, before he could go to Cleves. Sir Hugh waited his time, and all three then proceeded together.

Eugenia received her Father with a deliberate coldness that shocked him. He saw how profound was the impression made upon her mind, not merely of her personal evils, but of what she conceived to be the misconduct of her friends.

After a little general discourse, in which she bore no share, he proposed walking in the park; meaning there to take her aside, with less formality than he could otherwise desire to speak with her alone.

The ladies and Sir Hugh immediately looked for their hats or gloves: but Eugenia, saying she had a slight head-ache, walked away to her room.

'This, my dear brother,' cried Sir Hugh, sorrowfully following her with his eyes, 'is the very thing I wanted you for; she says she'll never more stir out of these doors as long as she's alive; which is a sad thing to say, considering her young years; and nobody knowing how Clermont may approve it. However, it's well I've had him brought up from the beginning to the classics, which I rejoice at every day more and more, it being the only wise thing I ever did of my own head; for as to talking Latin and Greek, which I suppose is what they will chiefly be doing, there's no doubt but they may do it just as well in a room as in the fields, or the streets.'

Mr. Tyrold, after a little consideration, followed her. He tapped at her door; she asked, in a tone of displeasure, who was there?—'Your Father, my dear,' he answered; and then, hastily opening it, she proposed returning with him down stairs.

'No,' he said; 'I wish to converse with you alone. The opinion I have long cherished of your heart and your understanding, I come now to put to the proof.'

Eugenia, certain of the subject to which he would lead, and feeling she could not have more to hear than to say, gave him a chair, and composedly seated herself next to him.

'My dear Eugenia,' said he, taking her passive hand, 'this is the moment that more grievously than ever I lament the absence of your invaluable Mother. All I have to offer to your consideration she could much better have laid before you; and her dictates would have met with the attention they so completely deserve.'

'Was my Mother, then, Sir,' said she, reproachfully, 'unapprized of the worldly darkness in which I have been brought up? Is she unacquainted that a little knowledge of books and languages is what alone I have been taught?'

'We are all but too apt,' answered Mr. Tyrold, mildly, though surprised, 'to deem nothing worth attaining but what we have missed, nothing worth possessing but what we are denied. How many are there, amongst the untaught and unaccomplished, who would think an escape such as yours, of all intellectual darkness, a compensation for every other evil!'

'They could think so only, Sir, while, like me, they lived immured always in the same house, were seen always by the same people, and were total strangers to the sensations they might excite in any others.'

'My dear Eugenia, grieved as I am at the present subject of your ruminations, I rejoice to see in you a power of reflection, and of combination, so far above your years. And it is a soothing idea to me to dwell upon the ultimate benevolence of Providence, even in circumstances the most afflicting: for if chance has been unkind to you, Nature seems, with fostering foresight, to have endowed you with precisely those powers that may best set aside her malignity.'

'I see, Sir,' cried she, a little moved, 'the kindness of your intention; but pardon me if I anticipate to you its ill success. I have thought too much upon my situation and my destiny to admit any fallacious comfort. Can you, indeed, when once her eyes are opened, can you expect to reconcile to existence a poor young creature who sees herself an object of derision and disgust? Who, without committing any crime, without offending any human being, finds she cannot appear but to be pointed at, scoffed and insulted!'

'O my child! with what a picture do you wound my heart, and tear your own peace and happiness! Wretches who in such a light can view outward deficiencies cannot merit a thought, are below even contempt, and ought not to be disdained, but forgotten. Make a conquest, then, my Eugenia, of yourself; be as superior in your feelings as in your understanding, and remember what Addison admirably says in one of the Spectators: 'A too acute sensibility of personal defects, is one of the greatest weaknesses of self-love.'

'I should be sorry, Sir, you should attribute to vanity what I now suffer. No! it is simply the effect of never hearing, never knowing, that so severe a call was to be made upon my fortitude, and therefore never arming myself to sustain it.'

Then, suddenly, and with great emotion clasping her hands: 'O if ever I have a family of my own,' she cried, 'my first care shall be to tell my daughters of all their infirmities! They shall be familiar, from their childhood, to their every defect—Ah! they must be odious indeed if they resemble their poor mother!'

'My dearest Eugenia! let them but resemble you mentally, and there is no person, whose approbation is worth deserving, that will not love and respect them. Good and evil are much more equally divided in this world than you are yet aware: none possess the first without alloy, nor the second without palliation. Indiana, for example, now in the full bloom of all that beauty can bestow, tell me, and ask yourself strictly, would you change with Indiana?'

'With Indiana?' she exclaimed; 'O! I would forfeit every other good to change with Indiana! Indiana, who never appears but to be admired, who never speaks but to be applauded.'

'Yet a little, yet a moment, question, and understand yourself before you settle you would change with her. Look forward, and look inward. Look forward, that you may view the short life of admiration and applause for such attractions from others, and their inutility to their possessor in every moment of solitude or repose; and look inward, that you may learn to value your own peculiar riches, for times of retirement, and for days of infirmity and age!'

'Indeed, Sir,—and pray believe me, I do not mean to repine I have not the beauty of Indiana; I know and have always heard her loveliness is beyond all comparison. I have no more, therefore, thought of envying it, than of envying the brightness of the sun. I knew, too, I bore no competition with my sisters; but I never dreamt of competition. I knew I was not handsome, but I supposed many people besides not handsome, and that I should pass with the rest; and I concluded the world to be full of people who had been sufferers as well as myself, by disease or accident. These have been occasionally my passing thoughts; but the subject never seized my mind; I never reflected upon it at all, till abuse, without provocation, all at once opened my eyes, and shewed me to myself! Bear with me, then, my father, in this first dawn of terrible conviction! Many have been unfortunate,—but none unfortunate like me! Many have met with evils—but who with an accumulation like mine!'

Mr. Tyrold, extremely affected, embraced her with the utmost tenderness: 'My dear, deserving, excellent child,' he cried, 'what would I not endure, what sacrifice not make, to soothe this cruel disturbance, till time and your own understanding can exert their powers?' Then, while straining her to his breast with the fondest parental commiseration, the tears, with which his eyes were overflowing, bedewed her cheeks.

Eugenia felt them, and, sinking to the ground, pressed his knees. 'O my father,' she cried, 'a tear from your revered eyes afflicts me more than all else! Let me not draw forth another, lest I should become not only unhappy, but guilty. Dry them up, my dearest father—let me kiss them away.'

'Tell me, then, my poor girl, you will struggle against this ineffectual sorrow! Tell me you will assert that fortitude which only waits for your exertion; and tell me you will forgive the misjudging compassion which feared to impress you earlier with pain!'

'I will do all, every thing you desire! my injustice is subdued! my complaints shall be hushed! you have conquered me, my beloved father! Your indulgence, your lenity shall take place of every hardship, and leave me nothing but filial affection!'

Seizing this grateful moment, he then required of her to relinquish her melancholy scheme of seclusion from the world: 'The shyness and the fears which gave birth to it,' said he, 'will but grow upon you if listened to; and they are not worthy the courage I would instil into your bosom—the courage, my Eugenia, of virtue—the courage to pass by, as if unheard, the insolence of the hard-hearted, and ignorance of the vulgar. Happiness is in your power, though beauty is not; and on that to set too high a value would be pardonable only in a weak and frivolous mind; since, whatever is the involuntary admiration with which it meets, every estimable quality and accomplishment is attainable without it: and though, which I cannot deny, its immediate influence is universal, yet in every competition and in every decision of esteem, the superior, the elegant, the better part of mankind give their suffrages to merit alone. And you, in particular, will find yourself, through life, rather the more than the less valued, by every mind capable of justice and compassion, for misfortunes which no guilt has incurred.'

Observing her now to be softened, though not absolutely consoled, he rang the bell, and begged the servant, who answered it, to request his brother would order the coach immediately, as he was obliged to return home; 'And you, my love,' said he, 'shall accompany me; it will be the least exertion you can make in first breaking through your averseness to quit the house.'

Eugenia would not resist; but her compliance was evidently repugnant to her inclination; and in going to the glass to put on her hat, she turned aside from it in shuddering, and hid her face with both her hands.

'My dearest child,' cried Mr. Tyrold, wrapping her again in his arms, 'this strong susceptibility will soon wear away; but you cannot be too speedy nor too firm in resisting it. The omission of what never was in our power cannot cause remorse, and the bewailing what never can become in our power cannot afford comfort. Imagine but what would have been the fate of Indiana, had your situations been reversed, and had she, who can never acquire your capacity, and therefore never attain your knowledge, lost that beauty which is her all; but which to you, even if retained, could have been but a secondary gift. How short will be the reign of that all! how useless in sickness! how unavailing in solitude! how inadequate to long life! how forgotten, or repiningly remembered in old age! You will live to feel pity for all you now covet and admire; to grow sensible to a lot more lastingly happy in your own acquirements and powers; and to exclaim, with contrition and wonder, Time was when I would have changed with the poor mind-dependent Indiana!'

The carriage was now announced; Eugenia, with reluctant steps, descended; Camilla was called to join them, and Sir Hugh saw them set off with the utmost delight.

CHAPTER VI

Strictures on Beauty

To lengthen the airing, Mr. Tyrold ordered the carriage by a new road; and to induce Eugenia to break yet another spell, in walking as well as riding, he proposed their alighting, when they came to a lane, and leaving the coach in waiting while they took a short stroll.

He walked between his daughters a considerable way, passing, wherever it was possible, close to cottages, labourers, and children. Eugenia submitted with a sigh, but held down her head, affrighted at every fresh object they encountered, till, upon approaching a small miserable hut, at the door of which several children were playing, an unlucky boy called out, 'O come! come! look!—here's the little hump-back gentlewoman!'

She then, clinging to her father, could not stir another step, and cast upon him a look of appeal and reproach that almost overset him; but, after speaking to her some words of kindness, he urged her to go on, and alone, saying, 'Throw only a shilling to the senseless little crew, and let Camilla follow and give nothing, and see which will become the most popular.'

They both obeyed, Eugenia fearfully and with quickness casting amongst them some silver, and Camilla quietly walking on.

'O, I have got a sixpence!' cried one; 'and I've got a shilling!' said another; while the mother of the little tribe came from her wash-tub, and called out, 'God bless your ladyship!' and the father quitted a little garden at the side of his cottage, to bow down to the ground, and cry, 'Heaven reward you, good madam! you'll have a blessing go with you, go where you will!'

The children then, dancing up to Camilla, begged her charity; but when, seconding the palpable intention of her father, she said she had nothing for them, they looked highly dissatisfied, while they redoubled their blessings to Eugenia.

'See, my child,' said Mr. Tyrold, now joining them, 'how cheaply preference, and even flattery, may be purchased!'

'Ah, Sir!' she answered, recovered from her terrour, yet deep in reflection, 'this is only by bribery, and gross bribery, too! And what pleasure, or what confidence can accrue from preference so earned!'

'The means, my dear Eugenia, are not beneath the objects: if it is only from those who unite native hardness with uncultured minds and manners, that civility is to be obtained by such sordid materials, remember, also, it is from such only it can ever fail you. In the lowest life, equally with the highest, wherever nature has been kind, sympathy springs spontaneously for whatever is unfortunate, and respect for whatever seems innocent. Steel yourself, then, firmly to withstand attacks from the cruel and unfeeling, and rest perfectly secure you will have none other to apprehend.'

The clear and excellent capacity of Eugenia, comprehended in this lesson, and its illustration, all the satisfaction Mr. Tyrold hoped to impart; and she was ruminating upon it with abated despondence, when, as they came to a small house, surrounded with a high wall, Mr. Tyrold, looking through an iron gate at a female figure who stood at one of the windows, exclaimed—'What a beautiful creature! I have rarely, I think seen a more perfect face.'

Eugenia felt so much hurt by this untimely sight, that, after a single glance, which confirmed the truth of what he said, she bent her eyes another way; while Camilla herself was astonished that her kind father should call their attention to beauty, at so sore and critical a juncture.

'The examination of a fine picture,' said he, fixing his eyes upon the window, and standing still at the iron gate, 'is a constant as well as exquisite pleasure; for we look at it with an internal security, that such as it appears to us to-day, it will appear again tomorrow, and tomorrow, and tomorrow; but in the pleasure given by the examination of a fine face, there is always, to a contemplative mind, some little mixture of pain; an idea of its fragility steals upon our admiration, and blends with it something like solicitude; the consciousness how short a time we can view it perfect, how quickly its brilliancy of bloom will be blown, and how ultimately it will be nothing.—'

'You would have me, Sir,' said Eugenia, now raising her eyes, 'learn to see beauty with unconcern, by depreciating its value? I feel your kind intention; but it does not come home to me; reasoning such as this may be equally applicable to any thing else, and degrade whatever is desirable into insignificance.'

'No, my dear child, there is nothing, either in its possession or its loss, that can be compared with beauty; nothing so evanescent, and nothing that leaves behind it a contrast which impresses such regret. It cannot be forgotten, since the same features still remain, though they are robbed of their effect upon the beholder; the same complexion is there, though faded into a tint bearing no resemblance with its original state; and the same eyes present themselves to the view, though bereft of all the lustre that had rendered them captivating.'

'Ah, Sir! this is an argument but formed for the moment. Is not the loss of youth the same to every body? and is not age equally unwelcome to the ugly and to the handsome?'

'For activity, for strength, and for purposes of use, certainly, my dear girl, there can be no difference; but for motives to mental regret, there can be no comparison. To those who are commonly moulded, the gradual growth of decay brings with it its gradual endurance, because little is missed from day to day; hope is not roughly chilled, nor expectation rudely blasted; they see their friends, their connections, their contemporaries, declining by the same laws, and they yield to the immutable and general lot rather imperceptibly than resignedly; but it is not so with the beauty; her loss is not only general, but peculiar; and it is the peculiar, not the general evil, that constitutes all hardship. Health, strength, agility, and animal spirits, she may sorrowing feel diminish; but she hears everyone complain of similar failures, and she misses them unmurmuring, though not unlamenting; but of beauty, every declension is marked with something painful to self-love. The change manifested by the mirror might patiently be borne; but the change manifested in the eyes of every beholder, gives a shock that does violence to every pristine feeling.'

'This may certainly, sir, be cruel; trying at least; but then,—what a youth has she first passed! Mortification comes upon her, at least, in succession; she does not begin the world with it,—a stranger at all periods to anything happier!'

'Ah, my child! the happiness caused by personal attractions pays a dear after-price! The soldier who enters the field of battle requires not more courage, though of a different nature, than the faded beauty who enters an assembly-room. To be wholly disregarded, after engaging every eye; to be unassisted, after being habituated to seeing crowds anxiously offer their services; to be unheard, after monopolising every ear—can you, indeed, persuade yourself a change such as this demands but ordinary firmness? Yet the altered female who calls for it, has the least chance to obtain it; for even where nature has endowed her with fortitude, the world and its flatteries have almost uniformly enervated it, before the season of its exertion.'

'All this may be true,' said Eugenia, with a sigh; 'and to me, however sad in itself, it may prove consolatory; and yet—forgive my sincerity, when I own—I would purchase a better appearance at any price, any expence, any payment, the world could impose!'

Mr. Tyrold was preparing an answer, when the door of the house, which he had still continued facing, was opened, and the beautiful figure, which had for some time retired from the window, rushed suddenly upon a lawn before the gate against which they were leaning.

Not seeing them, she sat down upon the grass, which she plucked up by hands full, and strewed over her fine flowing hair.

Camilla, fearing they should seem impertinent, would have retreated; but Eugenia, much struck, sadly, yet with earnestness, compelled herself to regard the object before her, who was young, fair, of a tall and striking figure, with features delicately regular.

A sigh, not to be checked, acknowledged how little either reasoning or eloquence could subdue a wish to resemble such an appearance, when the young person, flinging herself suddenly upon her face, threw her white arms over her head, and sobbed aloud with violence.

Astonished, and deeply concerned, Eugenia internally said, alas! what a world is this! even beauty so exquisite, without waiting for age or change, may be thus miserable!

She feared to speak, lest she should be heard; but she looked up to her father, with an eye that spoke concession, and with an interest for the fair afflicted, which seemed to request his assistance.

He motioned to her to be quiet; when the young person, abruptly half rising, burst into a fit of loud, shrill, and discordant laughter.

Eugenia now, utterly confounded, would have drawn her father away; but he was intently engaged in his observations, and steadily kept his place.

In two minutes, the laugh ceased all at once, and the young creature, hastily rising, began turning round with a velocity that no machine could have exceeded.

The sisters now fearfully interchanged looks that shewed they thought her mad, and both endeavoured to draw Mr. Tyrold from the gate, but in vain; he made them hold by his arms, and stood still.

Without seeming giddy, she next began to jump; and he now could only detain his daughters, by shewing them the gate, at which they stood, was locked.

In another minute, she perceived them, and, coming eagerly forward, dropt several low courtesies, saying, at every fresh bend—'Good day!—Good day!—Good day!'

Equally trembling, they now both turned pale with fear; but Mr. Tyrold, who was still immovable, answered her by a bow, and asked if she were well.

'Give me a shilling!' was her reply, while the slaver drivelled unrestrained from her mouth, rendering utterly disgusting a chin that a statuary might have wished to model.

'Do you live at this house!' said Mr. Tyrold.

'Yes, please—yes, please—yes, please,' she answered, twenty times following, and almost black in the face before she would allow herself to take another breath.

A cat now appearing at the door, she seized it, and tried to twine it round her neck with great fondling, wholly unresisting the scratches which tore her fine skin.

Next, capering forward with it towards the gate, 'Look! look!' she cried, 'here's puss!—here's puss!—here's puss!'

Then, letting it fall, she tore her handkerchief off her neck, put it over her face, strained it as tight as she was able, and tied it under her chin; and then struck her head with both her hands, making a noise that resembled nothing human.

'Take, take me away, my father!' cried Eugenia, 'I see, I feel your awful lesson! but impress it no further, lest I die in receiving it!'

Mr. Tyrold immediately moved off without speaking; Camilla, penetrated for her sister, observed the same silence; and Eugenia, hanging upon her father, and absorbed in profound rumination, only by the depth of her sighs made her existence known; and thus, without the interchange of a word, slowly and pensively they walked back to the carriage.

Eugenia broke the silence as soon as they were seated: 'O, my father!' she exclaimed, 'what a sight have you made me witness! how dread a reproof have you given to my repining spirit! Did you know this unhappy beauty was at that house? Did you lead me thither purposely to display to me her shocking imbecility?'

'Relying upon the excellence of your understanding, I ventured upon an experiment more powerful, I well knew, than all that reason could urge; an experiment not only striking at the moment, but which, by playing upon the imagination, as well as convincing the judgment, must make an impression that can never be effaced. I have been informed for some time, that this poor girl was in our neighbourhood; she was born an idiot, and therefore, having never known brighter days, is insensible to her terrible state. Her friends are opulent, and that house is taken, and a woman is paid, to keep her in existence and in obscurity. I had heard of her uncommon beauty, and when the news reached me of my dear Eugenia's distress, the idea of this meeting occurred to me; I rode to the house, and engaged the woman to detain her unfortunate charge at the window till we appeared, and then to let her loose into the garden. Poor, ill fated young creature! it has been, indeed, a melancholy sight.'

'A sight,' cried Eugenia, 'to come home to me with shame!—O, my dear Father! your prescription strikes to the root of my disease!—shall I ever again dare murmur!—will any egotism ever again make me believe no lot so hapless as my own! I will think of her when I am discontented; I will call to my mind this spectacle of human degradation—and submit, at least with calmness, to my lighter evils and milder fate.'

'My excellent child! this is just what I expected from the candour of your temper, and the rectitude of your sentiments. You have seen, here, the value of intellects in viewing the horrour of their loss; and you have witnessed, that beauty, without mind, is more dreadful than any deformity. You have seized my application, and left me nothing to enforce; my dear, my excellent child! you have left for your fond Father nothing but tender approbation! With the utmost thankfulness to Providence, I have marked from your earliest childhood, the native justness of your understanding; which, with your studious inclination to sedentary accomplishments, has proved a reviving source of consolation to your mother and to me, for the cruel accidents we have incessantly lamented. How will that admirable mother rejoice in the recital I have to make to her! What pride will she take in a daughter so worthily her own, so resembling her in nobleness of nature, and a superior way of thinking! Her tears, my child, like mine, will thank you for your exertions! she will strain you to her fond bosom, as your father strains you at this moment!'

'Yes, Sir,' cried Eugenia, 'your kind task is now completed with your vanquished Eugenia! her thoughts, her occupations, her happiness, shall henceforth all be centred in filial gratitude and contentment.'

The affectionate Camilla, throwing her arms about them both, bathed each with the tears of joy and admiration, which this soothing conclusion to an adventure so severe excited.

CHAPTER VII

The Pleadings of Pity

To oblige Mr. Tyrold, who had made the arrangement with Sir Hugh, Eugenia consented to dine and spend the day at Etherington, which she quitted at night in a temper of mind perfectly composed.

Camilla was deeply penetrated by the whole of this affair. The sufferings, so utterly unearned by fault or by folly, of a sister so dear to her, and the affecting fortitude which, so quickly upon her wounds, and at so early a period of life, she already began to display, made her blush at the dejection into which she was herself cast by every evil, and resolve to become in future more worthy of the father and the sister, who at this moment absorbed all her admiration.

Too reasonable, in such a frame of mind, to plan forgetting Mandlebert, she now only determined to think of him as she had thought before her affections became entangled; to think of him, in short, as he seemed himself to desire; to seek his friendly offices and advice, but to reject every offered establishment, and to live single for life.

Gratified by indulgent praise, and sustained by exerted virtue, the revived Eugenia had nearly reached Cleves, on her return, when the carriage was stopt by a gentleman on horseback, who, approaching the coach window, said, in a low voice, as if unwilling to be heard by the servants—'O, Madam! has Fate set aside her cruelty? and does Fortune permit me to live once more?'

She then recollected Mr. Bellamy. She had only her maid in the carriage, who was sent for her by Sir Hugh, Miss Margland being otherwise engaged.

All that had so lately passed upon her person and appearance being full upon her mind, she involuntarily shrunk back, hiding her face with her cloak.

Bellamy, by no means conceiving this mark of emotion to be unfavourable, steadied his horse, by leaning one hand on the coach-window, and said, in a yet lower voice—'O, Madam! is it possible you can hate me so barbarously?—will you not even deign to look at me, though I have so long been banished from your presence?'

Eugenia, during this speech, called to mind, that though new, in some measure, to herself, she was not so to this gentleman, and ventured to uncover her face; when the grief painted on the fine features of Bellamy, so forcibly touched her, that she softly answered—'No, Sir, indeed I do not hate you; I am incapable of such ingratitude; but I conjure—I beseech you to forget me!'

'Forget you?—O, Madam! you command an impossibility!—No, I am constancy itself, and not all the world united shall tear you from my heart!'

Jacob, who caught a word or two, now rode up to the other window, and as Eugenia began—'Conquer, Sir, I entreat you, this ill-fated partiality!—' told her the horses had been hard-worked, and must go home.

As Jacob was the oracle of Sir Hugh about his horses, his will was prescriptive law: Eugenia never disputed it, and only saying—'Think of me, Sir, no more!' bid the coachman drive on.

Bellamy, respectfully submitting, continued, with his hat in his hand, as the maid informed her mistress, looking after the carriage till it was out of sight.

A tender sorrow now stole upon the just revived tranquillity of the gentle and generous Eugenia. 'Ah!' thought she, 'I have rendered, little as I seem worthy of such power, I have rendered this amiable man miserable, though possibly, and probably, he is the only man in existence whom I could render happy!—Ah! how may I dare expect from Clermont a similar passion?'

Molly Mill, a very young girl, and daughter of a poor tenant of Sir Hugh, interrupted these reflections from time to time, with remarks upon their object. 'Dearee me, Miss,' she cried, 'what a fine gentleman that was!—he sighed like to split his heart when you said, don't think about me no more. He's some loveyer, like, I'm sure.'

Eugenia returned home so much moved by this incident, that Sir Hugh, believing his brother himself had failed to revive her, was disturbed all anew with acute contrition for her disasters, and feeling very unwell, went to bed before supper time.

Eugenia retired also; and after spending the evening in soft compassion for Bellamy, and unfixed apprehensions and distaste for young Lynmere, was preparing to go to bed, when Molly Mill, out of breath with haste, brought her a letter.

She eagerly opened it, whilst enquiring whence it came.

'O, Miss, the fine gentleman—that same fine gentleman—brought it himself: and he sent for me out, and I did not know who I was to go to, for Mary only said a boy wanted me; but the boy said, I must come with him to the stile; and when I come there, who should I see but the fine gentleman himself! And he gave me this letter, and he asked me to give it you—and see! look Miss! what I got for my trouble!'

She then exhibited a half-guinea.

'You have not done right, Molly, in accepting it. Money is bribery; and you should have known that the letter was improperly addressed, if bribery was requisite to make it delivered.'

'Dearee me, Miss, what's half-a-guinea to such a gentleman as that? I dare say he's got his pockets full of them!'

'I shall not read it, certainly,' cried Eugenia, 'now I know this circumstance. Give me the wax—I will seal it again.'

She then hesitated whether she ought to return it, or shew it to her uncle, or commit it to the flames.

That to which she was most unwilling, appeared, to the strictness of her principles, to be most proper: she therefore determined that the next morning she would relate her evening's adventure, and deliver the unread letter to Sir Hugh.

Had this epistle not perplexed her, she had meant never to name its writer. Persuaded her last words had finally dismissed him, she thought it a high point of female delicacy never to publish an unsuccessful conquest.

This resolution taken, she went to bed, satisfied with herself, but extremely grieved at the sufferings she was preparing for one who so singularly loved her.

The next morning, however, her uncle did not rise to breakfast, and was so low spirited, that fearing to disturb him, she deemed it most prudent to defer the communication.

But when, after she had taken her lesson from Dr. Orkborne, she returned to her room, she found Molly Mill impatiently waiting for her: 'O, Miss,' she cried, 'here's another letter for you! and you must read it directly, for the gentleman says if you don't it will be the death of him.'

'Why did you receive another letter?' said Eugenia, displeased.

'Dearee me, Miss, how could I help it? if you'd seen the taking he was in, you'd have took it yourself. He was all of a quake, and ready to go down of his two knees. Dearee me, if it did not make my heart go pit-pat to see him! He was like to go out of his mind, he said, and the tears, poor gentleman, were all in his eyes.'

Eugenia now turned away, strongly affected by this description.

'Do, Miss,' continued Molly, 'write him a little scrap, if it's never so scratched and bad. He'll take it kinder than nothing. Do, Miss, do. Don't be ill-natured. And just read this little letter, do, Miss, do;—it won't take you much time, you reads so nice and fast.'

'Why,' cried Eugenia, 'did you go to him again? how could you so incautiously entrust yourself to the conduct of a strange boy?'

'A strange boy! dearee me, Miss, don't you know it was Tommy Hodd? I knows him well enough; I knows all the boys, I warrant me, round about here. Come, Miss, here's pen and ink; you'll run it off before one can count five, when you've a mind to it. He'll be in a sad taking till he sees me come back.'

'Come back? is it possible you have been so imprudent as to have promised to see him again?'

'Dearee me, yes, Miss! he'd have made away with himself if I had not. He'd been there ever since six in the morning, without nothing to eat or drink, a riding up and down the road, till he could see me coming to the stile. And he says he'll keep a riding there all day long, and all night too, till I goes to him.'

Eugenia conceived herself now in a situation of unexampled distress. She forced Molly Mill to leave her, that she might deliberate what course to pursue.

Having read no novels, her imagination had never been awakened to scenes of this kind; and what she had gathered upon such subjects in the poetry and history she had studied with Dr. Orkborne, had only impressed her fancy in proportion as love bore the character of heroism, and the lover that of an hero. Though highly therefore romantic, her romance was not the common adoption of a circulating library: it was simply that of elevated sentiments, formed by animated credulity playing upon youthful inexperience.

'Alas!' cried she, 'what a conflict is mine! I must refuse a man who adores me to distraction, in disregard of my unhappy defects, to cast myself under the guidance of one who, perhaps, may estimate beauty so highly as to despise me for its want!'

This idea pleaded so powerfully for Bellamy, that something like a wish to open his letters, obtained pardon to her little maid for having brought them. She suppressed, however, the desire, though she held them alternately to her eyes, conjecturing their contents, and bewailing for their impassioned writer the cruel answer they must receive.

Though checked by shame, she had some desire to consult Camilla; but she could not see her in time, Mrs. Arlbery having insisted upon carrying her in the evening to a play, which was to be performed, for one night only, by a company of passing strollers at Northwick.

'My decision,' she cried, 'must be my own, and must be immediate. Ah! how leave a man such as this, to wander night and day neglected and uncertain of his fate! With tears he sent me his letters!—what must not have been his despair when such was his sensibility? tears in a man!—tears, too, that could not be restrained even till his messenger was out of sight!—how touching!—'

Her own then fell, in tender commiseration, and it was with extreme repugnance she compelled herself to take such measures as she thought her duty required. She sealed the two letters in an empty cover, and having directed them to Mr. Bellamy, summoned Molly Mill, and told her to convey them to the gentleman, and positively acquaint him she must receive no more, and that those which were returned had never been read. She bid her, however, add, that she should always wish for his happiness, and be grateful for his kind partiality; though she earnestly conjured him to vanquish a regard which she did not deserve, and must never return.

Molly Mill would fain have remonstrated; but Eugenia, with that firmness which, even in the first youth, accompanies a consciousness of preferring duty to inclination, silenced, and sent her off.

Relieved for herself, now the struggle was over, she secretly rejoiced that it was not for Melmond she had so hard a part to act: and this idea, while it rendered Bellamy less an object of regret, diminished also something of her pity for his conflict, by reminding her of the success which had attended her own similar exertions.

But when Molly returned, her distress was renewed: she brought her these words, written with a pencil upon the back of her own cover:

'I do not dare, cruellest of your sex, to write you another letter; but if you would save me from the abyss of destruction, you will let me hear my final doom from your own mouth. I ask nothing more! Ah! walk but one moment in the park, near the pales; deny not your miserable adorer this last single request, and he will fly this fatal climate which has swallowed up his repose for ever! But, till then, here he will stay, and never quit the spot whence he sends you these lines, till you have deigned to pronounce verbally his doom, though he should famish for want of food!

ALPHONSO BELLAMY.'

Eugenia read this with horrour and compassion. She imagined he perhaps thought her confined, and would therefore believe no answer that did not issue immediately from her own lips. She sent Molly to him again with the same message; but Molly returned with a yet worse account of his desperation, and a strong assurance, that if she would only utter to him a single word, he would obey, depart, and live upon it the rest of his life.

This completely softened her. Rather than imperiously suffer such a pattern of respectful constancy to perish, she consented to speak her own negative. But fearing she might be moved to some sympathy by his grief, she resolved to be accompanied by Camilla, and deferred, therefore, the interview till the next day.

Molly brought back his humble acknowledgments for this concession, and an account that, at last, slowly and sadly, he had ridden away.

Her feelings were now better satisfied than her understanding. She feared what she had granted was a favour; yet her heart was too tender to reproach a compliance made upon such conditions, and to prevent such evils.

CHAPTER VIII

The Disastrous Buskins

Camilla, though her personal sorrows were blunted by the view of the calamities and resignation of her sister, was so little disposed for amusement, that she had accepted the invitation of Mrs. Arlbery, only from wanting spirit to resist its urgency. Mr. Tyrold was well pleased that such a recreation came in her way, but desired Lavinia might be of the party: not only that she might partake of the same pleasure, but from a greater security in her prudence, than in that of her naturally thoughtless sister.

The town of Etherington afforded no theatre; and the room fitted up for the night's performance could contain but two boxes, one of which was secured for Mrs. Arlbery and her friends.

The attentive Major was ready to offer his hand to Camilla upon her arrival. The rest of the officers were in the box.

The play was Othello; and so miserably represented, that Lavinia would willingly have retired after the first scene: but the native spirits of Camilla revisited her in the view of the ludicrous personages of the drama. And they were soon joined by Sir Sedley Clarendel, whose quaint conceits and remarks assisted the risibility of the scene. She thought him the least comprehensible person she had ever known; but as he was totally indifferent to her, his oddity entertained without tormenting her.

The actors were of the lowest strolling kind, and so utterly without merit, that they had never yet met with sufficient encouragement to remain one week in the same place. They had only a single scene for the whole performance, which depictured a camp, and which here served for a street, a senate, a city, a castle, and a bed-chamber.

The dresses were almost equally parsimonious, everyone being obliged to take what would fit him, from a wardrobe that did not allow quite two dresses a person for all the plays they had to enact. Othello, therefore, was equipped as king Richard the third, save that instead of a regal front he had a black wig, to imitate wool: while his face had been begrimed with a smoked cork.

Iago wore a suit of cloaths originally made for Lord Foppington: Brabantio had borrowed the armour of Hamlet's Ghost: Cassio, the Lieutenant General in the christian army, had only been able to equip himself in Osmyn's Turkish vest; and Roderigo, accoutred in the garment of Shylock, came forth a complete Jew.

Desdemona, attired more suitably to her fate than to her expectations, went through the whole of her part, except the last scene, in the sable weeds of Isabella. And Amelia was fain to content herself with the habit of the first witch in Macbeth.

The gestures, both of the gentlemen and ladies, were as outrageous as if meant rather to intimidate the audience, than to shew their own animation; and the men approached each other so closely with arms a-kimbo, or double fists, that Sir Sedley, with pretended alarm, said they were giving challenges for a boxing match.

The ladies also, in the energy of their desire not to be eclipsed, took so much exercise in their action, that they tore out the sleeves of their gowns; which, though pinned up every time they left the stage, completely exposed their shoulders at the end of every act; and they raised their arms so high while facing each other, that Sir Sedley expressed frequent fears they meant to finish by pulling caps.

So imperfect were they also in their parts, that the prompter was the only person from whom any single speech passed without a blunder.

Iago, who was the master of the troop, was the sole performer who spoke not with a provincial dialect; the rest all betrayed their birth and parentage the first line they uttered.

Cassio proclaimed himself from Norfolk:

The Deuk dew greet yew, General,
Being not at yew're lodging to be feund—
The senate sent above tree several quests, &c.

Othello himself proved a true Londoner; and with his famed soldier-like eloquence in the senate-scene, thus began his celebrated defence.

Most potent, grawe, and rewerend Seignors,
My wery noble and approwed good masters,
That I have ta'en avay this old man's darter—

I vill a round, unwarnish'd tale deliver
Of my whole course of love; vhat drugs, vhat charms,
Vhat conjuration, and vhat mighty magic
I von his darter with—
Her father lov'd me, oft inwited me—
My story being done,
She gave me for my pains a vorld of sighs,
She svore in faith 'tvas strange, 'tvas passing strange,
'Tvas pitiful, 't'vas vondrous pitiful;
She vish'd she had not heard it; yet she vish'd
That Heawen had made her such a man.
This only is the vitchcraft I have us'd;
Here comes the lady, let her vitness it.

This happily making the gentle Desdemona recognised, notwithstanding her appearance was so little bridal, her Somersetshire father cried:

I preay you hear 'ur zpeak.
If a confez that a waz half the woer
Deztruction on my head, if my bead bleame
Light o' the mon!

His daughter, in the Worcestershire pronunciation, answered:

Noble father,
Hi do perceive ere a divided duty;
To you hi howe my life hand heducation,
My life hand heducation both do teach me
Ow to respect you. You're the lord hof duty;
Hi'm itherto your daughter: but ere's my usband!

The fond Othello then exclaimed:

Your woices, lords! beseech you let her vill
Have a free vay!—

And Brabantio took leave with

Look to'ur, Moor! if th' azt eyez to zee;
A haz deceiv'd 'ur veather, and may thee.

They were detained so long between the first and second act, that Sir Sedley said he feared poor Desdemona had lost the thread-paper from which she was to mend her gown, and recommended to the two young ladies to have the charity to go and assist her. 'Consider,' he said, 'the trepidation of a fair bride but just entered into her shackles. Who knows but Othello may be giving her a strapping, in private, for wearing out her cloaths so fast! you young ladies think nothing of these little conjugal freedoms.'

Mrs. Arlbery, though for some time she had been as well diverted by the play as Camilla, less new to such exhibitions, was soon tired of the sameness of the blunders, and, at the end of the fourth act, proposed retiring. But Camilla, who had long not felt so much entertained, looked so disappointed, that her good humour overcame her fatigue, and she was insisting upon staying; when a gentleman, who visited them from the opposite box, proposed that the young ladies should be carried home by his mother, a lady who lived at Etherington, and was acquainted at the rectory, and who intended to stay out not only the play but the farce. Lavinia consented; the son went with the proposition, and the business was soon arranged. Mrs. Arlbery, who had three miles to go beyond the parsonage-house, and who, though she delighted to oblige, was but little in the habit of practising self-denial, then consigned the young ladies to General Kinsale, to be conducted to the opposite box, and was handed by Colonel Andover to her coach.

The General guarded the eldest sister; the Major took care of Camilla: but they were all stopt in their passage by the sudden seizure of a pickpocket, and forced hastily back to the box they had quitted.

This commotion, though it had disturbed all the audience, had not stopt the performance; and Desdemona being just now discovered in bed, Camilla, not to lose the interesting scene, persuaded her sister to wait till the play was over, before they attempted again to cross to the opposite box; into which, in a few minutes after, she saw Mandlebert enter.

They had both already seated themselves as much out of sight as possible; and Camilla now began to regret she had not accompanied Mrs. Arlbery. She had thought only of the play and its entertainment, till the sight of Mandlebert told her that her situation was improper; and the idea only occurred to her by considering that it would occur to him.

Mandlebert had dined out with a party of men, and had stept in to see what was going forwards, without any knowledge whom he should meet: he instantly discerned Lavinia, and felt anxious to know why Camilla was not with her, and why she sat so much out of sight: but Camilla so completely hid herself, he could only see there was a female, whom he concluded to be some Etherington lady; and he determined to make further enquiry when the act should be over.

The performance now became so truly ludicrous, that Camilla, notwithstanding all her uneasiness, was excited to almost perpetual laughter.

Desdemona, either from the effect of a bad cold, or to give more of nature to her repose, breathed so hard, as to raise a general laugh in the audience; Sir Sedley, stopping his ears, exclaimed, 'O! if she snores I shall plead for her no more, if she tear her gown to tatters! Suffocation is much too lenient for her. She's an immense horrid personage! nasal to alarm!'

Othello then entered, with a tallow candle in his hand, staring and dropping grease at every step; and, having just declared he would not

Scar that vhiter skin of hers than snow,

perceived a thief in the candle, which made it run down so fast over his hand, and the sleeve of his coat, that, the moment not being yet arrived for extinguishing it, he was forced to lay down his sword, and, for want of better means, snuff it with his fingers.

Sir Sedley now protested himself completely disordered: 'I must be gone,' cried he, 'incontinently; this exceeds resistance: I shan't be alive in another minute. Are you able to form a notion of anything more annihilating? If I did not build upon the pleasure of seeing him stop up those distressing nostrils of the gentle Desdemona, I could not breathe here another instant.'

But just after, while Othello leant over the bed to say—

Vhen I've pluck'd the rose
I cannot give it wital growth again,
It needs must vither—

his black locks caught fire.

The candle now fell from his hand, and he attempted to pull off his wig; but it had been tied close on, to appear more natural, and his fright disabled him; he therefore flung himself upon the bed, and rolled the coverlid over his head.

Desdemona, excessively frightened, started up, and jumped out, shrieking aloud—'O, Lord! I shall be burnt!'

This noble Venetian Dame then exhibited, beneath an old white satin bedgown, made to cover her arms and breast, the dress in which she had equipped herself, between the acts, to be ready for trampling home; namely, a dirty red and white linen gown, an old blue stuff quilted coat, and black shoes and stockings.

In this pitiable condition, she was running, screaming, off the stage, when Othello, having quenched the fire, unconscious that half his curls had fallen a sacrifice to the flames, hastily pursued her, and, in a violent passion, called her a fool, and brought her back to the bed; in which he assisted her to compose herself, and then went behind the scenes to light his candle; which having done, he gravely returned, and, very carefully putting it down, renewed his part with the line.

Be thus vhen thou art dead, and I vill kill thee
And love thee after—

Amidst roars of laughter from the whole audience, who, when he kissed her, almost with one voice called out—'Ay ay, that's right—kiss and friends!'

And when he said—

I must veep—

'So must I too, my good friend,' cried Sir Sedley, wiping his eyes, 'for never yet did sorrow cost me more salt rheum! Poor Blacky! thou hast been most indissolubly comic, I confess. Thou hast unstrung me to a degree. A baby of half an hour might demolish me.'

And again, when Othello exclaimed—

She vakes!

'The deuce she does?' cried Sir Sedley, 'what! has she been asleep again already? She's a very caricatura of Morpheus. Ay, do thy worst, honest Mungo. I can't possibly beg her off. I would sooner snift thy farthing candle once a day, than sustain that nasal cadence ever more.'

'He's the finest fellow upon the face of the earth,' cried Mr. Macdersey, who had listened to the whole play with the most serious interest; 'the instant he suspects his wife, he cuts her off without ceremony; though she's dearer to him than his eye sight, and beautiful as an angel. How I envy him!'

'Don't you think 'twould have been as well,' said General Kinsale, 'if he'd first made some little enquiry?'

'He can do that afterwards, General; and then nobody will dare surmise it's out of weakness. For to be sure and certain, he ought to right her fame; that's no more than his duty, after once he has satisfied his own. But a man's honour is dearest to him of all things. A wife's a bauble to it—not worth a thought.'

The suffocating was now beginning but just as Desdemona begged to be spared—

But alf han our—

the door-keeper forced his way into the pit, and called out—'Pray, is one Miss Tyrold here in the play-house?'

The sisters, in much amazement hung back, entreating the gentlemen to screen them; and the man, receiving no answer, went away.

While wondering what this could mean, the play was finished, when one of the comedians, a brother of the Worcestershire Desdemona, came to the pit door, calling out—'Hi'm desired to hask hif Miss Camilla Tyrold's hany way ere hin the ouse, for hi'm hordered to call er hout, for her Huncle's hill and dying.'

A piercing shriek from Camilla now completed the interruption of all attention to the performance, and betrayed her hiding place. Concealment, indeed, was banished her thoughts, and she would herself have opened the box door to rush out, had not the Major anticipated her, seizing, at the same time, her hand to conduct her through the crowd.

CHAPTER IX

Three Golden Maxims

Lavinia, almost equally terrified, followed her sister; and Sir Sedley, burying all foppery in compassion and good nature, was foremost to accompany and assist. Camilla had no thought but to get instantly to Cleves; she considered not how; she only forced herself rapidly on, persuaded she could walk it in ten minutes, and ejaculating incessantly, 'My Uncle!—my dear Uncle!'—

They almost instantly encountered Edgar, who, upon the fatal call, had darted round to meet them, and finding each provided with an attendant, inquired whose carriage he should seek?

Camilla, in a broken voice, answered she had no carriage, and should walk.

'Walk?' he repeated; 'you are near five miles from Cleves!'

Scarce in her senses, she hurried on without reply.

'What carriage did you come in, Miss Tyrold?' said Edgar to Lavinia.

'We came with Mrs. Arlbery.'

'Mrs. Arlbery?—she has been gone this half hour; I met her as I entered.'

Camilla had now rushed out of doors, still handed by the Major.

'If you have no carriage in waiting,' said Edgar, 'make use, I beseech you, of mine!'

'O, gladly! O, thankfully!' cried Camilla, almost sobbing out her words.

He flew then to call for his chaise, and the door-keeper, for whom Sir Sedley had inquired, came to them, accompanied by Jacob.

'O, Jacob!' she cried, breaking violently from the Major, 'tell me!—tell me!—my Uncle!—my dearest Uncle!'

Jacob, in a tone of deep and unfeigned sorrow, said, his Master had been seized suddenly with the gout in his stomach, and that the doctor, who had been instantly fetched, had owned there was little hope.

She could hear no more; the shock overpowered her, and she sunk nearly senseless into the arms of her sister.

She was recovered, however, almost in a minute, and carried by Edgar into his chaise, in which he placed her between himself and the weeping Lavinia; hastily telling the two gentlemen, that his intimate connection with the family authorized his assisting and attending them at such a period.

This was too well known to be disputed; and Sir Sedley and the Major, with great concern, uttered their good wishes and retreated.

Jacob had already been for Mr. Tyrold, who had set off instantaneously on horseback.

Camilla spoke not a word the first mile, which was spent in an hysteric sobbing: but, recovering a little afterwards, and sinking on the shoulder of her sister, 'O, Lavinia!' she cried, 'should we lose my Uncle—'

A shower of tears wetted the neck of Lavinia, who mingled with them her own, though less violently, from having less connection with Sir Hugh, and a sensibility less ungovernable.

She called herself upon the postillion to drive faster, and pressed Edgar continually to hurry him; but though he gave every charge she could desire, so much swifter were her wishes than any possible speed, that twenty times she entreated to get out, believing she could walk quicker than the horses galloped.

When they arrived at the park gate, she was with difficulty held back from opening the chaise door; and when, at length, they stopt at the house porch, she could not wait for the step, and before Edgar could either precede or prevent her, threw herself into the arms of Jacob, who, having just dismounted, was fortunately at hand to save her from falling.

She stopt not to ask any question; 'My Uncle!—my Uncle!' she cried, impetuously, and, rushing past all she met, was in his room in a moment.

Edgar, though he could not obstruct, followed her close, dreading lest Sir Hugh might already be no more, and determined, in that case, to force her from the fatal spot.

Eugenia, who heard her footstep, received her at the door, but took her immediately from the room, softly whispering, while her arms were thrown round her waist—'He will live! he will live, my sister! his agonies are over—he is fallen asleep, and he will live!'

This was too sudden a joy for the desponding Camilla, whose breath instantly stopt, and who must have fallen upon the floor, had she not been caught by Edgar; who, though his own eyes copiously overflowed with delight, at such unexpected good news of the universally beloved Baronet, had strength and exertion sufficient to carry her downstairs into the parlour, accompanied by Eugenia.

There, hartshorn and water presently revived her, and then, regardless of the presence of Edgar, she cast herself upon her knees, to utter a fervent thanksgiving, in which Eugenia, with equal piety, though more composure, joined.

Edgar had never yet beheld her in a light so resplendent—What a heart, thought he, is here! what feelings, what tenderness, what animation!—O, what a heart!—were it possible to touch it!

The two sisters went both gently up stairs, encouraging and congratulating each other in soft whispers, and stationed themselves in an ante-room: Mr. Tyrold, by medical counsel, giving directions that no one but himself should enter the sick chamber.

Edgar, though he only saw the domestics, could not persuade himself to leave the house till near two o'clock in the morning: and by six, his anxiety brought him thither again. He then heard, that the Baronet had passed a night of more pain than danger, the gout having been expelled his stomach, though it had been threatening almost every other part.

Three days and nights passed in this manner; during which, Edgar saw so much of the tender affections, and softer character of Camilla, that nothing could have withheld him from manifesting his entire sympathy in her feelings, but the unaccountable circumstance of her starting forth from a back seat at the play, where she had sat concealed, attended by the Major, and without any matron protectress.

Miss Margland, meanwhile, scowled at him, and Indiana pouted in vain. His earnest solicitude for Sir Hugh surmounted every such obstacle to his present visits at Cleves; and he spent there almost the whole of his time.

On the fourth day of the attack, Sir Hugh had a sleep of five hours' continuance, from which he awoke so much revived, that he raised himself in his bed, and called out—'My dear Brother! you are still here?—you are very good to me, indeed; poor sinner that I am! to forgive me for all my bad behaviour to your Children.'

'My dearest Brother! my Children, like myself, owe you nothing but kindness and beneficence; and, like myself, feel for you nothing but gratitude and tenderness.'

'They are very good, very good indeed,' said Sir Hugh, with a deep sigh; 'but Eugenia!—poor little Eugenia has nearly been the death of me; though not meaning it in the least, being all her life as innocent as a lamb.'

Mr. Tyrold assured him, that Eugenia was attached to him with the most unalterable fondness. But Sir Hugh said, that the sight of her, returning from Etherington, with nearly the same sadness as ever, had wounded him to the heart, by shewing him she would never recover; which had brought back upon him all his first contrition, about the smallpox, and the fall from the plank, and had caused his conscience to give him so many twitches, that it never let him rest a moment, till the gout seized upon his stomach, and almost took him off at once.

Mr. Tyrold attributed solely to his own strong imagination the idea of the continuance of the dejection of Eugenia, as she had left Etherington calm, and almost chearful. He instantly, therefore, fetched her, intimating the species of consolation she could afford.

'Kindest of Uncles!' cried she, 'is it possible you can ever, for a moment, have doubted the grateful affection with which your goodness has impressed me from my childhood? Do me more justice, I beseech you, my dearest Uncle! recover from this terrible attack, and you shall soon see your Eugenia restored to all the happiness you can wish her.'

'Nobody has got such kind nieces as me!' cried Sir Hugh, again dissolving into tenderness; 'for all nobody has deserved so ill of them. My generous little Camilla, forgave me from the very first, before her young soul had any guile in it, which, God knows, it never has had to this hour, no more than your own. However, this I can tell you, which may serve to keep you from repenting being good, and that is, that your kindness to your poor Uncle may be the means of saving a christian's life; which, for a young person at your age, is as much as can be expected: for I think, I may yet get about again, if I could once be assured I should see you as happy as you used to be; and you've been the contentedest little thing, till those unlucky market-women, that ever was seen: always speaking up for the servants, and the poor, from the time you were eight years old. And never letting me be angry, but taking every body's part, and thinking them all as good as yourself, and only wanting to make them as happy.'

'Ah, my dear Uncle! how kind a memory is yours! retaining only what can give pleasure, and burying in oblivion whatever might cause pain!—'

'Is my Uncle well enough to speak?' cried Camilla, softly opening the door, 'and may I—for one single moment,—see him?—'

'That's the voice of my dear Camilla!' said Sir Hugh; 'come in, my little love, for I shan't shock your tender heart now, for I'm going to get better.'

Camilla, in an ecstasy, was instantly at his bedside, passionately exclaiming, 'My dear, dear Uncle! will you indeed recover?—'

Sir Hugh, throwing his feeble arms round her neck, and leaning his head upon her shoulder, could only faintly articulate, 'If God pleases, I shall, my little darling, my heart's delight and joy! But don't vex, whether I do or not, for it is but in the course of nature for a man to die, even in his youth; but how much more when he comes to be old? Though I know you can't help missing me, in particular at the first, because of all your goodness to me.'

'Missing you? O my Uncle! we can never be happy again without you! never never!—when your loved countenance no longer smiles upon us,—when your kind voice no longer assembles us around you!—'

'My dear child—my own little Camilla,' cried Sir Hugh, in a faint voice, 'I am ready to die!'

Mr. Tyrold here forced her away, and his brother grew so much worse, that a dangerous relapse took place, and for three days more, the physician, the nurse, and Mr. Tyrold, were alone allowed to enter his room.

During this time, the whole family suffered the truest grief, and Camilla was inconsolable.

When again he began to revive, he called Mr. Tyrold to him, and said that this second shake persuaded him he had but a short time more for this world; and begged therefore he would prepare him for his exit.

Mr. Tyrold complied, and found, with more happiness than surprise, his perfect and chearful resignation either to live or to die, rejoicing as much as himself, in the innocent benevolence of his past days.

Composed and strengthened by religious duties, he then desired to see Eugenia and Indiana, that he might give them his last exhortations and counsel, in case of a speedy end.

Mr. Tyrold would fain have spared him this touching exertion, but he declared he could not go off with a clear conscience, unless he told them the advice which he had been thinking of for them, between whiles, during all his illness.

Mr. Tyrold then feared that opposition might but discompose him, and summoned his youngest daughter and his niece, charging them both to repress their affliction, lest it should accelerate what they most dreaded.

Camilla, always upon the watch, glided in with them, supplicating her Father not to deny her admittance; though fearful of her impetuous sorrows, he wished her to retreat; but Sir Hugh no sooner heard her murmuring voice, than he declared he would have her refused nothing, though he had meant to take a particular leave of her alone, for the last thing of all.

Gratefully thanking him, she advanced trembling to his bedside; solemnly promising her Father that no expression of her grief should again risk agitating a life and health so precious.

Sir Hugh then desired to have Lavinia called also, because, though he had thought of nothing to say to her, she might be hurt, after he was gone, in being left out.

He was then raised by pillows and sat upright, and they knelt round his bed. Mr. Tyrold entreated him to be concise, and insisted upon the extremest forbearance and fortitude in his little audience. He seated himself at some distance, and Sir Hugh, after swallowing a cordial medicine, began:

'My dear Nieces, I have sent for you all upon a particular account, which I beg you to listen to, because, God only knows whether I may ever be able to give you so much advice again. I see you all look very melancholy, which I take very kind of you. However don't cry, my little dears, for we must all go off, so it matters but little the day or the hour; dying being, besides, the greatest comfort of us all, taking us off from our cares; as my Brother will explain to you better than me.

'The chief of what I have got to say, in regard to what I have been studying in my illness, is for you two, my dear Eugenia and Indiana; because, having brought you both up, I can't get it out of my head what you'll do, when I am no longer here to keep you out of the danger of bad designers.

'My hope had been to have seen you both married while I was alive and amongst you, and I made as many plans as my poor head knew how, to bring it about; but we've all been disappointed alike, for which reason we must put up with it properly.

'What I have now last of all, to say to you, my little dears, is three maxims, which may serve for you all four alike, though I thought of them, at first, only for you two.

'In the first place, Never be proud: if you are, your superiors will laugh at you, your equals won't love you, and your dependants will hate you. And what is there for poor mortal man to be proud of?—Riches!—why they are but a charge, and if we don't use them well, we may envy the poor beggar that has so much less to answer for.—Beauty!—why, we can neither get it when we haven't it; nor keep it when we have it.—Power!—why we scarce ever use it one way, but what we are sorry we did not use it another!

'In the second place, Never trust a Flatterer. If a man makes you a great many compliments, always suspect him of some bad design, and never believe him your friend, till he tells you of some of your faults. Poor little things! you little imagine how many you have, for all you're so good!

'In the third place, Do no harm to others, for the sake of any good it may do to yourselves; because the good will last you but a little while; and the repentance will stick by you as long as you live; and what is worse, a great while longer, and beyond any count the best Almanack-maker knows how to reckon.

'And now, my dear Nieces, this is all; except the recommending to my dear Eugenia to be kind to my poor servants, who have all used me so well, knowing I have nothing to leave them.'

Eugenia, suppressing her sobs, promised to retain them all, as long as they should desire to remain with her, and to provide for them afterwards.

'I know, you'll forget nobody, my dear little girl,' cried the Baronet, 'which makes me die contented; not even Mrs. Margland, a little particularity not being to be considered at one's last end: and much less Dr. Orkborne, who has so much a better right from you. As to Indiana, she'll have her own little fortune when she comes of age; and I dare say her pretty face will marry her before long.—And as to Clermont, he'll come off rather short, finding I leave him nothing; but you'll make up for the deficiency, by giving him the whole, as well as a good wife. As to Lionel, I leave him my blessing; and as to any other legacy I never happened to promise him any; which is very good luck for me, as well as my best excuse; and I may say the same to my dear Lavinia, which is the reason I called her in, because she may not often have an opportunity to hear a man speak upon his death-bed. However all I wish for is, that I could leave you all equal shares, as well as give Eugenia the whole.'

'O my dear Uncle!' exclaimed Eugenia, 'make a new Will immediately! do everything your tenderness can dictate!—or tell me what I shall do in your name, and every word, every wish shall be sacredly obeyed!'

'Dear, generous, noble girl! no! I won't take from you a shilling! keep it all—nobody will spend it so well;—and I can't give you back your beauty; so keep it, my dear, all, for my oath's sake, when I am gone; and don't make me die under a prevaricating; which would be but a grievous thing for a person to do; unless he was but a bad believer: which, God help us! there are enough, without my helping to make more.'

Mr. Tyrold now again remonstrated, motioning to the weeping group to be gone.

'Ah! my dear Brother!' said Sir Hugh, 'you are the only right person that ought to have had it all, if it had not been for my poor weak brain, that made me always be looking askew instead of strait forward. And indeed I always meant you to have had it for your life, till the smallpox put all things out of my head. However, I hope you won't object to preach my funeral sermon, for all my bad faults, for nobody else will speak of me so kindly; which may serve as a better lesson for those I leave behind.'

Tears flowed fast down the cheeks of Mr. Tyrold, as he uttered whatever he could suggest most tenderly soothing to his Brother: and the young mourners, not daring to resist, were all gliding away, except Camilla, whose hand was fast grasped in that of her Uncle.

'Ah, my Camilla,' cried he, as she would gently have withdrawn it, 'how shall I part with my little dear darling? this is the worst twitch to me of all, with all my contentedness! And the more because I know you love your poor old Uncle, just as well as if he had left you all he was worth, though you won't get one penny by his death!'

'O my dear, dearest Uncle—' exclaimed Camilla, in a passionate flood of tears; when Mr. Tyrold, assuring them both the consequences might be fatal, tore her away from the bed and the room.

VOLUME III

BOOK V

CHAPTER I

A Pursuer

Notwithstanding the fears so justly excited from the mixt emotions and exertions of Sir Hugh, Mr. Tyrold had the happiness to see him fall into a tranquil sleep, from which he awoke without any return of pain; his night was quiet; the next day was still better; and the day following he was pronounced out of danger.

The rapture which this declaration excited in the house, and diffused throughout the neighbourhood, when communicated to the worthy baronet, gave a gladness to his heart that recompensed all he had suffered.

The delight of Camilla exceeded whatever she had yet experienced: her life had lost half its value in her estimation, while she believed that of her uncle to be in danger.

No one single quality is perhaps so endearing, from man to man, as good-nature. Talents excite more admiration; wisdom, more respect; and virtue, more esteem: but with admiration envy is apt to mingle, and fear with respect; while esteem, though always honourable, is often cold: but good-nature gives pleasure without any allay; ease, confidence, and happy carelessness, without the pain of obligation, without the exertion of gratitude.

If joy was in some more tumultuous, content was with none so penetrating as with Eugenia. Apprised now that she had been the immediate cause of the sufferings of her uncle, his loss would have given to her peace a blow irrecoverable; and she determined to bend the whole of her thoughts to his wishes, his comfort, his entire restoration.

To this end all her virtue was called in aid; a fear, next to aversion, having seized her of Clermont, from the apprehension she might never inspire in him such love as she had inspired in Bellamy, nor see in him, as in young Melmond, such merit as might raise similar sentiments for himself.

Molly Mill had not failed to paint to her the disappointment of Bellamy in not seeing her; but she was too much engrossed by the dangerous state of her uncle, to feel any compunction in her breach of promise; though touched with the account of his continual sufferings, she became very gentle in her reprimands to Molly for again meeting him; and, though Molly again disobeyed, she again was pardoned. He came daily to the lane behind the park pales, to hear news of the health of Sir Hugh, without pressing either for an interview or a letter; and Eugenia grew more and more moved by his respectful obsequiousness. She had yet said nothing to Camilla upon the subject; not only because a dearer interest mutually occupied them, but from a secret shame of naming a lover at a period so ungenial.

But now that Sir Hugh was in a fair way of recovery, her situation became alarming to herself. Openly, and before the whole house, she had solemnly been assigned to Clermont Lynmere; and, little as she wished the connexion, she thought it, from circumstances, her duty not to refuse it. Yet this gentleman had attended her so long, had endured so many disappointments, and borne them so much to her satisfaction, that, though she lamented her concession as an injury to Clermont, and grew ashamed to name it even to Camilla, she believed it would be cruelty unheard of to break it. She determined, therefore, to see him, to pronounce a farewell, and then to bend all her thoughts to the partner destined her by her friends.

Molly Mill was alone to accompany her to give her negative, her good wishes, and her solemn declaration that she could never again see or hear of him more. He could deem it no indelicacy that she suffered Molly to be present, since she was the negociator of his own choice.

Molly carried him, therefore, this news, with a previous condition that he was not to detain her mistress one minute. He promised all submission; and the next morning, after breakfast, Eugenia, in extreme dejection at the ungrateful task she had to perform, called for Molly, and walked forth.

Camilla, who was then accidentally in her own room, was, soon after, summoned by three smart raps to her chamber door.

There, to her great surprise, she saw Edgar, who, after a hasty apology, begged to have a few minutes conference with her alone.

She descended with him into the parlour, which was vacant.

'You suspect, perhaps,' said he, in an hurried manner, though attempting to smile, 'that I mean to fatigue you with some troublesome advice; I must, therefore, by an abrupt question, explain myself. Does Mr. Bellamy still continue his pretensions to your sister Eugenia?'

Startled in a moment from all thoughts of self, that at first had been rushing with violence to her heart, Camilla answered, 'No! why do you ask?'

'I will tell you: In my regular visits here of late, I have almost constantly met him, either on foot or on horseback, in the vicinity of the park. I suspected he watched to see Eugenia; but I knew she now never left the house; and concluded he was ignorant of the late general confinement. This moment, however, upon my entrance, I saw him again; and, as he hastily turned away upon meeting my eye, I dismounted, gave my horse to my man, and determined to satisfy myself which way he was strolling. I then followed him to the little lane to the right of the park, where I perceived an empty post-chaise-and-four in waiting: he advanced, and spoke with the postillion—I came instantly into the house by the little gate. This may be accidental; yet it has alarmed me; and I ventured, therefore, thus suddenly to apply to you, in order to urge you to give a caution to Eugenia, not to walk out, just at present, unattended.'

Camilla thanked him, and ran eagerly to speak to her sister; but she was not in her room; nor was she with her uncle; nor yet with Dr. Orkborne. She returned uneasily to the parlour, and said she would seek her in the park.

Edgar followed; but they looked around for her in vain: he then, deeming the danger urgent, left her, to hasten to the spot where he had seen the post-chaise.

Camilla ran on alone; and, when she reached the park gate, perceived her sister, Molly Mill, and Bellamy, in the lane.

They heard her quick approach, and turned round.

The countenance of Bellamy exhibited the darkest disappointment, and that of Eugenia the most excessive confusion. 'Now then, Sir,' she cried, 'delay our separation no longer.'

'Ah, permit me,' said he, in a low voice, 'permit me to hope you will hear my last sad sentence, my final misery, another day!—I will defer my mournful departure for that melancholy joy, which is the last I shall feel in my wretched existence!'

He sighed so deeply, that Eugenia, who seemed already in much sorrow, could not utter an abrupt refusal; and, as Camilla now advanced, she turned from him, without attempting to say any thing further.

Camilla, in the delight of finding her sister safe, after the horrible apprehensions she had just experienced, could not speak to her for tears.

Abashed at once, and amazed, Eugenia faintly asked what so affected her? She gave no explanation, but begged her to turn immediately back.

Eugenia consented; and Bellamy, bowing to them both profoundly, with quick steps walked away.

Camilla asked a thousand questions; but Eugenia seemed unable to answer them.

In a few minutes they were joined by Edgar, who, walking hastily up to them, took Camilla apart.

He told her he firmly believed a villainous scheme to have been laid: he had found the chaise still in waiting, and asked the postillion to whom he belonged. The man said he was paid for what he did; and refused giving any account of himself. Bellamy then appeared: he seemed confounded at his sight; but neither of them spoke; and he left him and his chaise, and his postillion, to console one another. He doubted not, he said, but the design had been to carry Eugenia off, and he had probably only pretended to take leave, that the chaise might advance, and the postillion aid the elopement: though finding help at hand, he had been forced to give up his scheme.

Camilla even with rapture blest his fortunate presence; but was confounded with perplexity at the conduct of Eugenia. Edgar, who feared her heart was entangled by an object who sought only her wealth, proposed dismissing Molly Mill, that he might tell her himself the opinion he had conceived of Bellamy.

Camilla overtook her sister, who had walked on without listening to or regarding them; and, sending away Molly, told her Edgar wished immediately to converse with her, upon something of the utmost importance.

'You know my high esteem of him,' she answered; 'but my mind is now occupied upon a business of which he has no information, and I entreat that you will neither of you interrupt me.'

Camilla, utterly at a loss what to conjecture, joined Mandlebert alone, and told him her ill success. He thought every thing was to be feared from the present state of the affair, and proposed revealing at once all he knew of it to Mr. Tyrold: but Camilla desired him to take no step till she had again expostulated with her sister, who might else be seriously hurt or offended. He complied, and said he would continue in the house, park, or environs, incessantly upon the watch, till some decisive measure were adopted.

Joining Eugenia then again, she asked if she meant seriously to encourage the addresses of Bellamy.

'By no means,' she quietly answered.

'My dear Eugenia, I cannot at all understand you; but it seems clear to me that the arrival of Edgar has saved you from some dreadful violence.'

'You hurt me, Camilla, by this prejudice. From whom should I dread violence? from a man who—but too fatally for his peace—values me more than his life?'

'If I could be sure of his sincerity,' said Camilla, 'I should be the last to think ill of him: but reflect a little, at least, upon the risk that you have run; my dear Eugenia! there was a post-chaise in waiting, not twenty yards from where I stopt you!'

'Ah, you little know Bellamy! that chaise was only to convey him away; to convey him, Camilla, to an eternal banishment!'

'But why, then, had he prevailed with you to quit the park?'

'You will call me vain if I tell you.'

'No; I shall only think you kind and confidential.'

'Do me then the justice,' said Eugenia, blushing, 'to believe me as much surprised as yourself at his most unmerited passion: but he told me, that if I only cast my eyes upon the vehicle which was to part him from me for ever, it would not only make it less abhorrent to him, but probably prevent the loss of his senses.'

'My dear Eugenia,' said Camilla, half smiling, 'this is a violent passion, indeed, for so short an acquaintance!'

'I knew you would say that,' answered she, disconcerted; 'and it was just what I observed to him myself: but he satisfied me that the reason of his feelings being so impetuous was, that this was the first and only time he had ever been in love.—So handsome as he is!—what a choice for him to make!'

Camilla, tenderly embracing her, declared, 'the choice was all that did him honour in the affair.'

'He never,' said she, a little comforted, 'makes me any compliments; I should else disregard, if not disdain him: but indeed he seems, notwithstanding his own extraordinary manly beauty, to be wholly superior to external considerations.'

Camilla now forbore expressing farther doubt, from the fear of painful misapprehension; but earnestly entreated her to suffer Edgar to be entrusted and consulted: she decidedly, however, refused her consent. 'I require no advice,' cried she, 'for I am devoted to my uncle's will: to speak then of this affair would be the most cruel indelicacy, in publishing a conquest which, since it is rejected, I ought silently, though gratefully, to bury in my own heart.'

She then related the history of all that had passed to Camilla; but solemnly declared she would never, to any other human being, but him who should hereafter be entitled to her whole heart, betray the secret of the unhappy Bellamy.

CHAPTER II

An Adviser

The wish of Camilla was to lay this whole affair before her father; but she checked it, from an apprehension she might seem displaying her duty and confidence at the expence of those of her sister; whose motives for concealment were intentionally the most pure, however, practically, they might be erroneous; and whom she both pitied and revered for her proposed submission to her uncle, in opposition to her palpable reluctance.

She saw not, however, any obstacle to consulting with Edgar, since he was already apprised of the business, and since his services might be essentially useful to her sister: while, with respect to herself, there seemed, at this time, more of dignity in meeting than shunning his friendly intercourse, since his regard for her seemed to have lost all its peculiarity. He has precisely, cried she, the same sentiments for my sisters as for me,—he is equally kind, disinterested, and indifferent to us all! anxious alike for Eugenia with Mr. Bellamy, and for me with the detestable Major! Be it so!—we can no where obtain a better friend; and I should blush, indeed, if I could not treat as a brother one who can treat me as a sister.

Tranquil, though not gay, she returned to converse with him; but when she had related what had passed, he confessed that his uneasiness upon the subject was increased. The heart of Eugenia appeared to him positively entangled; and he besought Camilla not to lose a moment in acquainting Mr. Tyrold with her situation.

She pleaded against giving this pain to her sister with energetic affection: her arguments failed to convince, but her eloquence powerfully touched him; and he contented himself with only entreating that she would again try to aid him with an opportunity of conversing with Eugenia.

This she could not refuse; nor could he then resist the opportunity to inquire why Mrs. Arlbery had left her and Lavinia at the play. She thanked him for remembering his character of her monitor, and acknowledged the fault to be her own, with a candour so unaffected, that, captivated by the soft seriousness of her manner, he flattered himself his fear of the Major was a chimæra, and hoped that, as soon as Sir Hugh was able to again join his family, no impediment would remain to his begging the united blessings of the two brothers to his views.

When Camilla told her sister the request of Edgar, she immediately suspected the attachment of Bellamy had been betrayed to him; and Camilla, incapable of any duplicity, related precisely how the matter had passed. Eugenia, always just, no sooner heard than she forgave it, and accompanied her sister immediately down stairs.

'I must rest all my hope of pardon,' cried Edgar, 'for the part I am taking, to your conviction of its motive; a filial love and gratitude to Mr. Tyrold, a fraternal affection and interest for all his family.'

'My own sisterly feelings,' she answered, 'make me both comprehend and thank your kind solicitude: but, believe me, it is now founded in error. I am shocked to find you informed of this unhappy transaction; and I charge and beseech that no interference may wound its ill-fated object, by suffering him to surmise your knowledge of his humiliating situation.'

'I would not for the world give you pain,' answered Edgar: 'but permit me to be faithful to the brotherly character in which I consider myself to stand with you ... all.'

A blush had overspread his face at the word Brotherly; while at that of all, which recovered him, a still deeper stained the cheeks of Camilla: but neither of them looked at the other; and Eugenia was too self-absorbed to observe either.

'Your utter inexperience in life,' he continued, 'makes me, though but just giving up leading-strings myself, an adept in the comparison. Suffer me then, as such, to represent to you my fears, that your innocence and goodness may expose you to imposition. You must not judge all characters by the ingenuousness of your own; nor conclude, however rationally and worthily a mind such as yours might—may—and will inspire a disinterested regard, that there is no danger of any other, and that mercenary views are out of the question, because mercenary principles are not declared.'

'I will not say your inference is severe,' replied Eugenia, 'because you know not the person of whom you speak: but permit me to make this irrefragable vindication of his freedom from all sordid motives; he has never once named the word fortune, neither to make any inquiries into mine, nor any professions concerning his own. Had he any inducement to duplicity, he might have asserted to me what he pleased, since I have no means of detection.'

'Your situation,' said Edgar, 'is pretty generally known; and for his ... pardon me if I hint it may be possible that silence is no virtue. However, since I am unacquainted, you say, with his character, will you give me leave to make myself better informed?'

'There needs no investigation; to me it is perfectly known.'

'Forgive me if I ask how!'

'By his letters and by his conversation.'

A smile which stole upon the features of Edgar obliged him to turn his head another way; but presently recovering, 'My dear Miss Eugenia,' he cried, 'will it not be most consonant to your high principles, and scrupulous delicacy, to lay the whole of what has passed before Mr. Tyrold?'

'Undoubtedly, if my part were not strait forward. Had I the least hesitation, my father should be my immediate and decisive umpire. But ... I am not at liberty even for deliberation!—I am not ... I know ... at my own disposal!'—

She blushed and looked down, confused; but presently, with firmness, added, 'It is not, indeed, fit that I should be; my uncle completely merits to be in all things my director. To know his wishes, therefore, is not only to know, but to be satisfied with my doom. Such being my situation, you cannot misunderstand my defence of this unhappy young man. It is but simple justice to rescue an amiable person from calumny.'

'Let us allow all this,' said Edgar; 'still I see no reason why Mr. Tyrold....'

'Mr. Mandlebert,' interrupted she, 'you must do what you judge right. I can desire no one to abstain from pursuing the dictates of their own sense of honour. I leave you, therefore, unshackled: but there is no consideration which, in my opinion, can justify a female in spreading, even to her nearest connexions, an unrequited partiality. If, therefore, I am forced to inflict this undue mortification, upon a person to whom I hold myself so much obliged, an uneasiness will remain upon my mind, destructive of my forgetfulness of an event which I would fain banish from my memory.'

She then refused to be any longer detained.

'How I love the perfect innocence, and how I reverence the respectable singularity of that charming character!' cried Edgar; 'yet how vain are all arguments against such a combination of fearless credulity, and enthusiastic reasoning? What can we determine?'

'I am happy to retort upon you that question,' replied Camilla; 'for I am every way afraid to act myself, lest I should hurt this dear sister, or do wrong by my yet dearer father.'

'What a responsibility you cast upon me! I will not, however, shrink from it, for the path seems far plainer to me since I have had this conversation. Eugenia is at present safe; I see, now, distinctly, her heart is yet untouched. The readiness with which she met the subject, the openness with which she avows her esteem, the unembarrassed, though modest simplicity with which she speaks of his passion and his distress, all shew that her pity results from generosity, not from love. Had it been otherwise, with all her steadiness, all her philosophy, some agitation and anxiety would have betrayed her secret soul. The internal workings of hopes and fears, the sensitive alarms of repressed consciousness....' A deep glow, which heated his face, forced him here to break off; and, abruptly leaving his sentence unfinished, he hastily began another.

'We must not, nevertheless, regard this as security for the future, though it is safety for the present; nor trust her unsuspicious generosity of mind to the dangerous assault of artful distress. I speak without reserve of this man; for though I know him not, as she remonstrated, I cannot, from the whole circumstances of his clandestine conduct, doubt his being an adventurer.... You say nothing? tell me, I beg, your opinion.'

Camilla had not heard one word of this last speech. Struck with his discrimination between the actual and the possible state of Eugenia's mind, and with the effect the definition had produced upon himself, her attention was irresistibly seized by a new train of ideas, till finding he waited for an answer, she mechanically repeated his last word 'opinion?'

He saw her absence of mind, and suspected his own too palpable disturbance had occasioned it: but in what degree, or from what sensations, he could not conjecture. They were both some time silent; and then, recollecting herself, she said it was earnestly her wish to avoid disobliging her sister, by a communication, which, made by any one but herself, must put her into a disgraceful point of view.

Edgar, after a pause, said, they must yield, then, to her present fervour, and hope her sounder judgment, when less played upon, would see clearer. It appeared to him, indeed, that she was so free, at this moment, from any dangerous impression, that it might, perhaps, be even safer to submit quietly to her request, than to urge the generous romance of her temper to new workings. He undertook, meantime, to keep a constant watch upon the motions of Bellamy, to make sedulous inquiries into his character and situation in life, and to find out for what ostensible purpose he was in Hampshire: entreating leave to communicate constantly to Camilla what he might gather, and to consult with her, from time to time, upon what measures should be pursued: yet ultimately confessing, that if Eugenia did not steadily persist in refusing any further rejections, he should hold himself bound in conscience to communicate the whole to Mr. Tyrold.

Camilla was pleased, and even thankful for the extreme friendliness and kind moderation of this arrangement; yet she left him mournfully, in a confirmed belief his regard for the whole family was equal.

Eugenia, much gratified, promised she would henceforth take no step with which Edgar should not first be acquainted.

CHAPTER III

Various Confabulations

Mr. Tyrold saw, at first, the renewed visits of Edgar at Cleves with extreme satisfaction; but while all his hopes were alive from an intercourse almost perpetual, he perceived, with surprise and perplexity, that his daughter became more and more pensive after every interview: and as Edgar, this evening, quitted the house, he observed tears start into her eyes as she went up stairs to her own room.

Alarmed and disappointed, he thought it now high time to investigate the state of the affair, and to encourage or prevent future meetings, as it appeared to him to be propitious or hopeless.

Penetrated with the goodness, while lamenting the indifference of Edgar, Camilla had just reached her room; when, as she turned round to shut her door, Mr. Tyrold appeared before her.

Hastily, with the back of her hand, brushing off the tears from her eyes, she said, 'May I go to my uncle, Sir?... can my uncle admit me?'

'He can always admit you,' he answered; 'but, just now, you must forget him a moment, and consign yourself to your father.'

He then entered, shut the door, and making her sit down by him, said, 'What is this sorrow that assails my Camilla? Why is the light heart of my dear and happy child thus dejected?'

Speech and truth were always one with Camilla; who, as she could not in this instance declare what were her feelings, remained mute and confounded.

'Hesitate not, my dear girl,' cried he kindly, 'to unbosom your griefs or your apprehensions, where they will be received with all the tenderness due to such a confidence, and held sacred from every human inspection; unless you permit me yourself to entrust your best and wisest friend.'

Camilla now trembled, but could not even attempt to speak.

He saw her disorder, and presently added, 'I will forbear to probe your feelings, when you have satisfied me in one doubt;—Is the sadness I have of late remarked in you the effect of secret personal disturbance, or of disappointed expectation?'

Camilla could neither answer nor look up: she was convinced, by this question, that the subject of her melancholy was understood, and felt wholly overcome by the deeply distressing confusion, with which wounded pride and unaffected virgin modesty impress a youthful female, in the idea of being suspected of a misplaced, or an unrequited partiality.

Her silence, a suffocating sigh, and her earnest endeavour to hide her face, easily explained to Mr. Tyrold all that passed within; and respecting rather than wishing to conquer a shame flowing from fearful delicacy, 'I would spare you,' he said, 'all investigation whatever, could I be certain you are not called into any action; but, in that case, I know not that I can justify to myself so implicit a confidence, in youth and inexperience so untried in difficulties, so unused to evil or embarrassment as yours. Tell me then, my dear Camilla, do you sigh under the weight of any disingenuous conduct? or do you suffer from some suspence which you have no means of terminating?'

'My dearest father, no!' cried she, sinking upon his breast. 'I have no suspence!'

She gasped for breath.

'And how has it been removed, my child?' said Mr. Tyrold, in a mournful tone; 'has any deception, any ungenerous art....'

'O no, no!... he is incapable ... he is superior ... he....' She stopt abruptly; shocked at the avowal these few words at once inferred of her partiality, of its hopelessness, and of its object.

She walked, confused, to a corner of the room, and, leaning against the wainscot, enveloped her face in her handkerchief, with the most painful sensations of shame.

Mr. Tyrold remained in deep meditation. Her regard for Edgar he had already considered as undoubted, and her undisguised acknowledgment excited his tenderest sympathy: but to find she thought it without return, and without hope, penetrated him with grief. Not only his own fond view of the attractions of his daughter, but all he had observed, even from his childhood, in Edgar, had induced him to believe she was irresistibly formed to captivate him; and what had lately passed had seemed a confirmation of all he had expected. Camilla, nevertheless, exculpated him from all blame; and, while touched by her artlessness, and honouring her truth, he felt, at least, some consolation to find that Edgar, whom he loved as a son, was untainted by deceit, unaccused of any evil. He concluded that some unfortunate secret entanglement, or some mystery not yet to be developed, directed compulsatorily his conduct, and checked the dictates of his taste and inclination.

Gently, at length, approaching her, 'My dearest child,' he said, 'I will ask you nothing further; all that is absolutely essential for me to know, I have gathered. You will never, I am certain, forget the noble mother whom you are bound to revere in imitating, nor the affectionate father whom your ingenuousness renders the most indulgent of your friends. Dry up your tears then, my Camilla, and command your best strength to conceal for ever their source, and, most especially ... from its cause.'

He then embraced, and left her.

'Yes, my dearest father,' cried she, as she shut the door, 'most perfect and most lenient of human beings! yes, I will obey your dictates; I will hide till I can conquer this weak emotion, and no one shall ever know, and Edgar least of all, that a daughter of yours has a feeling she ought to disguise!'

Elevated by the kindness of a father so adored, to deserve his good opinion now included every wish. The least severity would have chilled her confidence, the least reproof would have discouraged all effort to self-conquest; but, while his softness had soothed, his approbation had invigorated her; and her feelings received additional energy from the conscious generosity with which she had represented Edgar as blameless. Blameless, however, in her own breast, she could not deem him: his looks, his voice, his manner, ... words that occasionally dropt from him, and meanings yet more expressive which his eyes or his attentions had taken in charge, all, from time to time, had told a flattering tale, which, though timidity and anxious earnestness had obscured from her perfect comprehension, her hopes and her sympathy had prevented from wholly escaping her. Yet what, internally, she could not defend she forgave; and, acquitting him of all intentional deceit, concluded that what he had felt for her, he had thought too slight and immaterial to deserve repressing on his own part, or notice on her's. To continue with him her present sisterly conduct was all she had to study, not doubting but that what as yet was effort, would in time become natural.

Strengthened thus in fortitude, she descended cheerfully to supper, where Mr. Tyrold, though he saw with pain that her spirits were constrained, felt the fondest satisfaction in the virtue of her exertion.

Her night passed in the consolation of self-applause. My dear father, thought she, will see I strive to merit his lenity, and that soothing consideration with the honourable friendship of Edgar, will be sufficient for the happiness of my future life, in the single and tranquil state in which it will be spent.

Thus comforted, she again met the eye of Mr. Tyrold the next day at breakfast; in the midst of which repast Edgar entered the parlour. The tea she was drinking was then rather gulped than sipped; yet she maintained an air of unconcern, and returned his salutation with apparent composure.

Edgar, while addressing to Mr. Tyrold his inquiries concerning Sir Hugh, saw, from the window, his servant, whom he had out-galloped, thrown with violence from his horse. He rushed out of the parlour; and the first person to rise, with involuntary intent to follow him, was Camilla. But, as she reached the hall-door, she saw that the man was safe, and perceived that her father was the only person who had left the room besides herself. Ashamed, she returned, and found the female party collected at the windows.

Hoping to retrieve the error of her eagerness, she seated herself at the table, and affected to finish her breakfast.

Eugenia told her they had discovered the cause of the accident, which had been owing to a sharp stone that had penetrated into the horse's hoof, and which Edgar was now endeavouring to extract.

A general scream, just then, from the window party, and a cry from Eugenia of 'O Edgar!' carried her again to the hall-door with the swiftness of lightning, calling out, 'Where?... What?... Good Heaven!...'

Molly Mill, accidentally there before her, said, as she approached, that the horse had kicked Mr. Mandlebert upon the shoulder.

Every thing but tenderness and terror was now forgotten by Camilla; she darted forward with unrestrained velocity, and would have given, in a moment, the most transporting amazement to Edgar, and to herself the deepest shame, but that Mr. Tyrold, who alone had his face that way, stopt, and led her back to the house, saying, 'There is no mischief; a bee stung the poor animal at the instant the stone was extracted, and the surprise and pain made it kick; but, fortunately, without any bad effect. I wish to know how your uncle is; I should be glad you would go and sit with him till I can come.'

With these words he left her; and, though abashed and overset, she found no sensation so powerful as joy for the safety of Edgar.

Still, however, too little at ease for conversing with her uncle, she went straight to her own chamber, and flew involuntarily to a window, whence the first object that met her eyes was her father, who was anxiously looking up. She retreated, utterly confounded, and threw herself upon a chair at the other end of the room.

Shame now was her only sensation. The indiscretion of her first surprise, she knew, he must forgive, though she blushed at its recollection; but a solicitude so pertinacious, an indulgence so repeated of feelings he had enjoined her to combat ... how could she hope for his pardon? or how obtain her own, to have forfeited an approbation so precious?

She could not go to her uncle; she would have remained where she was till summoned to dinner, if the house-maid, after finishing all her other work, had not a third time returned to inquire if she might clean her room.

She then determined to repair to the library, where she was certain only to encounter Eugenia, who would not torment, or Dr. Orkborne, who would not perceive her: but at the bottom of the stairs she was stopt by Miss Margland, who, with a malicious smile, asked if she was going to hold the bason?

'What bason?' cried she, surprised.

'The bason for the surgeon.'

'What surgeon?' repeated she, alarmed.

'Mr. Burton, who is come to bleed Mr. Mandlebert.'

She asked nothing more. She felt extremely faint, but made her way into the park, to avoid further conference.

Here, in the most painful suspence, dying for information, yet shirking whoever could give it her, she remained, till she saw the departure of the surgeon. She then went round by a back way to the apartment of Eugenia, who informed her that the contusion, though not dangerous, was violent, and that Mr. Tyrold had insisted upon immediate bleeding. The surgeon had assured them this precaution would prevent any ill consequence; but Sir Hugh, hearing from the servants what had happened, had desired that Edgar would not return home till the next day.

The joy of Camilla, that nothing was more serious, banished all that was disagreeable from her thoughts, till she was called back to reflections less consoling, by meeting Mr. Tyrold, as she was returning to her own room; who, with a gravity unusual, desired to speak with her, and preceded her into the chamber.

Trembling, and filled with shame, she followed, shut the door, and remained at it without daring to look up.

'My dear Camilla,' cried he with earnestness, 'let me not hope in vain for that exertion you have promised me, and to which I know you to be fully equal. Risk not, my dear girl, to others, those outward marks of sensibility which, to common or unfeeling observers, seem but the effect of an unbecoming remissness in the self-command which should dignify every female who would do herself honour. I had hoped, in this house at least, you would not have been misunderstood; but I have this moment been undeceived: Miss Margland has just expressed a species of compassion for what she presumes to be the present state of your mind, that has given me the severest pain.'

He stopt, for Camilla looked thunderstruck.

Approaching her, then, with a look of concern, and a voice of tenderness, he kindly took her hand, and added: 'I do not tell you this in displeasure, but to put you upon your guard. You will hear from Eugenia that we shall not dine alone; and from what I have dropt you will gather how little you can hope to escape scrutiny. Exert yourself to obviate all humiliating surmises, and you will amply be repaid by the balm of self-approbation.'

He then kissed her, and quitted the room.

She now remained in utter despair: the least idea of disgrace totally broke her spirit, and she sat upon the same spot on which Mr. Tyrold had left her, till the ringing of the second dinner bell.

She then gloomily resolved to plead an head-ache, and not to appear.

When a footman tapt at her door, to acquaint her every body was seated at the table, she sent down this excuse: forming to herself the further determination, that the same should suffice for the evening, and for the next morning, that she might avoid the sight of Edgar, in presence either of her father or Miss Margland.

Eugenia, with kind alarm, came to know what was the matter, and informed her, that Sir Hugh had been so much concerned at the accident of Edgar, that he had insisted upon seeing him, and, after heartily shaking hands, had promised to think no more of past mistakes and disappointments, as they had now been cleared up to the county, and desired him to take up his abode at Cleves for a week.

Camilla heard this with mixt pleasure and pain. She rejoiced that Edgar should be upon his former terms with her beloved uncle; but how preserve the caution demanded from her for so long a period, in the constant sight of her now watchful father, and the malicious Miss Margland?

She had added to her own difficulties by this present absconding, and, with severe self-blame, resolved to descend to tea. But, while settling how to act, after her sister had left her, she was struck with hearing the name of Mandlebert pronounced by Mary, the house-maid, who was talking with Molly Mill upon the landing place. Why it had been spoken she knew not; but Molly answered: 'Dearee me, never mind; I'll help you to do his room, if Nanny don't come in time. My little mistress would rather do it herself, than he should want for anything.'

'Why, it's natural enough,' said Mary, 'for young ladies to like young gentlemen; and there's none other comes a nigh 'em, which I often thinks dull enough for our young misses. And, to be certain, Mr. Mandlebert would be as pretty a match for one of 'em as a body could desire.'

'And his man,' said Molly, 'is as pretty a gentleman sort of person, to my mind, as his master. I'm sure I'm as glad as my young lady when they comes to the house.'

'O, as to Miss Eugeny,' said Mary, 'I believe, in my conscience, she likes our crack-headed old Doctor as well as e'er a young gentleman in Christendom; for there she'll sit with him, hour by hour, poring over such a heap of stuff as never was seed, reading, first one, then t'other, God knows what; for I believe never nobody heard the like of it before; and all the time never give the old Doctor a cross word.—'

'She never given nobody a cross word,' interrupted Molly; 'if I was Mr. Mandlebert, I'd sooner have her than any of 'em, for all she's such a nidging little thing.'

'For certain,' said Mary, 'she's very good, and a deal of good she does, to all as asks her; but Miss Camilla for my money. She's all alive and merry, and makes poor master young again to look at her. I wish Mr. Mandlebert would have her, for I have overheard Miss Margland telling Miss Lynmere she was desperate fond of him, and did all she could to get him.'

Camilla felt flushed with the deepest resentment, and could scarcely command herself to forbear charging Miss Margland with this persecuting cruelty.

Nanny, the under house-maid, now joining them, said she had been detained to finish altering a curtain for Miss Margland. 'And the cross old Frump,' she added, 'is in a worse spite than ever, and she kept abusing that sweet Mr. Mandlebert to Miss Lynmere all the while, till she went down to dinner, and she said she was sure it was all Miss Camilla's doings his staying here again, for she could come over master for any thing: and she said she supposed it was to have another catch at the young 'Squire's heart, but she hoped he would not be such a fool.'

'I'm sure I wish he would,' cried Molly Mill, 'if it was only to spite her, she's such a nasty old viper. And Miss Camilla's always so good-natured, and so affable, she'd make him a very agreeable wife, I dare say.'

'And she's mortal fond of him, that's true,' said Mary, 'for when they was both here, I always see her a running to the window, to see who was a coming into the park, when he was rode out; and when he was in the house, she never so much as went to peep, if there come six horses, one after t'other. And she was always a saying, "Mary, who's in the parlour? Mary, who's below?" while he was here; but before he come, duce a bite did she ask about nobody.'

'I like when I meets her,' said Molly Mill, 'to tell her Mr. Mandlebert's here, Miss; or Mr. Mandlebert's there, Miss;—Dearee me, one may almost see one self in her eyes, it makes them shine so.'

Camilla could endure no more; she arose, and walked about the room; and the maids, who had concluded her at dinner, hearing her step, hurried away, to finish their gossiping in the room of Mandlebert.

Camilla now felt wholly sunk; the persecutions of Miss Margland seemed nothing to this blow: they were cruel, she could therefore repine at them; they were unprovoked, she could therefore repel them: but to find her secret feelings, thus generally spread, and familiarity commented upon, from her own unguarded conduct, exhausted, at once, patience, fortitude, and hope, and left her no wish but to quit Cleves while Edgar should remain there.

Certain, however, that her father would not permit her to return to Etherington alone, a visit to Mrs. Arlbery was the sole refuge she could suggest; and she determined to solicit his permission to accept immediately the invitation of that lady.

CHAPTER IV

A Dodging

Camilla waited in the apartment of Mr. Tyrold till he came up stairs, and then begged his leave to spend a few days at the Grove; hinting, when he hesitated, though with a confusion that was hardly short of torture, at what had passed amongst the servants.

He heard her with the tenderest pity, and the kindest praise of her sincerity; and, deeply as he was shocked to find her thus generally betrayed, he was too compassionate to point out, at so suffering a moment, the indiscretions from which such observations must have originated. Yet he saw consequences the most unpleasant in this rumour of her attachment; and though he still privately hoped that the behaviour of Mandlebert was the effect of some transient embarrassment, he wished her removed from all intercourse with him that was not sought by himself, while the incertitude of his intentions militated against her struggles for indifference. The result, therefore, of a short deliberation was to accede to her request.

Camilla then wrote her proposition to Mrs. Arlbery, which Mr. Tyrold sent immediately by a stable-boy of the baronet's.

The answer was most obliging; Mrs. Arlbery said she would herself fetch her the next morning, and keep her till one of them should be tired.

The relief which this, at first, brought to Camilla, in the week's exertions it would spare, was soon succeeded by the most acute uneasiness for the critical situation of Eugenia, and the undoubted disapprobation of Edgar. To quit her sister at a period when she might serve her; ... to forsake Cleves at the moment Edgar was restored to it, seemed selfish even to herself, and to him must appear unpardonable. 'Alas!' she cried, 'how for ever I repent my hasty actions! Why have I not better struggled against my unfortunate feelings?'

She now almost hated her whole scheme, regretted its success, wished herself suffering every uneasiness Miss Margland could inflict, and all the shame of being watched and pitied by every servant in the house, in preference to deserting Eugenia, and making Mandlebert deem her unworthy. But self-upbraiding was all that followed her contrition: Mrs. Arlbery was to fetch her by appointment; and it was now too late to trifle with the conceding goodness of her father.

She did not dare excuse herself from appearing at breakfast the next morning, lest Mr. Tyrold should think her utterly incorrigible to his exhortations.

Edgar earnestly inquired after her health as she entered the room; she slightly answered she was better; and began eating, with an apparent eagerness of appetite: while he, who had expected some kind words upon his own accident, surprised and disappointed, could swallow nothing.

Mr. Tyrold, seeing and pitying what passed in her mind, gave her a commission, that enabled her, soon, to leave the room without affectation; and, happy to escape, she determined to go down stairs no more till Mrs. Arlbery arrived. She wished to have conversed first upon the affairs of Eugenia with Edgar: but to name to him whither she was herself going, when she could not possibly name why; to give to him a surprise that must recoil upon herself in disapprobation, was more than she could endure. She had invested him with full powers to counsel and to censure her; he would naturally use them to dissuade her from a visit so ill-timed; and what could she urge in opposition to his arguments that would not seem trifling or wilful?

The present moment was all that occupied, the present evil all that ever alarmed the breast of Camilla: to avoid him, therefore, now, was the whole of her desire, unmolested with one anxiety how she might better meet him hereafter.

She watched at her window till she saw the groom of Mrs. Arlbery gallop into the Park. She hastened then to take leave of Sir Hugh, whom Mr. Tyrold had prepared for her departure; but, at the door of his apartment, she encountered Edgar.

'You are going out?' cried he, perceiving an alteration in her dress.

'I am ... just going to ... to speak to my uncle,' cried she, stammering and entering the room at the same moment.

Sir Hugh kindly wished her much amusement, and hoped she would make him long amends when he was better. She took leave; but again, on the landing-place, met Edgar, who, anxious and perlexed, watched to speak to her before she descended the stairs. Eagerly advancing, 'Do you walk?' he cried; 'may I ask? or ... am I indiscreet?'

She answered she had something to say to Eugenia, but should be back in an instant. She then flew to the chamber of her sister, and conjured her to consult Edgar in whatever should occur during her absence. Eugenia solemnly consented.

Jacob presently tapped at the door, to announce that Mrs. Arlbery was waiting below in her carriage.

How to pass or escape Edgar became now her greatest difficulty; she could suggest nothing to palliate to him the step she was taking, yet could still less bear to leave him to wild conjecture and certain blame: and she was standing irresolute and thoughtful, when Mr. Tyrold came to summon her.

After mildly representing the indecorum of detaining any one she was to receive by appointment, he took her apart, and putting a packet into her hand, 'I would not,' he said, 'agitate your spirits this morning, by entering upon any topic that might disturb you: I have therefore put upon paper what I most desire you to consider. You will find it a little sermon upon the difficulties and the conduct of the female heart. Read it alone, and with attention. And now, my dearest girl, go quietly into the parlour, and let one brief and cheerful good-morrow serve for every body alike.'

He then returned to his brother.

She made Eugenia accompany her down stairs, to avoid any solitary attack from Edgar; he suffered them to pass; but followed to the parlour, where she hastily bid adieu to Miss Margland and Indiana; but was stopt from running off by the former, who said, 'I wish I had known you intended going out, for I designed asking Sir Hugh for the chariot for myself this morning, to make a very particular visit.'

Camilla, in a hesitating voice, said she should not use her uncle's chariot.

'You walk then?'

'No, ... ma'am ... but—there is—there is a carriage—I believe, now at the door.'

'O dear, whose?' cried Indiana; 'do, pray, tell me where you are going?' while Edgar, still more curious than either, held out his hand to conduct her, that he might obtain better information.

'I am very glad your head-ache is so well,' said Miss Margland; 'but, pray—is Mr. Mandlebert to be your chaperon?'

They both blushed, though both affected not to hear her: but, before they could quit the room, Indiana, who had run to a bow-window, exclaimed, 'Dear! if there is not Mrs. Arlbery in a beautiful high phaeton!'

Edgar, astonished, was now as involuntarily drawing back, as Camilla, involuntarily, was hurrying on: but Miss Margland, insisting upon an answer, desired to know if she should return to dinner?

She stammered out, No. Miss Margland pursued her to ask at what time the chariot was to fetch her; and forced from her a confession that she should be away for some days.

She was now permitted to proceed. Edgar, impressed with the deepest displeasure, leading her in silence across the hall: but, stopping an instant at the door, 'This excursion,' he gravely said, 'will rescue you from no little intended importunity: I had purposed tormenting you, from time to time, for your opinion and directions with respect to Miss Eugenia.'

And then, bowing coldly to Mrs. Arlbery, who eagerly called out to welcome her, he placed her in the phaeton, which instantly drove off.

He looked after them for some time, almost incredulous of her departure: but, as his amazement subsided into certainty, the most indignant disappointment succeeded. That she could leave Cleves at the very moment he was reinstated in its society, seemed conviction to him of her indifference; and that she could leave it in the present state of the affairs of Eugenia, made him conclude her so great a slave to the love of pleasure, that every duty and all propriety were to be sacrificed to its pursuit. 'I will think of her,' cried he, 'no more! She concealed from me her plan, lest I should torment her with admonitions: the glaring homage of the Major is better adapted to her taste,—She flies from my sincerity to receive his adulation,—I have been deceived in her disposition,—I will think of her no more!'

CHAPTER V

A Sermon

The kind reception of Mrs. Arlbery, and all the animation of her discourse, were thrown away upon Camilla. An absent smile, and a few faint acknowledgments of her goodness were all she could return: Eugenia abandoned when she might have been served, Edgar contemning when he might have been approving ... these were the images of her mind, which resisted entrance to all other.

Tired of fruitless attempts to amuse her, Mrs. Arlbery, upon their arrival at the Grove, conducted her to an apartment prepared for her, and made use of no persuasion that she would leave it before dinner.

Camilla then, too unhappy to fear any injunction, and resigned to whatever she might receive, read the discourse of Mr. Tyrold.

For Miss Camilla Tyrold.

It is not my intention to enumerate, my dear Camilla, the many blessings of your situation; your heart is just and affectionate, and will not forget them: I mean but to place before you your immediate duties, satisfied that the review will ensure their performance.

Unused to, because undeserving control, your days, to this period, have been as gay as your spirits. It is now first that your tranquillity is ruffled; it is now, therefore, that your fortitude has its first debt to pay for its hitherto happy exemption.

Those who weigh the calamities of life only by the positive, the substantial, or the irremediable mischiefs which they produce, regard the first sorrows of early youth as too trifling for compassion. They do not enough consider that it is the suffering, not its abstract cause, which demands human commiseration. The man who loses his whole fortune, yet possesses firmness, philosophy, a disdain of ambition, and an accommodation to circumstances, is less an object of contemplative pity, than the person who, without one real deprivation, one actual evil, is first, or is suddenly forced to recognise the fallacy of a cherished and darling hope.

That its foundation has always been shallow is no mitigation of disappointment to him who had only viewed it in its super-structure. Nor is its downfall less terrible to its visionary elevator, because others had seen it from the beginning as a folly or a chimæra; its dissolution should be estimated, not by its romance in the unimpassioned examination of a rational looker on, but by its believed promise of felicity to its credulous projector.

Is my Camilla in this predicament? had she wove her own destiny in the speculation of her wishes? Alas! to blame her, I must first forget, that delusion, while in force, has all the semblance of reality, and takes the same hold upon the faculties as truth. Nor is it till the spell is broken, till the perversion of reason and error of judgment become wilful, that Scorn ought to point 'its finger' or Censure its severity.

But of this I have no fear. The love of right is implanted indelibly in your nature, and your own peace is as dependant as mine and as your mother's upon its constant culture.

Your conduct hitherto has been committed to yourself. Satisfied with establishing your principles upon the adamantine pillars of religion and conscience, we have not feared leaving you the entire possession of general liberty. Nor do I mean to withdraw it, though the present state of your affairs, and what for some time past I have painfully observed of your precipitance, oblige me to add partial counsel to standing precept, and exhortation to advice. I shall give them, however, with diffidence, fairly acknowledging and blending my own perplexities with yours.

The temporal destiny of woman is enwrapt in still more impenetrable obscurity than that of man. She begins her career by being involved in all the worldly accidents of a parent; she continues it by being associated in all that may environ a husband: and the difficulties arising from this doubly appendant state, are augmented by the next to impossibility, that the first dependance should pave the way for the ultimate. What parent yet has been gifted with the foresight to say, 'I will educate my daughter for the station to which she shall belong?' Let us even suppose that station to be fixed by himself, rarely as the chances of life authorise such a presumption; his daughter all duty, and the partner of his own selection solicitous of the alliance: is he at all more secure he has provided even for her external welfare? What, in this sublunary existence, is the state from which she shall neither rise nor fall? Who shall say that in a few years, a few months, perhaps less, the situation in which the prosperity of his own views has placed her, may not change for one more humble than he has fitted her for enduring, or more exalted than he has accomplished her for sustaining? The conscience, indeed, of the father is not responsible for events, but the infelicity of the daughter is not less a subject of pity.

Again, if none of these outward and obvious vicissitudes occur, the proper education of a female, either for use or for happiness, is still to seek, still a problem beyond human solution; since its refinement, or its negligence, can only prove to her a good or an evil, according to the humour of the husband into whose hands she may fall. If fashioned to shine in the great world, he may deem the metropolis all turbulence; if endowed with every resource for retirement, he may think the country distasteful. And though her talents, her acquirements, may in either of these cases be set aside, with an only silent regret of wasted youth and application; the turn of mind which they have induced, the appreciation which they have taught of time, of pleasure, or of utility, will have nurtured inclinations and opinions not so ductile to new sentiments and employments, and either submission becomes a hardship, or resistance generates dissention.

If such are the parental embarrassments, against which neither wisdom nor experience can guard, who should view the filial without sympathy and tenderness?

You have been brought up, my dear child, without any specific expectation. Your mother and myself, mutually deliberating upon the uncertainty of the female fate, determined to educate our girls with as much simplicity as is compatible with instruction, as much docility for various life as may accord with invariable principles, and as much accommodation with the world at large, as may combine with a just distinction of selected society. We hoped, thus, should your lots be elevated, to secure you from either exulting arrogance, or bashful insignificance; or should they, as is more probable, be lowly, to instil into your understandings and characters such a portion of intellectual vigour as should make you enter into an humbler scene without debasement, helplessness, or repining.

It is now, Camilla, we must demand your exertions in return. Let not these cares, to fit you for the world as you may find it, be utterly annihilated from doing you good, by the uncombated sway of an unavailing, however well-placed attachment.

We will not here canvass the equity of that freedom by which women as well as men should be allowed to dispose of their own affections. There cannot, in nature, in theory, nor even in common sense, be a doubt of their equal right: but disquisitions on this point will remain rather curious than important, till the speculatist can superinduce to the abstract truth of the position some proof of its practicability.

Meanwhile, it is enough for every modest and reasonable young woman to consider, that where there are two parties, choice can belong only to one of them: and then let her call upon all her feelings of delicacy, all her notions of propriety, to decide: Since Man must choose Woman, or Woman Man, which should come forward to make the choice? Which should retire to be chosen?

A prepossession directed towards a virtuous and deserving object wears, in its first approach, the appearance of a mere tribute of justice to merit. It seems, therefore, too natural, perhaps too generous, to be considered either as a folly or a crime. It is only its encouragement where it is not reciprocal, that can make it incur the first epithet, or where it ought not to be reciprocal that can brand it with the second. With respect to this last, I know of nothing to apprehend:—with regard to the first—I grieve to wound my dearest Camilla, yet where there has been no subject for complaint, there can have been none for expectation.

Struggle then against yourself as you would struggle against an enemy. Refuse to listen to a wish, to dwell even upon a possibility, that opens to your present idea of happiness. All that in future may be realised probably hangs upon this conflict. I mean not to propose to you in the course of a few days to reinstate yourself in the perfect security of a disengaged mind. I know too much of the human heart to be ignorant that the acceleration, or delay, must depend upon circumstance: I can only require from you what depends upon yourself, a steady and courageous warfare against the two dangerous underminers of your peace and of your fame, imprudence and impatience. You have champions with which to encounter them that cannot fail of success, ... good sense and delicacy.

Good sense will shew you the power of self-conquest, and point out its means. It will instruct you to curb those unguarded movements which lay you open to the strictures of others. It will talk to you of those boundaries which custom forbids your sex to pass, and the hazard of any individual attempt to transgress them. It will tell you, that where allowed only a negative choice, it is your own best interest to combat against a positive wish. It will bid you, by constant occupation, vary those thoughts that now take but one direction, and multiply those interests which now recognise but one object: and it will soon convince you, that it is not strength of mind which you want, but reflection, to obtain a strict and unremitting control over your passions.

This last word will pain, but let it not shock you. You have no passions, my innocent girl, at which you need blush, though enough at which I must tremble!—For in what consists your constraint, your forbearance? your wish is your guide, your impulse is your action. Alas! never yet was mortal created so perfect, that every wish was virtuous, or every impulse wise!

Does a secret murmur here demand: if a discerning predilection is no crime, why, internally at least, may it not be cherished? whom can it injure or offend, that, in the hidden recesses of my own breast, I nourish superior preference of superior worth?

This is the question with which every young woman beguiles her fancy; this is the common but seductive opiate, with which inclination lulls reason.

The answer may be safely comprised in a brief appeal to her own breast.

I do not desire her to be insensible to merit; I do not even demand she should confine her social affections to her own sex, since the most innocent esteem is equally compatible, though not equally general with ours: I require of her simply, that, in her secret hours, when pride has no dominion, and disguise would answer no purpose, she will ask herself this question, 'Could I calmly hear that this elect of my heart was united to another? Were I to be informed that the indissoluble knot was tied, which annihilates all my own future possibilities, would the news occasion me no affliction?' This, and this alone, is the test by which she may judge the danger, or the harmlessness of her attachment.

I have now endeavoured to point out the obligations which you may owe to good sense. Your obligations to delicacy will be but their consequence.

Delicacy is an attribute so peculiarly feminine, that were your reflections less agitated by your feelings, you could delineate more distinctly than myself its appropriate laws, its minute exactions, its sensitive refinements. Here, therefore, I seek but to bring back to your memory what livelier sensations have inadvertently driven from it.

You may imagine, in the innocency of your heart, that what you would rather perish than utter can never, since untold, be suspected: and, at present, I am equally sanguine in believing no surmise to have been conceived where most it would shock you: yet credit me when I assure you, that you can make no greater mistake, than to suppose that you have any security beyond what sedulously you must earn by the most indefatigable vigilance. There are so many ways of communication independent of speech, that silence is but one point in the ordinances of discretion. You have nothing, in so modest a character, to apprehend from vanity or presumption; you may easily, therefore, continue the guardian of your own dignity: but you must keep in mind, that our perceptions want but little quickening to discern what may flatter them; and it is mutual to either sex to be to no gratification so alive, as to that of a conscious ascendance over the other.

Nevertheless, the female who, upon the softening blandishment of an undisguised prepossession, builds her expectation of its reciprocity, is, in common, most cruelly deceived. It is not that she has failed to awaken tenderness; but it has been tenderness without respect: nor yet that the person thus elated has been insensible to flattery; but it has been a flattery to raise himself, not its exciter in his esteem. The partiality which we feel inspires diffidence: that which we create has a contrary effect. A certainty of success in many destroys, in all weakens, its charm: the bashful excepted, to whom it gives courage; and the indolent, to whom it saves trouble.

Carefully, then, beyond all other care, shut up every avenue by which a secret which should die untold can further escape you. Avoid every species of particularity; neither shun nor seek any intercourse apparently; and in such meetings as general prudence may render necessary, or as accident may make inevitable, endeavour to behave with the same open esteem as in your days of unconsciousness. The least unusual attention would not be more suspicious to the world, than the least undue reserve to the subject of our discussion. Coldness or distance could only be imputed to resentment; and resentment, since you have received no offence, how, should it be investigated, could you vindicate? or how, should it be passed in silence, secure from being attributed to pique and disappointment?

There is also another motive, important to us all, which calls for the most rigid circumspection. The person in question is not merely amiable; he is also rich: mankind at large, therefore, would not give merely to a sense of excellence any obvious predilection. This hint will, I know, powerfully operate upon your disinterested spirit.

Never from personal experience may you gather, how far from soothing, how wide from honourable, is the species of compassion ordinarily diffused by the discovery of an unreturned female regard. That it should be felt unsought may be considered as a mark of discerning sensibility; but that it should be betrayed uncalled for, is commonly, however ungenerously, imagined rather to indicate ungoverned passions, than refined selection. This is often both cruel and unjust; yet, let me ask—Is the world a proper confident for such a secret? Can the woman who has permitted it to go abroad, reasonably demand that consideration and respect from the community, in which she has been wanting to herself? To me it would be unnecessary to observe, that her indiscretion may have been the effect of an inadvertence which owes its origin to artlessness, not to forwardness: She is judged by those, who, hardened in the ways of men, accustom themselves to trace in evil every motive to action; or by those, who, preferring ridicule to humanity, seek rather to amuse themselves wittily with her susceptibility, than to feel for its innocence and simplicity.

In a state of utter constraint, to appear natural is, however, an effort too difficult to be long sustained; and neither precept, example, nor disposition, have enured my poor child to the performance of any studied part. Discriminate, nevertheless, between hypocrisy and discretion. The first is a vice; the second a conciliation to virtue. It is the bond that keeps society from disunion; the veil that shades our weakness from exposure, giving time for that interior correction, which the publication of our infirmities would else, with respect to mankind, make of no avail.

It were better no doubt, worthier, nobler, to meet the scrutiny of our fellow-creatures by consent, as we encounter, per force, the all-viewing eye of our Creator: but since for this we are not sufficiently without blemish, we must allow to our unstable virtues all the encouragement that can prop them. The event of discovered faults is more frequently callousness than amendment; and propriety of example is as much a duty to our fellow-creatures, as purity of intention is a debt to ourselves.

To delicacy, in fine, your present exertions will owe their future recompence, be your ultimate lot in life what it may. Should you, in the course of time, belong to another, you will be shielded from the regret that a former attachment had been published; or should you continue mistress of yourself, from a blush that the world is acquainted it was not by your choice.

I shall now conclude this little discourse by calling upon you to annex to whatever I have offered you of precept, the constant remembrance of your mother for example.

In our joint names, therefore, I adjure you, my dearest Camilla, not to embitter the present innocence of your suffering by imprudence that may attach to it censure, nor by indulgence that may make it fasten upon your vitals! Imprudence cannot but end in the demolition of that dignified equanimity, and modest propriety, which we wish to be uniformly remarked as the attributes of your character: and indulgence, by fixing, may envenom a dart that as yet may be gently withdrawn, from a wound which kindness may heal, and time may close; but which, if neglected, may wear away, in corroding disturbance, all your life's comfort to yourself, and all its social purposes to your friends and to the world.

AUGUSTUS TYROLD.

CHAPTER VI

A Chat

The calm sadness with which Camilla had opened her letter was soon broken in upon by the interest of its contents, the view it displayed of her duties, her shame at her recent failures, and her fears for their future execution; and yet more than all, by the full decision in which it seemed written, that the unhappy partiality she had exposed, had been always, and would for ever remain unreturned.

She started at the intimation how near she stood to detection even from Edgar himself, and pride, reason, modesty, all arose to strengthen her with resolution, to guard every future conflict from his observation.

The article concerning fortune touched her to the quick. Nothing appeared to her so degrading as the most distant idea that such a circumstance could have any force with her. But the justice done to Edgar she gloried in, as an apology for her feelings, and exculpatory of her weakness. Her tears flowed fast at every expression of kindness to herself, her burning blushes dried them up as they were falling, at every hint of her feebleness, and the hopelessness of its cause; but wholly subdued by the last paragraph, which with reverence she pressed to her lips, she offered up the most solemn vows of a strict and entire observance of every injunction which the letter contained.

She was thus employed, unnoticing the passage of time, when Mrs. Arlbery tapped at her door, and asked if she wished to dine in her own room.

Surprised at the question, and ashamed to be thus seen, she was beginning a thousand apologies for not being yet dressed: but Mrs. Arlbery, interrupting her, said, 'I never listen to excuses. 'Tis the only battery that overpowers me. If, by any mischance, and in an evil hour, some country cousin, not knowing my ways, or some antediluvian prig, not minding them, happen to fall upon me with formal speeches, where I can make no escape, a fit of yawning takes me immediately, and I am demolished for the rest of the day.'

Camilla, attempting to smile, promised to play the country cousin no more. Mrs. Arlbery then observed she had been weeping; and taking her hand, with an examining look, 'My lovely young friend,' she cried, 'this will never do!'

'What, ma'am?... how?... what?...'

'Nay, nay, don't be frightened. Come down to dinner, and we'll talk over the hows? and the whats? afterwards. Never mind your dress; we go no where this evening; and I make a point not to suffer any body to change their attire in my house, merely because the afternoon is taking place of the morning. It seems to me a miserable compliment to the mistress of a mansion, to see her guests only equip themselves for the table. For my part, I deem the garb that is good enough for me, good enough for my geese and turkies ... apple and oyster-sauce included.'

Camilla then followed her down stairs, where she found no company but Sir Sedley Clarendel.

'Come, my dear Miss Tyrold,' said Mrs. Arlbery, 'you and I may now consider ourselves as tête-à-tête; Sir Sedley won't be much in our way. He hears and sees nothing but himself.'

'Ecstatically flattering that!' cried Sir Sedley; 'dulcet to every nerve!'

'O, I know you listen just now, because you are yourself my theme. But the moment I take another, you will forget we are either of us in the room.'

'Inhuman to the quick!' cried he; 'barbarous to a point!'

'This is a creature so strange, Miss Tyrold,' said Mrs. Arlbery, 'that I must positively initiate you a little into his character;—or, rather, into its own caricature; for as to character, he has had none intelligible these three years.—See but how he smiles at the very prospect of being portrayed, in defiance of all his efforts to look unconcerned! yet he knows I shall shew him no mercy. But, like all other egotists, the only thing to really disconcert him, would be to take no notice of him. Make him but the first subject of discourse, and praise or abuse are pretty much the same to him.'

'O shocking! shocking! killing past resuscitation! Abominably horrid, I protest!'

'O I have not begun yet. This is an observation to suit thousands. But do not fear; you shall have all your appropriations. Miss Tyrold, you are to be auditor and judge: and I will save you the time and the trouble which decyphering this animal, so truly a non-descript, might cost you.'

'What a tremendous exordium! distressing to a degree! I am agued with trepidation!

'O you wretch! you know you are enchanted. But no further interruption! I send you to Coventry for the next ten minutes.'

'This man, my dear Miss Tyrold, whom we are about to delineate, was meant by nature, and prepared by art, for something greatly superior to what he now appears: but, unhappily, he had neither solidity of judgment, nor humility of disposition, for bearing meekly the early advantages with which he set out in life; a fine person, fine parts, and a fine estate, all dashed into consciousness at the presuming age of one and twenty. By this aggregate of wealthy, of mental, and of personal prosperity, he has become at once self spoilt, and world spoilt. Had you known him, as I have done, before he was seized with this systematic affectation, which, I am satisfied, causes him more study than the united pedants of both universities could inflict upon him, you would have seen the most delightful creature breathing! a creature combining, in one animated composition, the very essences of spirit, of gaiety, and of intelligence. But now, with every thing within his reach, nothing seems worth his attainment. He has not sufficient energy to make use of his own powers. He has no one to command him, and he is too indolent to command himself. He has therefore turned fop from mere wantonness of time and of talents; from having nothing to do, no one to care for, and no one to please. Take from him half his wit, and by lessening his presumption, you will cure him of all his folly. Rob him of his fortune, and by forcing him into exertion, you will make him one of the first men of his day. Deface and maim his features and figure, and by letting him see that to appear and be admired is not the same thing, you will render him irresistible.'

'Have you done?' cried the baronet smiling.

'I protest,' said Mrs. Arlbery, 'I believe you are a little touched! And I don't at all want to reform you. A perfect character only lulls me to sleep.'

'Obliging in the superlative! I must then take as a consolation, that I have never given you a nap?'

'Never, Clarendel, I assure you; and yet I don't hate you! Vice is detestable; I banish all its appearances from my coteries; and I would banish its reality, too, were I sure I should then have any thing but empty chairs in my drawing-room—but foibles make all the charm of society. They are the only support of convivial raillery, and domestic wit. If formerly, therefore, you more excited my admiration, it is now, believe me, you contribute most to my entertainment.'

'Condoling to a phenomenon! I have really, then, the vastly prodigious honour to be exalted in your fair graces to the level of a mountebank? a quack doctor? his merry Andrew? or any other such respectable buffoon?'

'Piqued! piqued! I declare! this exceeds my highest ambition. But I must not weaken the impression by dwelling upon it.'

She then asked Camilla if she had any message for Cleves, as one of her servants was going close to the park gate.

Camilla, glad to withdraw, said she would write a few words to her father, and retired for that purpose.

'What in the world, my dear Clarendel,' said Mrs. Arlbery, 'can I do with this poor thing? She has lost all her sprightliness, and vapours me but to look at her. She has all the symptoms upon her of being in the full meridian of that common girlish disease, an hopeless passion.'

'Poor little tender dove!' cried the baronet. ''Twould be odious to cure her. Unfeeling to excess. What in nature can be half so mellifluously interesting? I shall now look at her with most prodigious softness. Ought one not to sigh as she approaches?'

'The matter to be sure is silly enough,' answered Mrs. Arlbery; 'but, this nonsense apart, she is a charming girl. Besides, I perceive I am a violent favourite with her; and flattery, my dear Clarendel, will work its way, even with me! I really owe her a good turn: Else I should no longer endure her; for the tender passion has terribly flattened her. If we can't restore her spirits, she will be a mere dead weight to me.'

'O a very crush! a cannon ball would be a butterfly in the comparison! But who is the irresistible? What form has the little blind traitor assumed?'

'O, assure yourself, that of the first young man who has come in her sight. Every damsel, as she enters the world, has some picture ready painted upon her imagination, of an object worthy to enslave her: and before any experience forms her judgment, or any comparison her taste, she is the dupe of the first youth who presents himself to her, in the firm persuasion of her ductile fancy, that he is just the model it had previously created.'

She then added, she had little doubt but young Mandlebert was the hero, from their private conferences after the raffle, and from her blushes when forced to name him.

'Nay, nay, this is not the first incongruity!' said the young baronet, 'not romantic to outrage. Beech Park has nothing very horrific in it. Nothing invincibly beyond the standard of a young lady's philosophy.'

'Depend upon it, that's the very idea its master has conceived of the matter himself. You wealthy Cavaliers rarely want flappers to remind you of your advantages. That Mandlebert, you must know, is my aversion. He has just that air and reputation of faultlessness that gives me the spleen. I hope, for her sake, he won't think of her; he will lead her a terrible life. A man who piques himself upon his perfections, finds no mode so convenient and ready for displaying them, as proving all about him to be constantly in the wrong. However, a character of that stamp rarely marries; especially if he is rich, and has no obstacles in his way. What can I do, then, for this poor thing? The very nature of her malady is to make her entertain false hopes. I am quite bent upon curing them. The only difficulty, according to custom, is how. I wish you would take her in hand yourself.'

'I?... preposterous in the extreme! what particle of chance should I have against Mandlebert?'

'O you vain wretch! to be sure you don't know, that though he is rich, you are richer? and, doubtless, you never took notice, that though he is handsome, you are handsomer? As to manners, there is little to choose between you, for he is as much too correct, as you are too fantastic. In conversation, too, you are nearly upon a par, for he is as regularly too right, as you are ridiculously too wrong,—but O the charm of dear amusing wrong, over dull commanding right! you have but to address yourself to her with a little flattering distinction, and Mandlebert ever after will appear to her a pedant.'

'What a wicked sort of sprite is a female wit!' cried Sir Sedley, 'breathing only in mischief! a very will-o'-the-wisp, personified and petticoated, shining but to lead astray. Dangerous past all fathom! Have the goodness, however, my fair Jack-o'-lanthorn, to intimate what you mean I should do with this languishing dulcinea, should I deliver her from thraldom? You don't advise me, I presume, to take unto myself a wife? I protest I am shivered to the utmost point north at the bare suggestion! frozen to an icicle!'

'No, no; I know you far too confirmed an egotist for any thing but an old bachelor. Nor is there the least necessity to yoke the poor child to the conjugal plough so early. The only sacrifice I demand from you is a little attention; the only good I aim at for her, is to open her eyes, which have now a film before them, and to let her see that Mandlebert has no other pre-eminence, than that of having been the first young man with whom she became acquainted. Never imagine I want her to fall in love with you. Heaven help the poor victim to such a complication of caprice!'

'Nay, now I am full south again! burning with shame and choler! How you navigate my sensations from cold to heat at pleasure! Cooke was a mere river water-man to you. My blood chills or boils at your command. Every sentence is a new climate. You waft me from extreme to extreme, with a rapidity absolutely dizzying. A balloon is a broad-wheeled wagon to you.'

'Come, come, jargon apart, will you make yourself of any use? The cure of a romantic first flame is a better surety to subsequent discretion, than all the exhortations of all the fathers, and mothers, and guardians, and maiden aunts in the universe. Save her now, and you serve her for life;—besides giving me a prodigious pleasure in robbing that frigid Mandlebert of such a conquest.'

'Unhappy young swain! I pity him to immensity. How has he fallen thus under the rigour of your wrath? Do you banish him your favour, like another Aristides, to relieve your ear from hearing him called the Just?'

'Was ever allusion so impertinent? or, what is worse, for aught I can determine, so true? for, certainly, he has given me no offence; yet I feel I should be enchanted to humble him. Don't be concerned for him, however; you may assure yourself he hates me. There is a certain spring in our propensities to one another, that involuntarily opens and shuts in almost exact harmony, whether of approbation or antipathy. Except, indeed, in the one article of love, which, distinguishing nothing, is ready to grasp at any thing.'

'But why have you not recourse to the gallant cockade?'

'The Major? O, I have observed, already, she receives his devoirs without emotion; which, for a girl who has seen nothing of the world, is respectable enough, his red coat considered. Whether the man has any meaning himself, or whether he knows there is such a thing, I cannot tell: but as I do not wish to see her surrounded with brats, while a mere brat herself, it is not worth inquiry. You are the thing, Clarendel, the very thing! You are just agreeable enough to annul her puerile fascination, yet not interesting enough to involve her in any new danger.'

'Flattering past imitability! divine Arlberiana!'

'Girls, in general,' continued she, 'are insupportable nuisances to women. If you do not set them to prate about their admirers, or their admired, they die of weariness;—if you do, the weariness reverberates upon yourself.'

Camilla here returned. She had written a few lines to Eugenia, to enforce her reliance upon Edgar, with an earnest request to be sent for immediately, if any new difficulty occurred. And she had addressed a few warmly grateful words to her father, engaging to follow his every injunction with her best ability.

Sir Sedley now rung for his carriage; and Camilla, for the rest of the evening, exerted herself to receive more cheerfully the kind civilities of her lively hostess.

CHAPTER VII

A Recall

After two days passed with tolerable, though not natural cheerfulness at the Grove, Camilla was surprised by the arrival of the carriage of Sir Hugh with a short note from Eugenia.

To Miss Camilla Tyrold.

An incident has happened that overpowers me with sadness and horror. I cannot write. I send the chariot. O! come and pass an hour or two at Cleves with your distressed.

EUGENIA!

Camilla could scarcely stop to leave a message for Mrs. Arlbery, before she flew to the carriage; nor even inquire for her uncle at Cleves, before she ran to the apartment of Eugenia, and, with a thousand tender caresses, desired to know what had thus cruelly afflicted her.

'Alas!' she answered, 'my uncle has written to Clermont to come over,—and informed him with what view!'

She then related, that Indiana, the preceding day, had prevailed with Sir Hugh to let her go to the Middleton races; and she found he would be quite unhappy if she refused to be also of the party. That they had been joined by Bellamy on the race ground, who only, however, spoke to Miss Margland, as Edgar, watchful and uneasy, scarce let him even see anyone else. But the horses having taken fright, while they were in a great crowd, Bellamy had persuaded Miss Margland to alight, while the coach passed a terrible concourse of carriages; and, in that interval, he had contrived to whisper a claim upon her tacit promise of viewing the chaise which was for ever to convey him away from her; and, though her engagement to Edgar made her refuse, he had drawn her, she knows not herself how, from her party, and, while she was angrily remonstrating, and he seemed in the utmost despair at her displeasure, Edgar, who had been at first eluded by being on horseback, dismounted, forced his way to her, and almost carried her back to the coach, leaving Bellamy, who she was sure had no sinister design, nearly dead with grief at being unworthily suspected. Edgar, she however added, was fixed in believing he meant to convey her away; and Jacob, asserting he saw him purposely frighten the horses, had told his surmises to Sir Hugh; which he had corroborated by an account that the same gentleman had stopt to converse with her in her last return from Etherington. Sir Hugh, terrified, had declared he would no longer live without Clermont upon the spot. She had felt too much for his disturbance to oppose him at the moment, but had not imagined his plan would immediately be put into execution, till, early this morning, he had sent for her, and produced his letter of recall, which had taken him, he said, the whole night to compose and finish. Urged by surprise and dissatisfaction, she was beginning a little remonstrance; but found it made him so extremely unhappy, that, in the fear of a relapse, she desisted; and, with a shock she knew not when she should overcome, saw the fatal letter delivered for the post.

Camilla, with much commiseration, inquired if she had consulted with Edgar. Yes, she answered; and he had extorted her permission to relate the whole transaction to her father, though in a manner wide from justice to the ill-fated Bellamy; whose design might be extraordinary, but whose character, she was convinced, was honourable.

Camilla, whose education, though private, had not like that of Eugenia, been secluded and studious, was far less credulous than her sister, though equally artless. She knew, too, with regard to this affair, the opinion of Edgar, and to know and be guided by it was imperceptibly one. She declared herself, therefore, openly against Bellamy, and made her motives consist in a commentary upon his proceedings.

Eugenia warmly defended him, declaring the judgment of Camilla, and that of all her friends, to be formed in the dark; for that none of them could have doubted a moment his goodness or his honour, had they seen the distracted suffering that was marked in his countenance.

'And what,' cried Camilla, 'says my father to all this?'

'He says just what Edgar says:—he is all that is kind and good, but he has never beheld Bellamy—how, then, should he know him?'

A message came now from Sir Hugh to Camilla, that he would see her before she went, but that he was resting at present from the fatigue of writing a letter. He sent her, however, with his love, the foul copy, to amuse her till she could come to him.

To Clermont Lynmere Esq.

Dear Nephew,

I have had a very dangerous illness, and the doctors themselves are all surprised that I recovered; but a greater doctor than them was pleased to save me, for which I thank God. But as this attack has made me think more than ever I thought before, I am willing to turn my thoughts to good account.

Now, as I have not the gift of writing, at which, thank God, I have left off repining, from the reason of its great troublesomeness in acquiring, I can't pretend to any thing of a fine letter, but shall proceed to business.

My dear Clermont, I write now to desire you would come over out of hand; which I hope you won't take unkind, foreign parts being no great pleasure to see, in comparison of old England; besides which, I have another apology to offer, which is, having a fine prize in view for you; which is the more essential, owing to some unlucky circumstances, in which I did not behave quite as well as I wish, though very unwillingly; which I mention to you as a warning. However, you have no need to be cast down, for this prize will set all right, and make you as rich as a lord, at the same time that you are as wise as a philosopher. And as learning, though I have the proper respect for it, won't serve to make the pot boil, you must needs be glad of more substantial fuel; for there's no living upon air, however you students may affect to think eating mere gluttony.

Now, this prize is no other than your cousin Eugenla Tyrold, whom I don't tell you is a beauty; but if you are the sensible lad I take you for, you won't think the worse of her for wanting such frail perfections. Besides, we should not be too nice amongst relations, for if we are, what can we expect from the wide world? So I beg you to come over with all convenient speed, for fear of her falling a prey to some sharper, many such being to be found; especially at horse-races, and so forth. I remain,

Dear nephew,
Your affectionate uncle,

HUGH TYROLD.

Eugenia, from motives of delicacy and of shame, declined reading the copy as she had declined reading the letter; but looked so extremely unhappy, that Camilla offered to plead with her uncle, and use her utmost influence that he would countermand the recall.

'No,' answered she, 'no! 'tis a point of duty and gratitude, and I must bear its consequences.'

She was now called down to Mr. Tyrold. Camilla accompanied her.

He told her he had gathered, from the kind zeal and inquiries of Edgar, that Bellamy had certainly laid a premeditated plan for carrying her off, if she went to the races; which, as the whole neighbourhood was there, might reasonably be expected.

Eugenia, with fervour, protested such wickedness was impossible.

'I am unwilling, my dear child,' he answered, 'to adulterate the purity of your thoughts and expectations, by inculcating suspicions; but, though nature has blessed you with an uncommon understanding, remember, in judgment you are still but fifteen, and in experience but a child. One thing, however, tell me candidly, is it from love of justice, or is it for your happiness you combat thus ardently for the integrity of this young man?'

'For my justice, Sir!' said she firmly.

'And no latent reason mingles with and enforces it?'

'None, believe me! save only what gratitude dictates.'

'If your heart, then, is your own, my dear girl, do not be uneasy at the letter to Clermont. Your uncle is the last man upon earth to put any constraint upon your inclinations; and need I add to my dearest Eugenia, I am the last father to thwart or distress them? Resume, therefore, your courage and composure; be just to your friends, and happy in yourself.'

Reason was never thrown away upon Eugenia. Her mind was a soil which received and naturalized all that was sown in it. She promised to look forward with more cheerfulness, and to dwell no longer upon this agitating transaction.

Edgar now came in. He was going to Beech Park to meet Bellamy. He was charged with a long message for him from Sir Hugh; and an order to inform him that his niece was engaged; which, however, he declined undertaking, without first consulting her.

This was almost too severe a trial of the duty and fortitude of Eugenia. She coloured, and was quitting the room in silence: but presently turning back, 'My uncle,' she cried, 'is too ill now for argument, and he is too dear to me for opposition:—Say, then, just what you think will most conduce to his tranquillity and recovery.'

Her father embraced her; Camilla shed tears; and Edgar, in earnest admiration, kissed her hand. She received their applause with sensibility, but looked down with a secret deduction from its force, as she internally uttered, 'My task is not so difficult as they believe! touched as I am with the constancy of Bellamy—It is not Melmond who loves me! it is not Melmond I reject!—'

Edgar was immediately setting off, but, stopping him—'One thing alone I beg,' she said; 'do not communicate your intelligence abruptly. Soften it by assurances of my kind wishes.—Yet, to prevent any deception, any future hope—say to him—if you think it right—that I shall regard myself, henceforward, as if already in that holy state so sacred to one only object.'

She blushed, and left them, followed by Camilla.

'If born but yesterday,' cried Mr. Tyrold, while his eyes glistened, 'she could not be more perfectly free from guile.'

'Yet that,' said Edgar, 'is but half her praise; she is perfectly free, also, from self! she is made up of disinterested qualities and liberal sensations. To the most genuine simplicity, she joins the most singular philosophy; and to knowledge and cultivation, the most uncommon, adds all the modesty as well as innocence of her extreme youth and inexperience.'

Mr. Tyrold subscribed with frankness to this just praise of his highly-valued daughter; and they then conferred upon the steps to be taken with Bellamy, whom neither of them scrupled to pronounce a mere fortune-hunter. All the inquiries of Edgar were ineffectual to learn any particulars of his situation. He said he was travelling for his amusement; but he had no recommendation to anyone; though, by being constantly well-dressed, and keeping a shewy footman, he had contrived to make acquaintance almost universally in the neighbourhood. Mr. Tyrold determined to accompany Edgar to Beech Park himself, and there, in the most peremptory terms, to assure him of the serious measures that would ensue, if he desisted not from his pursuit.

He then went to take leave of Camilla, who had been making a visit to her uncle, and was returning to the Grove.

He had seen with concern the frigid air with which Edgar had bowed to her upon his entrance, and with compassion the changed countenance with which she had received his formal salutation. His hope of the alliance now sunk; and so favourite a wish could not be relinquished without severe disappointment; yet his own was immaterial to him when he looked at Camilla, and saw in her expressive eyes the struggle of her soul to disguise her wounded feelings. He now regretted that she had not accompanied her mother abroad; and desired nothing so earnestly as any means to remove her from all intercourse with Mandlebert. He seconded, therefore, her speed to be gone, happy she would be placed where exertion would be indispensable; and gently, yet clearly, intimated his wish that she should remain at the Grove, till she could meet Edgar without raising pain in her own bosom, or exciting suspicions in his. Cruelly mortified, she silently acquiesced. He then said whatever was most kind to give her courage; but, dejected by her conscious failure, and afflicted by the change in Edgar, she returned to Mrs. Arlbery in a state of mind the most melancholy.

And here, nothing could be less exhilarating nor less seasonable than the first news she heard.

The regiment of General Kinsale was ordered into Kent, in the neighbourhood of Tunbridge: It was the season for drinking the water of that spring; and Mr. Dennel was going thither with his daughter. Sir Sedley Clarendel conceived it would be serviceable also to his own health; and had suddenly proposed to Mrs. Arlbery forming a party to pass a few weeks there. With a vivacity always ready for any new project, she instantly agreed to it, and the journey was settled to take place in three days. When Camilla was informed of this intended excursion, the disappointment with which it overpowered her was too potent for disguise: and Mrs. Arlbery was so much struck with it, that, during coffee, she took Sir Sedley apart, and said; 'I feel such concern for the dismal alteration of that sweet girl, that I could prevail with myself, all love-lorn as she is, to take her with me to Tunbridge, if you will aid my hardy enterprise of driving that frozen composition of premature wisdom from her mind. If you are not as invulnerable as himself, you cannot refuse me this little sleight of gallantry.'

Sir Sedley gave a laughing assent, declaring, at the same time, with the strongest professed diffidence, his conscious inability. Mrs. Arlbery, in high spirits, said she scarce knew which would most delight her, to mortify Edgar, or restore Camilla to gaiety and independance. Yet she would watch, she said, that matters went no further than just to shake off a whining first love; for the last thing upon earth she intended was to entangle her in a second.

Camilla received the invitation with pleasure yet anxiety: for though glad to be spared returning to Cleves in a state of disturbance so suspicious, she was bitterly agitated in reflecting upon the dislike of Edgar to Mrs. Arlbery, the pains he had taken to prevent her mingling with this society, and the probably final period to his esteem and good-will, that would prove the result of her accompanying such a party to a place of amusement.

CHAPTER VIII

A Youth of the Times

Mrs. Arlbery accompanied Camilla the next day to Cleves, to ask permission of Mr. Tyrold for the excursion. She would trust the request to none but herself, conscious of powers of persuasion unused to repulse.

Mr. Tyrold was distressed by the proposition: he was not satisfied in trusting his unguarded Camilla to the dissipation of a public place, except under the wing of her mother; though he felt eager to remove her from Edgar, and rejoiced in any opportunity to allow her a change of scene, that might revive her natural spirits, and unchain her heart from its unhappy subjection.

Perceiving him undetermined, Mrs. Arlbery called forth all her artillery of eloquence and grace, to forward her conquest. The licence she allowed herself in common of fantastic command, gave way to the more feminine attraction of soft pleading: her satire, which, though never malignant, was often alarming, was relinquished for a sportive gaiety that diffused general animation; and Mr. Tyrold soon, though not caught like his daughter, ceased to wonder that his daughter had been caught.

In this indecision he took Camilla apart, and bade her tell him, without fear or reserve, her own feelings, her own wishes, her own opinion upon this scheme. She held such a call too serious and too kind for disguise: she hid her face upon his shoulder and wept; he soothed and encouraged her to confidence; and, in broken accents, she then acknowledged herself unequal, as yet, to fulfilling his injunctions of appearing cheerful and easy, though sensible of their wisdom.

Mr. Tyrold, with a heavy heart, saw how much deeper was her wound, than the airiness of her nature had prepared him to expect, and could no longer hesitate in granting his consent. He saw it was her wish to go; but he saw that the pleasures of a public place had no share in exciting it. To avoid betraying her conscious mortification was her sole and innocent motive; and though he would rather have sent her to a more private spot, and have trusted her to a more retired character; he yet thought it possible, that what opportunity presented unsought, might, eventually, prove more beneficial than what his own choice would have dictated; for public amusements, to the young and unhackneyed, give entertainment without requiring exertion; and spirits lively as those of Mrs. Arlbery create nearly as much gaiety as they display.

Fixed, now, for the journey, he carried Camilla to her uncle to take leave. The prospect of not seeing her again for six weeks was gloomy to Sir Hugh; though he bore it better at this moment, when his fancy was occupied by arranging preparations for the return of Clermont, than he could have done at almost any other. He put into her hand a fifty pound Bank note for her expences, and when, with mingled modesty and dejection, she would have returned the whole, as unnecessary even to her wishes, Mr. Tyrold, interfering, made her accept twenty pounds. Sir Hugh pressed forward the original sum in vain; his brother, though always averse to refuse his smallest desire, thought it here a duty to be firm, that the excursion, which he granted as a relief to her sadness, might not lead to pleasures ever after beyond her reach, nor to their concomitant extravagance. She could not, he knew, reside at Tunbridge with the oeconomy and simplicity to which she was accustomed at Etherington; but he charged her to let no temptation make her forget the moderate income of which alone she was certain; assuring her, that where a young woman's expences exceeded her known expectations, those who were foremost to praise her elegance, would most fear to form any connection with her, and most despise or deride her in any calamity.

Camilla found no difficulty in promising the most exact observance of this instruction; her heart seemed in sackcloth and ashes, and she cared not in what manner her person should be arrayed.

Sir Hugh earnestly enjoined her not to fail to be at Cleves upon the arrival of Clermont, intimating that the nuptials would immediately take place.

She then sought Eugenia, whom she found with Dr. Orkborne, in a state of mind so perfectly calm and composed, as equally to surprise and rejoice her. She saw with pleasure that all Bellamy had inspired was the most artless compassion; for since his dismission had now positively been given, and Clermont was actually summoned, she devoted her thoughts solely to the approaching event, with the firm, though early wisdom which distinguished her character.

Indiana joined them; and, in a low voice, said to Camilla, 'Pray, cousin, do you know where Mr. Macdersey is? because I am sadly afraid he's dead.'

Camilla, surprised, desired to know why she had such an apprehension?

'Because he told me he'd shoot himself through the brains if I was cruel—and I am sure I had no great choice given me: for, between ourselves, Miss Margland gave all the answers for me, without once stopping to ask me what I should chuse. So if he has really done it, the fault is more her's than mine.'

She then said, that, just after Camilla's departure the preceding day, Mr. Macdersey arrived, and insisted upon seeing her, and speaking to Sir Hugh, as he was ordered into Kent, and could not go so far in suspence. Sir Hugh was not well enough to admit him; and Miss Margland, upon whom the office devolved, took upon her to give him a positive refusal; and though she went into the room while he was there, never once would let her make an answer for herself.

Miss Margland, she added, had frightened Sir Hugh into forbidding him the house, by comparing him with Mr. Bellamy; but Mr. Macdersey had frightened them all enough, in return, as he went away, by saying, that as soon as ever Sir Hugh was well, he would call him out, because of his sending him word down stairs not to come to Cleves any more, for he had been disturbed enough already by another Irish fortune-hunter, that came after another of his nieces; and he was the more sure Mr. Macdersey was one of them, because of his being a real Irishman, while Mr. Bellamy was only an Englishman. 'But don't you think now, cousin,' she continued, 'Miss Margland might as well have let me speak for myself?'

Camilla inquired if she was sorry for the rejection.

'N ... o,' she answered, with some hesitation; 'for Miss Margland says he's got no rent-roll; besides, I don't think he's so agreeable as Mr. Melmond; only Mr. Melmond's worth little or no fortune they say: for Miss Margland inquired about it, after Mr. Mandlebert behaved so. Else I can't say I thought Mr. Melmond disagreeable.'

Mrs. Arlbery now sent to hasten Camilla, who, in returning to the parlour, met Edgar. He had just gathered her intended excursion, and, sick at heart, had left the room. Camilla felt the consciousness of a guilty person at his sight; but he only slightly bowed; and coldly saying, 'I hope you will have much pleasure at Tunbridge,' went on to his own room.

And there, replete with resentment for the whole of her late conduct, he again blessed Dr. Marchmont for his preservation from her toils; and, concluding the excursion was for the sake of the Major, whose regiment he knew to be just ordered into Kent, he centered every former hope in the one single wish that he might never see her more.

Camilla, shocked by such obvious displeasure, quitted Cleves with still increasing sadness; and Mrs. Arlbery would heartily have repented her invitation, but for her dependance upon Sir Sedley Clarendel.

At Etherington they stopt, that Camilla might prepare her package for Tunbridge. Mrs. Arlbery would not alight.

While Camilla, with a maid-servant, was examining her drawers, the chamber door was opened by Lionel, for whom she had just inquired, and who, telling her he wanted to speak to her in private, turned the maid out of the room.

Camilla begged him to be quick, as Mrs. Arlbery was waiting.

'Why then, my dear little girl,' cried he, 'the chief substance of the matter is neither more nor less than this: I want a little money.'

'My dear brother,' said Camilla, pleasure again kindling in her eyes as she opened her pocket-book, 'you could never have applied to me so opportunely. I have just got twenty pounds, and I do not want twenty shillings. Take it, I beseech you, any part, or all.'

Lionel paused and seemed half choaked. 'Camilla,' he cried presently, 'you are an excellent girl. If you were as old and ugly as Miss Margland, I really believe I should think you young and pretty. But this sum is nothing. A drop of water to the ocean.'

Camilla now, drawing back, disappointed and displeased, asked how it was possible he should want more.

'More, my dear child? why I want two or three cool hundred.'

'Two or three hundred?' repeated she, amazed.

'Nay, nay, don't be frightened. My uncle will give you two or three thousand, you know that. And I really want the money. It's no joke, I assure you. It's a case of real distress.'

'Distress? impossible! what distress can you have to so prodigious an amount?'

'Prodigious! poor little innocent! dost think two or three hundred prodigious?'

'And what is become of the large sums extorted from my uncle Relvil?'

'O that was for quite another thing. That was for debts. That's gone and over. This is for a perfectly different purpose.'

'And will nothing—O Lionel!—nothing touch you? My poor mother's quitting England ... her separation from my father and her family ... my uncle Relvil's severe attack ... will nothing move you to more thoughtful, more praise-worthy conduct?'

'Camilla, no preaching! I might as well cast myself upon the old ones at once. I come to you in preference, on purpose to avoid sermonising. However, for your satisfaction, and to spur you to serve me, I can assure you I have avoided all new debts since the last little deposit of the poor sick hypochondriac miser, who is pining away at the loss of a few guineas, that he had neither spirit nor health to have spent for himself.'

'Is this your reasoning, your repentance, Lionel, upon such a catastrophe?'

'My dear girl, I am heartily concerned at the whole business, only, as it's over, I don't like talking of it. This is the last scrape I shall ever be in while I live. But if you won't help me, I am undone. You know your influence with my uncle. Do, there's a dear girl, use it for your brother! I have not a dependance in the world, now, but upon you!'

'Certainly I will do whatever I can for you,' said she, sighing; 'but indeed, my dear Lionel, your manner of going on makes my very heart ache! However, let this twenty pounds be in part, and tell me your very smallest calculation for what must be added?'

'Two hundred. A farthing less will be of no use; and three will be of thrice the service. But mind!... you must not say it's for me!'

'How, then, can I ask for it?'

'O, vamp up some dismal ditty.'

'No, Lionel!' exclaimed she, turning away from him; 'you propose what you know to be impracticable.'

'Well, then, if you must needs say it's for me, tell him he must not for his life own it to the old ones.'

'In the same breath, must I beg and command?'

'O, I always make that my bargain. I should else be put into the lecture room, and not let loose again till I was made a milk-sop. They'd talk me so into the vapours, I should not be able to act like a man for a month to come.'

'A man, Lionel?'

'Yes, a man of the world, my dear; a knowing one.'

Mrs. Arlbery now sent to hasten her, and he extorted a promise that she would go to Cleves the next morning, and procure a draft for the money, if possible, to be ready for his calling at the Grove in the afternoon.

She felt this more deeply than she had time or courage to own to Lionel, but her increased melancholy was all imputed to reflections concerning Mandlebert by Mrs. Arlbery.

That lady lent her chaise the next morning, with her usual promptitude of good humour, and Camilla went to Cleves, with a reluctance that never before accompanied her desire to oblige.

Her visit was received most kindly by all the family, as merely an additional leave taking; in which light, though she was too sincere to place it, she suffered it to pass. Having no chance of being alone with her uncle by accident, she was forced to beg him, in a whisper, to request a tête-à-tête with her: and she then, covered with all the confusion of a partner in his extravagance, made the petition of Lionel.

Sir Hugh seemed much surprised, but protested he would rather part with his coat and waistcoat than refuse anything to Camilla. He gave her instantly a draft upon his banker for two hundred pounds; but added, he should take it very kind of her, if she would beg Lionel to ask him for no more this year, as he was really so hard run, he should not else be able to make proper preparations for the wedding, till his next rents became due.

Camilla was now surprised in her turn; and Sir Hugh then confessed, that, between presents and petitions, his nephew had had no less than five hundred pounds from him the preceding year, unknown to his parents; and that for this year, the sum she requested made the seventh hundred; without the least account for what purpose it was given.

Camilla now heartily repented being a partner in a business so rapacious, so unjustifiable, and so mysterious; but, kindly interrupting her apology, 'Don't be concerned, my dear,' he cried, 'for there's no help for these things; though what the young boys do with all their money now-a-days, is odd enough, being what I can't make out. However, he'll soon be wiser, so we must not be too severe with him; though I told him, the last time, I had rather he would not ask me so often; which was being almost too sharp, I'm afraid, considering his youngness; for one can't expect him to be an old man at once.'

Camilla gave voluntarily her word no such application should find her its ambassadress again: and though he would have dispensed with the promise, she made it the more readily as a guard against her own facility.

'At least,' cried the baronet, 'say nothing to my poor brother, and more especially to your mother; it being but vexatious to such good parents to hear of such idleness, not knowing what to think of it; for it is a great secret, he says, what he does with it all; for which reason one can't expect him to tell it. My poor brother, to be sure, had rather he should be studying hic, hæc, hoc; but, Lord help him! I believe he knows no more of that than I do myself; and I never could make out much meaning of it, any further than it's being Latin; though I suppose, at the time, Dr. Orkborne might explain it to me, taking it for granted he did what was right.'

Camilla was most willing to agree to concealing from her parents what she knew must so painfully afflict them, though she determined to assume sufficient courage to expostulate most seriously with her brother, against whom she felt sensations of the most painful anger.

Again she now took leave; but upon re-entering the parlour, found Edgar there alone.

Involuntarily she was retiring; but the counsel of her father recurring to her, she compelled herself to advance, and say, 'How good you have been to Eugenia! how greatly are we all indebted for your kind vigilance and exertion!'

Edgar, who was reading, and knew not she was in the house, was surprised, both by her sight and her address, out of all his resolutions; and, with a softness of voice he meant evermore to deny himself, answered, 'To me? can any of the Tyrold family talk of being indebted to me?—my own obligations to all, to every individual of that name, have been the pride, have been—hitherto—the happiness of my life!—'

The word 'hitherto,' which had escaped, affected him: he stopt, recollected himself, and presently, more drily added, 'Those obligations would be still much increased, if I might flatter myself that one of that race, to whom I have ventured to play the officious part of a brother, could forget those lectures, she can else, I fear, with difficulty pardon.'

'You have found me unworthy your counsel,' answered Camilla, gravely, and looking down; 'you have therefore concluded I resent it: but we are not always completely wrong, even when wide from being right. I have not been culpable of quite so much folly as not to feel what I have owed to your good offices; nor am I now guilty of the injustice to blame their being withdrawn. You do surely what is wisest, though not—perhaps—what is kindest.'

To these last words she forced a smile; and, wishing him good morning, hurried away.

Amazed past expression, and touched to the soul, he remained, a few instants, immoveable; then, resolving to follow her, and almost resolving to throw himself at her feet, he opened the door she had shut after her: he saw her still in the hall, but she was in the arms of her father and sisters, who had all descended, upon hearing she had left Sir Hugh, and of whom she was now taking leave.

Upon his appearance, she said she could no longer keep the carriage; but, as she hastened from the hall, he saw that her eyes were swimming in tears.

Her father saw it too, with less surprise, but more pain. He knew her short and voluntary absence from her friends could not excite them: his heart ached with paternal concern for her; and, motioning everybody else to remain in the hall, he walked with her to the carriage himself, saying, in a low voice, as he put her in, 'Be of better courage, my dearest child. Endeavour to take pleasure where you are going—and to forget what you are leaving: and, if you wish to feel or to give contentment upon earth, remember always, you must seek to make circumstance contribute to happiness, not happiness subservient to circumstance.'

Camilla, bathing his hand with her tears, promised this maxim should never quit her mind till they met again.

She then drove off.

'Yes,' she cried, 'I must indeed study it; Edgar cares no more what becomes of me! resentment next to antipathy has taken place of his friendship and esteem!'

She wrote down in her pocket-book the last words of her father; she resolved to read them daily, and to make them the current lesson of her future and disappointed life.

Lionel, too impatient to wait for the afternoon, was already at the Grove, and handed her from the chaise. But, stopping her in the portico, 'Well,' he cried, 'where's my draft?'

'Before I give it you,' said she, seriously, and walking from the servants, 'I must entreat to speak a few words to you.'

'You have really got it, then?' cried he, in a rapture; 'you are a charming girl! the most charming girl I know in the world! I won't take your poor twenty pounds: I would not touch it for the world. But come, where's the draft? Is it for the two or the three?'

'For the two; and surely, my dear Lionel—'

'For the two? O, plague take it!—only for the two?—And when will you get me the odd third?'

'O brother! O Lionel! what a question! Will you make me repent, instead of rejoice, in the pleasure I have to assist you?'

'Why, when he was about it, why could he not as well come down like a gentleman at once? I am sure I always behaved very handsomely to him.'

'How do you mean?'

'Why, I never frightened him; never put him beside his poor wits, like t'other poor nuncle. I don't remember I ever did him an ill turn in my life, except wanting Dr. Pothook, there, to flog him a little for not learning his book. It would have been a rare sight if he had!—Don't you think so?'

'Rare, indeed, I hope!'

'Why, now, what could he have done, if the Doctor had really performed it? He could not in justice have found fault, when he put himself to school to him. But he'd have felt a little queer. Don't you think he would?'

'You only want to make me laugh, to prevent my speaking to the purpose; but I am not disposed to laugh; and therefore—'

'O, if you are not disposed to laugh, you are no company for me. Give me my draft, therefore.'

'If you will not hear, I hope, at least, Lionel, you will think; and that may be much more efficacious. Shall I put up the twenty? I really do not want it. And it is all, all, all I can ever procure you! Remember that!'

'What?—all?—this all?—what, not even the other little mean hundred?'

'No, my dear brother! I have promised my uncle no further application—'

'Why what a stingy, fusty old codger, to draw such a promise from you!'

'Hold, hold, Lionel! I cannot endure to hear you speak in such a manner of such an uncle! the best, the most benevolent, the most indulgent—'

'Lord, child, don't be so precise and old maidish. Don't you know it's a relief to a man's mind to swear, and say a few cutting things when he's in a passion? when all the time he would no more do harm to the people he swears at, than you would, that mince out all your words as if you were talking treason, and thought every man a spy that heard you. Besides, how is a man the worse for a little friendly curse or two, provided he does not hear it? It's a very innocent refreshment to a man's mind, my dear; only you know nothing of the world.'

Mrs. Arlbery now approaching, he hastily took the draft, and, after a little hesitation, the twenty pounds, telling her, if she would not ask for him, she must ask for herself, and that he felt no compunction, as he was certain she might draw upon her uncle for every guinea he was worth.

He then heartily embraced her; said she was the best girl in the world, when she did not mount the pulpit, and rode off.

Camilla felt no concern at the loss of her twenty pounds: lowered and unhappy, she was rather glad than sorry that her means for being abroad were diminished, and that to keep her own room would soon be most convenient.

The next day was fixed for the journey.

BOOK VI

CHAPTER I

A Walk by Moonlight

Mrs. Arlbery and Camilla set off in the coach of Mr. Dennel, widower of a deceased sister of the husband of Mrs. Arlbery, whom she was induced to admit of the party that he might aid in bearing the expenses, as she could not, from some family considerations, refuse taking her niece into her coterie. Sir Sedley Clarendel drove his own phaeton; but instead of joining them, according to the condition which occasioned the treaty, cantered away his ponies from the very first stage, and left word, where he changed horses, that he should proceed to the hotel upon the Pantiles.

Mrs. Arlbery was nearly provoked to return to the Grove. With Mr. Dennel she did not think it worth while to converse; her niece she regarded as almost an idiot; and Camilla was so spiritless, that, had not Sir Sedley acceded to her plan, this was the last period in which she would have chosen her for a companion.

They travelled very quietly to within a few miles of Tunbridge, when an accident happened to one of the wheels of the carriage, that the coachman said would take some hours to repair. They were drawn on, with difficulty, to a small inn upon the road, whence they were obliged to send a man and horse to Tunbridge for chaises.

As they were destined, now, to spend some time in this place, Mrs. Arlbery retired to write letters, and Mr. Dennel to read newspapers; and, invited by a bright moon, Camilla and Miss Dennel wandered from a little garden to an adjoining meadow, which conducted them to a lane, rendered so beautiful by the strong masses of shade with which the trees intercepted the resplendent whiteness of the moon, that they walked on, catching fresh openings with fresh pleasure, till the feet of Miss Dennel grew as weary with the length of the way, unbroken by any company, as the ears of Camilla with her incessant prattling, unaided by any idea. Miss Dennel proposed to sit down, and, while relieving herself by a fit of yawning and stretching, Camilla strolled a little further in search of a safe and dry spot.

Miss Dennel, following in a moment, on tiptoe, and trembling, whispered that she was sure she heard a voice. Camilla, with a smile, asked if only themselves were privileged to enjoy so sweet a night? 'Hush!' cried she, 'hush! I hear it again!' They listened; and, in a minute, a soft plaintive tone reached their ears, too distant to be articulate, but undoubtedly female.

'I dare say it's a robber!' exclaimed Miss Dennel shaking; 'If you don't run back, I shall die!'

Camilla assured her, from the gentleness of the sound, she must be mistaken; and pressed her to advance a few steps further, in case it should be anybody ill.

'But you know,' said Miss Dennel, speaking low, 'people say that sometimes there are noises in the air, without its being anybody? Suppose it should be that?'

Still, though almost imperceptibly, Camilla drew her on, till, again listening, they distinctly heard the words, 'My lovely friend.'

'La! how pretty!' said Miss Dennel; 'let's go a little nearer.'

They advanced, and presently, again stopping heard, 'Could pity pour balm into my woes, how sweetly would they be alleviated by your's, my lovely friend?'

Miss Dennel now looked enchanted, and eagerly led the way herself.

In a few minutes, arriving at the end of the lane, which opened upon a wild and romantic common, they caught a glimpse of a figure in white.

Miss Dennel turned pale. 'Dear!' cried she, in the lowest whisper, 'what is it?'

'A lady,' answered Camilla, equally cautious not to be heard, though totally without alarm.

'Are you sure of that?' said Miss Dennel, shrinking back, and pulling her companion to accompany her.

'Do you think it's a ghost?' cried Camilla, unresisting the retreat, yet walking backwards to keep the form in sight.

'Fie! how can you talk so shocking? all in the dark so, except only for the moon?'

'Your's, my lovely friend!' was now again pronounced in the tenderest accent.

'She's talking to herself!' exclaimed Miss Dennel; 'Lord, how frightful!' and she clung close to Camilla, who, mounting a little hillock of stones, presently perceived that the lady was reading a letter.

Miss Dennel, tranquillised by hearing this, was again content to stop, when their ears were suddenly struck by a piercing shriek.

'O Lord! we shall be murdered!' cried she, screaming still louder herself.

They both ran back some paces down the lane, Camilla determining to send somebody from the inn to inquire what all this meant: but presently, through an opening in the common, they perceived the form in white darting forwards, with an air wild and terrified. Camilla stopt, struck with compassion and curiosity at once; Miss Dennel could not quit her, but after the first glance, hid her face, faintly articulating, 'O, don't let it see us! don't let it see us! I am sure it's nothing natural! I dare say it's somebody walking!'

The next instant, they perceived a man, looking earnestly around, as if to discover who had echoed the scream; the place they occupied was in the shade, and he did not observe them. He soon rushed hastily on, and seized the white garment of the flying figure, which appeared, both by its dress and form, to be an elegant female. She clasped her hands in supplication, cast up her eyes towards heaven, and again shrieked aloud.

Camilla, who possessed that fine internal power of the thinking and feeling mind to adopt courage for terror, where any eminent service may be the result of immediate exertion, was preparing to spring to her relief; while Miss Dennel, in extreme agony holding her, murmured out, 'Let's run away! let's run away! she's going to be murdered!' when they saw the man prostrate himself at the lady's feet, in the humblest subjection.

Camilla stopt her flight; and Miss Dennel, appeased, called out; 'La! his kneeling! how pretty it looks! I dare say it's a lover. How I wish one could hear what he says!'

An exclamation, however, from the lady, uttered in a tone of mingled affright and disgust, of 'leave me! leave me!' was again the signal to Miss Dennel of retreat, but of Camilla to advance.

The rustling of the leaves, caused by her attempt to make way through the breach, caught the ears of the suppliant, who hastily arose; while the lady folded her arms across her breast, and seemed ejaculating the most fervent thanks for this relief.

Camilla now forced a passage through the hedge, and the lady, as she saw her approach, called out, in a voice the most touching, 'Surely 'tis some pitying Angel, mercifully come to my rescue!'

The pursuer drew back, and Camilla, in the gentlest words, besought the lady to accompany her to the friends she had just left, who would be happy to protect her.

She gratefully accepted the proposal, and Camilla then ventured to look round, to see if the object of this alarm had retreated: but, with an astonishment that almost confounded her, she perceived him, a few yards off, taking a pinch of snuff, and humming an opera air.

The lady, then, snatching up her letter, which had fallen to the ground, touched it with her lips, and carefully folding, put it into her bosom, tenderly ejaculating, 'I have preserved thee!... O from what danger! what violation!'

Then pressing the hand of Camilla, 'You have saved me,' she cried, 'from the calamity of losing what is more dear than I have words to express! Take me but where I may be shielded from that wretch, and what shall I not owe to you?'

The moon now shining full upon her face, Camilla saw seated on it youth, sensibility, and beauty. Her pleasure, involuntarily rather than rationally, was redoubled that she had proved serviceable to her, as, in equal proportion, was her abhorrence of the man who had caused the disturbance.

The three females were now proceeding, when the offender, with a careless air, and yet more careless bow, advancing towards them, negligently said, 'Shall I have the honour to see you safe home, ladies?'

Camilla felt indignant; Miss Dennel again screamed; and the stranger, with a look of horror and disgust, said; 'Persecute me no more!'

'O hang it! O curse it!' cried he, swinging his cane to and fro, 'don't be serious. I only meant to frighten you about the letter.'

The lady deigned no answer, but murmured to herself 'that letter is more precious to me than life or light!'

They now walked on; and, when they entered the lane, they had the pleasure to observe they were not pursued. She then said to Camilla, 'You must be surprised to see any one out, and unprotected, at this late hour; but I had employed myself, unthinkingly, in reading some letters from a dear and absent friend, and forgot the quick passage of time.'

A man in a livery now appearing at some distance, she hastily summoned him, and demanded where was the carriage?

In the road, he answered, where she had left it, at the end of the lane.

She then took the hand of Camilla, and with a smile of the utmost softness said, 'When the shock I have suffered is a little over, I must surely cease to lament I have sustained it, since it has brought to me such sweet succour. Where may I find you tomorrow, to repeat my thanks?'

Camilla answered, 'she was going to Tunbridge immediately, but knew not yet where she should lodge.'

'Tunbridge!' she repeated; I am there myself; I shall easily find you out tomorrow morning, for I shall know no rest till I have seen you again.'

She then asked her name, and, with the most touching acknowledgments, took leave.

Camilla recounted her adventure to Mrs. Arlbery, with an animated description of the fair Incognita, and with the most heart-felt delight of having, though but accidentally, proved of service to her. Mrs. Arlbery laughed heartily at the recital, assuring her she doubted not but she had made acquaintance with some dangerous fair one, who was playing upon her inexperience, and utterly unfit to be known to her. Camilla warmly vindicated her innocence, from the whole of her appearance, as well as from the impossibility of her knowing that her scream could be heard: yet was perplexed how to account for her not naming herself, and for the mystery of the carriage and servant in waiting so far off. These latter she concluded to belong to her father, as she looked too young to have any sort of establishment of her own.

'What I don't understand in the matter is, that there reading of letters by the light of the moon;' said Mr. Dennel. 'Where's the necessity of doing that, for a person that can afford to keep her own coach and servants?'

Mr. Dennel was a man as unfavoured by nature as he was uncultivated by art. He had been accepted as a husband by the sister of Mr. Arlbery, merely on account of a large fortune, which he had acquired in business. The marriage, like most others made upon such terms, was as little happy in its progression as honourable in its commencement; and Miss Dennel, born and educated amidst domestic dissention, which robbed her of all will of her own, by the constant denial of one parent to what was accorded by the other, possessed too little reflexion to benefit by observing the misery of an alliance not mentally assorted; and grew up with no other desire but to enter the state herself, from an ardent impatience to shake off the slavery she experienced in singleness. The recent death of her mother had given her, indeed, somewhat more liberty; but she had not sufficient sense to endure any restraint, and languished for the complete power which she imagined a house and servants of her own would afford.

When they arrived at the hotel, in Tunbridge, Mrs. Arlbery heard, with some indignation, that Sir Sedley Clarendel was gone to the rooms, without demonstrating, by any sort of inquiry, the smallest solicitude at her non-appearance.

CHAPTER II

The Pantiles

A servant tapt early at the door of Camilla, the next morning, to acquaint her that a lady, who called herself the person that had been so much obliged to her the preceding day, begged the honour of being admitted.

Camilla was sorry, after the suspicions of Mrs. Arlbery, that she did not send up her name; yet, already partially disposed, her prepossession was not likely to be destroyed by the figure that now appeared.

A beautiful young creature, with an air of the most attractive softness, eyes of the most expressive loveliness, and a manner which by every look and every motion announced a soul 'tremblingly alive,' glided gently into the room, and advancing, with a graceful confidence of kindness, took both her hands, and pressing them to her heart, said, 'What happiness so soon to have found you! to be able to pour forth all the gratitude I owe you, and the esteem with which I am already inspired!'

Camilla was struck with admiration and pleasure; and gave way to the most lively delight at the fortunate accident which occasioned her walking out in a place entirely unknown to her; declaring she should ever look back to that event as to one of the marked blessings of her life.

'If you,' answered the fair stranger, 'have the benevolence thus to value our meeting, how should it be appreciated by one who is so eternally indebted to it? I had not perceived the approach of that person. He broke in upon me when least a creature so ungenial was present to my thoughts. I was reading a letter from the most amiable of friends, the most refined—perhaps—of human beings!'

Camilla, impatient for some explanation, answered, 'I hope, at least, that friend will be spared hearing of your alarm?'

'I hope so! for his own griefs already overwhelm him. Never may it be my sad lot to wound where I mean only to console.'

At the words his own, Camilla felt herself blush. She had imagined it was some female friend. She now found her mistake, and knew not what to imagine next.

'I had retired,' she continued, 'from the glare of company, and the weight of uninteresting conversation, to read, at leisure and in solitude, this dear letter—heart-breaking from its own woes, heart-soothing to mine! In a place such as this, seclusion is difficult. I drove some miles off, and ordered my carriage to wait in the high road, while I strolled alone upon the common. I delight in a solitary ramble by moonlight. I can then indulge in uninterrupted rumination, and solace my melancholy by pronouncing aloud such sentences, and such names, as in the world I cannot utter. How exquisitely sweet do they sound to ears unaccustomed to such vibrations!'

Camilla was all astonishment and perplexity. A male friend so beloved, who seemed to be neither father, brother, nor husband; a carriage at her command, though without naming one relation to whom either that or herself might belong; and sentiments so tender she was almost ashamed to listen to them; all conspired to excite a wonder that painfully prayed for relief: and in the hope to obtain it, with some hesitation, she said, 'I should have sought you myself this morning, for the pleasure of inquiring after your safety, but that I was ignorant by what name to make my search.'

The fair unknown looked down for a moment, with an air that shewed a perfect consciousness of the inquiry meant by this speech; but turning aside the embarrassment it seemed to cause her, she presently raised her head, and said, 'I had no difficulty to find you, for my servant, happily, made his inquiry at once at this hotel.'

Disappointed and surprised by this evasion, Camilla saw now an evident mystery, but knew not how to press forward any investigation. She began, therefore, to speak of other things, and her fair guest, who had every mark of an education rather sedulously than naturally cultivated, joined readily in a conversation less personal.

They did not speak of Tunbridge, of public places, nor diversions; their themes, all chosen by the stranger, were friendship, confidence, and sensibility, which she illustrated and enlivened by quotations from favourite poets, aptly introduced and feelingly recited; yet always uttered with a sigh, and an air of tender melancholy. Camilla was now in a state so depressed, that, notwithstanding her native vivacity, she fell as imperceptibly into the plaintive style of her new acquaintance, who seemed habitually pensive, as if sympathy rather than accident had brought them together.

Yet when chance led to some mention of the adventure of the preceding evening, and the lady made again an animated eulogium of the friend whose letter she was perusing; she hazarded, with an half smile, saying: 'I hope—for his own sake, this friend is some sage and aged personage?'

'O no!' she answered; 'he is in the bloom of youth.'

Camilla, again a little disconcerted, paused; and the lady went on.

'It was in Wales I first met him; upon a spot so beautiful that painting can never do it justice. I have made, however, a little sketch of it, which, some day or other, I will shew you, if you will have the goodness to let me see more of you.'

Camilla could not refrain from an eager affirmative; and the conversation was then interrupted by a message from Mrs. Arlbery, who always breakfasted in her own room, to announce that she was going out lodging-hunting.

Camilla would rather have remained with her new acquaintance, better adapted to her present turn of mind than Mrs. Arlbery; but this was impossible, and the lovely stranger hastened away, saying she would call herself the next morning to shew the way to her house, where she hoped they might pass together many soothing and consolatory hours.

Camilla found Mrs. Arlbery by no means in her usual high spirits. The opening of her Tunbridge campaign had so far from answered its trouble and expence, that she heartily repented having quitted the Grove. The Officers either were not arrived in the neighbourhood, or were wholly engaged in military business; Camilla, instead of contributing to the life of the excursion, seemed to hang heavily both upon that, and upon herself; and Sir Sedley Clarendel, whose own proposition had brought it to bear, had not yet made his appearance, though lodging in the same hotel.

Thus vexatiously disappointed, she was ill-disposed to listen with pleasure to the history Camilla thought it indispensable to relate of her recent visit: and in answer to all praise of this fair Incognita, only replied by asking her name and connexions. Camilla felt extremely foolish in confessing she had not yet learnt them. Mrs. Arlbery then laughed unmercifully at her commendations, but concluded with saying: 'Follow, however, your own humour; I hate to torment or be tormented: only take care not to be seen with her.'

Camilla rejoiced she did not exact any further restriction, and hoped all raillery would soon be set aside, by an honourable explanation.

They now repaired to the Pantiles, where the gay company and gay shops afforded some amusement to Camilla, and to Miss Dennel a wonder and delight, that kept her mouth open, and her head jerking from object to object, so incessantly, that she saw nothing distinctly, from the eagerness of her fear lest anything should escape her.

Mrs. Arlbery, meeting with an old acquaintance in the bookseller's shop, there sat down with him, while the two young ladies loitered at the window of a toy-shop, struck with just admiration of the beauty and ingenuity of the Tunbridge ware it presented to their view; till Camilla, in a party of young men who were strolling down the Pantiles, and who went into the bookseller's shop, distinguished the offender of the fair unknown.

To avoid following, or being recollected by a person so odious to her, she entered the toy-shop with Miss Dennel, where she amused herself, till Mrs. Arlbery came in search of her, in selecting such various little articles for purchase as she imagined would amount to about half a crown; but which were put up for her at a guinea. This a little disconcerted her: though, as she was still unusually rich, from Mr. Tyrold's having advanced her next quarterly allowance, she consoled herself that they would serve for little keep-sakes for her sisters and her cousin: yet she determined, when next she entered a shop for convenience, to put nothing apart as a buyer, till she had inquired its price.

The assaulter, Lord Newford, a young nobleman of the ton, after taking a staring survey of every thing and every body around, and seeing no one of more consequence, followed Mrs. Arlbery, with whom formerly he had been slightly acquainted, to the toy-shop. He asked her how she did, without touching his hat; and how long she had been at Tunbridge, without waiting for an answer; and said he was happy to have the pleasure of seeing her, without once looking at her.

To his first sentence, Mrs. Arlbery made a civil answer; but, repenting it upon the two sentences that succeeded, she heard them without seeming to listen, and fixing her eyes upon him, when he had done, coolly said, 'Pray have you seen any thing of my servant?'

Lord Newford, somewhat surprised, replied, 'No.'

'Do look for him, then,' cried she, negligently, 'there's a good man.'

Lord Newford, a little piqued, and a little confused at feeling so, said he should be proud to obey her; and turning short off to his companion, cried, 'Come, Offy, why dost loiter? where shall we ride this morning?' And, taking him by the arm, quitted the Pantiles.

Mrs. Arlbery, laughing heartily, now felt her spirits a little revive; 'I doat,' she cried, 'upon meeting, now and then, with insolence, for I have a little taste for it myself, which I make some conscience of not indulging unprovoked.'

They then proceeded to the milliner's, to equip themselves for going to the rooms at night. Mrs. Arlbery and Miss Dennel, who were both rich, gave large orders: Camilla, indifferent to every thing except to avoid appearing in a manner that might disgrace her party, told the milliner to choose for her what she thought fashionable that was most reasonable. She was soon fitted up with what was too pretty to disapprove, and desiring immediately to pay her bill, found it amounted to five guineas; though she had imagined she should have change out of two.

She had only six, and some silver; but was ashamed to dispute, or desire any alteration; she paid the money; and only determined to apply to another person than the seller, when next she wanted any thing reasonable.

Mrs. Arlbery now ordered the carriage, and they drove to Mount Pleasant, where she hired a house for the season, to which they were to remove the next day.

In the evening, they went to the Rooms, where the decidedly fashionable mien and manner of Mrs. Arlbery, attracted more general notice and admiration than the youthful captivation of Camilla, or the pretty face and expensive attire of Miss Dennel.

Dressed by the milliner of the day, Camilla could not fail to pass uncensured, at least, with respect to her appearance; but her eyes wanted their usual lustre, from the sadness of her heart, and she never looked less herself, nor to less advantage.

The master of the ceremonies brought to her Sir Theophilus Jarard; but as she had seen him the companion of Lord Newford, to whom she had conceived a strong aversion, she declined dancing. He looked surprised, but rather offended than disappointed, and with a little laugh, half contemptuous, as if ashamed of having offered himself, stalked away.

Sir Sedley Clarendel was now sauntering into the room. Mrs. Arlbery, willing to shew her young friend in a favourable point of view to him, though more from pique at his distance, than from any thought at that moment of Camilla, told her she must positively accept Sir Theophilus, whose asking her must be regarded as a particular distinction, for he was notoriously a man of the ton. And, heedless of her objections, told Mr. Dennel to call him back.

'How can I do that,' said Mr. Dennel, 'after seeing her refuse him with my own eyes?'

'O, nobody cares about a man's eyes,' said Mrs. Arlbery; 'go and tell him Miss Tyrold has changed her mind, and chooses to dance.'

'As to her changing her mind,' he answered, 'that's likely enough; but I don't see how it's any reason I should go of a fool's errand.'

'Pho, pho, go directly; or you sha'n't dine before eight o'clock for the whole Tunbridge season.'

'Nay,' said Mr. Dennel, who had an horror of late hours, 'if you will promise we shall dine more in reason'—

'Yes, yes,' cried Mrs. Arlbery, hurrying him off, notwithstanding the reiterated remonstrances of Camilla.

'See, my dear,' she then added, laughing, 'how many weapons you must have in use, if you would govern that strange animal called man! yet never despair of victory; for, depend upon it, there is not one of the race that, with a little address, you may not bring to your feet.'

Camilla, who had no wish but for one single votary, and whose heart was sunk from her failure in obtaining that one, listened with so little interest or spirit, that Mrs. Arlbery, quite provoked, resolved not to throw away another idea upon her for the rest of the evening. And therefore, as her niece went completely and constantly for nothing with her, she spoke no more, till, to her great relief, she was joined by General Kinsale.

Mr. Dennel returned with an air not more pleased with his embassy, than her own appeared with her auditress. The gentleman, he said, had joined two others, and they were all laughing so violently together, that he could not find an opportunity to deliver his message, for they seemed as if they would only make a joke of it.

Mrs. Arlbery then saw that he had got between Lord Newford and Sir Sedley, and that they were all three amusing themselves, without ceremony or disguise, at the expense of every creature in the room; up and down which they strolled, arm in arm, looking familiarly at every body, but speaking to nobody; whispering one another in hoarse low voices, and then laughing immoderately loud: while nothing was distinctly heard, but from time to time, 'What in the world is become of Mrs. Berlinton to-night?' or else, 'How stupid the Rooms are without Lady Alithea.'

Mrs. Arlbery, who, like the rest of the world, saw her own defects in as glaring colours, and criticised them with as much animated ridicule as those of her neighbours, when exhibited by others, no sooner found she was neglected by this set, than she raved against the prevailing ill manners of the leaders in the ton, with as much asperity of censure, as if never for a moment betrayed herself, by fashion, by caprice, nor by vanity, to similar foibles. 'Yet, after all,' cried she presently, 'to see fools behave like fools, I am well content. I have no anger, therefore, against Lord Newford, nor Sir Theophilus Jarard; if they were not noticed for being impertinent, how could they expect to be noticed at all? When there is but one line that can bring them forward, I rather respect them that they have found it out. But what shall we say to Sir Sedley Clarendel? A man as much their superior in capacity as in powers of pleasing? 'Tis a miserable thing, my dear General, to see the dearth of character there is in the world. Pope has bewailed it in women; believe me, he might have extended his lamentation. You may see, indeed, one man grave, and another gay; but with no more "mark or likelihood," no more distinction of colouring, than what simply belongs to a dismal face or a merry one: and with just as little light and shade, just as abrupt a skip from one to the other, as separates inevitably the old man from the young one. We are almost all, my good General, of a nature so pitifully plastic, that we act from circumstances, and are fashioned by situation.'

Then, laughing at her own pique, 'General,' she added, 'shall I make you a confession? I am not at all sure, if that wretched Sir Sedley had behaved as he ought to have done, and been at my feet all the evening, that I should not, at this very moment, be amused in the same manner that he is himself! yet it would be very abominable, I own.'

'This is candid, however.'

'O, we all acknowledge our faults, now; 'tis the mode of the day: but the acknowledgment passes for current payment; and therefore we never amend them. On the contrary, they take but deeper root, by losing all chance of concealment. Yet I am vexed to see that odious Sir Sedley shew so silly a passion for being a man of the ton, as to suffer himself to be led in a string by those two poor paltry creatures, who are not more troublesome as fops, than tiresome as fools, merely because they are better known than himself upon the turf and at the clubs.'

Here, she was joined by Lord O'Lerney and the honourable Mr. Ormsby. And, in the next saunter of the tonnish triumvirs, Lord Newford, suddenly seeing with whom she was associated, stopt, and looking at her with an air of surprise, exclaimed, 'God bless me! Mrs. Arlbery! I hope you are perfectly well?'

'Infinitely indebted to your lordship's solicitude!' she answered, rather sarcastically. But, without noticing her manner, he desired to be one in her tea-party, which she was then rising to form.

She accepted the offer, with a glance of consciousness at the General, who, as he conducted her, said: 'I did not expect so much grace would so immediately have been accorded.'

'Alas! my dear General, what can one do? These tonnish people, cordially as I despise them, lead the world; and if one has not a few of them in one's train, 'twere as well turn hermit. However, mark how he will fare with me! But don't judge from the opening.'

She now made his lordship so many gay compliments, and mingled so much personal civility with the general entertainment of her discourse, that, as soon as they rose from tea, he professed his intention of sitting by her, for the rest of the evening.

She immediately declared herself tired to death of the Rooms, and calling upon Miss Dennel and Camilla, abruptly made her exit.

The General, again her conductor, asked how she could leave thus a conquest so newly made.

'I leave,' she answered, 'only to secure it. He will be piqued that I should go, and that pique will keep me in his head till to-morrow. 'Tis well, my dear General, to put any thing there! But if I had stayed a moment longer, my contempt might have broken forth into satire, or my weariness into yawning: and I should then inevitably have been cut by the ton party for the rest of the season.'

Miss Dennel, who had been dancing, and was again engaged to dance, remonstrated against retiring so soon; but Mrs. Arlbery had a regular system never to listen to her. Camilla, whom nothing had diverted, was content to retreat.

At the door stood Sir Sedley Clarendel, who, as if now first perceiving them, said to Mrs. Arlbery, 'Ah! my fair friend!—And how long have you been at the Wells?'

'Intolerable wretch!' cried she, taking him apart, 'is it thus you keep your conditions? did you draw me into bringing this poor love-sick thing with me, only to sigh me into the vapours?'

'My dear madam!' exclaimed he, in a tone of expostulation, 'who can think of the same scheme two days together? Could you possibly form a notion of anything so patriarchal?'

Before they retired to their chambers at the hotel, Camilla told Mrs. Arlbery how shocking to her was the sight, much more any acquaintance with Lord Newford, who was the person that had so much terrified the lady she had met on their journey. Mrs. Arlbery assured her he should be exiled her society, if, upon investigation, he was found the aggressor; but while there appeared so much mystery in the complaint and the conduct of this unknown lady, she should postpone his banishment.

Camilla was obliged to submit: but scarce rested till she saw again her new favourite the next morning.

CHAPTER III

Mount Ephraim

This expected guest arrived early. Camilla received her with the only sensation of pleasure she had experienced at Tunbridge. Yet what she excited seemed still stronger: the fair stranger besought her friendship as a solace to her existence, and hung upon her as upon a treasure long lost, and dearly recovered. Camilla soon caught the infection of her softness, and felt a similar desire to cultivate her regard. She found her beauty attractive, her voice melodious, and her manners bewitchingly caressing.

Fearing, nevertheless, while yet in ignorance of her connexions, to provoke further ridicule from Mrs. Arlbery by going abroad with her, she proposed deferring to return her visit till another day: the lady consented, and they spent together two hours, which each thought had been but two minutes, when Mrs. Arlbery summoned Camilla to a walk.

The fair unknown then took leave, saying her servant was in waiting; and Camilla and Mrs. Arlbery went to the bookseller's.

Here, that lady was soon joined by Lord O'Lerney and General Kinsale, who were warm admirers of her vivacity and observations. Mr. Dennel took up the Daily Advertiser; his daughter stationed herself at the door to see the walkers upon the Pantiles; Sir Theophilus Jarard, under colour of looking at a popular pamphlet, was indulging in a nap in a corner; Lord Newford, noticing nothing, except his own figure as he past a mirrour, was shuffling loud about the floor, which was not much embellished by the scraping of his boots; and Sir Sedley Clarendel, lounging upon a chair in the middle of the shop, sat eating bon bons.

Mrs. Arlbery, for some time, confined her talents to general remarks: but finding these failed to move a muscle in the face of Sir Sedley, at whom they were directed, she suddenly exclaimed: 'Pray, my Lord O'Lerney, do you know any thing of Sir Sedley Clarendel?'

'Not so much,' answered his Lordship, 'as I could wish; but I hope to improve my acquaintance with him.'

'Why then, my lord, I am much afraid you will conclude, when you see him in one of those reveries, from the total vacancy of his air, that he is thinking of nothing. But pray permit me to take his part. Those apparent cogitations, to which he is so much addicted, are moments only of pretended torpor, but of real torment, devoted, not as they appear, to supine insipidity, but to painful secret labour how next he may call himself into notice. Nevertheless, my lord, don't let what I have said hurt him in your opinion; he is quaint, to be sure, but there's no harm in him. He lives in my neighbourhood; and, I assure your lordship, he is, upon the whole, what may be called a very good sort of man.'

Here she yawned violently; and Sir Sedley, unable to maintain his position, twice crossed his legs, and then arose and took up a book: while Lord Newford burst into so loud a laugh, that he awakened Sir Theophilus Jarard, by echoing, 'A good sort of man! O poor Clary!... O hang it!... O curse it!... poor Clary!'

'What's the matter with Clary?' cried Sir Theophilus, rubbing his eyes; 'I have been boring myself with this pamphlet, till I hardly know whether I am awake or asleep.'

'Why, he's a good sort of man!' replied Lord Newford.

Sir Sedley, though he expected, and even hoped for some pointed strictures, and could have defied even abuse, could not stand this mortifying praise; and, asking for the subscription books, which, already, he had twice examined, said: 'Is there any body here one knows?'

'O, ay, have you any names?' cried Lord Newford, seizing them first; and with some right, as they were the only books in the shop he ever read.

'Come, I'll be generous,' said Mrs. Arlbery, 'and add another signature against your lordship's next lecture.'

She then wrote her name, and threw down half-a-guinea. Camilla, to whom the book was next presented, concluded this the established custom, and, from mere timidity, did the same; though somewhat disturbed to leave herself no more gold than she gave. Miss Dennel followed; but her father, who said he did not come to Tunbridge to read, which he could do at home, positively refused to subscribe.

Sir Theophilus now, turning, or rather, tossing over the leaves, cried: 'I see no name here one knows any thing of, but Lady Alithea Selmore.'

'Why, there's nobody else here,' said Lord Newford, 'not a soul!'

Almost every body present bowed; but wholly indifferent to reproof, he again whistled, again streamed up and down the room, and again took a bold and full survey of himself in the looking-glass.

'On the contrary,' cried Sir Sedley, 'I hear there is a most extraordinary fine creature lately arrived, who is invincible to a degree.'

'O that's Mrs. Berlinton;' said Sir Theophilus; 'yes, she's a pretty little thing.'

'She's very beautiful indeed,' said Lord O'Lerney.

'Where can one see her?' cried Mrs. Arlbery.

'If she is not at the Rooms to-night,' said Sir Sedley, 'I shall be stupified to petrifaction. They tell me she is a marvel of the first water; turning all heads by her beauty, winning all hearts by her sweetness, fascinating all attention by her talents, and setting all fashions by her elegance.'

'This paragon,' cried Mrs. Arlbery, to Camilla, 'can be no other than your mysterious fair. The description just suits your own.'

'But my fair mysterious,' said Camilla, 'is of a disposition the most retired, and seems so young, I don't at all think her married.'

'This divinity,' said Sir Sedley, 'for the blessing of everyone, yet

Lord of Himself, uncumber'd by a Wife [1],

[Footnote 1: Dryden]

is safely noosed; and amongst her attributes are two others cruel to desperation; she excited every hope by a sposo properly detestable—yet gives birth to despair, by a coldness the most shivering.'

'And what,' said Mrs. Arlbery, 'is this Lady Alithea Selmore?'

'Lady Alithea Selmore,' drily, but with a smile, answered General Kinsale.

'Nay, nay, that's not to be mentioned irreverently,' returned Mrs. Arlbery; 'a title goes for a vast deal, where there is nothing else; and, where there is something, doubles its value.

Mr. Dennel, saying he found, by the newspaper, a house was to be sold upon Mount Ephraim, which promised to be a pretty good bargain, proposed walking thither, to examine what sort of condition it was in.

Lord O'Lerney inquired if Camilla had yet seen Mount Ephraim. No, she answered; and a general party was made for an airing. Sir Sedley ordered his phaeton; Mrs. Arlbery drove Camilla in her's; Miss Dennel walked with her father; and the rest of the gentlemen went on horseback.

Arrived at Mount Ephraim, they all agreed to alight, and enjoy the view and pure air of the hill, while Mr. Dennel visited the house. But, just as Mrs. Arlbery had descended from the phaeton, her horses, taking fright at some object that suddenly struck them, reared up, in a manner alarming to the spectators, and still more terrific to Camilla, in whose hands Mrs. Arlbery had left the reins: and the servant, who stood at the horses' heads, received a kick that laid him flat on the ground.

'O, jump out! jump out!' cried Miss Dennel, 'or else you'll be murdered!'

'No! no! keep your seat, and hold the reins!' cried Mrs. Arlbery: 'For heaven's sake, don't jump out!'

Camilla, mentally giddy, but personally courageous, was sufficiently mistress of herself to obey the last injunction, though with infinite labour, difficulty, and terror, the horses plunging and flouncing incessantly.

'Don't you think she'll be killed?' cried Lord Newford, dismounting, lest his own horse should also take fright. 'Do you think one could help her?' said Sir Theophilus Jarard, steadily holding the bridle of his mare from the same apprehension.

Lord O'Lerney was already on foot to afford her assistance, when the horses, suddenly turning round, gave to the beholders the dreadful menace of going down the steep declivity of Mount Ephraim full gallop.

Camilla now, appalled, had no longer power to hold the reins; she let them go, with an idea of flinging herself out of the carriage, when Sir Sedley, who had darted like lightning from his phaeton, presented himself at the horses' heads, on the moment of their turning, and, at the visible and imminent hazard of his life, happily stopt them while she jumped to the ground. They then, with a fury that presently dashed the phaeton to pieces, plunged down the hill.

The fright of Camilla had not robbed her of her senses, and the exertion and humanity of Sir Sedley seemed to restore to him the full possession of his own: yet one of his knees was so much hurt, that he sunk upon the grass.

Penetrated with surprise, as well as gratitude, Camilla, notwithstanding her own tremor, was the first to make the most anxious inquiries: secretly, however, sighing to herself: Ah! had Edgar thus rescued me! yet struck equally with a sense of obligation and of danger, from the horrible, if not fatal mischief she had escaped, and from the extraordinary hazard and kindness by which she had been saved, she expressed her concern and acknowledgments with a softness, that even Sir Sedley himself could not listen to unmoved.

He received, indeed, from this adventure, almost every species of pleasure of which his mind was capable. His natural courage, which he had nearly annihilated, as well as forgotten, by the effeminate part he was systematically playing, seemed to rejoice in being again exercised; his good nature was delighted by the essential service he had performed; his vanity was gratified by the publicity of the praise it brought forth; and his heart itself experienced something like an original feeling, unspoilt by the apathy of satiety, from the sensibility he had awakened in the young and lovely Camilla.

The party immediately flocked around him, and he was conveyed to a house belonging to Lord O'Lerney, who resided upon Mount Ephraim, and his lordship's carriage was ordered to take him to his apartment at the hotel.

Mrs. Arlbery, whose high spirits were totally subdued by the terror with which she had been seized at the danger of Camilla, was so delighted by her rescue, and the courage with which it was effected, that all her spleen against Sir Sedley was changed into the warmest approbation. When he was put into the coach, she insisted upon seeing him safe to the hotel; Camilla, with her usual inartificial quickness, seconding the motion, and Lord O'Lerney, a nobleman far more distinguished by benevolence and urbanity than by his rank, taking the fourth place himself. The servant, who was considerably hurt, he desired might remain at his house.

In descending Mount Ephraim, Camilla turned giddy with the view of what she had escaped, and cast her eyes with doubled thankfulness upon Sir Sedley as her preserver. Fragments of the phaeton were strewed upon the road; one of the horses lay dead at the bottom of the hill; and the other was so much injured as to be totally disabled for future service.

When they came to the hotel, they all alighted with the young baronet, Camilla with as little thought, as Mrs. Arlbery with little care for doing any thing that was unusual. They waited in an adjoining apartment till they were assured nothing of any consequence was the matter, and Lord O'Lerney then carried them to their new lodging upon Mount Pleasant.

Mrs. Arlbery bore her own share in this accident with perfect good-humour, saying it would do her infinite good, by making her a rigid oeconomist; for she could neither live without a phaeton, nor yet build one, and buy ponies, but by parsimonious savings from all other expenses.

At night they went again to the Rooms. But Mrs. Arlbery found in them as little amusement as Camilla. Sir Sedley was not there, either to attack or to flatter; the celebrated Mrs. Berlinton still appeared not to undergo a scrutiny; and Lady Alithea Selmore sat at the upper end of the apartment, attended by all the beaux, except the General, now at Tunbridge.

This was not to be supported. She arose, and declaring she would take her tea with the invalid, bid the General escort her to his room.

In their way out, she perceived the assembly books. Recollecting she had not subscribed, she entered her name, but protested she could afford but half-a-guinea, upon her present new and avaricious plan.

Camilla, with much secret consternation, concluded it impossible to give less; and a few shillings were now all that remained in her purse. Her uneasiness, however, presently passed away, upon recollecting she should want no more money, as she was now free of the rooms, and of the library, and equipped in attire for the whole time she should stay.

Miss Dennel put down a guinea; but her father, telling her half-a-crown would have done, said, for that reason, he should himself pay nothing.

Sir Sedley received them with the most unaffected pleasure: forced upon solitude, and by no means free from pain, he had found no resource but in reading, which of late had been his least occupation, except the mere politics of the day. Even reflection had discovered its way to him, though a long banished guest, which had quitted her post, to make room for affectation, vanity, and every species of frivolity. Reduced, however, to be reasonable, even by this short confinement, he now felt the obligation of their charitable visit, and set his foppery and conceit apart, from a desire to entertain them. Camilla had not conceived he had the power of being so pleasantly natural; and the strong feeling of gratitude in her ever warm heart made her contribute what she was able to the cheerfulness of the evening.

Some time after, General Kinsale was called out, and presently returned with Major Cerwood, just arrived from the regiment; who, with some apology to Sir Sedley, hoped he might be pardoned for the liberty he took, upon hearing who was at the hotel, of preferring such society to the Rooms.

As the Major had nothing in him either brilliant or offensive, his sight, after the first salutations, was almost all of which the company was sensible.

Camilla, his sole object, he could not approach; she sat between the baronet and Mrs. Arlbery; and all her looks and all her attention were divided between them.

Mrs. Arlbery, emerging from the mortifications of neglect, which she had experienced, almost for the first time in her life, at the Rooms, was unusually alive and entertaining; Sir Sedley kept pace with her, and the discourse was so whimsical, that Camilla, amused, and willing to encourage a sensation so natural to her, after a sadness till now, for so long a time unremitting, once more heard and welcomed the sound of her own laughter.

It was instantly, however, and strangely checked; a sigh, so deep that it might rather be called a groan, made its way through the wainscot of the next apartment.

Much raillery followed the sight of her changed countenance; the hotel was pronounced to be haunted, and by a ghost reduced to that plight from her cruelty. But the good-humour and gaiety of the conversation soon brought her again to its tone; and time passed with general hilarity, till they observed that Miss Dennel, who, having no young female to talk with of her own views and affairs, was thoroughly tired, had fallen fast asleep upon her chair.

Her father was already gone home to a hot supper, which he had ordered in his own room, and meant to eat before their return; Mrs. Arlbery, to his great discomfort, allowing nothing to appear at night but fruit or oysters.

They now took leave, Mrs. Arlbery conducted by the General, and Camilla, by the Major; while Miss Dennel, unassisted and half asleep, stumbled, screamed, and fell, just before she reached the staircase.

The General was first to aid her; the Major, not choosing to quit Camilla; who, looking round at a light which came from the room whence the sigh they had heard had issued, perceived, as it glared in her eyes, it was held by Edgar.

Astonishment, pleasure, hope, and shame, took alternate rapid possession of her mind; but the last sensation was the first that visibly operated, and she snatched her hand involuntarily from the Major.

Mrs. Arlbery exclaimed, 'Bless me, Mr. Mandlebert! are you the ghost we heard sighing in that room yonder?'

Mandlebert attempted to make some slight answer; but his voice refused all sound.

She went on, then, to the carriage of Mr. Dennel, followed by her young ladies, and drove off for Mount Pleasant.

CHAPTER IV

Knowle

The last words of Camilla to Mandlebert, in quitting Cleves, and the tears with which he saw her eyes overflowing, had annihilated all his resentment, and left him no wish but to serve her. Her distinction between what was wisest and what was kindest, had penetrated him to the quick. To be thought capable of severity towards so sweet a young creature, the daughter of his guardian, his juvenile companion, and earliest favourite, made him detestable in his own eyes. He languished to follow her, to apologise for what had hurt her, and to vow to her a fair and disinterested friendship for the rest of his life: and he only forced himself, from decency, to stay out his promised week with the baronet, before he set out for Tunbridge.

Upon his arrival, which was late, he went immediately to the Rooms; but he only saw her name in the books, and learnt, upon inquiring for Mrs. Arlbery, that she and her party were already retired.

Glad to find her so sober in hours, he went to the hotel, meaning quietly to read till bed-time, and to call upon her the next morning.

In a few moments, a voice struck his ear that effectually interrupted his studies. It was the voice of Camilla. Camilla at an hotel at past eleven o'clock! He knew she did not lodge there; he had seen, in the books, the direction of Mrs. Arlbery at Mount Pleasant. Mrs. Arlbery's voice he also distinguished, Sir Sedley Clarendel's, General Kinsale's, and, least of all welcome, ... the Major's.

Perhaps, however, some lady, some intimate friend of Mrs. Arlbery, was just arrived, and had made them spend the evening there. He rang for his man, and bid him inquire who had taken the next room, ... and learnt it was Sir Sedley Clarendel.

To visit a young man at an hotel; rich, handsome, and splendid; and with a chaperon so far from past her prime, so elegant, so coquetish, so alluring, and still so pretty; and to meet there a flashy Officer, her open pursuer and avowed admirer—'Tis true, he had concluded, Tunbridge and the Major were one; but not thus, not with such glaring impropriety; his love, he told himself, was past; but his esteem was still susceptible, and now grievously wounded.

To read was impossible. To hold his watch in his hand, and count the minutes she still stayed, was all to which his faculties were equal. No words distinctly reached him; that the conversation was lively, the tone of every voice announced, but when that of Camilla struck him by its laughter, the depth of his concern drew from him a sigh that was heard into the next apartment.

Of this, with infinite vexation, he was himself aware, from the sudden silence and pause of all discourse which ensued. Ashamed both of what he felt and what he betrayed, he grew more upon his guard, and hoped it might never be known to whom the room belonged.

When, however, as they were retiring, a scream reached his ear, though he knew it was not the voice of Camilla, he could not command himself, and rushed forth with a light; but the lady who screamed was as little noticed as thought of: the Major was holding the hand of Camilla, and his eye could take in no more: he saw not even that Mrs. Arlbery was there; and when roused by her question, all voice was denied him for answer; he stood motionless even after they had descended the stairs, till the steps of the General and the Major, retiring to their chambers, brought to him some recollection, and enabled him to retreat.

Fully now, as well as cruelly convinced, of the unabated force of his unhappy passion, he spent the night in extreme wretchedness; and all that was not swallowed up in repining and regret, was devoted to ruminate upon what possible means he could suggest, to restore to himself the tranquillity of indifference.

The confusion of Camilla persuaded him she thought she was acting wrong; but whether from disapprobation of the character of the Major, or from any pecuniary obstacles to their union, he could not devise. To assist the marriage according to his former plan, would best, he still believed, sooth his internal sufferings, if once he could fancy the Major at all worthy of such a wife. But Camilla, with all her inconsistencies, he thought a treasure unequalled: and to contribute to bestow her on a man who, probably, only prized her for her beauty, he now persuaded himself would rather be culpable than generous.

Upon the whole, therefore, he could resolve only upon a complete change of his last system; to seek, instead of avoiding her; to familiarise himself with her faults, till he ceased to doat upon her virtues; to discover if her difficulties were mental or worldly; to enforce them if the first, and ... whatever it might cost him—to invalidate them if the last.

This plan, the only one he could form, abated his misery. It reconciled him to residing where Camilla resided, it was easy to him, therefore, to conclude it the least objectionable.

Camilla, meanwhile, in her way to Mount Pleasant, spoke not a syllable. Dismay that Edgar should have seen her so situated, while in ignorance how it had happened, made an uneasiness the most terrible combat the perplexed pleasure, that lightened, yet palpitated in her bosom, from the view of Edgar at Tunbridge, and from the sigh which had reached her ears. Yet, was it for her he sighed? was it not, rather, from some secret inquietude, in which she was wholly uninterested, and might never know? Still, however, he was at Tunbridge; still, therefore, she might hope something relative to herself induced his coming; and she determined, with respect to her own behaviour, to observe the injunctions of her father, whose letter she would regularly read every morning.

Mrs. Arlbery, also, spoke not; the unexpected sight of Mandlebert occupied all her thoughts; yet, though his confusion was suspicious, she could not, ultimately, believe he loved Camilla, as she could suggest no possible impediment to his proclaiming any regard he entertained. His sigh she imagined as likely to be mere lassitude as love; and supposed, that having long discovered the partiality of Camilla, his vanity had been confounded by the devoirs of the Major.

Miss Dennel, therefore, was the only one whose voice was heard during the ride; for now completely awaked, she talked without cessation of the fright she had endured. 'La, I thought,' cried she, 'when I tumbled down, somebody threw me down on purpose, and was going to kill me! dear me! I thought I should have died! And then I thought it was a robber; and then I thought that candle that come was a ghost! O la! I never was so frightened in my life!'

The next morning they went, as usual, to the Pantiles, and Mrs. Arlbery took her seat in the bookseller's shop, where the usual beaux were encountered; and where, presently, Edgar entering, addressed to her some discourse, and made some general inquiries after the health of Camilla.

It was a cruel drawback to her hopes to see him first thus in public: but the manner of Mrs. Arlbery at the hotel, he had thought repulsive; he had observed that she seemed offended with him since the rencounter at the breakfast given for Miss Dennel; and he now wished for some encouragement for renewing his rights to the acquaintance.

Sir Sedley, though with the assistance of a stick he had reached the library, was not sufficiently at his ease to again mount his horse; a carriage expedition was therefore agitating for the morning, and to see Knowle being fixed upon, equipages and horses were ordered.

While they waited their arrival. Lady Alithea Selmore, and a very shewy train of ladies and gentlemen, came into the library. Sir Sedley, losing the easy, natural manner which had just so much pleased Camilla, resumed his affectation, indolence, and inattention, and flung himself back in his chair, without finishing a speech he had begun, or listening to an inquiry why he stopt short. His friends, Lord Newford and Sir Theophilus Jarard, shuffled up to her ladyship; and Sir Sedley, muttering to himself life would not be life without being introduced to her, got up, and seizing Lord Newford by the shoulder, whispered what he called the height of his ambition, and was presented without delay.

He then entered into a little abrupt, half articulated conversation with Lady Alithea, who, by a certain toss of the chin, a short and half scornful laugh, and a supercilious dropping of the eye, gave to every sentence she uttered the air of a bon mot; and after each, as regularly stopt for some testimony of admiration, as a favourite actress in some scene in which every speech is applauded. What she said, indeed, had no other mark than what this manner gave to it; for it was neither good nor bad, wise nor foolish, sprightly nor dull. It was what, if naturally spoken, would have passed, as it deserved, without censure or praise. This manner, however, prevailed not only upon her auditors, but herself, to believe that something of wit, of finesse, of peculiarity, accompanied her every phrase. Thought, properly speaking, there was none in any thing she pronounced: her speeches were all replies, which her admirers dignified by the name of repartees, and which mechanically and regularly flowed from some word, not idea, that preceded.

Mrs. Arlbery, having listened some time, turned entirely away, though with less contempt of her ladyship than of her hearers. Her own auditors, however, except the faithful General, had all deserted her. Even the Major, curious to attend to a lady of some celebrity, had quitted the chair of Camilla; and Edgar himself, imagining, from this universal devotion, there was something well worth an audience, had joined the group.

'We are terribly in the back ground, General!' cried Mrs. Arlbery, in a low voice. 'What must be done to save our reputations?'

The General, laughing, said, he feared they were lost irretrievably; but added that he preferred defeat with her, to victory without her.

'Your gallantry, my dear General,' cried she, with a sudden air of glee, 'shall be rewarded! Follow me close, and you shall see the fortune of the day reversed.'

Rising then, she advanced softly, and with an air of respect, towards the party, and fixing herself just opposite to Lady Alithea, with looks of the most profound attention, stood still, as if in admiring expectation.

Lady Alithea, who had regarded this approach as an intrusion that strongly manifested ignorance of high life, thought much better of it when she remarked the almost veneration of her air. She deemed it, however, wholly beneath her to speak when thus attended to; till, observing the patient admiration with which even a single word seemed to be hoped for, she began to pardon what appeared to be a mere tribute to her fame; and upon Sir Theophilus Jarard's saying, 'I don't think we have had such a bore of a season as this, these five years;' could not refuse herself the pleasure of replying: 'I did not imagine, Sir Theophilus, you were already able to count by lustres.'

Her own air of complacency announced the happiness of this answer. The company, as usual, took the hint, and approbation was buzzed around her. Lord Newford gave a loud laugh, without the least conception why; and Sir Theophilus, after paying the same compliment, wished, as it concerned himself, to know what had been said; and glided to the other end of the shop, to look for the word lustre in Entick's dictionary.

But this triumph was even less than momentary; Mrs. Arlbery, gently raising her shoulders with her head, indulged herself in a smile that favoured yet more of pity than derision; and, with a hasty glance at the General, that spoke an eagerness to compare notes with him, hurried out of the shop; her eyes dropt, as if fearful to trust her countenance to an instant's investigation.

Lady Alithea felt herself blush. The confusion was painful and unusual to her. She drew her glove off and on; she dabbed a highly scented pocket handkerchief repeatedly to her nose; she wondered what it was o'clock; took her watch in her hand, without recollecting to examine it; and then wondered if it would rain, though not a cloud was to be discerned in the sky.

To see her thus completely disconcerted, gave a weight to the mischievous malice of Mrs. Arlbery, of which the smallest presence of mind would have robbed it. Her admirers, one by one, dwindled away, with lessened esteem for her talents; and, finding herself presently alone in the shop with Sir Theophilus Jarard, she said, 'Pray, Sir Theophilus, do you know anything of that queer woman?'

The words queer woman were guides sufficient to Sir Theophilus, who answered, 'No! I have seen her, somewhere, by accident, but—she is quite out of our line.'

This reply was a sensible gratification to Lady Alithea, who, having heard her warmly admired by Lord O'Lerney, had been the more susceptible to her ridicule. Rudeness she could have despised without emotion; but contempt had something in it of insolence; a commodity she held herself born to dispense, not receive.

When Mrs. Arlbery arrived, laughing, at the bottom of the Pantiles, she found Edgar making inquiries of the time and manner of drinking the mineral water.

Camilla heard him, also, and with deep apprehensions for his health. He did not however look ill; and a second sadness, not less deep, ensued, that she could now retain no hope of being herself his inducement to this journey.

But egotism was no part of her composition; when she saw, therefore, the next minute, Sir Sedley Clarendel advance limping, and heard him ask if his phaeton were ready, she approached him, saying, 'Will you venture, Sir Sedley, in your phaeton?'

'There's no sort of reason why not,' answered he, sensibly flattered; 'yet I had certainly rather go as you go!'

'Then that,' said Mrs. Arlbery, 'must be in Dennel's coach, with him and my little niece here: and then I'll drive the General in your phaeton.'

'Agreed!' cried Sir Sedley, seating himself on one of the forms; and then, taking from a paper some tickets, added; 'I want a few guineas.'

'So do I!' exclaimed Mrs. Arlbery; 'do you know where such sort of things are to be met with?'

'Lady Alithea Selmore has promised to disperse some twenty tickets for the master of the ceremonies' ball, and she commands me to help. How many shall I give you?'

'Ask Mr. Dennel,' answered she negligently; 'he's the only paymaster just now.'

Mr. Dennel turned round, and was going to walk away; but Mrs. Arlbery, taking him by the arm, said: 'My good friend, how many tickets shall Sir Sedley give you?'

'Me!—none at all.'

'O fie! every body goes to the master of the ceremonies' ball. Come, you shall have six. You can't possibly take less.'

'Six! What should I do with them?'

'Why, you and your daughter will use two, and four you must give away.'

'What for?'

'Was ever such a question? To do what's proper and right, and handsome and gallant.'

'O, as to all that, it's what I don't understand. It's out of my way.'

He would then have made off; but Mrs. Arlbery, piqued to succeed, held him fast, and said: 'Come, if you'll be good, I'll be good too, and you shall have a plain joint of meat at the bottom of the table every day for a fortnight.'

Mr. Dennel softened a little here into something like a smile; and drew two guineas from his purse; but more there was no obtaining.

'Come,' cried Sir Sedley, 'you have canvassed well so far. Now for your fair self.'

'You are a shocking creature!' cried she; 'don't you know I am turned miser?'

Yet she gave her guinea.

'But the fair Tyrold does not also, I trust, assume that character?'

Camilla had felt very uneasy during this contest; and now, colouring, said she did not mean to go to the ball.

'Can you ever expect, then,' said Mrs. Arlbery, 'to have a partner at any other? You don't know the rules of these places. The master of the ceremonies is always a gentleman, and every body is eager to shew him every possible respect.'

Camilla was now still more distressed; and stammered out, that she believed the fewer balls she went to, the better her father would be pleased.

'Your father, my dear, is a very wise man, and a very good man, and a very excellent preacher: but what does he know of Tunbridge Wells? Certainly not so much as my dairy maid, for she has heard John talk of them; but as to your father, depend upon it, the sole knowledge he has ever obtained, is from some treatise upon its mineral waters; which, very possibly, he can analyse as well as a physician: but for the regulation of a country dance, be assured he will do much better to make you over to Sir Sedley, or to me.'

Camilla laughed faintly, and feeling in her pocket to take out her pocket handkerchief, by way of something to do, Mrs. Arlbery concluded she was seeking her purse, and suddenly putting her hand upon her arm to prevent her, said, 'No, no! if you don't wish to go, or choose to go, or approve of going, I cannot, in sober earnestness, see you compelled. Nothing is so detestable as forcing people to be amused. Come, now for Knowle.'

Sir Sedley was then putting up his tickets; but the Major, taking one of them out of his hand, presented it to Camilla, saying: 'Let the ladies take their tickets now, and settle with us afterwards.'

Camilla felt extremely provoked, yet not knowing how to resist, took the ticket; but, turning pointedly from the Major to Sir Sedley, said: 'I am your debtor, then, sir, a guinea—the smallest part, indeed, of what I owe you, though all I can pay!' And she then resolved to borrow that sum immediately of Mrs. Arlbery.

Sir Sedley began to think she grew handsomer every moment: and, contrary to his established and systematic inattention, upon hearing the sound of the carriages, conducted her himself to Mr. Dennel's coach, which he ascended after her.

Edgar, unable to withstand joining the party, had ordered his horse during the debate about the tickets.

Lords O'Lerney and Newford, and Sir Theophilus Jarard, and Major Cerwood, went also on horseback.

Sir Sedley made it his study to procure amusement for Camilla during the ride; and while he humoured alternately the loquacious folly of Miss Dennel, and the under-bred positiveness of her father, intermingled with both comic sarcasms against himself, and pointed annotations upon the times, that somewhat diverted her solicitude and perplexity.

She forgot them however, more naturally, in examining the noble antique mansion, pictures, and curiosities of Knowle; and in paying the tribute that taste must ever pay to the works exhibited there of Sir Joshua Reynolds.

The house viewed, they all proceeded to the park, where, enchanted with the noble old trees which venerably adorn it, they strolled delightedly, till they came within sight of an elegant white form, as far distant as their eyes could reach, reading under an oak.

Camilla instantly thought of her moonlight friend; but Sir Theophilus called out, 'Faith, there's the divine Berlinton!'

'Is there, faith?' exclaimed Lord Newford, suddenly rushing forward to satisfy himself if it were true.

Deeming this an ill-bred and unauthorised intrusion, they all stopt. The studious fair, profoundly absorbed by her book, did not hear his lordship's footsteps, till his coat rustled in her ears. Raising then her eyes, she screamed, dropt her book, and darting up, flew towards the wood, with a velocity far exceeding his own, though without seeming to know, or consider, whither her flight might lead her.

Camilla, certain now this was her new friend, felt an indignation the most lively against Lord Newford, and involuntarily sprung forward. It was evident the fair fugitive had perceived none of the party but him she sought to avoid; notwithstanding Lord Newford himself, when convinced who it was, ceased his pursuit, and seemed almost to find out there was such a sensation as shame; though by various antics, of swinging his cane, looking up in the air, shaking his pocket handkerchief, and sticking his arms a-kimbo, he thought it essential to his credit to disguise it.

Camilla had no chance to reach the flying beauty, but by calling to her to stop; which she did instantly at the sound of her voice, and, turning round with a look of rapture, ran into her arms.

The Major, whose devoirs to Camilla always sought, not avoided the public eye, eagerly pursued her. Edgar, cruelly envying a licence he concluded to result from his happy situation, looked on in silent amaze; but listened with no small attention to the remarks that now fell from Mrs. Arlbery, who said she was sure this must be the fair Incognita that Miss Tyrold had met with upon the road; and gave a lively relation of that adventure.

He could not hear without delight the benevolent courage thus manifested by Camilla, nor without terror the danger to which it might have exposed her. But Lord O'Lerney, with an air of extreme surprise, exclaimed: 'Is it possible Lord Newford could give any cause of alarm to Mrs. Berlinton?'

'Is she then, my lord, a woman of character?' cried Mrs. Arlbery.

'Untainted!' he answered solemnly; 'as spotless, I believe, as her beauty: and if you have seen her, you will allow that to be no small praise. She comes from a most respectable family in Wales, and has been married but a few months.'

'Married, my lord? my fair female Quixote assured me she was single.'

'No, poor thing! she was carried from the nursery to the altar, and, I fear, not very judiciously nor happily.'

'Dear!' cried Miss Dennel, 'i'n't she happy?'

'I never presume to judge,' answered his lordship, smiling; 'but she has always something melancholy in her air.'

'Pray how old is she?' said Miss Dennel.

'Eighteen.'

'Dear! and married?—La! I wonder what makes her unhappy!'

'Not a husband, certainly!' said Mrs. Arlbery, laughing, 'that is against all chance and probability.'

'Well, I'm resolved when I'm married myself, I won't be unhappy.'

'And how will you help it?'

'O, because I'm determined I won't. I think it's very hard if I may'nt have my own way when I'm married.'

''Twill at least be very singular!' answered Mrs. Arlbery.

Camilla now returned to her party, having first conducted her new friend towards a door in the park where her carriage was waiting.

'At length, my dear,' said Mrs. Arlbery, 'your fair mysterious has, I suppose, avowed herself?'

'I made no inquiry,' answered she, painfully looking down.

'I can tell you who she is, then, myself,' said Miss Dennel; 'she is Mrs. Berlinton, and she's come out of Wales, and she's married, and she's eighteen.'

'Married!' repeated Camilla, blushing from internal surprise at the conversations she had held with her.

'Yes; your fair Incognita is neither more nor less,' said Mrs. Arlbery, 'than the honourable Mrs. Berlinton, wife to Lord Berlinton's brother, and, next only to Lady Alithea Selmore, the first toast, and the reigning cry of the Wells for this season.'

Camilla, who had seen and considered her in almost every other point of view, heard this with less of pleasure than astonishment. When a further investigation brought forth from Lord O'Lerney that her maiden name was Melmond, Mrs. Arlbery exclaimed: 'O, then, I cease to play the idiot, and wonder! I know the Melmonds well. They are all half crazy, romantic, love-lorn, studious, and sentimental. One of them was in Hampshire this summer, but so immensely "melancholy and gentleman-like [2]," that I never took him into my society.'

[Footnote 2: Ben Jonson]

"Twas the brother of this young lady, I doubt not,' said Lord O'Lerney; 'he is a young man of very good parts, and of an exemplary character; but strong in his feelings, and wild in pursuit of whatever excites them.'

'When will you introduce me to your new friend, Miss Tyrold?' said Mrs. Arlbery; 'or, rather,' (turning to Lord Newford,) 'I hope your lordship will do me that honour; I hear you are very kind to her; and take much care to convince her of the ill effects and danger of the evening air.'

'O hang it! O curse it!' cried his lordship; 'why does a woman walk by moon-light?'

'Why, rather, should man,' said Lord O'Lerney, 'impede so natural a recreation?'

The age of Lord O'Lerney, which more than doubled that of Lord Newford, made this question supported, and even drew forth the condescension of an attempted exculpation. 'I vow, my lord,' he cried, 'I had no intention but to look at a letter; and that I thought, she only read in public to excite curiosity.'

'O but you knelt to her!' cried Miss Dennel, 'you knelt to her! I saw you! and why did you do that, when you knew she was married, and you could not be her lover?'

The party being now disposed to return to the Wells, Mrs. Arlbery called upon the General to attend her to the phaeton. Camilla, impatient to pay Sir Sedley, followed to speak to her; but, not aware of her wish, Mrs. Arlbery hurried laughingly on, saying, 'Come, General, let us be gone, that the coach may be last, and then Dennel must pay the fees! That will be a good guinea towards my ponies!'

CHAPTER V

Mount Pleasant

The shame and distress natural to every unhackneyed mind, in any necessity of soliciting a pecuniary favour, had now, in that of Camilla, the additional difficulty of coping against the avowed desire of Mrs. Arlbery not to open her purse.

When they arrived at Mount Pleasant, she saw all the horsemen alighted, and in conversation with that lady; and Edgar move towards the carriage, palpably with a design to hand her out: but as the Major advanced, he retreated, and, finding himself unnoticed by Mrs. Arlbery, remounted his horse.

Provoked and chagrined, she sprung forwards alone, and when pursued by the Major, with some of his usual compliments, turned from him impatiently and went up stairs.

Intent in thinking only of Edgar, she was not herself aware of this abruptness, till Mrs. Arlbery, following her to her chamber, said, 'Why were you so suddenly haughty to the Major, my dear Miss Tyrold? Has he offended you?'

Much surprised, she answered, no; but, forced by further questions, to be more explicit, confessed she wished to distance him, as his behaviour had been remarked.

'Remarked! how? by whom?'

She coloured, and was again hardly pressed before she answered, 'Mr. Mandlebert—once—named it to me.'

'O, ho, did he?' said Mrs. Arlbery, surprised in her turn; 'why then, my dear, depend upon it, he loves you himself.'

'Me!—Mr. Mandlebert!—' exclaimed Camilla, doubting what she heard.

'Nay, why not?'

'Why not?' repeated she in an excess of perturbation; 'O, he is too good! too excelling! he sees all my faults—points them out himself—'

'Does he?...' said Mrs. Arlbery thoughtfully, and pausing: 'nay, then,—if so—he wishes to marry you!'

'Me, ma'am!' cried Camilla, blushing high with mingled delight at the idea, and displeasure at its free expression.

'Why, else, should he caution you against another?'

'From goodness, from kindness, from generosity!—'

'No, no; those are not the characteristics of young men who counsel young women! We all heard he was engaged to your beautiful vacant-looking cousin; but I suppose he grew sick of her. A very young man seldom likes a silly wife. It is generally when he is further advanced in life that he takes that depraved taste. He then flatters himself a fool will be easier to govern.'

She now went away to dress; leaving Camilla a new creature; changed in all her hopes, though overwhelmed with shame at the freedom of this attack, and determined to exert her utmost strength of mind, not to expose to view the secret pleasure with which it filled her.

She was, however, so absent when they met again, that Mrs. Arlbery, shaking her head, said: 'Ah, my fair friend! what have you been thinking of?'

Excessively ashamed, she endeavoured to brighten up. The General and Sir Sedley had been invited to dinner. The latter was engaged in the evening to Lady Alithea Selmore, who gave tea at her own lodgings. 'The Rooms, then, will be quite empty,' said Mrs. Arlbery; 'so we had better go to the play.'

Mr. Dennel had no objection, and Sir Sedley promised to attend them, as it would be time enough for her ladyship afterwards.

So completely was Camilla absorbed in her new ideas, that she forgot both her borrowed guinea, and the state of her purse, till she arrived at the theatre. The recollection was then too late; and she had no resource against completely emptying it.

She was too happy however, at this instant, to admit any regret. The sagacity of Mrs. Arlbery she thought infallible; and the sight of Edgar in a box just facing her, banished every other consideration.

The theatre was almost without company. The assembly at Lady Alithea Selmore's had made it unfashionable, and when the play was over, Edgar found easily a place in the box.

Lord Newford and Sir Theophilus Jarard looked in just after, and affected not to know the piece was begun. Sir Sedley retired to his toilette, and Mr. Dennel to seek his carriage.

Some bills now got into the box, and were read by Sir Theophilus, announcing a superb exhibition of wild beasts for the next day, consisting chiefly of monkies who could perform various feats, and a famous ourang outang, just landed from Africa.

Lord Newford said he would go if he had but two more days to live. Sir Theophilus echoed him. Mr. Dennel expressed some curiosity; Miss Dennel, though she protested she should be frightened out of her wits, said she would not stay at home; Mrs. Arlbery confessed it would be an amusing sight to see so many representations of the dear human race; but Camilla spoke not: and scarce heard even the subject of discourse.

'You,' cried the Major, addressing her, 'will be there?'

'Where?' demanded she.

'To see this curious collection of animals.'

'It will be curious, undoubtedly,' said Edgar, pleased that she made no answer; 'but 'tis a species of curiosity not likely to attract the most elegant spectators; and rather, perhaps, adapted to give pleasure to naturalists, than to young ladies.'

Softened, at this moment, in every feeling of her heart towards Edgar, she turned to him, and said, 'Do you think it would be wrong to go?'

'Wrong,' repeated he, surprised though gratified, 'is perhaps too hard a word; but, I fear, at an itinerant show, such as this, a young lady would run some chance of finding herself in a neighbourhood that might seem rather strange to her.'

'Most certainly then,' cried she, with quickness, 'I will not go!'

The astonished Edgar looked at her with earnestness, and saw the simplicity of sincerity on her countenance. He looked then at the Major; who, accustomed to frequent failures in his solicitations, exhibited no change of features. Again he looked at Camilla, and her eyes met his with a sweetness of expression that passed straight to his heart.

Mrs. Arlbery now led the way to the coach; the forwardness of the Major, though in her own despight, procured him the hand of Camilla; but she had left upon Edgar an impression renovating to all his esteem. She is still, he thought, the same; candid, open, flexible; still, therefore, let me follow her, with such counsel as I am able to give. She has accused me of unkindness;—She was right! I retreated from her service at the moment when, in honour, I was bound to continue in it. How selfish was such conduct! how like such common love as seeks only its own gratification, not the happiness or welfare of its object! Could she, though but lately so dear to me, that all the felicity of my life seemed to hang upon her, become as nothing, because destined to another? No! Her father has been my father, and so long as she retains his respected name, I will watch by her unceasingly.

In their way home, one of the horses tired, and could not be made to drag the carriage up to Mount Pleasant. They were therefore obliged to alight and walk. Mrs. Arlbery took the arm of Mr. Dennel, which she did not spare, and his daughter, almost crying with sleep and fatigue, made the same use of Camilla's. She protested she had never been so long upon her feet in her life as that very morning in Knowle Park, and, though she leant upon her companion with as little scruple as upon a walking stick, she frequently stopt short, and declared she should stay upon the road all night, for she could not move another step: and they were still far from the summit, when she insisted upon sitting down, saying fretfully, 'I am sure I wish I was married! Nobody minds me. I am sure if I was, I would not be served so. I'm resolved I'll always have two coaches, one to come after me, and one to ride in; for I'm determined I won't marry a man that has not a great fortune. I'm sure papa could afford it too, if he'd a mind; only he won't. Every body vexes me. I'm sure I'm ready to cry!'

Mr. Dennel and Mrs. Arlbery, who neither of them, at any time, took the smallest notice of what she said, passed on, and left the whole weight both of her person and her complaints to Camilla. The latter, however, now reached the ears of a fat, tidy, neat looking elderly woman, who, in a large black bonnet, and a blue checked apron, was going their way; she approached them, and in a good-humoured voice, said: 'What! poor dear! why you seem tired to death? come, get up, my dear; be of good heart, and you shall hold by my arm; for that t'other poor thing's almost hauled to pieces.'

Miss Dennel accepted both the pity and the proposal; and the substantial arm of her new friend, gave her far superior aid to the slight one of Camilla.

'Well, and how did you like the play, my dears?' cried the woman.

'La!' said Miss Dennel, 'how should you know we were at the play?'

'O, I have a little bird,' answered she, sagaciously nodding, 'that tells me everything! you sat in the stage box?'

'Dear! so we did! How can you tell that? Was you in the gallery?'

'No, my dear, nor yet in the pit neither. And you had three gentlemen behind you, besides that gentleman that's going up the Mount?'

'Dear! So we had! But how do you know? did you peep at us behind the scenes?'

'No, my dear; I never went behind the scenes. But come, I hope you'll do now, for you ha'n't much further to go.'

'Dear! how do you know that?'

'Because you live at that pretty house, there, up Mount Pleasant, that's got the little closet window.'

'La, yes! who told you so?'

'And there's a pretty cat belonging to the house, all streaked brown and black?'

'O, la!' exclaimed Miss Dennel, half screaming, and letting go her arm, 'I dare say you're a fortune-teller! Pray, don't speak to me till we get to the light!'

She now hung back, so terrified that neither Camilla could encourage, nor the woman appease her; and she was going to run down the hill, forgetting all her weariness, to seek refuge from the servants, when the woman said, 'Why what's here to do? Why see, my dear, if I must let you into the secret—you must know—but don't tell it to the world!—I'm a gentlewoman!' She then removed her checked apron, and shewed a white muslin one, embroidered and flounced.

Miss Dennel was now struck with a surprise, of which Camilla bore an equal share. Their new acquaintance appeared herself in some confusion, but having exacted a promise not to be discovered to the world, she told them, she lodged at a house upon Mount Pleasant, just by their's, whence she often saw them; that, having a ticket given her, by a friend, for the play, she dressed herself and went into a box, with some very genteel company, who kept their coach, and who sat her down afterwards at another friend's, where she pretended she should be fetched: 'But I do my own way,' continued she, 'and nobody knows a word of the matter: for I keep a large bonnet, and cloak, and a checked apron, and a pair of clogs, or pattens, always at this friend's; and then when I have put them on, people take me for a mere common person, and I walk on, ever so late, and nobody speaks to me; and so by that means I get my pleasure, and save my money; and yet always appear like a gentlewoman when I'm known.'

She then again charged them to be discreet, saying that if this were spread to the world, she should be quite undone, for many ladies that took her about with them, would notice her no more. At the same time, as she wished to make acquaintance with such pretty young ladies, she proposed that they should all three meet in a walk before the house, the next morning, and talk together as if for the first time.

Camilla, who detested all tricks, declined entering into this engagement; but Miss Dennel, charmed with the ingenuity of her new acquaintance, accepted the appointment.

Camilla had, however, her own new friend for the opening of the next day. 'Ah! my sweet protectress!' cried she, throwing her arms about her neck, 'what am I not destined to owe you? The very sight of that man is horror to me. Amiable, generous creature! what a sight was yours, when turning round, I met your eyes, and beheld him no more!'

'Your alarm, at which I cannot wonder,' said Camilla, 'prevented your seeing your safety; for Lord Newford was with a large party.'

'O, he is obnoxious to my view! wherever I may see him, in public or in private, I shall fly him. He would have torn from me the loved characters of my heart's best correspondent!—'

Camilla now felt a little shocked, and colouring and interrupting her, said: 'Is it possible, Mrs. Berlinton—' and stopt not knowing how to go on.

'Ah! you know me, then! You know my connexions and my situation!' cried she, hiding her face on Camilla's bosom: 'tell me, at least, tell me, you do not therefore contemn and abhor me?'

'Heaven forbid!' said Camilla, terrified at such a preparation; 'what can I hear that can give you so cruel an idea?'

'Alas! know you not I have prophaned at the altar my plighted vows to the most odious of men? That I have formed an alliance I despise? and that I bear a name I think of with disgust, and hate ever to own?'

Camilla, thunderstruck, answered; 'No, indeed! I know nothing of all this!'

'Ah! guard yourself, then, well,' cried she, bursting into tears, 'from a similar fate! My friends are kind and good, but the temptation of seeing me rich beguiled them. I was disinterested and contented myself, but young and inexperienced; and I yielded to their pleadings, unaware of their consequences. Alas! I was utterly ignorant both of myself and the world! I knew not how essential to my own peace was an amiable companion; and I knew not, then,—that the world contained one just formed to make me happy!'

She now hung down her head, weeping and desponding. Camilla sought to sooth her, but was so amazed, so fearful, and so perplext, she scarce knew what either to say or to think.

The fair mourner, at length, a little recovering, added: 'Let me not agitate your gentle bosom with my sorrows. I regard you as an angel sent to console them; but it must be by mitigating, not partaking of them.'

Camilla was sensibly touched; and though strangely at a loss what to judge, felt her affections deeply interested.

'I dreaded,' she continued, 'to tell you my name, for I dreaded to sink myself into your contempt, by your knowledge of an alliance you must deem so mercenary. 'Twas folly to hope you would not hear it; yet I wished first to obtain, at least, your good will. The dear lost name of Melmond is all I love to pronounce! That name, I believe, is known to you; so may be, also, perhaps, my brother's unhappy story?'

Melmond, she then said, believing Miss Lynmere betrothed to Mr. Mandlebert, had quitted Hampshire in misery, to finish his vacation in Wales, with their mutual friends. There he heard that the rumour was false; and would instantly have returned and thrown himself at the feet of the young lady, by whose cousin, Mr. Lionel Tyrold, he had been told she was to inherit a large fortune; when this second report, also, was contradicted, and he learnt that Miss Lynmere had almost nothing; 'My brother,' added she, 'with the true spirit of true sentiment, was but the more urgent to pursue her; but our relations interfered—and he, like me, is doomed to endless anguish!'

The accident, she said, of the preceding morning, was owing to her being engaged in reading Rowe's letters from the dead to the living; which had so infinitely enchanted her, that, desiring to peruse them without interruption, yet fearing to again wander in search of a rural retreat, she had driven to Knowle; where, hearing the noble family was absent, she had asked leave to view the park, and there had taken out her delicious book, which she was enjoying in the highest luxury of solitude and sweet air, when Lord Newford broke in upon her.

Camilla enquired if she feared any bad consequences, by telling Mr. Berlinton of his impertinence.

'Heaven forbid,' she answered, 'that I should be condemned to speak to Mr. Berlinton of anything that concerns or befalls me! I see him as little as I am able, and speak to him as seldom.'

Camilla heard this with grief, but durst not further press a subject so delicate. They continued together till noon, and then reluctantly parted, upon a message from Mrs. Arlbery that the carriages were waiting. Mrs. Berlinton declined being introduced to that lady, which would only, she said, occasion interruptions to their future tête-à-têtes.

Neither the thoughtlessness of the disposition, nor the gaiety of the imagination of Camilla, could disguise from her understanding the glaring eccentricity of this conduct and character: but she saw them with more of interest than blame; the various attractions with which they were mixed, blending in her opinion something between pity and admiration, more captivating, though more dangerous, to the fond fancy of youth, than the most solid respect, and best founded esteem.

CHAPTER VI

The Accomplished Monkies

When Camilla descended, she found Sir Sedley Clarendel and General Kinsale in attendance; and saw, from the parlour window, Miss Dennel sauntering before the house, with the newly made acquaintance of the preceding evening.

The Baronet, who was to drive Mrs. Arlbery, enquired if Camilla would not prefer, also, an open carriage. Mrs. Arlbery seconded the motion. Miss Dennel, then, running to her father, exclaimed, 'Pray, papa, let's take this lady I've been talking with in the coach with us. She's the good-naturedest creature I ever knew.'

'Who is she? what's her name?'

'O, I don't know that, papa; but I'll go and ask her.'

Flying then back, 'Pray, ma'am,' she cried, 'what's your name? because papa wants to know.'

'Why, my dear, my name's Mittin. So you may think of me when you put on your gloves.'

'Papa, her name's Mittin,' cried Miss Dennel, scampering again to her father.

'Well, and who is she?'

'O, la, I'm sure I can't tell, only she's a gentlewoman.'

'And how do you know that?'

'She told me so herself.'

'And where does she live?'

'Just by, papa, at that house you see there.'

'O, well, if she's a neighbour, that's enough. I've no more to say.'

'O, then, I'll ask her!' cried Miss Dennel, jumping, 'dear! I'm so glad! 'twould have been so dull, only papa and I. I'm resolved, when I've a house of my own, I'll never go alone any where with papa.'

This being muttered, the invitation was made and accepted, and the parties set forward.

The ride was perfectly pleasing to Camilla, now revived and cheerful; Sir Sedley was free from airs; Mrs. Arlbery drew them into conversation with one another, and none of them were glad when Mr. Dennel, called 'stop! or you'll drive too far.'

Camilla, who, supposing she was going, as usual, to the Pantiles, had got into the phaeton without inquiry; and who, finding afterwards her mistake, concluded they were merely taking an airing, now observed she was advancing towards a crowd, and presently perceived a booth, and an immense sign hung out from it, exhibiting a man monkey, or ourang outang.

Though excessively fluttered, she courageously, and at once, told Mrs. Arlbery she begged to be excused proceeding.

Mrs. Arlbery, who had heard, at the play, the general objections of Mandlebert, though she had not attended to her answer, conjectured her reason for retreating, and laughed, but said she would not oppose her.

Camilla then begged to wait in Mr. Dennel's carriage, that she might keep no one else from the show. Sir Sedley, saying it would be an excruciatingly vulgar sight, proposed they should all return; but she pleaded strongly against breaking up the party, though, while she was handed out, to go back to the coach, the Dennels and Mrs. Mittin had alighted, and it had driven off.

The chagrin of Camilla was so palpable, that Mrs. Arlbery herself agreed to resign the scheme; and Sir Sedley, who drew up to them, said he should rejoice in being delivered from it: but Miss Dennel, who was waiting without the booth for her aunt, was ready to cry at the thought of losing the sight, which Mrs. Mittin had assured her was extremely pretty; and, after some discussion, Camilla was reduced to beg she might do no mischief, and consent to make one.

A more immediate distress now occurred to her; she heard Mr. Dennel call out to the man stationed at the entrance of the booth, 'What's to pay?' and recollected she had no money left.

'What your Honor pleases,' was the answer, 'but gentlefolks gives half-a-crown.'

'I'm sure it's well worth it,' said Mrs. Mittin, 'for it's one of the most curious things you ever saw. You can't give less, sir.' And she passed nimbly by, without paying at all: but added, 'I had a ticket the first day, and now I come every day for nothing, if it don't rain, for one only need to pay at first.'

Mr. Dennel and his daughter followed, and Camilla was beginning a hesitating speech to Mrs. Arlbery, as that lady, not attending to her, said to Mr. Dennel: 'Well, frank me also; but take care what you pay; I'm not at all sure I shall ever return it. All I save goes to my ponies.' And, handed by the General, she crossed the barrier; not hearing the voice of her young friend, which was timidly beseeching her to stop.

Camilla was now in extreme confusion. She put her hand into her pocket, took it out, felt again, and again brought forth the hand empty.

The Major, who was before her, and who watched her, begged leave to settle with the booth-keeper; but Camilla, to whom he grew daily more irksome, again preferred a short obligation to the Baronet, and blushingly asked if he would once more be her banker?

Sir Sedley, by no means suspecting the necessity that urged this condescension, was surprised and delighted, and almost without knowing it himself, became all that was attentive, obliging, and pleasing.

Before they were seated, the young Ensign, Mr. Macdersey, issuing from a group of gentlemen, addressed himself to Camilla, though with an air that spoke him much discomposed and out of spirits. 'I hope you are well, Miss Camilla Tyrold,' he cried; 'and have left all your family well? particularly the loveliest of your sex, that angel of beauty, the divine Miss Lynmere?'

'Except the company present!' said Mrs. Arlbery; 'always except the company present, when you talk of beauty to women.'

'I would not except even the company absent!' replied he, with warmth; but was interrupted from proceeding, by what the master of the booth called his Consort of Musics: in which not less than twenty monkies contributed their part; one dreadfully scraping a bow across the strings of a vile kit, another beating a drum, another with a fife, a fourth with a bagpipe, and the sixteen remainder striking together tongs, shovels, and pokers, by way of marrowbones and cleavers. Every body stopt their ears, though no one could forbear laughing at their various contortions, and horrible grimaces, till the master of the booth, to keep them, he said, in tune, dealt about such fierce blows with a stick, that they set up a general howling, which he called the Wocal part of his Consort, not more stunning to the ear, than offensive to all humanity. The audience applauded by loud shouts, but Mrs. Arlbery, disgusted, rose to quit the booth. Camilla eagerly started up to second the motion, but her eyes still more expeditiously turned from the door, upon encountering those of Edgar; who, having met the empty coach of Mr. Dennel, had not been able to refrain from inquiring where its company had been deposited; nor, upon hearing it was at the accomplished Monkies, from hastening to the spot, to satisfy himself if or not Camilla had been steady to her declaration. But he witnessed at once the propriety of his advice, and its failure.

The master of the booth could not endure to see the departure of the most brilliant part of his spectators, and made an harangue, promising the company, at large, if they would submit to postponing the Consort, in order to oblige his friends the Quality, they should have it, with the newest squalls in taste, afterwards.

The people laughed and clapped, and Mrs. Arlbery sat down.

In a few minutes, the performers were ready for a new exhibition. They were dressed up as soldiers, who, headed by a corporal, came forward to do their exercises.

Mrs. Arlbery, laughing, told the General, as he was upon duty, he should himself take the command: the General, a pleasant, yet cool and sensible man, did not laugh less; but the Ensign, more warm tempered, and wrong headed, seeing a feather in a monkey's cap, of the same colour, by chance, as in his own, fired with hasty indignation, and rising, called out to the master of the booth: 'What do you mean by this, sir? do you mean to put an affront upon our corps?'

The man, startled, was going most humbly to protest his innocence of any such design; but the laugh raised against the Ensign amongst the audience gave him more courage, and he only simpered without speaking.

'What do you mean by grinning at me, sir?' said Macdersey; 'do you want me to cane you?'

'Cane me!' cried the man enraged, 'by what rights?'

Macdersey, easily put off all guard, was stepping over the benches, with his cane uplifted, when his next neighbour, tightly holding him, said, in a half whisper, 'If you'll take my advice, you'd a deal better provoke him to strike the first blow.'

Macdersey, far more irritated by this counsel than by the original offence, fiercely looked back, calling out 'The first blow! What do you mean by that, sir?'

'No offence, sir,' answered the person, who was no other than the slow and solemn Mr. Dubster; 'but only to give you a hint for your own good; for if you strike first, being in his own house, as one may say, he may take the law of you.'

'The law!' repeated the fiery Ensign; 'the law was made for poltroons: a man of honour does not know what it means.'

'If you talk at that rate, sir,' said Dubster, in a low voice, 'it may bring you into trouble.'

'And who are you, sir, that take upon you the presumption to give me your opinion?'

'Who am I, sir? I am a gentleman, if you must needs know.'

'A gentleman! who made you so?'

'Who made me so? why leaving off business! what would you have make me so? you may tell me if you are any better, if you come to that.'

Macdersey, of an ancient and respectable family, incensed past measure, was turning back upon Mr. Dubster; when the General, taking him gently by the hand, begged he would recollect himself.

'That's very true, sir, very true, General!' cried he, profoundly bowing; 'what you say is very true. I have no right to put myself into a passion before my superior officer, unless he puts me into it himself; in which case 'tis his own fault. So I beg your pardon, General, with all my heart. And I'll go out of the booth without another half syllable. But if ever I detect any of those monkies mocking us, and wearing our feathers, when you a'n't by, I sha'n't put up with it so mildly. I hope you'll excuse me, General.'

He then bowed to him again, and begged pardon of all the ladies; but, in quitting the booth, contemptuously said to Mr. Dubster: 'As to you, you little dirty fellow, you a'n't worth my notice.'

'Little dirty fellow!' repeated Mr. Dubster, when he was gone; 'How come you to think of that? why I'm as clean as hands can make me!'

'Come, sir, come,' said Mrs. Mittin, reaching over to him, and stroking his arm, 'don't be angry; these things will happen, sometimes, in public companies; but gentlemen should be above minding them. He meant no harm, I dare say.'

'O, as to that, ma'am,' answered Mr. Dubster proudly, 'I don't much care if he did or not: it's no odds to me. Only I don't know much what right he has to defame me. I wonder who he thinks he is that he may break the peace for nothing. I can't say I'm much a friend to such behaviour. Treating people with so little ceremony.'

'I protest,' cried Sir Sedley to Camilla, ''tis your favourite swain from the Northwick assembly! wafted on some zephyr of Hope, he has pursued you to Tunbridge. I flatter myself he has brought his last bran new cloaths to claim your fair hand at the master of the ceremonies' ball.'

'Hush! hush!' cried Camilla, in a low voice; 'he will take you literally should he hear you!'

Mr. Dubster, now perceiving her, bowed low from the place where he stood, and called out, 'How do you do, ma'am? I ask pardon for not speaking to you before; but I can't say as I see you.'

Camilla was forced to bow, though she made no answer. But he continued with his usual steadiness; 'Why, that was but a unked morning we was together so long, ma'am, in my new summer-house. We was in fine jeopardy, that's the truth of it. Pray, how does the young gentleman do as took away our ladder?'

'What a delectable acquaintance!' cried Sir Sedley; 'would you have the cruelty to keep such a treasure to yourself? present me, I supplicate!'

'O, I know you well enough, sir,' said Mr. Dubster, who overheard him; 'I see you at the hop at the White Hart; and I believe you know me pretty well too, sir, if I may take account by your staring. Not that I mind it in the least.'

'Come, come, don't be touchy,' said Mrs. Mittin; 'can't you be good-natured, and hold your tongue? what signifies taking things amiss? It only breeds ill words.'

'That's very sensibly observed upon!' said Mr. Dennel; 'I don't know when I've heard any thing more sensibly said.'

'O, as to that, I don't take it amiss in the least,' cried Mr. Dubster; 'if the gentleman's a mind to stare, let him stare. Only I should like to know what it's for. It's no better than child's play, as one may say, making one look foolish for nothing.'

The ourang outang was now announced, and Mrs. Arlbery immediately left the booth, accompanied by her party, and speedily followed by Edgar.

Neither of the carriages were in waiting, but they would not return to the booth. Sir Sedley, to whom standing was still rather inconvenient, begged a cast in the carriage of a friend, who was accidentally passing by.

Macdersey, who joined them, said he had been considering what that fellow had proposed to him, of taking the first blow, and found he could not put up with it: and upon the appearance of Mr. Dubster, who in quitting the booth was preparing, with his usual leisurely solemnity, to approach Camilla, darted forward and seizing him by the collar, exclaimed, 'Retract, sir! Retract!'

Mr. Dubster stared, at first, without speech or opposition; but being released by the Major, whom the General begged to interfere, he angrily said: 'Pray, sir, what business have you to take hold of a body in such a manner as that? It's an assault, sir, and so I can prove. And I'm glad of it; for now I can serve you as I did another gentleman once before, that I smarted out of a good ten pound out of his pocket, for a knock he gave me, for a mere nothing, just like this here pulling one by the collar, nobody knows why.'

The Major, endeavouring to quiet Macdersey, advised him to despise so low a person.

'So I will, my dear friend,' he returned, 'as soon as ever I have given him the proper chastisement for his ignorance. But I must do that first. You won't take it ill, Major.'

'I believe,' cried Mr. Dubster, holding up both his hands, 'the like of this was never heard of! Here's a gentleman, as he calls himself, ready to take away my life, with his own good will, for nothing but giving him a little bit of advice! However, it's all one to me. The law is open to all. And if any one plays their tricks upon me, they shall pay for their fun. I'm none of your tame ones to put up with such a thing for nothing. I'm above that, I promise you.'

'Don't talk, sir, don't talk!' cried Macdersey; 'it's a thing I can't bear from a mean person, to be talked to. I had a hundred thousand times rather stand to be shot at.'

'Not talk, sir? I should be glad to know what right you has to hinder me, provided I say nothing against the law? And as to being a mean person, it's more than you can prove, for I'm sure you don't know who I am, nor nothing about me. I may be a lord, for any thing you know, though I don't pretend to say I am. But as to what people take me for, that behave so out of character, it's what I sha'n't trouble my head about. They may take me for a chimney-sweeper, or they may take me for a duke; which they like. I sha'n't tell them whether I'm one or t'other, or whether I'm neither. And as to not talking, I shall hold my tongue when I think proper.'

'Ask my pardon this instant, fellow!' cried the Ensign, whom the Major, at the motion of the General, now caught by the arm, and hurried from the spot: Mrs. Mittin, at the same moment pulling away Mr. Dubster, and notably expounding to him the advantages of patience and good humour.

Mrs. Arlbery, wearied both of this squabble and of waiting, took the arm of the General, and said she would walk home; Miss Dennel lovingly held by Mrs. Mittin, with whom her father also assorted, and by whom Mr. Dubster was drawn on.

Camilla alone had no immediate companion, as the Major was occupied by the Ensign. Edgar saw her disengaged. He trembled, he wavered; he wished the Major back; he wished him still more at a distance too remote ever to return; he thought he would instantly mount his horse, and gallop towards Beech Park; but the horse was not ready, and Camilla was in sight;—and, in less than a minute, he found himself, scarce knowing how, at her side.

Camilla felt a pleasure that bounded to her heart, though the late assertions of Mrs. Arlbery prepared her to expect him. He knew not, however, what to say; he felt mortified and disappointed, and when he had uttered something scarce intelligible about the weather, he walked on in silence.

Camilla, whose present train of thoughts had no discordant tendency, broke through this strangeness herself, and said: 'How frivolous I must appear to you! but indeed I was at the very door of the booth, before I knew whither the party was going.'

'You did not, I hope, at least,' he cried, 'when you had entered it, deem me too rigid, too austere, that I thought the species, both of company and of entertainment, ill calculated for a young lady?'

'Rigid! austere!' repeated she; 'I never thought you either! never—and if once again—' she stopt; embarrassed, ashamed.

'If once again what?' cried he in a tremulous voice; 'what would Miss Camilla say?—would she again—Is there yet—What would Miss Camilla say?—'

Camilla felt confounded, both with ideas of what he meant to allude to, and what construction he had put upon her half finished sentence. Impatient, however, to clear that, 'If once more,' she cried, 'you could prevail with yourself—now and then—from time to time—to give me an hint, an idea—of what you think right—I will promise, if not a constant observance, at least a never-failing sense of your kindness.'

The revulsion in the heart, in the whole frame of Edgar, was almost too powerful for restraint: he panted for an immediate explanation of every past and every present difficulty, and a final avowal that she was either self-destined to the Major, or that he had no rival to fear: But before he could make any answer, a sudden and violent shower broke up the conference, and grouped the whole party under a large tree.

This interruption, however, had no power upon their thoughts; neither of them heard a word that was saying; each ruminated intently, though confusedly, upon what already was passed. Yet where the wind precipitated the rain, Edgar stationed himself, and held his hat to intercept its passage to Camilla; and as her eye involuntarily was caught by the shower that pattered upon his head and shoulders, she insensibly pressed nearer to the trunk of the tree, to afford more shelter to him from its branches.

The rest of the party partook not of this taciturnity: Mr. Dubster, staring Mrs. Mittin full in the face, exclaimed: 'I think I ought to know you, ma'am, asking your pardon?'

'No matter for that!' cried she, turning with quickness to Camilla; 'Lord, miss—I don't know your name,—how your poor hat is all I don't know how! as limp, and as flimzy, as if it had been in a wash-tub!'

'I've just bethought me,' continued he, 'where it was we used to see one another, and all the whole manner of it. I've got it as clear in my head as if it was but yesterday. Don't you remember—'

'Can't you stand a little out, there?' interrupted she; 'what signifies a man's old coat? don't you see how you let all the rain come upon this young lady? you should never think of yourself, but only of what you can do to be obliging.'

'A very good rule, that! a very good one indeed!' said Mr. Dennel; 'I wish everybody would mind it.'

'I'm as willing to mind it, I believe,' said Mr. Dubster, 'as my neighbours; but as to being wet through, for mere complaisance, I don't think it fair to expect such a thing of nobody. Besides, this is not such an old coat as you may think for. If you was to see what I wear at home, I promise you would not think so bad of it. I don't say it's my best; who'd be fool then, to wear it every day? However, I believe it's pretty nigh as good as that I had on that night I saw you at Mrs. Purdle's, when, you know, one of your pattens—'

'Come, come, what's the man talking about? one person should not take all the conversation up so. Dear miss ... do tell me your name?... I am so sorry for your hat, I can't but think of it; it looks as dingy!...'

'Why, now, you won't make me believe,' said Mr. Dubster, 'you've forgot how your patten broke; and how I squeezed my finger under the iron? And how I'd like to have lost the use of it? There would have been a fine job! And how Mrs. Purdle....'

'I'm sure the shower's over,' cried Mrs. Mittin, 'and if we stay here, we shall have all the droppings of the leaves upon us. Poor miss thing-o-me's hat is spoilt already. There's no need to make it worse.'

'And how Mrs. Purdle,' he continued, 'was obliged to lend you a pair of shoes and stockings, because you was wet through your feet? And how they would not fit you, and kept tumbling off? And how, when somebody come to fetch you in their own coach, you made us say you was taken ill, because you was so daubed with mud and mire, you was ashamed to shew yourself? And how....'

'I can't think what you are talking of,' said Mrs. Mittin; 'but come, let's you and I go a little way on, to see if the rain's over.' She then went some paces from the tree, and said: 'What signifies running on so, Mr. Dubster, about things nobody knows anything of? It's tiring all the company to death. You should never talk about your own fingers, and hap-hazards, to genteel people. You should only talk about agreeable subjects as I do. See how they all like me! That gentleman brought me to the monkies in his own coach.'

'As to that,' answered he, gravely, 'I did not mean, in the least, to say anything disagreeable; only I thought it odd you should not seem to know me again, considering Mrs. Purdle used—'

'Why you've no nous, Mr. Dubster; Mrs. Purdle's a very good sort of woman and the best friend I have in the world, perhaps, at the bottom; but she i'n't a sort of person to talk of before gentlefolks. You should talk to great people about their own affairs, and what you can do to please them, and find out how you can serve them, if you'd be treated genteelly by them, as I am. Why, I go every where, and see every thing, and it costs me nothing. A friend, a lady of great fashion, took me one day to the monkies, and paid for me; and I've gone since, whenever I will, for nothing.'

'Nobody treats me to nothing,' answered he, in a melancholy voice, 'whatever's the reason: except when I make friends with somebody that can let me in free, sometimes. And I get a peep, now and then, at what goes forward, that way.'

'But you are rich enough to pay for yourself now, Mr. Dubster; good lack! if I had such a fortune as yours, I'd go all the world over, and thanks to nobody.'

'And how long would you be rich then, Mrs. Mittin? Who'd give you your money again when you'd spent it? I got mine hard enough. I sha'n't fool it away in a hurry, I promise you!'

'I can't say I see that, Mr. Dubster, when two of your wives died so soon, and left you so handsome.'

'Why, yes, I don't say to the contrary of that; but then, think of the time before, when I was 'prentice!—'

The shower was now over, and the party proceeded as before.

Edgar, uncertain, irresolute, walked on in silence: yet attentive, assiduous, even tenderly watchful to guide, guard, and assist his fair companion in her way. The name of the Major trembled perpetually upon his lips; but fear what might be the result of his inquiries stopt his speech till they approached the house; when he commanded voice to say: 'You permit, then, the renewal of my old privilege?—'

'Permit! I wish for it!'

They were now at the door. Edgar, not daring to speak again to Camilla, and not able to address any one else, took his leave; enchanted that he was authorized, once more, to inform himself with openness of the state of her affairs, and of her conduct. And Camilla, dwelling with delight upon the discernment of Mrs. Arlbery, blest the happy penetration that had endowed her with courage to speak again to Edgar in terms of friendship and confidence.

Mrs. Mittin, declaring she could not eat till she had seen what could be done for the hat of Miss Tyrold, accompanied her upstairs, took it off herself, wiped it, smoothed, and tried to new arrange it; and, at last, failing to succeed, insisted upon taking it home, to put it in order, and promised to return it in the morning time enough for the Pantiles. Camilla was much ashamed; but she had no means to buy another, and she had now lost her indifference to going abroad. She thought, therefore, this new acquaintance at least as useful as she was officious, and accepted her civility with thanks.

CHAPTER VII

The Rooms

The evening, as usual, was destined to the Rooms. The first object Camilla perceived upon her entrance was Edgar, and the smile with which she met his eye brought him instantly to her side. That smile was not less radiant for his nearer approach; nor was his pleasure in it less animated for observing that Major Cerwood was not of her party, nor as yet in the room. The opportunity seemed inviting to engage her himself; to suggest and to find it irresistible was the same thing, and he inquired if her whole evening were arranged, or she would go down two dances with an old friend.

The softness of her assent was even exquisite delight to him; and, as they all walked up and down the apartment, though he addressed her but little, and though she spoke but in answer, every word he uttered she received as couching some gentle meaning, and every syllable she replied, he thought conveyed something of flattering interest: and although all was upon open and unavoidable subjects, he had no eyes but for her, she had no attention but for him.

This quiet, yet heart-felt intercourse, was soon a little interrupted by the appearance of a large and striking party, led on by Lady Alithea Selmore; for which every body made way, to which every body turned, and which, passing by all the company without seeming conscious there was any to pass, formed a mass at the upper end of the room, with an air and manner of such exclusive attention to their chief, or to one another, that common observation would have concluded some film before their eyes obstructed their discerning that they were not the sole engrossers of the apartment.

But such was not the judgment formed of them by Mrs. Arlbery, who, forced by the stream to give them passage, paid herself for the condescension by a commentary upon the passengers. 'Those good people,' said she, 'strive to make us believe we are nothing to them. They strive even to believe it themselves. But this is the mere semblance worn by pride and affectation, to veil internal fatigue.

They come hither to recruit their exhausted powers, not, indeed, by joining in our society, but by a view of new objects for their senses, and the flattering idea, for their minds, of the envy or admiration they excite. They are all people of some consequence, and many of them are people of title: but these are far the most supportable of the group; their privileged superiority over the rest is so marked and indisputable, that they are saved the trouble either of claiming or ascertaining it: but those who approach their rank without reaching it, live in a constant struggle to make known their importance. Indeed, I have often seen that people of title are less gratified with the sound of their own honours, than people of no title in pronouncing them.'

Sir Sedley Clarendel was of this set. Like the rest he passed Mrs. Arlbery without seeming to notice her, and was passing Camilla in the same manner; but not aware this was only to be fine, like the party to which he belonged, she very innocently spoke to him herself, to hope he got safe to his lodgings, without feeling any further ill effect from his accident.

Sir Sedley, though internally much gratified by this interest in his safety, which in Camilla was the result of having herself endangered it, looked as if he scarce recollected her, and making hastily a kind of half bow, walked on with his company.

Camilla, who had no view, nor one serious thought concerning him, was rather amused than displeased by his caprices; and was preparing to relate the history of his lameness to Edgar, who seemed surprised and even hurt by her addressing him, and by his so slightly passing her, when the entrance of another splendid party interrupted all discourse.

And here, to her utter amaze, she beheld, as chief of the group, her romantic new friend; not leading, indeed, like Lady Alithea Selmore, a train, but surrounded by admirers, who, seeking no eye but hers, seemed dim and humble planets, moving round a radiant sun.

Camilla now, forgetting Sir Sedley, would have taken this moment to narrate her adventure with Mrs. Berlinton, had not her design been defeated by the approach of the Major. He belonged to this last group, but was the only one that separated from it. He spoke to Camilla with his usual air of devotion, told her he had dined with Mrs. Berlinton, to whose husband, whom he had taken for her grandfather, he had been just introduced; and begged to know of Mrs. Arlbery if he might have the pleasure of bringing them all acquainted; an offer which Camilla, unauthorised by Mrs. Berlinton, had not ventured to make. Mrs. Arlbery declined the proposal; not anxious to mix where she had small chance of presiding.

The party, after traversing the room, took full and exclusive possession of a considerable spot just below that occupied by Lady Alithea.

These two companies completely engrossed all attention, amply supplying the rest of the assembly with topics for discourse. The set with Lady Alithea Selmore was, in general, haughty, supercilious, and taciturn; looking around with eyes determined to see neither any person nor any thing before them, and rarely speaking, except to applaud what fell from her ladyship; who far less proud, because a lover of popularity, deigned herself, from time to time, a slight glance at the company, to see if she was observed, and to enjoy its reverence.

The party to which Mrs. Berlinton was the loadstone, was far more attractive to the disciples of nature, though less sedulously sought by those whom the manners and maxims of the common world had sophisticated. They were gay, elegant, desirous to please, because pleased themselves; and though some of them harboured designs deeper and more dangerous than any formed by the votaries of rank, they appeared to have nothing more in view than to decorate with flowers the present moment. The magnetic influence of beauty was, however, more powerful than that of the ton; for though Mrs. Berlinton, from time to time, allured a beau from Lady Alithea Selmore, her ladyship, during the whole season, had not one retaliation to boast. But, on the other hand, the females, in general, strove to cluster about Lady Alithea; Mrs. Berlinton leaving them no greater chance of rival-ship in conversation than in charms.

Edgar had made way upon the approach of the Major, who wore an air of superior claim extremely unpleasant to him; but, since already engaged to Camilla, he meant to return to her when the dancing began.

She concluded he left her but to speak to some acquaintance, and was, herself, amply occupied in observing her new friend. The light in which she now beheld her, admired, pursued, and adulated, elegantly adorned in her person, and evidently with but one rival for fame and fashion in Tunbridge, filled her with astonishment. Nothing could less assort with her passion for solitude, her fondness for literary and sentimental discussions, and her enthusiasm in friendship. But her surprise was mixed with praise and admiration, when she reflected upon the soft humility, and caressing sweetness of her manners, yet found her, by general consent, holding this elevated rank in society.

The Major earnestly pressed to conduct Camilla to this coterie, assuring her Mrs. Berlinton would not have passed, had she seen her, for, during dinner, and at coffee, she had talked of nobody else. Camilla heard this with pleasure, but shrunk from all advances, and strove rather to hide than shew herself, that Mrs. Berlinton might have full liberty either to seek or avoid her. She wished to consult Edgar upon this acquaintance; though the present splendour of her appearance, and the number of her followers, made her fear she could never induce him to do justice to the sweetness and endearment of her social powers.

When the Major found he pleaded in vain, he said he would at least let Mrs. Berlinton know where to look for her; and went himself to that lady.

Edgar, who had felt sensibly mortified to observe, when he retreated, that the eyes and attention of Camilla had been wholly bestowed upon what he considered merely as a new scene, was now coming forward; when he saw Mrs. Berlinton hastily rise, suddenly break from all her adulators, and, with quick steps and animated gestures, traverse the apartment, to address Camilla, whom, taking by both her hands, which she pressed to her heart, she conjured, in the most flattering terms, to accompany her back.

Camilla was much gratified; yet, from delicacy to Mrs. Arlbery, stimulated by the fear of missing her expected partner in the country dances, declined the invitation: Mrs. Berlinton looked disappointed; but said she would not be importunate, and returned alone.

Camilla, a little disturbed, besought the Major to follow, with an offer of spending with her, if she pleased, the whole of the ensuing day.

'Charming!' cried the Major, 'for I am engaged to her myself already.'

To Camilla this hearing was distressing; to Edgar it was scarcely endurable. But she could not retract, and Edgar was stopt in the inquiries he meant to make concerning this striking new acquaintance, by an abrupt declaration from Mrs. Arlbery, that the Rooms were insufferable, and she would immediately go home. She then gave her hand to the General, and Miss Dennel took the arm of Camilla, murmuring, that she would never leave the Rooms at such an early hour again, when once she was married.

To quit Edgar thus, at the very moment of renewed intercourse and amity, seemed too cruel; and Camilla, though with blushes, and stammering, whispered Mrs. Arlbery, 'What can I do, ma'am? most unfortunately I have engaged myself to dance?'

'With whom?'

'With—Mr.—Mandlebert.'

'O, vastly well! Stay, then by all means: but, as he has not engaged me too, allow me, I beseech you, to escape. Mrs. Berlinton will, I am sure, be happy to take care of you.'

This scheme was, to Camilla, the most pleasant that could be proposed; and, at the same instant, the Major returned to her, with these words written with a pencil upon the back of a letter.

'To-morrow, and next day, and next day, come to me, my lovely friend; every thing, and every body fatigues me but yourself.'

Camilla, obliged again to have recourse to the Major, wrote, upon the same paper, 'Can you have the goodness to convey me to Mount Pleasant to-night, if I stay?' and begged him to bring her an answer. She entreated, also, Mrs. Arlbery to stop till it arrived, which was almost in the same minute; for the eye of Mrs. Berlinton had but glanced upon the words, ere her soft and lovely form was again with their fair writer, with whom, smiling and delighted, she walked back, arm in arm, to her place.

Mrs. Arlbery and the General, and Mr. and Miss Dennel, now left the room.

Edgar viewed all this with amazement. He found that the young lady she joined was sister-in-law to a peer, and as fashionable as she was beautiful; but could not fathom how so great an intimacy had so suddenly been formed.

Camilla, thus distinguished, became now herself an object of peculiar notice; her own personal claim to particular attention, her dejection had forfeited, for it had robbed her eyes of their animation, and her countenance of its play; but no contagion spreads with greater certainty nor greater speed than that of fashion; slander itself is not more sure of promulgation. She was now looked at by all present as if seen for the first time; every one discovered in her some charm, some grace, some excellence; those who, the minute before, had passed her with perfect indifference, said it was impossible to see and not be struck with her; and all agreed she could appear upon no spot under the sun, and not instinctively be singled out, as formed to shine in the highest sphere.

But he by whom this transaction was observed with most pleasure, was Sir Sedley Clarendel. The extraordinary service he had performed for Camilla, and the grateful interest she had shewn him in return, had led him to consider her with an attention so favourable, that, without half her merit, or half her beauty, she could not have failed rising in his estimation, and exciting his regard: and she had now a superior charm that distanced every other; she had been asked to dance, yet refused it, by a man of celebrity in the ton; and she was publicly sought and caressed by the only rival at Tunbridge, in that species of renown, to Lady Alithea Selmore.

He felt an increased desire to be presented to Mrs. Berlinton himself; and, gliding from his own circle as quietly as he could contrive, not to offend Lady Alithea, who, though she laughed at the little

Welsh rustic, was watchful of her votaries, and jealous of her rising power, came gently behind Lord O'Lerney and whispered his request.

He was received by the young beauty with that grace, and that sweetness which rendered her so generally bewitching, yet with an air that proved her already accustomed to admiration, and untouched by its intoxicating qualities. All that was voluntary of her attention was bestowed exclusively upon Camilla, though, when addressed and called upon by others, she answered without impatience, and looked without displeasure.

This conduct, at the same time that it shewed her in a point of view the most amiable, raised Camilla higher and higher in the eyes of the by-standers: and, in a few minutes more, the general cry throughout the assembly was, to inquire who was the young lady thus brought forward by Mrs. Berlinton.

Edgar heard this with increased anxiety. Has she discretion, has she fortitude, thought he, to withstand public distinction? Will it not spoil her for private life; estrange her from family concerns? render tasteless and insipid the conjugal and maternal characters, meant by Nature to form not only the most sacred of duties, but the most delicious of enjoyments?

Very soon after, this anxiety was tinctured with a feeling more severe; he saw her spoken to negligently by Sir Sedley; he required, after what he had already himself deemed impertinence from the Baronet, that she should have assumed to him a distant dignity; but he perceived, on the contrary, that she answered him with pleasant alacrity, and, when not engaged by Mrs. Berlinton, attended to him, even with distinction.

Alas! thought he, the degradation from the true female character is already begun! already the lure of fashion draws her from what she owes to delicacy and propriety, to give a willing reception to insolence and foppery!

Camilla, meanwhile, unsuspicious of his remarks, and persuaded every civility in her power was due to Sir Sedley, was gay, pleased, and pleasing; happy to consider herself under the guidance, and restored to the amity of Edgar, and determined to acquaint him with all her affairs, and consult him upon all her proceedings.

The dancing, for which mutually they languished, as the mutual means of reunion, seemed not to be the humour of the evening, and those who were ready for it, were not of sufficient consequence to bring it forward. But when Mrs. Berlinton mentioned, that she had been taking some lessons in a cotillon, a universal cry was raised by all her party, to try one immediately. She pleaded in vain her inexperience in such dances; they insisted there was nobody present that could criticise, that her form alone would compensate for every mistake of rule, and that the best lesson was easy practice.

She was soon gained, for she was not addicted to denials; but the application which ensued to Camilla was acceded to less promptly. As there were but two other ladies in the circle of Mrs. Berlinton, her assistance was declared to be indispensable. She pleaded inability of every sort, though to dance without Edgar was her only real objection; for she had no false shame in being ignorant of what she never had learnt. But Mrs. Berlinton protested she would not rise if she were the only novice to be exhibited; and the Major then prepared to prostrate himself at the feet of Camilla; who, hastily, and ashamed, stood up, to prevent an action that Edgar might misinterpret.

Hoping, however, now, to at least draw him into their set, she ventured to acknowledge to Mrs. Berlinton, that she was already engaged, in case she danced.

The Major, who heard her, and who knew it was not to himself, strenuously declared this could only be for country dances, and therefore would not interfere with a cotillon.

'Will country dances, then,' said she, blushing, 'follow?'

'Certainly, if any one has spirit to begin them.'

The cotillon was now played, and the preceding bow from the opposite Major forced her courtsie in return.

The little skill in this dance of one of the performers, and the total want of it in another, made it a mere pleasantry to all, though the youth and beauty of the two who did the worst, rendered them objects of admiration, that left nearly unnoticed those who did best.

To Camilla what belonged to pleasantry in this business was of short duration. When the cotillon was over, she saw nothing of Edgar. She looked around, mortified, disappointed. No one called for a country dance; and the few who had wished for it, concluding all chance over when a cotillon was begun, had now retired, or given it up.

What was this disappointment, compared with the sufferings of Edgar? Something of a contest, and of entreaties, had reached his ears, while he had hovered near the party, or strolled up and down the room. He had gathered the subject was dancing, and he saw the Major most earnest with Camilla. He was sure it was for her hand, and concluded it was for a country dance; but could she forfeit her engagement? were matters so far advanced, as to make her so openly shew him all prevailing, all powerful, not only over all rivals, but, according to the world's established customs upon these occasions, over all decorum?

Presently, he saw the Major half kneel; he saw her rise to prevent the prostration; and he heard the dance called.

He could bear no more; pain intolerable seized, distracted him, and he abruptly quitted the ballroom, lest the Major should approach him with some happy apology, which he was unfitted to receive.

He could only settle his ideas by supposing she really loved Major Cerwood, and had suffered her character to be infected by the indelicacy that made a part of his own. Yet why had she so striven to deny all regard, all connection? what an unaccountable want of frankness! what a miserable dereliction of truth!

His first impulse was to set off instantly from Tunbridge; but his second thoughts represented the confession this would make. He was too proud to leave the Major, whom he despised, such a triumph, and too much hurt to permit Camilla herself to know him so poignantly wounded. She could not, indeed, but be struck by his retreat; he resolved, however, to try to meet with her the next day, and to speak to her with the amity they had so lately arranged, yet in a way that should manifest him wholly free from all other interest or view.

CHAPTER VIII

All pleasure to Camilla was completely over from the moment that Edgar disappeared.

When she returned to Mount Pleasant, Mrs. Arlbery, whom she found alone, said, 'Did I not understand that you were going to dance with Mr. Mandlebert? How chanced he to leave you? We were kept ages waiting for the coach; and I saw him pass by, and walk off.'

Camilla, colouring, related the history of the cotillon; and said, she feared, not knowing how she had been circumstanced, he was displeased.

'Displeased!' cried Mrs. Arlbery, laughing; 'and do you, at seventeen, suffer a man to be displeased? How can you do worse when you are fifty? Know your own power more truly, and use it better. Men, my dear, are all spoilt by humility, and all conquered by gaiety. Amuse and defy them!—attend to that maxim, and you will have the world at your feet.'

'I have no such ambition: ... but I should be sensibly hurt to make an old friend think ill of me.'

'When an old friend,' said Mrs. Arlbery, archly, 'happens to be a young man, you must conduct yourself with him a little like what you are; that is, a young woman. And a young woman is never in her proper place, if such sort of old friends are not taught to know their own. From the instant you permit them to think of being offended, they become your masters; and you will find it vastly more convenient to make them your slaves.'

Camilla pretended to understand this in a mere general sense, and wished her good night.

The next morning, at an early hour, her chamber door was opened with great suddenness, and no preparation, and Mrs. Mittin tript nimbly into the room, with a hat in her hand.

'Look here! my dear Miss Tyrold,' cried she, 'for now that other young lady has told me your name, and I writ it down upon paper, that I might not forget it again: look at your hat now! Did you ever see anything so much improved for the better? I declare nobody would know it! Miss Dennel says it's as pretty again as it was at first. I'll go and shew it to the other lady.'

Away she went, triumphant, with the trophy of her notability; but presently returned, saying, 'Do, pray, Miss Tyrold, write me down that other lady's name upon a scrap of paper. It always goes out of my head. And one looks as if one knew nobody, when, one forgets people's names.'

Camilla complied, and expressed her shame to have caused her so much trouble.

'O, my dear, it's none at all. I got all the things at Mrs. Tillden's.'

'Who is Mrs. Tillden?' cried Camilla, staring.

'Why the milliner. Don't you know that?'

'What things?' asked Camilla, alarmed.

'Why these, my dear; don't you see? Why it's all new, except just the hat itself, and the feathers.'

Camilla was now in extreme embarrassment. She had concluded Mrs. Mittin had only newly arranged the ornaments, and had not the smallest idea of incurring a debt which she had no means to discharge.

'It all comes to quite a trifle,' continued Mrs. Mittin, 'for all it's so pretty. Mrs. Tillden's things are all monstrous cheap. I get things for next to nothing from her, sometimes, when they are a little past the mode. But then I recommend her a heap of customers. I get all my friends, by hook or by crook, to go to her shop.'

'And what,' stammered out Camilla, 'besides my thanks, do I owe you?'

'Oh nothing. She would not be paid; she said, as you was her customer, and had all your things of her at first, she'd put it down in your bill for the season.'

This was, at least, some respite; though Camilla felt the disagreeable necessity of increasing her intended demand upon Mrs. Arlbery.

Miss Dennel came with a summons from that lady to the Pantiles, whither, as the day was fine, she proposed they should walk.

'O,' cried Mrs. Mittin, 'if you are going upon the Pantiles, you must go to that shop where there's the curious ear-rings that are be to raffled for. You'll put in to be sure.'

Camilla said no, with a sigh attributed to the ear-rings, but due to a tender recollection of the raffle in which Edgar had procured her the trinket she most valued. Mrs. Mittin proposed accompanying them, and asked Camilla to introduce her to Mrs. Arlbery. This was very disagreeable; but she knew not how, after the civility she owed her, to refuse.

Mrs. Arlbery received her with much surprize, but perfect unconcern; conscious of her own importance, she feared no disgrace from being seen with one in a lower station; and she conceived it no honour to appear with one in a higher.

When they came to the Pantiles, Mrs. Mittin begged to introduce them to a view of the ear-rings, which belonged, she said, to one of her particular friends; and as Mrs. Arlbery caught the eye of Sir Sedley Clarendel in passing the window, she entered the shop.

'Well,' cried Mrs. Mittin, to its master, 'don't say I bring you no company. I am sure you ought to let me throw for nothing, if it's only for good luck; for I am sure these three ladies will all put in. Come, Miss Dennel, do lead the way. 'Tis but half a guinea, and only look what a prize.'

'Ask papa to pay for me!' cried Miss Dennel.

'Come, good sir, come, put down the half guinea for the young lady. I'm sure you can't refuse her. Lord! what's half a guinea?'

'That's a very bad way of reasoning,' answered Mr. Dennel; 'and what I did not expect from a woman of your sense.'

'Why you don't think, sir, I meant that half a guinea's a trifle? No indeed! I know what money is better than that. I only mean half a guinea is nothing in comparison to ten guineas, which is the price of the ear-rings; and so that makes me think it's pity the young lady should lose an opportunity of getting them so cheap. I'm sure if they were dear, I should be the last to recommend them, for I think extravagance the greatest sin under the sun.'

'Well, now you speak like the sensible woman I took you for.'

A very little more eloquence of this sort was necessary, before Mr. Dennel put down half a guinea.

'Well, I declare,' cried Mrs. Mittin, 'there's only three more names wanted; and when these two ladies have put in, there will be only one! I'm sure if I was rich enough, that one would not be far off. But come, ma'am, where's your half guinea? Come, Miss Tyrold, don't hold back; who knows but you may win? there's only nineteen against you. Lord, what's that?'

Camilla turned away, and Mrs. Arlbery did not listen to a word; but when Sir Sedley said, 'They are really very pretty; won't you throw?' she answered, 'I must rather make a raffle with my own trinkets, than raffle for other people's. Think of my ponies! However, I'll put in, if Mr. Dennel will be my paymaster.'

Mr. Dennel, turning short off, walked out of the shop.

'This is a bad omen!' cried she, laughing; and then desired to look at the list of rafflers; when seeing amongst the names those of Lady Alithea Selmore and the Hon. Mrs. Berlinton, she exclaimed: ''Tis a coalition of all fashion and reputation! We shall be absolutely scouted, my dear Miss Tyrold, if we shrink. My poor ponies must wait half a guinea longer! Let us put in together.'

Camilla answered, she had no intention to try for them.

'Well, then, lend me half a guinea; for I never trust myself, now, with my purse.'

'I have not a half guinea ... I have ... I have no ... gold ... in my purse,' answered Camilla, with a face deeply tinged with red.

Major Cerwood, who joined the party during this discussion, intreated to be banker for both the ladies. Camilla positively refused any share; but Mrs. Mittin said it would be a shame for such a young lady to go without her chance, and wrote down her name next to that of Mrs. Arlbery; while the Major, without further question, put down a guinea upon the counter.

Camilla could not endure this; yet, from a youthful shame of confessing poverty, forced herself to the ear of Mrs. Arlbery, and whispered an entreaty that she would pay the guinea herself.

Mrs. Arlbery, surprized, answered she had really come out without her purse; but seeing her seriously vexed, added, 'If you do not approve of the Major for a banker till we go home, what say you to Sir Sedley?'

'I shall prefer him a thousand times!'

Mrs. Arlbery, in a low voice, repeated this to the young Baronet, and receiving his guinea, threw it down; making the Major, without the smallest excuse or ceremony, take back his own.

This was by no means lost upon Sir Sedley; he felt flattered ... he felt softened; he thought Camilla looked unusually lovely; he began to wonder at the coldness of Mandlebert, and to lament that the first affections of so fair a creature should be cast away.

Mandlebert himself was an object of nothing less than envy. He had entered the shop during the contest about the raffle, and seen Major Cerwood pay for Camilla as well as for Mrs. Arlbery. Confirmed in his notions of her positive engagement, and sick at heart from the confirmation, he walked further into the shop, upon pretence of looking at some other articles, before he could assume sufficient composure to speak to her.

Mrs. Mittin now began woefully to repine that she could not take the last share for the ear-rings; and, addressing herself to Mr. Dennel, who re-entered as soon as he saw the money was paid for Mrs. Arlbery, she said, 'You see, sir, if there was somebody ready to take the last chance at once, this gentleman might fix a day for the throwing immediately; but else, it may be dawdled on, nobody knows how long; for one will be gone, and t'other will be gone, and there'll be no getting the people together; and all the pleasure of the thing is being here to throw for one's self: for I don't much like trusting money matters out of sight.'

'If I'd thought of all that,' said Mr. Dennel, 'I should not have put in.'

'True, sir. But here, if it was not that I don't happen to have half a guinea to spare just now, how nicely it might all be finished in a trice! For, as I have been saying to Miss Dennel, this may turn out a real bargain; for they'll fetch their full value at any time. And I tell Miss Dennel that's the only way to lay out money, upon things that will bring it back again if it's wanted; not upon frippery froppery, that's spoilt in a minute, and then i'n't worth a farthing.'

'Very sensibly said,' cried Mr. Dennel; 'I'm sure she can't hear better advice; I'm much obliged to you for putting such sensible thoughts into her head.' And then, hoping she would continue her good lessons to his daughter, he drew out his purse, and begged her to accept a chance from it for the prize.

Mrs. Mittin was in raptures; and the following week was settled for the raffle.

Mrs. Arlbery, who had attended to this scene with much amusement, now said to General Kinsale, who had taken a seat by her: 'Did I not tell you well, General, that all men are at the disposition of women? If even the shrewd monied man cannot resist, what heart shall we find impenetrable? The connoisseur in human characters knows, that the pursuit of wealth is the petrifaction of tenderness: yet yonder is my good brother-in-law, who thinks cash and existence one, allured even to squander money, merely by the address of that woman, in allowing that money should be the first study of life! Let even Clarendel have a care of himself! or, when least he suspects any danger, some fair dairy-maid will praise his horsemanship, or take a fancy to his favourite spaniel, or any other favourite that happens to be the foible of the day, and his invulnerability will be at her feet, and Lady Clarendel be brought forward in a fortnight.'

Lord O'Lerney now entered the shop, accompanying a lady whose countenance and appearance were singularly pleasing, and who, having made some purchase, was quietly retiring, when the master of the shop inquired if she wished to look at the ear-rings; adding, that though the number was full, he knew of one person, who would give up her chance, in case it would oblige a customer.

She answered she had no present occasion for ear-rings, and would not therefore take up either his time or her own unnecessarily; and then walked gently away, still attended by Lord O'Lerney.

'Bless me,' cried Mrs. Arlbery, 'who is that? to hear a little plain common sense is so rare, it strikes one more than wit.'

'It's Lady Isabella Irby, madam,' answered the master of the shop.

Here Lord O'Lerney, who had only handed her to her carriage, returned.

'My Lord,' cried Mrs. Arlbery, 'do you know what a curiosity you brought in amongst us just now? A woman of rank who looks round upon other people just as if she thought they were her fellow creatures?'

'Fie, fie!' answered Lord O'Lerney, laughing, 'why will you suppose that so rare? If we have not as many women who are amiable with titles as without, it is only because we have not the same number from which to select them. They are spoilt or unspoilt, but in the same proportion as the rest of their sex. Their fall, or their escape, is less local than you imagine; it does not depend upon their titles, but upon their understandings.'

'Well, my lord, I believe you are right. I was adopting a narrow prejudice, merely from indolence of thought.'

'But why, my lord,' cried Sir Sedley, 'does this paragon of a divinity deny her example to the world? Is it in contempt of our incorrigibility? or in horror of our contagion?'

'My dear Sir Sedley,' said Mrs. Arlbery, 'don't flatter yourself with being so dangerous. Her ladyship does not fly you from fear, take my word for it. There is nothing in her air that looks as if she could only be good by being shut up. I dare believe she could meet you every day, yet be mistress of herself! Nevertheless, why, my lord, is she such a recluse? Why does one never see her at the Rooms?'

'Never see her there, my dear madam! she is there almost every night; only being unintruding, she is unnoticed.'

'The satire, then, my lord,' said Mrs. Arlbery, 'falls upon the company. Why is she not surrounded by volunteer admirers? Why, with a person and manner so formed to charm, joined to such a character, and such rank, has she not her train?'

'The reason, my dear madam, you could define with more sagacity than myself; she must be sought! And the world is so lazy, that the most easy of access, however valueless, is preferred to the most perfect, who must be pursued with any trouble.'

Admirable Lord O'Lerney! thought Edgar, what a lesson is this to youthful females against the glare of public homage, the false brilliancy of unfeminine popularity!

This conversation, however, which alone of any he had heard at Tunbridge promised him any pleasure, was interrupted by Mr. Dennel, who said the dinner would be spoilt, if they did not all go home.

Camilla felt extremely vexed to quit the shop, without clearing up the history of the dance; and Edgar, seeing the persevering Major at her side as she departed, in urgency to put any species of period to his own sufferings, followed the party, and precipitately began a discourse with Lord O'Lerney upon making the tour of Europe. Camilla, for whom it was designed, intent upon planning her own defence, heard nothing that was said, till Lord O'Lerney asked him if his route would be through Switzerland, and he answered: 'My route is not quite fixed, my lord.'

Startled, she now listened, and Mrs. Arlbery, whom she held by the arm, was equally surprised, and looked to see how she bore this intimation.

'If you will walk with me to my lodgings,' replied Lord O'Lerney, 'I will shew you my own route, which may perhaps save you some difficulties. Shall you set out soon?'

'I fancy within a month,' answered Edgar; and, arm in arm, they walked away together, as Camilla and her party quitted the Pantiles for Mount Pleasant.

CHAPTER IX

Counsels for Conquest

Fortunately for Camilla, no eye was upon her at this period but that of Mrs. Arlbery; her changed countenance, else, must have betrayed still more widely her emotion. Mrs. Arlbery saw it with real concern, and saying she had something to consult her about, hurried on with her alone.

Camilla scarce knew that she did, or what she suffered; the suddenness of surprise, which involved so severe a disappointment, almost stupified her faculties. Mrs. Arlbery did not utter one word by the way, and, when they arrived at home, saw her to her chamber, pressed her hand, and left her.

She now, from a sense of shame, came to her full recollection. She was convinced all her feelings were understood by Mrs. Arlbery; she thought over what her father had said upon such exposures, and hopeless of any honorable end to her suspences, earnestly wished herself back at Etherington, to hide in his revered breast her confusion and grief.

Even Mrs. Arlbery she now believed had been mistaken; Edgar appeared never to have loved her; his attentions, his kindness, had all flowed from friendship; his solicitude, his counsel had been the result of family regard.

When called to dinner, she descended with downcast eyes. She found no company invited; she felt thankful, yet abashed; and Mrs. Arlbery let her retire when the meal was over, but soon followed to beg she would prepare for the play.

She saw her hastily putting away her handkerchief, and dispersing her tears. 'Ah! my dear,' cried she, taking her hand, 'I am afraid this old friend of yours does not much contribute to make Tunbridge Wells salubrious to you!'

Camilla, affecting not to understand her, said she had never been in better health.

'Of mind, do you mean, or body?' cried Mrs. Arlbery, laughing; but seeing she only redoubled her distress, more seriously added, 'Will you suffer me, my dear Miss Tyrold, to play the old friend, also, and speak to you with openness?'

Camilla durst not say no, though she feared to say yes.

'I must content myself with a tacit compliance, if I can obtain no other. I am really uneasy to talk with you; not, believe me, from officiousness nor impertinence, but from a persuasion I may be able to promote your happiness. You won't speak, I see? And you judge perfectly right; for the less you disclaim, the less I shall torment you. Permit me, therefore, to take for granted that you are already aware I am acquainted with the state of your heart.'

Camilla, trembling, had now no wish but to fly; she fastened her eyes upon the door, and every thought was devoted to find the means of escape.

'Nay, nay, if you look frightened in sober sadness, I am gone. But shall I think less, or know less, for saying nothing? It is not speech, my dear Miss Tyrold, that makes detections: It only proclaims them.'

A sigh was all the answer of Camilla: though, assured, thus, she had nothing to gain by flight, she forced herself to stay.

'We understand one another, I see, perfectly. Let me now, then, as unaffectedly go on, as if the grand explanation had been verbally made. That your fancy, my fair young friend, has hit upon a tormentor, I will not deny; yet not upon an ingrate; for this person, little as you seem conscious of your power, certainly loves you.'

Surprised off all sort of guard, Camilla exclaimed, 'O no!—O no!'

Mrs. Arlbery smiled, but went on. 'Yes, my dear, he undoubtedly does you that little justice; yet, if you are not well advised, his passion will be unavailing; and your artlessness, your facility, and your innocence, with his knowledge, nay, his very admiration of them, will operate but to separate you.'

Glowing with opposing yet strong emotions at these words, the countenance of Camilla asked an explanation, in defiance of her earnest desire to look indifferent or angry.

'You will wonder, and very naturally, how such attractions should work as repulses; but I will be plain and clear, and you must be candid and rational, and forgive me. These attractions, my dear, will be the source of this mischief, because he sees, by their means, that you are undoubtedly at his command.'

'No, madam! no, Mrs. Arlbery!' cried Camilla, in whose pride now every other feeling was concentrated, 'he does not, cannot see it!—'

'I would not hurt you for the world, my very amiable young friend; but pardon me if I say, that not to see it—he must be blinder than I imagine him!—blinder than ... to tell you the truth, I am much inclined to think any of his race.'

Confounded, irritated, and wounded, Camilla remained a moment silent, and then, though scarce articulately, answered: 'If such is your opinion ... at least he shall see it ... fancy it, I mean ... no more!...'

'Keep to that resolution, and you will behold him ... where he ought to be ... at your feet.'

Irresistibly, though most unwillingly, appeased by this unexpected conclusion, she turned away to hide a blush in which anger had not solely a place, and suffered Mrs. Arlbery to go on.

'There is but one single method to make a man of his ruminating class know his own mind: give him cause to fear he will lose you. Animate, inspirit, inspire him with doubt.'

'But why, ma'am,' cried Camilla, in a faltering voice; 'why shall you suppose I will take any method at all?'

'The apprehension you will take none is the very motive that urges me to speak to you. You are young enough in the world to think men come of themselves. But you are mistaken, my dear. That happens rarely; except with inflamed and hot-headed boys, whose passions are in their first innocence as well as violence. Mandlebert has already given the dominion of his to other rulers, who will take more care of his pride, though not of his happiness. Attend to one who has travelled further into life than yourself, and believe me when I assert, that his bane, and yours alike, is his security.'

With a colour yet deeper than ever, Camilla resentfully repeated, 'Security!'

'Nay, how can he doubt? with a situation in life such as his....'

'Situation in life! Do you think he can ever suppose that would have the least, the most minute weight with me?'

'Why, it would be a very shocking supposition, I allow! but yet, somehow or other, that same sordid thing called money, does manage to produce such abundance of little comforts and pretty amusements, that one is apt ... to half suspect ... it may really not much add to any matrimonial aversion.'

The very idea of such a suspicion offended Camilla beyond all else that had passed; Mrs. Arlbery appeared to her indelicate, unkind, and ungenerous, and regretting she had ever seen, and repenting she had ever known her, she sunk upon a chair in a passionate burst of tears.

Mrs. Arlbery embraced her, begged her pardon a thousand times; assured her all she had uttered was the effect of esteem as well as of affection, since she saw her too delicate, and too inexperienced, to be aware either of the dangers or the advantages surrounding her; and that very far from meaning to hurt her, she had few things more at heart than the desire of proving the sincerity of her regard, and endeavouring to contribute to her happiness.

Camilla thanked her, dried her eyes, and strove to appear composed; but she was too deeply affected for internal consolation: she felt herself degraded in being openly addressed as a love-sick girl; and injured in being supposed, for a moment, capable of any mercenary view. She desired to be excused going out, and to have the evening to herself; not on account of the expence of the play; she had again wholly forgotten her poverty; but to breathe a little alone, and indulge the sadness of her mind.

Mrs. Arlbery, unfeignedly sorry to have caused her any pain, would not oppose her inclination; she repeated her apologies, dragged from her an assurance of forgiveness, and went down stairs alone to a summons from Sir Sedley Clarendel.

The first moments of her departure were spent by Camilla in the deepest dejection; from which, however, the recollection of her father, and her solemn engagement to him, soon after awakened her. She read again his injunctions, and resolving not to add to her unhappiness by any failure in her duty, determined to make her appearance with some spirit before Mrs. Arlbery set out.

'My dear Clarendel,' cried that lady, as she entered the parlour, 'this poor little girl is in a more serious plight than I had conjectured. I have been giving her a few hints, from the stores of my worldly knowledge, and they appear to her so detestably mean and vulgar, that they have almost broken her heart. The arrival of this odious Mandlebert has overthrown all our schemes. We are cut up, Sir Sedley! completely cut up!'

'O, indubitably to a degree!' cried the Baronet, with an air of mingled pique and conceit; 'how could it be otherwise? Exists the wight who could dream of competition with Mandlebert!'

'Nay, now, my dear Clarendel, you enchant me. If you view his power with resentment, you are the man in the world to crumble it to the dust. To work, therefore, dear creature, without delay.'

'But how must I go about it? a little instruction, for pity!'

'Charming innocent! So you don't know how to try to make yourself agreeable?'

'Not in the least! I am ignorant to a redundance.'

'And were you never more adroit?'

'Never. A goth in grain! Witless from the first muling in my nurse's arms!'

'Come, come, a truce for a moment, with foppery, and answer me seriously; Were you ever in love, Clarendel? speak the truth. I am just seized with a passionate desire to know.'

'Why ... yes ...' answered he, pulling his lips with his fingers, 'I think—I rather think ... I was once.'

'O tell! tell! tell!'

'Nay, I am not very positive. One hears it is to happen; and one is put upon thinking of it, while so very young, that one soon takes it for granted. Define it a little, and I can answer you more accurately. Pray, is it any thing beyond being very fond, and very silly, with a little touch of melancholy?'

'Precise! precise! Tell me, therefore, what it was that caught you. Beauty? Fortune? Flattery? or Wit? Speak! speak! I die to know!'

'O, I have forgotten all that these hundred years! I have not the smallest trace left!'

'You are a terrible coxcomb, my dear Clarendel! and I am a worse myself for giving you so much encouragement. But, however, we must absolutely do something for this fair and drooping violet. She won't go even to the play tonight.'

'Lovely lily! how shall we rear it? Tell her I beg her to be of our party.'

'You beg her? My dear Sir Sedley! what do you talk of?'

'Tell her 'tis my entreaty, my supplication!'

'And you think that will make her comply?'

'You will see.'

'Bravo, my dear Clarendel, bravo! However, if you have the courage to send such a message, I have not to deliver it: but I will write it for you.'

She then wrote,

'Sir Sedley Clarendel asserts, that if you are not as inexorable as you are fair, you will not refuse to join our little party tonight at the theatre.'

Camilla, after a severe conflict from this note, which she concluded to be the mere work of Mrs. Arlbery to draw her from retirement, sent word she would wait upon her.

Sir Sedley heard the answer with exultation, and Mrs. Arlbery with surprise. She declared, however, that since he possessed this power, she should not suffer it to lie dormant, but make it work upon her fair friend, till it either excited jealousy in Mandlebert, or brought indifference to herself. 'My resolution,' cried she, 'is fixt; either to see him at her feet, or drive him from her heart.'

Camilla, presently descending, looked away from Mrs. Arlbery; but, unsuspicious as she was undesigning, thanked the Baronet for his message, and told him she had already repented her solitary plan. The Baronet felt but the more flattered, from supposing this was said from the fear of flattering him.

In the way to the theatre, Camilla, with much confusion, recollected her empty purse; but could not, before Mr. and Miss Dennel and Sir Sedley, prevail with herself to make it known; she could only determine to ask Mrs. Arlbery to pay for her at present, and defer the explanation till night.

But, just as she alighted from the coach, Mrs. Arlbery, in her usual manner, said: 'Do pay for me, good Dennel; you know how I hate money.'

Camilla, hurrying after her, whispered, 'May I beg you to lend me some silver?'

'Silver! I have not carried any about with me since I lost my dear ponies and my pet phaeton. I am as poor as Job; and therefore bent upon avoiding all temptation. Somebody or other always trusts me. If they get paid, they bless their stars. If not,—do you hear me, Mr. Dennel?—'twill be all the same an hundred years hence; so what man of any spirit will think of it? hey, Mr. Dennel?'

'But—dear madam!—pray—'

'O, they'll change for you, here, my dear, without difficulty.'

'But ... but ... pray stop!... I ... I have no gold neither!'

'Have you done like me, then, come out without your purse?'

'No!...'

This single negative, and the fluttered manner, and low voice in which it was pronounced, gave Mrs. Arlbery the utmost astonishment. She said nothing, however, but called aloud to Mr. Dennel to settle for the whole party.

Mr. Dennel, during the dialogue, had paid for himself and his daughter, and walked on into the box.

'What a Hottentot!' exclaimed Mrs. Arlbery. 'Come, then, Clarendel, take pity on two poor distressed objects, and let us pass.'

Sir Sedley, little suspicious of the truth, yet flattered to be always called upon to be the banker of Camilla, obeyed with alacrity.

Mrs. Arlbery placed Camilla upon a seat before her, and motioned to the Baronet to remain in a row above; and then, in a low voice, said: 'My dear Clarendel, do you know they have let that poor girl come to Tunbridge without a sixpence in her pocket!'

'Is it possible?'

''Tis a fact. I never suspected it till suspicion was followed by confirmation. She had a guinea or two, I fancy, at first, just to equip her with one set of things to appear in; which, probably, the good Parson imagined would last as clean and as long at a public place as at his parsonage-house, where my best suit is worn about twice in a summer. But how that rich old uncle of hers could suffer her to come without a penny, I can neither account for nor forgive. I have seen her shyness about money-matters for some days past; but I so little conjectured the possibility of her distress, that I have always rather increased than spared it.'

'Sweet little angel!' exclaimed the Baronet, in a tone of tenderness; 'I had indeed no idea of her situation. Heavens! I could lay half my fortune at her feet to set her at ease!'

'Half, my dear Clarendel!' cried Mrs. Arlbery, laughing; 'nay, why not the whole? where will you find a more lovely companion?'

'Pho, pho!—but why should it be so vastly horrid an incongruity that a man who, by chance, is rich, should do something for a woman who, by chance, is poor? How immensely impertinent is the prejudice that forbids so natural a use of money! why should the better half of a man's actions be always under the dominion of some prescriptive slavery? 'Tis hideous to think of. And how could he more delectably spend, or more ecstatically enjoy his fortune, than by so equitable a participation?'

'True, Sir Sedley. And you men are all so disinterested, so pure in your benevolence, so free from any spirit of encroachment, that no possible ill consequence could ensue from such an arrangement. When once a fair lady had made you a civil courtesy, you would wholly forget you had ever obliged her. And you would let her walk her ways, and forget it also: especially if, by chance, she happened to be young and pretty.'

This raillery was interrupted by the appearance of Edgar in an opposite box. 'Ah!' cried Mrs. Arlbery, 'look but at that piece of congelation that nothing seems to thaw! Enter the lists against him, dear Clarendel! He has stationed himself there merely to watch and discountenance her. I hate him heartily; yet he rolls in wealth, and she has nothing. I must bring them, therefore, together, positively: for though a husband ... such a fastidious one especially ... is not what I would recommend to her for happiness, 'tis better than poverty. And, after his cold and selfish manner, I am convinced he loves her. He is evidently in pursuit of her, though he wants generosity to act openly. Work him but with a little jealousy, and you will find me right.'

'Me, my dear madam? me, my divine Mrs. Arlbery? Alas! with what chance? No! see where enters the gallant Major. Thence must issue those poignant darts that newly vivify the expiring embers of languishing love.'

'Now don't talk such nonsense when I am really serious. You are the very man for the purpose: because, though you have no feeling, Mandlebert does not know you are without it. But those Officers are too notoriously unmeaning to excite a moment's real apprehension. They have a new dulcinea wherever they newly quarter, and carry about the few ideas they possess from damsel to damsel, as regularly as from town to town.'

The Major was now in the box, and the conversation ended.

He endeavoured, as usual, to monopolize Camilla; but while her thoughts were all upon Edgar, the whole she could command of her attention was bestowed upon Sir Sedley.

This was not unobserved by Edgar, who now again wavered in believing she loved the Major: but the doubt brought with it no pleasure; it led him only the more to contemn her. Does she turn, thought he, thus, from one to the other, with no preference but of accident or caprice? Is her favour thus light of circulation? Is it now the mawkish Major, and now the coxcomb Clarendel? Already is she thus versed in the common dissipation of coquetry?... O, if so, how blest has been my escape! A coquette wife!...

His heart swelled, and his eye no longer sought her.

At night, as soon as she went to her own room, Mrs. Arlbery followed her, and said: 'My dear Miss Tyrold, I know much better than you how many six-pences and three-pences are perpetually wanted at places such as these. Do suffer me to be your banker. What shall we begin our account with?'

Camilla felt really thankful for being spared an opening upon this subject. She consented to borrow two guineas; but Mrs. Arlbery would not leave her with less than five, adding, 'I insist upon doubling it in a day or two. Never mind what I say about my distress, and my phaeton, and my ponies; 'tis only to torment Dennel, who trembles at parting with half-a-crown for half an hour; or else, now and then, to set other people a staring; which is not unamusing, when nothing else is going forward. But believe me, my dear young friend, were I really in distress, or were I really not to discharge these petty debts I incur, you would soon discover it by the thinness of our parties! These men that now so flock around us; would find some other loadstone. I know them pretty well, dear creatures!...'

Though shocked to appear thus destitute, Camilla was somewhat relieved to have no debt but with Mrs. Arlbery; for she resolved to pay Sir Sedley and the milliner the next day, and to settle with Mrs. Arlbery upon her return to Etherington.

CHAPTER X

Strictures upon the Ton

The next day was appointed for the master of the ceremonies' ball; which proved a general rendezvous of all parties, and almost all classes of company.

Mrs. Mittin, in a morning visit to Camilla, found out that she had only the same cap for this occasion that she had worn upon every other; and, assuring her it was grown so old-fashioned, that not a lady's maid in Tunbridge would now be seen in it, she offered to pin her up a turban, which should come to next to nothing, yet should be the prettiest, and simplest, and cheapest thing that ever was seen.

Camilla, though a stranger to vanity, and without any natural turn to extravagance, was neither of an age, nor a philosophy, to be unmoved by the apprehension of being exposed to ridicule from her dress: she thankfully, therefore, accepted the proposal; and Mrs. Mittin, taking a guinea, said, she would pay Mrs. Tillden for the hat, at the same time that she bought a new handkerchief for the turban.

When she came back, however, she had only laid out a few shillings at another shop, for some articles, so cheap, she said it would have been a shame not to buy them; but without paying the bill, Mrs. Tillden having desired it might not be discharged till the young lady was leaving the Wells.

As the turban was made up from a pattern of one prepared for Mrs. Berlinton, Camilla had every reason to be satisfied of its elegance. Nor did Mrs. Mittin involve her in much distress how her own trouble might be recompensed; the cap she found unfit for Camilla, she could contrive, she said, to alter for herself; and as a friend had given her a ticket for the ball, it would be mighty convenient to her, as she had nothing of the kind ready.

Far different were the sensations with which Edgar and Camilla saw each other this night, from those with which, so lately they had met in the same apartment. Edgar thought her degenerating into the character of a coquette, and Camilla, in his intended tour, anticipated a period to all their intercourse.

She was received, meanwhile, in general, with peculiar and flattering attention. Sir Sedley Clarendel made up to her, with public smiles and courtesy; even Lord Newford and Sir Theophilus Jarard, though they passed by Mrs. Arlbery without speaking to her, singled out Camilla for their devoirs. The distinction paid her by the admired Mrs. Berlinton had now not only marked her as an object whom it would not be derogatory to treat with civility, but as one who might, hence-forward, be regarded herself as admitted into certain circles.

Mrs. Arlbery, though every way a woman of fashion, they conceived to be somewhat wanting in ton, since she presided in no party, was unnoticed by Lady Alithea Selmore, and unknown to Mrs. Berlinton.

Ton, in the scale of connoisseurs in the certain circles, is as much above fashion, as fashion is above fortune: for though the latter is an ingredient that all alike covet to possess, it is courted without being respected, and desired without being honoured, except only by those who, from earliest life, have been taught to earn it as a business. Ton, meanwhile, is as attainable without birth as without understanding, though in all the certain circles it takes place of either. To define what it is, would be as difficult to the most renowned of its votaries, as to an utter stranger to its attributes. That those who call themselves of the ton either lead, or hold cheap all others, is obtrusively evident: but how and by what art they attain such pre-eminence, they would be perplexed to explain. That some whim has happily called forth imitators; that some strange phrase has been adopted; that something odd in dress has become popular; that some beauty, or some deformity, no matter which, has found annotators; may commonly be traced as the origin of their first public notice. But to whichever of these accidents their early fame may be attributed, its establishment and its glory is built upon vanity that knows no deficiency, or insolence that knows no blush.

Notwithstanding her high superiority both in capacity and knowledge, Mrs. Arlbery felt piqued by this behaviour, though she laughed at herself for heeding it. 'Nevertheless,' cried she, 'those who shew contempt, even though themselves are the most contemptible, always seem on the higher ground. Yet 'tis only, with regard to these animals of the ton, that nobody combats them. Their presumption is so notorious, that, either by disgust or alarm, it keeps off reprehension. Let anyone boldly, and face to face, venture to be more uncivil than themselves, and they would be overpowered at once. Their valour is no better than that of a barking cur, who affrights all that go on without looking at him, but who, the moment he is turned upon with a stamp and a fierce look, retreats himself, amazed, afraid, and ashamed.'

'If you, Mrs. Arlbery,' said the General, 'would undertake to tutor them, what good you might do!'

'O, Heavens, General, suspect me not of such reforming Quixotism! I have not the smallest desire to do them any good, believe me! If nature has given them no sense of propriety, why should I be more liberal? I only want to punish them; and that not, alas! from virtue, but from spite!'

The conversation of the two men of the ton with Camilla was soon over. It was made up of a few disjointed sentences, abusing Tunbridge, and praising the German Spa, in cant words, emphatically and conceitedly pronounced, and brought round upon every occasion, and in every speech, with so precise an exclusion of all other terms, that their vocabulary scarce consisted of forty words in totality.

Edgar occupied the space they vacated the moment of their departure; but not alone; Mrs. Mittin came into it with him, eager to tell Camilla how everybody had admired her turban; how sweetly she looked in it; how everybody said, they should not have known her again, it became her so; and how they all agreed her head had never been so well dressed before.

Edgar, when he could be heard, began speaking of Sir Sedley Clarendel; he felt miserable in what he thought her inconsiderate encouragement of such impertinence; and the delicacy which restrained him from expressing his opinion of the Major, had no weight with him here, as jealousy had no share in his dislike to the acquaintance: he believed the young Baronet incapable of all love but for himself, and a decidedly destined bachelor: without, therefore, the smallest hesitation, he plainly avowed that he had never met with a more thoroughly conceited fop, a more elaborate and self-sufficient coxcomb.

'You see him only,' said Camilla, 'with the impression made by his general appearance; and that is all against him: I always look for his better qualities and rejoice in finding them. His very sight fills me with grateful pleasure, by reminding me of the deliverance I owe to him.'

Edgar, amazed, intreated an explanation; and, when she had given it, struck and affected, clasped his hands, and exclaimed: 'How providential such a rescue! and how differently shall I henceforth behold him!' And, almost involuntarily turning to Mrs. Arlbery, he intreated to be presented to the young Baronet.

Sir Sedley received his overtures with some surprise, but great civility; and then went on with a ludicrous account he was giving to Lord Newford and Sir Theophilus, of the quarrel of Macdersey with Mr. Dubster.

'How awake thou art grown, Clary?' cried Sir Theophilus; 'A little while ago thou wast all hip and vapour; and now thou dost nothing but patronise fun.'

'Why, yes,' answered the Baronet, 'I begin to tire of ennui. 'Tis grown so common. I saw my footman beginning it but last week.'

'O, hang it! O, curse it!' cried Lord Newford, 'your footman!'

'Yes, the rogue is not without parts. I don't know if I shan't give him some lessons, upon leaving it off myself. The only difficulty is to find out what, in this nether world, to do without it. How can one fill up one's time? Stretching, yawning, and all that, are such delicious ingredients for coaxing on the lazy hours!'

'O, hang it, O, curse it,' cried Lord Newford; 'who can exist without them? I would not be bound to pass half an hour without yawning and stretching for the Mogul's empire. I'd rather snap short at once.'

'No, no, don't snap short yet, little Newy,' cried Sir Sedley. 'As to me, I am never at a loss for an expedient. I am not without some thoughts of falling in love.'

He looked at Edgar; who, not aware this was designed to catch his attention, naturally exclaimed: 'Thoughts! can you choose, or avoid at pleasure?'

'Most certainly. After four-and-twenty a man is seldom taken by surprise; at least, not till he is past forty: and then, the fear of being too late, sometimes renovates the eagerness of the first youth. But, in general, your willing slaves are boys.'

Edgar, laughing, begged a little information, how he meant to put his thoughts in execution.

'Nothing so facile! 'Tis but to look at some fair object attentively, to follow her with your eyes when she quits the room; never to let them rest without watching for her return; filling up the interval with a few sighs; to which, in a short time, you grow so habituated, that they become natural; and then, before you are aware, a certain solicitude and restlessness arise, which the connoisseurs in natural history dub falling in love.'

'These would be good hints,' said Edgar, 'to urge on waverers, who wish to persuade themselves to marry.'

'O no, my dear sir! no! that's a mistake of the first magnitude; no man is in love when he marries. He may have loved before; I have even heard he has sometimes loved after: but at the time never. There is something in the formalities of the matrimonial preparations that drive away all the little cupidons. They rarely stand even a demand of consent—unless they doubt obtaining it; but a settlement! Parchments! Lawyers!—No! there is not a little Love in the Island of Cyprus, that is not ready to lend a wing to set passion, inspiration, and tenderness to flight, from such excruciating legalities.'

'Don't prose, Clary; don't prose,' cried Sir Theophilus, gaping till his mouth was almost distorted.

'O, killing! O, murder!' cried Lord Newford; 'what dost talk of marriage for?'

'It seems, then,' said Edgar, 'to be much the same thing what sort of wife falls to a man's lot; whether the woman of his choice, or a person he should blush to own?'

'Blush!' repeated Sir Sedley, smiling; 'no! no! A man of any fashion never blushes for his wife, whatever she may be. For his mistress, indeed, he may blush: for if there are any small failings there, his taste may be called in question.'

'Blush about a wife!' exclaimed Lord Newford; 'O, hang it! O, curse it! that's too bad!'

'Too bad, indeed,' cried Sir Theophilus; 'I can't possibly patronise blushing for a wife.'

''Tis the same, then, also,' said Edgar, 'how she turns out when the knot is tied, whether well or ill?'

'To exactitude! If he marry her for beauty, let her prove what she may, her face offers his apology. If for money, he needs none. But if, indeed, by some queer chance, he marries with a view of living with her, then, indeed, if his particularity gets wind, he may grow a little anxious for the acquittal of his oddity, in seeing her approved.'

'Approved! Ha! ha!' cried Lord Newford; 'a wife approved! That's too bad, Clary; that's too bad!'

'Poor Clary, what art prosing about?' cried Sir Theophilus. 'I can't possibly patronise this prosing.'

The entrance of the beautiful Mrs. Berlinton and her train now interrupted this conversation; the young Baronet immediately joined her; though not till he had given his hand to Edgar, in token of his willingness to cultivate his acquaintance.

Edgar, returning to Camilla, confessed he had too hastily judged Sir Sedley, when he concluded him a fool, as well as a fop; 'For,' added he, with a smile, 'I see, now, one of those epithets is all he merits. He is certainly far from deficient in parts, though he abuses the good gifts of nature with such pedantry of affectation and conceit.'

Camilla was now intent to clear the history of the cotillon; when Mrs. Berlinton approaching, and, with graceful fondness, taking her hand, entreated to be indulged with her society: and, since she meant not to dance, for Edgar had not asked her, and the Major she had refused, she could not resist her invitation. She had lost her fear of displeasing Mrs. Arlbery by quitting her, from conceiving a still greater, of wearying by remaining with her.

Edgar, anxious both to understand and to discuss this new connexion, hovered about the party with unremitting vigilance. But, though he could not either look at or listen to Mrs. Berlinton, without admiring her, his admiration was neither free from censure of herself, nor terrour for her companion: he saw her far more beautiful than prudent, more amiable than dignified. The females in her group were few, and little worthy notice; the males appeared, to a man, without disguise, though not without restraint, her lovers. And though no one seemed selected, no one seemed despised; she appeared to admit their devoirs with little consideration; neither modestly retiring from power, nor vainly displaying it.

Camilla quitted not this enchantress till summoned by Mrs. Arlbery; who, seeing herself again, from the arrival of Lady Alithea Selmore, without any distinguished party, that lady drawing into her circle all people of any consequence not already attracted by Mrs. Berlinton, grew sick of the ball and the rooms, and impatient to return home. Camilla, in retiring, presented, folded in a paper, the guinea, half-guinea, and silver, she had borrowed of Sir Sedley; who received it without presuming at any contest; though not, after what he had heard from Mrs. Arlbery, without reluctance.

Edgar watched the instant when Camilla moved from the gay group; but Mrs. Mittin watched it also; and, approaching her more speedily, because with less embarrassment, seized her arm before he could reach her: and before he could, with any discretion, glide to her other side, Miss Dennel was there.

'Well now, young ladies,' said Mrs. Mittin, 'I'm going to tell you a secret. Do you know, for all I call myself Mrs. I'm single?'

'Dear, la!' exclaimed Miss Dennel; 'and for all you're so old!'

'So old, Miss! Who told you I was so old? I'm not so very old as you may think me. I'm no particular age, I assure you. Why, what made you think of that?'

'La, I don't know; only you don't look very young.'

'I can't help that, Miss Dennel. Perhaps you mayn't look young yourself one of these days. People can't always stand still just at a particular minute. Why, how old, now, do you take me to be? Come, be sincere.'

'La! I'm sure I can't tell; only I thought you was an old woman.'

'An old woman! Lord, my dear, people would laugh to hear you. You don't know what an old woman is. Why it's being a cripple, and blind, and deaf, and dumb, and slavering, and without a tooth. Pray, how am I like all that?'

'Nay, I'm sure I don't know; only I thought, by the look of your face, you must be monstrous old.'

'Lord, I can't think what you've got in your head, Miss Dennel! I never heard as much before, since I was born. Why the reason I'm called Mrs. is not because of that, I assure you; but because I'd a mind to be taken for a young widow, on account everybody likes a young widow; and if one is called Miss, people being so soon to think one an old maid, that it's quite disagreeable.'

This discourse brought them to the carriage.

CHAPTER XI

Traits of Character

The following morning, Mrs. Mittin came with eager intelligence, that the raffle was fixed for one o'clock; and, without any scruple, accompanied the party to the shop, addressing herself to every one of the set as to a confirmed and intimate friend. But her chief supporter was Mr. Dennel, whose praise of her was the vehicle to his censure of his sister-in-law. That lady was the person in the world whom he most feared and disliked. He had neither spirit for the splendid manner in which she lived, nor parts for the vivacity of her conversation. The first, his love of money made him condemn as extravagant, and the latter his self-love made him hate, because he could not understand. He persuaded himself, therefore, that she had more words than meaning; and extolled all the obvious truths uttered by Mrs. Mittin, to shew his superior admiration of what, being plain and incontrovertible, he dignified with the panegyric of being sensible.

When they came upon the Pantiles, they were accosted by Mr. Dubster; who having solemnly asked them, one by one, how they all did, joined Mrs. Mittin, saying: 'Well, I can't pretend as I'm over sorry you've got neither of those two comical gentlemen with you, that behaved so free to me for nothing. I don't think it's particular agreeable being treated so; though it's a thing I don't much mind. It's not worth fretting about.'

'Well, don't say any more about it,' cried Mrs. Mittin, endeavouring to shake him off; 'I dare say you did something to provoke 'em, or they're too genteel to have taken notice of you.'

'Me provoke them! why what did I do? I was just like a mere lamb, as one may say, at the very time that young Captain fell abusing me so, calling of me a little dirty fellow, without no provocation. If I'm little, or big, I don't see that it's any business of his. And as to dirty, I'd put on all clean linen but the very day before, as the people can tell you at the inn; so the whole was a mere piece of falsehood from one end to t'other.'

'Well, well, what do you talk about it for any more? You should never take anything ill of a young gentleman. It's only aggravating him so much the worse.'

'Aggravating him, Mrs. Mittin! why what need I mind that? Do you think I'm to put up with his talking of caning me, and such like, because of his being a young gentleman? Not I, I assure you! I'm no such person. And if once I feel his switch across these here shoulders, it won't be so well for him!'

The party now entered the shop where the raffle was to be held.

Edgar was already there; he had no power to keep away from any place where he was sure to behold Camilla; and a raffle brought to his mind the most tender recollections. He was now with Lord O'Lerney, in whose candour and benevolence of character he took great delight, and with whom he had joined Lady Isabella Irby, who had been drawn, as a quiet spectatress, to the sight, by a friend, who, having never seen the humours of a raffle, had entreated, through her means, to look on. He languished to see Camilla presented to this lady, in whose manners and conversation, dignity and simplicity were equally blended.

While he was yet, though absently, conversing with them, Lord O'Lerney pointed out Camilla to Lady Isabella.

'I have taken notice of her already at the Rooms;' answered her Ladyship; 'and I have seldom, I think, seen a more interesting young creature.'

'The character of her countenance,' said Lord O'Lerney, 'strikes me very peculiarly. 'Tis so intelligent, yet so unhackneyed, so full of meaning, yet so artless, that, while I look at her, I feel myself involuntarily anxious for her welfare.'

'I don't think she seems happy,' said Lady Isabella; 'Do you know who she is, my Lord?'

Edgar, here, with difficulty suppressed a sigh. Not happy! thought he; ah! wherefore? what can make Camilla unhappy?

'I understand she is a niece of Sir Hugh Tyrold,' answered his Lordship; 'a Yorkshire Baronet. She is here with an acquaintance of mine, Mrs. Arlbery, who is one of the first women I have ever known, for wit and capacity. She has an excellent heart, too; though her extraordinary talents, and her carelessness of opinion make it sometimes, but very unjustly, doubted.'

Edgar heard this with much pleasure. A good word from Lord O'Lerney quieted many fears; he hoped he had been unnecessarily alarmed; he determined, in future, to judge her more favourably.

'I should be glad,' continued his Lordship, 'to hear this young lady were either well established, or returned to her friends without becoming an object of public notice. A young woman is no where so rarely respectable, or respected, as at these water-drinking places, if seen at them either long or often. The search of pleasure and dissipation, at a spot consecrated for restoring health to the sick, the infirm, and the suffering, carries with it an air of egotism, that does not give the most pleasant idea of the feeling and disposition.'

'Yet, may not the sick, my Lord, be rather amended than hurt by the sight of gaiety around them?'

'Yes, my dear Lady Isabella; and the effect, therefore, I believe to be beneficial. But as this is not the motive why the young and the gay seek these spots, it is not here they will find themselves most honoured. And the mixture of pain and illness with splendor and festivity, is so unnatural, that probably it is to that we must attribute that a young woman is no where so hardly judged. If she is without fortune, she is thought a female adventurer, seeking to sell herself for its attainment; if she is rich, she is supposed a willing dupe, ready for a snare, and only looking about for an ensnarer.'

'And yet, young women seldom, I believe, my Lord, merit this severity of judgment. They come but hither in the summer, as they go to London in the winter, simply in search of amusement, without any particular purpose.'

'True; but they do not weigh what their observers weigh for them, that the search of public recreation in the winter is, from long habit, permitted without censure; but that the summer has not, as yet, prescription so positively in its favour; and those who, after meeting them all the winter at the opera, and all the spring at Ranelagh, hear of them all the summer at Cheltenham, Tunbridge, &c. and all the autumn at Bath, are apt to inquire, when is the season for home.'

'Ah, my Lord! how wide are the poor inconsiderate little flutterers from being aware of such a question! How necessary to youth and thoughtlessness is the wisdom of experience!'

Why does she not come this way? thought Edgar; why does she not gather from these mild, yet understanding moralists, instruction that might benefit all her future life?

'There is nothing,' said Lord O'Lerney, 'I more sincerely pity than the delusions surrounding young females. The strongest admirers of their eyes are frequently the most austere satirists of their conduct.'

The entrance of Lord Newford, Sir Theophilus Jarard, and Sir Sedley Clarendel, all noisily talking and laughing together, interrupted any further conversation. The two former no sooner saw Camilla, and perceived neither Lady Alithea Selmore, nor Mrs. Berlinton, than they made up to her; and Sir Sedley, who now found she was completely established in the bon ton, felt something of pride mix with pleasure in publicly availing himself of his intimacy with her; and something like interest mix with curiosity, in examining if Edgar were struck with her ready attention to him.

Upon Edgar, however, it made not the slightest impression. While Sir Sedley had appeared to him a mere fop, he had thought it degraded her; but how he regarded him as her preserver, it seemed both natural and merited.

Sir Sedley, not aware of this reasoning, was somewhat piqued; and taking him to another part of the shop, whispered: 'I am horribly vapoured! Do you know I have some thoughts of trying that little girl? Do you think one could make anything of her?'

'How? what do you mean?' cried Edgar, with sudden alarm.

Sir Sedley, a little flattered, affectedly answered: 'O, if you have any serious designs that way, incontestably I won't interfere.'

'Me!' cried Edgar, surprised and offended; 'believe me, no! I have all my life considered her—as my sister.'

Sir Sedley saw this was spoken with effort; and negligently replied: 'Nay you are just at the first epocha for marrying from inclination; but you are in the right not to perform so soon the funeral honours of liberty. 'Tis what you may do at any time. So many girls want establishments, that a man of sixty can just as easily get a wife of eighteen, as a man of one-and-twenty. The only inconvenience in that sort of alliance is, that though she begins with submitting to her venerated husband as prettily as to her papa, she is terribly apt to have a knack of running away from him, afterwards, with equal facility.'

'That is rather a discouraging article, I confess,' cried Edgar, 'for the tardy votaries of Hymen!'

'O, no! 'tis no great matter!' answered he, patting his snuffbox; 'we are impenetrable in the extreme to those sort of grievances now-a-days. We are at such prodigious expence of sensibility in public, for tales of sorrow told about pathetically, at a full board, that if we suffered much for our private concerns to boot, we must always meet one another with tears in our eyes. We never weep now, but at dinner, or at some diversion.'

Lord Newford, pulling him by the arm, called out: 'Come, Clary, what art about, man? we want thee.'

'Come, Clary! don't shirk, Clary,' cried Sir Theophilus; 'I can't possibly patronise this shirking.' And they hauled him to a corner of the shop, where all three resumed their customary laughing whispers.

'You will not, perhaps, suspect, Lady Isabella,' said Lord O'Lerney, smiling, 'that one of that triumvirate is by no means deficient in parts, and can even, when he desires it, be extremely pleasing?'

'Your Lordship judges right, I confess! I had not, indeed, done him such justice!'

'See then,' said his Lordship, 'how futile an animal is man, without some decided character and principle!

He's every thing by turns, and nothing long [3].

[Footnote 3: Dryden's Absalom and Achitophel.]

Wise, foolish; virtuous, vicious; active, indolent; prodigal and avaricious! No contrast is too strong for him while guided but by accident or impulse. This gentleman also, in common with the rest of his tonnish brethren, is now daily, though unconsciously, hoarding up a world of unprepared-for mortification, by not foreseeing that the more he is celebrated in his youth, for being the leader of the ton, and the man of the day, the earlier he will be regarded as a creature out of date, an old beau, and a fine gentleman of former times. But 'tis by reverses, such as these, that folly and impropriety pay their penalties. We might spare all our anger against the vanity of the beauty, or the conceit of the coxcomb. Are not wrinkles always in waiting to punish the one, and age, without honour, to chastise and degrade the other?'

All the rafflers were now arrived, except Mrs. Berlinton, who was impatiently expected. Lady Alithea Selmore had already sent a proxy to throw for her in her own woman; much to the dissatisfaction of most part of the company. A general rising and inquietude to look out for Mrs. Berlinton, gave Edgar, at length, an opportunity to stand next to Camilla. 'How I grieve,' he cried 'you should not know Lady Isabella Irby! she seems to me a model for a woman of rank in her manners, and a model for a woman of every station in her mind. The world, I believe, could scarce have tempted her to so offensive a mark of superiority as has just been exhibited by Lady Alithea Selmore, who has ingeniously discovered a method of being signalised as the most important person out of twenty, by making herself nineteen enemies.'

'I wonder,' said Camilla, 'she can think the chance of the ear-rings worth so high a price!'

A footman, in a splendid livery, now entering, inquired for Miss Tyrold. She was pointed out to him by Major Cerwood, and he delivered her a letter from Mrs. Berlinton.

The contents were to entreat she would throw for that lady, who was in the midst of Akenside's Pleasures of the Imagination, and could not tear herself away from them.

Camilla blushed excessively in proclaiming she was chosen Mrs. Berlinton's proxy. Edgar saw with tenderness her modest confusion, and, with a pleasure the most touching, read the favourable impression it made upon Lord O'Lerney and Lady Isabella.

This seemed an opportunity irresistible for venting his fears and cautions about Mrs. Berlinton; and, taking the bustling period in which the rafflers were arranging the order and manner of throwing, he said, in a low, and diffident tone of voice, 'You have committed to me an important and, I fear, an importunate office; yet, while I hold, I cannot persuade myself not to fulfil it; though I know that to give advice which opposes sentiment and feeling, is repugnant to independence and to delicacy. Such, therefore, I do not mean to enforce; but merely to offer hints—intimations—and observations—that without controlling, may put you upon your guard.'

Camilla, affected by this unexpected address, could only look her desire for an explanation.

'The lady,' he continued, 'whom you are presently to represent, appears to be uncommonly engaging?—'

'Indeed she is! She is attractive, gentle, amiable.'

'She seems, also, already to have caught your affection?'

'Who could have withheld it, that had seen her as I have seen her? She is as unhappy as she is lovely....'

'I have heard of your first meeting, with as much pleasure in the presence of mind it called forth on one side, as with doubt and perplexity, upon every circumstance I can gather, of the other.—'

'If you knew her, you would find it impossible to hold any doubts; impossible to resist admiring, compassionating, and loving her!'

'If my knowledge of her bribed an interest in her favour, without convincing me she deserved it, I ought, rather, to regret that you have not escaped falling into such a snare, than that I could have escaped it myself.'

'I believe her free, nay incapable of all ill!' cried Camilla warmly; 'though I dare not assert she is always coolly upon her guard.'

'Do not let me hurt you,' said Edgar, gently; 'I have seen how lovely she is in person, and how pleasing in manners. And she is so young that, were she in a situation less exposed, want of steadiness or judgment might, by a little time, be set right. But here, there is surely much to fear from her early possession of power.... O, that some happier chance had brought about such a peculiar intercourse for you with Lady Isabella Irby! There, to the pleasure of friendship, might be added the modesty of retired elegance, and the security of established respectability.'

'And may not this yet happen, with Mrs. Berlinton? Lady Isabella, though still young, is not in the extreme youth of Mrs. Berlinton: a few more years, therefore, may bring equal discretion; and as she has already every other good quality, you may hereafter equally approve her.'

'Do you think, then,' said Edgar, half smiling, 'that the few years of difference in their age were spent by Lady Isabella in the manner they are now spent by Mrs. Berlinton? do you think she paved the way for her present dignified, though unassuming character, by permitting herself to be surrounded by professed admirers? by letting their sighs reach her ears? by suffering their eyes to fasten with open rapture on her face? and by holding it sufficient not to suppress such liberties, so long as she does not avowedly encourage them?'

Camilla was startled. She had not seen her conduct in this light: yet her understanding refused to deny it might bear this interpretation.

Charmed with the candour of her silence, Edgar continued, 'How wide from all that is open to similar comment, is the carriage and behaviour of Lady Isabella! how clear! how transparent, how free from all conjecture of blemish! They may each, indeed, essentially be equally innocent; and your opinion of Mrs. Berlinton corroborates the impression made by her beautiful countenance: yet how far more highly is the true feminine character preserved, where surmise is not raised, than where it can be parried! Think but of those two ladies, and mark the difference. Lady Isabella, addressed only where known, followed only because loved, sees no adulators encircling her, for adulation would alarm her; no admirers paying her homage, for such homage would offend her. She knows she has not only her own innocence to guard, but the honour of her husband. Whether she is happy with him or not, this deposit is equally sacred.—'

He stopt; for Camilla again started. The irrepressible frankness of her nature revolted against denying how much this last sentence struck her, and she ingenuously exclaimed: 'O that this most amiable young creature were but more aware of this duty!'

'Ah, my dear Miss Camilla,' cried Edgar, with energy, 'since you feel and own ... and with you, that is always one ... this baneful deficiency, drop, or at least suspend an intercourse too hazardous to be indulged with propriety! See what she may be sometime hence, ere you contract further intimacy. At present, unexperienced and unsuspicious, her dangers may be yours. You are too young for such a risk. Fly, fly from it, my dear Miss Camilla!... as if the voice of your mother were calling out to caution you!'

Camilla was deeply touched. An interest so warm in her welfare was soothing, and the name of her mother rendered it awful; yet, thus united, it appeared to her more strongly than ever to announce itself as merely fraternal. She could not suppress a sigh; but he attributed it to the request he had urged, and, with much concern, added: 'What I have asked of you, then, is too severe?'

Again irresistibly sighing, yet collecting all her force to conceal the secret cause, she answered, 'If she is thus exposed to danger ... if her situation is so perilous, ought I not rather to stay by, and help to support her, than by abandoning, perhaps contribute to the evil you think awaiting her?'

'Generous Camilla!' cried he, melted into tender admiration, 'who can oppose so kind a design? So noble a nature!...'

No more could be said, for all preliminaries had been settled, and the throwing being arranged to take place alphabetically, she was soon summoned to represent Mrs. Berlinton.

From this time, Edgar could speak to her no more: even the Major could scarcely make way to her: the two men of the ton would not quit her, and Sir Sedley Clarendel appeared openly devoted to her.

Edgar looked on with the keenest emotion. The proof he had just received that her intrinsic worth was in its first state of excellence, had come home to his heart, and the fear of seeing her altered and spoilt, by the flatteries and dangers which environed her, with his wavering belief in her engagement with Major Cerwood, made him more wretched than ever. But when, some time after, she was called upon to throw for herself, the recollection that, from the former raffle, her half-guinea, even when the prize was in her hand, had been voluntarily withdrawn to be bestowed upon a poor family, so powerfully affected him, that he could not rest in the shop; he was obliged to breathe a freer air, and to hide his disturbance by a retreat.

Her throw was the highest the dice had yet afforded. A Miss Williams alone came after her, whose throw was the lowest; Miss Camilla Tyrold, therefore, was proclaimed to be the winner.

This second testimony of the favour of fortune was a most pleasant surprise to Camilla, and made the room resound with felicitations, till they were interrupted by a violent quarrel upon the Pantiles, whence the voice of Macdersey was heard, hollooing out: 'Don't talk, I say sir! don't presume to say a word!' and that of Mr. Dubster angrily answering, he would talk as long as he thought proper, whether it was agreeable or not.

Sir Sedley advanced to the combatants, in order to help on the dispute; but Edgar, returning at the sound of high words, took the Ensign by the arm, and prevailed with him to accompany him up and down the Pantiles; while Mrs. Mittin ran to Mr. Dubster, and pulling him into the shop, said: 'Mr. Dubster, if I'm not ashamed of you! how can you forget yourself so? talking to gentlemen at such a rate!'

'Why what should hinder me?' cried he; 'do you think I shall put up with every thing as I used to do when you first knew me, and we used to meet at Mr. Typton's, the tallow chandler's, in Shug-lane? no, Mrs. Mittin, nor no such a thing; I'm turned gentleman myself, now, as much as the best of 'em; for I've nothing to do, but just what I choose.'

'I protest, Mr. Dubster,' cried Mrs. Mittin, taking him into a corner 'you're enough to put a saint into a pet! how come you to think of talking of Mr. Typton here? before such gentlefolks? and where's the use of telling every body he's a tallow chandler? and as to my meeting with you there once or so, in a way, I desire you'll mention it no more; for it's so long ago, I have no recollection of it.'

'No! why don't you remember—'

'Fiddle, faddle, what's the good of ripping up old stories about nothing? when you're with genteel people, you must do as I do; never talk about business at all.'

Macdersey now entered the shop, appeased by Edgar from shewing any further wrath, but wantonly inflamed by Sir Sedley, in a dispute upon the passion of love.

'Do you always, my dear friend,' said the Baronet, 'fall in love at first sight?'

'To be sure I do! If a man makes a scruple of that, it's ten to one but he's disappointed of doing it at all; because, after two or three second sights, the danger is you may spy out some little flaw in the dear angel, that takes off the zest, and hinders you to the longest day you have to live.'

'Profoundly cogitated that! you think then, my vast dear sir, the passion had more conveniently be kindled first, that the flaws may appear after, to cure it?'

'No, sir! no! when a man's once in love, those flaws don't signify, because he can't see them; or, if he could, at least he'd scorn to own them.'

'Live for ever brave Ireland!' exclaimed Mrs. Arlbery; 'what cold, phelgmatic Englishman would have made a speech of so much gallantry?'

'As to an Englishman,' said Macdersey, 'you must never mind what he says about the ladies, because he's too sheepish to speak out. He's just as often in love as his neighbours, only he's so shy he won't own it, till he sees if the young fair one is as much in love as himself; but a generous Irishman never scruples to proclaim the girl of his heart, though he should have twenty in a year.'

'But is that perfectly delicate, my dearest sir, to the several Dulcineas?'

'Perfectly! your Irishman is the delicatest man upon earth to the fair sex; for he always talks of their cruelty, if they are never so kind. He knows every honest heart will pity him, if it's true; and if it i'n't, he is too much a man of honour not to complain all one; he knows how agreeable it is to the dear creatures; they always take it for a compliment.'

'Whether avowedly or clandestinely,' said Mrs. Arlbery, 'still you are all in our chains. Even where you play the tyrant with us, we occupy all your thoughts; and if you have not the skill to make us happy, your next delight is to make us miserable; for though, now and then, you can contrive to hate, you can never arrive at forgetting us.'

'Contrive to hate you!' repeated Macdersey; 'I could as soon contrive to turn the world into a potato; there is nothing upon earth, nothing under the whole firmament I value but beauty!'

'A cheerful glass, then,' said Sir Sedley, 'you think horridly intolerable?'

'A cheerful glass, sir! do you take me for a milk-sop? do you think I don't know what it is to be a man? a cheerful glass, sir, is the first pleasure in life; the most convivial, the most exhilarating, the most friendly joy of a true honest soul! what were existence without it? I should choose to be off in half an hour; which I should only make so long, not to shock my friends.'

'Well, the glass is not what I patronise,' said Sir Theophilus; 'it hips me so consumedly the next day; no, I can't patronise the glass.'

'Not patronise wine?' cried Lord Newford; 'O hang it! O curse it! that's too bad, Offy! but hunting! what dost think of that, little Offy?'

'Too obstreperous! It rouses one at such aukward hours; no, I can't patronise hunting.'

'Hunting!' cried Macdersey; 'O, it leaves everything behind it; 'tis the thing upon the earth for which I have the truest taste. I know nothing else that is not a bauble to it. A man is no more, in my estimation, than a child, or a woman, that don't enjoy it.'

'Cards, then,' said Sir Sedley, 'you reprobate?'

'And dice?'—cried Lord Newford—

'And betting?'—cried Sir Theophilus.

'Why what do you take me for, gentlemen?' replied Macdersey, hotly; 'Do you think I have no soul? no fire? no feeling? Do you suppose me a stone? a block? a lump of lead? I scorn such suspicions; I don't hold them worth answering. I am none of that torpid, morbid, drowsy tribe. I hold nobody to have an idea of life that has not rattled in his own hand the dear little box of promise. What ecstasy not to know if, in two seconds, one mayn't be worth ten thousand pounds! or else without a farthing! how it puts one on the rack! There's nothing to compare with it. I would not give up that moment to be sovereign of the East Indies! no, not if the West were to be put into the bargain.'

'All these things,' said Mr. Dennel, 'are fit for nothing but to bring a man to ruin. The main chance is all that is worth thinking of. 'Tis money makes the mare to go; and I don't know any thing that's to be done without it.'

'Money!' exclaimed Macdersey, 'tis the thing under heaven I hold in the most disdain. It won't give me a moment's concern never to see its colour again. I vow solemnly, if it were not just for the pleasures of the table, and a jolly glass with a friend, and a few horses in one's stable, and a little ready cash in one's purse, for odd uses, I should not care if the mint were sunk under ground to-morrow; money is what I most despise of all.'

'That's talking out of reason,' said Mr. Dennel, walking out of the shop with great disgust.

'Why, if I was to speak,' said Mr. Dubster, encouraged to come forward, by an observation so much to his own comprehension and taste as the last; 'I can't but say I think the same; for money—'

'Keep your distance, sir!' cried the fiery Ensign, 'keep your distance, I tell you! if you don't wish I should say something to you pretty cutting.'

This broke up the party, which else the lounging spirit of the place, and the general consent by which all descriptions of characters seem determined to occupy any spot whatever, to avoid a moment's abode in their lodgings, would still have detained till the dinner hour had forced to their respective homes. To suppress all possibility of further dissention, Mrs. Arlbery put Miss Dennel under the care of Macdersey, and bid him attend her towards Mount Pleasant.

Mr. Dubster, having stared after them some time in silence, called out: 'Keep my distance! I can't but say but what I think that young Captain the rudest young gentleman I ever happened to light upon! however, if he don't like me, I shan't take it much to heart; I can't pretend to say I like him any better; so he may choose; it's much the same to me; it breaks no squares.'

Edgar, almost without knowing it, followed Camilla, but he could displace neither the Baronet nor the Major, who, one with a look of open exultation, and the other with an air of determined perseverance, retained each his post at her side.

He saw that all her voluntary attention was to Sir Sedley, and that the Major had none but what was called for and inevitable. Was this indifference, or security? was she seeking to obtain in the Baronet a new adorer, or to excite jealousy, through his means, in an old one? Silent he walked on, perpetually exclaiming to himself: 'Can it be Camilla, the ingenuous, the artless Camilla, I find it so difficult to fathom, to comprehend, to trust?'

He had not spirits to join Mrs. Arlbery, though he lamented he had not, at once, visited her; since it was now awkward to take such a step without an invitation, which she seemed by no means disposed to offer him. She internally resented the little desire he had ever manifested for her acquaintance; and they had both too much penetration not to perceive how wide either was from being the favourite of the other.

CHAPTER XII

Traits of Eccentricity

Thus passed the first eight days of the Tunbridge excursion, and another week succeeded without any varying event.

Mrs. Arlbery now, impelled with concern for Camilla, and resentment against Edgar, renewed the subject of her opinion and advice upon his character and conduct. 'My dear young friend,' cried she, 'I cannot bear to see your days, your views, your feelings, thus fruitlessly consumed: I have observed this young man narrowly, and I am convinced he is not worth your consideration.'

Camilla, deeply colouring, was beginning to assure her she had no need of this counsel; but Mrs. Arlbery, not listening, continued.

'I know what you must say; yet, once more, I cannot refrain venturing at the liberty of lending you my experience. Turn your mind from him with all the expedition in your power, or its peace may be touched for the better half of your life. You do not see, he does not, perhaps, himself know, how exactly he is calculated to make you wretched. He is a watcher; and a watcher, restless and perturbed himself, infests all he pursues with uneasiness. He is without trust, and therefore without either courage or consistency. To-day he may be persuaded you will make all his happiness; to-morrow, he may fear you will give him nothing but misery. Yet it is not that he is jealous of any other; 'tis of the object of his choice he is jealous, lest she should not prove good enough to merit it. Such a man, after long wavering, and losing probable happiness in the terror of possible disappointment, will either die an old batchelor, with endless repinings at his own lingering fastidiousness, or else marry just at the eve of confinement for life, from a fit of the gout. He then makes, on a sudden, the first prudent choice in his way; a choice no longer difficult, but from the embarrassment of its ease; for she must have no beauty, lest she should be sought by others, no wit, lest others should be sought by herself; and no fortune, lest she should bring with it a taste of independence, that might curb his own will, when the strength and spirit are gone with which he might have curbed her's.'

Camilla attempted to laugh at this portrait; but Mrs. Arlbery entreated her to consider it as faithful and exact. 'You have thought of him too much,' cried she, 'to do justice to any other, or you would not, with such perfect unconcern, pass by your daily increasing influence with Sir Sedley Clarendel.'

Excessively, and very seriously offended, Camilla earnestly besought to be spared any hints of such a nature.

'I know well,' cried she, 'how repugnant to seventeen is every idea of life that is rational. Let us, therefore, set aside, in our discussions, any thing so really beneficial, as a solid connection formed with a view to the worldly comforts of existence, and speak of Sir Sedley's devoirs merely as the instrument of teaching Mandlebert, that he is not the only rich, young, and handsome man in this lower sphere, who has viewed Miss Camilla Tyrold with complacency. Clarendel, it is true, would lose every charm in my estimation by losing his heart; for the earth holds nothing comparable for deadness of weight, with a poor soul really in love—except when it happens to be with oneself!—yet, to alarm the selfish irresolution of that impenetrable Mandlebert, I should really delight to behold him completely caught.'

Camilla, distressed and confused, sought to parry the whole as raillery: but Mrs. Arlbery would not be turned aside from her subject and purpose. 'I languish, I own,' cried she, 'to see that frozen youth worked up into a little sensibility. I have an instinctive aversion to those cold, haughty, drawing-back characters, who are made up of the egotism of looking out for something that is wholly devoted to them, and that has not a breath to breathe that is not a sigh for their perfections.'

'O! this is far ...' Camilla began, meaning to say, far from the character of Mandlebert; but ashamed of undertaking his defence, she stopt short, and only mentally added, Even excellence such as his cannot, then, withstand prejudice!

'If there is any way,' continued Mrs. Arlbery, 'of animating him for a moment out of himself, it can only be by giving him a dread of some other. The poor Major does his best; but he is not rich enough to be feared, unless he were more attractive. Sir Sedley will seem more formidable. Countenance, therefore, his present propensity to wear your chains, till Mandlebert perceives that he is putting them on; and then ... mount to the rising ground you ought to tread, and shew, at once, your power and your disinterestedness, by turning from the handsome Baronet and all his immense wealth, to mark ... since you are determined to indulge it ... your unbiassed preference for Mandlebert.'

Camilla, irresistibly appeased by a picture so flattering to all her best feelings, and dearest wishes, looked down; angry with herself to find she felt no longer angry with Mrs. Arlbery.

Mrs. Arlbery, perceiving a point gained, determined to enforce the blow, and then leave her to her reflections.

'Mandlebert is a creature whose whole composition is a pile of accumulated punctilios. He will spend his life in refining away his own happiness: but do not let him refine away yours. He is just a man to bewitch an innocent and unguarded young woman from forming any other connexion, and yet, when her youth and expectations have been sacrificed to his hesitation, ... to conceive he does not use her ill in thinking of her no more, because he has entered into no verbal engagement. If his honour cannot be arraigned of breaking any bond, ... What matters merely breaking her heart?'

She then left the room; but Camilla dwelt upon nothing she had uttered except the one dear and inviting project of proving disinterestedness to Edgar. 'O! if once,' she cried, 'I could annihilate every mercenary suspicion! If once I could shew Edgar that his situation has no charms for me ... and it has none! none! then, indeed, I am his equal, though I am nothing, ... equal in what is highest, in mind, in spirit, in sentiment!

From this time the whole of her behaviour became coloured by this fascinating idea; and a scheme which, if proposed to her under its real name of coquetry, she would have fled and condemned with antipathy, when presented to her as a means to mark her freedom from sordid motives, she adopted with inconsiderate fondness. The sight, therefore, of Edgar, wherever she met him, became now the signal for adding spirit to the pleasure with which, already, and without any design, she had attended to the young Baronet. Exertion gave to her the gaiety of which solicitude had deprived her, and she appeared, in the eyes of Sir Sedley, every day more charming. She indulged him with the history of her adventure at the house of Mr. Dubster, and his prevalent taste for the ridiculous made the account enchant him. He cast off, in return, all airs of affectation, when he conversed with her separately; and though still, in all mixt companies, they were resumed, the real integrity, as well as indifference of her heart, made that a circumstance but to stimulate this new species of intercourse, by representing it to be equally void of future danger to them both.

All this, however, failed of its desired end. Edgar never saw her engaged by Sir Sedley, but he thought her youthfully grateful, and esteemed her the more, or beheld her as a mere coquette, and ceased to esteem her at all. But never for a moment was any personal uneasiness excited by their mutually increasing intimacy. The conversations he had held, both with the Baronet and herself, had satisfied him that neither entertained one serious thought of the other; and he took, therefore, no interest in their acquaintance, beyond that which was always alive,—a vigilant concern for the manner in which it might operate upon her disposition.

With respect to the Major, he was by no means so entirely at his ease. He saw him still the declared and undisguised pursuer of her favour; and though he perceived, at the same time, she rather avoided than sought him, he still imagined, in general, his acceptance was arranged, from the many preceding circumstances which had first given him that belief. The whole of her behaviour, nevertheless, perplexed as much as it grieved him, and frequently, in the same half hour, she seemed to him all that was most amiable for inspiring admiration, and all that was least to be depended upon, for retaining attachment.

Yet however, from time to time, he felt alarmed or offended, he never ceased to experience the fondest interest in her happiness, nor the most tender compassion for the dangers with which he saw her environed. He knew, that though her understanding was excellent, her temper was so inconsiderate, that she rarely consulted it; and that, though her mind was of the purest innocence, it was unguarded by caution, and unprotected by reflexion. He thought her placed where far higher discretion, far superior experience, might risk being shaken; and he did not more fervently wish, than internally tremble, for her safety. Wherever she appeared, she was sure of distinction: ''Tis Miss Tyrold, the friend of Mrs. Berlinton,' was buzzed round the moment she was seen; and the particular favour in which she stood with some votaries of the ton, made even her artlessness, her retired education, and her ignorance of all that pertained to the certain circles, past over and forgiven, in consideration of her personal attractions, her youth, and newness.

Still, however, even this celebrity was not what most he dreaded: so sudden and unexpected an elevation upon the heights of fashionable fame might make her head, indeed, giddy, but her heart he thought formed of materials too pure and too good to be endangered so lightly; and though frequently, when he saw her so circumstanced, he feared she was undone for private life, he could not reflect upon her principles and disposition, without soon recovering the belief that a short time might restore her mind to its native simplicity and worth. But another rock was in the way, against which he apprehended she might be dashed, whilst least suspicious of any peril.

This rock, indeed, exhibited nothing to the view that could have affrighted any spectator less anxiously watchful, or less personally interested in regarding it. But youth itself, in the fervour of a strong attachment, is as open-eyed, as observant, and as prophetic as age, with all its concomitants of practice, time, and suspicion. This rock, indeed, far from giving notice of danger by any sharp points or rough prominences, displayed only the smoothest and most inviting surface: for it was Mrs. Berlinton, the beautiful, the accomplished, the attractive Mrs. Berlinton, whom he beheld as the object of the greatest risk she had to encounter.

As he still preserved the character with which she had consented to invest him of her monitor, he seized every opportunity of communicating to her his doubts and apprehensions. But in proportion as her connexion with that lady increased, use to her manners and sentiments abated the wonderment they inspired, and they soon began to communicate an unmixt charm, that made all other society, that of Edgar alone excepted, heartless and uninteresting. Yet, in the conversations she held with him from time to time, she frankly related the extraordinary attachment of her new friend to some unknown correspondent, and confessed her own surprise when it first came to her knowledge.

Edgar listened to the account with the most unaffected dismay, and represented the probable danger, and actual impropriety of such an intercourse, in the strongest and most eloquent terms; but he could neither appal her confidence, nor subdue her esteem. The openness with which all had originally and voluntarily been avowed, convinced her of the innocence with which it was felt, and all that his exhortations could obtain, was a remonstrance on her own part to Mrs. Berlinton.

She found that lady, however, persuaded she indulged but an innocent friendship, which she assured her was bestowed upon a person of as much honour as merit, and which only with life she should relinquish, since it was the sole consolation of her fettered existence.

Edgar, to whom this was communicated, saw with terror the ascendance thus acquired over her judgment as well as her affections, and became more watchful and more uneasy in observing the progress of this friendship, than all the flattering devoirs of the gay Baronet, or the more serious assiduities of the Major.

Mrs. Berlinton, indeed, was no common object, either for fear or for hope, for admiration or for censure. She possessed all that was most softly attractive, most bewitchingly beautiful, and most irresistibly captivating, in mind, person, and manners. But to all that was thus most fascinating to others, she joined unhappily all that was most dangerous for herself; an heart the most susceptible, sentiments the most romantic, and an imagination the most exalted. She had been an orphan from earliest years, and left, with an only brother, to the care of a fanatical maiden aunt, who had taught her nothing but her faith and her prayers, without one single lesson upon good works, or the smallest instruction upon the practical use of her theoretical piety. All that ever varied these studies were some common and ill selected novels and romances, which a young lady in the neighbourhood privately lent her to read; till her brother, upon his first vacation from the University, brought her the works of the Poets. These, also, it was only in secret she could enjoy; but, to her juvenile fancy, and irregularly principled mind, that did not render them more tasteless. Whatever was most beautifully picturesque in poetry, she saw verified in the charming landscapes presented to her view in the part of Wales she inhabited; whatever was most noble or tender in romance, she felt promptly in her heart, and conceived to be general; and whatever was enthusiastic in theology, formed the whole of her idea and her belief with respect to religion.

Brought up thus, to think all things the most unusual and extraordinary, were merely common and of course; she was romantic without consciousness, and excentric without intention. Nothing steady or rational had been instilled into her mind by others; and she was too young, and too fanciful to have formed her own principles with any depth of reflection, or study of propriety. She had entered the world, by a sudden and most unequal marriage, in which her choice had no part, with only two self-formed maxims for the law of her conduct. The first of these was, that, from her early notions of religion, no vestal should be more personally chaste; the second, that, from her more recently imbibed ones of tenderness, her heart, since she was married without its concurrence, was still wholly at liberty to be disposed of by its own propensities, without reproach and without scruple.

With such a character, where virtue had so little guide even while innocence presided; where the person was so alluring, and the situation so open to temptation, Edgar saw with almost every species of concern the daily increasing friendship of Camilla. Yet while he feared for her firmness, he knew not how to blame her fondness; nor where so much was amiable in its object, could he cease to wish that more were right.

Thus again lived and died another week; and the fourth succeeded with no actual occurrence, but a new change of opinion in Mrs. Arlbery, that forcibly and cruelly affected the feelings of Camilla.

Uninformed of the motive that occasioned the indifference with which Edgar beheld the newly awakened gallantry of Sir Sedley, and the pleasure with which Camilla received it, Mrs. Arlbery observed his total unconcern, first with surprise, next with perplexity, and finally with a belief he was seriously resolved against forming any connection with her himself. This she took an early opportunity to intimate to Camilla, warmly exhorting her to drive him fast from her mind.

Camilla assured her that no task could be more easy; but the disappointment of the project with respect to Sir Sedley, which she blushed to have adopted, hurt her in every possible direction. Coquetry was as foreign to the ingenuousness of her nature, as to the dignity of all her early maternal precepts. She had hastily encouraged the devoirs of the Baronet, upon the recommendation of a woman she loved and admired; but now, that the failure of her aim brought her to reflexion, she felt penitent and ashamed to have heeded any advice so contrary to the singleness of the doctrines of her father, and so inferior to the elevation of every sentiment she had ever heard from her mother. If Edgar had seen her design, he had surely seen it with contempt: and though his manner was still the most gentle, and his advice ever ready and friendly, the opinion of Mrs. Arlbery was corroborated by all her own observations, that he was decidedly estranged from her.

What repentance ensued! what severity of regret! how did she canvass her conduct, how lament she had ever formed that fatal acquaintance with Mrs. Arlbery, which he had so early opposed, and which seemed eternally destined to lead her into measures and conduct most foreign to his approbation!

The melancholy that now again took possession of her spirits made her decline going abroad, from a renewed determination to avoid all meetings with Edgar. Mrs. Arlbery felt provoked to find his power thus unabated, and Sir Sedley was astonished. He still saw her perpetually, from his visits at Mount Pleasant; but his vanity, that weakest yet most predominant feature of his character, received a shock for which no modesty of apprehension or fore-thought had prepared him, in finding that, when he saw her no more in the presence of Mandlebert, he saw her no more the same. She was ready still to converse with him; but no peculiar attention was flattering, no desire to oblige was pointed. He found he had been merely a passive instrument, in her estimation, to excite jealousy; and even as such had been powerless to produce that effect. The raillery which Mrs. Arlbery spared not upon the occasion added greatly to his pique, and his mortification was so visible, that Camilla perceived it, and perceived it with pain, with shame, and with surprise. She thought now, for the first time, that the public homage he had paid her had private and serious motives, and that what she imagined mere sportive gallantry, arose from a growing attachment.

This idea had no gratifying power; believing Edgar without care for her, she could not hope it would stimulate his regard; and conceiving she had herself excited the partiality by wilful civilities, she could feel only reproach from a conquest, unduly, unfairly, uningenuously obtained.

In proportion as these self-upbraidings made her less deserving in her own eyes, the merits of the young Baronet seemed to augment; and in considering herself as culpable for having raised his regard, she appeared before him with a humility that gave a softness to her look and manners, which soon proved as interesting to Sir Sedley as her marked gaiety had been flattering.

When she perceived this, she felt distressed anew. To shun him was impossible, as Mrs. Arlbery not only gave him completely the freedom of her house, but assiduously promoted their belonging always to the same group, and being seated next to each other. There was nothing she would not have done to extenuate her error, and to obviate its ill effect upon Sir Sedley; but as she always thought herself in the wrong, and regarded him as injured, every effort was accompanied with a timidity that gave to every change a new charm, rather than any repulsive quality.

In this state of total self-disapprobation, to return to Etherington was her only wish, and to pass the intermediate time with Mrs. Berlinton became her sole pleasure. But she was forced again into public to avoid an almost single intercourse with Sir Sedley.

In meeting again with Edgar she saw him openly delighted at her sight, but without the least apparent solicitude, or notice, that the young Baronet had passed almost the whole of the interval upon Mount Pleasant.

This was instantly noticed, and instantly commented upon by Mrs. Arlbery, who again, and strongly pointed out to Camilla, that to save her youth from being wasted by fruitless expectation, she must forget young Mandlebert, and study only her own amusement.

Camilla dissented not from the opinion; but the doctrine to which it was easy to agree, it was difficult to put in practice; and her ardent mind believed itself fettered for ever, and for ever unhappy.

CHAPTER XIII

Traits of Instruction

The sixth and last week destined for the Tunbridge sojourn was begun, when Mrs. Arlbery once more took her fair young guest apart, and intreated her attention for one final half hour. The time, she said, was fast advancing in which they must return to their respective homes; but she wished to make a full and clear representation of the advantages that might be reaped from this excursion, before the period for gathering them should be past.

She would forbear, she said, entering again upon the irksome subject of the insensibility of Mandlebert, which was, at least, sufficiently glaring to prevent any delusion. But she begged leave to speak of what she believed had less obviously struck her, the apparent promise of a serious attachment from Sir Sedley Clarendel.

Camilla would here instantly have broken up the conversation, but Mrs. Arlbery insisted upon being heard.

Why, she asked, should she wilfully destine her youth to a hopeless waste of affection, and dearth of all permanent comfort? To sacrifice every consideration to the honours of constancy, might be soothing, and even glorious in this first season of romance; but a very short time would render it vapid; and the epoch of repentance was always at hand to succeed. With the least address, or the least genuine encouragement, it was now palpable she might see Sir Sedley, and his title and fortune at her feet.

Camilla resentfully interrupted her, disclaiming with Sir Sedley, as with everyone else, all possibility of alliance from motives so degrading; and persisted, in declaring, that the most moderate subsistence with freedom, would be preferable to the most affluent obtained by any mercenary engagement.

Mrs. Arlbery desired her to recollect that Sir Sedley, though rich even to splendour, was so young, so gay, so handsome, and so pleasant, that she might safely honour him with her hand, yet run no risk of being supposed to have made a merely interested alliance. 'I throw out this,' she cried, 'in conclusion, for your deepest consideration, but I must press it no further. Sir Sedley is evidently charmed with you at present; and his vanity is so potent, and, like all vanity, so easily assailable, that the smallest food to it, adroitly administered, would secure him your slave for life, and rescue you from the antediluvian courtship of a man, who, if he marries at all, is so deliberate in his progress, that he must reach his grand climacteric before he can reach the altar.'

Far from meditating upon this discourse with any view to following its precepts, Camilla found it necessary to call all her original fondness for Mrs. Arlbery to her aid, to forgive the plainness of her attack, or the worldliness of her notions: and all that rested upon her mind for consideration was, her belief in the serious regard of Sir Sedley, which, as she apprehended it to be the work of her own designed exertions, she could only think of with contrition.

These ruminations were interrupted by a call down stairs to see a learned bullfinch. The Dennels and Sir Sedley were present; she met the eyes of the latter with a sensation of shame that quickly deepened her whole face with crimson. He did not behold it without emotion, and experienced a strong curiosity to define its exact cause.

He addressed himself to her with the most marked distinction; she could scarcely answer him; but her manner was even touchingly gentle. Sir Sedley could not restrain himself from following her in every motion by his eyes; he felt an interest concerning her that surprised him; he began to doubt if it had been indifference which caused her late change; her softness helped his vanity to recover its tone, and her confusion almost confirmed him that Mrs. Arlbery had been mistaken in rallying his failure of rivalry with Mandlebert.

The bird sung various little airs, upon certain words of command, and mounted his highest, and descended to his lowest perch; and made whatever evolutions were within the circumference of his limited habitation, with wonderful precision.

Camilla, however, was not more pleased by his adroitness, than pained to observe the severe aspect with which his keeper issued his orders. She inquired by what means he had obtained such authority.

The man, with a significant wag of the head, brutally answered, 'By the true old way, Miss; I licks him.'

'Lick him!' repeated she, with disgust; 'how is it possible you can beat such a poor delicate little creature?'

'O, easy enough, Miss,' replied the man, grinning; 'everything's the better for a little beating, as I tells my wife. There's nothing so fine set, Miss, but what will bear it, more or less.'

Sir Sedley asked with what he could strike it, that would not endanger its life.

'That's telling, sir!' cried the man, with a sneer; 'howbeit, we've plenty of ill luck in the trade. No want of that. For one that I rears, I loses six or seven. And sometimes they be so plaguy sulky, they tempt me to give 'em a knock a little matter too hard, and then they'll fall you into a fit, like, and go off in a twinkle.'

'And how can you have the cruelty,' cried Camilla, indignantly, 'to treat in such a manner a poor little inoffensive animal who does not understand what you require?'

'O, yes, a does, miss, they knows what I wants as well as I do myself; only they're so dead tiresome at being shy. Why now this one here, as does all his larning to satisfaction just now, mayhap won't do nothing at all by an hour or two. Why sometimes you may pinch 'em to a mummy before you can make 'em budge.'

'Pinch them!' exclaimed she; 'do you ever pinch them?'

'Do I? Ay, miss. Why how do you think one larns them dumb creturs? It don't come to 'em natural. They are main dull of themselves. This one as you see here would do nothing at all, if he was not afraid of a tweak.'

'Poor unhappy little thing!' cried she! 'I hope, at least, now it has learnt so much, its sufferings are over!'

'Yes, yes, he's pretty well off. I always gives him his fill when he's done his day's work. But a little squeak now and then in the intrum does 'em no harm. They're mortal cunning. One's forced to be pretty tough with 'em.'

'How should I rejoice,' cried Camilla, 'to rescue this one poor unoffending and oppressed little animal from such tyranny!' Then, taking out her purse, she desired to know what he would have for it.

The man, as a very great favour, said he would take ten guineas; though it would be his ruin to part with it, as it was all his livelihood; but he was willing to oblige the young lady.

Camilla, with a constrained laugh, but a very natural blush, put up her purse, and said: 'Thou must linger on, then, in captivity, thou poor little undeserving sufferer, for I cannot help thee!'

Every body protested that ten guineas was an imposition; and the man offered to part with it for five.

Camilla, who had imagined it would have cost half a guinea, was now more ashamed, because equally incapable to answer such a demand; she declined, therefore, the composition, and the man was dismissed.

At night, when she returned to her own room from the play, she saw the little bullfinch, reposing in a superb cage, upon her table.

Delighted first, and next perplexed, she flew to Mrs. Arlbery, and inquired whence it came.

Mrs. Arlbery was as much amazed as herself.

Questions were then asked of the servants; but none knew, or none would own, how the bird became thus situated.

Camilla could not now doubt but Sir Sedley had given this commission to his servant, who could easily place the cage in her room, from his constant access to the house. She was enchanted to see the little animal relieved from so painful a life, but hesitated not a moment in resolving to refuse its acceptance.

When Sir Sedley came the next day, she carried it down, and, with a smile of open pleasure, thanked him for giving her so much share in his generous liberality; and asked if he could take it home with him in his carriage, or, if she should send it to his hotel.

Sir Sedley was disappointed, yet felt the propriety of her delicacy and her spirit. He did not deny the step he had taken, but told her that having hastily, from the truth of reflection her compassion had awakened, ordered his servant to follow the man, and buy the bird, he had forgotten, till it arrived, his incapability of taking care of it. His valet was as little at home as himself, and there was small chance, at an inn, that any maid would so carefully watch, as to prevent its falling a prey to the many cats with which it was swarming. He hoped, therefore, till their return to Hampshire, she would take charge of a little animal that owed its deliverance from slavery to her pitying comments.

Camilla, instinctively, would with unfeigned joy, have accepted such a trust: but she thought she saw something archly significant in the eye of Mrs. Arlbery, and therefore stammered out, she was afraid she should herself be too little at home to secure its safety.

Sir Sedley, looking extremely blank, said, it would be better to re-deliver it to the man, brute as he was, than to let it be unprotected; but, where generosity touched Camilla, reflection ever flew her; and off all guard at such an idea, she exclaimed she would rather relinquish going out again while at Tunbridge, than render his humanity abortive; and ran off precipitately with the bird to her chamber.

Mrs. Arlbery, soon following, praised her behaviour; and said, she had sent the Baronet away perfectly happy.

Camilla, much provoked, would now have had the bird conveyed after him; but Mrs. Arlbery assured her, inconsistency in a woman was as flattering, as in a man it was tedious and alarming; and persuaded her to let the matter rest.

Her mind, however, did not rest at the same time: in the evening, when the Baronet met them at the Rooms, he was not only unusually gay, but looked at her with an air and manner that seemed palpably to mark her as the cause of his satisfaction.

In the deepest disturbance, she considered herself now to be in a difficulty the most delicate; she could not come forward to clear it up, without announcing expectations from his partiality which he had never authorised by any declaration; nor yet suffer such symptoms of his believing it welcome to pass unnoticed, without risking the reproach of using him ill, when she made known, at a later period, her indifference.

Mrs. Arlbery would not aid her, for she thought the embarrassment might lead to a termination the most fortunate. To consult with Edgar was her first wish; but how open such a subject? The very thought, however, gave her an air of solicitude when he spoke to her, that struck him, and he watched for an opportunity to say, 'You have not, I hope, forgotten my province?... May I, in my permitted office, ask a few questions?'

'O, yes!' cried she, with alacrity; 'And, when they are asked, and when I have answered them, if you should not be too much tired, may I ask some in my turn?'

'Of me!' cried he, with the most gratified surprise.

'Not concerning yourself!' answered she, blushing; 'but upon something which a little distresses me.'

'When, and where may it be?' cried he, while a thousand conjectures rapidly succeeded to each other; 'may I call upon Mrs. Arlbery to-morrow morning?'

'O, no! we shall be, I suppose, here again at night,' she answered; dreading arranging a visit Mrs. Arlbery would treat, she knew, with raillery the most unmerciful.

There was time for no more, as that lady, suddenly tired, led the way to the carriage. Edgar followed her to the door, hoping and fearing, at once, every thing that was most interesting from a confidence so voluntary and so unexpected.

Camilla was still more agitated; for though uncertain if she were right or wrong in the appeal she meant to make, to converse with him openly, to be guided by his counsel, and to convince him of her superiority to all mercenary allurements were pleasures to make her look forward to the approaching conference with almost trembling delight.

CHAPTER XIV

A Demander

The next night, as the carriage was at the door, and the party preparing for the Rooms, the name of Mr. Tyrold was announced, and Lionel entered the parlour.

His manner was hurried, though he appeared gay and frisky as usual; Camilla felt a little alarmed; but Mrs. Arlbery asked if he would accompany them.

With all his heart, he answered, only he must first have a moment's chat with his sister. Then, saying they should have a letter to write together, he called for a pen and ink, and was taking her into another apartment, when Mr. Dennel objected to letting his horses wait.

'Send them back for us, then,' cried Lionel, with his customary ease, 'and we will follow you.'

Mr. Dennel again objected to making his horses so often mount the hill; but Lionel assuring him nothing was so good for them, ran on with so many farrier words and phrases of the benefit they would reap from such light evening exercise, that, persuaded he was master of the subject, Mr. Dennel submitted, and the brother and sister were left tête-à-tête.

At any other time, Camilla would have proposed giving up the Rooms entirely: but her desire to see Edgar, and the species of engagement she had made with him, counterbalanced every inconvenience.

'My dear girl,' said Lionel, 'I am come to beg a favour. You see this pen and ink. Give me a sheet of paper.'

She fetched him one.

'That's a good child,' cried he, patting her cheek; 'so now sit down, and write a short letter for me. Come begin. Dear Sir.'

She wrote—Dear Sir.

'An unforeseen accident,—write on,—an unforeseen accident has reduced me to immediate distress for two hundred pounds....'

Camilla let her pen drop, and rising said, 'Lionel! is this possible?'

'Very possible, my dear. You know I told you I wanted another hundred before you left Cleves. So you must account it only as one hundred, in fact, at present.'

'O Lionel, Lionel!' cried Camilla, clasping her hands, with a look of more remonstrance than any words she durst utter.

'Won't you write the letter?' said he, pretending not to observe her emotion.

'To whom is it to be addressed?'

'My uncle, to be sure, my dear! What can you be thinking of? Are you in love, Camilla?'

'My uncle again? no Lionel, no!—I have solemnly engaged myself to apply to him no more.'

'That was, for me, my dear; but where can your thoughts be wandering? Why you must ask for this, as if it were for yourself.'

'For myself!'

'Yes, certainly. You know he won't give it else.'

'Impossible! what should I want two hundred pounds for?'

'O, a thousand things; say you must have some new gowns and caps, and hats and petticoats, and all those kind of gear. There is not the least difficulty; you can easily persuade him they are all worn out at such a place as this. Besides, I'll tell you what is still better; say you've been robbed; he'll soon believe it, for he thinks all public places filled with sharpers.'

'Now you relieve me,' said she, with a sort of fearful smile, 'for I am sure you cannot be serious. You must be very certain I would not deceive or delude my uncle for a million of worlds.'

'You know nothing of life, child, nothing at all. However, if you won't say that, tell him it's for a secret purpose. At least you can do that. And then, you can make him understand he must ask no questions about the matter. The money is all we want from him.'

'This is so idle, Lionel, that I hope you speak it for mere nonsense. Who could demand such a sum, and refuse to account for its purpose?'

'Account, my dear? Does being an uncle give a man a right to be impertinent? If it does, marry out of hand yourself, there's a good girl, and have a family at once, that I may share the same privilege. I shall like it of all things; who will you have?'

'Pho, pho!'

'Major Cerwood?'

'No, never!'

'I once thought Edgar Mandlebert had a sneaking kindness for you. But I believe it is gone off. Or else I was out.'

This was not an observation to exhilarate her spirits. She sighed: but Lionel, concluding himself the cause, begged her not to be low-spirited, but to write the letter at once.

She assured him she could never again consent to interfere in his unreasonable requests.

He was undone, then, he said; for he could not live without the money.

'Rather say, not with it,' cried she; 'for you keep nothing!'

'Nobody does, my dear; we all go on the same way now-a-days.'

'And what do you mean to be the end of it all, Lionel? How do you purpose living when all these resources are completely exhausted?'

'When I am ruined, you mean? why how do other people live when they're ruined? I can but do the same; though I have not much considered the matter.'

'Do consider it, then, dear Lionel! for all our sakes, do consider it!'

'Well,—let us see.'

'O, I don't mean so; I don't mean just now; in this mere idle manner.—'

'O, yes, I'll do it at once, and then it will be over. Faith I don't well know. I have no great gusta for blowing out my brains. I like the little dears mighty well where they are. And I can't say I shall much relish to consume my life and prime and vigour in the king's bench prison. 'Tis horribly tiresome to reside always on the same spot. Nor I have no great disposition to whisk off to another country. Old England's a pretty place enough. I like it very well; ... with a little rhino understood! But it's the very deuce, with an empty purse. So write the letter, my dear girl.'

'And is this your consideration, Lionel? And is this its conclusion?'

'Why what signifies dwelling upon such dismalties? If I think upon my ruin beforehand, I am no nearer to enjoyment now than then. Live while we live, my dear girl! I hate prophesying horrors. Write, I say, write!'

Again she absolutely refused, pleading her promise to her uncle, and declaring she would keep her word.

'Keep a fiddlestick!' cried he, impatiently; 'you don't know what mischief you may have to answer for! you may bring misery upon all our heads! you may make my father banish me his sight, you may make my mother execrate me!—'

'Good Heaven!' cried Camilla interrupting him, 'what is it you talk of? what is it you mean?'

'Just what I say; and to make you understand me better, I'll give you a hint of the truth; but you must lose your life twenty times before you reveal it—There's—there's—do you hear me?—there's a pretty girl in the case!'

'A pretty girl!—And what has that to do with this rapacity for money?'

'What an innocent question! why what a baby thou art, my dear Camilla!'

'I hope you are not forming any connexion unknown to my father?'

'Ha, ha, ha!' cried Lionel laughing loud: 'Why thou hast lived in that old parsonage-house till thou art almost too young to be rocked in a cradle.'

'If you are entering into any engagement,' said she, still more gravely, 'that my father must not know, and that my mother would so bitterly condemn,—why am I to be trusted with it?'

'You understand nothing of these things, child. 'Tis the very nature of a father to be an hunks, and of a mother to be a bore.'

'O Lionel! such a father!—such a mother!—'

'As to their being perfectly good, and all that, I know it very well. And I am very sorry for it. A good father is a very serious misfortune to a poor lad like me, as the world runs; it causes one such confounded gripes of the conscience for every little awkward thing one does! A bad father would be the joy of my life; 'twould be all fair play there; the more he was choused the better.'

'But this pretty girl, Lionel!—Are you serious? Are you really engaging yourself? And is she so poor? Is she so much distressed, that you require these immense and frequent sums for her?'

Lionel laughed again, and rubbed his hands; but after a short silence assumed a more steady countenance, and said, 'Don't ask me any thing about her. It is not fit you should be so curious. And don't give a hint of the matter to a soul. Mind that! But as to the money, I must have it. And directly: I shall be blown to the deuce else.'

'Lionel!' cried Camilla, shrinking, 'you make me tremble! you cannot surely be so wicked ... so unprincipled.... No! your connexions are never worse than imprudent!—you would not else be so unkind, so injurious as to place in me such a confidence!'

The whole face of Lionel now flashed with shame, and he walked about the room, muttering: ''Tis true, I ought not to have done it.' And soon after, with still greater concern, he exclaimed: 'If this appears to you in such a heinous light, what will my father think of it? And how can I bear to let it be known to my mother?'

'O never, never!' cried she emphatically; 'never let it reach the knowledge of either! If indeed you have been so inconsiderate, and so wrong—break up, at least, any such intercourse before it offends their ears.'

'But how, my dear, can I do that, if it gets blazed abroad?'

'Blazed abroad!'

'Yes; and for want, only, of a few pitiful guineas.'

'What can you mean? How can it depend upon a few guineas?'

'Get me the guineas;—and leave the how to me.'

'My dear Lionel,' cried she, affectionately, 'I would do any thing that is not absolutely improper to serve you; but my uncle has now nothing more to spare; he has told me so himself; and with what courage, then, in this dark, mysterious, and, I fear, worse than mysterious business, can I apply to him?'

'My dear child, he only wants to hoard up his money to shew off poor Eugenia at her marriage; and you know as well as I do what a ninny he is for his pains; for what a poor little dowdy thing will she look, dizened out in jewels and laces?'

'Can you speak so of Eugenia? the most amiable, the most deserving, the most excellent creature breathing!'

'I speak it in pure friendship. I would not have her exposed. I love dear little Greek and Latin as well as you do. Only the difference is I don't talk so like an old woman; and really when you do it yourself, you can't think the ridiculous effect it has, when one looks at your young face. However, only write the request as if from yourself, and tell him you'll acquaint him with the reason next letter; but that the post is just going out now, and you have time for no more. And then, just coax him over a little, with, how you long to be back, and how you hate Tunbridge, and how you adore Cleves, and how tired you are for want of his bright conversation,—and you may command half his fortune.—My dear Camilla, you don't know from what destruction you will rescue me! Think too of my father, and what a shock you will save him: And think of my mother, whom I can never see again if you won't help me!'

Camilla sighed, but let him put the pen into her hand, whence, however, the very next moment's reflection was urging her to cast it down, when he caught her in his arms in a transport of joy, called her his protectress from dishonour and despair, and said he would run to the Rooms while she wrote, just to take the opportunity of seeing them, and to un-order the carriage, that she might have no interruption to her composition, which he would come back to claim before the party returned, as he must set off for Cleves, and gallop all night, to procure the money, which the loss of a single day would render useless.

All this he uttered with a rapidity that mocked every attempt at expostulation or answer; and then ran out of the room and out of the house.

Horrour at such perpetual and increasing ill conduct, grief at the compulsive failure of meeting Edgar, and perplexity how to extricate herself from her half given, but wholly seized upon engagement to write, took for a while nearly equally shares in tormenting Camilla. But all presently concentred in one domineering sentiment of sharp repentance for what she had apparently undertaken.

To claim two hundred pounds of her uncle, in her own name, was out of all question. She could not, even a moment, dwell upon such a project; but how represent what she herself so little understood as the necessity of Lionel? or how ask for so large a sum, and postpone, as he desired, all explanation? She was incapable of any species of fraud, she detested even the most distant disguise. Simple supplication seemed, therefore, her only method; but so difficult was even this, in an affair so dark and unconscionable, that she began twenty letters without proceeding in any one of them beyond two lines.

Thus far, however, her task was light to what it appeared to her upon a little further deliberation. That her brother had formed some unworthy engagement or attachment, he had not, indeed, avowed clearly, but he had by no means denied, and she had even omitted, in her surprise and consternation, exacting his promise that it should immediately be concluded. What, then, might she be doing by endeavouring to procure this money? Aiding perhaps vice and immorality, and assisting her misguided, if not guilty brother, to persevere in the most dangerous errors, if not crimes?

She shuddered, she pushed away her paper, she rose from the table, she determined not to write another word.

Yet, to permit parents she justly revered to suffer any evil she had the smallest chance to spare them, was dreadful to her; and what evil could be inflicted upon them, so deeply, so lastingly severe, as the conviction of any serious vices in any of their children?

This, for one minute, brought her again to the table; but the next, her better judgment pointed out the shallowness and fallacy of such reasoning. To save them present pain at the risk of future anguish, to consult the feelings of her brother, in preference to his morality, would be forgetting every lesson of her life, which, from its earliest dawn, had imbibed a love of virtue, that made her consider whatever was offensive to it as equally disgusting and unhappy.

To disappoint Lionel was, however, terrible. She knew well he would be deaf to remonstrance, ridicule all argument, and laugh off whatever she could urge by persuasion. She feared he would be quite outrageous to find his expectations thus thwarted; and the lateness of the hour when he would hear it, and the weight he annexed, to obtaining the money expeditiously, redoubled at once her regret for her momentary compliance, and her pity for what he would undergo through its failure.

After considering in a thousand ways how to soften to him her recantation, she found herself so entirely without courage to encounter his opposition, that she resolved to write him a short letter, and then retire to her room, to avoid an interview.

In this, she besought him to forgive her error in not sooner being sensible of her duty, which had taught her, upon her first reflexion, the impossibility of demanding two hundred pounds for herself, who wanted nothing, and the impracticability of demanding it for him, in so unintelligible a manner.

Thus far only she had proceeded, from the length of time consumed in regret and rumination, when a violent ringing at the door, without the sound of any carriage, made her start up, and fly to her chamber; leaving her unfinished letter, with the beginnings of her several essays to address Sir Hugh, upon the table, to shew her various efforts, and to explain that they were relinquished.

CHAPTER XV

An Accorder

Thus, self-confined and almost in an agony, Camilla remained for a quarter of an hour, without any species of interruption, and in the greatest amazement that Lionel forbore pursuing her, either with letter or message.

Another violent ringing at the bell, but still without any carriage, then excited her attention, and presently the voice and steps of Lionel resounded upon the stairs, whence her name was with violence vociferated.

She did not move; and in another minute, he was rapping at her chamber door, demanding admittance, or that she would instantly descend.

Alarmed for her open letter and papers, she inquired who was in the parlour.

'Not a soul,' he answered; 'I have left them all at the Rooms.'

'Have you returned, then, twice?'

'No. I should have been here sooner, but I met two or three old cronies, that would not part with me. Come, where's your letter?'

'Have you not seen what I have written?'

Down upon this intimation he flew, without any reply; but was presently back, saying he found nothing in the parlour, except a letter to herself.

Affrighted, she followed him; but not one of her papers remained. The table was cleared, and nothing was to be seen but a large packet, addressed to her in a hand she did not know.

She rang to inquire who had been in the house before her brother.

The servant answered, only Sir Sedley Clarendel, who he thought had been there still, as he had said he should wait till Mrs. Arlbery came home.

'Is it possible,' cried she, 'that a gentleman such as Sir Sedley Clarendel, can have permitted himself to touch my papers?'

Lionel agreed that it was shocking; but said the loss of time to himself was still worse; without suffering her, therefore, to open her packet, he insisted that she should write another letter directly; adding, he had met the Baronet in his way from the Rooms, but had little suspected whence he came, or how he had been amusing himself.

Camilla now hung about her brother in the greatest tribulation, but refused to take the pen he would have put into her hands, and, at last, not without tears, said: 'Forgive me, Lionel! but the papers you ought to have found would have explained—that I cannot write for you to my uncle.'

Lionel heard this with the indignation of an injured man. He was utterly, he said, lost; and his family would be utterly disgraced, for ruin must be the lot of his father, or exile or imprisonment must be his own, if she persisted in such unkind and unnatural conduct.

Terrour now bereft her of all speech or motion, till the letter, which Lionel had been beating about in his agitation, without knowing or caring what he was doing, burst open, and some written papers fell to the floor, which she recognised for her own.

Much amazed, she seized the cover, which had only been fastened by a wafer that was still wet, and saw a letter within it to herself, which she hastily read, while a paper that was enclosed dropt down, and was caught by Lionel.

To Miss Camilla Tyrold.

Forgive, fairest Camilla, the work of the Destinies. I came hither to see if illness detained you; the papers which I enclose from other curious eyes caught mine by accident. The pathetic sisterly address has touched me. I have not the honour to know Mr. Lionel Tyrold; let our acquaintance begin with an act of confidence on his part, that must bind to him for ever his lovely sister's.

Most obedient and devoted
SEDLEY CLARENDEL.

The loose paper, picked up by Lionel, was a draft, upon a banker, for two hundred pounds.

While this, with speechless emotion, was perused by Camilla, Lionel, with unbounded joy, began jumping, skipping, leaping over every chair, and capering round and round the room in an ecstasy.

'My dearest Lionel,' cried she, when a little recovered, 'why such joy? you cannot suppose it possible this can be accepted.'

'Not accepted, child? do you think me out of my senses? Don't you see me freed from all my misfortunes at once? and neither my father grieved, nor my mother offended, nor poor numps fleeced?'

'And when can you pay it? And what do you mean to do? And to whom will be the obligation? Weigh, weigh a little all this.'

Lionel heard her not; his rapture was too buoyant for attention, and he whisked every thing out of its place, from frantic merriment, till he put the apartment into so much disorder, that it was scarce practicable to stir a step in it; now and then interrupting himself to make her low bows, scraping his feet all over the room, and obsequiously saying: 'My sister Clarendel! How does your La'ship do? my dear Lady Clarendel, pray afford me your La'ship's countenance.'

Nothing could be less pleasant to Camilla than raillery which pointed out, that, even by the unreflecting Lionel, this action could be ascribed to but one motive. The draft, however, had fallen into his hands, and neither remonstrance nor petition, neither representation of impropriety nor persuasion, could induce him to relinquish it; he would only dance, sing, and pay her grotesque homage, till the coach stopt at the door; and then, ludicrously hoping her Ladyship would excuse his leaving her, for once, to play the part of the house-maid, in setting the room to rights, he sprang past them all, and bounded down the hill.

Mrs. Arlbery was much diverted by the confusion in the parlour, and Miss Dennel asked a thousand questions why the chairs and tables were all thrown down, the china jars removed from the chimney-piece into the middle of the room, and the sideboard apparatus put on the chimney-piece in their stead.

Camilla was too much confounded either to laugh or explain, and hastily wishing them good-night, retired to her chamber.

Here, in the extremest perturbation, she saw the full extent of her difficulties, without perceiving any means of extrication. She had no hope of recovering the draft from Lionel, whom she had every reason to conclude already journeying from Tunbridge. What could she say the next day to Sir Sedley? How account for so sudden, so gross an acceptance of pecuniary obligation? What inference might he not draw? And how could she undeceive him, while retaining so improper a mark of his dependence upon her favour? The displeasure she felt that he should venture to suppose she would owe to him such a debt, rendered but still more palpable the species of expectation it might authorise.

To destroy this illusion occupied all her attention, except what was imperiously seized upon by regret of missing Edgar, with whom to consult was more than ever her wish.

In this disturbed state, when she saw Mrs. Arlbery the next morning, her whole care was to avoid being questioned: and that lady, who quickly perceived her fears by her avoidance, took the first opportunity to say to her, with a laugh, 'I see I must make no inquiries into the gambols of your brother last night: but I may put together, perhaps, certain circumstances that may give me a little light to the business: and if, as I conjecture, Clarendel spoke out to him, his wildest rioting is more rational than his sister's gravity.'

Camilla protested they had not conversed together at all.

'Nay, then, I own myself still in the dark. But I observed that Clarendel left the Rooms at a very early hour, and that your brother almost immediately followed.'

Camilla ventured not any reply; and soon after retreated.

Mrs. Arlbery, in a few minutes, pursuing her, laughingly, and with sportive reproach, accused her of intending to steal a march to the altar of Hymen; as she had just been informed, by her maid, that Sir Sedley had actually been at the house last night, during her absence.

Camilla seriously assured her, that she was in her chamber when he arrived, and had not seen him.

'For what in the world, then, could he come? He was sure I was not at home, for he had left me at the Rooms?'

Camilla again was silent; but her tingling cheeks proclaimed it was not for want of something to say. Mrs. Arlbery forbore to press the matter further; but forbore with a nod that implied I see how it is! and a smile that published the pleasure and approbation which accompanied her self-conviction.

The vexation of Camilla would have prompted an immediate confession of the whole mortifying transaction, had she not been endued with a sense of honour, where the interests of others were concerned, that repressed her natural precipitance, and was more powerful even than her imprudence.

She waited the greatest part of the morning in some little faint hope of seeing Lionel: but he came not, and she spent the rest of it with Mrs. Berlinton. She anxiously wished to meet Edgar in the way, to apologise for her non-appearance the preceding evening; but this did not happen; and her concern was not lessened by reflecting upon the superior interest in her health and welfare, marked by Sir Sedley, who had taken the trouble to walk from the Rooms to Mount Pleasant to see what was become of her.

She returned home but barely in time to dress for dinner, and was not yet ready, when she saw the carriage of the Baronet drive up to the door.

In the most terrible confusion how to meet him, what to say about the draft, how to mention her brother, whether to seem resentful of the liberty he had so unceremoniously taken, or thankful for its kindness, she had scarce the force to attire herself, nor, when summoned down stairs, to descend.

This distress was but increased upon her entrance, by the sight and the behaviour of the Baronet; whose address to her was so marked, that it covered her with blushes, and whose air had an assurance that spoke a species of secret triumph. Offended as well as frightened, she looked every way to avoid him, or assumed a look of haughtiness, when forced by any direct speech to answer him. She soon, however, saw, by his continued self-complacency, and even an increase of gaiety, that he only regarded this as coquetry, or bashful embarrassment, since every time she attempted thus to rebuff him, an arch smile stole over his features, that displayed his different conception of her meaning.

She now wished nothing so much as a prompt and positive declaration, that she might convince him of his mistake and her rejection. For this purpose, she subdued her desire of retreat, and spent the whole afternoon with Mrs. Arlbery and the Dennels in his company.

Nevertheless, when Mrs. Arlbery, who had the same object in view, though with a different conclusion, contrived to draw her other guests out of the apartment and to leave her alone with Sir Sedley, modesty and shame both interfered with her desire of an explanation, and she was hastily retiring; but the Baronet, in a gentle voice, called after her, 'Are you going?'

'Yes, I have forgotten something....'

He rose to follow her, with a motion that seemed purporting to take her hand; but, gliding quickly on, she prevented him, and was almost at the same moment in her own chamber.

With augmented severity, she now felt the impropriety of an apparent acceptance of so singular and unpleasant an obligation, which obviously misled Sir Sedley to believe her at his command.

Shocked in her delicacy, and stung in her best notions of laudable pride, she could not rest without destroying this humiliating idea; and resolved to apply to Edgar for the money, and to pay the Baronet the next day. Her objections to betraying the extravagance of Lionel, though great and sincere, yielded to the still more dangerous evil of letting Sir Sedley continue in an errour, that might terminate in branding her in his opinion, with a character of inconsistency or duplicity.

Edgar, too, so nearly a brother to them both, would guard the secret of Lionel better, in all probability, than he would guard it himself; and could draw no personal inferences from the trust and obligation when he found its sole incitement was sooner to owe an obligation to a ward of her father, than to a new acquaintance of her own.

Pleased at the seeming necessity of an application that would lead so naturally to a demand of the counsel she languished to claim, she determined not to suffer Sir Sedley to wait even another minute under his mistake; but, since she now could speak of returning the money, to take courage for meeting what might either precede or ensue in a conference.

Down, therefore, she went; but as she opened the parlour door, she heard Sir Sedley say to Mrs. Arlbery, who had just entered before her: 'O, fie! fie! you know she will be cruel to excruciation! you know me destined to despair to the last degree.'

Camilla, whose so speedy re-appearance was the last sight he expected, was too far advanced to retreat; and the resentment that tinged her whole complexion shewed she had heard what he said, and had heard it with an application the most offensive.

An immediate sensibility to his own impertinence now succeeded in its vain display; he looked not merely concerned, but contrite; and, in a voice softened nearly to timidity, attempted a general conversation, but kept his eyes, with an anxious expression, almost continually fixed upon her's.

Anger with Camilla was a quick, but short-lived sensation; and this sudden change in the Baronet from conceit to respect, produced a change equally sudden in herself from disdain to inquietude. Though mortified in the first moment by his vanity, it was less seriously painful to her than any belief that under it was couched a disposition towards a really steady regard. With Mrs. Arlbery she was but slightly offended, though certain she had been assuring him of all the success he could demand:

her way of thinking upon the subject had been openly avowed, and she did justice to the kindness of her motives.

No opportunity, however, arose to mention the return of the draft; Mrs. Arlbery saw displeasure in her air, and not doubting she had heard what had dropt from Sir Sedley, thought the moment unfavorable for a tête-à-tête, and resolutely kept her place, till Camilla herself, weary of useless waiting, left the room.

Following her then to her chamber, 'My dear Miss Tyrold,' she cried, 'do not let your extreme youth stand in the way of all your future life. A Baronet, rich, young, and amiable, is upon the very point of becoming your slave for ever; yet, because you discover him to be a little restive in the last agonies of his liberty, you are eager, in the high-flown disdain of juvenile susceptibility, to cast him and his fortune away; as if both were such every-day baubles, that you might command or reject them without thought of future consequence.'

'Indeed no, dear madam; I am not actuated by pride or anger; I owe too much to Sir Sedley to feel either above a moment, even where I think them ... pardon me!... justly excited. But I should ill pay my debt, by accepting a lasting attachment, where certain I can return nothing but lasting, eternal, unchangeable indifference.'

'You sacrifice, then, both him and yourself, to the fanciful delicacy of a first love?'

'No, indeed!' cried she blushing. 'I have no thought at all but of the single life. And I sincerely hope Sir Sedley has no serious intentions towards me; for my obligations to him are so infinite, I should be cruelly hurt to appear to him ungrateful.'

'You would appear to him, I confess, a little surprising,' said Mrs. Arlbery, laughing; 'for diffidence certainly is not his weak part. However, with all his foibles, he is a charming creature, and prepossession only can blind you to his merit.'

Camilla again denied the charge, and strove to prevail with her to undeceive the Baronet from any false expectations. But she protested she would not be accessary to so much after-repentance; and left her.

The business now wore a very serious aspect to Camilla. Mrs. Arlbery avowed she thought Sir Sedley in earnest, and he knew she had herself heard him speak with security of his success. The bullfinch had gone far, but the draft seemed to have riveted the persuasion. The bird it was now impossible to return till her departure from Tunbridge; but she resolved not to defer another moment putting upon her brother alone the obligation of the draft, to stop the further progress of such dangerous inference.

Hastily, therefore, she wrote to him the following note:

To Sir Sedley Clarendel, Bart.

SIR,

Some particular business compelled my brother so abruptly to quit Tunbridge, that he could not have the honour to first wait upon you with his thanks for the loan you so unexpectedly put into his hands; by mine, however, all will be restored to-morrow morning, except his gratitude for your kindness.

I am, sir, in both our names,
your obliged humble servant,
CAMILLA TYROLD.

MOUNT PLEASANT,
Thursday Evening.

She now waited till she was summoned down stairs to the carriage, and then gave her little letter to a servant, whom she desired to deliver it to Sir Sedley's man.

Sir Sedley did not accompany them to the Rooms, but promised to follow.

Camilla, on her arrival, with palpitating pleasure, looked round for Edgar. She did not, however, see him. She was accosted directly by the Major; who, as usual, never left her, and whose assiduity to seek her favour seemed increased.

She next joined Mrs. Berlinton; but still she saw nothing of Edgar. Her eyes incessantly looked towards the door, but the object they sought never met them.

When Sir Sedley entered, he joined the group of Mrs. Berlinton.

Camilla tried to look at him and to speak to him with her customary civility and chearfulness, and nearly succeeded; while in him she observed only an expressive attention, without any marks of presumption.

Thus began and thus ended the evening. Edgar never appeared.

Camilla was in the utmost amaze and deepest vexation. Why did he stay away? was his wrath so great at her own failure the preceding night, that he purposely avoided her? what, also, could she do with Sir Sedley? how meet him the next morning without the draft she had now promised?'

In this state of extreme chagrin, when she retired to her chamber, she found the following letter upon her table:

To Miss Camilla Tyrold.

Can you think of such a trifle? or deem wealth so truly contemptible, as to deny it all honourable employment? Ah, rather, enchanting Camilla! deign further to aid me in dispensing it worthily!

SEDLEY CLARENDEL.

Camilla now was touched, penetrated, and distressed beyond what she had been in any former time. She looked upon this letter as a positive intimation of the most serious designs; and all his good qualities, as painted by Mrs. Arlbery, with the very singular obligation she owed to him, rose up formidably to support the arguments and remonstrances of that lady; though every feeling of her heart, every sentiment of her mind, and every wish of her soul, opposed their smallest weight.

CHAPTER XVI

A Helper

The next morning, as Camilla had accompanied Mrs. Arlbery, in earnest discourse, from her chamber to the hall, she heard the postman say Miss Tyrold as he gave in a letter. She seized it, saw the hand-writing of Lionel, and ran eagerly into the parlour, which was empty, to read it, in some hopes it would at least contain an acknowledgment of the draft, that might be shewn to Sir Sedley, and relieve her from the pain of continuing the principal in such an affair.

The letter, however, was merely a sportive rhapsody, beginning; My dear Lady Clarendel; desiring her favour and protection, and telling her he had done what he could for her honour, by adding two trophies to the victorious car of Hymen, driven by the happy Baronet.

Wholly at a loss how to act, she sat ruminating over this letter, till Mrs. Arlbery opened the door. Having no time to fold it, and dreading her seeing the first words, she threw her handkerchief, which was then in her hand, over it, upon the table, hoping presently to draw it away unperceived.

'My dear friend,' said Mrs. Arlbery, 'I am glad to see you a moment alone. Do you know any thing of Mandlebert?'

'No!' answered she affrighted, lest any evil had happened.

'Did he not take leave of you at the Rooms the other night?'

'Leave of me? is he gone any where?'

'He has left Tunbridge.'

Camilla remained stupified.

'Left it,' she continued, 'without the poor civility of a call, to ask if you had any letters or messages for Hampshire.'

Camilla coloured high; she felt to her heart this evident coldness, and she knew it to be still more marked than Mrs. Arlbery could divine; for he was aware she wished particularly to speak with him; and though she had failed in her appointment, he had not inquired why.

'And this is the man for whom you would relinquish all mankind? this is the grateful character who is to render you insensible to every body?'

The disturbed mind of Camilla needed not this speech; her debt to Sir Sedley, cast wholly upon herself by the thoughtless Lionel; her inability to pay it, the impressive lines the Baronet had addressed to her, and the cruel and pointed indifference of Edgar, all forcibly united to make her wish, at this moment, her heart at her own disposal.

In a few minutes, the voice of Sir Sedley, gaily singing, caught her ear. He was entering the hall, the street door being open. She started up; Mrs. Arlbery would have detained her, but she could not endure to encounter him, and without returning his salutation, or listening to his address, crossed him in the hall, and flew up stairs.

There, however, she had scarcely taken breath, when she recollected the letter which she had left upon the table, and which the afflicting intelligence that Edgar had quitted Tunbridge, had made her forget she had received. In a terror immeasurable, lest her handkerchief should be drawn aside, and betray the first line, she re-descended the stairs, and hastily entered the room. Her shock was then inexpressible. The handkerchief, which her own quick motion in retiring had displaced, was upon the floor, the letter was in full view; the eyes of Sir Sedley were fixed upon his own name, with a look indefinable between pleasure and impertinence, and Mrs. Arlbery was laughing with all her might.

She seized the letter, and was running away with it, when Mrs. Arlbery slipt out of the room, and Sir Sedley, shutting the door, half archly, half tenderly repeated, from the letter, 'My dear Lady Clarendel!'

In a perfect agony, she hid her face, exclaiming: 'O Lionel! my foolish ... cruel brother!...'

'Not foolish, not cruel, I think him,' cried Sir Sedley, taking her hand, 'but amiable ... he has done honour to my name, and he will use it, I hope, henceforth, as his own.'

'Forget, forget his flippancy,' cried she, withdrawing impatiently her hand; 'and pardon his sister's breach of engagement for this morning. I hope soon, very soon, to repair it, and I hope....'

She did not know what to add; she stopt, stammered, and then endeavoured to make her retreat.

'Do not go,' cried he, gently detaining her; 'incomparable Camilla! I have a thousand things to say to you. Will you not hear them?'

'No!' cried she, disengaging herself; 'no, no, no! I can hear nothing!...'

'Do you fascinate then,' said he, half reproachfully, 'like the rattlesnake, only to destroy?'

Camilla conceived this as alluding to her recent encouragement, and stood trembling with expectation it would be followed by a claim upon her justice.

But Sir Sedley, who was far from any meaning so pointed, lightly added; 'What thus agitates the fairest of creatures? can she fear a poor captive entangled in the witchery of her loveliness, and only the more enslaved the more he struggles to get free?'

'Let me go,' cried she, eager to stop him; 'I beseech you, Sir Sedley!'

'All beauteous Camilla!' said he, retreating yet still so as to intercept her passage; 'I am bound to submit; but when may I see you again?'

'At any time,' replied she hastily; 'only let me pass now!'

'At any time! adorable Camilla! be it then to-night! be it this evening!... be it at noon!... be it....'

'No, no, no, no!' cried she, panting with shame and alarm; 'I do not mean at any time! I spoke without thought ... I mean....'

'Speak so ever and anon,' cried he, 'if thought is my enemy! This evening then....'

He stopt, as if irresolute how to finish his phrase, but soon added: 'Adieu, till this evening, adieu!' and opened the door for her to pass.

Triumph sat in his eye; exultation spoke in every feature; yet his voice betrayed constraint, and seemed checked, as if from fear of entrusting it with his sentiments. The fear, however, was palpably not of diffidence with respect to Camilla, but of indecision with regard to himself.

Camilla, almost sinking with shame now hung back, from a dread of leaving him in this dangerous delusion. She sat down, and in a faltering voice, said: 'Sir Sedley! hear me, I beg!...'

'Hear you?' cried he, gallantly casting himself at her feet; 'yes! from the fervid rays of the sun, to the mild lustre of the moon!... from.

Frances Burney – A Short Biography

Frances Burney was born on June 13th, 1752 in Lynn Regis (now King's Lynn).

Her mother, Esther, was described as of "warmth and intelligence," the daughter of a French refugee, she had been brought up a Catholic.

Frances's father, Charles Burney, was a noted musician, musicologist and composer as well as being a man of letters.

In 1760 the family moved to Poland Street, In London's Soho, giving them an entrée to a wider circle of the cultural elite.

A difficult situation arose in 1766 when Charles Burney eloped to marry for a second time. Elizabeth Allen, was the wealthy widow of a King's Lynn wine merchant and already the mother of three children.

The two families were now merged into one and tensions were always simmering as Elizabeth established her rules in an overbearing way, always with the threat of anger near to the surface.

Her father had always favoured her sisters Esther and Susanna over Frances. By the age of 8 Frances had still not learned the alphabet and couldn't read. Her sisters were sent to be educated in Paris whilst Frances educated herself, reading from the family library, which she then devoured as her ambitions began to take hold. She now also began her own 'scribblings'.

In 1762, her mother, Esther, died and it was a loss that Frances was to feel deeply for the rest of her life.

However, there was one family friend who had spotted Frances's talents. He was Samuel Crisp. He encouraged Frances to write, mainly by requesting frequent journal-letters from her that recounted the family goings-on and also that of her social circle in London.

Frances was fifteen by the time her father eventually remarried in 1767. Pressure was also being exerted for her to give up writing; it was "unladylike" and "might vex Mrs. Allen."

Feeling that she had been improper, she burnt her first manuscript, The History of Caroline Evelyn, which she had written in secret. However, Frances did keep an account of the emotions that led up to this in her diaries which she thereafter continued to write, a practice she kept faith with for 72 years.

Frances was a talented storyteller with a strong sense of character, she often wrote these "journal-diaries" as correspondence to her family and friends, recounting events from her life and her observations upon them. Her diary contains the extensive reading in her father's library, as well the visits and behaviour of the various important arts personalities who came to their home. Frances and her sister Susanna were particularly close, and it was to her that Frances would correspond throughout her adult life, in the form of such journal-letters.

In 1775 Frances received a proposal from Thomas Barlow, whom she had met only once before, and which she recounts amusingly in her journals.

By 1778 Frances Burney was ready to be acknowledged as an author. The publication that year of Evelina or the History of a Young Lady's Entrance into the World, was published anonymously in 1778, without her father's knowledge or permission, by Thomas Lowndes, who, after reading the first volume, agreed to publish it upon receipt of the finished work.

This was a time when having a novel published by a young woman was almost unthinkable. In fact, she had her brother pose as its author. Unfortunately, he was also the negotiator and despite its critical success and praise from such luminaries as Edmund Burke and Dr Johnson she received only twenty guineas.

Its comic depictions of English society and realistic use of accents among the working class brought it to the attention of her father who was at first surprised and then supportive that his daughter had published a novel and enhanced the family's standing. With the books rare use of a female teenage protagonist Frances was already pushing the boundaries of the novel.

It also brought Frances an invitation to the home of patron of the arts Hester Thrale. Here she met Dr Johnson, who would remain her friend and correspondent throughout the period of her visits, from 1779 to 1783. Mrs Thrale wrote to Dr Burney on July 22nd, stating that: "Mr. Johnson returned home full of the Prayes of the Book I had lent him, and protesting that there were passages in it which might do honour to Richardson: we talk of it for ever, and he feels ardent after the dénouement; he could not get rid of the Rogue, he said." Dr Johnson's best compliments were eagerly transcribed in Frances's diary.

Sojourns at Streatham could occupy months at a time, and on several occasions the guests, including Frances, made trips to Brighton and Bath. As with other notable events, these experiences were faithfully recorded.

In 1779, encouraged by the public's warm reception of comic material in Evelina, and with offers of help from Arthur Murphy and Richard Brinsley Sheridan, Frances began to write a dramatic comedy called The Witlings. The play satirised London society, including the literary world and its pretensions.

It was not published at the time as her father and Samuel Crisp thought it would offend some of the public by seeming to mock the Bluestockings, and also their reservations about the propriety of a woman writing comedy. The play is the story of Celia and Beaufort, lovers kept apart by their families due to "economic insufficiency".

In 1781 Samuel Crisp died. Much of her subsequent work, Cecilia, or Memoirs of an Heiress, was written after much discussion with Crisp. The novel was published the following year. Her advance was now £250 and the first edition ran to 2000 copies, the first of several printings that year alone.

The narrative of Cecilia tells of Cecilia Beverley, whose inheritance from her uncle comes on the condition that she marries but keeps the family name.

In 1784 one of her greatest supporters, and her frequent correspondent, Dr Johnson, died. Her promising relationship with a clergyman, George Owen Cambridge, was also over. Frances was 33 years old but she had made a great deal of her life already.

In 1785, thanks to her association with Mary Granville Delany, a woman influential in both literary and royal circles, Frances travelled to the court of King George III and Queen Charlotte. There she was offered the post of "Keeper of the Robes", and a salary of £200 per annum. Frances hesitated. She had no wish to be separated from her family, nor to anything that would restrict her time in writing. But, unmarried at 34, she felt obliged to accept and thought that improved social status and income might allow her greater freedom to write.

She developed a warm relationship with the queen and princesses that lasted into her later years, yet her worries were prophetic: the position exhausted her and left her little, if any, time to write. She was unhappy and her feelings were amplified by a poor relationship with her colleague, Elizabeth Schwellenburg, co-Keeper of the Robes.

But despite writing little in the way of novels she still kept at her journals recounting life at court and the various political and social events.

By 1790, frustrated at her lack of writing, her further failed relationships, and with her health failing she asked to be released from service. The request was granted.

She returned to her father's house in Chelsea, but continued to receive a yearly pension of £100. She maintained a friendship with the royal family and received letters from the princesses until her death.

Between 1790–91 Frances wrote four blank-verse tragedies: Hubert de Vere, The Siege of Pevensey, Elberta and Edwy and Elgiva. Only the last was performed but met with public failure and played for only one night.

The French Revolution which had begun in 1789 brought support from many English literates for the ideals of equality and social justice. It was now that Frances became acquainted with a group of French exiles known as "Constitutionalists", who had fled France and were living at Juniper Hall, near Mickleham, where Frances's sister Susanna lived.

Frances quickly became attached to General Alexandre D'Arblay, an artillery officer who had been adjutant-general to Lafayette, a hero of the French Revolution.

Frances's father disapproved because of Alexandre's poverty, his Catholicism, and his ambiguous social status as an émigré. In spite of these objections they were married on July 28th, 1793.

On December 18th, 1794, Frances gave birth to their only child, a son, Alexander.

The impoverished couple were saved from poverty in 1796 by the publication of her next novel Camilla, or a Picture of Youth, a story of frustrated love and impoverishment. She made £1000 on the novel and sold the copyright for another £1000. This was enough to enable them to build a house in Westhumble; Camilla Cottage. Their life was now happy on all fronts.

Sadly, the news that her sister Susanna and her family were moving to Ireland that year caused her, and her father, some consternation, as did her sister Charlotte's remarriage in 1798 to the pamphleteer Ralph Broome.

Between 1797–1801 Frances wrote three further comedies; Love and Fashion, A Busy Day and The Woman Hater. All were unpublished during her lifetime.

The illness and death of Susanna in 1800 brought an end to their lifelong correspondence. Frances was devastated and only resumed her journal writing at the request of her husband, for the benefit of their son.

In 1801 D'Arblay was offered service with the government of Napoleon in France, and in 1802 Frances and her son followed him to Paris, where they expected to remain for a year. The outbreak of the war between France and England meant their stay extended for ten years. Although the conditions of their time left her isolated from her family, Frances was supportive of her husband's decision to move.

In August 1810 Frances developed pains in her breast. Her husband suspected breast cancer. Through her royal network of acquaintances, she was treated by leading physicians and, a year later, on September 30th, 1811, she underwent a mastectomy performed by "7 men in black". The operation was performed by M. Dubois, the accoucheur (midwife or obstetrician) to the Empress Marie Louise, Duchess of Parma, and widely considered the best doctor in France. Frances was later able to write about the operation in detail, since she was conscious through most of it, anesthetics not yet being in use.

Frances survived, even though she was still in recovery and not back to full health, returned to England in 1812 to visit her ailing father and also to avoid young Alexander's conscription into the French army

In 1814, Frances published her fourth novel, The Wanderer or, Female Difficulties, a few days before her father's death. A story of love and misalliance set in the French Revolution", it criticises the English treatment of foreigners during the war.

Frances made £1500 from the first run, but it did not go into a second English printing, although it met her immediate financial needs.

In 1815 Napoleon escaped from Elba. D'Arblay was then serving with the King's Guard, and he became involved in the military actions that followed. Frances joined her wounded husband at Trèves, and together they returned to Bath, England. Frances wrote an account of this and of her Paris years in her Waterloo Journal, written between 1818 and 1832. D'Arblay was rewarded with promotion to lieutenant-general but died shortly afterwards, in 1818, of cancer.

Frances now moved to London to be nearer to her son, a fellow at Christ's College. In honour of her father she gathered and in 1832 published, in three volumes, the Memoirs of Doctor Burney. The memoirs overly praised her father's accomplishments and character. Always protective of her father and the family's reputation, she deliberately destroyed evidence of facts that were painful or unflattering.

She now lived almost in retirement, outliving her son, Alexander, who died in 1837, and her sister, Charlotte, who died in 1838.

Frances continued to receive many visits from younger members of the Burney family, who gathered to listen to her fascinating accounts and her talents for imitating the people she described. She continued to write in her journals but alas her canon of novels and plays received no further additions.

Frances Burney died on January 6th, 1840.

She was buried with her son and her husband in Walcot cemetery in Bath.

There is a Royal Society of Arts blue plaque to record her period of residence at 11 Bolton Street, Mayfair.

Frances Burney – A Concise Bibliography

Fiction

The History of Caroline Evelyn, (manuscript destroyed by author, 1767.)
Evelina: or, The History of a Young Lady's Entrance into the World. 1778.
Cecilia: or, Memoirs of an Heiress. 1782.
Camilla: or, A Picture of Youth. 1796.
The Wanderer: or, Female Difficulties. 1814.

Non Fiction

Brief Reflections Relative to the French Emigrant Clergy. 1793.
Memoirs of Doctor Burney. 1832.

Journals & Letters

The Early Diary of Frances Burney 1768–1778. 2 volumes. 1889.
The Diary and Letters of Madame D'Arblay. 1904.
The Diary of Fanny Burney.
Dr. Johnson & Fanny Burney by Fanny Burney.
The Early Journals and Letters of Fanny Burney, 1768–1786. 5 volumes.
The Court Journals and Letters of Frances Burney. 4 volumes. (to date).
The Journals and Letters of Fanny Burney (Madame D'Arblay) 1791–1840. 12 volumes.

Plays

The Witlings, 1779 (satirical comedy).
Edwy and Elgiva, 1790 (verse tragedy). Produced at Drury Lane, 21 March 1795.
Hubert de Vere, 1788–91 (verse tragedy).
The Siege of Pevensey, 1788–91 (verse tragedy).
Elberta, (fragment) 1788–91 (verse tragedy).
Love and Fashion, 1799 (satirical comedy).
The Woman Hater, 1800–1801 (satirical comedy).

A Busy Day, 1800–1801 (satirical comedy).

Printed in Great Britain
by Amazon